THE
RAINSHADOW
ORPHANS

THE
RAINSHADOW
ORPHANS

NAOMI ISHIGURO

solstice

London · New York · Amsterdam/Antwerp · Sydney/Melbourne · Toronto · New Delhi

First published in Great Britain by Solstice Books,
an imprint of Simon & Schuster UK Ltd, 2026

1 3 5 7 9 10 8 6 4 2

Simon & Schuster UK Ltd, 1st Floor
222 Gray's Inn Road, London WC1X 8HB

Simon & Schuster Australia, Sydney
Simon & Schuster India, New Delhi

www.simonandschuster.co.uk
www.simonandschuster.com.au
www.simonandschuster.co.in

The authorised representative in the EEA is Simon & Schuster Netherlands BV,
Herculesplein 96, 3584 AA Utrecht, Netherlands. info@simonandschuster.nl

A CIP catalogue record for this book is available from the British Library

Hardback ISBN: 978-1-3985-4499-4
Trade Paperback ISBN: 978-1-3985-4500-7
eBook ISBN: 978-1-3985-4501-4
Audio ISBN: 978-1-3985-4502-1

Typeset in Baskerville by M Rules
Map credit © Virginia Allyn Illustration
Internal artwork India Minter/S&S Art Dept. & © Shutterstock
Printed and Bound in the UK using 100% Renewable Electricity at CPI Group (UK) Ltd

MIX
Paper | Supporting
responsible forestry
FSC
www.fsc.org
FSC® C013604

For all the wonderful students who let me be their teacher, and for all my own wonderful teachers.

In memory of Chris Barton.

RAINSHADOW

NAVISHIM

TO EARDLAND

UP TO FIVE MONTHS' SAILING

COMMERCIAL OFFICE DIST

THE IMPERIAL PALACE

OLD TOWN

Golden Moon
Square

Golden
Bake

Shadow Column

Library

Rainsha
Univers

The Covered Market

THE SANDSLIP PLAINS

Starfruit
Wharf

The Docks

Western Gate

Eastern

THE KEEPER'S CRESCENT

Northern Gate

The Lucky Crows
Warehouses

The Southern Corner

Mailee's Cafe

The Gods' Road

TO HANASAKI ISLAND

Southern Gate

TWO WEEKS' SAILING

SLAND

Arimoto
Granitarium Mines

MOUNTAIN LOWLANDS

ARIMOTO RESIDENCE

Main Imperial
Power Station

River Navis

Arimoto
Power Station

SUBURBS

ONSEN VILLAGE

Kawakamis'
partment Building

Tramways

TO AURIA

SIX DAYS' SAILING

TO VILMIA

THREE DAYS' SAILING

TO MURALANIA

TEN DAYS' SAILING

THE
RAINSHADOW
ORPHANS

BOOK ONE

OF

THE RAINSHADOW
ORPHANS SERIES

PART I

THE FIRST SIGNS
OF AUTUMN

CHAPTER ONE

Turning Leaves

Hiding in a ginkgo tree in the Imperial Palace's gardens, Toshiko Kawakami did wonder if she might be out of her depth. She'd been looking forward to this mission, excited to put herself to the test, spying on Emperor Asayo Soramoto and her guests as they celebrated the Turning Leaf Festival.

It had been a difficult evening already, though, involving a hard climb over the walls into the Imperial Palace's grounds, and then a desperate dash past the cameras and alarm systems, which Mei had helpfully disabled. Encountering the Palace's guard dogs had certainly been alarming, too, although Jun had prepared her well, with a giant backpack of chicken gyoza that had done a surprisingly good job of distracting them. She'd faced a breathless scramble over the inner garden wall after that, before a last, hand-over-hand climb through hanging lanterns and leaves to make it all the way up here, to where she was perched high in the tree canopy.

She'd been so sure she was ready for tonight. After all, she'd recently turned seventeen, which surely counted as practically adult. Now, though, her palms and fingertips were raw, and she could feel herself shaking, only just maintaining her grip on the branch beneath her. She also couldn't rid herself of the thought that her Auntie Reiko most certainly wouldn't have been happy with any of this.

Taking a moment to catch her breath as she watched the stars and the Three Sister Moons shine out from the sky's deep evening blue, Toshiko found that she could fully picture Auntie Reiko now, in her mind's eye – Auntie Reiko with her eyebrows rising higher and higher up her lined forehead. *You think this is a good way to behave?* she might have said, accompanying the words with a slow, disappointed shake of the head. *Look at this girl. She thinks she can just go off and do whatever she likes. No worry for safety. No cares for the consequences of breaking the law …*

Reiko, however, was gone. Toshiko let the mental picture dissipate into the dusk and sighed, prompting a 'What's up, Tosh?' from Mei, in her earpiece – Mei, her sister in every way but blood, and who, at twenty-one years old, was annoyingly unflappable. Mei always acted like she'd seen it all before and, irritatingly enough, more often than not it seemed she actually had.

Mei, unlike Auntie Reiko, was a family member who was, emphatically, still here. She was even perhaps *too* here sometimes, Toshiko reflected now, given that her older sister had predictably used the earpiece to provide a constant and generally critical commentary on all of her actions throughout this mission so far. Of course, though, Mei wasn't actually physically anywhere nearby. Always hostile to the idea of leaving the comfort of her tech lab and its vast stockpile of snacks, she never risked her own skin, or did anything strenuous enough to chip her long acrylic nails.

'What can you see?' she piped up again in Toshiko's ear, interrupting these mutinous thoughts. 'You've made it into the gardens properly by now, right? Also, we need to discuss those dogs. I couldn't tell from all the barking – were they cute scary or just *scary* scary?'

Judging the question sufficiently ridiculous to ignore, Toshiko took an extra moment to collect her thoughts.

'Come in, Tosh? You could start speaking to me any time ... now? Are you okay?'

'Yes, I'm fine,' Toshiko hissed, scowling into the froth of gold-tinged leaves around her. 'This may come as a surprise to you, but those of us who do things physically instead of virtually sometimes need a moment to breathe.'

She heard a pop on the other end of the line – the sound of Mei bursting her bubble gum. The sharp clarity of the noise was both a reminder of how little Mei cared about the physical versus virtual snipe, and of just how good the tech she built really was. Mei had earned her place at home with the snacks. Toshiko found herself rolling her eyes, only to have a passing squirrel flash her what was surely a look of reproach.

'You're getting flustered,' Mei told her. 'Come on, you're doing great so far. How about you just tell me what can you see?'

Like most of her citizens, Emperor Asayo Soramoto made the most of summer's lingering heat to celebrate the Turning Leaf Festival – Rainshadow City's official first night of autumn, when the leaves were just beginning to change their colours – with a lavish outdoor banquet. As Toshiko shimmied forwards along her branch to peer through the leaves, she was rewarded with her first clear view of the banquet table below, not twenty feet in front of her, set out beneath the avenue of trees. She also got her first glimpse of the Emperor herself.

It was almost a surprise to discover that Emperor Asayo looked, in person, almost exactly as she did in the daily telecasts. Sitting towards the centre of the long, laden table, she was dressed to perfection as usual in a sharply tailored trouser suit, its material the burnt-orange colour of an autumn forest.

Toshiko had just begun to shift further along her branch, hoping to see who the Emperor was talking to across the table, when her foot caught on an unexpected knot in the wood and then slipped against the tree's ridged bark.

She managed to recover her balance, but the movement set the many paper lanterns that were suspended from the tree swinging gently back and forth, the whole cluster of them moving like a cloud of outsize fireflies. Toshiko held her breath, certain she must have revealed her presence to the whole gathering.

Everyone sitting at the table below, though, still seemed too intent on each other and on the spread of festival food before them to even think of looking up into the branches. The stewards serving them also appeared far too focused on carrying out their duties to the Emperor's satisfaction to expect anything more than a gentle breeze at work in the treetops above – thank the Gods. Toshiko let her breath out, slowly, feeling her heartbeat settle.

The sound of Mei popping her gum came crisp and clear again over the earpiece. 'Well?' she asked Toshiko.

Toshiko looked back down through the ginkgo leaves, and considered how she might describe the scene to Mei. There were perhaps as many as fifty people seated at the long table below, being waited on by a mixture of stewards in Imperial livery and simple Service-bots on wheels. The table itself was laid out with a magnificent spread of different types of food, and set with more gleaming cups, plates and glasses than Toshiko would have known what to do with.

Many of Emperor Asayo's guests seemed to be high-ranking ministers or advisors: the kind of people responsible for delivering her agenda in running day-to-day life in this island city state of Rainshadow City, as well as for managing the city's relationship with the other islands that made up its wider Empire of the Rainshadow Archipelago. These were all people in nondescript middle age, looking elegantly professional in well-cut suits and dresses, which were all of subtly rich shades of dark blue, grey and black. Scattered amidst these guests were others dressed in the colourful reds, oranges and golds that were more typical of the Turning Leaf Festival. Toshiko guessed these might be members of the Emperor's extended family.

With a start, then, she registered that the Emperor's young son was here, sitting next to his mother on her left-hand side. Like his mother, the Crown Prince, a boy of ten, looked just as he did in the telecasts. He wasn't the only child at this banquet, either. There were a couple of small girls sitting a few seats further down from him, who Toshiko thought might be his cousins, and a small cluster of even younger children at the table's far end.

Somehow, Toshiko hadn't expected any children to be here tonight at all, though she realized now how foolish that had been of her. While there were big political dinners and events at the Palace almost every evening of the week, the Turning Leaf Festival was one of the city's most family-focused celebrations. It was sometimes all too easy to forget, given the enormous power that Emperor Asayo Soramoto held in her position as autocrat of the whole Rainshadow Archipelago, that she was also in fact a real human being, with a family of her own.

Family festival or not, Toshiko knew there would surely still be a high degree of political manoeuvring taking place between the adults at the table – something that was obviously contributing to rising levels of restlessness and boredom amidst the gathering's youngest members. If she were going to be spotted tonight, she realized, it would most likely be by one of them.

'So, did you fall out of the tree, or . . . ?' Mei's words were accompanied by an impatient tapping sound, and Toshiko could just picture her drumming her lime-green nails on the shiny surface of her desk.

'As if you'd care.'

'Of course I care. I have a vested interest in this mission going well. Now, stay focused. Is the target there?'

Tearing her eyes away from all the beautiful clothes, raden-worked rice bowls, lacquered chopsticks and platters of sushi, tempura, golden sweet potato tartlets and huge grilled matsutake mushrooms, Toshiko made herself remember the real reason she'd come here tonight, and began studying the guests at the table with more intention. To begin with, she thought that maybe he wasn't here and Jun's information had been faulty. Then, finally, she clocked him: Ken Saito of the Lucky Crows, sitting next to the Crown Prince, just one place away from the Emperor herself on her left-hand side.

The Lucky Crows were the biggest, most formidable, and officially the only organized crime syndicate on the island, controlling the whole of Rainshadow City's underground economy. Mei was certain, too, that they also pulled the strings of all sorts of elements within the island city state's ruling elite. Back when the Kawakamis had still lived in the Keeper's Crescent – the fenced-off arc of shanty towns that ran along the southern section of the island's coast, and a place that none of the city's legal citizens liked to think about – Ken Saito had served as the gang's head of operations there. Known as 'the Captain', he'd managed the exploitation of the Crescent's residents as cheap labour for Rainshadow City proper. He'd also been responsible for the collection of the 'taxes' that the Lucky Crows demanded from everyone who lived within the Crescent's confines, as well as for the gang's brisk trade in kakogan dust.

At first, Toshiko was amazed she hadn't recognized Saito immediately. Then again, it had been a full five years now since Auntie Reiko had done the unthinkable and defied him, refusing to let him take her adopted children into the city for a job in the granitarium mines so dangerous there would have been a good chance of them not coming back. It had been five years too, of course, since the night following that act of defiance, when Reiko had looked out of their little house's front door and announced that Saito was approaching.

Toshiko and Mei had huddled with Jun, the third Kawakami sibling and their adoptive brother, under the large wooden table that had formed the centrepiece of their home – the same table at which the three of them had eaten all their meals together, and at which Reiko had taught them their lessons. Concealed by its overlarge tablecloth, they had clung together in the gloom as a cut-short scream from Reiko had torn through the very air around them. As Mei had started to sob, Toshiko had slipped her siblings' protective grip to peek out from their hiding place. First, she'd seen Ken Saito, and had noticed immediately how completely out of place he'd seemed in their small but cosy main room. Then, she'd registered that he was wiping a dagger on a pocket-handkerchief and looking down at the floor – at Reiko's body, lying twisted at his feet.

Jun had it on good authority that Saito had since risen to

become a General in the gang, and was now one of the closest advisors to the Sensei – the Lucky Crows' leader, who was never seen in public but was often whispered about in the city's shadier corners. To be at the Sensei's right hand was a high position indeed, and Saito's rise had been remarkably swift. As Jun said, you had to wonder what he'd done to get so far so fast – and whether it had left him with nightmares.

Toshiko took a moment now to simply watch Saito, taking in all the details of this man who had killed the closest person to a parent she'd ever known, studying him in a way she hadn't been able to back in the half-light and horror of the last time she'd seen him.

Her first thought was that he was younger than she'd expected – still in his late twenties, maybe. With a confusing jolt, she realized that this surely meant he couldn't have been much older than Mei and Jun were now when he'd killed Auntie Reiko. It was a jarring idea to consider, since he always seemed so adult in her memories. There were other small differences, too, between Saito as he sat at the banquet table tonight and the image of him that had haunted her thoughts so relentlessly over these past five years. When he'd worked as the Captain, Saito had always kept his hair shorn short, in a dark fuzz over his scalp. He wore it longer now, in a typical business cut. He'd acquired a new scar – a vicious little apostrophe just above his left cheekbone – and his jawline seemed sharper, his shoulders even broader than Toshiko remembered, too. His cold grey eyes, though, were just the same as they always were in her nightmares.

She continued to observe him closely, watching those same hands that had killed Reiko as they reached now through the general dance of movement continuously unfolding over the table's surface – an improvised ballet of chopsticks, bracelets, rings, cups, dumplings, sashimi and tempura – to settle on a decanter of whiskey.

As Saito poured himself a drink, she noticed the hint of Lucky Crows sleeve tattoos just visible at the tops of his shirt cuffs, along with the Comms-Disc on his left wrist. These wrist-strapped devices were Lucky Crows tech, worn by all of the gang's higher-ranking members. While preparing for this mission, Mei had discovered that the Crows could use them to communicate with each other via a closed network which covered most of Rainshadow island.

Saito's Comms-Disc would have looked like a fairly typical model for the gang, had it not been studded with bright gem-stones. Clearly, he had a taste for the ostentatious. His fingers, too, were loaded with gleaming, heavy-looking rings, and he wore a large, luminescent pearl on a gold chain around his neck. The pearl gleamed against the black T-shirt he'd paired with his suit jacket like a miniature moon – a luminous, unearthly medallion.

'I've found him. He's here,' was all Toshiko said to Mei.

'You're absolutely sure it's him?' Mei was still trying to put on a bored voice, but Toshiko knew her well enough to detect a new agitation in her tone.

'It's Saito. I'm certain.'

There was nothing else from Mei for a moment, but Toshiko could sense the ticking clockwork of her thoughts. 'How friendly does he seem with Emperor Asayo?' Mei asked eventually.

'Well, it's a cosy-enough gathering,' Toshiko replied, a little unsure of what Mei was getting at now in asking this. 'Wait, she's talking to him now. And he's smiling, kind of. Looks a bit like a shark.'

'Is her kid there?' Mei asked.

'You mean the Crown Prince?'

'No, I meant an obscure nephew on the Emperor's mother's side.' Mei's voice dripped with sarcasm. 'Yes, clearly the Crown Prince.'

'He's here,' Toshiko told her, biting back a retort.

'And where is he sitting, in relation to Saito?'

'Right next to him, actually.'

'Gods,' Mei replied, her voice suddenly tight. 'You know, it's enough to make anyone sick, the extent to which she's so obviously in Saito's pocket, and in the Lucky Crows' pocket by implication. Inviting him to a Turning Leaf dinner with her family, and seating him next to her only child? Could she honour him any more highly?'

Toshiko never quite knew how to reply when Mei talked like this about the Emperor and the politics of Rainshadow City's ruling powers.

'Right,' Mei was continuing, though, sounding suddenly businesslike. 'I think we should move on to the next phase. It's time to steal the ring.'

'What? Now? Weren't we going to wait to do that?'

'No time like the present.'

'But this is my first time properly on my own on a mission,' Toshiko hissed, getting louder now, forgetting to care whether those below could hear her. 'You promised this was just recon.'

'We hadn't found him yet, when I said that. I didn't know how I would feel.'

'You're serious? You really want me to do this?'

'Unless you want to be all scared about it. Is he actually wearing the ring?'

'I'm not scared,' Toshiko huffed. 'You're the one who never leaves the apartment.'

'Stay focused. Is he wearing the ring?'

Still grumbling at Mei in her head, Toshiko went back to watching Ken Saito's hands. There it was – a flash of gold on the little finger of his left hand. It was distinctive in being the simplest and plainest ring of all of those he was wearing tonight – the only one, in fact, that didn't look as if it had been designed to double as a weapon.

'Yes, he's wearing it,' she told Mei.

'Perfect.'

Toshiko could hear in her sister's voice just how much she wanted that ring. According to Jun's investigations, this apparently simple piece of jewellery contained a chip that held access codes to almost every closed network in Rainshadow City, as well as to the Lucky Crows' private accounts, including bank accounts. There was no copy, and Saito never let it leave his person. For a hacker like Mei, that ring was the key to whole new realms of possibility, reaching even beyond the next stage in their current scheme of skimming credits from the gang's reserves. After everything they'd suffered at the Lucky Crows' hands, the Kawakamis were only too happy to steal as much as they needed from the gang in order to fund the life they'd managed to grasp for themselves beyond the Keeper's Crescent in the years following Reiko's death.

'Any advice on how I get hold of it?' Toshiko asked Mei. 'It seems pretty firmly on his finger.'

'I got you in there,' Mei replied, and Toshiko could just visualize her shrugging as the sound of her nails tapping against the desk came over the earpiece again. 'Didn't you decide fieldwork was going to be your area of expertise?'

'Fine,' Toshiko sighed. 'But you're cooking me dinner for the rest of the week.'

'Jun will cook dinner. You know he loves cooking dinner.'

'You're on washing-up duty, then.'

'Just get on with it,' Mei said.

Sisters. Were they more trouble than they were worth? Rolling her eyes, Toshiko wriggled back through the densely clustered leaves, towards the ginkgo tree's trunk, then began to climb down. She moved noiselessly, naturally, able to shift her weight and centre of balance with a dancer's grace, barely having to think at all about where she put her feet.

She took just a moment to check that everyone at the table was still fully immersed in their various conversations before dropping, catlike, onto the paving below without so much as rustling a leaf. A grin spread over her face in spite of her nerves. Mei might have all the talent for computing, but Toshiko could climb like it was a skill that had been gifted to her by the Gods.

'And they don't teach that at high school,' she whispered, triumphant, at exactly the same moment that the Crown Prince looked up from his place at the table and caught her eye.

'Oh shiitake mushrooms,' she hissed.

'What is it? What have you done?' said Mei.

'It's fine, just give me a minute.'

Toshiko darted behind the tree's trunk, hoping the midnight blue of her jacket and trousers would help her blend into the night. And yet the child was obviously not that stupid or easily distracted, because when she looked out from behind the tree again a moment later, he was still staring.

This was fine, Toshiko told herself. She would just have to give up on the idea of getting Mei to do the washing-up for the week. She would back away, slowly, and retreat, hoping the dogs would remember her as the blessed giver of gyoza and so refrain from attacking her as she climbed back over the wall. Yes, she would have to face Jun's concern and Mei's superior attitude for a few days, and yes, she might have slightly confirmed her older siblings' views of her as young and inexperienced, but she would also be home, safe and alive. They could find another way of locating Ken Saito and steal the ring when they'd actually had time to formulate a proper plan for getting it off his finger. All would be well.

She turned, crept to hide behind the delicate fronds of a maple tree, then dropped behind a low, ornamental wall, crawling forward on the ground in its shelter, forearm over forearm.

She didn't get very far before a pair of small blue slippers, embroidered with silver cats, stepped into view in front of her. She looked up to see the Crown Prince.

'Who are you?' the boy asked Toshiko. 'What are you doing here?'

He hadn't bothered to modulate the volume of his voice at all, and Toshiko found herself making hushing movements at him with her hands.

He was still very much a child – she might yet be able to get away with this, so long as she didn't scare him, or reveal any sign that she wasn't simply a regular, law-abiding citizen. As she considered how best to answer, she shifted her arm to hide the small tattoo that danced across her wrist, of three terns in flight over the watery curves of a river. There was no reason the Crown Prince would recognize it, but all the same – all three Kawakamis had one, and it didn't hurt to be cautious.

'Tosh?' Mei's voice piped up in her ear. 'Who's that? Who are you talking to?'

'Not now,' she hissed at Mei.

'What?' said the Crown Prince.

'What?' said Mei.

'Be quiet, both of you,' Toshiko snapped, wishing Mei had installed an off-switch in the earpiece.

'You weren't invited, were you?' said the Crown Prince. 'My mother didn't invite you.'

'Wow, is the Emperor really your mother?' Toshiko asked, playing for time, frantically trying to think of the best way out of this.

The boy only frowned at her. 'Yes. And I can tell she didn't invite you. I bet she doesn't like you.'

Pushing herself up to her elbows now, so as to face him more properly while still remaining hidden from the banquet table, Toshiko decided there could be worse ideas than running with his interpretation of her as a spurned party guest.

'Is it a fun party?' she asked, trying to sound as plaintive as possible.

The Crown Prince kicked one of his slippers against the paving of the path. 'Not really,' he said. 'Just grown-ups talking about boring things.'

Toshiko nodded sympathetically. 'Sounds rough. What kinds of boring things?'

'Like . . .' The boy looked up to the starred sky, as if that might provide some explanation for the adults' behaviour, then sighed heavily. 'You know. Like taxes and stuff.'

'I see,' Toshiko said. 'And what kinds of things do you prefer to talk about?'

'I don't know,' the boy replied. 'I like stories, I suppose. Good ones, with lots of adventures and fighting. And I like games.'

'I know a game you could play with me,' Toshiko told him then.

'Oh?' said the boy, sceptical but interested.

'Yeah, it's a really fun game,' she said. 'You see that guy over there?' She shifted herself on the ground to point at Saito.

'My uncle?' asked the boy, pointing over to the table too, but at a completely different man.

'No,' Toshiko tried again. 'The younger one, who you were sitting next to. With the scar and the giant pearl around his neck.'

'Ohhhh, him,' said the boy. 'Mr Winter. I don't like Mr Winter.'

Mr Winter. Toshiko mentally filed away the alias. 'Why not?'

The Crown Prince didn't seem to want to reply to that, and only scuffed his slipper into the path again.

'Well, this is a game to play a trick on Mr Winter,' Toshiko continued.

'Okay.' He was listening.

'You have to try and get Mr Winter to give you his ring.'

'His ring?'

'Yes. That small gold one, there. You see? On his little finger.'

'Oh,' the Crown Prince said. 'You mean the one with the dragon on it?'

'I don't know, I can't see that from here.'

'Well, it does have a dragon on it.'

'That's really good knowledge,' Toshiko said, flattering the boy. 'I bet you're going to be great at this game.'

'How do I get him to give it to me though?' the Crown Prince asked.

'That's the challenge,' said Toshiko. 'Tell him you want to play with it. Or that you want to see the dragon.'

'What happens if I do get the ring?'

'You'd win this round,' Toshiko said. 'Then you'd have to set me a challenge for the next round. The only thing to be careful of is that in order to win, you have to manage to get the ring all the way back here, to where I am, without Mr Winter trying to take it back.'

The boy frowned for a moment, his head on one side, thinking about it. Then – 'Okay,' he said, and trotted back towards the guests.

'What are you doing?' Mei demanded in Toshiko's ear.

'Improvising,' she hissed back.

Still sheltering behind the low wall, Toshiko watched the events at the table. For a while, things seemed to proceed mostly as before, except that the meal was obviously now drawing to a close. Soon, it wasn't only the Crown Prince who had gotten down from the table and was roving the gardens; several of the other young children began doing this too, and Toshiko found herself trying not to breathe, almost, in her efforts to blend in with the night.

She watched as the Crown Prince pottered over to two small girls who had gone to sit beside an ornamental pond, and then as the three of them started throwing pebbles into the water. After this had continued for several minutes, Toshiko began to wonder if the boy might have forgotten all about the ring. The children seemed to be trying to see whose throw could generate the biggest splash, and as Toshiko found herself growing increasingly impatient, a startled frog sprang from the water, setting all three children off in shrieking and recoiling, giggling loudly.

The noise caught the Emperor's attention. She glanced up from the conversation she'd been deep in with Ken Saito, who had shifted into the Crown Prince's empty seat, right next to her.

'What's going on over there?' the Emperor called, a note of sternness in her tone.

'It was a frog!' the smallest girl spluttered.

'Please do excuse the children, Mr Winter,' the Emperor said, turning to Saito, her voice catching a little knowingly on the false name. 'They are unaccustomed to the formality of occasions such as these. They were too young to be present for the Turning Leaf celebrations last year, you see.'

'It is no trouble, of course, Majesty,' Saito replied. His voice had the timbre of rust, of gravel, of the hardest rock found in the depths of the mountains – and he spoke stiffly, seeming unaccustomed to contorting his words into such pleasantries.

'Oof,' said Mei in Toshiko's ear. 'Someone sounds grisly.'

Toshiko sighed. Of course the mic attached to her earpiece was somehow so good that Mei could pick up the nuances of Saito's voice from twenty feet away. If Mei had been born with a legitimate Rainshadow City ID card, she'd surely have been able to get any job she wanted at any tech company on the island.

'Mr Winter,' piped up the Emperor's son then, as he stood up from where he'd been sitting with the girls and began to trot back over towards the table. 'Do you like games?'

Oh no. Toshiko closed her eyes and sent out a prayer to any God who might be nearby that the boy wouldn't reveal her.

'It depends on the game,' replied Ken Saito, not sounding very playful at all.

'Can I see the dragon, Mr Winter?' the boy tried again. 'The dragon on your ring?'

'On my ring?' said Saito, as a hush began to fall over the banquet table.

'I'm so interested in dragons, you see. I'd love to see the dragon on your ring more clearly.'

Saito didn't move. No one else spoke. The boy smiled winningly and held out his hand.

'Well?' said the Emperor. With a skip of her heartbeat, Toshiko saw that the Emperor was looking at Saito expectantly. 'Surely he can see it for a moment.'

'I would rather not part with it, if avoidable, Majesty.'

'You would deny my son this small request? Please, we are among friends, Mr Winter, and children need these little kind-nesses, as flowers require the light of the sun.'

'I'll be careful with it, Mr Winter, I promise.' The boy blinked up at him.

Under the combined gaze of the Emperor and the whole table of guests now, Ken Saito slipped his golden dragon ring off his little finger and placed it in the palm of the child.

'Yesss,' the boy said as his small fingers closed in a fist around it. He did a little jump on the spot and then, watched by every-one at the Emperor's Turning Leaf celebration, ran right back to where Toshiko was still hiding behind her low wall.

'Got it!' he cried when he reached her, and handed her the ring. It felt cold and strangely heavy in her palm. 'I won! Now I have to set a challenge for you.'

With the eyes of the whole table surely watching now, the time for subterfuge had clearly passed. In the awful, silent moment that followed, Toshiko stood up to her full height and stepped out from behind the wall, revealing herself to the guests and to the Palace stewards serving them. She made sure to raise up her hands, open-palmed, to show she was holding no weapons – only the ring, gleaming incriminatingly from between the thumb and forefinger of her right hand. Toshiko watched as the Emperor's sharp gaze took in every inch of her. Saito's jaw tightened, too, his hands curling into fists.

'Arrest her,' called the Emperor at last.

Mei shrieked Toshiko's name down the earpiece as, in a clatter of crockery, five of the stewards who had been attending the table dropped their trays and hurtled towards Toshiko like the trained Imperial Guards they clearly were. *Of course*, Toshiko almost groaned aloud. She should have realized that for all the show of this dinner being an intimate family affair, the Emperor would never host any kind of event without security on hand.

'Until the next time,' Toshiko called back to the Crown Prince as she turned and fled. 'I owe you another round of the game.'

And then she was away, a gust of wind loose through the gardens, even before the expression of triumph on the boy's face had had time to change to puzzlement.

She flew over potted plants, a stream, a path of stepping stones and a little bridge, acutely aware all the time of the Emperor's Guards behind her – of the sounds of their shoes on stone, then on gravel, and then of a crash as one of them kicked over what was probably a flowerpot. She didn't stop for breath until she reached the empty gatehouse by the side of the garden wall. Ducking around it, she paused to slip the ring into her pocket, freeing up her hands for the climb out of the gardens.

It was in this moment of distraction that Ken Saito stepped around the gatehouse's other side to appear before her, blocking her path. Standing in front of her like this, he seemed somehow bigger than she'd expected – a harsh, hulking figure against the glow of the evening sky. She couldn't help but note that there was nothing in his expression to suggest he recognised her. But why should he remember the face of one frightened child in the dark, she supposed? He'd probably seen hundreds of them.

Saito grinned and reached into his jacket, unsheathing a hidden blade. It wasn't the same one he'd used to take Reiko's life. If anything, it looked even more lethal, being longer and having a curve to it which made the whole knife flash like an unpleasant grin in the moonlight. Toshiko found herself stumbling backwards only to collide with hard brick. Saito had her trapped here, between the gatehouse and the wall.

'Hand it over,' he growled, sounding far more comfortable in this situation than he had at the dinner table. 'I won't wait.'

Toshiko could hear the Emperor's Guards coming closer, too, making their way towards her through the gardens. She chanced a glance in their direction, trying to gauge how long she had before they reached her – and as she did so, she took her eyes off Saito. In that instant of her attention being elsewhere, he seized her by the shoulder and brought his knife up to her throat.

Toshiko gasped in shock as he ran the very edge of his blade over the fine skin covering her larynx, drawing just the whisper of a thin, beaded trail of blood. Even at this proximity, so close that she could see the full intensity of menace concentrated within his gaze, he still showed no signs of recognition. How insignificant she was to him, when he had taken so much from her.

'Fine,' she spat. 'You can have it.' She reached into her pocket for the ring and threw it at his feet.

She couldn't really say what possessed her to do what she did next. The only possible reasons were that she hated losing, especially against Ken Saito, and that she had no time to think clearly. As he lowered his blade, lurching to stoop for the ring, she reached out and closed her fist around the oversized pearl suspended from the chain around his neck. It fit neatly into the hollow of her palm – as if it were somehow meant to be there – and felt surprisingly cool on her skin.

She pulled hard and the chain snapped, the pearl coming away in her hand. Saito's fingers flew to his neck, but he was distracted, still not having retrieved his precious ring from where it had rolled between the stones of the path.

Toshiko took advantage of his hesitation to spring away from him, bracing her left hand and left foot against the gatehouse behind her, while her right hand and right foot flew up the garden wall opposite. Moving crabwise like this up the vertical, she hoisted herself over the wall to drop into the darkness of the wider grounds beyond.

She landed hard, but somehow remained blessedly uninjured. With the stolen pearl still clutched in her fist, she set off running again for the Palace grounds' outer walls, sending a prayer of thanks as she went to any nearby God who might be looking out for her.

She was surely being followed, but she was fast, and when it came to running on smooth, paved paths like these, no one could match her for speed. Before long, she was nearing the walls, where she was met by the Palace's guard dogs.

Mercifully, they didn't attack, perhaps remembering her from the gyoza bonanza earlier. They did still bark at her enthusiastically, but it wasn't as if the noise mattered much anymore, since everyone in the Palace likely already knew she was here. As she clambered up the wall, she decided she'd tell Mei that the dogs were overall more cute than scary.

After a quick scramble down the wall's other side, Toshiko was finally out of the Palace's confines and plunging into the city beyond. Rainshadow City was a place so dense with people, buildings and activity that surely no one would be able to catch her now. Especially not tonight, with the streets and squares so busy with Turning Leaf celebrations. Everywhere, hawkers were selling maple leaf cakes, children were playing with kites and paper flags, and neighbours were eating together in lantern-lit outdoor gatherings, most of which seemed filled with far more laughter and liveliness than the Emperor's celebration had been, regardless of its grandeur. Toshiko could easily disappear among all this. Or she could for tonight at least.

CHAPTER TWO

A Night of Darkness and Light

1.

Haru knew that the name his mother had chosen for him was meant to signify springtime, clear skies and light for the future of the whole Rainshadow Archipelago. Locked up again in his room, however, with just the leaves of the maple tree outside tapping his window for company, he found it hard to feel anything but darkness.

Closing his eyes against the dim glow of the wall lanterns, he lay listening to the sounds of the tree and of water flowing through the garden fountains, until he began to grow drowsy. He forced his eyes back open then, and shuffled around on his bed to lie on his stomach to look out of the window. He couldn't see much from here, only the tangled branches of the tree as it swayed in the wind. The bright gold, green and orange tints of its shifting leaves were barely visible now in the darkness that was gathering fast, in spite of the glow of the Three Sister Moons. He found he felt almost worse, though, watching the tree and the sky like this. The sight seemed so redolent of the whole, vast world beyond the window – forbidden to him, until his mother forgave him.

The first few times his mother had locked him in his room like this, declaring, as she always did, that punishment was the only way to stop him from becoming as useless as his father had been, Haru had tried asking her favourite God for help – Yuto, God of Ambition. She had always insisted, after all, on his keeping a little gold-framed talisman to Yuto on the table by his bed, and while this was just a slip of paper bearing the God's name in neat calligraphy, Yuto's priests did say that it was charged with something of the God's essential essence. Haru had tried his luck in addressing himself to this talisman anyway – talking to Yuto with as much respect as he could muster, asking for help. And yet the God hadn't seemed to want to listen, and the hours had stretched longer and lonelier than ever. Haru hadn't felt much like talking to any of the Gods after that.

He groaned now and buried his face in his pillow. Probably he should have known not to listen to the stranger when she'd suggested the game, and yet he'd been so bored after sitting for such a long time at the dinner, with none of the adults around him willing to talk to him about anything interesting. Mr Winter, next to him, had barely said a word to him at all – except to tell him off as they'd all been sitting down together, when Haru had reached out to touch the huge pearl hanging around his neck.

Keep your hands to yourself, he'd snarled, slapping Haru's fingers away – and his heavy rings had caught Haru's knuckles, making him flinch.

When Haru's mother had asked why he'd reached like that for Mr Winter's pearl, Haru hadn't been able to give her a good answer. He certainly hadn't intended to steal it, as the stranger had tricked him into doing later on with the ring. The pearl had just seemed like such a beautiful thing – as if it had been calling out, almost, for his fingers to brush the shifting colours of its surface. When he'd muttered something to that effect, though, his mother had only glared at him with a coldness to match Mr Winter's.

Don't be ridiculous, she'd said, her voice infused with disappointment that had stung. *Honestly, you become more like your father every day.*

Haru never quite knew what his mother meant when she accused him of this particular offence. His father had died when he'd been only three, and while he did have a faint recollection of deft fingers setting a paper boat sailing on the Palace gardens' frog pond, as well as of a man with untidy hair, playing a curious stringed instrument which had looked a bit like a wooden box, that was about all he could remember. He definitely couldn't recall anything detailed enough for him to want to be anything like his father. Really, he only wished to help his mother and do what was expected of him as heir to the Empire.

And yet it was so difficult to know how to please her when all she ever seemed to care about these days were her plans for the LIFE-Hub. Sometimes it felt to Haru that whole seasons of his life had passed while she'd been locked in meetings about the LIFE-Hub with Mr Winter and the others. The problem was, too, that Haru never did understand what the LIFE-Hub was going to be *for*, exactly. Any time his mother had talked to him about it, she'd spoken only in terms of grand concepts, like *progress, society* and *future* – flashy words that seemed to do the opposite of actually explaining anything, in how their dazzle distracted from any real details of what they might actually mean.

Another thing Haru couldn't understand was why his mother was so keen on Mr Winter in the first place. It seemed clear to Haru, even from simple encounters with the man around the Palace, that Mr Winter had a peculiar darkness of spirit about him. Perhaps his mother just wasn't able to sense it.

Haru did have a particular talent for understanding people, he knew – a talent that seemed to be sharpening all the time, in fact. These days, he was often able to sense something about who a person was just from watching them for a while, or even from simply passing them in a corridor. The impression he always got from Mr Winter was that of a storm – it was as if a storm cloud were filling the space around Mr Winter's body, hovering above his skin. Maybe, Haru considered now, that was something of why he'd reached for his pearl. It had seemed like such a bright thing, trapped within the thunder and the rain of him.

Still, though, it hadn't been Mr Winter who'd landed him in trouble tonight. It had been the stranger, and the way she'd tricked him. He almost hated her for it, with her blue jacket and bird tattoo, and the way her eyes had filled with sparkle as she'd told him about the game. And yet she hadn't struck Haru as a cheat or a liar, and she hadn't seemed anything like Mr Winter either, consumed as he was by storm clouds. Instead, she had felt . . . Haru wriggled around again on his bed to lie on his back, tipping his head to look upside down at the waving branches of the maple as he tried to recall the impression he'd sensed from her. She had seemed like a lantern, its glowing flame burning steady through the frosty dark of a cold night.

His thoughts were interrupted then by the tree. Perhaps it was only because he was staring at it upside down, but its five-pointed leaves had started to seem more like small hands to him than ever, waving for attention. He flipped over so that he was on his stomach again, looking at it the right way up, only to find that the leaves still waved. As he watched, one of them even appeared to reach forward and tap the window. It didn't do this in quite the same way that the branches had always rattled and scraped against the glass before, the other times he'd been locked in here. Instead, it did it like a person asking to be let in.

Haru stared in surprise. Surely he couldn't be imagining things? Frowning, he pushed himself up to his knees, then climbed off the bed to go over to the window.

'I'm sorry,' he told the tree, feeling a little foolish as he did so. 'It's locked. I've tried to open it, but it's always locked.'

The tree kept tapping.

'I would open it for you, but I can't. See?' Haru mimed trying and failing to open the window, then put on a stern face, which he hoped might approximate his mother, and mimed locking it up.

The tree stopped tapping, going back to swaying gently, and Haru was reminded of someone taking a moment to think, scratching their head.

Just then, a flash of light caught him by surprise, and he squeezed his eyes shut. When he opened them again, he found his vision speckled with bright, coloured spots. He was busy blinking these away when his gaze caught on a shadow flitting over the top of the window frame. He blinked again, shaking his head, trying to banish any confusion. His eyes had returned to normal now, but the shadow hadn't disappeared. Instead, it sprang from the window up onto the nearest of the ceiling's wooden beams and proceeded from there to leap from beam to beam across the ceiling, away from Haru, only finally coming to rest on the edge of a beam in the room's furthest and darkest corner.

Haru squinted. The shadow had moved so fast that he hadn't been able to catch much more than glimpses of it, and he could still only just make out a small, indistinct shape, roughly the size of a mouse. He took a step closer. It flinched back.

'It's okay,' he said. 'It's just me, see? I won't hurt you.'

He tried another step forward. The shape trembled, but didn't move.

'See?' he said again. 'It's okay.'

Ever so slowly, he advanced towards it. Still, its appearance seemed to remain vague, almost formless. Passing his bedside cabinet, Haru reached for a lantern, raising it to light more of the room. The shape, though, leapt away from the light, jumping between the beams again to come to a stop once more in the ceiling's shadows.

'Okay, so no lantern,' Haru said. 'You don't like that. I get it. I've put it down.' He held up his open palms to underscore the point. 'Why won't you let me see you, though? I only want . . .' he trailed off, not sure what he could possibly want from this small, mysterious shape in the night. He took a breath and started again. 'I only thought it might be nice to have a friend here with me. I feel lonely up here by myself sometimes.'

The shape was still for a moment and then ever so slowly it edged along its beam, out of the shadows. Even as it did so, its form seemed to shift. At one moment, the room's soft lantern glow fell on it in such a way that Haru was sure it was a mouse. The next moment, it looked more like a lizard – and then he thought it might be a songbird, as it flitted towards him again across the ceiling's beams to come to a stop just above where he was standing, his eyes wide with astonishment. Perched here and fully in the light now, the shape seemed to definitively decide what it was, settling in the form of a squirrel.

The squirrel hopped down to land squarely in the middle of the bed, and Haru couldn't stop his jaw from falling open. Even now, it didn't resemble any ordinary squirrel he'd ever seen before. Instead of grey or russet fur, it was aflame with all the brightest shades of early autumn, and when its strikingly alert little eyes blinked, Haru saw they looked exactly like liquid gold.

2.

After escaping the Palace, Toshiko decided she wouldn't go home immediately. Even with all the festival celebrations making it harder for anyone to trace her through the city's streets, it never hurt to be cautious. So she wandered through the main, central shopping area and then rode the tram all the way west to the end of the line, to where wide stone steps led down to the ocean.

This whole waterside promenade was sparkling with lanterns tonight, alive with the sounds of drums. As Toshiko wove in and out of crowds that moved like tides around her, she nodded along to the musicians and watched street performers on stilts, their head-dresses glowing with the reds and oranges of autumn leaves and their cheekbones studded with glowing patterns of amber gems. Eventually she bought herself an onigiri rice ball from one of the many food stalls and sat down in a quieter spot by the water's edge to chew it slowly, letting the salt breeze from the ocean cool her cheeks as she watched the lights of party boats out on the waves.

After an hour or so by the water, she took a stroll through the covered market, and then at last caught a tram back to the east of the city, and home. Saito's pearl stayed hidden in her pocket the whole way.

The sky-blue door to the unassuming apartment building she returned to that night looked perfectly ordinary. Inside was a lobby, which led to a staircase, which could be followed down to what seemed to be a simple utility room filled with communal washing machines and dryers for the block. Only someone studying the room carefully would take notice of the wide, floor-to-ceiling metal sheet fixed to the far wall, next to the third dryer from the left.

Yawning as she finally allowed herself to feel the lateness of the hour and the strain of the night's events, Toshiko went over to this third dryer. A sequence of taps to its side popped open a panel, underneath which was a keypad. She punched in a code before replacing the panel, making the dryer look entirely ordinary again – and it did function very well as an ordinary dryer, too; Mei had made sure of that. After a five-second wait, the metal sheet on the wall next to it slid back to reveal a dim corridor ending in another door, also painted sky-blue. Toshiko gave a nod to the camera fixed to the corridor's ceiling as she headed down it to unlock the second door, using the key she always wore on a chain around her neck.

'Hungry?' Her feet had barely hit the doormat when Jun's voice greeted her from over in the kitchen. 'I'm making pancakes.'

'What happened to asking for a passcode?' Toshiko called through to him as she locked the apartment's door behind her.

'I recognize your walk. You always shuffle in here like no one told you how to pick up your feet. Plus, I saw you on Mei's camera.'

The pancakes did smell good. Slipping off her boots, Toshiko inhaled the buttery smell of frying batter.

The room around her was small but comfortable. In front of her, two worn but inviting couches were arranged in an L-shape, the floor between them covered with a midnight-blue, shag-pile rug on which two little silver Mouse-bots, the abandoned playthings of Mochi, the Kawakamis' cat, circled mechanically. Opposite the couches by the kitchen door stood a battered, dark wood dining table, which boasted a bowl of lychees, and also a wrought-iron candelabra that Toshiko had picked up years ago in the covered market, now filled with gently flickering candles.

Tonight, she immediately went to collapse into the nearest couch and grabbed one of its many cushions, a large proportion of which were shaped like non-specific creatures with giant, kawaii eyes – something that was very much Mei's influence. For a moment, Toshiko simply sat back, basking in the familiar sights and smells of this sanctuary that she and her siblings had built for themselves. Then, before long, Jun popped his head around the kitchen door.

Jun was twenty years old, tall and lanky. Right now, his hair was standing up at odd angles, made frizzy by the heat of the kitchen and shoved carelessly back into the headband he always wore while cooking. This disordered hair combined with his eyes – bright and blinking behind round glasses – to lend him, in this moment, the unmistakable air of a chick only just hatched from its egg.

'You know, I think I *would* like pancakes,' Toshiko told him. 'I think I'd like a whole stack of them, topped with blueberries and maple syrup and butter.'

'Difficult night?'

She shrugged.

'Mei told me,' Jun nodded. 'Didn't get the ring, huh?'

'Tonight wasn't even supposed to be about getting the ring, though,' Toshiko huffed. 'It was only meant to be an information-gathering trip. Mei got greedy.'

'Well, she who dares wins,' Jun said. 'Maybe just not all of the time.'

He cast Toshiko a concerned look. She tried to smile, but it felt wrong on her face.

'Don't worry,' he told her. 'Pancakes can fix this.'

Toshiko sighed. 'Thanks, Jun. I don't know if they can, though.'

'Hmm, they do tend to fix most things, you know.'

Toshiko smiled as Jun ducked into the kitchen again, to see to the frying pan. It was typical of her brother to try to cheer her up, even after she'd made such a mess of everything. For as long as she'd known him, Jun had always enjoyed taking care of people. Even back when he'd been a young child who didn't know a word of Navishian – Navishian being the language everyone spoke here in Rainshadow City, even predominantly in the Crescent – he'd still looked out for her, and for Mei and for Auntie Reiko too, with countless small and thoughtful gestures, never demanding praise, or even acknowledgement.

Dragging herself up out of the sofa, Toshiko followed Jun to the kitchen, where, leaning on the doorframe, she watched him flip the pancake. Of course, he could have used their Baker-bot to do it for him. The bot was, at this moment, perched in front of him on the counter, stirring the bowl of pancake batter round and round, somewhat redundantly. Jun took pride in perfecting these kinds of skills himself, though, and could flip a pancake as effortlessly as any professional chef.

'The Lucky Crows won't let this rest,' she told him. 'Saito knows I tried to steal the ring, and he can probably guess why. He certainly realizes I know it's more than just a regular ring.'

Jun slid the pancake onto a plate before pouring a fresh disk of batter into the pan to make the next one. 'Did he get a look at your face?'

Toshiko shivered at the memory of Ken Saito looming

over her next to the gatehouse, his curved blade held to her throat.

'Yes,' was all she said to Jun. 'It was dark, but yes, he did.'

'Still, what's one face in the night?' Jun replied lightly, and she wouldn't even have noticed his frown had he not been her adopted brother now for a full fourteen years. 'It's not like he knows who you are. Unless—' He turned round to her again, more serious this time. 'You weren't followed, were you? You made sure you weren't followed?'

Toshiko rolled her eyes, though she knew Jun was right to ask the question. 'Of course I made sure I wasn't followed. I'm not a kid.'

Jun nodded, turning back to the stove. 'That's all you can do, then,' he said. 'We try things in life – sometimes they work out, sometimes they don't. We'll lie low for a week and it'll blow over. I'm sure Saito has people coming after him all the time.' He pulled out a chair at the kitchen table and gestured for Toshiko to sit. She did, flopping down to drop her head in her hands, rubbing her eyes.

'There's something else though, Jun,' she began.

Jun took a moment to flip the pancake before replying. 'What something else?'

'Something Mei couldn't have heard on the audio. Something we didn't plan to do.'

'Go on.'

'I took something from him. After he saw my face.'

Toshiko reached into her pocket for Saito's pearl and held it out for Jun to see. The broken chain glinted in the low kitchen lights, while the pearl itself positively radiated a sense of presence, its surface seeming to gleam with cool impenetrability.

'Wow,' Jun said, his attention finally completely drawn from the stove. 'What in the world is that?'

3.

'Who in the names of all the Gods are these Kawakamis?'

Struggling to lift a crate far too heavy for his slight build, Theo gratefully allowed himself to be distracted by this overheard snatch of conversation. Abandoning his efforts, he ducked around the stack of crates in front of him, looking for the speaker amid the gloomy vista of the docks at night.

Over the past few hours, a bank of unseasonable cloud had blown in from over the water, blocking the light of the Three Sister Moons and obscuring the stars from view. To one side of him, through the murk, Theo could make out the wooden platforms of the docks, slick with sea water, extending from the concrete quay on which he was standing to stretch out into the ocean. Six large cargo barges bobbed alongside these platforms, with their tall sails furled. Their long, wooden bodies sat low down in the dark waves, overloaded as they were with hundreds of sealed crates identical to the one with which he'd just been struggling, each emblazoned with the Lucky Crows' emblem of two birds back-to-back, with spread wings crossing. A large team of Crows – mostly made up of footsoldiers in the gang, like Theo – was methodically unloading these crates from the barges, carrying them inland to stack them up on the quay.

About a thousand feet away, set back from the ocean and separated from the quay and the docks by a wide stretch of the waterfront that was dotted with old boathouses and smaller storage sheds, stood the warehouse where Theo and the rest of the Crows here tonight had been charged with taking these crates. It was the last in a line of warehouses all owned by the gang, and was the only one with its lights on and doors open. It had started the evening completely empty.

Of course, none of them had been told the first thing about what was actually in all these crates. The Lucky Crows tended to operate on a need-to-know basis, and most of Theo's fellow footsoldiers seemed to have readily reconciled themselves to ignorance. Streams of them were moving doggedly back and forth over the waterfront, shifting the crates unquestioningly. They were indistinct figures in the dark, hunched under the weight of their burdens as they headed out, only to come back swaggering, inflated with affected casualness as they tried not to show the strain of the work.

It took Theo a moment of scanning these figures to locate Daichi Santos, the man whose question, a moment ago, had caught his attention. He had recognized Daichi's voice over the undercurrents of noise from the sea and the wind, and now he finally picked him out in the darkness as one of a pair of Crows making their return journey back to the docks.

The man walking next to Daichi was his older brother, Hiroto. Daichi was part of Theo's immediate team of footsoldiers, just as Hiroto had been too, up until a couple of weeks ago, when he'd been given the promotion that had taken him away from a life of manual labour and into the Crows' offices, in the gleaming waterside skyscraper known as the Shadow Column. Theo supposed that Hiroto must have been drafted back in tonight as extra help for the footsoldiers. This was a big job, after all, especially considering they'd been ordered to get it done before first light.

'Is it just me,' Daichi was saying to Hiroto now, 'or had no one even heard of the Kawakamis until tonight?'

'Whoever they are,' Hiroto replied, 'there are mugshots of them up on every screen back at headquarters. The Sensei really wants them tracked down, fast.'

'Wait,' said Daichi, stopping in his tracks, disrupting the flow of the returning Crows behind him in order to turn to Hiroto and register his incredulity. 'There are photos of them up on *every* screen in the Shadow Column?'

'That's what I said, isn't it?' Hiroto replied as he stopped walking too to turn to his brother – attracting grunts of annoyance from the Crows around them.

Daichi whistled, oblivious to any irritation from his fellow gang members. 'But I mean, that's a lot of screens. It's a lot of focus for the Crows to be giving what seems like just a bunch of upstarts. They should be honoured, really. What d'you reckon they did to deserve it?'

Hiroto only shrugged before giving Daichi a light punch on the shoulder, signalling it was time they got moving again.

'Word at the Shadow Column,' he told Daichi as they walked, drawing closer to Theo now, 'is that they've set themselves up as a rival gang in the city to the Crows, and even stole something from Saito. Something pretty important from the sounds of it.'

Daichi whistled. 'I mean, who does that though? Who *steals* from Saito? These Kawakamis must have a death wish. Did you hear what it was they stole?'

Hiroto shook his head. 'You know no one tells me anything up there. I don't make the plans, I just make the coffee.'

That last phrase tripped off his tongue like it was something he frequently said, and both brothers laughed, perhaps a little cynically. Soon they'd reached the wall of crates right in front of Theo, and he ducked out of sight, still listening.

'At least you get to go up there, to the Column,' Daichi was saying now, a touch moodily. 'Some of us are still stuck down here all day.'

'All in good time, little brother,' Hiroto told him. 'If they promoted me, they'll definitely be willing to do the same for you too.

We just need to find the right thing to really catch their attention and impress them.'

With that, Hiroto grasped the topmost crate of the stack in front of him and heaved it into his arms – an action that, unfortunately, exposed Theo to the full glare of his and Daichi's attention.

'Bluejay,' Daichi growled immediately, his eyes narrowing with suspicion. 'What are you doing, lurking back there?'

Theo had only been in the Lucky Crows a couple of days when the foreman of their team of footsoldiers had begun calling him *Bluejay*. It was a name that seemed designed to draw attention to his difference – to his small, birdlike frame, and to his eyes, which were a distinctive bright blue of a sort that was rarely seen here in the Archipelago. *Bluejay* had stuck, anyway, to the extent that at this point, ten long months later, he wasn't sure anyone in the Crows even remembered his real name.

Faced with Daichi glowering at him now, Theo shook his head. 'I wasn't . . . I was . . .' He began to mime being exhausted from lifting the crates, pretending to tug at one and then exaggeratedly wiping his brow.

He often mimed like this with his fellow footsoldiers, even though by now he'd picked up more than enough Navishian to easily get by here on Rainshadow island. It was simply an instinct with Theo – or it was these days, anyway – to conceal the full extent of any abilities or knowledge he might possess. He'd learnt from experience that life was often safer that way.

Hiroto rolled his eyes and laughed. 'Look at him.' Scorn dripped from his voice as he rested his crate down on another nearby stack to nod over towards Theo, catching his brother's eye as he did so. 'Useless, skinny, freeloading kid.'

It was a struggle for Theo to act like he wasn't able to

understand the insult. At nineteen, he was hardly a kid anymore, and whether or not he was particularly efficient, he certainly worked hard every day for his place in the Crows. In any case, he must have kept his face sufficiently blank to convince Daichi, who raised his voice now, speaking the Navishian words to Theo with exaggerated slowness:

'You can get to work now, Bluejay. Like the rest of us.'

Theo nodded and ducked behind the pile of remaining crates, doing his best to look extra busy as he tried again to lift one. He managed to heave it up onto one knee, and then attempted to wrestle it fully into his arms.

The truth was, it wasn't only the weight of these crates that was causing Theo so much difficulty. The specific nature of his particular abilities meant that he was able to sense something about their contents, too – and whatever it was inside of them, he could feel it giving off an unusual hum of energy, which seemed both alarming and compelling by turns. Whichever it was, it was so strong that it left him feeling off-balance, and even a little nauseous.

After a moment of grappling with the crate, he lost his grip on it, sending it tumbling down onto the concrete quay with a crash so resounding that Theo was surprised the whole wooden structure of it remained intact. Even some of the usually cautious, wilfully ignorant footsoldiers looked up from their trudging at the noise to scan the docks warily.

The Santos brothers only laughed.

'Pathetic,' Daichi said, and spat at Theo's feet.

The two of them then hefted their own crates into their arms with apparent ease and sauntered off along the quay, towards the beckoning lights of the warehouse. Theo glowered after them into the gloom, watching their receding figures as they fell once again into shadow.

It seemed so completely unfair to him that the Santos brothers felt they could taunt him like this. While no one would think it now, he'd actually been in the Crows for a couple of months longer than they had, and while Hiroto may have been promoted lightning fast, Daichi was still very much a footsoldier. It wasn't as if they were much older him either – and they were outsiders here on Rainshadow island too, no more natives of this place than he was.

He couldn't help but feel that the Santos brothers based a lot of their sense of superiority on the fact that, unlike him, they'd arrived here from another of the Archipelago's islands – Theo couldn't remember which one. It was something that meant, anyway, that they fitted in a lot better here than he did in terms of looks, and that they'd grown up, too, knowing a good amount of Navishian, and with a much broader working knowledge than he had about how things worked within the Rainshadow Empire.

He supposed it also probably helped that they were both taller and stronger than he was, and so considerably better at the kind of manual labour footsoldiers tended to be charged with. Privately, in his more despairing moments, Theo did sometimes wonder what the Captain could have been thinking, when she'd recruited him into the gang.

He sighed, leaning on his fallen crate now to breathe in the salt of the sea air. At the edges of his hearing, he could make out occasional snatches of chattering crowds and drumbeats drifting in on the wind all the way from the Turning Leaf celebrations in Rainshadow City. You almost wouldn't know that, in between here and those celebrations, there lay a whole stretch of the island that most of the city's well-heeled citizens normally tried to forget even existed – the Sandslip Plains, on which stood the Keeper's Crescent. The Crescent's confines were pointedly defined by twin barbed-wire security fences, one encircling the other, with the outermost boasting the added feature of an electrified wire running through its centre.

The fences themselves weren't the most formidable things in the world. There was a narrow gap under each of them, perhaps big enough to wriggle through if you were feeling very brave, or very stupid. The fences, though, acted as a clear visual declaration that anyone who wasn't a legal, ID card-carrying citizen wasn't welcome in Rainshadow City. They were also a reminder of the brutal fact of there being Imperial Guards in each of the towers dotting their perimeter, armed with tall, powerful bows – meaning that anyone foolhardy enough to try to make a break across the plains for the city risked being shot on sight.

In marked contrast to the city's Turning Leaf celebrations, the Crescent was dark and quiet tonight. Theo knew that this was partly just down to its limited electricity supply, which would mean earlier nights now that the year was getting older and the sun setting earlier. It was also true, though, that the Keeper's Crescent never celebrated the same festivals as Rainshadow City itself. It was almost a tacit act of defiance – an insistence that the Crescent wasn't just the city's shadow, but a separate place in its own right.

In any case, the only hint tonight of any settlement out there in the darkness of the Sandslip Plains was the fluttering in the wind of Keeper's Garlands – the knotted lengths of coloured ribbons and scraps of material that people in the Crescent hung up over their doorways to attract the blessings of the Keeper into their dwellings. That, and the sound of a single dog barking.

After any particularly hard days of working for the Crows, Theo did sometimes wonder if perhaps he never should have left the Crescent to join the gang. He'd lived there himself, of course, in those first hard weeks after arriving here on the island. It was simply where the city authorities dumped everyone like him who turned up on these shores without any recognized claim to the precious Rainshadow City ID card that would have allowed them to build a life in the city proper.

And yet, as he'd discovered while living in the Crescent, this didn't mean that all of its residents – or 'Keeper's Children', as they called themselves – were recent blow-ins from overseas, like him. In actual fact, recent arrivals only made up a fraction of the Crescent's population. Most of the people there had lived trapped behind its barbed-wire fences for years. After all, the Crescent had existed on the Sandslip Plains in some form for generations, kept there by Rainshadow City's tacit reliance on its residents for cheap labour, as well as by the fact of its being the Crows' main market for kakogan dust. Many of its younger residents had even been born there.

A lot of the Keeper's Children Theo had talked to while living in the Crescent had been holding tight to the dream that some-day something would change and the Emperor would finally welcome them as citizens. Others had been sunk in a paralysis of cynicism – trapped there through having nowhere else safe to go, or any funds with which to travel even if a safe place had existed for them. Then, of course, there had been those Keeper's Children who'd desperately hoped for the same kind of opportu-nity that had somehow found its way to Theo when, after eleven long weeks of living life on his own in the Crescent, the Captain had swept into his life with her surprising offer of recruitment – not for another terrible job in the city this time, but for entry into the ranks of the Lucky Crows. It had seemed like the luckiest of breaks, at the time.

Theo sighed and straightened up. He really should at least try to get down to work or someone would notice he wasn't pulling his weight – and being taunted by the Santos brothers would be the least of his worries. He gave his fingers one last warm-up flex before bending his knees, preparing to have another go at the crate.

'I can't help but notice that you seem to be struggling,' said an unexpected yet chillingly familiar female voice behind him. 'Do you really think this is good enough, to justify your place in our ranks?'

Abandoning the crate once again, Theo turned towards the voice, dread now knotting in his stomach.

4.

'Who in the world are you?' Haru blurted out to the golden squirrel, before catching himself. His voice had seemed to resonate too loudly in the silence of his room – and what if one of his mother's staff, or even his mother herself, had heard him speaking? It would surely only lead to more trouble if anyone were to come and investigate now, only to find this creature here.

Never taking his eyes off the squirrel, Haru ran to press his ear against his bedroom door, listening for anyone in the corridor. Everything beyond, though, seemed just as quiet and still as ever. He swallowed. Of course, he should have known not to worry. No one had ever come to check on him when he'd been locked up for punishment before.

Watching him listening there at the door, the squirrel twitched its head to one side. Then, seeming to judge him as otherwise occupied, it jumped back onto the windowsill.

'No, wait! Please don't go,' Haru called after it.

The squirrel stopped where it was, poised in front of the

window. Seeing it there, Haru couldn't help but realize just how similar its colouring was to the mingled shades of orange and gold in the leaves of the maple tree just behind it, outside the window. In fact, from what he could make out in the moonlight, the flame colours at the tips of the maple's leaves were almost an exact match for the squirrel's fur.

'You're from the tree,' he said.

The squirrel gave a triumphant leap along the length of the windowsill – surely an admission of agreement.

'You *are* from the tree!' Haru cried out in excitement, before feeling suddenly self-conscious, wishing he had more to offer this extraordinary and unexpected visitor. He didn't even have any snacks.

'I don't have any food, I'm afraid,' he said to the squirrel with a frown. 'I don't even know what you eat.'

The squirrel gave a reassuring twitch of its nose.

'Still, I do wish I had something to give you,' Haru told it. 'I'm not shut up here without snacks by choice. Next time, I'll make sure there's something for you in my pockets. Do you like nuts?'

The squirrel twitched its nose again, then leapt off the windowsill and onto the floor to run in an enthusiastic circle.

'I'll take that as a yes.' Haru found he couldn't help but smile. 'What's your name, anyway?' he asked. 'I'm Haru.' He placed a hand in the centre of his chest and said it again very clearly and slowly. '*Haru.*'

The squirrel hopped from foot to foot, making a chirruping sound, but didn't seem to be able to talk.

'That's okay,' Haru said. 'You're a squirrel, right?'

The squirrel put its head on one side.

'Okay, but you're a squirrel *now*, at least. So I'll call you Risu. It's Mainlander for *Squirrel*. Is that okay?'

The squirrel seemed to consider this for a moment, then gave a small, happy jump.

'Risu! That's settled then. Hi, Risu!' Haru waved. 'Now you have to say, *Hi, Haru!*'

Instead, Risu squeaked, then scurried forward to run in another loop, this time around Haru's feet.

'Hey!' Haru cried out, spinning to keep the squirrel in view, and very nearly tripping himself up in the process. Risu stopped, adopting what seemed to be a particularly innocent expression, and in spite of everything that had happened this evening, Haru laughed.

'You're funny,' he told Risu. 'Will you stay here with me until I fall asleep?'

As Haru sat back down on his bed, giggling at the way Risu leapt up onto the covers next to him, he caught sight again of the maple outside. It was almost too dark to see anything properly now – and yet it still seemed clear to Haru that all the life and animation he'd sensed in the tree earlier had disappeared, leaving him looking at only simple leaves and branches again. The tree was beautiful, certainly, but blank, and definitely not like someone he could talk to. All of the tree's magic was here, he realized then. It was in Risu.

5.

The pearl gleamed in the lamplight of the Kawakamis' kitchen, still dangling on its chain from Toshiko's fingers. As Jun stared at it, eyes growing wider, Toshiko tried desperately to think of how she might make an explanation of how she'd come by it sound halfway reasonable. She didn't even get the chance to begin, though, because Mei chose that moment to emerge from her tech cave.

'I thought I smelled pancakes,' Mei said, coming to lounge against the kitchen doorframe.

Toshiko knew, of course, that she had bigger things to worry about in this moment, but as she looked at Mei, framed there in the kitchen doorway, she felt suddenly very aware of how scruffy she was in comparison with her sister – uncomfortably conscious of her worn-out tunic and trousers, and of her hair, too, tied back randomly and then made all windswept by the chaos of the evening.

Mei's long, dark hair, streaked with fluorescent pink and neon green, was piled on top of her head tonight in a style that managed to look both complicated and effortless. Her long, glossy nails matched the colours in her hair, and then she'd set all of this off by contrasting it with a black T-shirt and jeans. Her make-up was immaculate, as ever – an expert, photo-ready job of contouring and winged eyeliner, even though Toshiko knew for a fact she hadn't left the apartment all day. Her whole look only seemed enhanced, too, by the fact that Mochi, the Kawakamis' fourteen-year-old Vilmian Blue cat, was draped in his favourite position around her shoulders. His squashed-up features were arranged in his trademark expression of disgruntled alarm, while his thick, grey fur was as fluffy as ever. Despite Mochi's dangerous proximity to Mei's dangling hoop earrings, he didn't seem at all inclined to play with them.

Mei and Mochi had always shared a special kind of understanding that extended far beyond even this unlikely accord over her earrings. Toshiko had been so young when Auntie Reiko had brought Mochi home as a kitten that she barely remembered it happening. Mei, on the other hand, had been old enough to be delighted by their new arrival, and had looked after him, fiercely, from the very beginning.

Sometimes, Toshiko did have to wonder whether Mei's intense attachment to the cat had something to do with how much she missed Auntie Reiko, and the life they'd all lived together before Ken Saito had torn it to pieces. Other times, it seemed just as likely that Mei simply found Mochi's perpetual moodiness irrationally endearing.

Mei's eyes found their way then, at last, from the pancake batter frying on the stove to the pearl hanging from Toshiko's fingers.

'What in all the Gods is that?' she asked, her voice seeming to drop a full octave, as it always did when she was very serious about something. 'You'd better explain this, sister. Quickly.'

'Let her relax and eat something first,' Jun cut in.

'No, it's fine,' said Toshiko. 'It was around Saito's neck. I grabbed it just before I ran, when he forced me to give back the ring. I don't quite know why I did it now.'

Mei's eyes narrowed as she reached out for the pearl. She weighed it experimentally in one hand, and then, before Toshiko could stop her, she was trying it with her teeth, biting down on it – a pirate testing the authenticity of a gold coin. Seeming to learn nothing from this experiment, Mei frowned and held the pearl up to Mochi. Mochi gave it two very delicate sniffs, then seemed to recoil, his amber eyes narrowing in an expression that seemed even more disdainful than the usual sulkiness of his typical resting face.

'It doesn't seem like a real pearl,' Mei said. 'It's too big, for one thing. And too heavy. Too dense.'

'Maybe it has a chip inside it, like the ring?' Toshiko ventured.

'Maybe,' said Mei. 'Mind if I take a look at it in the lab?'

Toshiko shrugged. 'Go ahead.'

'Pancakes?' Jun called after Mei as she prowled out of the kitchen, pearl in hand.

'You know it,' she replied without turning round. 'Matcha and mango.'

Jun nodded as he finished frying the third pancake. He popped it onto the plate with the other two, doused the whole thing in maple syrup, added some blueberries from the stasis box and presented it to Toshiko with a flourish and a fork.

'For you, madame.'

Toshiko smiled in spite of herself. Every day she gave thanks to the Keeper that she and Mei had found Jun on the Crescent's scrubland all those years ago, when he'd been just a six-year-old boy, lost and suddenly alone in the world, with tears tracking through the dirt stains on his cheeks. She was grateful, too, that somehow, in a moment of uncharacteristic openness, Mei had reached out her hand and asked him to come with them, back to Auntie Reiko's. Perhaps it had been solidarity more than anything else – one orphan recognizing the need of another. Perhaps, too, Mei had understood something of what it must be like to arrive in the Crescent knowing no one, and speaking no Navishian. While Mei herself had been born there, her mother had come from Auria, one of the Archipelago's southern islands.

'Did you mean what you said before?' Toshiko asked Jun now as he rummaged in the cupboard for Mei's matcha. 'That you think this is something that could blow over?'

Jun smiled, but it didn't reach his eyes. 'There's no sense worrying about it now,' was all he said. 'I'll go into town tomorrow and find out what I can, and we can go from there.'

Toshiko nodded. 'Thanks, Jun. We really don't deserve you, you know.'

'We're the Kawakamis. We help each other. It's what we do.'

'It is.' Toshiko nodded. 'But still – thank you.'

She chatted to Jun about some more normal things after that, as she ate her pancakes. He wasn't convinced that Mei's quest to invent the ultimate boba machine – her 'side project' as she kept calling it – was an appropriate use of the family's tech budget, but he also wasn't sure how to broach this with her. Toshiko offered some tentative advice, and, licking the maple syrup from her plate, almost succeeded in letting the warmth of home convince her that all of the evening's earlier events weren't anything too serious after all.

Soon, she was yawning and padding to her bedroom, slipping off her jacket and throwing it on her bed. She was just about to go and brush her teeth when she stopped. Something had fallen out of one of the jacket's pockets and was floating to the floor. She knelt to find a long, straight, black feather.

She'd seen feathers like this before. One had landed on Auntie Reiko's pillow the night before Ken Saito had arrived to take her from them forever. They'd been a common-enough sight back in the Keeper's Crescent, appearing whenever anyone crossed the Crows – whether that was by openly defying Saito, as Reiko had done, or simply falling behind on the monthly payments that the Crows extorted from every household. The feathers were the Lucky Crows' calling card, and while the type and extent of the punishment they promised did vary, they never meant anything good.

Toshiko shuddered, dropping the feather as if it were poisoned.

6.

'Do you really think this is good enough, to justify your place in our ranks?'

The woman who had appeared on the docks in front of Theo

was maybe a little older than he was, though her dark glasses made it difficult to tell. She had short hair, wore a long coat that fluttered around her ankles in the breeze, and held herself, as she always did, with an air of being fully confident of belonging completely in the space she occupied. Right now, she was leaning with a marked nonchalance against the stacked crates, her arms crossed, showing off the gleaming silver buttons on the wide cuffs of her coat.

This was the Captain – the woman in charge of the Crows' affairs in the Crescent and also the one who'd been responsible for recruiting Theo into their ranks on that moonless night ten months ago. She'd always been a distant figure in Theo's life, before and since then, yet impossible to ignore as she stalked the narrow streets of the Keeper's Crescent, striking dread into the hearts of all who saw her.

Immediately, Theo dropped into a respectful bow.

The Captain only waved a dismissive hand. 'Don't worry, I'm kidding,' she said. 'I mean, you were always going to be useless as a footsoldier – look at you.' She barked a careless laugh at that, which Theo found he didn't much appreciate. 'No. That was never what you were for really. But it's time to find out whether or not I was right in thinking you might be useful to us elsewhere. Stand up straight.'

Theo followed the order without hesitation or question, unbending from his bow to blink back at her, too wary to formulate an appropriate sentence in Navishian.

The Captain only sighed, then said, 'You heard the boys back there talking about the Kawakamis.'

'Oh . . .' Theo stammered, hedging now. 'I can't . . . Navishian, well. I try but . . .' He made a show of reaching for the words.

'You were listening to them, you heard them, and you

understood them. Don't lie, Bluejay. You speak Navishian as well as I do, and you're always paying attention. Don't think we haven't noticed.'

Theo swallowed, mouth turning dry.

'I wasn't asking you a question, just now,' the Captain continued. 'It was a statement of fact. You heard them talking.'

Theo nodded.

'Have you heard of these Kawakamis before?'

He shook his head.

'You may as well reply properly. I know you can. There's no point in trying to pretend with me.'

'No, I haven't heard of them before,' he told her, in perfect Navishian.

The Captain nodded. 'Good. Well, you've heard of them now. Come to the Shadow Column tomorrow at sunset to find out some more. Tell them Eleanor Minami sent you. And you never know – you might find this new job more suited to your particular talents than footsoldier work.'

Theo just had time to wonder if she was serious – a small, petty part of himself brightening at the idea of his being chosen for something more important than the Santos brothers could conceive of – when in one swift movement, the Captain straightened up from where she'd been leaning, turned in a swirl of her coat and gave a hard shove to the topmost crate in the stack behind her. She must have been strong, though she looked relatively slight. First, the crate teetered, then it began to fall, tumbling right towards Theo.

'Catch!' she called out, with an almost jovial note in her voice.

Theo's reaction was pure instinct – there wasn't time for anything else. Even as the crate fell, threatening to crush him

entirely, he reached inside himself, cutting through the surface
churn of thoughts direct to the steady hum of energy at his core,
sending it surging outwards and upwards.

He caught the crate just in time, harnessing the vibrations
of energy moving through the natural fibres of its wood to hold
the whole, lethally heavy mass of it perfectly still – suspended in
mid-air, just above his head.

He stepped to one side then, before allowing the crate to continue its trajectory in a controlled fall.

When he looked up, the Captain was already walking away,
her coat billowing behind her. He had no way of knowing
whether she'd witnessed what he'd just done, though apparently she'd entertained no doubts about his survival. That was
certainly concerning, especially combined with her use of that
phrase, *particular talents.*

Theo was distracted from his unease, however, by a sudden
and overwhelming feeling of nausea. He staggered, feeling almost
as if he were afflicted with vertigo, and only just managed a quick
glance around to check that no one had noticed what he'd just
done – blessedly, it seemed they hadn't – before collapsing to sit
on his crate, head spinning.

In the moment he'd saved himself, he'd felt something far
beyond the ordinary vibrations of the wood of the crate – a dis-
quietingly large surge of power, in fact, coming from whatever
was inside, seeming like an amplified version of the same, unfamiliar part-attraction, part-repulsion he'd been feeling towards
the crates all night, ever since arriving here at the docks.

The fact was that different sources of energy had different signa-
tures to them. It was true that he was able to sense energy flowing
through everything, but there were definite qualitative differences – variations in timbre, texture and amplitude – depending

on what it was that the energy happened to be flowing through. Back home, in what now felt like another life, Theo had tried to explain this variety to Susanna by comparing it to the different bird calls of the dawn chorus. Over time, and with her help, he'd become able to differentiate between the calls of all sorts of different things – plants, earth, rivers, and even air currents. The feeling he was getting from these crates tonight wasn't like anything he'd encountered before. The vibrations were simply too strong, too lacking in the usual ebbs and flows of natural variation, and too concentrated into an unfamiliar, headache-inducing intensity.

He tried to pull himself together, taking a series of slow, deep breaths of ocean air – and only found himself beginning to worry again about just how much the Captain might have seen.

It was dark out here though, he told himself, and everything had happened so fast. Even if she had seen something unusual, she could hardly properly accuse him of anything. Anyway, all he'd done was save his own life from an unprovoked attack. No one could object to that, could they?

Not feeling nearly as sure of the answer to that as he'd have liked, Theo rubbed his eyes and then finally got to his feet, looking around once more to check he was still unobserved.

When he'd begun this job at the docks, he'd promised himself that he would try his best to do everything ordinarily, just as any other footsoldier might. And yet now that he'd already used his abilities once tonight, he couldn't help but feel that there wouldn't be too much more harm in risking using them again. Anyway, if he was being realistic, it was probably the only way he was going to get any of these crates to the warehouse.

He closed his eyes and, far more calmly and steadily now than when he'd been faced with the falling crate, began the process of mentally sorting through all his surface thoughts to reach the warm steadiness that, for as long as he could remember, had burned somewhere beneath all of that noise, like a low, vibrating hum at his core.

The Gift had been the name Susanna had given to it back home in Eardland, in the days before the awful night that had formed such a hinge in his life, marking the beginning of his exile. While he knew, of course, that Susanna wouldn't think of his abilities as being anything so benign as a 'gift' anymore, he found himself persisting in clinging to the name. A part of him hadn't quite stopped hoping, perhaps, that if he simply refused to let go of it, it might still one day come to fit.

When he was able to access the Gift peacefully and in his own time like this, tuning into it could be an almost meditative process. Now, Theo did his best to ignore the intense pulse of the crates' contents and instead focused solely on the more pliable strands of energy that moved through the wooden exterior of his crate, as well as through the air surrounding it.

From there, what he needed to do was simple. He sent just the smallest surge of his own power towards those vibrations in the wood and in the air, together with a wish for lightness, and for flight – and when he tried lifting the crate again, it was easy.

Gripping it without any trouble now, he made his way over to the warehouse, even giving the Santos brothers a nod as they passed him by on their way back to the barges once more. He knew it was a risk to draw their attention. There was a chance, after all, that they would notice the curious golden glow that would surely be ringing the blue irises of his eyes by now, as it always did when he tapped into the Gift's power. It would have taken a far stronger man than he was, though, to pass up the chance of seeing the shock on their smug faces.

As Theo stepped through the warehouse's entrance, his gaze flickered over the walls of identical crates now stacked up inside. For a moment, he was tempted to try probing their contents, risking a further, more extensive use of the Gift.

He soon reminded himself, however, of what all his unquestioning colleagues outside clearly knew all too well – that where the activities of the Crows were concerned, it was usually safest to remain in the dark.

CHAPTER THREE

A Kind of Magic

1.

Eyes snapping open into darkness, Toshiko was instantly alert, tense under the blankets of her cosy futon bed. She lay quiet, working to keep her breathing slow and steady, as if she were still sleeping. From what she could make out in the gloom, her bedroom was just as it had been when she'd slipped into unsettled dreams a few hours earlier. If everything truly was undisturbed, though, what could have shocked her awake like that? She was a famously heavy sleeper, oblivious through storms, arguments and the sounds of Mei crashing around the apartment in the small hours, fixing tea and snacks after late-night sessions in her tech lab.

A few more seconds of silence passed and she began to breathe a little easier. Could it simply be her own nerves that had woken her? Even just the memory of holding the Crows' black feather between her thumb and forefinger, after all, was enough to make her want to pull the covers right up over her head and muffle her worries in the warmth of the bedding around her. She was poised to do exactly this when a scratching sound on the far side of the room signalled that she hadn't just been imagining things. She swallowed, mouth suddenly dry. Someone must have tracked her from the party and somehow got past Mei's security measures.

Trying to avoid thinking about what such a person might have come here to do, Toshiko scanned her mind for possible courses of action. Mei and Jun were asleep in the adjacent rooms. She could call out to them, but that would instantly reveal to the intruder that she was awake and knew they were here – and anyway, her siblings wouldn't be able to reach her quickly enough to help. It was up to her, it seemed , to deal with this threat on her own.

She forced herself to sit up then, ever so quietly, and look around. Nothing in the darkness was moving so far; all of the shadows and shapes in the room were just where they should be.

Noiselessly, she slid from the bed onto the floor, drawing herself up into the low, defensive stance that years of Hido training made automatic, before beginning to creep across the room.

The scratching started again, and Toshiko paced towards it, preparing to confront whatever was waiting for her in the shadows before it could surprise her first – until she fell heavily over a discarded sandal, and Mochi came shooting out from behind the hulking shape of an armchair to leap onto her back, where she lay sprawled on the floor. *Mochi.* Of course. Toshiko brushed the cat off and sat up groaning, trying not to think about the bruises she'd surely have tomorrow, or about how Mei would definitely be hooting with laughter had she been witness to that particular display of idiocy.

Mochi, usually standoffish with Toshiko, surprised her now by curling himself around her legs and purring. His slow-blinking eyes seemed to glow in the dark – twin points of amber light in the gloom.

'What are you doing?' Toshiko asked him, scratching his ears. 'Did you come in here just to scare me?'

Mochi turned a look on her that could equally have conveyed great depths of thought or total, utter blankness, before giving something between a meow and a yawn. Toshiko sighed. It seemed typical that even when Mei herself was asleep, her cat was still here, messing with her. Even so, one thing Mochi had revealed to her was just how tightly wound she really was. The tiniest familiar sound in the room had woken her and led her to presume that an assassin from the Crows had broken in to kill her.

She got to her feet, turned on the light and scooped Mochi into her arms, before padding out of her room, heading back to the living-room couches.

Earlier, the way the evening had turned out had felt so much better than the disaster into which it could have descended that she'd almost been ready to pass the mission off as a relative success. Now though, in what was not quite yet the cold light of day, reality was beginning to reassert itself. She'd failed, was the truth of it, and worse – she'd put both herself and her family in danger. Everyone on Rainshadow island knew that if you crossed the Crows they'd never let it go, even if it had only been a small infraction – and what she'd done in stealing Saito's pearl certainly wouldn't count as that anyway. The Crows had ample means of being able to seek redress, too. The Sensei, whoever they were, probably held almost as much power on the island as the Emperor.

Collapsing into the couch by the wall, Toshiko groaned and curled herself into a ball with Mochi – who seemed just about willing to put up with her holding him like this, even if he didn't look particularly pleased with the situation. It wasn't just Saito and the Crows she had to worry about, either: she'd also been seen quite clearly by the Emperor, and while the Emperor might have less of a public reputation for grisly revenge than the Sensei did, Rainshadow City certainly hadn't become the ruthlessly ordered and controlled place it was today without its head of state strictly enforcing her authority.

Toshiko had been so sure that she would be able to hold her own in a mission with Mei and Jun – that she was finally ready to find her feet and her place in this family as an equal to the two of them, instead of always being the baby of the group, needing to be looked after and worried over. How had she managed to mess things up so badly?

Her inward scolding of herself was interrupted by Mochi, wriggling to dig his claws into her shoulder.

'Hey!' Toshiko cried at the sudden sting of pain, before looking around, worried she'd woken Mei or Jun. That would be all she needed to do now – deprive them of sleep after ruining their lives. Their doors stayed firmly shut, though, the rooms beyond quiet. Mochi mewled and turned his stare on her again. Was she imagining it, or did he look even more accusing than usual?

'Fine,' she whispered to the cat. 'I'll pull myself together and stop trying to get you to comfort me. Will that make you happy?'

Mochi merely turned away, licking a paw. Whether the cat was as wise as an elder or as blank as a void, it was true that this was no way to behave. Toshiko was a Kawakami. She couldn't sit here moping. She needed to snap out of all this worrying and actually do something.

Kawakami. Toshiko could still hear the name spoken in Reiko's voice, with the particular, clear intonation Reiko had always used when she'd been talking to her three adopted charges about this favourite subject of their family name, back in their old life in the Keeper's Crescent.

'Our language, Navishian,' Reiko might have begun, warming up to her topic, 'may well seem like one seamless thing to all of you, as if it has always been this way. And yet it is quite the opposite. It is, in fact, a hotchpotch language of borrowings, drawn from many different places. You see, Rainshadow island's population and culture were actually formed from a huge variety of different peoples, all finding their way to this small island in past centuries – though you'd never know it today of course, with the way the Emperor behaves, acting as if her existing citizens are the only ones who could ever have a right to belong here. In any case, as far as the Navishian language goes, the lion's share of linguistic borrowings is from Mainlander, and even our name, Kawakami, came originally from the Mainland. Now, who can tell me what it means?'

It was a question she was liable to ask them at any point in the day – while they were preparing dinner, or cleaning their small home, or even randomly in the middle of their lessons. She always asked it, too, with the twinkling air of a teacher who has perfect confidence that her students will be able to come up with just the answer she's looking for – which they always could, of course. The meaning behind their family name had long been an old story for the three of them, this conversation repeated by Reiko so often that none of them could even remember when they'd first learnt its beats by heart.

'Above the river,' Mei was usually the first to pipe up.

'Exactly,' Reiko would smile. 'And does that simply mean that we're from the top part of a river, from upstream, near the source? Or perhaps that we live on a hill overlooking a river?'

'No,' Mei would reply. 'It means that we aren't caught up in things. That we have control.'

Reiko would always nod like this information was new and interesting to her, quite as if she hadn't been the one to drill the message into each of them from their first days of living under her roof.

'Precisely,' she would say. 'The name Kawakami is closely related to another form of the name. *Kawaue*. And that doesn't only mean to live upstream. It could also mean to fly above the river, like the birds. And if you fly above the river like the birds, you don't have to be swept up in the current below. You can choose to follow it, and find out where the river leads, or not. You can go the other way, if that is what you think is best. You have control over your own life.'

None of them, not even Jun, whose first language was Mainlander, could figure out how much of this interpretation of their name was based on any real linguistic integrity or family legacy, and how much Reiko herself had simply dreamed up on her own. Knowing Reiko, a lot of the definition had probably been embroidered, embellished and simply invented to suit her own purposes. And yet perhaps that didn't matter, Toshiko thought to herself now – perhaps that simply wasn't the important thing about it.

'*Above the river,*' she said to the cat, forcing herself up from the sofa. 'I don't just have to wait for whatever's going to happen to me. I can choose.'

Mochi only mewled vaguely and continued licking his paw.

2.

Haru yawned, watching his pebble skip across the surface of the carp pond in the Palace gardens. He hadn't slept well last night. To begin with, excitement at Risu's arrival had kept him awake.

Then, when he'd woken in the early hours only to find Risu had disappeared, he'd been so upset that he'd been unable to go back to sleep. Now, he just felt vaguely hollow and exhausted.

He rubbed his eyes, squinting as the pink dawn light played over the water, making it glitter. He was just selecting a new pebble from the path to throw at its surface when Kei appeared.

Despite how he was feeling today, Haru had to admit he was happy to see her. Kei was his favourite of the Palace's servants by far. She'd arrived on the staff three years ago, when he'd been only seven – and they'd been firm friends ever since. Gradually, over the years, she'd taken on most of the jobs that involved looking after him, and that had made Haru's life an awful lot more fun.

There were just so many things he liked about Kei. Unlike the other servants, she enjoyed games and stories – and then she had freckles, and a laugh like a startled duck that could splutter out at the most unexpected moments, and a chipped front tooth, which only made her face friendlier by messing up its otherwise symmetrical prettiness. Haru had often begged her to tell him how that tooth had been damaged, but she would only make up a more ridiculous story each time. The last one being that she'd done it falling from a ladder while painting a mural on the wall of a local tonkatsu shop. The impression Haru picked up from Kei, too, couldn't be more different from the storm he sensed from Mr Winter. It felt, in fact, exactly like splashing in puddles after spring rain.

'Today's telecast is going to be a big one,' Kei told him now as she approached the carp pond. 'There's going to be an important announcement, apparently, and the Emperor herself has requested that you be made presentable for it. Between you and me, Princeling, I wouldn't mess up this chance to redeem yourself after last night.'

Her words on their own might have sounded strict, but Kei leavened them with a grin and a wink.

Haru followed her, still yawning, back to his room, where he stood sleepy on a stool, rubbing his eyes in the bright morning light as she deftly accomplished the complicated series of knots and folds that were needed to fasten the formal robe he usually wore for special occasions. Haru never enjoyed wearing clothes like this. They made it difficult to move, and he felt old and stiff, like an adult.

'Kei,' he began as she tied a knot at his shoulder, her tongue sticking out slightly in concentration. 'Have you ever had a friend who just ... disappeared?'

For a moment he thought she hadn't heard him. She carried on with the knot until she was finished, brushed down the silk that was now covering both of his shoulders, and gave a satisfied nod.

'That's a strange thing for you to be asking about,' she replied at last. 'Do you have a friend who disappeared?'

'That's not answering the question,' Haru told her. 'I wanted to know if *you* had.'

She smiled at that. 'You're getting sharper by the day, you know. How old are you now, twenty-four? Did I miss a bunch of birthdays?'

Not to be so easily distracted, Haru folded his arms. 'But have you, though, had a friend who disappeared?'

Gently, Kei guided Haru to unfold his arms, and straightened the silk of his robe. 'I've had lots of friends, over the years,' she said. 'Some are still my friends, but a lot of them ...' She shrugged. 'We drifted apart.'

'How did you drift apart?'

'Well, some of them still live back home.'

'On Muralania?'

She nodded. 'On Muralania.'

Haru frowned. 'Muralania is really quite far away, isn't it?'

'It is indeed. Just beyond the Archipelago's southernmost edge, and over a week's sailing from Rainshadow City, even in good weather.' Kei smiled, but still managed to look a little sad.

'But you do still know where those friends are, though?' Haru persisted. 'They haven't disappeared from where you left them?'

'Well, perhaps they chose to try out life beyond the walls of Muralania too. Who knows what they did, after I left? I've been here a long time, now, after all. Probably longer than you can imagine.'

'But you're not *that* old.'

'Is that right? How old am I, then?'

Haru thought. 'On your last birthday, you were ... thirty-five.'

'Good memory,' Kei grinned. 'And at my great age I've had plenty of time to live lots of lives, and to have had lots of different friends. One of them even followed me here, all the way from home. Though I still don't get to see him as much as I'd like to.'

Her face took on an interesting expression at this, a mix of thoughtful, dreamy and regretful all at once. Haru was going to ask her who she was talking about, when the expression vanished again, as she held out one of his blue embroidered slippers.

'Foot,' she demanded with mock-sternness, and Haru balanced with one hand on her shoulder as she slid the slipper on.

'You know though, Kei,' he said at last, 'I don't think any of that is the kind of disappearing friend I meant.'

'No?' Slippers now neatly on Haru's feet, Kei sat back on her heels to look at him. 'What kind of disappearing friend did you mean then, Princeling?'

Haru looked away, suddenly unable to meet her eye. 'It'll sound ridiculous.'

'And most of what you say doesn't sound ridiculous at all.'

'Hey!'

'I'm only kidding,' she smiled. 'Try me. I say a lot of ridiculous things too.'

'It was last night.' Haru frowned, wondering how to begin.

'After the banquet?'

Haru nodded. 'When I was sent up to my room. I could have been dreaming, I suppose. But I don't think I was.'

'What happened?' Kei prompted. She looked concerned now. Haru knew she hated when he was locked up alone in his room. That was another thing he liked about her.

'Nothing bad,' Haru assured her, his eyes straying to the window, over to the bright, autumn-tipped leaves of the maple tree outside, as they waved back and forth in the breeze. The tree still looked resolutely like nothing more than a simple tree, as it had done every time Haru had checked it since waking up to find Risu gone from his room. 'It was like . . . there was a squirrel.'

'A squirrel?' said Kei, nose wrinkling.

'Not a regular squirrel.' Haru tried again. 'It was as if, suddenly, for a while, I could see the characters in things. For instance, if there was a tree, I could see who it would be if it were a person, or an animal.' His voice tailed off as he finished the sentence. 'See – I told you it would sound stupid.'

Kei was looking at him differently now though. Her usual playful expression had vanished. 'I don't think this sounds stupid at all,' she said. 'A tree's personality, you say?'

'Yes.'

'And what was this tree's personality like?'

'It was fun. Like a friend. It . . . hopped about.'

'Hopped about?'

'Yes.'

'And then what did it do, after the hopping?'

'We talked a bit. Or – I did the talking. But I'm sure it understood. Then I fell asleep, and when I woke up this morning it wasn't there anymore.'

Kei nodded deeply at that.

'Has anything like that ever happened to you?' Haru asked her hopefully.

'Not to me exactly,' she said, giving him a curious look. 'It seems there's more to you than meets the eye, Princeling.'

'What do you mean?'

Kei checked the chronometer she always wore around her neck. 'We're not late for your mother quite yet. Take a seat.' She gestured at the stool on which he was standing. 'Without creasing your robes, please.'

Haru sat carefully and folded his hands neatly in his lap, ready to listen.

'What do you know about Sun Spirits?' Kei asked him.

3.

Toshiko hesitated outside the closed door to Mei's tech lab, while Mochi immediately scratched to be let in. In truth, he was allowed into the lab much more often than she was, and Mei certainly wouldn't have liked the idea of her snooping about in it unsupervised. If Toshiko was going to come up with a plan to get them out of this situation though, then she would need to see the object at the heart of the problem – Ken Saito's pearl.

Tentatively, she pushed the door open. Mei's tech lab – or

tech cave, as Toshiko always privately thought of it – was a surprisingly large room, and even when cast in night-time gloom like this, it exuded an intimidatingly organized and streamlined atmosphere. One part of it was taken up by a bank of computers, keyboards and screens, while another wall was dense with cubby holes and drawers, each holding a different type of bot part, circuit board or adaptor. The rest of the space was filled with a work bench, a desk and a swivel chair.

Flicking the lights on tonight, the first thing to draw Toshiko's eye was a little Camera-bot, advancing across Mei's desk on spindly tripod feet to fix Toshiko with its lens. Toshiko sighed and gave the bot a wave. She could argue with Mei about this later.

She'd expected to have to search through drawers and cabinets for the pearl, but surprisingly, there it was – its appearance completely at odds with the rest of the room's orderliness in that it was lying, chain splayed, right out in the open on the desk. Next to it was a metal detector, a screwdriver, a hammer, a glass of water, a pair of pliers and a box of matches. The whole scene had an air of frustration and abandonment, as if Mei had just got sick of it all and walked off.

While Mochi jumped right onto the desk to curl up alongside this mess – the very picture of contentment – Toshiko was more hesitant. She pulled out Mei's chair and sat down carefully, imagining that her sister might stick her head around the door at any moment, thundering at her to stop touching her things. Mei didn't, though – clearly the Camera-bot was just a camera, and wasn't fitted up with any kind of fancy alert system.

Reassured by the quiet around her, Toshiko picked up the pearl and held it in her palm. It simply sat there, perfect and quiet, with the ghosts of colours shifting over its opalescent surface in the room's dim light. Again, she was struck by the sensation she'd had in the moment before she'd grabbed it from around Saito's neck – a feeling of coolness, and also of contained, controlled power, almost as if the pearl had a whole life its own, and had never truly been Saito's at all.

'Did you make me steal you?' she asked it. 'I won't be impressed if you did. I have a family, you know. You've put us all in danger.'

She turned her attention to its chain then, bending the catch back into shape from where she'd warped it, in ripping it from Saito's neck. Before long, she'd got it working perfectly again, and almost without thinking, fastened it around her own neck, slipping the pearl beneath her shirt. It felt heavy in a way that seemed disproportionate even to its considerable size, but was still far from being a burden. Instead, its weight had a reassuring quality to it, making her feel anchored. She stood and tried out what it would feel like to walk around wearing it, ignoring her sense of how Mei would surely react to see her do something so ridiculous.

'What *are* you?' she asked it, as she paced.

And then Mochi stretched out on the desk, his paw jutting out to knock Mei's spindly Camera-bot off its edge – and before Toshiko knew what she was doing, she'd leapt across the space on dancer's feet to stretch out her hands and catch the bot inches from the floor.

She blinked, frozen in position, tripod leg in hand. She shouldn't have been able to do that, she realized. After all, she'd been on the other side of the room entirely. She straightened up, anyway, and replaced the bot on the desk. It seemed completely unharmed.

'What was that?' she breathed.

Mochi only looked bored, before shifting his attention to grooming his front legs.

Toshiko lowered her gaze to her hands, turning them this way and that. Yes, she was fast, everybody said so, but what she'd just done had been surely impossible. She drew the pearl out from under her shirt again and stared at it, hard. It didn't seem to look any different. And yet, now that she thought about it, it was possible she could even have been a little faster than usual, as she'd fled the Palace with it in her pocket. At the time, she'd assumed it was only fear of Ken Saito and his blade that was spurring her onwards. Now, she couldn't help but wonder.

Letting the pearl fall back against her skin, she shot her feet and hands out into her favourite fighting stance. She threw a series of punches, and felt an easy strength and power behind them that she'd never quite felt before. From there, she spun herself first into a low kick, and then into whirling drop-kick, which took her leaping high into vertical space.

Time, then, seemed to slow down into an eternal instant through which she levitated, a creature of pure movement. All at once, she realized that she could now sense the currents of the air, swirling around her like constantly flowing chords of energy. She could even almost physically see them, at the very edge of what it was possible for her eyes to perceive: hints of shimmering gold, moving past her in sweeping curves and spirals. And suddenly she simply *knew* that if she chose, she would be able to surf any of these currents as she pleased – that she might even try seizing them, and bending the flow of their energies to her will.

Reaching for a handful of these bright chords of air, she gathered them in to support her descent as she flew downwards to finish her drop-kick with a level of precision that had never before been hers, despite years of practice.

Mochi let out a mewl of surprise, startling Toshiko into laughter. The cat was staring at her like he'd never seen her before, his fur standing on end.

'See?' she said. 'Mei's not always the only interesting one around here.'

She relaxed out of her fighting stance and tried a few simple leaps across the room, testing what new levels of height and speed she could achieve. And then, slowly, she began to realize that this was something she could use. She might not understand exactly how the pearl worked, but what she did know was that it somehow enhanced all her existing combat skills to make her a genuine force to contend with – a girl who really could fly above the river, choosing which way she wanted to go.

Toshiko had still been so young when Auntie Reiko had been murdered. She'd felt so powerless then, completely reliant on her older siblings to look after them. She still felt so shaken, too, by how little she'd been able to do to protect Auntie Reiko, the strength of her love so mismatched with how helpless she'd been. The Crows might have given them another feather, she considered now, but this time, thanks to this pearl, everything else would be different. She would take control, and she would find the Crows before they could find her. She, not they, would make the first move.

She realized, too, that she happened to have at her finger-tips the perfect means by which to plan what that move would be. Before she'd botched things with Saito at the Palace, the Kawakamis' plan had been to use his ring to hack into the Crows' bank accounts – and they'd realized, of course, that taking on the Crows like this would be a highly risky endeavour by any meas-ure, unless they had a smart way to keep one step ahead of them. Enter Mei, with what she'd dubbed her 'Birdcatcher' database.

Mei might have hated people being in her space, but just as Mei's tech lab door didn't have a lock, there were no real secrets in the Kawakami operation, and all passwords were shared. In a matter of minutes, Toshiko had logged into Mei's computer and passed through the three layers of security that were required to access the Birdcatcher. The screen flashed a deep indigo, before lighting up with the database, which took the form of a map showing all of the familiar contours, streets and tramways of Rainshadow City.

The Birdcatcher tracked the movements of eight key members of the Crows whose Comms-Discs Mei had been able to hack. Ken Saito himself, unfortunately, wasn't among them. His whereabouts were notoriously difficult to trace. The movements of these eight key players, though, were a reasonably reliable indicator of the gang's broader activities – and then the Birdcatcher had a secondary feature, too. It scanned the City Web for any mentions of the Crows, and then generated automatic alerts based on what it found, tied to the relevant locations on the map.

Looking at the Birdcatcher now, one thing was immediately obvious: something big was going on at the docks. All eight tracked Crows were there, and all but one of the activity alerts were concentrated there, too. It seemed, then, that Toshiko knew where she was going.

She returned to her room to pack a bag and get dressed, slipping on light trousers and a jacket, both loose enough to allow her the maximum freedom of movement possible. After a moment's thought, she strapped her pair of crescent moon-bladed knives to her belt, too. In spite of how dangerous they surely could be, she'd always found these knives to be quite beautiful, each one formed of two perfect, crossing arcs of sharp, polished steel, the handles in the centres of the outer blades. She'd never actually used them before, except in her Hido training, but, remembering Ken Saito's lethal-looking blade at the banquet, she figured now that they might come in useful if she did need to defend herself. She didn't pack much else – just the feather

from the Crows, along with her forged ID card and a silk purse
Mei had once gifted her, now holding a mixed handful of cloud,
moon and sun credits, both of which she shoved into her jacket's
inside pocket. From the kitchen, she grabbed a canteen of water
and a pack of rice crackers. Whatever strength and power the
pearl might give her, she knew she was still nothing without
snacks.

On her way out, she scribbled a note to Mei and Jun.

Couldn't sleep. I've gone to fix this mess. Back soon. Don't worry.

At the threshold of the apartment, she paused to whisper a
goodbye to each of her siblings' closed bedroom doors. They
would be okay, of course. They were more than capable of looking after themselves and each other. She was the one who still
needed to prove herself.

Just as she was finally turning to leave, Mochi emerged from
the shadows. After winding himself around her ankles a few
times, he used his claws to climb uncomfortably up her legs, only
to settle, a dead weight, on the top of her backpack.

'What are you doing?' Toshiko hissed at the cat. 'You can't
come with me. And you're *Mochi*. You don't want to come with
me. You don't even like me.'

Mochi meowed, but stayed put.

Toshiko shrugged. Mei would be annoyed with her anyway,
and while of course she'd been fully ready to strike out by herself,
she supposed she wouldn't say no to a bit of company. Mochi
could always find his own way home if things got too dangerous.

Closing the Kawakamis' front door softly behind her,
Toshiko made her way back out through the apartment's gaunt-
let of security measures, and into the misty chill of Rainshadow
City's streets in the early morning – one girl and a cat against
the most powerful gang on the island. With the pearl around

her neck, though, she didn't feel afraid, she realized. She felt powerful.

4.

'What do I know about Sun Spirits?' Haru frowned, blinking at Kei in the early-morning light that was still streaming from his windows.

Kei nodded, affirming her question as she shuffled around on the floor to sit cross-legged opposite him, looking up to where he was still perched on his stool. 'Have you heard of them before?'

'I think I did have some books about them when I was very small.' Haru chewed his lip. 'But my mother got rid of those. I don't think she likes Sun Spirits very much. She told me not to talk about them.'

'Well,' said Kei, 'then I suppose we'll just have to make sure she doesn't hear us.' She cast a glance around the room, empty but for the two of them. 'Do you know what Sun Spirits really are?'

Haru shook his head. 'I don't remember much.'

'That's okay,' Kei told him. 'Sun Spirits are very special beings, in that they come from the ancient life force that flows constantly through every natural element of our world, animating living things, and governing all the growth, movement and change around us – and within us, too. Ultimately, this life force comes from the sun, because all life and energy in our world starts with the sun. And that's where it gets its name – *Sola*. You've heard of Sola before, haven't you?'

Haru nodded. 'The priests talk about it in my lessons, sometimes. Though they never really explained what it is, properly.' He frowned. 'They certainly never said anything about a flowing life force, or about Sola being everywhere, in all living things.'

Kei sighed. 'That doesn't surprise me. No one here in Rainshadow City understands much about Sola, especially not those priests. On Muralania, though, we keep to the older ways, and so we've held on to knowledge that's been lost, almost everywhere through the Archipelago. Why don't you try saying it?' She nodded to Haru, then. 'Go on. *Sola*.'

'Sola,' Haru repeated.

She smiled. 'Very good. Even if the Rainshadow priests might not know much about it, they probably do still understand a few basic things. For instance, when they're talking about Sola in your lessons, who do they say are made from it?'

Haru furrowed his brow, thinking, then sprang up from his stool, buoyed with the excitement of knowing the answer.

'The Gods!' he cried – and then paused, suddenly uncertain. 'I'm not sure I understand how Gods can actually be made from Sola, though,' he said, as Kei took his hand and helped him to sit back down, without creasing his robes too badly. 'I mean, surely it isn't possible for anyone to be completely made out of life force, or sun energy – or whatever you said Sola is.'

'It's not impossible for the Gods,' Kei told him. 'You could even think of Gods as what comes into being when there are surges or spikes in the intensity of the world's Sola field.'

'Spikes?' Haru frowned.

Kei nodded. 'Yes. By which I mean such high concentrations of Sola that all the energy has to go somewhere, or do something.'

'And so . . . it goes into making a God?' Haru puzzled out, as Kei nodded again. 'But what makes a spike happen?' he asked.

'You know, I don't think there are any strict rules about it,' mused Kei. 'High concentrations of Sola seem to come from lots of different things. A spike could happen because of something slow and simple, for instance, like a tree living for a remarkably long period of time, or from something sudden and powerful, like a powerful storm, or even a hurricane. I've even heard of spikes happening because of how we interact with the world, as humans – as a result of someone making an object with a great deal of love, for instance. Or because a strong emotion as been felt particularly intensely in a particular place – like extreme happiness. Or sadness, too.'

Haru considered it. 'I think I sort of understand,' he told her, eventually. 'But what does Sola have to do with Sun Spirits?'

'Well, you see it's not just Gods who are made from Sola,' Kei told him. 'All Sun Spirits are.'

'Wait,' Haru interrupted, confused again. 'But if Sun Spirits are made from Sola, wouldn't that mean they're just the same as Gods?'

'In a way, yes,' Kei smiled. 'Not all Sun Spirits are worshipped as Gods, though – but then again, that's not up to them. That's up to us – and what we humans choose to do.'

Haru frowned, his mind getting tangled, now, in everything she was saying. 'So you're saying all Gods are Sun Spirits, and all Sun Spirits could be Gods, if humans chose to see them that way?'

Kei nodded.

Haru shook his head. 'That doesn't seem right, though,' he told her. 'If Sun Spirits are just like the Gods, then my mother wouldn't dislike them so much, would she? I mean, she loves the Gods. Yuto, especially. Yuto, God of Ambition.' Even just saying Yuto's name out loud reminded Haru to stop slouching on his stool.

Kei gave him a curious look at that, and Haru realized then that they'd never really discussed particular Gods like this before. It felt strange to think that perhaps Kei didn't love Yuto the way his mother did.

'But why would my mother not like Sun Spirits, though,' Haru asked again, 'if they really are just like Gods?'

Kei seemed to consider this carefully before answering. 'I think maybe,' she began, speaking very evenly now, 'it could be because your mother sees it as her job to keep control of everything in her Empire. Perhaps she only likes Gods whose priests answer to her, and who she knows will pass on messages she's approved to everyone who worships at their shrines.'

'I don't know about that.' Haru shook his head. Everything Kei was saying seemed too much to consider all at once. 'Anyway though, do you mean you think it was a Sun Spirit that I saw in my room last night?' he asked, bringing the conversation back onto more solid ground.

'It sounds like it to me,' Kei told him. 'That's definitely what anyone from Muralania would say, anyway, if you told them what you told me, about that squirrel. And if it really was a Sun Spirit, you'll be interested to know that's a sign of you being a very special person, Princeling.'

'How do you mean?' Haru asked.

'Not just anyone can see Sun Spirits. In fact, practically no one can. To see one, you'd have to be deeply in tune with the particular flows of Sola which animate them. Even people who've spent their lives becoming expert in channelling Sola can struggle to achieve such levels of perception.' Kei gave him a puzzled look. 'Have you ever seen any creatures like that squirrel before?'

'I don't think so.' Haru frowned. Then he shifted his gaze to watch the tree again, outside the window. 'If I really do have a special talent, though, then why would the squirrel – the Sun Spirit – just disappear? Why would it leave like that?'

Kei only shook her head, eyes filling with sympathy. 'I'm sorry,

Princeling. I really couldn't say. It's a very rare and lucky thing to have seen one at all.'

'But I miss it,' Haru said. 'I felt lonely, and it came to help me. I thought we were friends.'

'Sun Spirits can be mischievous,' Kei told him. 'You can't always trust them.'

Haru shook his head. 'This was a friendly one, I'm sure of it.' He thought for a moment, staring hard at the tree. 'Maybe it's hiding, for some reason. Or maybe it's me who's forgotten how to see it.' He jumped down from where he'd been perched on the stool to sit opposite Kei on the floor. 'How many Sun Spirits are there?'

Kei laughed. 'In total? Maybe thousands? Maybe hundreds of thousands? Probably more.'

Haru gasped. 'No one knows?'

Kei smiled. 'No one knows.'

'Have you ever seen any?'

Kei seemed to be about to answer, but then glanced down at her chronometer. The day had been heating up as they'd been talking – the sun, outside the windows, edging up from the horizon over the water.

'I should take you to your mother,' she said. 'She'll want to check you over, before the telecast.'

Haru made a face. 'Only if you tell me if you've ever seen a Sun Spirit, too,' he said. 'Or if you've met anyone else who's seen one, back on Muralania. Please.'

Kei checked her chronometer again. 'Okay,' she said. 'Just quickly then. When I was only a little bit older than you, maybe about eleven or twelve, a dragon came to the lake in our village.'

'You've seen a *dragon*?' Haru stared, trying to figure out whether she was being serious.

Of course he'd heard the stories that there were still dragons living on Muralania – everyone had – but there were certainly no dragons anywhere near Rainshadow island, and it seemed almost unreal to Haru that someone who he knew as well as Kei, who combed his hair and organized his clothes and whom he spoke to every day, could actually have seen one.

'I have indeed seen a dragon,' Kei said, smiling broadly at his incredulity. 'They're actually not all that uncommon, on Muralania. They're still very special, though, and it's considered the luckiest thing possible if you see one. Can you think why?'

Haru considered. 'Because dragons are so strong?'

Kei laughed. 'Kind of, yes. But also because dragons are Sun Spirits too. They're the kings and queens of the Sun Spirits, in fact – the strongest and proudest of them all. They're the only kind of Sun Spirit most people will ever see, because they're the exception to what I told you earlier, about Sun Spirits being very difficult for humans to perceive. Dragons are born from such enormous surges of Sola that they're difficult to miss.'

'So that's how you saw the one that came to your village,' Haru said.

Kei nodded. 'That's not the only amazing thing about dragons, either,' she continued. 'They're actually able to channel and guide flows of Sola, using the power of special pearls that they all have at their throats – and like this, they can do such incredible things you'd hardly believe it. They can even use their pearls to draw extra Sola out of a type of rock that only exists deep within the Muralanian mountains. We call it draconic ore, because it seems that there's frozen Sola locked up within its deposits – Sola which only the dragons know how to draw out and set flowing again, harnessing its energy to increase their strength and abilities.'

'So dragons really are kind of . . . magic?' Haru reddened. He did feel a little ridiculous, asking such a question.

Until Kei nodded, and he couldn't help but grin back at her with delight.

'I wish a dragon would come here,' he said, 'to Rainshadow island. Or that I could go to Muralania, to see the dragons there.'

At that, Kei gave him a slightly sad smile. 'Maybe one day I'll take you,' she told him.

'Really?' Haru gasped. 'You would do that?' He couldn't hide his excitement at the idea.

'Maybe,' was all she replied, though – and suddenly Haru wasn't sure if she'd meant it at all.

'Now, Princeling,' she continued. 'We'd better get on, or we'll be late for your mother. Stand up and give me a twirl.'

Haru only scowled and stayed put, cross-legged on the floor.

'Do you want to get us both in trouble?' Kei looked more serious now, like she did whenever she was too busy with other work around the Palace and he tried to distract her into playing a game. All the talk of dragons and Sun Spirits was definitively at an end, then.

Haru sighed. 'No, I don't want to get us in trouble,' he said, and pushed himself to his feet. He gave her a half-hearted spin, so she could see his outfit.

'Perfect,' Kei told him. 'Now all you need is a smile.'

5.

Early morning at the docks had a particular kind of bleached-out beauty. The sky over the ocean was washed in patterns of pale yellows and golds as the sun tried to burn through the morning mist. The waves were tipped with light, and the wet surfaces of the quayside and the slatted platforms leading out to sea reflected the marbled sky.

What must have been about forty people – all of them Crows, Toshiko suspected – sat, or lounged, or simply stared out to the ocean. A few drank from canteens of water while others dragged on cigarettes, blowing smoke out into the dawn. All of them looked exhausted.

Alongside them was a hint of the night's hard labour they'd just passed. Six large cargo barges were moored by the docks, all empty now, with their crews preparing to depart – all except for the outermost barge in the row, from which two tired-looking Crows were still removing one last wooden crate. Toshiko watched as they grappled with it. These men looked strong, all muscle and swagger, yet this seemed a challenge even for them. Working together, the two of them managed to heft it into their arms before beginning a slow and awkward journey towards the open doors of a waiting warehouse, all the way down the quay. Toshiko clocked the Crows' logo on the crate's side as they passed the spot where she was hiding with Mochi, crouched behind a hillock in the scrubland that separated the docks from the Keeper's Crescent behind her.

She hadn't been so close to the Crescent's barbed-wire fences since she'd lived on the other side of them. Being physically closer to this place where they'd lost Auntie Reiko, and had lived so completely in the shadow of the Crows' menace, seemed to make it all feel rawer to her now – as if it were a lot more recently than five years ago that all of this had happened. She shivered, and sent a silent apology to the Keeper that she wasn't able to feel gladder to visit him today, just in case he was listening. Then she turned her attention back to the Crows.

'What do you suppose they're up to?' she muttered to Mochi, who had chosen, as his preferred means of travel, to sit heavily in her backpack with his head poking out from the undone zip at the top. The cat, unsurprisingly, elected to remain silent, simply digging his claws into Toshiko's back as he shifted into a comfier position in the bag.

She sighed in resignation, then began to edge along the length of the hillock that was keeping her hidden, trying as she did to keep pace with the two men and their crate as they made their way towards the warehouse door. The pearl, at least, gave her the ability to move so lightly on her feet that she was almost noiseless.

None of the alerts on Mei's database had managed to communicate anything about what the Crows' business here might be, and try as she might, Toshiko couldn't even begin to guess at anything specific. One thing was already clear, though: while everything the Crows did was shady, this whole operation definitely had a particular air of secrecy about it. If she could just find out what was in those crates, and, what's more, what it was *for*, she'd bet on that being useful knowledge to use against Ken Saito.

She'd been taking care to keep within the relative shelter of the scrubland, but as the men with the crate moved up alongside the Crows' line of warehouses, it became impossible to stay where she was and also keep watching them. A quick glance back to the waterfront told her that most of the Crows here were distracted – either lost to their own weariness or, in the case of one group, which was talking loudly and throwing stones out into the waves, to their keenness to prove that they weren't actually weary at all. Bending low, to keep herself out of anyone's eyeline as far as was possible, Toshiko dashed out of the scrubland's safety and into the warehouse's shadow.

What are you doing? she imagined Mei hissing into her ear then, as she surely would have been doing, had this been a regular Kawakami mission, with Toshiko wearing an earpiece. *So this is the plan, then? Just being out in the open? Could you be any more obvious?*

Fine, Toshiko thought, unaccountably missing Mei's constant interfering a little now, and wishing, just for a moment, that she really did have her sister there to provide her typical commentary.

As she looked around, scanning the area for possible better options, her gaze lighted on a fisherman's oilskin coat, thrown over a quayside railing. It would probably be a little big for her, but it was a nicely unassuming dark green, and would undoubtedly help her blend in better within the dockland setting. It also didn't look as if anyone was keeping an eye on it, having the air of a garment cast off in the midst of a busy night only to be subsequently forgotten. Staying low, she scuttled over to the coat, grabbed it, and shrugged it on, covering both her backpack and Mochi, who let out a yowl of surprise.

'Shhhh,' she told him. 'It's better if you're hidden.'

Amazingly, he didn't protest any further. Perhaps she was finally seeing some positive effects from his lifelong habit of burrowing into clothes and bedding.

The coat wasn't just big – it drowned her, falling heavily to her ankles. It also smelled strongly of an unappetizing blend of fish and chewing tobacco. She wrinkled her nose but decided to stick with it, rolling up the sleeves so that she could at least use her hands, and then throwing the hood up over her head.

Disguise now sorted as best as possible, she made her way back over to the warehouse. The entrance was wide, and there only seemed to be two Crows there on duty to stand guard. With so many Crows going in and out tonight, high security evidently hadn't seemed practical.

Trying to move with an air of nonchalant confidence, Toshiko wandered right up to the side of the entrance that was furthest from the Crows' security guards. They seemed absorbed, in any case, in an argument about which Fighter-bot was sure to win the current Bot-Battles tournament: clearly, it had been both a long and a slow night for them. Making an effort not to quicken her pace so much as to make herself conspicuous, Toshiko walked right past them, and stepped inside.

The warehouse's interior was dim, the long aisles of stacked crates inside illuminated only by overhead strips of granitarium-powered electric light. In spite of their struggling with that last crate outside on the quay, the men she'd seen earlier had obviously made their way deep inside by now. She could hear the distant, faint sounds of their voices and shuffling feet.

The whole place was otherwise very quiet and very still, and yet it also felt somehow expectant to Toshiko, as if it weren't filled with something so mundane as simply crates at all, and instead housed some sort of large creature – currently sleeping, but still quite ready to be woken at any moment. Taking care to tread lightly, she began moving between two walls of crates.

She'd only managed a few steps, though, before she froze again at the sound of two new voices, echoing towards her out of the hush. These people, it sounded like, were walking down the aisle to her left. They didn't seem like footsoldier Crows, somehow. Both voices – one belonging to a woman, the other to a man – carried certain levels of assurance to them, as if whoever these people might be, they were more accustomed to giving orders than to manual labour.

'It's a possibility,' the female voice was saying. 'We should be taking precautions, is all I'm saying. It could still be hazardous, when stored in these quantities.'

'Those mountain-dwellers seem fine, by all accounts.'

'But you would never find it in this kind of concentration in the mountains. It would be diluted, scattered amidst normal rock.'

'What do you propose we do, though? Tell the Sensei this

whole operation was a mistake, and that we have to send it all back to Muralania?'

'I'm not saying it's necessarily a mistake to have brought it here. Only that it's powerful stuff. We don't know enough about it yet to be complacent.'

Toshiko turned on the spot and silently retraced her steps to the end of her aisle of crates. Then, ever so carefully, she peered around to see who was talking.

A woman in a lab coat and a man in a business suit were coming slowly down the shadowed aisle towards her. The woman was all earnest hand gestures, while the man had his hands in his pockets, and was walking a little more quickly than she was. He looked distracted, as if he knew there was somewhere else he needed to be, but couldn't quite remember where that was.

'Look,' he was saying to the woman now. 'The Sensei seems certain this is necessary, and important for the future of the Crows. Isn't that enough?'

'Maybe,' the woman sounded anxious, 'but after what happened on Hanasaki Island ...' she sighed. 'I know that we're following a different process now, but it still makes me uncomfortable. I can't help but wonder if it shouldn't be here, like this. It doesn't seem safe. It's just—' she paused, seeming to search for the right word. 'It's *unnatural*.'

The man stopped walking, and whirled to face her. 'You should be careful who hears you say that.'

The woman took a step back, away from him, and in doing so the scope of her gaze widened sufficiently to take in the shadowed form of Toshiko, watching from the end of the aisle. Toshiko immediately ducked back out of sight, but it was too late.

'Hey, you, footsoldier. You shouldn't be in here,' the woman was saying now, her steps ringing out on the warehouse floor as she quickened her pace towards where Toshiko was crouched, trying to disappear into the shadows, into the fisherman's coat, into the air.

6.

The morning found Jun sewing – hunched in a chair in the circle of pale, early-morning light filtering in from his high bedroom window, as he mended the torn shoulder of a jacket he'd worn during the Kawakamis' Granitarium Investments heist, last year.

Couldn't sleep. I've gone to fix this mess. Back soon. Don't worry.

The words of Toshiko's note circled in his head as he moved the silver needle in and out of the midnight-blue fabric, trying to calm his breathing. Usually, sewing calmed him down. After leaving the Keeper's Crescent, he'd quietened his grief and soothed the worries he'd felt at their new life's dangerous uncertainty by stitching scraps and mending second-hand clothes, until slowly, incrementally, he'd found himself becoming more expert at it.

From the beginning of the Kawakamis' new life outside of the Crescent, Jun had been their on-the-ground intelligence gatherer, using his skills with people to obtain any key information that they hadn't been able to get through Mei's hacking skills, but had still needed in order to pull off the various heists which had finally given them the financial foundation they'd needed to survive in the city, just the three of them. It hadn't been long before it had seemed like the natural thing to appoint him as the family's resident costume maker, too – and so Jun had begun a sideline in disguises, turning whatever rags and cast-offs he could find around the city into clothes which could win him confidences, and open important doors.

Jun's prowess at sewing, however, hadn't started with stitching costumes at all. It had begun, in fact, with stitching wounds. Back in the Keeper's Crescent, Jun had always assumed that he might grow up to have a career as a healer. He'd shown a talent for it, helping out the community's only real healer, and unofficial matriarch – a woman called Mailee, who, in her life before the Crescent, had worked as a nurse in the hospital over on Vilmia, an island in the Archipelago's south-west. Mailee had never told Jun precisely what it was that had driven her to leave her old home, and Jun hadn't pried. Mailee, like a lot of the Keeper's Children, clearly hadn't wanted to dwell on her past.

When she'd arrived here on Rainshadow island, in any case, Mailee hadn't been in possession of the crucial ID card that would have allowed her to get a job in the city's hospital. And so, as she'd waited for her application to be processed, she'd begun healing those in the Crescent around her who'd needed medical help, giving them treatment in return for whatever they could afford to pay – or even for free, sometimes, if they couldn't afford anything. She hadn't expected to be living like this for too long. As a trained medical professional, surely she'd be welcomed into Rainshadow City soon enough?

And yet, when Jun had first met Mailee twenty-seven years later, she'd still been in the Crescent, setting broken bones, stitching wounds and treating fevers, coughs and colds. In that time, she'd become invaluable to the Keeper's Children. After all, there were no hospitals in the Crescent, and so for the sick and injured, she was the only real alternative to the kakogan dust that was sold everywhere by the Crows. A by-product of granitarium production, kakogan dust did happen to be a powerful painkiller, but it was also dangerously addictive and, unlike Auntie Mailee, as everyone in the Crescent called her, it couldn't actually heal anything.

When Mei and Toshiko had found Jun, all alone as a

six-year-old child on the scrubland, he'd been very sick, still suffering from the fever that had afflicted most of the passengers on the boat he'd taken over from the Mainland – the same fever that had killed his mother, who'd been the only one travelling with him. Auntie Reiko had taken him straight to Mailee, and after days of her care and attention, Jun's sickness had passed. As he'd recovered his strength, he'd sat by her, so that she could keep a close eye on him while she did her work in treating others.

Unable to follow the language of any of the conversations around him, Jun had instead focused his attention on watching Mailee work, and gradually, as he'd learnt more Navishian, he'd fallen into helping her. Before long, it had become clear that he had a way with people – a natural sensitivity to how they might be feeling, as well as to the nature of their suffering. He had a talent, too, for observing people closely and giving them the full, unwavering focus of his attention, often finding the true source of their sickness or pain, even before they were aware of it themselves.

As an undocumented person though, Jun, like Mailee, would never be able to work as a healer here in Rainshadow City proper. While Mei had done a good job of mocking them up false ID cards, which were fine for duping shopkeepers, along with the odd over-curious Imperial Guard, these still only partially connected to the all-important Citizenry Database, which remained, even with Mei's continued efforts, largely un-hackable. If anyone scanned Jun's false card and did any digging whatsoever into his profile, they would soon discover that, according to city records, its bearer didn't officially exist – and the consequences of that kind of discovery in Rainshadow City would be far worse than simply being barred from getting a job. Undocumented people who were found beyond the Crescent's fences were liable to disappear permanently.

And so Jun had left behind ambitions in the Crescent, too,

alongside responsibilities when he'd chosen to leave Mailee on her own once again to take care of all the people who came to her for help. And yet, as he reminded himself whenever guilt at this decision threatened to overwhelm him, he'd only been fifteen when Auntie Reiko had died – surely far too young to be held to such a large commitment as helping Mailee look after everyone in the Keeper's Crescent forever, regardless of what might be happening in his own life. Ultimately, too, he'd had to do what was best for his sisters. For Jun, family always came first, as he hoped was the case for all the Kawakamis.

Couldn't sleep. I've gone to fix this mess. Back soon. Don't worry.

Jun had rolled up his sleeves before beginning his work on the jacket, and his gaze caught now on the tattoo of three terns in flight over a river, which was clearly visible on his arm, just above his right wrist. Three birds, flying together. And yet now Toshiko had gone and put herself in the position of being alone somewhere out in the city, with the Crows, of all people, hunting her. Toshiko – his baby sister and the girl he'd sworn to Auntie Reiko he'd always protect.

'Wow, you're really mending that jacket.' Mei finally appeared in Jun's bedroom doorway, still in pyjamas and with her hair knotted into an uncharacteristically haphazard bun on the top of her head. Jun had woken her a few minutes ago, Toshiko's note in hand, the panic of its discovery having shocked him awake far more efficiently than coffee had ever managed to do. Mei didn't have any of her trademark make-up on yet, and generally looked decidedly groggy. It was still only just after dawn, and she often rose as late as noon.

Jun blinked at her, pushing his glasses up his nose from where they'd been slipping. 'How do you mean?'

Mei smiled, though she looked worried, too. 'You're just doing a very thorough job of mending it, is all. Does it really need quite so many stitches in the same place?'

Jun blinked and looked down. She was right. In his distraction he maybe had gone a little overboard. He sighed. 'What do you think we should do, though?' he asked. 'I don't even know where to start looking for her. She could be anywhere.'

Mei bit her lip. 'I shouldn't have asked her to steal the ring. Or I shouldn't have sprung it on her, at least. Then none of this would have happened.'

Jun sighed. 'Don't beat yourself up.'

'It's my fault, though. I pushed her too hard, before she was ready.'

'No one's perfect, I suppose,' he told her.

Mei rubbed her eyes and looked annoyed.

'Though I could have done things differently, too,' Jun added then, hurriedly. 'I could have been stricter with her last night, for instance. I could have made sure she didn't try anything stupid.'

Mei smiled. 'You're never strict.'

'No, that's your job.'

'I'm not strict. Strict implies a level of being responsible. I'm scary.'

Jun frowned down at the jacket on his lap. There was no point, really, in their going over how things could have been different. A plan was what they needed, but Mei's usually formidable brain power didn't seem to have kicked in yet, so far out of her usual waking hours.

'Maybe I'll start at the covered market,' he told her. 'I could ask the traders if they've seen or heard anything that could give us a lead as to where she might have gone. They're always up so early, there's a chance they may have done.'

'If you take the earpiece, I could talk to you. Give suggestions.'

Jun nodded. 'That would be good. Did you make any progress on the pearl last night, by the way?'

Mei shook her head, sending several loose strands of hair escaping from her messy bun. 'I stayed up for hours, and tried all sorts. I scanned it for bugs and explosives, used a metal detector, tried X-raying it, and I even used my new electromagnetic scanner. That was weird. This little light came on that I've never seen before. It seemed like a glitch, though, as it seemed to be saying that the pearl was giving off thermal radiation, which didn't even make sense, as it still felt cool to touch. So, then I just tried smashing the pearl with a hammer, anyway, to see if there was anything inside – but I couldn't even scratch it. And then I had a go at setting it on fire.' She rolled her eyes at Jun's look of alarm. 'Oh don't worry,' she told him. 'Of course it wouldn't burn. It didn't even char. It just sat there like, *whatever dude, you think I care about flames?* And then I tried leaving it in a glass of water for a bit.'

'And?'

'It just ... does nothing. I can't scratch it, break it, burn it, open it, discover anything about it. Apart from that weird little light on the scanner, which didn't even make any logical sense, it's like the pearl's just completely inert. Like nothing in the world can interact with it sufficiently to have any lasting effect.'

'Can I see it?'

Mei shrugged. 'Sure.'

A moment later she was back, looking spooked. 'It's gone,' she told him.

Jun stared. 'Did Tosh take it?'

'I don't know. Maybe? Could someone have broken in?'

'We could check the cameras.'

The footage from the CCTV covering the front entrance and all of the windows showed nothing happening all night until just before 5am, when the front door camera had caught Toshiko leaving. Mei let out a low hiss as they sat at the dining table and watched.

'She took the cat,' she growled. 'I can't believe she would take the cat.'

The footage from the Camera-bot that Mei had set up in her tech lab managed to frustrate her even more, if that were possible. It all seemed to be there, recorded, but after showing Toshiko coming through the door, all it had captured was a bright, white blankness, almost as if something had burned out the image. Mei took the battery panel off the back of the bot and checked its levels of granitarium, which seemed to be fine, before replacing the panel and testing the camera again, taking some footage of the bowl of lychees on the table. It seemed to be working completely normally, now.

'None of this makes any sense,' she huffed. 'I hate it. And I want my cat back.'

'Mochi will be okay,' Jun tried to reassure her. 'I don't think the Lucky Crows are very interested in cats.'

Mei sighed. 'We can do this, can't we, brother? We can keep Tosh safe and show the Crows that they can't mess with us – right?'

Jun shrugged. 'If anyone's coming after my family, I'm certainly not going to make it easy for them.'

Mei nodded – a solemn, sharp movement that set her messy hair quivering. 'You're right,' she said. 'Above the river.' And then she helped herself to a lychee.

7.

The two Crows kept coming towards Toshiko through the shadowed warehouse, the sounds of their quickening footsteps bouncing off the towers of crates.

'You stay where you are, you hear me?' called out the woman in the lab coat, as she advanced down the aisle.

Feeling oddly calm in the pungent swathes of her fisherman's coat, Toshiko realized she had a clear decision before her. She could try to run, and carry on sneaking and spying, or she could do something different. And, ultimately, she hadn't come here this morning just to lurk in the shadows, had she?

What did you come here to do then, sister? she imagined Mei asking her.

It was lucky Mei wasn't actually in her ear, as Toshiko definitely didn't feel ready to answer that question yet.

What she did feel ready to do, though, thanks to the pearl, was stop hiding. She drew herself up tall and stepped forward into the dim glow of the strip lighting overhead. The two Crows had almost reached her now.

'What are you doing in here?' the man asked. 'The job is finished. No more footsoldiers allowed.'

Toshiko took another step closer towards them. 'What makes you think I'm a footsoldier?' she asked, her voice ringing out loud amid the hush of the warehouse.

'What?' said the man. 'What did you say?'

Toshiko answered by lowering her hood, then shedding the coat entirely. 'I told you, I'm not a footsoldier.'

'Hey,' said the woman. 'It's that girl. From the photograph. The girl Saito wanted.'

'You're going straight to Saito,' said the man. 'Don't you even try to run.'

And then they were on her, rough hands seizing her shoulders – their earlier argument forgotten as they worked together to secure her arms behind her back. Mochi, whom Toshiko had suspected of snoozing beneath the coat, yowled then with all the frustration of the unexpectedly woken. He climbed up fully onto her shoulders and began swiping at the Crows with his claws, tearing at the woman's lab coat and sending both Crows into fits of cursing.

A part of Toshiko's mind was screaming for her to do something to resist, too. These two didn't look like fighters, and she was sure she could take them, especially with the pearl to help her. So why was she struggling in only the most cursory way – pretending, really, while actually letting them take her prisoner?

Instead of listening to these thoughts, though, Toshiko hushed the cat. Mochi gave the man one more nasty scratch on the forehead, but then managed to settle into a tense mass of bristling fur and wary eyes. Without Mochi to concern them, the two Crows doubled down in their efforts to pin Toshiko's arms behind her back – and, after only the merest wriggle of protest, Toshiko let them.

The man spat on the warehouse floor. 'I can't wait to see what Saito does when he gets hold of you,' he rasped, as blood dripped a jagged trail down his forehead from where Mochi had slashed at him.

Toshiko did her best to arrange her face into a convincing expression of terror. It wasn't hard. She just summoned up all the fear and powerlessness she'd felt in that moment five years before, when Saito had murdered her aunt and broken their family. It certainly seemed to convince the two Crows holding her. They broke into matching grins.

'Oh, don't look like that, sweetie,' the woman said. 'He'll be so happy to see you.'

CHAPTER FOUR

Ruffling Feathers

1.

Couldn't sleep. I've gone to fix this mess. Back soon. Don't worry.
For what felt like the hundredth time that morning, Jun cursed Toshiko's note as he paced up and down the waterfront, scowling at the terns as they dipped their wings over the water. This simply wasn't what the Kawakamis did. They worked together, and always would. It was what Reiko had wanted, and what they'd sworn to each other they'd do after she'd been killed. It was even why they'd got the tattoos. It was the *whole point.*

'Wait, I'm onto something,' Mei said in his ear, sounding suddenly alert.

'You are? What is it?'

'I've just checked the activity log on my computer. Looks like Tosh logged in last night and accessed the Birdcatcher.'

'The Birdcatcher? Why would she do that?'

'Maybe because she was looking for a way to "fix this mess", as she puts it,' Mei said. 'There was increased Crows activity down at the docks overnight. You could try looking around that way, if you're careful?'

Jun was already pacing down the promenade, over to the little knot of four boatmen standing smoking by a clutch of rowing boats, moored by the nearest landing stage. Not so long ago – surely within the lifetimes of these four boatmen's parents – fishing had been the main industry on the island. Now that everything had changed, boatmen like these did as much work as an unofficial water-taxi service, ferrying citizens to and fro, as they did any actual fishing.

'I need to go to the docks,' Jun told them. 'Who can take me?'

The fishermen looked non-committal. One of them shrugged.

'I can pay,' Jun said.

'Seven cloud credits,' declared the oldest of them – a skinny, weather-beaten man, hardened enough to days on the ocean to be wearing only a thin, threadbare shirt with no coat or jacket, despite the early-morning chill.

'Excuse me, *how* much?' Mei was saying, incredulous down the earpiece, but Jun didn't have it in him to bargain this morning.

'Fine,' he told the old man. 'Just take me there.'

2.

The woman in the lab coat and the man in the business suit marched Toshiko down the docks to what looked like a simple boathouse. When the doors swung open, though, they revealed a doorman – a young man in bottlecap glasses and a hanten jacket – and then behind him, an interior that was about as far from any ordinary boathouse as the Imperial Palace was from a Keeper's Crescent dwelling.

Toshiko's first impressions were those of candlelight and cigar smoke. As her eyes blinked through the haze and adjusted to the relative darkness, she took in polished floors leading up to a raised, central platform, on which stood a huge table – round, heavy-looking and carved from dark wood. Around it lounged a handful of individuals who were all stylishly if ostentatiously dressed in sharp suits, expensive-looking silks and conspicuous jewellery. They seemed to be playing cards – gambling for the large piles of sun and moon credits scattered on the tabletop. At the centre of the group sat a familiar figure whose eyes flicked up to meet her own.

'You,' Ken Saito said, immediately discarding his hand of cards. He laughed, in a way that couldn't have sounded any further from friendly. 'Nice cat.'

He seemed a lot more at home here than he had in the Palace gardens. The raw aggression with which he carried himself – evident even in the way that he now cracked his knuckles over his discarded hand of cards – seemed allowed to fully spread out here, unhindered by the confining demands of gentility and diplomacy. And yet Toshiko did notice, too, that he definitely looked a little more frayed at the edges than he had last night. He had dark shadows under his eyes, and as she watched him, a muscle jumped restlessly in his right eyelid. Briefly, incongruously, she found herself wondering if she might not be the only one who had struggled to sleep last night.

The other Crows were looking back and forth between him and Toshiko, where she still stood in the doorway with the two

Crows who'd brought her here still gripping her arms. Careful not to move her gaze away from Saito, Toshiko counted six of them in the periphery of her vision. Together with the two Crows still holding her, and the young guy who'd opened the door, that made nine adversaries in total. She swallowed. *Above the river*, she reminded herself. She refused to let Saito treat her as prey – as if she were someone he could terrorize with such simple things as feathers, whenever he saw fit.

'I have something of yours,' she told him. 'I came to return it.'

Saito's eyes flashed hungry, the muscle in his eyelid seeming to jump with greater ferocity. 'Now this is a surprise,' he said. 'Good girl.'

'You'll have to tell your lackeys to let go of my arms though, if you want it back,' she said. 'It's in my backpack.'

'Ah yes,' he grinned. 'Keiko and Rico. The Sensei's pet scientists.' He gave them both a nod. 'Until now, I have to say I didn't understand why we kept you around, but it seems you can be good for more than just messing about with obscure minerals. Let her go. And enjoy knowing that in bringing her to me, you've finally done something useful. I can take it from here.'

As they dropped Toshiko's arms, she could sense the relief emanating from both of them, at no longer having to be so near Mochi – who immediately leapt off her backpack to take up a defensive position at her feet. As Toshiko slipped out of her bag's straps, she wondered what possible use the Sensei could have for scientists. And what did Saito mean, *obscure minerals*?

She didn't have time to ponder this now, though. She was busy rummaging in her backpack, making a show of the process. 'It's in here somewhere . . .' she said.

'Get on with it,' said Saito.

'Got it!' she cried out, triumphant, as she pulled out the black feather, holding it up into the light of a nearby candle so that he couldn't miss what it was. Then, she lowered it into the flame.

Saito and the Crows around him watched the feather singe and curl. When finally she dropped it, embers flared bright against the darkness of its charred remains, as it caught the breeze from the open door and then drifted, smoking, to her feet.

Saito's expression soured. He stood, pushing his chair back to give Toshiko a clear view of the long, curved knife at his belt, which she remembered only too well from last night at the Palace.

'You shouldn't have done that,' he told her.

3.

A fine mist lurked over the waves as the boatman rowed Jun around Rainshadow island's coast to the docks.

'Lots of strange things happening over at the docks, these days,' the old man observed as they went. 'What's a youngster like you got to do with it?'

'Not much,' said Jun. 'What kinds of strange things?'

'You don't know?'

'Not unless you tell me.'

The old man adopted a studiedly blank expression and stared out to sea.

Jun rolled his eyes and slipped him another cloud credit. The man grinned, showing his teeth.

'Boats have been leaving for Muralania for weeks,' he told Jun. 'Big ones, too. Last night, eight came back, and they weren't empty, no. Full loads of cargo, all taken from behind Muralania's walls, it seems.'

'What kind of boats? Whose were they? What did they bring?'

'I don't know,' the old man said. 'What could I know about such things? I'm just a fisherman.'

His face had taken on a different kind of blankness now. This seemed to Jun more like a genuine shutting down of the topic than a hint for more credits. He tried a different tack.

'Fine, so that's all you can tell me about the cargo boats, I get it. You haven't heard anything about a girl, though, have you? A teenage girl coming this way or, I don't know' – he made himself say it – 'getting captured?'

'Offer him more money,' Mei hissed in Jun's ear.

Jun held out another cloud credit, but the boatman merely looked over his shoulder to gauge the boat's trajectory. 'You can ask all you want. I told you, I'm only a fisherman. What do I know about teenage girls?'

They were silent for the rest of the trip over, Jun trying not to fret too visibly.

He asked the boatman to drop him about half a mile along the waterfront from the docks, thinking to approach on foot. It paid to be as discreet as possible, after all, when dealing with such dangerous operators as the Lucky Crows.

As Jun walked, it didn't seem to him that anything particularly unusual was happening, not on this stretch of coast, anyway. All around him was a tranquil scene of fan palms rustling in sea breezes, and of empty fishing boats, moored and bobbing in the waves. There were a few people making their ways down the waterfront, but most only looked like dock-workers, tired after a night shift.

'I'm nearly there,' he told Mei. 'What does the Birdcatcher say now, about the Crows' activity at the docks?'

'That there's still quite a lot of it, basically,' Mei said. 'Be careful, and don't do anything rash.'

Jun was scanning the scrubland by the side of the main promenade for a potentially more hidden route onwards, when he heard a shout up ahead. Two young men were coming his way.

'Hey,' one of them called. 'Kawakami. Stop right there.'

Jun froze.

'Oh no,' Mei said. 'They shouldn't know that name. Run, Jun. Get out of there.'

Jun wasn't sure he would make it though, even if he tried. They were too close, and while he might be accomplished at many things, sprinting didn't happen to be one of them.

4.

'Where's my pearl?' Saito spat at Toshiko, the rage in his voice barely under control.

This was fine, Toshiko told herself. She had the pearl's powers to help her, and also she was armed, just as much as he was. Keiko and Rico might be excellent at science, for all she knew, but their skills of observation hadn't extended to noticing the crescent moon knives on her belt.

She dropped her backpack and paced forward into the boathouse, Mochi moving alongside her now, showing off his best unimpressed prowl. Immediately, everyone around the table with Saito jumped to their feet and drew weapons – all knives, except for a pair of throwing stars. It could have been worse, Toshiko reflected. There were no bows to deal with at least.

'You don't remember me, do you?' she asked Ken Saito.

'You're the girl who stole my pearl,' he replied. There was a new vein jumping in his temple now, and he was flexing his fingers, too, clearly itching to put his hands to use in addressing his frustration.

'No,' Toshiko asserted. 'I meant that you don't remember me from before.'

'Thanks to you, I remember everything now,' Ken Saito growled then, surprising her. 'I remember the old woman, and I remember you watching from under the table. Just because I remember, though, it doesn't mean I have to care.'

Suddenly, Toshiko found herself picturing Reiko sitting across from her at the dining table of their old house in the Crescent, not so far from here – Reiko as she'd been while reading one of the stories that Toshiko had liked to write for her when she'd been small, laughing appreciatively at all the parts she'd tried to make funny. Reiko had been Toshiko's rescuer, her parent and her teacher. She'd been the adult to whom she'd brought all of her disappointments and achievements. And then this man in front of her had shattered all of that. And even if he did seem to remember, now, the moment he'd done it, that almost made his refusal to show any remorse more awful. He didn't even know Reiko's name.

Toshiko drew her knives from her belt, swinging the half-moon blades up into her hands to level them at him. The scientists gasped as she did so, realizing simultaneously just how much of a misstep they'd made in bringing an armed and angry girl into Saito's personal gambling circle.

'Get her,' Saito ordered the Crows around him as he leapt up onto the tabletop, boots scattering cards and credits.

The Crows around him still looked caught out and confused as he thundered across the table towards Toshiko, blade flashing in his hand.

Thanks to the pearl, though, Toshiko was quicker than he was – immediately launching herself into a great, spinning leap that took her all the way over his head, to land in a crouch behind him on the tabletop, poised to defend herself on all sides, although none of the other Crows had even begun to react yet. Saito skidded to a stop at the table's edge and whirled to face her, but she was already on the attack, the curved tip of the half-moon blade in her right hand arcing towards his throat.

5.

Jun tried not to panic as the two Crows advanced towards him down the waterfront. They seemed about his own age, but they certainly looked tougher than he was, and would surely be faster, too. Toshiko was the one who enjoyed athletics and martial arts. Aside from his healing work, Jun's hobbies had always been books, languages, theatre and cooking – none of which were immediately useful in this situation, he reflected now.

'Gentlemen,' he ventured as they drew nearer. 'I don't believe we've met. Who's Kawakami?'

'You are, asshole,' said the shorter one.

'I'm afraid you have the wrong person, gentlemen,' Jun tried again. 'This must be a misunderstanding.'

'Jun,' Mei hissed in his ear. 'What are you doing? Get out of there. *Now.*'

'The only misunderstanding here is that we're not gentlemen,' grinned the second Crow, the taller and more wiry of the two. 'Right, Daichi?' He turned to his partner.

'Right, Hiroto,' Daichi replied with a grin.

Now that these two men were closer, Jun could see how similar their features were – though Daichi definitely had a younger face than Hiroto. Jun wondered if they could be brothers.

'This definitely is one of them, right?' Daichi was saying now, gesturing at Jun.

'Matches the photo the boss sent round. Even the same clothes.'

'Photo?' Mei said immediately in the earpiece, voice sharp.

'What photo?' Jun asked the two men.

'The photos all over the Shadow Column of you and the rest of your little gang,' Hiroto told him. 'Seems like you've got yourselves on the wrong side of the Sensei.'

Daichi laughed at that. Then, without warning and alarmingly in sync, the two brothers moved into action. Hiroto pulled a short length of weighted chain from his pocket, swinging it deftly around Jun's wrists, while Daichi raised a fist – suddenly adorned with a spiked and gleaming knuckle-duster – to hold it uncomfortably close to Jun's temple.

'Come on, we're taking you to Saito,' Hiroto said.

'This will be great,' Daichi enthused. 'Saito will love us. Maybe I'll get a promotion now too, and get to join you up in the Shadow Column.'

'You can hope,' Hiroto said. 'But then who'll do all the work down here?'

'This idiot can, once Saito's finished with him,' Daichi replied, making Jun flinch as he gestured at him with his knuckle-duster. 'I'm done with footsoldier work.'

'I don't know if he'll be fit for footsoldier work, once Saito's finished with him. He seemed pretty angry.'

Jun shivered.

'Fair enough,' said Daichi, with blunt matter-of-factness. 'Come on, I'm tired. Let's go.'

Jun let himself be led as his mind worked frantically to think of a way out of this. On the earpiece, he could hear Mei typing furiously while crunching through snacks. He prayed the snacks were good ones for providing inspiration. For his part, he was drawing a terrifying blank.

'Honestly, who steals from Ken Saito?' wondered Daichi as they carried on along the waterfront, their progress made slightly awkward by Hiroto's chain, still looped around Jun's wrists. 'What are you, stupid?'

'Bingo,' Mei said at last through the earpiece. 'I've found these guys. Hiroto and Daichi Santos. Undocumented migrants – though weirdly there's nothing I can find anywhere about where they're actually *from*. They only seem to have been on Rainshadow island for just over nine months, anyway, so they can't have been with the Crows very long. Wait. Let me check something.'

Jun grimaced as he listened to Mei typing again, willing her to make this quick.

'It's as I suspected,' Mei announced. 'They're from Hanasaki Island. Came over after the lab disaster.'

Jun had to fight to keep from showing any reaction in his expression.

'No wonder they covered their tracks about where they came from,' Mei continued. 'Especially now, with all that talk about infection and sickness, and then those weird rumours about the ghosts, too. Hang on' – more typing – 'Oof. Looks like they lost their sister to the immediate explosion, according to the death records in the Hanasaki Disaster database.'

While it was impossible, of course, for Jun to consider this new information about what the Santos brothers had suffered to be good news, exactly, it might still provide him with some much-needed help. He might be useless at running and fighting, but he was excellent at talking to people, and winning their sympathies. Making a swift calculation, he decided now to give up on any attempt at denial.

'Okay, sure,' he told the two brothers. 'So we stole from Saito, and it was stupid. I know it was. I personally would never dream of crossing the Crows. The issue is, it was my little sister who did it.'

6.

Saito parried Toshiko's blow, but only just – stopping her blade closer to his skin than would have felt comfortable even to the most reckless fighter. He used simple brute strength to force her crescent knife backwards and away from him, then lashed out with a powerful kick.

Toshiko dodged, disengaging their blades before whirling to use the knife in her left hand to deflect a blow from one of the Crows at the table's edge, who'd finally snapped into action. Thanks to the pearl, she'd felt the shift his knife had caused in the air currents behind her, even before he'd built up any momentum behind the swing.

She danced through the Crows' attacks, weaving chaos among them as she used her knowledge of Hido's teachings, together with her new strength and speed from the pearl, to keep herself grounded yet a constantly moving target – defying all of them with her unpredictable shifts in direction more than with her weapons. The Crows were the Crows, and she was angry with them all, but she didn't even know these people's names. She reserved all the bite of her attacks for Saito, forcing him to the centre of the table with her swinging knives, her whirling kicks, her anger.

He was good, though, deflecting every blow she swung his way while coming at her with unexpected attacks of his own, his curved blade flashing forward to threaten her throat, her stomach, her heart. He caught her at last with a boot to the kidneys, sending pain shooting through her lower back. As she reeled, he seized her wrist and squeezed hard – trying to get her to drop the knife she held in that hand.

She yelled out, feeling the fine bones of her wrist surely about to snap in his grip, before managing to swing her other blade around, straight towards his eyes, forcing him to let go of her to avoid it. She lashed out again, aiming once more for his throat, but he was ready for her this time, catching her shoulder and trying to throw her.

She allowed herself to be lifted just far enough into the air to fully feel the golden strands of air currents all around her. Then, gathering in all these currents to form an improvised net of air with which to catch herself, she broke the momentum of his throw, launching herself off his shoulders to hang suspended in mid-air for a moment, before twisting to land a kick square in the centre of his chest. He managed to slice a thin, shallow cut on her calf as she flew into him, but she still sent him sprawling, his knife clattering away from him over the tabletop, cards scattering as he fell heavily onto his back.

Toshiko landed gently next to him. Blood was dripping from the cut on her leg, but she still felt almost invincible. As she advanced on him now, her blades gleaming in the candlelight, that image flashed into her mind again, of him wiping his bloody dagger on his handkerchief as Reiko lay dead at his feet.

He pushed himself up to his elbows, watching her now with a hunger in his eyes that seemed completely ill-suited to the position of vulnerability he found himself in.

'You have it with you now, don't you?' he said. 'That's how you're doing this. I can see it in the colour of your eyes – the way they've turned gold, at the edges. You have my pearl.'

She didn't answer him. She didn't owe him any answers.

'You don't deserve it,' he told her. He began shifting back and away from her as she approached, but didn't stop watching her with that same, covetous look. 'I fought for it myself, you know. I won it – and I *need* it. You might be using its power, but you don't understand it. You don't know where it comes from. You don't know what it does.'

'I know what it does,' Toshiko said, her voice steady, in spite of the sliver of uncertainty she'd felt at his words. 'It helps me get revenge on murderers.'

She leaned over him, the tip of the crescent blade in her right hand held to his throat. Could she really do this? she wondered. Did she even want to?

'She has the pearl!' Saito yelled out then to the staring Crows grouped around them. 'Get her! What are you doing, you useless fools? Get the pearl!'

Still hesitating, Toshiko heard a warning howl from Mochi as all six members of Saito's gambling circle flew at her at once.

7.

'Your little sister?' said Hiroto Santos, the weighted chain he was still using to tow Jun down the waterfront beginning to chafe painfully now against Jun's wrists.

'She's only just turned seventeen,' Jun replied. 'She didn't know what she was doing, stealing from Saito. She doesn't even really understand about who the Crows are, on this island. You know how girls that young can be.'

'Don't I just,' said Daichi, and Jun could have sworn a sad sort of smile played over his lips as he did so. He found himself hoping it was some memory of the Santos sister, lost to the disaster, then felt guilty at the thought.

'She just saw something pretty,' he continued anyway, 'and she decided she wanted it, and so she took it. What seventeen-year-old-girl wouldn't?'

'A sensible, rational one,' Hiroto said.

'Have you ever met a truly sensible, rational seventeen-year-old girl, though?' Jun asked, cringing inwardly at how he knew Toshiko would surely react if she were ever to find out he'd said that, even in spite of the desperate situation.

Daichi actually laughed. 'Good point,' he said.

'And now I'm in this world of trouble,' Jun sighed. 'Of course, I'd defend her to the end, though,' he added. 'She is my little sister, after all.'

'Family's family,' said Daichi, yawning again, carelessly sending his spiked knuckle-duster lurching closer to Jun's temple as he did so.

'You two got any sisters?' Jun carried on, trying to swallow his alarm at the knuckle-duster's proximity. 'You guys are surely brothers, right?'

Hiroto's jaw tightened, setting Jun's nerves even more on edge than they had been already. Perhaps he'd miscalculated, and prying into family affairs was a step too far, too fast.

'It's just the two of us, these days,' Daichi replied. 'We get by, though.'

Jun sighed. 'Even so, you can still imagine how worried I am for my sister. I mean, what will happen to her? On the run in the city, the Crows after her. Just seventeen. So young, really. We lost our parents long ago, you see' – and this wasn't technically a lie, Toshiko and Jun both being orphans, just from different parents – 'and of course, now that you two have caught me, I won't even be around to take care of her either.'

Hiroto suddenly stopped in his tracks, sending both Jun and

Daichi stumbling. Jun swallowed, inwardly imploring any God who might be paying attention to grant him the luck he sorely needed now.

When Hiroto spoke, he didn't look at Jun. 'Fine,' was what he said, and then with a flick of the wrist he swung his chain off, and away from Jun's wrists. He caught its links neatly in one hand and slipped it back into his pocket, before folding his arms to glare at Jun. 'I'm going to give you one chance,' he said. 'For your sister, you hear me? Just one chance.'

It took Jun a moment to figure out what he meant. Daichi still looked confused. Hiroto shot him a look, and then Daichi lowered his fist. Jun allowed himself a breath of relief at the knuckle-duster's departure.

'This is for your sister,' Hiroto said again to Jun. 'So make sure you're not this stupid again, or she really will be left on her own.'

'Thank you,' Jun breathed. 'I owe you one.'

And before either of the brothers could change their minds, Jun turned and ran as fast as he could, away down the waterfront. His pounding feet kept pace with Mei's chant of 'Go, go, go!' in the earpiece as he went.

'What the hell, dude?' he just heard Daichi saying to Hiroto, behind him, before he made it out of earshot. 'That was going to be my big chance.'

'You'll have other chances.'

'Yeah. And I guess I am kind of tired. Those crates were *heavy*.'

Jun kept running until he was completely out of breath, though the brothers clearly weren't following him. Even after he'd slowed to a walk, he decided not to risk asking another boatman to take him back to Rainshadow City proper. If the Crows were circulating pictures of him, it would be better to walk the rest of the journey, keeping to the quieter areas.

'So they know our surname,' Mei said in the earpiece then, as he went, 'and they know what we look like. What else do you think they know?'

'Hopefully not where the apartment is,' he replied. 'Keep a close eye on all the cameras.'

'As if I'm ever *not* keeping a close eye on the cameras.'

'Don't have a nap, is what I mean.'

Mei drew in a mock-outraged gasp. 'I would never.'

'I'm heading to the covered market,' Jun told her. 'I need to do my best to transform into someone else – someone they don't recognize – before coming home. Then we can figure out a new plan for what to do about Tosh.'

'I hope she's okay.'

'She's smart and she's resourceful,' Jun said. 'I'm sure she's fine.' He didn't sound convinced, though, even to himself.

Mei fell silent for a time, and Jun could imagine her chewing her lip, as she always did when she was worried.

'Come back quickly,' was all she said, eventually. 'It's lonely here without the cat.'

8.

The coordinated advance of Saito's followers left Toshiko distracted, and Saito made use of the moment to knock her hand holding the crescent knife away from him, and shove her backwards on the tabletop. She landed in a strong defensive stance, dodging the attacks of the other Crows around the table as she did so, but his continued cries of 'Get the pearl! She has the pearl!' seemed to spur on his followers, and they kept coming for her.

In the melee, she **made** out the bottlecap glasses of the man who'd opened the door, together with flashes of the luxury silk, red lipstick and intricate tattoos worn by the gamblers. The pearl still gave her the edge over these people, but she'd lost sight of Saito.

She had an instant's warning from a snag in the golden web of air currents around her – too late even for her sharpened reflexes to do anything about it – before Saito's knife came at her from behind, biting deep into the flesh above her shoulder.

Immediately, she felt blood, wet and warm and sticky, tangling with her hair. She didn't yet feel any pain. That would surely come later. Doing her best to convince herself that the wound probably felt worse than it was, she spun to face him, blades up, only to recoil, shocked, at what she saw now in his face.

He'd been vicious before, but there was a new kind of brutal, ruthless desperation in his expression as he loomed over her. This was the look of a man whose whole essence was bent on reclaiming what he saw as his own, and who was willing to take it back by any means necessary, however brutal or monstrous. Toshiko found she couldn't even meet his gaze, it was too awful.

Instead, she looked wildly around at the other advancing Crows, and then at the wider room, with its flickering candles. There was Mochi, standing in the light of the still-open door, looking poised to run out into the brightness of the morning. It was this sight of Mochi here, familiar creature of home, in the smoky, violent gloom of this environment, that finally shook the last of her resolve.

As Saito raised his knife once more, she took a breath and, against every instinct, closed her eyes. The sea breeze from the open door was sending a wider, brighter arc of energy through the room than any of the smaller shifts in the air. She concentrated, separating this strand out from the web of all the others.

Then she seized upon it, and leapt. The pearl served her well –
Toshiko found herself soaring far further than was normal or
natural, up and out from the circle of Crows on the tabletop,
towards the doors, the light and Mochi.

She landed in a crouch, halfway across the polished wood
floor, and sprinted the rest of the way, dropping her knives so to
be able to scoop Mochi into her arms as she went. A throwing
star hit the boards of the floor behind her as she ran, but the pearl
helped her here, too, sending her swift and light out of the doors,
along the quayside, and from there, finally into the scrubland
that led to the Keeper's Crescent.

She wriggled with practiced grace under its twin barbed-wire
fences to emerge into the Crescent's morning bustle. For all of
Saito's years as the Captain, running the Crows' operations
here, he could never know this place better than she did. It
had been nothing more than a professional project for him, she
knew, simply a means to the end of rising in the ranks of the
gang. To her, by contrast, this place had been everything. It had
been home.

9.

From where he was hidden on the waterfront, crouched behind
a concrete planter boasting an array of uncomfortably spiky fan
palms, Theo let go his awareness of the Gift.

He frowned as he watched Hiroto and Daichi Santos stroll
off, still bickering, in the direction of the cramped, moth-eaten
apartment on the city's outskirts where Daichi lived, along
with Theo and the rest of their team of footsoldiers. It was far
from being a homely place, but the fact of its being owned and
managed by the Crows meant it was at least protected from the

eyes of the Imperial Guard, ever-sharp when it came to finding undocumented people who dared stray independently outside of the Crescent, but always blind to the Crows' operations.

Theo had been heading back to the apartment, too, trailing behind the Santos brothers at what he'd hoped was a safe distance to avoid their scorn, when he'd witnessed them accost the man from the Kawakamis. Of course, he'd immediately ducked out of sight, ready to make use of the Gift in any way he could to frustrate their efforts in keeping hold of their prisoner. Capturing one of the Crows' most-wanted would have been a real opportunity for Hiroto and Daichi to pursue what he'd assumed was their ultimate goal of advancement within the ranks of the gang. It followed, then, that sabotaging that opportunity had seemed to Theo like the perfect revenge for the months of taunting to which they'd subjected him. What he really hadn't expected, though, was for the Santos brothers to foil their golden opportunity all by themselves.

He wasn't sure he liked the idea of these two people he'd dismissed as little more than malignant thugs suddenly showing signs of mercy and humanity – especially when they thought no one was watching. It was a disconcerting contrast to how they usually behaved, around the rest of the Crows. He found himself doubly surprised, too, that it had been Hiroto who had relented and let the man go. Hiroto had always seemed like the harsher and more humourless of the brothers, something that Theo had automatically assumed made him the more ruthless. And yet Hiroto had looked almost haunted when the man from the Kawakamis had started talking about his sister.

For the first time in all these months of existing miserably alongside the Santos brothers, Theo began to wonder, then, what their story really was. Why had they come to Rainshadow

City – just the two of them, without anybody else from their family? Sure, he'd heard them boasting about coming to seek their fortunes in the Crows, like all the footsoldiers did, but that would be an easy lie to tell. Could they have been running from something, just as he had been? And if that had been the case, who might they have left behind? A sister of their own, maybe.

For all its air of gleaming promise on a morning like this, full of whispering palms and sunlight breaking through haze to dance on the surface of the sea, Theo felt more clearly than ever just how strong the systems of power really were which flowed beneath Rainshadow City's surface, making it such a perfectly calibrated place for turning desperate people vicious.

With the Santos brothers almost out of sight now, he straightened up behind the planter and stretched into the morning light. He was just about to set off again after them, when he spotted a particularly well-shaped flat stone at the base of one of the fan palms next to him. After a quick glance around to check he really was alone now, he picked up the stone, feeling its smooth surface between his fingers. Then, he allowed himself to tune back into the Gift.

Growing up, other people in Theo's village had called his abilities a curse, and a sign of the Devil – and for a time, he'd believed them. All of that had changed, though, when Susanna had stepped into his life, starting from that single, electrifying moment three years ago, when, carelessly, he'd let his eyes stray over to her at the village dance on Midsummer's Eve – and, instead of looking away like everyone else, she'd met his gaze, and held it.

It wasn't just that in dubbing his strange powers, 'the Gift', she'd given them a miraculous new name. Susanna had fully changed everything about how he saw them. Gradually, and with her help, he'd stopped trying to suppress the Gift, and, instead, had begun to try to understand it, and even to use it. He'd learnt to perceive not only the nuances of the unusual energy that existed within him, but also how this energy related to the answering flows and frequencies that spooled through everything else, animating and driving the world. The more he'd learnt about the Gift, too, the more *right* it had come to feel, glowing there within him like a hidden song, or a wonderful secret – certainly not like anything demonic. Until, of course, everything had changed.

In those first awful months after leaving home, during his voyage across the oceans to the Archipelago, Theo had gone so far as to wish, with full sincerity, that he'd never listened to Susanna at all. He'd even sworn to himself that he'd never use the Gift again, believing that everyone had been right, after all, when they'd told him he was cursed.

And yet now, over a year later, and even though Susanna herself surely feared and even despised him, some part of Theo couldn't let go of the hope that, in spite of how wrong everything had gone back home, she might still have been right – at least in some small, imperfect way. He hadn't been able to keep denying himself the use of the Gift, anyway. It had so quickly come to feel like a completely natural part of him, a muscle that needed to be used.

This morning, on the waterfront, he used it to sense the energy moving within the substance of the stone now resting in his palm – to feel all the vibrations, humming through its trace minerals and porous rock. As soon as he felt fully attuned to them, Theo took a breath, fed the stone a surge of his own energy, and sent it flying through the air, out towards the ocean.

Instead of trying to control its flight, he simply used the Gift to experience it – to live inside the stone as it freely skimmed the water's surface, skipping over the waves a full four times, sending up sparks that caught the sunlight, turning gold. He didn't reel his awareness back in until the stone struck the water its final, fifth time, and began to sink.

He took a deep breath of salt-filled air then, and let himself linger in that sensation of the stone dancing away from the island, moving as if it really might be able to keep on going, far beyond sight of these shores. And then he turned back, to continue on down the waterfront.

Of course he understood how illusory the feeling had been. He knew very well that, in reality, neither he nor that stone was remotely capable of leaving Rainshadow island. The stone was, in all likelihood, even now being washed back in by the tide – and as far as he was concerned, he'd never been less free in his life, since pledging his allegiance to the Crows. He hadn't only pledged allegiance, either. He'd accepted their wages, as well as the roof they'd put over his head.

Living the way he had in the Crescent, Theo hadn't felt as if he'd had any freedom left to give up, in joining the gang. His life had seemed so out of his own control, being barely able to scrape together enough credits on which to survive, and so having to accept a pittance for doing all the terrible jobs the Crows recruited for in the Crescent – the only jobs available to Keeper's Children, with their lack of ID cards. Feeding the huge, industrial crushers in Rainshadow City's granitarium plants had been a regular one, as well as cleaning toxic chemicals from the processing equipment which those same plants used in granitarium extraction. And then, of course, there had been simply being sent down into the mines themselves. If ever there was a job that needed doing in the City so dangerous and unpleasant that no legitimate citizen would ever agree to it, then without doubt the Crows would come rounding people up in the Crescent – with the tacit approval of the Emperor and her Imperial Guard, of course.

It was the process of being marched back through the City to the Crescent after finishing one of these jobs that had always felt particularly galling to Theo. He'd hated seeing all of those glassy office blocks, gleaming in the sun, as he'd trudged back under the supervision of the Crows, to a life of salvaged odds and ends; of root vegetables grown alongside the barbed wire, and of kakogan dust to treat any sicknesses and injuries he might pick up instead of real healers, in a hospital. If ever Theo began to have doubts about whether he'd made the right choice in joining the Crows, he made himself think back to how those walks had felt – as well as to the other main reason he'd had for joining the gang, of course.

This other reason was something none of the Keeper's Children had ever wanted to discuss, when he'd lived among them, for fear of courting bad luck: people had been disappearing regularly from the Crescent at night. Some had simply never made it to the end of a walk home. Others had even vanished from inside their own houses.

Most of these people hadn't vanished forever. Many, in fact, had been found wandering the scrubland by the barbed wire just a few weeks after they'd gone missing. Without exception, they'd been thinner, paler, and looking markedly older than when they'd disappeared, and Theo had heard more than one rumour, too, that they were covered with strange wounds and scars – with puncture marks that traced maps of harm up the lengths of their spines. None of them had had any memory at all of what had been done to them, or even of where they'd been, all that time they'd been gone. Theo, for one, felt certain that something awful had happened to them.

As he'd witnessed more of these vanishings and reappear-
ances, he'd become increasingly, creepingly aware of the fact
that the people who'd gone missing had all tended to occupy the
fringes of life and society in the Crescent – just as he himself had
done. He did definitely sleep easier at night these days, for all that
he disliked some elements of his life in the Crows. Joining them
had undoubtedly been the best choice he could have made in a
bad set of circumstances.

He actually stopped walking, then, to laugh at that last
thought – not cheerfully. How many people within the Crows'
extensive ranks, he wondered, had started out by saying exactly that?

To distract himself from the idea, as well as from the guilt
that was creeping in now, inevitably, as it always did these days
whenever he used the Gift, Theo made himself think back once
more to the interaction he'd just witnessed, between the Santos
brothers and the man from the Kawakamis.

The Kawakamis were an interesting prospect. They didn't
quite fit with the mental picture he'd built up so far of how life
worked here, on Rainshadow island. Usually, the Crows or the
Crescent really were the only two options for those who were undocumented, or down on their luck. Running a crime operation
outside of the Crows' hegemony was something more perilous
than he'd heard of anyone on the island daring to attempt before.

Come to the Shadow Column tomorrow at sunset to find out some more,
the Captain had said, seeming to appraise him from behind her
dark glasses.

Of course, Theo understood that no summons to the Shadow
Column came without attendant dangers. And yet, how dangerous could anything really be to him now, when he had so little
left to lose?

CHAPTER FIVE

The Bigger Picture

1.

Haru and Kei approached the entrance to the Emperor's rooms, only to find General Kubo talking to the group of Guards stationed at the door.

General Kubo was the most recently appointed member of the Ten Generals – the council of the Imperial Guard's most elite commanders, which advised the Emperor on all military matters. Haru knew from talk around the Palace that General Kubo was by far the youngest on this council – uncommonly young, in fact, to have made the rank of General at all. And yet Haru always found this knowledge hard to square with the fact that General Kubo seemed to him, anyway, like someone who had never been young in his life.

The General was a man who held himself rigidly at all times, as if constantly standing to attention. He wore his hair buzzed even closer to his scalp than military regulation required, and his pale grey eyes were difficult to make out behind small, round glasses that always seemed to pick up and reflect the light of their surroundings. He wore the same type of dark purple uniform, of course, as all the Imperial Guards did, decorated with the same silver braid and badges of rank as those worn by the other Generals – and yet, to Haru's eyes, Kubo's uniform always seemed somehow both neater and sharper than any of the other Guards', though none of them ever looked scruffy.

It wasn't just General Kubo's surface appearance, either, that made Haru uneasy. While the General had been polite enough to him the few times they'd chanced to meet around the Palace, the deeper impression Haru always picked up from him was cold, hard and metallic – like the parts of some ruthlessly efficient machine.

Today, Haru hung back behind Kei as General Kubo looked up from his conversation with the Guards to acknowledge their approach with a bow.

'Crown Prince,' General Kubo said, greeting Haru before he turned to Kei. 'The Emperor is in a meeting,' he told her. 'She has a lot to prepare before the telecast.'

This was typical, Haru reflected. When was his mother not in a meeting? She was in meetings so often these days that she barely had time left over for her other favourite hobby of telling him off.

'That's why we're here, though,' Kei was saying to General Kubo now, with a frown. 'We've come because of the telecast. I've been getting Prince Haru ready for it. I was told to bring him here as soon as we were finished.'

The other Guards present would surely know the truth of this. As the unit charged with protecting the Emperor's private rooms, they would have been primed with a list of everyone expected this morning. Haru noticed, though, that they seemed almost as wary of General Kubo as he was himself. Certainly none of them seemed willing to say anything that might be interpreted as contradicting the General. All of them, even the Captain, were now standing still, with their eyes fixed straight ahead, as if by maintaining this neutral, formal stance they might somehow blend into the background of the corridor's interior of sliding panels and polished wood.

'And you're sure you weren't mistaken?' General Kubo said to Kei, using the few extra inches of height he had on her to loom over her now, in a way Haru didn't like at all. 'Servants of your rank aren't usually permitted to approach the Emperor directly like this, even with the Crown Prince temporarily placed in your charge.'

Steeling his nerves, Haru stepped out from behind Kei to put himself between her and the General.

'I'm here to see my mother,' he announced, doing his best to sound firm. 'Let us through. We'll wait for her in the Jasmine Room.'

General Kubo's expression registered irritation – and suddenly, Haru found himself completely unsure of what he should do, if the General should try to oppose him. He didn't know what would make his mother angrier, his failing to assert himself and uphold the authority of the Imperial family, or his showing defiance to one of her favoured representatives.

General Kubo, though, seemed to realize the irregularity of arguing with royalty moments after Haru did. His obvious displeasure melted away, as he adopted a conciliatory smile.

'My apologies, Crown Prince,' he said. 'I didn't mean to imply you weren't welcome to visit your mother whenever you pleased. I was simply passing on what information I had from recently leaving her presence myself.'

At last, he stepped to one side, allowing Haru a clear path to the door.

Haru bent to remove his blue slippers – forbidden, of course, on the tatami floors of his mother's rooms – and looked up again just in time to see the leader of the unit of Guards glance over to General Kubo, as if seeking his direct permission to open the door. The General nodded back his assent, for all the world as if access to the Emperor's rooms was a favour that was within his power to grant – when as far as Haru knew, anyway, it was nothing of the sort. Haru frowned, as the Guards finally slid open the door.

They bowed low to him as he passed, while the most junior member of their number shuffled forward to pick up his slippers and place them in the little wooden shoerack just inside the door, before the step up onto the tatami.

Haru had just turned back towards Kei when Kubo interrupted them again.

'The Prince is surely old enough to wait in the Jasmine Room by himself,' he told the Guards. 'I'm sure, too, that this servant here' – he cast a pointed look in Kei's direction – 'will have more pressing demands on her time than simply sitting at the Crown Prince's leisure.'

Haru tried to stand as tall as he could – which was still a lot shorter than General Kubo. 'Kei can go wherever I go,' he told him. 'She's been allowed in here before, you know.'

'It's okay, Haru,' Kei interrupted. 'The General is right, I do have plenty of other work to do, around the Palace. I'll meet you back here once you've seen your mother, okay?'

'Okay,' Haru sighed. He never liked when other Palace officials treated Kei as if she didn't matter. Her expression now, though, was practically begging him not to make a scene.

Under the cold stare of General Kubo, he managed to wave her a quick goodbye before the Guards slid the doors shut again between them, leaving him alone in the Jasmine Room's lamplight.

Haru shook his head to dismiss the unease he felt following the encounter with the General, then went to sit on one of the uncomfortable floor cushions that were arranged around the room's central tea table.

The Jasmine Room was by far the smallest of Haru's mother's suite of rooms, functioning as a kind of antechamber to the maze-like network of spaces beyond, all interconnected through sliding doors made from paper and wood. The Jasmine Room boasted two sets of these doors. The ones on Haru's left led through to the Council Room, which was where his mother held meetings with her advisors and the Generals from the Imperial Guard. The doors ahead of him led straight through to the cosier, more intimate space of the Silver Laurel Room, beyond which extended his mother's private lounge and sleeping quarters.

From what General Kubo had said, Haru had expected to find his mother in the Council Room. Instead, though, it was the paper doors to the Silver Laurel Room that were illuminated by lanterns within, the shadows falling in such a way that Haru was able to watch his mother's seated silhouette discuss camera angles and lighting for the upcoming telecast with the silhouette of another woman, who was standing alongside her with an awkward, hovering posture. While his mother's voice was only slightly muffled by the doors and distance between them, Haru couldn't hear what the other woman was saying at all, she was replying so meekly.

Settling in to his cushion now, Haru yawned. He hated the telecasts. He never usually understood anything of what his mother announced during them, and all the cameras made him feel self-conscious.

After what felt like ages, the timid woman's silhouette bowed to his mother's, and then disappeared sideways, through the Silver Laurel Room's far set of doors.

'Haru,' the Emperor called out then, her voice carrying easily through into the Jasmine Room.

Haru stiffened, and sat a little straighter on his cushion.

'Come in, little one,' she commanded. 'Come in so I can see you.'

Little one. She only usually called him that when she was in a good mood, at least.

Haru got to his feet, padding over to the screen doors and sliding them aside to reveal the bright interior of the Silver Laurel Room, and his mother. The particular impression Haru had always picked up from her was one of gleaming and glittering reflective surfaces, and the way he found her today complemented the feeling perfectly.

She was sitting in the room's far corner, at a highly polished mother-of-pearl dressing table, which boasted an enormous trifold mirror. Her new suit was the rich blue of lapis lazuli, diamonds glittered at her throat, and jade glinted from her ears, bringing out the green tones in her light-brown eyes.

In one hand, she held a make-up brush, and Haru could see in the mirrors in front of her that while one eye was a finished piece of art, heavily shaded with a blend of dark eyeshadows, she had not yet begun work on the other. He shivered at the striking asymmetry of her face, at how it didn't match the gleaming perfection of the rest of her.

The polish of her appearance always had a hard edge to it in any case, though, as a result of the vein of deadly strength running detectably through it, implanted there by her father – Haru's grandfather, and the Emperor before her. He had been sceptical about a daughter being strong enough to lead the Rainshadow

Empire. Having had no son, though, he'd attempted to compensate for what he perceived as her feminine weakness by insisting
on her being trained by his top Generals to be as formidable as
any elite Guard. This training regime was something Haru's
mother continued to this day, and however much she smiled and
adorned herself with jewellery, even Haru could see the under-
lying potential for violence in how she carried herself.

'Quickly now, little one,' she said, as if coaxing a kitten, meeting Haru's eye in the dressing table's central mirror. 'And close
the door behind you.'

In spite of his disgrace at the banquet last night, she didn't
sound particularly angry, and Haru found himself feeling almost
more disconcerted by this than if she'd seemed obviously furious.
Of course, though, he did as she said in spite of his misgivings,
shutting the doors and advancing into the room, stopping just shy
of arm's length from her, where he bowed deeply.

When he'd straightened up, he found she'd turned in her chair
to look at him directly, and also that she was frowning. 'A little
creased,' was all she said, with a gesture at the silk of his robe.

Still, though, she showed no clear signs of anger towards him,
about last night. It really wasn't like her at all to forgive him so
quickly for such a large transgression, but as Haru studied her, confused, a small smile even played about her lips. She turned back to
the mirror then, and began painting make-up onto her naked eyelid.

For a wild moment, Haru caught himself wondering what it
might be like to tell his mother about Risu, even in spite of her
dislike of Sun Spirits. He found, as he considered the question,
that he could hardly even begin to imagine doing such a thing.
She was so caught up in the polished world of her leadership that
even talking to her about the regular squirrels outside in the gardens would feel incongruous and unwelcome – let alone trying to

explain to her about Risu. At best, she'd only dismiss all notion of the magic he'd felt from the little squirrel, and tell him he'd been dreaming. At worst, she'd be angry with him, and accuse him of lying, before likening him to his father again.

Haru shook off the thought of telling her anything. Even to begin was impossible.

'Do you realize, little one,' she continued now, serenely oblivious to his thoughts, 'that today's telecast might be the most important of either of our lifetimes?'

Haru shook his head in answer to the question, watching as she began to blend the dark colours at her lash-line into the lighter, shadowed shades above. As long as he could remember, she'd always done her own make-up, never interested in the help of stylists or servants for this task. Presentation was almost a creative art form, for her.

'I thought not,' she said, with a sigh, as if he'd disappointed her simply by answering truthfully. 'Well, today, I am going to be announcing to our citizens that we are finally ready to build the LIFE-Hub.'

Haru tried to force his expression into showing some enthusiasm.

'You should be more excited,' his mother told him, seeing through his efforts immediately. 'The LIFE-Hub will be my life's greatest achievement. We might think bots are advanced now, after all, but the Hub will transform them into something else entirely. It will be the biggest change to life in Rainshadow City since the discovery of granitarium.' She finished applying the eyeliner, and shifted around again in her chair to face him. 'I don't suppose you understand what any of that really means, though. How old are you, now?'

'I'm ten,' Haru reminded her.

'Yes, well,' she said. 'Whether you understand the significance of today's announcement or not, everything will move very quickly now. The LIFE-Hub will be my legacy. The Rainshadow Archipelago I hand over to you will be quite transformed from the one we have today.'

Haru stayed quiet. He was never sure how to talk to his mother, when she was in this kind of mood. She was difficult to understand in any kind of mood, really. Whenever he tried to intuit what she might be thinking or feeling, he only ever found himself obstructed by that same impression of reflective surfaces again. It felt impossible to see anything definite, beneath all the dizzying scatterings of light. She projected so many images which dazzled, and yet none ever seemed like true originals. Today, as the silence stretched between them, he only looked away from her to stare down at his stockinged feet on the tatami.

'Aren't you going to say anything?' she finally asked. 'It's not just *my* legacy. I've also built your future – your inheritance.' She raised a neatly plucked eyebrow. 'You're going to show me today that you're worthy to be heir of all this, aren't you? That you take after me, and the Emperors before me, not the waste of space that was your father?'

Haru nodded again, more vigorously this time.

'So then, tell me – how will you conduct yourself during this announcement, child? What will you do, and what will you not do?'

Haru was spared having to think of an appropriate answer by a knock on the doors to the Jasmine Room. They slid open to reveal one of the Guards from the corridor outside.

'Apologies for the interruption, Majesty,' the Guard said. 'It's, well ...' he shot a quick glance at Haru. 'It's *Mr Winter*, here to speak with you. I thought you'd want to know.'

While Haru was only too familiar with the apprehension he

always felt at any mention of Mr Winter's name, he was surprised to see a frown also creasing his mother's perfectly made-up face. She was normally only too happy to see Mr Winter. What could have changed? The idea of there somehow now being a rift between the two of them felt almost impossible for Haru to imagine.

'He wasn't meant to come this morning,' his mother told the Guard. 'There isn't long before the telecast.'

'He was insistent, Majesty,' said the Guard.

His mother closed her eyes briefly, then put her make-up brush down on the dressing table. 'Then I suppose you'd better let him in.'

The doors sighed shut behind the Guard, only to open again a moment later to reveal Mr Winter himself, looking too hulking and large for the Palace's interior. He advanced towards them, stepping from the soft shadows of the Jasmine Room into the brighter lamplight, eyes narrowing at the sight of Haru. He looked even stormier, perhaps, than he had done last night, with dark circles under his eyes. Haru wondered if he might be here to punish him for his attempt to take the ring – whether he should now try to pre-empt Mr Winter's anger, even, and apologize.

When Mr Winter spoke, though, he did as the Guard had done, addressing only Haru's mother. 'The Sensei sent me,' he said shortly, with a cursory nod of greeting. 'There are certain things we need to discuss.'

Haru blinked in surprise. No one ever spoke to his mother like that. They addressed her as 'Majesty' – or as 'Emperor Asayo', at the very least – and they bowed low whenever they approached her.

He turned to see how his mother would react, but incredibly, she didn't seem about to make any move to correct Mr Winter at all, though she was watching him through wary, narrowed eyes.

'I trust you have your script ready for the announcement?'

Mr Winter continued, as Haru stared. 'The Sensei wishes for me to look over it. I also have the final forms for you to sign, for our agreement concerning the site for the LIFE-Hub.' He spoke those last two words, *LIFE-Hub*, slightly awkwardly, as if his voice didn't fit naturally around the slick, commercial-sounding contours of the name.

Haru's mother sighed, then, and turned to Haru. 'Mr Winter is here to discuss the telecast,' she told him, suddenly sounding all business, the playful talk of 'little one' clearly over. 'Run along. We don't have much time.'

After a quick glance between the two of them – at his mother's formal smile and Mr Winter's stormy scowl – Haru dropped a swift bow in each of their directions, and scurried over to the doors. He could feel the rain clouds of Mr Winter's gaze as he passed him, slipping back into the Jasmine Room, and then to the corridor outside.

It was a relief to find Kei waiting there for him with his blue slippers. He never liked visiting his mother's rooms. For someone so defined by reflective surfaces, she seemed too incautious about the types of people she chose to keep close to her.

2.

Morning in the Keeper's Crescent was in full swing, and all the streets Toshiko and Mochi ventured down were filled with people chopping wood, washing clothes, cooking over open fires, throwing out garbage, or heading to the river to wash and fill barrels with clean water for the day's supply. Everyone was busy, and for a place filled with people who were essentially stuck, unable to venture legally beyond its barbed wire, the Keeper's Crescent felt surprisingly light on its feet. When you were living in these conditions, Toshiko knew, with no running water, no access to bots to help with basic tasks, and only an extremely erratic electricity supply mainly stolen from the electrified wire in the outer security fence, just staying alive was a full-time occupation.

First, she simply focused on plunging as deep as she could into the winding network of narrow dirt roads lined with houses, losing herself in the familiar scents of woodsmoke, soapy water, roasting meat, and the distant yet pungent waft of the open sewer that ran the length of the Crescent's far side. It felt surprisingly jarring, to be back amid these sights and smells that reminded her so strongly of the old life that she, her siblings and Auntie Reiko had led here. Toshiko pushed all of those thoughts firmly away now, though. She couldn't let herself get distracted, when for all she knew, the Crows could still be on her tail.

Picking up her pace, she took a series of turnings through the streets, moving fast, with Mochi still at her heels. The lack of any overall planning to the organization and layout of the Crescent meant that it was easy even for those who knew the place fairly well to get lost. She was banking on this, to escape any Crows who might have considered following her.

Before long, she and Mochi came to the wide road that ran through the Crescent's heart – the Gods' Road, as it was called by all the Keeper's Children, and had been for as long as anyone here could remember. Along it could be found the closest things the Crescent could offer to shops and public buildings, which meant that as well as being this place's main throughfare, the Gods' Road also served as a focal point for the community – as an extended town square, of a kind.

As Toshiko and Mochi trudged up it now, walking inland, a group of boys on bikes zipped past in the opposite direction towards the sea, shouting to each other in a language she didn't understand, their momentum sending the loose strands of her hair flying. In spite of the morning she'd had, she found herself smiling at their vitality, until a barefoot toddler waddled into view in a nearby doorway, and on catching sight of her, burst instantly into noisy, frightened tears. Toshiko supposed she couldn't blame the child. She must look a sight, after all – sweaty, dirty and dishevelled, with blood dripping both from the lesser wound on her leg, and from the gash on her shoulder, which she was trying very hard, if not entirely successfully, not to find too alarming.

Carrying on up the Gods' Road, she soon realized that apart from the crying toddler, it was as if no one here could see her at all. She couldn't blame anyone for this, she supposed. She looked like trouble, she knew, and everyone here lived with quite enough of that already, without courting more. It wasn't that the Keeper's Children didn't help their neighbours – they did, fiercely and regularly – it was just that after five years of absence, it seemed she was almost a stranger here now.

She was scanning the roadside for a place where she might sit for a moment to recuperate and catch her breath, when Mochi suddenly seemed to sense something on the breeze, and dashed forward, disappearing between the legs of a group of children balancing a large metal basin of water between them. Toshiko swore. There was no way to follow the cat without knocking over both the children and the water which they'd surely carried all the way here from the river, a daily chore she remembered only too well, her own arms even seeming to ache in sympathy as she watched them. She ducked around the group instead, only to find that Mochi had disappeared in all the bustle of the Gods' Road. Of course – Mochi had grown up here, just as much as she had. Who was he to realize that this was not a good time to revisit old haunts?

'Mochi,' she called out, up the street. 'Mochi, get back here.'

This only succeeded in attracting a few alarmed glances.

Pushing through the pain in her shoulder, she dodged her way through the bustle on the road. She passed a man selling barbecued chicken skewers, and a group of girls of about her age, selling miscellaneous bot-parts, circuitry and fragments of granitarium battery, laid out on patterned blankets on the street – but certainly no Mochi.

She was close to simply sitting down by the side of the road in despair, when a flash of a familiar, upraised tail weaving through the crowds ahead caught her eye. She sighed with a mixture of exhaustion and relief, and started after it, grateful that even despite her tiredness, the pearl gave her the speed she needed to catch up with the cat.

Soon, her irritation with Mochi dissolved as she finally realized where he was heading. He was going to Mailee's café, which was, very possibly, exactly where she needed to be. As people often said around here – if the Gods' Road was the heart of the Crescent, then Mailee's café was the heart of the Gods' Road.

This café wasn't much like any ordinary café Toshiko knew of, in the world beyond the Crescent. For a start, it took the form of a huge tent, made from red, chequered oilcloth, and of a size large enough to fit a full wedding party. Also, while Toshiko remembered there always being a hot cup of tea and a warm welcome for her at the café, there hadn't always been food. The prevalence of food could never be relied upon in the Crescent, after all, especially during the winter and early spring months when it was next to impossible to grow anything here, even in the polytunnels which the Keeper's Children kept in some of the more sheltered areas. Unlike in regular cafés, too, during the times when she was serving food, the café's owner – Auntie Mailee, as everyone called her – would never name a specific price for it. Instead, she simply trusted the Keeper's Children to pay whatever they could. She often fed people for free, if they needed it.

The other thing about Mailee, Toshiko remembered now, was that she was a healer. While Toshiko herself had always been a healthy child, she remembered Mailee taking care of Jun, when he'd first arrived in their family. Mailee had always been the one, too, to whom Auntie Reiko had gone for help if ever she herself fell sick. They'd been old friends, after all, and then of course Reiko trusted Mailee to never touch kakogan dust, which both women considered as nothing more than poison, despite its being so coveted by so many Keeper's Children.

As Toshiko watched Mochi disappear through the red, chequered oilcloth of the café's entrance, she found herself wondering if Mei could be right, and Mochi was far more intelligent than he let on. Had he somehow realized she needed a healer for her shoulder, and brought her here deliberately? Or perhaps he just remembered spending happy afternoons snoozing in the café's sunspots, while Mailee and Reiko played chess.

Inside, everything was much as Toshiko remembered, largely unchanged in the five years since she'd last been here. The red oilcloth of the walls and ceiling, and the vibrant oranges, reds and blues of the Keeper's Garlands criss-crossing overhead, lent the place a brightness which endured even on cloudy days. It was filled with mismatched tables and chairs, where anyone could sit, meet friends and share tea, news and gossip – and there was even a fire pit at the café's far end, with a slit in the ceiling above for the smoke to escape. While the fire wasn't lit now, on this warm, early autumn morning, having the fire pit here meant that people could gather in the café during winter and still be warm. It meant you could linger here after dark, too, wrapped in blankets, talking late into the night.

The café also housed an important landmark that had no rival of its kind on the whole of Rainshadow island. In the opposite corner to the fire stood a small shrine to the Keeper – the God from whom the Crescent took its name. It didn't much resemble the Imperial-sponsored shrines in Rainshadow City proper, set up for the more widely worshipped Gods. Instead, the Keeper's shrine took the form of a small wooden structure made from pale cypress wood, looking somewhere between a cabinet and a miniature house, and decorated with dark sprays of waxy, evergreen leaves. Within this structure was a framed painting of the barefoot child-God in his distinctive indigo-blue robe, as well as a small table for offerings, a stand for incense sticks and a round pewter tray on which visitors placed lit candles.

Modest as it all might appear to an outside eye, this was the Keeper's only shrine on Rainshadow island, and it was unique in other ways, too. All the offerings, decorations and features of the shrine formed a living, constantly changing amalgam of the varying religious and cultural traditions brought to the Crescent by the peoples who found themselves here. After all, new arrivals were appearing all the time from the other Archipelagan islands, and beyond – and everyone wanted to show their appreciation for the Keeper in their own ways.

While this mingling of traditions was certainly an unconventional approach to showing respect for a God – and one which may well have appalled some of the more devout worshippers at the major shrines in the city – it was also a practice that had always felt strangely fitting to Toshiko. It suited the mixed nature of the Crescent, as well as the fact that, according to the stories, the Keeper himself wasn't actually native to Rainshadow City either, or even to the Archipelago. Instead, the stories told of him coming here himself long ago, from a faraway land all the way beyond the mountains of the Mainland.

Toshiko had always found that his presence in the corner here cast a pleasant feeling of safety through the café – he was, after all, the God responsible for looking after lost children and travellers. The Keeper's Children's persistence in leaving offerings and tokens of worship at his shrine always made her feel more protected too, in how it revealed that, in spite of all the hardships of life in the Crescent, there were plenty of people here who still believed that a God really might be looking out for them – who believed it strongly enough, in fact, to give him precious food and coins they could little afford to lose.

Today, Toshiko was glad to see that the offerings hadn't faltered in her absence. Next to several flickering candles that smelled to her of juniper and sandalwood, the Keeper's little wooden table bore gifts of water, salt and rice, as well as a generous pile of beancakes – reputed to be his favourite – and a temari ball and a spinning top. As the guardian of lost children and an eternal child himself, the Keeper was a God who loved to play.

The café was largely quiet this morning, with few tables occupied. Mailee was here, though, just as Toshiko remembered her, sitting at her usual table near the Keeper's Shrine, with two large tea urns set up before her, along with an array of chipped cups. Mochi looked remarkably content and at home as he leapt from chair to chair through the café towards her.

Toshiko, though, only hung back in the shadows of the doorway, suddenly feeling a little shy as she watched Mailee break into a wrinkled smile and reach out to stroke Mochi. She hadn't minded too much that no one else in the Crescent had remembered her, as she'd walked through its streets. She'd changed a lot, after all. Back when she'd lived here, all anyone would have seen of her would have been a frightened young girl, hiding behind her older siblings, always clutching at her sister's hand. If

Mailee didn't remember her now, though, then that would feel like something final, and definitive – a clear sign that she really was no longer of this place.

'Hello, you,' Mailee was saying to the cat now, as he nuzzled her palm. 'Where did you come from?' She didn't lift her eyes from Mochi as she directed her voice over to where Toshiko was still hovering in the doorway. 'I know this cat,' she said. 'Did he come here with you?'

'He did.'

Mailee did look up at her then. It was a hard look, which took in everything and softened nothing, and yet didn't seem hostile. It was simply the look of a woman who couldn't afford to trust every stranger who wandered into her café. And then, finally, she smiled.

'Reiko's girl,' she said. 'I know you. You're taller, but you have the same awkward shyness. And the same fire, too, hiding beneath all that.' Her brow creased, and she pulled a pair of glasses from the breast pocket of her tunic, putting them on to squint again at Toshiko. 'What's wrong with you, though?' she said.

'What do you mean, what's wrong with me?'

'Well,' Mailee shrugged, 'I have to say, you look a mess.'

3.

Theo only managed to grab a few hours of broken rest before dragging his sleep-deprived self back to the docks for another day of footsoldier work for the Crows. He was almost annoyed when the foreman turned him away with a dismissive shake of the head.

'You aren't needed here anymore, Bluejay,' he said. 'They've got another job for you, so I'm told.' He grimaced, as if to suggest this job might be a particularly grim one.

'But what should I do, in that case?' Theo asked. 'Where shall I go now?'

'I don't know, do I? You, Bluejay, are not my problem any-more, thank the Gods.' The foreman barked a laugh at this, and the other Crows joined in, Daichi among them, all signs of yesterday's unexpected moment of mercy absent, his laughter just as openly contemptuous as that of all the others.

Theo had a whole afternoon, then, to use as his own before his sunset appointment at the Shadow Column – and there was only one thing he ever did, these days, in the meagre time off that the Crows allowed him. He went to Rainshadow University's library.

He set off today with the laughter of his fellow footsoldiers ringing in his ears, to walk north-west up the seafront, away from the docks. He would follow the ocean as far as the covered market, where he'd turn inland and make for the Old Town, where the University's grand buildings – all carved wooden facades and sweeping, tiled roofs – jostled for space amid the winding streets of traditional shops and cafes.

As a naturally curious person, of course Theo valued books and libraries for their own sake, as a general principle. His repeated visits to this library, though, were not simply for idle browsing. When he'd finally accepted, after arriving here on Rainshadow island, that his efforts of returning to a life of suppressing the Gift had failed, he'd decided that learning more about it might be the next best thing, with a view towards containing it, so that he couldn't accidentally hurt anyone else, at least. Surely, he'd thought, there had to be records of other people who'd experienced something similar to what he could do. The idea that he might be the only one in all of history with anything like the Gift seemed too lonely an idea to accept without evidence, and the library had seemed the best place on the island to begin his research.

Of course, he wasn't officially allowed into it. He did have a fake ID card, given to him when he'd joined the Crows, but it was abundantly clear that the gang had used the bare minimum of effort and funds on his false documentation. The card was the wrong type of grey, to start with, noticeably a shade lighter than the legitimate ones were, and his photo had the look of having been pasted in with shoddy, dated software – which he supposed it probably had been. The card was usually adequate to persuade the city's Imperial Guards, all used to turning a blind eye to the Crows, to wave him through the various checkpoints around the island, but it wouldn't be good enough to get him through the doors of the University – an institution, of course, that was only open to legal Rainshadow citizens.

So he'd had to get creative. The Gift could be useful, in these circumstances.

Reaching the covered market now, Theo took a moment to pause at a seafront fruit stand, spending the last cloud credits in his pocket on a cup of deep red watermelon juice poured over crushed ice – badly needed now in the direct sun, coming up on the hottest part of the day. Trying to ignore the guarded, suspicious look that the vendor gave him as he handed over the money, as if the man feared this strange-looking foreigner making a grab for the rest of the contents of his stall, Theo turned away from the sea – which was sparkling, now, with an almost obnoxious vivacity, the sun having fully burned through any last hint of mist and cloud – to begin his walk through the city.

He navigated the covered market as quickly as he could, keeping his head down, trying to ignore the ladies who clutched protectively at their bags as he passed, as well as the insults hurled after him by the big group of kids lurking close to the food stalls, targeting his hair, his eyes, his obvious alienness.

Back out in the sun, he pulled the navy blue beanie hat he always carried with him from his jacket pocket, and slipped it on. It wouldn't be pleasant, wearing it in this heat, but at least it would cover his conspicuously bright hair. Then he downed the remainder of the cool, sweet watermelon juice in a few last grateful gulps, before starting on through the churn of late-morning activity filling the main road ahead of him.

Pedestrians, weaving bicycles, highly decorated palanquins and irresponsibly speeding rickshaws all competed for space, surging over and around the thick, metal tram rails which formed the road's spine. This whole chaotic vista was thrown into dizzyingly stark contrasts of glare and shadow, too, by the office blocks that towered at the road's either side – monoliths of reflective glass, many of them connected through palm-strewn walkways in the sky.

As Theo made his way through all of this, he wondered what trick he would pull today to sneak past the University's security into the library. He had to be careful not to repeat methods at a frequency that could attract suspicion. Over these past months of visiting, he'd created countless colourful distractions – falling roof tiles, sudden leaks, and an earthquake-like rumbling in the far courtyard, to name a few. He'd also used plenty of more traditional means of breaking and entering, such as employing the Gift to manipulate the catches on windows and the solid oak of heavy doors, as well as to silence any treacherously creaky stairs and floorboards.

Sometimes, he would imagine that Susanna was somehow there with him, watching and laughing along as he successfully got the better of the Guards again and again. Susanna, that is, from the days before everything had gone so badly wrong back in Eardland – just as she'd been in that near-perfect time at the beginning of their golden year and a half together, when he'd just started to believe it when she told him she loved him.

In any case, at this point, he'd certainly learnt far more about the Gift from his efforts in breaking into the library than from any actual research he'd managed to carry out within its walls. For all his explorations so far, not a single volume on those shelves, housing centuries worth of experience and wisdom, had so much as mentioned anyone who'd had any remotely similar experiences to those which so defined and afflicted his life. And yet, he couldn't give up. There were still whole shelves, even rooms, that he hadn't explored, and whatever the kids here in Rainshadow City might shout at him in the streets, he still wasn't willing to accept that he was an anomaly, some kind of freak. In all the years of history that the library encapsulated, there had to have been at least one other person like him who had left behind some trace of their experiences – some kind of legacy, however small, that he would be able to learn from.

4.

Toshiko opened her mouth to speak, only to find herself immediately unsure of how to explain to Mailee what had happened with Ken Saito. 'My shoulder,' was all she managed, gesturing at the wound.

Mailee beckoned her to come closer. 'I thought Reiko would have taught you not to be so timid,' she said. 'Come into the light. No one would be able to see you properly, lurking over there, and I have bad eyes.'

Toshiko began to edge forward, then promptly sped up as Mailee began to tut impatiently in a way that reminded her with sudden, unexpected force of Auntie Reiko.

Mailee sucked in a breath when she saw the shoulder wound.

'You've got yourself into some trouble, I see,' she said. 'You've not been followed, have you? I won't have whoever did this chasing you into my café.'

'I haven't been followed,' Toshiko told her, with a private, inner appeal to the Keeper that this was true. Surely, though, if Saito and the Crows had chased her into the Crescent, there would be some sign of it by now. Saito was well known around here, feared from his years as the Captain. It would be difficult for him to step back into the Keeper's Crescent without leaving some level of commotion in his wake.

'In that case, you'd better sit down,' Mailee said, suddenly all business, getting to her feet and bustling off towards the bags and boxes she kept by the Keeper's Shrine, filled with her healing supplies. 'Let's get you sorted you out.'

As Mailee washed her hands and then rummaged through her bags, finding what she needed, Toshiko pulled out a chair and sat, with Mochi winding back and forth around her ankles. By the time Mailee was coming back over, she still hadn't decided whether it was her imagination, or if the cat really was looking particularly smug at having successfully brought her here.

'What did you do, to get a cut like this?' Mailee asked, as she donned a pair of medical gloves and began to clean Toshiko's wound. 'Are you mixed up in something shady?'

'No,' Toshiko said, stroking Mochi as he leapt into her lap and curled up into a heavy and contented mass of grey fur. 'At least not by choice.'

'So someone came after you?'

'No. Or – kind of.'

'What are you talking about, girl? Make sense or I'll stop helping.'

'You remember what happened to my auntie,' Toshiko said, then.

It wasn't a question. Of course Mailee remembered. Everyone who'd lived in the Crescent at the time knew what Ken Saito had done to Reiko, as punishment simply for protecting her orphans.

Mailee's expression turned graver, tighter around the eyes. She nodded.

'Well,' Toshiko continued. 'Something happened, last night, which made me think Saito might come for me, too, and for my brother and sister. So I decided I'd take matters into my own hands. I wanted to be in control, I suppose. You remember what Auntie Reiko used to say – *above the river*? I wanted to show him he couldn't just hunt us as he pleased anymore. And ... I don't know. I suppose I wanted revenge.'

'Revenge?' Mailee's eyebrows shot up, and she paused in her dabbing of Toshiko's shoulder. 'Against Ken Saito? Are we talking the same Ken Saito here, Reiko's girl?'

Toshiko nodded, and Mailee whistled. 'But you're a small girl to be thinking about getting revenge on a man like that,' she told her.

'I know,' Toshiko said. 'You're going to tell me it was impulsive and stupid.'

Mailee didn't reply immediately. Instead, she continued tending to Toshiko's shoulder, her tongue now sticking out slightly in concentration.

'I suppose I could tell you that,' she said, eventually. 'But since it seems you know it already, what would be the point? Really, I think I am more interested in this question of revenge.'

She finished cleaning Toshiko's wound, covered it with a strip of gauze, and then began to bind it with a length of cloth bandage.

'For instance,' she said, as she worked, 'do you think you would feel better now, if you had succeeded in getting your revenge?'

It was an interesting question. Toshiko thought back to the moment she'd crouched over Saito, holding her blade to his throat. She could have done it then, but she'd hesitated.

'I didn't want to be a killer,' she said out loud. 'I didn't want him to make me into one. It would have felt like he'd won, in some way. Does that make sense?'

'So revenge wouldn't make you feel better?'

'I guess not.'

Mailee finished tying off the cloth she'd been winding around Toshiko's shoulder. 'How does that feel?' she asked.

Gingerly, Toshiko tried to move her arm. 'Not bad,' she said. 'Thank you. Will it – will I be okay?'

She felt like a child, asking this. And yet it suddenly felt so reassuring to have found Mailee – an adult, who knew how to take care of her – that she hadn't been able to stop herself. She supposed this was how it was for all of the people in the Crescent, who Mailee healed. The Keeper's Children were tough because they had to be, but perhaps that only made Mailee's determination to look after them more precious.

Mailee tutted at Toshiko's question, but she did give her a smile. 'You'll be fine,' she told her. 'It looked a lot worse than it was.'

Toshiko hoped that was true. She reached into her pocket for some credits to offer Mailee, but in spite of how short money always was here in the Crescent, the older woman waved them away.

'Take it as a favour to my old friend,' she said. 'By which, of course, I mean this cat.' She smiled a slightly sad smile as she pulled off the gloves, wiped her hands with an alcohol wipe, and then poured out a cup of tea, which she handed to Toshiko. 'Back to this revenge of yours, though. Are you giving up on it, now?'

Toshiko remembered this tea, she realized, made from the mint leaves and nettles that grew on the scrublands by the fences.

'I don't think I can give up,' she replied. 'I mean, I'm not actually sure I have a choice now, I'm in so deep. But – no. Even if I could walk away, I wouldn't.'

'Then this is what I think,' Mailee told her, suddenly sounding firm. 'I don't think you truly want that "like for like" kind of revenge at all. I think what you want is to win. And these are not the same things, you understand?'

Toshiko nodded slowly, not quite sure yet if she did understand.

'Perhaps you need to give more thought to *how* you win,' Mailee elaborated. 'Young kids like you, you think it's easy. No thinking required. He killed someone, so you kill him, and on it goes.' She shook her head. 'But that isn't winning, you know. Not at all. If you want to win, and so get *real* revenge, you have to think about what that winning would actually look like, to you. The bigger picture. What you truly want, and how to get it.' She flashed a crooked smile.

Toshiko couldn't help but laugh. 'Are you secretly some sort of revenge strategy expert?'

Mailee shrugged, suddenly all casual. 'Don't forget I used to play chess with your auntie,' she said, as she pointed to a nearby table. 'Over there. Every Friday. She was very good, your auntie. But I was even better.'

Toshiko smiled. A part of her had worried, stepping into the tent, that seeing this old friend of Reiko's could be painful. It felt now, though, more like unearthing a piece of long-buried treasure, to be reminded of those Friday chess games, and, too, to see Auntie Reiko through different eyes for a moment, and imagine her as Mailee must remember her – as a contemporary, and a friend.

'So how would you win against the Crows?' Toshiko asked Mailee. 'How would you get "real revenge"? I mean, if trying to kill Saito isn't the way to win, then what is?'

'Saito was the Captain here, but he was also just the Captain. We have a new Captain now, and she is just as bad. And after her, there'll be another one. Always think. What is the bigger picture, here? What is bigger than any of these smaller people?'

'You sound like my sister,' Toshiko said. 'She wanted to hack into the Crows' accounts and skim cash from them. I think that was her version of revenge. That was how this whole thing started, really.'

'I remember your sister,' Mailee said, with an approving nod. 'She is a sensible girl. Her idea is better already, but we can do more than a little stealing, surely. In all of these matters, you have one important thing to consider: how is it you might stop your opponent from getting what they want?'

Toshiko shrugged. 'What do the Crows want?'

'I don't know, Reiko's girl,' Mailee batted at her sleeve. 'I'm just an old woman with bad knees, whose old friend's children ran off with her favourite cat. But you could find out.'

'Oh.' Toshiko must have looked disappointed, because Mailee spoke up again.

'They've been sniffing around here a lot, you know,' she said. 'I don't know why, or what they're looking for, but there are more of them than usual, and they aren't bullying like normal, either. They're poking around, making sketches, going back and forth with those measuring wheels, even digging up bits of the dirt, and taking it away in sealed canisters . . . I don't like it.' She shook her head. 'That could be a place to start.'

Toshiko sipped her tea, its taste immediately taking her back to her childhood. All this that Mailee was describing now was definitely new behaviour from the Crows.

Toshiko frowned. 'I wonder what they're planning.'

Mailee's expression had clouded, though, into even deeper uncertainty. 'There is something else, too, Reiko's girl,' she continued, with a glance around at the scattering of people at the café's other tables, her voice dropping lower. 'No one knows yet whether this is the work of the Crows, or if it's something else, but after you left – maybe over the last year or two – people here have been going missing.'

'Missing?' Toshiko lowered her tea.

Mailee nodded. 'One person every month or so. Most come back again, though, eventually. People find them, stumbling about out there' – she gestured towards somewhere beyond her tent, past the busy sweep of the Gods' Road. 'They bring them to me, for healing. Often, there is nothing much I can do. They just need food and rest. The bad thing is, though, that they can never seem to remember what it was that happened to them.'

As Mailee gave a visible shudder, Toshiko frowned, tasting a new bitterness on her tongue that had nothing to do with the herb tea. 'How long has this been happening for?' she asked. 'Has anyone done anything to stop it?'

'What can we do, Reiko's girl? Who is going to help us? I watch and I wait, and I check on my neighbours. I warn those who visit my café.' Mailee shrugged, an effort towards dismissiveness, though her expression told a different story.

'You should try to be careful,' Toshiko told her. 'Maybe don't walk home by yourself at night, after closing up here.'

Mailee only smiled at that. 'Ah, no need to worry about me, Reiko's girl. The Crows have been up to no good in the Crescent for years, and I'm still here, aren't I?'

'You are,' Toshiko smiled back, though she couldn't pretend she wasn't still uneasy. 'Thank you for helping me.'

Mailee chuckled. 'For my old chess rival, anything. Even if she kept adopting orphan children who made her late for chess with Auntie Mailee.' She reached down to scratch Mochi between the ears, where he was snoring softly in Toshiko's lap. 'But you'd best get along now, Reiko's girl. It's not safe for you here, if you've been fighting with Crows. The Captain is never far away, and she's a sharp one – just as sharp as Ken Saito was, in your time.'

Toshiko returned the teacup, and bade Mailee farewell.

With Mochi curled in the crook of her good arm, she wandered back into the hot sunlight of the morning, before pausing, stuck, on the Gods' Road, wondering where to go. She wasn't ready to face Saito again, tired and injured as she was, and besides, she wasn't even sure anymore if that was what she wanted. Talking about the situation with Mailee had felt like finding a window, albeit a fogged, distorted one, onto how Auntie Reiko herself might have thought about all of this. And it certainly seemed to Toshiko now, anyway, as if taking control of events and flying above the river might be more complicated than she'd first assumed. But what *was* the bigger picture here, really? How could she win the chess game, instead of just taking one piece on the board?

Toshiko frowned, starting on the trudge up the Gods' Road to the stretch of barbed wire closest to the city. She didn't anticipate getting much trouble from the Guards at the Crescent's border. After all, in her pocket, she had the excellent fake ID card Mei had made for her, which connected to a corresponding false profile that her sister had managed to enter into the Citizenry Database. This profile, of course, wouldn't stand up to anything beyond the most surface level of scrutiny, given that even Mei couldn't hack into the Database fully. It would, though, be enough to get her past the Guards, and out of the Crescent. Over the years, Toshiko had complained so often about the limitations of the Kawakamis' ID cards, but this morning, she felt more keenly than ever just how much more of a chance her card really did give her, in comparison to everyone else here in the Crescent. The sheer unfairness of this, too, felt to her like it might somehow be a part of it all – part of that 'bigger picture' that Mailee had told her to think about. She kicked a foot into the dust as she went, feeling her thoughts seeming to tangle in ever-tighter knots.

As she walked, she returned to pondering the question of just what it was that the Crows wanted. What were they up to, in that warehouse? From what the scientists had been saying before they'd caught her, all those crates she'd seen in there contained something dangerous. And then the gang's behaviour here in the Crescent sounded strange, too – unsettlingly so, in spite of Mailee's reassurances. How was it all connected? And where did those disappearances fit in, too? And, more to the point, what could she do about any of it?

She needed to think, *really* think. She couldn't go home – not yet. Her siblings would be unhappy with her for leaving this morning without telling them, and there would be a massive commotion as soon as she arrived back, she knew. She needed to be somewhere calm, where she could let her thoughts roam freely.

Suddenly, she realized she knew just the place.

'Fancy a trip to Rainshadow University?' she asked Mochi.

Mochi only turned his face away, looking unimpressed.

CHAPTER SIX

Golden Moon Square

1.

As Theo walked, the architecture around him began to change rapidly from glassy office blocks, all built in the past hundred years since the granitarium boom, to much smaller and more homely buildings built from wood and bamboo, decked out with tiled awnings and patterned noren curtains. He was finally in Rainshadow City's Old Town, the district that contained the University, and which, as a result, was favoured by artists and students.

He was beginning to feel hungry now – which wasn't ideal, given he'd spent the last of the credits in his pockets on watermelon juice. It was a problem that was also compounded by the fact that most of the shops in this area seemed to be dedicated to selling different types of food. Theo was offered coconut fish curry with roti prata flatbread, as well as siu mai dumplings, spicy fried noodles, bao buns and turmeric chicken wings by the various traders standing in their doorways, hoping to lure in customers. He merely smiled and shook his head at each as he carried on walking.

If he'd been a true citizen of Rainshadow City, it wouldn't even have mattered that he was out of cash. Real citizens used their ID cards to buy things on credit all the time. It was easy. Merchants need only scan an ID card to log the amount owed in the Citizenry Database, and if the balance was cleared by the end of the month, then there were no repercussions. Of course, in spite of his fake ID card, Theo didn't have an entry in the Database. Even the most dedicated service to the Crows couldn't earn you so much.

He successfully made it, anyway, past all of these shops to Golden Moon Square. This was the shady, tree-lined, cobbled square at the Old Town's heart, dominated on all sides by the tall, wooden structures of the University buildings – all beams, pillars, struts and rafters, each roof a gentle upward curve, covered with the University's distinctive dark blue ceramic tiles. Golden Moon Square would have looked straight out of an old painting, Theo thought, had it not been for the banks of telecast screens positioned at its either end, and the electronic speakers on the lampposts. Theo had learnt, too, from his reading in the library, that despite the University's traditional appearance, the library itself was the only building to predate the granitarium boom. There hadn't been much call for in-depth academic research when this had been an island of loggers and fisherman, who had studied the woods and the ocean instead of software and circuitry. The discovery of granitarium, and the need for highly trained engineers and scientists to capitalize on its possibilities, had changed all that, of course.

Theo was just about to hurry over to the carved wooden doors of the library, when the square's speakers gave the clanging, one-minute warning that signalled the screens were about to flare into life for the daily noon telecast.

He stopped walking, cursing inwardly. He hated watching these things. They were just propaganda from the Emperor, pure and simple – and despite the citizens' quiet compliance, he doubted whether even they could enjoy them much, either. The telecasts might be the most-viewed broadcasts in the city, but that was only because they were screened in all public spaces, offices, trams and shops, and failing to watch was a civil offence.

He dropped to sit, anyway, in a spot in the shade on the edge of the raised sidewalk that bordered the square, and settled in, ready for another few minutes of nonsense from the Imperial Palace. It was a relief to be out of the sun, at least. He let himself enjoy the feeling of the light breeze on his skin, as it rustled the already crisped leaves of the trees on the square's perimeter. And as he did so, he scanned his surroundings, watching the students, researchers and teachers who'd been milling around, or sitting at the outside tables of the University's café, talking over baked goods and bubble tea. All of them now, to a citizen, were falling silent, obediently turning their full attention to the telecast screens around them.

Theo's gaze caught, then, on a girl on the opposite side of the square, also sitting on the sidewalk's edge. Like him, too, she didn't seem all that interested in the idea of the telecast, apparently more focused on the pastry she was eating out of one of the University café's bakery bags. This wasn't really what had drawn Theo's attention, though. He had noticed her, instead, for three particular reasons. First, she seemed to be injured, her shoulder covered with a large, white bandage. Second, she had a sizeable grey cat at her feet, with whom she currently seemed to be sharing her pastry – and third, she was, to his eyes at least, completely and unignorably beautiful.

2.

Toshiko often visited Golden Moon Square like this. Its old-fashioned buildings made it feel like something of a sanctuary to her within the rest of the towering, gleaming city. It was usually busy and bustling enough, too, that she never had to worry too much about the pairs of Imperial Guards stationed in front of the University's library, as well as its various science and technology buildings. She even felt, in fact, like she might be able to blend in a little with the particular crowd that frequented the square – and it was this, really, that kept her coming back here, time and again. More than anything, Toshiko loved the idea that someone might mistake her for a student.

She wasn't even fully sure what the University's students did, sequestered away in their grand old buildings. What she did know, though, is that all of them seemed to move through their surround-ings with the ease and certainty of people on a clear and productive path in life, confident that they were doing valuable and valued work, and would go on to lead successful lives, full of reward and satisfaction. It did feel a little disloyal to her family, but more than anything sometimes, she wanted to be like that, too.

Occasionally, she was strict with herself, and tried to stop coming here. That had been Jun's advice, when she'd dared to tell him just a little of what she felt about this place. He'd said that being so close to a life that she could never have might only make it feel more distant – and she knew he was wise, and probably right. And yet every time she swore she'd give up the habit, she'd be back here a few weeks later, ordering a pastry in the café with the affected nonchalance she'd cultivated over her many visits, all for the thrill of wondering whether the counter staff might just have taken her for someone who belonged in these surroundings.

And then she would shuffle away, too nervous to keep up the charade for long enough to actually sit down at one of the café's tables. *Maybe next time*, she always told herself, as she retreated to her usual spot on the sidewalk, beneath the whispering leaves of one of the square's ginkgo trees. And the café did do very good pastry, at least.

She looked up from the wintermelon cake she'd chosen today to notice a boy – or a young man, really, seeing as he was definitely a few years older than she was – sitting across from her on the other side of the square, just along from the library building. He'd been watching her, it seemed – and yet, instead of looking hurriedly and awkwardly away when she caught his eye, as she surely would have done had their situations been reversed, he only seemed startled for a moment, before giving her a smile.

Toshiko's first thought was that he looked very odd. He seemed completely ill-fitting, in fact, in these surroundings. He was wearing a woollen hat, for a start, in spite of the warm weather, as well as rough work clothes that seemed the opposite of all the University people's stylish, well-cut garments, which somehow always hung in casual yet artistic folds, and always appeared to be meticulously clean, as if their owners really did do nothing but study. Even the way this young man was sitting – a little hunched, with his elbows resting on his knees – seemed to give off a part defensive, part insolent air, which couldn't have seemed more at odds with everyone else here in Golden Moon Square.

His was a funny kind of smile, too. Ironical. It was a smile that seemed to laugh a little at the scene around them – at the earnestness of all the students and lecturers here, already waiting in silence for the telecast to begin, and even at the ornate grandeur of the University buildings themselves.

She had never seen anyone with eyes of his colour before, she realized then. They were the same bright blue of the ocean on a spring morning. Or of the wingtips of the kingfishers she sometimes watched behind the power station across town, as they dived, sharp-beaked and brilliant, over the River Navis.

A little cautiously, she found herself smiling back.

And then the two banks of screens on either side of the square flashed into life, showing Rainshadow City's crest – a traditional woodcut image of a fishhook crossed with a trident in relief against a background of dark blue waves. The crest was a dual reference to the island's two traditional industries of timber and fishing, and one of the very few enduring elements in the city's iconography that still made reference to its largely forgotten older ways.

Without thinking, Toshiko had turned to look at the screens. It was simply a reflex to her – after all, watching the telecasts was compulsory for all citizens, and the fact she wasn't exactly one of them herself only made it especially important that she continued acting as if she were. The boy with the blue eyes, though, didn't seem to be following suit. As she glanced back at him, he only raised what was definitely a sceptical eyebrow. She laughed – and then caught herself, looking around in alarm.

Thankfully, no one seemed to have noticed she hadn't been paying attention, and she still couldn't see many dark purple Imperial Guard uniforms here in the square, at all. Even so, as Mei and Jun had always drilled into her, you never could be too careful.

Still feeling a little nervous, as if this were a considerable transgression, though it was only looking away from the screens for a moment before the telecast had even started, Toshiko widened her eyes at the boy. *See what you made me do?* she tried to convey to him, with that look. *You should be more careful.*

He nodded back at her, as if he'd understood, then tipped his head on one side. The gesture seemed almost birdlike, and sent a lock of bright golden hair spilling out from his strange woollen hat. He definitely couldn't be from Rainshadow City, with hair like that. Where had he come from? she wondered. And was he a citizen? As the breeze picked up, sending the leaves of the square's trees rustling again, he gave her another smile. *Watch this*, he seemed to be telling her.

First, he performed an exaggerated version of what she'd just done in scanning their surroundings for potential threats – then he got to his feet, turned, and walked right up to the wooden fire escape stairs that snaked up the side of the library building.

Everyone else in the square, even the Guards at the library's front entrance, had their attention fixed on the telecast screens. She was the only one, it seemed, who noticed the blue-eyed boy trip lightly up that winding flight of stairs, only to step through the sliding wooden door at the top. She frowned. She knew all too well from the undercover work she'd done with her siblings that security was rarely lax throughout the city, especially in state-owned buildings like the University's. Surely that door shouldn't have been possible to open so easily from the outside.

And then the fanfare signalling the start of the telecast blared from the square's speakers, and Toshiko turned back to the screens, still feeling a little dazed by what she'd just witnessed.

She was just in time to see the image of the city's crest dissolve into the usual scene of the Emperor and the Crown Prince.

The two of them were standing, as ever, in front of two crossed flags – one for Rainshadow City, and the other for the broader Rainshadow Archipelago. As usual, they were standing stiffly, staring straight ahead, with the Emperor slightly in front of her son.

Toshiko's lingering sense of shock at the behaviour of the young man with the ocean-blue eyes, though, seemed to throw this familiar image of the Emperor's family into new light for her today, and it suddenly struck her as looking a little lonely. Of course there were extended branches and offshoots of the wider Imperial family, but in the most immediate sense, it really was only Asayo Soramoto and her son left. It felt like a long time now since the Crown Prince's father had also been there, alongside them.

Toshiko found she could barely remember him, in fact – a no-bleman from somewhere overseas, whom the Palace's priests had chosen and brought over, to be the Imperial consort and father to the Imperial children. He'd always remained a silent figure, bowing and waving formally to the populace from the Emperor's shadow, and had disappeared from the public eye when his son had still been very young. The Palace had given no explanation other than announcing, two weeks after he'd stopped appearing for telecasts and public engagements, that he'd died after a short illness. It suddenly seemed rather sad to Toshiko, to see these two survivors of that family tragedy facing the public like this, the Emperor smiling her telecast-friendly smile, and her child so small and quiet next to her.

Seeing the Crown Prince again like this, Toshiko realized she did feel bad about the way she'd used him, at the Turning Leaf banquet. She'd only been trying to follow Mei's instructions, and do what was best for her family, but it probably hadn't been fair of her. At least the boy didn't look as if he'd been too harshly punished, seeming just as clean and as well dressed as when Toshiko had seen him last night. Now that she'd met him in person, though, and had seen the way his eyes had lit up when she'd suggested a game, she found herself a little unsettled by the way he was staring straight ahead now, unsmiling, not meeting the camera's eye.

'Good afternoon, citizens of Rainshadow City, from my family to yours,' began the Emperor, her voice ringing crisp and clear from the loudspeakers. 'As we celebrate the start of a new season, I have some exciting news for you. It is my great pleasure to be able to announce a huge step forward in our plans for the LIFE-Hub.'

She paused here, as if anticipating applause, and quite a few people in the square did actually clap. Toshiko was amazed they could work up the excitement. The Emperor was always talking about the LIFE-Hub. She'd mentioned it so many times over the years that Toshiko had long forgotten what the individual letters in the acronymized name even stood for. She was barely clearer on what the LIFE-Hub's actual purpose was intended to be. The Emperor was always making grandiose yet entirely vague statements about how it would be the future of bot-manufacturing technology. The only thing Toshiko understood for certain, was what Mei always said – that it was, quite clearly, Asayo Soramoto's attempt to replicate the seismic shift in the island's fortunes over which her grandfather, Goro Soramoto, had presided.

When he had inherited the throne, Goro Soramoto had been a King, not an Emperor, and the island over which he had ruled had been called Navishima. Navishima itself had been unre-markable – just one of an archipelago of independent islands quietly existing in the Mainland's shadow, humbly self-sustaining in being a nation of fisherman, farmers and loggers. The discovery of granitarium in Navishima's mountains, however, coupled with new understandings of the huge possibilities offered by granitarium batteries, had led to a technology boom unlike anything any of the islands had ever seen.

In the handful of years that followed, Navishima had gone from being a place of thick forests, sweeping rice paddies, tidy vegetable fields and modest buildings of bamboo and wood, to a gleaming, sprawling urban jungle. Soon, the last few patches of wilderness seemed to cower in the shade of factories and vast office blocks, all dedicated to the completely new industries of manufacturing electrical parts, building computers and designing software. As if to confirm and complete the change, the King had announced that the island would henceforth have a new name – *Rainshadow City* – which he deemed 'independent, confident and modern' in how it seemed to shake off the last shades of the Mainland's influence, etymologically at least. And so just like that, old Navishima had vanished, and a new city state was born.

The immense wealth which the granitarium industries had brought to Rainshadow City had also allowed its king to expand his Guard. With the help of this increased military might, Goro Soramoto had swiftly brought one island after the next under his control, and so began outsourcing Rainshadow City's farming, wood and food production to his colonies, dedicating ever more of his home island's population and limited space to the highly lucrative tech and computer industries. Like this, he began transforming the whole Archipelago around him into a resource to support his beloved Rainshadow City – the nerve-centre of his new Empire, and the seat of his power – and soon, every one of the Archipelago's islands had fallen to his control. Every one of them, that is, apart from the distant, curiously unbreakable walled island fortress of Muralania.

'I am delighted to inform you all,' said his granddaughter now, beaming out from the telecast screen, 'that Rainshadow City has finally acquired and brought onto our shores a critical amount of a newly discovered, rare mineral which years of experiments have highlighted as the single most essential resource for our LIFE-Hub's success. And that is not all,' she continued. 'I can also announce that a suitable site for the LIFE-Hub has been secured. To reassure you – our scientific advisory board is unanimous in its certainty that the amount of land surrounding the site is sufficient to ensure that no citizen need have any fear of their immediate environment becoming contaminated, or indeed being at all affected in any negative way by the LIFE-Hub's activities.'

Toshiko put out a hand to still Mochi's paw, where he'd begun playing with one of the buttons on her jacket, probably hoping for more wintermelon cake. This was something new from the Emperor now, surely. It sounded, for once, like actual progress towards the LIFE-Hub's establishment, and the whole thing unsettled her somehow, the Emperor's words tugging on threads of worry in her mind.

Still smiling broadly, the Emperor spread her hands wide, as if to demonstrate her magnanimity, before continuing.

'Now that we have established that you need not fear being adversely affected by the LIFE-Hub, let us move to consider: what benefits might you look forward to enjoying? Well, my citizens, I can reveal to you today just what it is that our outstanding scientists have been working on. They have developed a whole new generation of bot, which we have decided to call – ALISE.'

As she spoke, an information box popped up on the screen next to her. The word 'ALISE' was spelled out at the top, along with a longer name, 'Artificially Living Intelligent Service Executive'. Below the text spun a basic 3D outline of a woman's body.

'ALISE might be a bot, but she is not a bot as you know them. Bots, as we have them now, help us with the mundane tasks of the day, or perform little tricks to entertain our children, and pets. They are simple things, capable only of carrying out certain repetitive actions which we, ourselves, have pre-programmed. ALISE is different. ALISE can learn. She is adaptable, and she takes initiative of her very own. She is even sensitive to emotions.'

The Emperor paused, giving her populace time to digest this information.

'ALISE may not be human,' she continued, 'but she is the person we all wish we had in our lives, to remove the need for any foreign labour on our shores, while still allowing you, my citizens, to dedicate your time and your minds to the higher task of pursuing more interesting and economically productive forms of work. ALISE is happy to do any task, no matter how menial, gruelling, or even dangerous. She is trustworthy when looking after children, and is a highly competent cook. She does not require breaks, she does not herself require food, and she does not care where she rests her head to sleep. Crucially, of course, she does not demand a salary or citizenship, as many of our workers in these kinds of roles currently do' – the Emperor paused for a grimace, participating in what she clearly considered a shared moment of acknowledgement of a pervasive evil, before continuing. 'ALISE is also now, in her final model, made from completely inorganic substances. This further means that, unlike a lot of our current menial workforce, you need not worry about her reproducing, or generating any unpleasant waste throughout her life – or indeed when it is over. Once the energy powering an

ALISE has run out, we can choose to simply re-start her with a fresh dose from our miracle mineral, or to recycle her parts into a new ALISE entirely.'

The Emperor snapped her fingers, and the image of the single rotating female body on the screen became many.

'The Living Intelligence Formation and Extermination Hub, or LIFE-Hub, as you will know it, will generate ALISE in her thousands, and in her hundreds of thousands. She will be born in the LIFE-Hub's Beginnings Complex, she will grow in its Learning and Testing Complex, and she will reside in the Workforce Basecamp, waiting to be called into service. Many years later, when she has done her duty in supporting you, my citizens, to lead more focused and productive lives out here in Rainshadow City, she will be returned to the LIFE-Hub's Retirement Complex.' The Emperor's expression grew more serious again, as her voice took on an almost plaintive note. 'You will all know just how stretched our city's resources are, as a result of all the labour we are currently being forced to recruit from beyond our shores via our recruitment tests in overseas test centres, and by various other means, too' – Toshiko felt a kick of resentment at this fleeting, almost airy acknowledgement of the city's reliance on the labour of the Keeper's Children. 'ALISE will eliminate the need for all of that. As I say, she really will require none of the resources that our foreign workers currently consume.'

The Emperor waved a hand, and the spinning bodies on the screen disappeared, leaving just herself and the Crown Prince again, standing in front of the flags.

'While we will have to wait until the LIFE-Hub is complete and producing ALISE at scale for us to see a full, transformative change to our society, there are, in fact, already a number of

ALISEs in existence.' She paused again, eyebrows raised, as if anticipating a collective gasp. 'Seven of them, to be precise. These first pioneering ALISE bots will be unveiled to my invited guests at the Palace tonight, at a party that I will be hosting to celebrate ALISE's introduction into our lives. From there, I promise it will not be long before you have all had the chance to meet her, as she begins to deliver Rainshadow City into a new age. I hope you, my citizens, are as thrilled about this prospect as I am. It only remains for me to wish you luck, health and a good afternoon. The Soramoto family are, as ever, your servants.'

As the Emperor gave a small, farewell bow to the camera, signalling the end of the telecast, Toshiko found her attention drifting back to the Crown Prince, as he quickly copied his mother's gesture. The Prince's eyes roved as he straightened up, giving him the air, suddenly, of someone in search of an escape – and then the screen cut back to the Rainshadow City crest again, before going dark.

Toshiko felt as if her thoughts were whirling now, like confused weather systems in her mind. This announcement seemed to her to be charged with ominous significance, even if she couldn't yet grasp exactly what that significance was.

Frowning, still lost to her thoughts, she turned away from the screens – only to see the boy with the blue eyes making his way back down the wooden steps of the library's fire escape – now with a large, old-looking book in his hands.

This was absurd. She'd never before seen such outrageous deviation from all the rules, written and unwritten, of Rainshadow City – except by her two siblings, of course, who she'd believed to be renegades, completely unique. She wanted to find out who he thought he was, that he could dare to behave like this. And she wanted him to notice her again, maybe, too, and to continue that conversation it had seemed they'd begun, with that silent exchange across the cobbles.

The whole square around her now had erupted into conversation – all the citizens buzzing with excitement and questions about the new ALISE bots, and what their introduction might mean for the future of the city. In spite of her yearning to belong here, at the University, Toshiko couldn't quite match the cold dread she'd personally felt at the Emperor's words with the delighted animation of all these people around her.

Perhaps it was something in that disjunct that made her reckless. She took one last glance over at the few Guards who were here in the square, none of whom, thankfully, seemed to have noticed her at all amid everything else going on. Then she finished her last bite of wintermelon cake, and with its sweetness still lingering on her tongue, and Mochi at her heels, she got to her feet and marched across the square to intercept the blue-eyed boy with the book.

It was only when he'd already seen her coming, stopping in his tracks to watch her approach with an expression that was almost a straight cross between guilt and amusement, that it occurred to Toshiko that she should be more careful. Hadn't those scientists back in the Crows' warehouse said something about a picture of her being circulated amid the ranks of the gang? What if this boy was one of them? What if he was on Crows' business now, and that was why he felt so confident to steal from the University, and ignore the telecast so blithely?

And yet appropriating single books didn't seem like the Lucky Crows' style. And he didn't look like a Crow to her, either. The Crows were tough and cold, like Ken Saito – dead on the inside as a result of all the awful things they'd done. They didn't look like this, filled with curiosity and humour – did they?

3.

'Hey! You stole that book, didn't you?'

Faced with the directness of the girl's accusation, Theo found himself unsure of how to reply. She'd seemed friendly enough a moment ago, smiling back at him across the square. It was probably stupid of him to have attracted her attention like that, he knew, let alone allowing her to see him break into the library, and yet he'd had an instinct about her – something hard to explain, even to himself. It had felt as if he'd spotted, in her, another person like himself, who stood outside the schedule of demands that the social contract of Rainshadow City placed upon its citizens.

Maybe, though, that had been illusion, born from loneliness on the one hand, and a desire to show off to a pretty girl on the other. Terrible reasons, both, for landing up in trouble, he knew. If she genuinely was a law-abiding citizen about to turn him into the Guards, this would find its way to the senior rankings of the Crows – and he didn't like to guess at what kind of retribution they'd inflict on him for causing them trouble.

He should probably try to distract her, and then run. And yet, even though her dark eyes were flashing and the colour in her cheeks was raised slightly, as if in irritation or anger – and even if her cat, too, was now giving him one of the most hostile looks he'd received in his life, even since arriving here in Rainshadow City – Theo still found himself somehow unwilling to believe that this girl really was quite the simple, outraged and loyal citizen she appeared to be. She just didn't seem to fit into that paradigm.

'You didn't watch the telecast, either,' she added to her initial accusation – a touch defensively, as if she thought he might try to contradict her.

'I didn't,' he replied. 'Well observed.'

Her eyes narrowed with suspicion. 'What is that book, anyway?' she asked, taking a step closer to look at it. *Ten Principles of Objects in Motion*. She wouldn't be able to learn much from that, at least. As she leaned closer to the cover, reading the characters of the title upside down, the loose strands of her hair caught the breeze to disrupt the lines of her heart-shaped face. There was something particular about the way she moved, Theo realized then. Her back was straight as bamboo, but there was nothing at all rigid about her. Instead, she was exceptionally light on her feet, moving through the air as loose and free as an ocean breeze, looking poised at any moment to leap, or run, or break into dance.

She frowned, tucking the loose strands of her hair back behind her ears as she straightened up again, to glare at him.

'Why would you steal it, though?' she asked.

'Well, it was this one, or *Seven Ways to Show off to Girls without Breaking into Libraries*,' he told her, cringing inwardly at the awkwardness of his own joke. 'I couldn't decide.'

Thankfully though, she laughed. Laughter seemed within easy reach for her, in spite of all the show of confrontation.

The shadow of a bird passing overhead fell over them then, and they both looked up, allowing the fragile camaraderie of the moment to fade. Abruptly, Theo felt a stab of guilt at the thought of himself here, standing in a sunlit cobbled square and flirting with a pretty girl over a stolen library book. He knew he had no right, after leaving Susanna, and after breaking her heart the way he had. He still loved Susanna, of course he did. What would she think if she could see him now? Or perhaps she wouldn't care.

'Sorry,' he said to the girl, now. 'You shouldn't have seen any of this. Please, don't tell the Guards.' He turned to go.

'Wait,' she said, though – and in spite of himself he turned back. 'You're new to the city, aren't you?' she asked.

Theo nodded.

'Then you should be more careful. Don't just think you can just steal whatever you want here and get away with it. You can't. They'll come after you.'

'Who will?'

'The Crows. Or the Imperial Guard, if the Crows haven't got you first.' She looked over her shoulder, checking for anyone watching. 'Surely you know this already, though? Everybody here does.'

'Well, maybe I'm not everybody,' he simply said, before walking away. He knew it was rude, probably – not to mention risky. She could very easily just tell the Guards what she'd seen, and having the book on his person like this would count as clear evidence. And yet he couldn't stay here anymore, with Susanna seeming to drift further away from him with every new sentence he uttered.

The girl didn't call after him this time as he crossed the square, though he was sure he heard her cat give out a warning hiss.

And don't come back, that hiss seemed to say.

4.

Toshiko blinked after the strange, blue-eyed boy. She felt, unaccountably, a little like she'd just been slapped in the face. For a fleeting moment, after all, she'd thought she might have found someone else – someone outside her tiny trusted circle of herself and her two siblings – who also questioned the rules and norms of this city, and dared to try carving their own path through them. And then he'd simply walked away. Part of her did still worry that he could be working for the Crows, but if he had been and he'd recognized her, then why not try to grab her, and take her to Saito?

Still feeling irrationally upset by the whole encounter, Toshiko gathered Mochi into her arms and sat back down on the kerb. Could it even be possible that he was another escaped Keeper's Child, just like she and her siblings were, and that he'd dashed away so abruptly out of fear, worried that she might have figured him out?

Her thoughts turned back to the Crescent again, and from there, to what Mailee had said earlier, about the Crows sniffing around its streets, doing odd things like measuring the land. And suddenly, she felt as though something very important might have been set out before her while she'd been distracted by the boy with the blue eyes – something she should have figured out by now. She'd barely begun to wonder what it might be, though, when Mochi leapt out of her lap to stalk over the cobbles back towards the University café, and then stopped to look back at her pointedly, wearing his best plaintive expression.

Toshiko sighed. 'Fair enough,' she told the cat. 'You do probably deserve another treat. And I suppose I am still a little hungry.'

She followed the cat back into the café's wonderfully refreshing, granitarium-powered air conditioning, and took her place in the queue for the counter behind a group of three girls in sundresses, all just a little older than her. They giggled at Mochi, and then noticed Toshiko properly, their shared ease transforming immediately to suspicion as they took in her worn clothes and conspicuous shoulder bandage.

Probably, Toshiko thought then, she would never be able to fit in properly here at the University, and any attempt to playact that she might be a student was laughable – a joke that had always been obvious to everyone but her.

She picked up Mochi again, squeezing him tightly for comfort as she waited behind the girls. They had all turned to face away from her now, going back to their conversation – discussing the ALISE bots, and why the Emperor might have chosen to make all of them look female.

The girls seemed to think it was a clever decision on the Emperor's behalf, given that most citizens probably would be more inclined to trust female-looking bots to take care of their children and their homes. Toshiko did wonder, though, what broader influence the fact of all those Service-bots looking like women might have on people, and whether it could even mark a step back in the direction of the island's pre-granitarium days, when, from what she'd been able to make out, women had been seen as little more than domestic slaves.

In being the Archipelago's first female Emperor, Asayo Soramoto was herself a pioneer. Of course, Toshiko had listened to Mei's many diatribes against her, and so did understand how the Emperor, together with the office she held, was to blame for so much of the unfairness and violence that underpinned Rainshadow City. She still couldn't help but feel a little disappointed in her now, though.

She also couldn't help but wonder, too, if such accurately human-looking bots might just be a little too creepy for comfort. After all, while there were plenty of bots here in Rainshadow City already, none were fully humanoid – and the idea did unsettle her.

She frowned as she moved forward a step in the queue and the girls in front of her began ordering their bubble teas and cups of Kopi C. The truth was, she couldn't even begin to predict all the different kinds of impacts the bots might have. Hundreds of thousands of them in Rainshadow City seemed almost too huge to imagine. And then the LIFE-Hub itself, too, was going to have to be much bigger than she'd ever expected, if it was going to make so many bots, and also include all those separate places within it – the Beginnings Complex, the Workforce Basecamp, and the rest.

Toshiko scratched Mochi's ears. 'Where on the island would there even be room for something like that?' she wondered aloud.

As far as she knew, all of the space on which it was possible to build had already been used. Rainshadow island wasn't a big place by any measure, and since the granitarium boom, the city had grown to cover almost the whole of it, even spreading up the sides of its low mountains, which were all now dominated by granitarium mines. There wasn't any wilderness left to destroy, or build over.

Toshiko's eyes drifted to the Kawakami tattoo on her wrist, and, hitching Mochi up in her arms, she began tracing its familiar pattern of three terns over the water with her fingertips. Was it finally time to admit that she wanted her family's help, and advice? For all that Mei exasperated her sometimes, Toshiko would give a lot, right now, for her and Jun's thoughts. Besides, Mochi might currently be perfectly docile here in the queue for the bakery counter, but there was only so long that giving him scraps of pastry was going to keep him happy. Mei knew the real trick to that, too.

CHAPTER SEVEN

None of Us Are Safe

1.

As soon as Toshiko stepped through the front door to the Kawakamis' apartment, she was seized upon by Mei and Jun. That was one of the downsides of the security cameras – there was no way to enter discreetly.

'What in all the Gods did you think you were doing?' Mei shrieked, grabbing her by the shoulders and shaking her, sending a breath-taking spark of pain through her shoulder injury. 'Where *were* you?'

'I'm so glad you're safe, Tosh,' was all Jun said, prying her away from Mei's grip and folding her into a hug that was almost as effective as Mei's aggravation of her wound at bringing tears to her eyes.

'Oh, make no mistake,' Mei said. 'She's not safe. None of us are *safe*. But at least she's here, which is one huge lot better than not here. But *why* were you not here, little sister? And why did you take my cat?'

'He's not your cat, he's our cat,' Toshiko replied, and then immediately wished this hadn't been the first thing she'd chosen to say to her sister after disappearing the way she had.

'Don't even try me,' said Mei. She gathered Mochi up into the kind of squeezing embrace that he'd surely have greeted with claws to the face had it come from anyone other than her, and then turned again to fix Toshiko with her blue-eyeliner-lined gaze. 'You're in disgrace for weeks. For *years*. The only way you could be deader to me is if you were actually dead. Which you could have been. Easily. Do you realize how worried we were?'

'It's true, Tosh,' Jun cut in then. His voice was softer, but the look in his eyes was more serious. 'We took some risks, too, trying to find you.'

'Jun took some risks, is what he means,' Mei said. 'He was nearly captured by the Crows, you know.'

'I'm sorry,' said Toshiko. 'I'm so sorry. I ...' Looking at their expressions of reproach, she found she couldn't even begin to explain. 'I got pastry,' she tried instead, holding out the paper bag of goodies she'd brought home for her siblings.

This didn't have the desired effect at all. Jun's gaze turned sad, seeing the University logo on the bag – clearly thinking, as ever, of how it would be better for her not to spend so much time watching a life none of them could ever lead. Mei, in contrast, didn't seem to care where the bag was from, but seemed affronted by its very existence, focusing on it now with all the concentrated intensity of her anger.

'*That's* why you were missing for hours? That's why your

brother here risked his actual life to try and rescue you? You
went out for *pastry*?'

'No,' Toshiko said, feeling suddenly so tired, and wishing her
siblings would move aside so she could collapse onto the couch.
'The pastry was a side effect. Do you want it or not?'

Mei's eyebrows rose at Toshiko's temerity. Then, in a flash of
neon pink and green nails, she shot out a hand from where she
was holding the contented furball that was Mochi, and seized the
bag. 'What kind of side effect? What did you get?'

With Mei distracted, Jun at last laid a gentle hand on Toshiko's
arm and guided her to the couch. She sank into the cushions with
gratitude, slipping off her shoes and allowing her toes to burrow
into the thick blue rug.

'What happened?' she asked Jun. 'What does she mean, you
were nearly captured by the Crows?'

Toshiko expected Jun to shrug it off and say that Mei was
exaggerating as usual, but he looked serious as he came to sit on
the adjacent couch by the wall. 'That's what happened,' he told
her. 'The Crows recognized me as a Kawakami. They knew I
was connected to you.'

'How?' Toshiko asked, feeling her eyes go wide.

'Clearly we aren't always as clever at covering our tracks as
we think.'

'Do they know about the Granitarium Investments job?'

'Potentially not, since they weren't coming after us before you
stole the pearl' – Toshiko winced at the reminder – 'but they must
know we're part of the same gang somehow, and that was our
most conspicuous job.'

'Gang? Since when were we a gang?' said Toshiko. 'We're a
family.'

'They're calling us a gang,' Jun said. 'And circulating our

pictures in the Shadow Column, apparently. We have to be especially careful now, out there in the city. Really, you should have had a disguise, coming home.'

'I came back the long way,' Toshiko told him. 'And there was no one on the street when I entered the building. I waited to make sure.'

Jun sighed. 'Then that'll have to be enough.' He still didn't look happy, though. 'What happened to your shoulder?'

Toshiko shook her head. 'It's a long story. Listen, Jun. I'm sorry. I'm so sorry you nearly got captured. I didn't think you'd go looking for me.'

Jun frowned. 'What else was I going to do?'

Toshiko shrugged.

'You have to remember that we care about you, Tosh. You're our sister. We're family, and there's only the three of us. I promised Reiko I would look after you. I wasn't just going to let you disappear on your own. Not with the Crows after you.'

Toshiko only bit her lip and grabbed one of Mei's round, kawaii creature cushions. She felt so stupid for not thinking about what her siblings would do, what they would risk to keep her safe. She'd thought only of herself, of her wounded pride at messing up the Turning Leaf Festival mission, and her desire to prove herself. It all felt so small, now.

'I'm sorry,' she said again. It came out as a whisper.

'It's okay,' Jun told her. 'Just don't do it again, all right?'

'Hey, you didn't do too bad on this pastry,' Mei piped up then. She was still poking around in the bakery bag's contents, Mochi now back in his traditional position of being draped around her shoulders, like a grouchy scarf. 'The University might be full of stuck-up, Emperor-obsessed drones, but I do love the café's azuki bean cakes.'

'I know,' Toshiko replied. 'Mochi reminded me.'

'Did he actually?'

'No, of course he didn't. What do you think? He's a cat.'

Mei rolled her eyes. 'It could totally have been possible. Mochi's a very intelligent cat. More intelligent than some sisters around here, in fact. Though, in honour of you remembering my love of azuki bean paste, I have decided that you are granted the privilege of witnessing the unveiling of my side project.'

'Your side project? You don't mean—'

'The ultimate boba machine? Yes, sister, I do. It's ready.'

Suddenly, Mei was herding both Toshiko and Jun off the sofas.

'Every flavour and every flavour combination you could possibly imagine,' she was saying. 'And don't tell me it wasn't a good use of the tech budget. It's providing essential team-building opportunities and refreshment for this, our crucial strategy-making, ground-breaking, plan-forming gang meeting.'

'Our what?' Toshiko blinked as Mei steered them to the kitchen doorway.

'Our gang meeting,' Mei repeated. 'We need a plan. Boba will help.'

Shouldering past her siblings into the kitchen, bag of pastry still in hand, Mei gestured grandly towards the counter, where stood a vast, gleaming gadget boasting an impressive array of levers, nozzles, bottles and tubes. It stood out against the ceramic kitchen tiles like a spaceship in a grandma's living room. It was also somewhat incongruously covered with entertaining cat stickers. The cat, striking a different pose in each sticker, looked so much like Mochi that Toshiko was sure Mei must have had them made custom.

'Oh,' Jun said, staring at the machine, looking a little dazed.

'There it is. Our tech budget. And we're leaning into the "gang" thing now, I see.'

Mei shrugged. 'We steal things, we break the law, we do heists. We can be both a family and a gang, right? Also, being in a gang sounds fun, and we're never allowed to be anything fun in this stupid city. I *like* being in a gang.'

'The Crows are meant to be the only gang in town,' Jun reminded her. 'It could be dangerous to call ourselves that.'

'They already think we're a gang,' Mei said. 'And everything's dangerous now. Stop worrying and tell me what flavour you want.'

'What flavours do you have?' Jun asked, still sounding grudging.

Mei tapped impatient fingernails on the kitchen counter. 'I told you, it's ultimate. Anything you could imagine.'

'Could it do a simple milk tea with plain tapioca pearls?'

'Excuse me?' Mei and Mochi were staring at Jun with twin expressions of outrage. 'I offer you any flavour on the planet and *that's* what you choose?'

2.

Travellers to the Archipelago often said that the view over the ocean from Rainshadow City at sundown was one of the most beautiful sights in the world. Unlike the quick, blink-and-you-miss-them sunsets of the islands further south, Rainshadow City took its time to say farewell to each day. Oranges and reds bled out over the sea as the sun began its descent, washing like paint over the water's surface. If you stood on the seafront promenade at this time of year, you could watch terns silhouetted against the display of colour, dancing over the waves and dipping in and out of the floating city of fishing boats and traders on their ways back and forth from the covered market. It seemed a ghost vista, almost, from the pre-granitarium days of old Navishima.

Looking out to sea as he sat on the stone steps of the promenade in front of the Shadow Column this evening, though, Theo found himself barely noticing the seductive beauty of the evening. He held in his hand one of this afternoon's paper news bulletins, several more of which were blowing over the steps, around his boots.

ALISE to revolutionize our city! declared the headline.

He'd laughed, when he'd first read the summary of the Emperor's plans. Of course the citizens of Rainshadow City would find hyper-intelligent bots more palatable than foreigners like him. At least, at a push, all these new bots might mean a little less hideous, dangerous work for the Keeper's Children to do. His initial amusement had faded quickly however, leaving him scowling at the ocean. It was calm this evening, presenting an innocent face that belied the ferocity of the winter swells that were surely just around the corner. He rubbed his eyes, sighed, and crumpled the bulletin into his pocket.

Sunset, he considered. What kind of person chose that, as a time to meet? Did the Captain not own a chronometer? The whole unnecessary drama and vagueness of it all was intentional, surely. It had to be an attempt to disconcert him, and put him at a disadvantage – just like that stunt with the crate. He still couldn't figure out whether she'd guessed he would save himself with the Gift. If she had, then it was possible this meeting could bring him something that all his searches of the library had failed to. He wasn't sure if he felt more excited or apprehensive about the idea. Either way, it was probably best not to get his expectations up. There was a good chance, after all, that the Captain simply enjoyed messing with people.

He drew in a deep breath, inhaling the scents around him – sea salt and fresh fish from the sea, jasmine from the vines trailing over the steps, and lemongrass, frying ginger and coconut from the food stalls behind him. It was all collectively such a distinctively Rainshadow City aroma that, breathing it in, Theo found himself hit by a sudden pang of homesickness. He dug his fingernails into his palms. He, of all people, could not afford to be nostalgic.

The sun had sunk, now, to hovering not much more than an inch above the horizon – which seemed close enough, he decided. He pushed himself to his feet, dusted off his perennially filthy footsoldier trousers, and began heading up the steps, towards the looming heights of the Shadow Column.

One of the tallest skyscrapers in Rainshadow City, the Shadow Column was also one of the most distinctive features of the skyline, with its jagged spire gesturing menacingly up to the heavens. It took its name from the reflective, charcoal-coloured glass of its walls, which gave passers-by the momentary illusion of transparency, before foiling any overly enquiring eyes with its gloomy opacity. Theo had never been inside before, but he'd heard from those few footsoldiers who'd been admitted past its daunting façade that the interior was like a vision of the future, with everything state-of-the-art, from the coffee machines to the weapons.

The weapons certainly did look fancy, Theo noted as he approached the lines of security officials stationed outside the building. All of them wore long, curving katana on their belts – the hilts wrapped in silk cords, and the sleek, dark wood scabbards inlaid with gleaming silver versions of the Crows' double-bird insignia. Theo kept his head held high as he approached, trying not to think about how quickly those sharp blades could surely be drawn, or about the last time he'd walked up to security officials like this, at the border checkpoint where he'd been refused a City ID card.

'Eleanor Minami sent me,' he said, repeating what the Captain had said, exactly.

Amazingly, those words operated like a magic ticket, making everything work more smoothly than any other process he'd experienced yet, since arriving on Rainshadow island. He found himself whisked past all the security guards and electronic body scanners, and was soon stepping into the vast atrium at the building's heart.

The Shadow Column was nothing if not true to its name. Almost everything inside seemed to have been made from the same dark, reflective glass as the building's exterior, giving Theo the impression of having stepped into an uncanny world, located in the heart of a raincloud. Hundreds of people in dark business suits moved through this muted yet sleek environment, walking purposefully through the vast space, only to disappear behind closed doors, or into the central bank of elevators that stretched skywards to the seemingly thousands of floors unfolding above.

'If it isn't Bluejay,' a familiar voice rang out before he could take in much more of his surroundings. 'Didn't expect to see you here.'

Theo looked away from one of the many screens on the atrium's wall – which had been showing an image of the same man from the Kawakamis that he'd witnessed the Santos brothers let go this morning – only to see Hiroto Santos himself coming towards him now, peeling off from a group emerging from one of the elevators. With a coffee in hand, and wearing a sharply tailored suit, Hiroto bore very little resemblance to that haunted young man from the waterfront.

'How did you even get in here?' Hiroto sneered now, looking Theo up and down. 'I didn't think they let people like you through the front doors.'

'Eleanor Minami sent me,' Theo hazarded.

Hiroto whistled. 'Very confident, aren't you? Can't think what you've done to earn a punishment this grand. I knew you were useless, Bluejay, but useless enough to attract the attention of the top brass? Now that's some achievement.'

'Come this way please,' said a calm, female voice next to Theo then. 'Ignore the fool with the coffee.'

It was the Captain, and she'd certainly spoken loud enough for Hiroto to hear. Her seniority here in the Crows' headquarters was obvious, even in spite of her youth. Turning to her now, Theo noticed how everyone who so much as walked past her through the foyer seemed to bow slightly, lowering their heads in deference. Even her choice of clothing – an emerald green trouser suit – seemed to elevate her above the rest of the comparatively nondescript Crows. She wore the same dark glasses as always, of course. As far as Theo knew, she was never seen without them. Looking at them now, close up and in daylight, he wondered if they could even be made from the same distinctive glass that was so ubiquitous here in the Shadow Column. He glanced back at Hiroto then, and felt a spark of satisfaction to see him looking as if he'd been slapped in the face. Theo flashed him a grin as he stood up to follow the Captain. Hiroto only glowered back.

No one else joined them in the elevator, and they stood in silence as they shot upwards, past more floors than Theo would have ever thought it was possible for a building to have.

'Who even is Eleanor Minami?' he asked the Captain eventually, to break the silence more than anything else. 'Is it you?'

'Don't be ridiculous,' was all she replied.

3.

After Mei had finally accepted that Jun really did want plain milk tea, and then had made drinks for them all, and had given Mochi his dinner, the three Kawakamis gathered around their large, wooden dining table for their planning meeting. They each had a cup of their favourite bubble tea in front of them, the iron candelabra was lit, and Toshiko had cut up the azuki bean and lotus seed paste pastries that she'd brought home from the University, setting out these bite-sized chunks on a plate in the table's centre, ready to be shared.

For the moment, everything seemed to her almost exactly as it should be. Here she was with her siblings again, the three of them working together to protect their small family. And yet, looking at Mei and Jun now – Mei poking at the pearls in her tea with her straw while Jun set out paper and pens on the tabletop – Toshiko was hit with a sense of bittersweetness as she found herself taken back, suddenly, to a memory of them all sitting around a different table in another time, ready to begin the day's lessons. Reiko had always started the mornings by giving each of them a math problem to solve. Mei had loved this, of course, because she was good at math. Toshiko had come to love it too, though, because no matter how many times she got a problem wrong, Reiko would always sit by her, and patiently talk her through all the steps to solving it correctly, never letting the older two interrupt until she was sure Toshiko really did understand.

'You okay, Tosh?' Jun asked, breaking through her thoughts.

She only nodded, and helped herself to a chunk of lotus seed paste pastry, hoping its sweetness would distract her from the sudden sadness that had come over her.

'Right,' Mei said, seizing a sheet of paper from Jun and ignoring his frown as she wrote the characters for *"gang strategy meeting"* across the top of it, and double-underlined them. 'First things first,' she turned to Toshiko. 'What happened to you this morning? Explain.'

Sipping her passionfruit tea for courage, Toshiko recounted what had happened, though she left out the details of some of the more dangerous-sounding parts, as well as the confusing encounter with the boy with the ocean-blue eyes. She minimized the seriousness of her shoulder injury, too, reassuring them that Auntie Mailee had seen to it, and tried not to notice Jun's mouth still turning to a thin line of worry as he eyed the bandage. When she got to explaining about the pearl, both Mei and Jun's eyes widened.

'Do you still have it now?' Jun asked.

Toshiko nodded, pulling it out on its chain from under her shirt to show them. 'Want it?'

Jun shook his head. 'You keep it. If it helps with fighting, you should have it. You're the only one of us who knows how.'

'It doesn't feel like it's only about fighting, though,' Toshiko said. She stared into her tea, searching for the right way to explain the golden web of light she experienced when she drew on the pearl's power. 'It's like ... it helps me see the energy in everything. And I can then use that for fighting. But it might help with other things, too.'

'It didn't help me last night, when I was trying to figure out what it was,' frowned Mei. 'If you can make the pearl work, you keep it for now.' She jotted a note about the pearl on her sheet of paper. 'So, as far as I see it,' she continued, 'the upshot of everything you did this morning is that the Crows are still coming for us and for the pearl, but now Saito will be even angrier, and he won't underestimate you again as he knows that you can fight. Right?'

Toshiko sighed, wishing that just sometimes Mei wouldn't be quite so blunt. 'I suppose so, yes.'

'Good.' Mei jotted some more notes, capturing what she'd just said. 'So what we need to do is to stop him, and the Crows he's put on our tail.'

'I think so,' Toshiko said, feeling a little nervous now. Everything finally felt so calm here, in spite of the threats outside, and she didn't want to disrupt that feeling. And yet she knew she had to tell them about all the puzzle pieces that had been sliding together in her mind ever since she'd left Golden Moon Square, to form an ominous picture. 'Except that I was thinking,' she began, with a wary glance at Mei, 'that maybe we could try to think bigger than just escaping the Crows. That we could try to address the bigger picture.'

'What do you mean, the bigger picture?' Mei immediately shot back, as Jun began to look even more worried.

'You've heard the news about those new ALISE bots?' she asked her siblings.

Both of them nodded. 'It would have been hard to miss,' Jun said. 'Even if we hadn't seen the telecast, it's all over the afternoon bulletin.'

'Well,' Toshiko continued, 'I think those bots might be linked to the Crows.'

'Go on,' said Mei, looking interested now.

Toshiko took another fortifying sip of tea, before voicing the fear that she'd come to feel more and more certain was the truth. 'The Emperor said in the telecast that she's got this new mineral, which she can use to power the ALISE bots. I think that might be what's in that warehouse that the Crows have taken over, at the docks. I heard two scientists, earlier, talking.'

'But why would the Emperor get the Crows to import it for her, though?' Jun asked. 'Surely she has people of her own to do that.'

'Unless it was obtained illegally,' Mei cut in. 'Jun, you said that the boatman who gave you a lift this morning mentioned ship-loads of something coming from Muralania. Muralania stands outside the Empire, so good old Emperor Asayo may well have decided that there were easier and cheaper ways of getting hold of whatever this is than those offered by legal and legitimate trade.'

'You're saying that whatever is in that warehouse might be stolen,' Jun finished her thought.

'Precisely,' said Mei. 'And if that's the case, of course the Emperor would choose to import it through the Crows, to keep her hands clean. We know how she always uses them to do her dirty work.'

'That's the other thing,' Toshiko spoke up again. 'I think I know where she's going to build the LIFE-Hub.'

'How do you mean?' asked Jun, as Mei watched her closely, brow furrowed.

Toshiko thought back again to what Mailee had told her this morning, about the Crows measuring up land in the Crescent, and testing the soil. She was right about this, surely – even if she really didn't want to be.

'I think she's going to build the LIFE-Hub on the Keeper's Crescent,' she told her siblings, the words coming out in a rush.

'What?' Mei said immediately, her pen held suspended in mid-air above her sheet of paper, forgotten in her alarm. 'But what will happen to the Keeper's Children?'

'Exactly,' Toshiko told her sister. 'That's what I'm worried about. I'm not sure what the Emperor and the Crows have got planned for them, but I'd bet a lot of credits that it's nothing good.'

Both Mei and Jun were looking just as she felt, now, at the idea.

'That's what I meant by *the bigger picture*,' she told them. 'And that's why I think that maybe now we should decide to do more than just retreat, and keep on running and hiding from Ken Saito – that we should go on the offensive instead, and actually try to do something about all this.'

An uncertain silence filled the room, only to be finally broken by Mei.

'Hear, hear,' she said, simply. 'I see you've grown up, little sister. I agree.'

'Jun?' Toshiko asked.

'I see your point,' he said, carefully, 'but is it really up to us to try and fix something so big? It's just not safe, for one thing – and you're still so young, Toshiko.'

'But it's just like Mei said earlier,' Toshiko told him, surprised to find herself actually agreeing with her sister, for once. 'I'm not safe, anyway. And I'm not sure I ever have been – not even before I stole the pearl. I certainly wasn't safe as a baby, before Reiko took me in. I was abandoned in the scrublands by the Crescent. And then I was hardly safe in the Crescent, either – none of us living there could be, with the Crows about. I haven't even been safe since we left, living by a forged ID, and being forced to steal for a living. I'll never be safe, none of us will be, while the Crows can decide to come for us at any moment, whenever it suits them. And that will always be the case, unless we do something to stop them.'

Even Mochi was staring at her now. Toshiko ploughed on, her voice rising from tentative to passionate as she surprised even herself with the full extent of the new conviction she felt.

'I mean, this is just more of the same old thing, isn't it?' she said. 'If I'm right, and they are planning to build the LIFE-Hub where the Crescent is, this whole plan of theirs is just like what happened to Reiko, all over again. It's that same sense they have, that they can just do what they like to anyone who's undocumented, and no one will challenge them. But we can't keep letting the Crows, or the Emperor, attack the tiny amounts of freedom and land and *life* that the Keeper's Children have managed to carve out for themselves – Keeper's Children like Reiko was, and like we were, back then. I think that's the bigger picture, really. And I think that's how we get real revenge for what happened to Reiko – and how we finally properly protect ourselves, too. We dare to do something big, that would definitely stop them from just taking what they want from people like us, again and again – something that would help us to get what we want, instead.'

'And what do we want?' asked Mei, quietly.

'Just for us, and for any other Keeper's Child, to have as much of a chance at life as everyone else on this Godsdamned island,' Toshiko answered, simply.

'Hell yeah,' Mei said to that. 'You know, I think I love this real revenge idea. Sign me up.'

Toshiko looked over again at Jun. He seemed to hesitate, before he took a deep breath, and nodded. 'Okay,' he said. 'I suppose I'm with you, too. It's just . . . I promised Reiko I'd protect you.'

'I know,' Toshiko told him. 'Thank you, Jun.' She reached across to grasp his shoulder, and smiled.

The moment was broken by the aggressively loud, wet sounds of Mei sucking at the dregs of her bubble tea with her straw.

'Mochi agrees, too,' she said, 'which makes it unanimous.' Then she grinned, a little maniacally. 'So we're actually doing this? We're taking on the Crows and the Emperor?'

'You're definitely enjoying this way too much,' Jun told her, 'but yes, I suppose we're agreed.' He managed a smile. 'Even if I did want to do anything else, I'd be outvoted anyway, since we seem to be counting Mochi.'

Mei gave a whoop and knocked over her empty cup in excitement. 'Trust me, if you think this is me enjoying something too much, you haven't seen anything yet. So – how are we going to do this?'

Both Toshiko and Jun looked blankly back at her across the table.

'Seriously?' Mei threw up her hands. 'Seriously, Toshiko? After all those big speeches, you have literally no plan for how we're even going to start?' She sighed. 'Honestly, you two expect me to do all the work around here.'

Tutting now, Mei jumped to her feet, disappearing into her tech cave. Moments later, she was back with her laptop. Staring alternately between her screen and the notes she'd scribbled throughout the meeting, she began to type, furiously.

'Mei, what are you . . . ?' Toshiko began, before Mei made a noise of warning.

'Don't interrupt a genius at work,' she said, her eyes never leaving her screen. 'Unless it's to feed me sustenance.'

Toshiko obligingly passed over a slice of azuki bean pastry, before sitting back to wait in silence.

'So,' Mei said eventually, looking up just when Toshiko and Jun were beginning to shift awkwardly in their seats. 'The Emperor is unveiling the first of her ALISE bots at another party at the Palace tonight, and my extremely useful hacking skills have allowed me to find a lovely image of the invitation, which I think I could use to make a convincing enough counterfeit to get us through the gates.'

She spun her laptop screen around to show them an image of an invitation written out in ornate script, decorated with illustrations of boats, waves, tridents and seabirds – a gesture to the island's past, when its people's fortunes had risen or fallen with the moods of the sea. It felt strangely incongruous to Toshiko, given the reason for the party.

'I say we crash this party,' Mei declared. 'Kind of like how Toshiko did with the one last night, except this time without getting caught.'

Toshiko made a face at her sister across the table. Mei only raised a sarcastic eyebrow, before continuing.

'The way I see it,' she told Toshiko and Jun, 'is that we need more information. We don't know anything for certain yet really, and if Asayo Soramoto is launching the whole ALISE enterprise to her cronies and inner circle tonight, the chances are that she'll tell them where the planned location for the LIFE-Hub is. If she does, then we'll know one way or another whether Toshiko's theory is correct, and even if she doesn't actually announce the location, surely someone at the party will know where the LIFE-Hub's going to be – it's going to be a huge complex, after all, so it can't be that big of a secret. And then I could also try and get a scan of one of the ALISE bots, too, to try to find out what this mineral is that's powering them, which we think is now filling up that warehouse. And that could provide us with some ideas for how to mess things up for the Crows, too.'

'But, wait,' Toshiko interrupted. 'Even if we have a convincing mock-up of the invitation, the Guards will still recognize us, won't they? If the Emperor is working as closely with the Crows as we think, they'll surely have given her people our pictures by now. And everyone last night at the banquet saw me, anyway.'

'Oh but they won't recognize us' – Mei gave her a mysterious raise of the eyebrows – 'because we have a master costumier right here.' She turned to face Jun, across the table. 'Reckon you can whip us up three new disguises by tonight?'

'Wait,' Jun was already frowning. '*Three* new characters? You mean you're coming with us? You never do fieldwork.'

'I do sometimes.'

Toshiko and Jun exchanged a look.

'Okay fine, I never come, but usually you need tech support,' Mei folded her arms. 'But this is a tech party. You need me there to investigate the bots. And I can't even remember the last time I went to a party, anyway. I never get the chance to dress fancy.'

'I'm not saying you can't come,' Jun laughed. 'I'm just surprised. What will you do, so far away from snacks?'

'There'll be snacks there,' Mei assured him. 'Fancy canapés, probably. There always are, at these kinds of events.'

Toshiko giggled. 'And how would you know?'

'Oh, I know,' Mei said. 'There's more to me than meets the eye, little sister.'

'Sure there is,' said Jun. 'But how will you cope without Mochi? You've already been separated for nearly a whole day.'

The Kawakamis turned to observe the cat – who was now a round, contentedly snoring bundle of fur on the sofa.

'Oh, but Mochi's coming with us,' said Mei. 'Sorry, Jun. I probably should have said *four* new disguises. Your tailoring skills extend to making costumes for cats, right?'

Jun groaned. 'You're joking, aren't you?'

CHAPTER EIGHT

Preparations for a Party

1.

It was afternoon, and the shadows were lengthening in the Palace gardens. Haru's mother was in another meeting, conferring with her officials about the announcement she'd made in the telecast, and Kei was off in the laundry wing, busy with some chore. Everywhere in the gardens, stewards were putting up lights and decorations in preparation for the evening's big party, and Haru, left largely to his own devices, had come out to watch them. He always liked the decorations they put up for his mother's parties much more than he liked the events themselves.

Sitting down on the grassy bank by the frog pond to watch two stewards on ladders string a chain of lanterns through the boughs of a magnolia tree, he found his eyelids drooping almost immediately in the warmth of the low sun. He kicked off his slippers to enjoy the coolness of the neatly shorn grass between his toes, and then curled up on the bank, thinking he would close his eyes just for a moment, and let the sun play on their lids.

As Haru's breathing settled into the steady, calm rhythm of the soundly asleep, he began to dream of Kei's home, on Muralania. He had only left the Palace a handful of times in his life and had certainly never been to Muralania, but he knew this place in his dream had to be it, because of the dragon.

Haru couldn't see the dragon as clearly as he would have liked, because while he was sitting on the shores of a vast lake, it was swimming far out in the water, where the lake was shrouded in thick, white mist. He could only just make out the shadowed silhouette of its vast, serpentine body as it twisted through the water, along with hints of the bright turquoise colour of its scales, and a pale glow like moonlight coming from somewhere close to its throat. Dragons had pearls at their throats, Kei had told him, which they could use to draw extra Sola from a special type of rock in the mountains. Maybe the silvery glow meant this dragon was channelling Sola right now.

He called out for Kei to come and see, and all at once she was there next to him on the banks of the lake.

'Dragons are the kings and queens of the Sun Spirits,' she said again, just as she'd told him that morning.

For one glorious instant as Kei's words seemed to settle around him, Haru saw one of the dragon's eyes glowing bright gold through the mist. Then the dragon blinked, slowly, and turned away, to disappear beneath the surface of the water.

'Did you see that, Kei?' Haru breathed, in his dream.

'Did I see what?' Kei's voice replied.

Strangely, it had sounded as if she'd been standing somewhere above him when she'd spoken, instead of where she should have been, next to him on the banks of the lake.

Haru's eyes fluttered open to see the real Kei smiling down at him. The magnolia tree behind her was now fully decked out with lanterns, and the two stewards with their ladders had disappeared.

'Kei!' Haru cried out in surprise, sitting up. 'You were in my dream.'

'Was I, really? Was it a good dream?'

'I think so,' Haru replied, rubbing his eyes. 'I can't remember all of it, now.'

She laughed. 'Then it can't have been a terrible one, at least. Come on, it's time to get you fed before you have to get ready for the party.'

Haru groaned, flopping back down on the grass. 'Do I have to go?'

Kei nodded. 'Sorry, Princeling. Your mother demands it. But you can wear your favourite blue robe, and I happen to know that the cooks have prepared inari sushi as part of your dinner. Does any of that make it better?'

Haru considered it, head tipped to one side, before nodding.

'I thought it might,' said Kei.

He let her pull him to his feet, and begin leading him back to the Palace.

'Kei,' he asked as they went. 'Did the dragon that came to your village have turquoise scales and golden eyes?'

'It did indeed,' she said, blinking down at him. 'But how would you ever be able to guess a thing like that, Princeling?'

Haru didn't know how to answer her though, so he only shrugged and ran on ahead, humming the little song he always sang when there was inari sushi for dinner.

2.

There was one more room in the Kawakamis' flat, aside from
the bedrooms, kitchen, living room, bathroom and Mei's tech
lab. Over the years, this room had gradually been taken over by
Jun, as a home for all the disguises and outfits that he'd lovingly
restored, for use in all their various heists. He referred to it as
'the dressing-up box,' always using massively exaggerated air
quotes as he did so, as if to underline the extent to which that
unassuming name completely failed to capture the room's un-
surpassed majesty.

Stepping through the doorway, a visitor to Jun's 'dressing-
up box' was met with an open central area marked out by a
gold-embroidered rug. On either side stood a series of clothing
racks, thick with an array of costumes. A large mirror with
an ornate jade edge rested against the far wall, next to which
stood Jun's beloved sewing machine and three tailoring dummies, all dressed in half-finished sleeves and collars, colourfully
mismatched.

Today, though, Toshiko found her gaze drawn to a small
wooden cabinet next to these dummies, which she hadn't noticed
before. Like all the furniture Jun chose, usually from the covered
market, this cabinet was beautiful – adorned with mother-of-
pearl inlay, depicting interweaving leaves and vines. It wasn't the
cabinet's beauty, though, that had caught her attention – it was
what Jun had arranged on top of it. First, there was a sketch of the
Keeper, which Toshiko was sure she remembered Jun drawing
as a child, in the Crescent. Next to this sketch stood a stack of
incense sticks and a small stand, and then alongside these was a
small, framed painting of Auntie Reiko.

Jun's painting captured Reiko exactly as Toshiko remembered

her – in a familiar pose, standing in the sunlight in their old house's doorway. She seemed to be laughing at something a neighbour had just said, gesturing with one hand, while holding a cup of tea in the other. Seeing this image for the first time now, Toshiko realized how little she ever came into this room, too often leaving Jun to himself. She'd forgotten what a good artist her brother was, and more than that, too – Jun hardly ever talked about his grief, and always seemed so steady, and so mild in his temperament. Suddenly, Toshiko found herself realizing anew just how much he must miss Reiko, too, even if he did choose to express it in quieter ways than she or Mei tended to.

Following his sisters into 'the dressing-up box' this afternoon, Jun went over to the cabinet and struck a match to light one of the incense sticks. It was a Keeper's Crescent custom – evolved from older, Mainlander traditions – to burn incense for anyone you wanted to keep in your heart, whether they be living or dead, human or God. Growing up, the Crescent's elders had always told the three Kawakamis that the smoke from the incense would diffuse outwards, carrying their thoughts and wishes with it to whomever it was they wanted to reach, regardless of where that person may be, in this world or the next.

This afternoon, Jun let the incense stick burn for a moment, before he shook out the flame to set a richly scented curl of smoke twisting out into the lamplit room.

'One for the Keeper,' he said, placing the incense stick carefully in the stand as the warm, familiar smells of mandarin peel and cinnamon began to fill the space around them. 'Thank you for watching over our family.'

He repeated the process with a second incense stick, setting it next to the first just as the smoke began rising from its tip. 'And one for our beloved Reiko,' he said. 'We miss you, and hope you're doing well in the next world. Thank you for watching over us, too.'

'It's a beautiful painting,' Mei told Jun, after a moment of quiet.

He looked up from arranging the incense sticks to study it himself, and from the way his smile tinged sad at the edges, Toshiko knew he wasn't really examining the quality of his handiwork.

'Well, you know,' was all he said, though. 'I had to make sure I never forgot a single thing about her. That none of us would. Anyway. We should probably get to work.'

'Yes, we should,' Mei agreed, blinking fast as she turned away from the picture, her tone suddenly more determined and efficient than ever. She glanced around the room, scowling at all the many different pieces of clothing. 'Where do we start?'

'Well,' Jun said, 'I've been thinking: since it's a party, we might need to do more than simply look the part. We'll have to go properly undercover, inventing full characters for ourselves, so that we're ready to speak to people, too. And I think it'll probably work best if we don't pretend to be from Rainshadow island itself. So how do the two of you feel about the idea of doing some acting?'

Toshiko frowned. Jun was probably right. The upper echelons of Rainshadow City's high society were so small that within them, everyone would surely already know everyone else. It was very possible, too, that Jun himself might well actually be able to convince as a foreign aristocrat for the evening. He'd always had a theatrical streak, ever since they'd been children making up plays together for Auntie Reiko to watch, back in their little house in the Crescent. He was good with languages too, able to speak pretty fluent Mainlander from having grown up on the Mainland until he was six, and then he'd also learnt quite a bit of Vilmian from Mailee, as well as passable amounts of at least three other Archipelagan languages, just from talking to people while going about his healing work, which often involved helping new arrivals to the Crescent. By contrast, Toshiko couldn't speak a single other language, and wasn't even very sure about accents – even those from the nearest of the neighbouring islands. Neither she nor Mei had left Rainshadow island in their lives.

'I feel great about acting,' Mei was already declaring, though. 'It's easy, right?' She put on a thick, vastly unconvincing Aurian accent – 'I am a noblewoman from Auria. I live in a mansion and have my own private pool.'

Jun raised an eyebrow. 'Really?'

'What?' Mei said, affronted, sticking with the accent. If anything, it seemed now to be getting worse. 'But I actually am from Auria.'

'Um – I mean, your mother was,' Jun said. 'But that doesn't mean you are.'

Mei rolled her eyes. 'Well, it's hardly like I'm from Rainshadow City, is it?' she retorted, back to her normal voice, now. 'After all, Asayo Soramoto and her citizens would only try to throw me out if they ever found out I was here.'

3.

Up on the fiftieth floor of the Shadow Column, the sleek metal doors facing Theo and the Captain slid open. The room they revealed bore such little resemblance to the rest of the building's interior that for a moment Theo found himself wondering, irrationally, if the laws of reality might have made some mistake. In contrast to all the dark, reflective glass filling the building below, Theo was faced now with something that looked like a somewhat dated, but still rather homely living room. A floor of rough wooden boards stretched to a large rug, embroidered with blue and silver flowers, in the centre of which stood a low, lacquered coffee table, bearing a traditional Navishian clay-fired tea set.

Sitting side by side at this table in mismatched armchairs were a small, elderly lady and a much younger man. A far more spindly-looking chair stood empty opposite them. Both looked up as Theo and the Captain entered, and Theo shivered, recognizing the man as Ken Saito.

The old woman's identity still sparked his curiosity, even despite the ominous presence of Saito next to her. Theo gave her a quick, assessing glance while still managing to look as if he were meekly focused on the ground just ahead of his feet – a skill he'd learnt back home in Eardland, surrounded by his neighbours' hostility. She wore gold-framed glasses and a light, padded house jacket, with a silk scarf knotted around her neck. Beneath the jacket, she had on a cream rollneck jumper and loose but tailored slacks. She couldn't have been more than five feet tall, and laughter lines creased the corners of her light grey eyes as she smiled at their approach. She absolutely looked, Theo thought, like a picture-book drawing of someone's grandma.

Ken Saito, next to her, formed a striking contrast. The piercing look he turned on Theo, together with the way he held himself, as a coiled spring of potential violence, did little to set Theo at his ease. Saito had pushed up the sleeves of his black suit jacket, too, leaving his extensive Lucky Crows sleeve tattoos on show. The intricate, interlocking patterns, filled with details of dark birds' wings, red peonies and twisting vines, acted as a clear reminder of the high rank he held within the gang – not that Theo needed one. Like the old woman, Saito stayed seated as Theo gave them both hurried, awkward bows of greeting.

'Ah,' the old woman began. 'So this is the Bluejay, as they call him.'

Her voice was lower and more authoritative than Theo would have expected. He hesitated as she began to beckon him forward.

'Come on,' she said. 'Yes, just like that. Don't be shy.'

Theo glanced sideways at the Captain. She didn't seem fazed in the slightest, and even gave him a shrug. He stepped forward, cautiously, towards the edge of the room's blue and silver rug, wincing as a floorboard shrieked under his tread.

The old lady gave Theo a twinkling smile. 'My, my,' she said. 'What lovely, bright blue eyes. You're a long way from home, Bluejay, aren't you?'

'Indeed, madam,' he managed to say evenly, in reply.

'And do you miss your home?' she probed.

'I do, madam.'

'Leave anyone behind?'

'No one in particular, madam.' He hadn't told anyone on Rainshadow island about Susanna. His memories of her felt both too precious and too painful.

The old lady, though, was nodding. 'I thought so,' she said, as if she'd read his thoughts anyway. She waved a hand at the empty chair at the tea table, across from her. 'Take a seat, go on. Not you though, Hana dear. My thanks, however, for bringing the Bluejay.'

The Captain gave a short bow, and turned to leave through the double doors, which opened and then shut again behind her just as silently as before.

'My granddaughter Hana, you know,' the old lady smiled after her. 'A most impressive young person, in my opinion. What do you think, Bluejay?'

'Most impressive, madam,' he agreed.

The woman's eyes narrowed. 'Yes, we'll loosen your tongue soon enough. But look – you still haven't sat down.'

'My apologies.' Feeling the intensity of her stare, as well as that of scowling Ken Saito next to her, Theo edged over to the empty chair and lowered himself into it.

'There,' the old woman said, placidly. 'That wasn't so hard, was it? Now, would you like some tea?'

'I . . . really couldn't say,' was all Theo managed to reply.

'It would be rude to refuse,' she told him.

'In that case,' Theo said, 'I shall have some tea.'

'Excellent,' she nodded. 'Ken here will pour it for us.'

Next to her, Saito gave a grunt of acknowledgement and began arranging and pouring three steaming cups of tea from the little teapot, accomplishing the process with surprising speed and dexterity, though the cups looked almost comically miniature in his hands. Theo noted the ropes of muscle around his wrists, the roughness of his skin, and the gold signet ring stamped with a dragon that he wore on his little finger. It danced back and forth across the table, catching the light as he distributed the cups and placemats. He served the old lady first, Theo last.

'My consigliere,' the old woman smiled, waving a hand in Saito's direction. 'He's such a good boy. I don't know what I would do without him.'

Saito remained entirely impassive as she patted one of his immense shoulders. The old woman took a sip of her tea then, and gave a contented sigh before setting the cup back down.

'Now, Bluejay,' she said. 'You must be curious as to where you've found yourself, and why. Of all the things I've heard about you, after all, the most frequently repeated is that you are curious, though you do try to hide it. When Hana recruited you, though, she did tell me a little more than that, too: that you managed to learn to speak Navishian, for instance, in a little over two months. A remarkable feat, given that it takes most new arrivals to our shores at least two years to accomplish basic proficiency. And then of course she mentioned that you were light on your feet, and could be light-fingered, too, when you wanted to be, as I believe that jacket of yours can attest ...'

Theo worried the cuffs guiltily. It was true that he'd stolen it from a visiting sailor, posing as a hawker and selling him hot tea on a warm day, only to sneak back and whip the jacket away when the sailor had taken it off. He'd only done that, though, because those first nights when he'd arrived on the island had been so cold.

'Now, I agreed with Hana that these were traits that could absolutely mark you out as someone who might be particularly useful to me, should the right job come up. What really got me interested in your case, though, was when I discovered about all the books.'

'The books?' Theo asked, guiltily.

'Yes,' the old woman smiled. 'The books. All stolen, of course. Now, the simple fact of your reading them at all was remarkable in the first place, among my footsoldiers. I'm sorry to say that the purpose of such a pursuit baffles even my dear consigliere, here.' She patted Saito's hand – and again, amazingly, Saito didn't visibly react. 'I soon began to keep a closer eye, though, on *what* you were reading,' she continued. 'At first, it seemed an entirely random selection of titles. Then, I began to see a possible pattern. And I began to wonder.'

She left the words hanging between them, and Theo found himself uncertain as to whether or not he wanted her to go on. It was true that he'd come here this evening wondering if this might be how he'd finally learn more about the Gift. Some secret part of him may have even considered the idea that, if there was going to be a pocket of acceptance for his strange, possibly cursed abilities anywhere in the world, it surely might be here, amid the notorious criminal underworld of Rainshadow City. And yet, poised now on the precipice of finding himself fully discovered and exposed . . . he felt suddenly afraid.

After all, if this woman did know about the Gift, it could be the beginning of a fresh wave of the same persecution he'd suffered in Eardland. It could be the beginning of disaster. And with very few credits in his pocket and having sworn allegiance to the Crows, it would be a lot harder to run this time, if he needed to.

'Do try some tea before it gets cold,' she instructed now, inter-rupting his thoughts. 'Go on, it's not poisoned.'

She waited until Theo had lifted the cup to his lips and taken a sip. It was immediately and clearly the most delicious thing he'd tasted in months – a flavour that reminded him of summer baked earth, and of jasmine flowers in the evening.

'The truth is, that a long time ago, before any of this' – she gestured vaguely around herself – 'I used to be a teacher, and I still do take an interest in every single one of the promising young people who comes into my care. And the plain fact is that I now have a job that needs doing – and from everything I've learnt about you, I believe you might just be the perfect young man to do it.'

A teacher. Finally it dawned on Theo. 'You're . . .'

'The Sensei, yes. That is what they call me, down below.' She waved a casual hand at the floor as she spoke, seeming to invoke all of the Shadow Column's many floors beneath her, filled with people all working busily in her name. 'People up here tend to just call me Ms Minami, though, or Eleanor. Apart from dear Hana, of course. She calls me Grandma.'

'It's a . . . well. It's an honour to meet you,' Theo stammered, turning to include Ken Saito in the statement too. 'Both of you.'

'Now then, Bluejay,' the Sensei continued. 'Do not speak too soon. I haven't told you what the job will be yet, have I?'

Theo shook his head.

'Exactly. Ken, perhaps you would like to explain.'

4.

Contrary to all of her initial hopes of 'dressing fancy', Mei ended up in the plain, dark blue tunic and trousers of an Imperial Palace steward, her distinctive streaked hair tucked neatly under the uniform's cap.

'I knew that uniform would come in handy one day,' Jun said, delighted. 'If you really want to find things out, be one of the staff.'

'I am unconvinced,' Mei told him.

'Well, unless you can suddenly sway me with a better Aurian accent, or think of some way to conceal Mochi that isn't in a laundry bag filled with towels, then I will respectfully have to ignore your being unconvinced.'

'Why did I suggest this mission again?' Mei sulked.

'Remember the canapés,' Toshiko told her. 'You'll still be able to grab some, as staff.'

'I am more than just my stomach, Toshiko.'

'Allegedly.'

'Shush,' Jun hushed them. 'Toshiko, are you feeling happy with your outfit?'

Toshiko stepped up to the mirror and gave a slow twirl, considering. She was wearing a bright red kimono which Mei had bought on impulse a few years back and then had never worn, 'because no one around here ever gives me a reason to wear anything special.'

In spite of its long, flowing sleeves, this wasn't a full furisode-style kimono of course – not with all the traditional layers of silk, and the heavy, ornate obi sash. Even now, after the Granitarium Investments heist, the Kawakamis simply didn't have that kind of money. This was a more modern, Rainshadow-era design – the kind which could be purchased in the city for a moon credit or two, if you knew the right places to look. However, its pattern of a flock of white cranes soaring over the golden swirls of a river was intricately detailed and undeniably beautiful, and the tracery of gold embroidery on the slimmer version of the sash, too, was of a quality that would surely impress even the most expert eye.

Overall, given that this was a garden party they were attending, Jun had decided that as a disguise for Toshiko, this might just pass muster. From his observations while doing undercover work in Rainshadow City's high society, the younger women were tending to favour these lighter, adapted kimono designs these days anyway, especially in the warmer months – often preferring ease of movement over tradition.

Studying herself in the mirror, Toshiko found herself oddly disarmed by her reflection. The rich shades of red and gold in the kimono's pattern seemed to draw out the darkness of her eyes and hair, as did the matching white, red and pink floral pins that she now wore twisted up into her elaborately plaited chignon. The kimono's collar managed to completely cover all signs of her shoulder injury, too, while the flowing silk sleeves were already encouraging her to carry herself differently, she noticed – straighter, and more gracefully. Like a young woman with presence.

'You look hot,' said Mei, simply, setting Toshiko blushing to the roots of her elaborately styled hair.

'Leave her alone,' said Jun. 'She's not *hot*, she's Aya Ikeda. She's the daughter of an elderly granitarium magnate from Vilmia, attending the party with her dear uncle' – he struck a pose, gesturing at himself – 'to represent her sickly father's interest in investing in the LIFE-Hub. And I'll not have my niece spoken to that way by a mere steward.'

He was clearly enjoying himself now, in spite of his earlier misgivings about this whole plan. While Toshiko had been trying on potential disguises, he'd even dug out some old stage make-up he'd used during their Granitarium Investments heist last year, when he'd spent an afternoon pretending to be a Mainlander banker in his mid-30s, who he'd named Akio Birch. He was already getting excited about inventing the new character he would play at the party this evening – planning to grey his hair, and use his artistic skills to paint a scattering of fine lines around his eyes and mouth.

He turned back to Toshiko, now. 'How do you feel about your costume?' he asked her, again.

She tore her gaze away from the unfamiliar new version of herself in the mirror to look back at him. 'I'm worried about the shoes,' was all she said. 'I don't think I can run, or fight in these.'

She was wearing traditional wooden platform sandals to go with the kimono. She'd never worn them before, and they felt unfamiliar on her feet, forcing her to take awkward, fumbling steps that didn't seem to fit at all with the new fiery red self she saw in the mirror.

'Hopefully you won't need to fight,' Jun told her. 'But if you do, just kick them off. You're still wearing the pearl, right?'

Toshiko nodded, reaching for the golden chain around her

neck. Both Mei and Jun watched closely as she pulled it from the kimono's folds, their curiosity clear.

'Out of interest,' Jun asked her, 'can you feel it doing anything, while you're just standing there, not fighting anyone?'

'I don't think so.' Toshiko shook her head. 'I can still feel that it's there, though, and that I could use it, if I needed it. It's ... kind of like holding an umbrella.'

'Excuse me?' said Mei.

'I just mean that you don't feel very different holding an umbrella when it's all folded up, apart from the fact that you know that if it starts raining, you can put it up, and you'll be protected.'

'I have never seen anything that looked less like an umbrella,' Mei told her.

'May I?' Jun asked then, holding out a hand for the pearl. 'Just for a moment?'

'Of course. I mean – you don't need to ask. It's not really mine, after all.' Toshiko unclipped the catch on the chain, and passed the pearl over. Immediately, its anchoring feeling of potential protection, of safety and power, diminished.

Jun pushed his glasses up his nose, examining the pearl closely on his open palm. Then, after a moment, he folded it in his fingers, and closed his eyes. He took a long, slow breath before opening them again. When he did, he turned to Toshiko.

'I think—' he began, then hesitated. 'I think I can see your pain.'

'My what?' said Toshiko.

'Over your shoulder. Does it still hurt?'

Of course it still hurt – she'd been making light of it, because she'd known he'd worry.

'I suppose maybe a bit,' she hedged. 'But what do you mean, you can *see* it?'

'I honestly don't understand it myself,' Jun said. 'It's like ... there's a disruption in the balance of everything, just around your shoulder. Like a snag. As if someone was knitting and then dropped a stitch.'

He took a step towards Toshiko, and laid a hand ever-so-gently on her bandage, before closing his eyes again, brow furrowed in concentration. And then Toshiko realized she could feel what he was doing. It was exactly like he'd said – an untangling, as if the different knotted strands of pain were unwinding and smoothing out into clear, cool threads of light, before weaving themselves back together again, into the way they were meant to be.

When Jun's eyes opened, her pain was gone, and the irises of his brown eyes were ringed with gold. And then the gold faded, and he let go of her shoulder. Tentatively then, Toshiko loosened the kimono's collar to peel back a corner of her bandage. Instead of the ugly gash Ken Saito had left there with his curved knife, there was only new, smooth skin.

'Thank you,' she breathed.

'Okay, so what in all the Gods just happened?' said Mei.

'My shoulder's better,' Toshiko told her. 'It's healed.'

'So this is literally a magic pearl, then? It can help *you* fight, make *you* heal wounds – what can't it do?'

'I don't think it could make me heal wounds,' said Toshiko. 'I mean, I never felt as if I could do that, when I had it. Maybe it's just that Jun's good at taking care of sick people anyway. Like how I'm good at Hido, and martial arts, generally. Do you feel like it could help you fight?' she asked Jun.

He frowned, then backed up the short length of the room to the clothing rail behind him, and tried an experimental kick. Just as his leg was swinging around, he overbalanced and tripped over a pile of coats on the floor.

'Ouch,' he said, landing awkwardly.

'Good thing you can heal your own injuries, then,' said Mei. 'But how come it gives both of you special powers, and it gave me nothing? I had it with me for *hours* last night in the tech lab. I tried everything on it. I would have dissected it, if it hadn't been completely, weirdly indestructible. Why would it give me nothing?'

Toshiko ignored her. 'This is amazing,' she said to Jun. 'You can heal injuries, and cure pain? Jun, this could literally change the world.'

And then she stopped. She'd noticed something. A single streak of Jun's dark hair – at the front, just near his parting – had turned completely white.

'Jun,' she said, pointing. 'Look!'

He turned to the mirror, all the wonder that had previously lit his expression fading as he stared. 'At least I won't have to grey that bit artificially, now,' he said, with a stab at jauntiness, though he did sound quite shaken.

'I'm sorry,' Toshiko told him. 'D'you think it's because you helped me? I never had anything like that happen to me, when I used the pearl to fight. I'd have warned you, if I had.'

'I knew that pearl wasn't to be trusted!' Mei snatched at Jun's fist that was still holding it, tugging at his fingers to release it.

He opened them, revealing it there, sitting in his palm, so quiet and still and impassive.

'We should lock it up,' Mei said. 'I have this box, in my lab. It's lined with lead, for when I work with granitarium isotopes—'

'No,' Toshiko interrupted. 'I don't want to leave it unattended anywhere, and it could still help us. I could use it to defend us, if anything goes wrong at this party.'

Mei opened her mouth, clearly about to argue. Her objection to the pearl ran deeper, Toshiko understood, than the responsibility it held for turning that streak of Jun's hair white. Whatever strange power it drew on and channelled was anathema to Mei, and everything she believed in – a direct counter to the logical world of science and technology to which she'd devoted her whole intellectual life.

'Could you use your make-up skills to disguise me?' Toshiko asked her sister now, before she could speak again. 'These outfits are one thing, but I think we could still use your help to achieve the full transformations we need.'

Mei hesitated. Jun might enjoy inventing new characters to play, but Mei was the one who seriously loved make-up, for its own sake – loved the armour and artistry of it. She also loved being flattered. Clearly, she felt caught now between arguing further about the pearl, and accepting Toshiko's very well-chosen distraction. 'Fine,' she said, at last. 'But the second that pearl does anything else I don't like, it's going straight into my lead box.'

With that, she turned on her heel and walked out of the room.

'She's right,' Jun said, handing the pearl back to Toshiko. 'We should be careful.'

Toshiko nodded, clipping the chain again around her neck, and hiding the pearl once more amid the folds of her kimono.

A moment later, Mei returned bearing a full make-up bag, literally bursting its seams with various powders and paints.

Before letting Mei get to work, Toshiko paused to take one last glance at herself in the mirror. As she did, she found herself wondering if the boy with the blue eyes who she'd seen in the square would have reacted any differently to her, had she looked like this, earlier. Would he have lingered to talk to her, instead of rushing off like that? Or perhaps her conspicuous scruffiness had been the only reason he'd noticed her at all.

Maybe one day, she thought to herself, she would find herself getting ready for a party like this for real, preparing to go to an event where she really would get to meet other people, and talk to them as herself, as Toshiko – and not as some made-up granitarium magnate's daughter.

'Ready to turn into a completely different person?' Mei asked her with a grin, brandishing a make-up brush.

'Never been readier,' she said, letting the fantasy go as she turned away from the mirror, ready to submit to her sister.

5.

Theo suppressed a shudder as, in a voice which sounded like the human vocal equivalent of rusty nails being churned with gravel, Ken Saito began to explain the job the Crows now wanted him to do.

'Last night, a girl of about your age stole a precious artefact from my possession. It is essential to the wider aims of the Crows, and valuable to me, personally.'

'Poor Ken,' the Sensei cut in, with an almost sly sideways look at her consigliere. 'He was far younger than you are now, Bluejay, when he first came into my care, and at first, I thought he'd be able to do anything without experiencing any pangs of conscience. Then, I realized that even my Ken has his limits.' She looked, indulgently, in Saito's direction. 'It's why I let him keep hold of the pearl, you know. To suppress the nightmares.'

Saito's eyes closed briefly – though whether in acknowledgement of what she'd said, or in anger at her disclosure, Theo couldn't tell.

'The girl who stole the artefact,' he continued, sounding perhaps just a little more tense than before the Sensei had spoken, 'is part of a small gang of youths who, according to our intelligence services, call themselves the Kawakamis. Your task is to befriend the girl, infiltrate these Kawakamis, steal back the artefact to return to us personally, and then activate this explosive device' – he pulled a small lacquer box from his jacket pocket and set it on the table by the teapot – 'and leave it in their home while they are all present.'

'Wait – you want me to kill them?'

'Only after you've safely retrieved the artefact.'

'But . . . I can't just *murder* people like that.'

'Bluejay,' the Sensei cut in then. 'Do not pretend with me.'

'What? I'm not pretending.'

'We know that you have killed before,' she said, looking at him over her glasses.

Theo's mouth went suddenly dry.

'Because, Bluejay, Ken here isn't the only one who knows how night can bring with it all sorts of unwanted visions and memories, is he?' She raised her eyebrows at Theo. 'Even still, let me reassure you that in many ways, once you've killed once, it does become easier to do it again. Just like many other things in this life.'

Theo could feel her eyes still on him as he turned away to look out of the black glass of the windows, to where, outside, the day's final rays of sun were dipping below the waves. She was right; he did get nightmares. They came for him regularly, in spite of how hard he tried not to think back to that night so many months ago now, when the Watch had come for him, armed with batons and clubs – and with what had felt like the whole village in tow, too, everyone hungry to finally see his blood spilt, and brandishing everything from pitchforks and sickles, to flaming torches.

Two of the women had grabbed Susanna, holding her back as she'd tried to persuade them to leave him alone. As the crowd had surrounded him, Theo had been able to hear her calling out, begging everyone to stop as they'd begun kicking, striking and burning him with their torches from all sides.

In his panic, terrified he might never wake up again if he lost consciousness there on the ground, Theo had reached out through the room with the Gift. The first vibrations he'd been able to sense had come from the wooden handle of an axe, held in the hands of one of the villagers who was bearing down on him.

Immediately that Theo had begun using the Gift to exercise even the smallest control over the axe's handle, the man wielding it had dropped it, as if it were poisoned. He'd then fixed Theo with a look of such disgust that all of Theo's fear had combusted into rage – rage at this man, and at the Watch, and at all of these people who'd come here tonight, believing they knew what he was, and that they therefore had a right to break down his door, and to threaten and hurt him, and take Susanna away from him. He'd felt fury at himself, too, for having somehow been born with the Gift, when he'd never wanted to be different. And so he'd lashed out, using the Gift almost reflexively to lift the man's discarded axe into the air, and send it flying almost randomly into the melee – where it had come to rest, buried deep in the chest of an older man, who just at that moment had been making his way through the crowd, unarmed.

Seth, his name had been, and he was Susanna's uncle. While he'd never been fond of Theo, and hadn't been shy in letting him know it, Susanna had been the light of his life, since he'd never had a child of his own. In the days afterwards, Theo had tortured himself with wondering whether Seth might even have been coming forward through the mob that night to try and help him – for Susanna's sake, if not for his own. Regardless, he knew for a certainty that a part of him would never stop reliving that moment when Seth had fallen, toppling like a fallen tree to begin bleeding out on the flagstones.

He'd never forget Susanna's expression, either – how she'd stopped calling out, and had stopped resisting the two women still holding tight to her arms. How she'd looked right at him, too, the horror and fury in her expression suddenly a perfect match for those of all the other villagers.

Theo turned away from the Shadow Column's windows, pushing the memory away again as he forced himself to meet the Sensei's still and rather watchful gaze.

'How do you know so much about me?' he asked, his voice coming out as little more than a whisper.

She only gave him a slight smile – pleased, perhaps, to see how well she'd hit her mark. 'I told you,' she replied. 'I take an interest in all the promising young people in my care. Now can we agree that, in spite of your affectation of delicate sensibilities, you are in fact perfectly capable of fulfilling this task?'

Theo rubbed his eyes. 'You said there was an artefact,' he said. 'What exactly is it? And what makes you think I'll be able to steal it?'

'The artefact in question is a dragon pearl,' the Sensei explained. 'It was taken from Muralania at great risk by Ken here, some years ago. And as we have mentioned, it has certain ... peculiar properties. You will find yourself able to steal it, because the Kawakamis will trust you. They were raised in the Keeper's Crescent, where, unless I am very much mistaken, you yourself lived until relatively recently. It will be easy for you to persuade them to see you as one of their own.'

'Do they really have to die?'

'I am afraid so.' The Sensei's tone was tinged with something almost convincingly like real regret.

'No one crosses the Crows without consequences,' Saito cut in, to underline the point.

'And if I say no to the task?' Theo asked, then.

'No one crosses the Crows without consequences,' Saito said again, with a grin. This was the first time he'd ever seen Saito smile, Theo realized, and it was not a pleasant sight. He felt a sudden flare of anger at how they dared threaten him like this, just assuming he was totally theirs to control.

'So, you see,' the Sensei continued, 'it really is all quite lovely and neat. Having said that, though, I do like to be fair. You would like to return home, yes?'

'I don't see how that's your business,' Theo said.

'Be careful of your tongue, young man. Ken here is a dab hand at breaking fingers, and you'll note that it isn't necessary for you to have all of yours in working order to accomplish this task for me. A couple of broken bones, in fact, might even augment the seeming authenticity of your pose as a needy Keeper's Crescent dweller. Let's try that again. You want to return home.'

'I can't,' Theo said. 'I can never return home.'

'Never?' the Sensei asked. 'Goodness, Bluejay. That seems somewhat dramatic.'

'It would be too dangerous for me to risk going back,' he said, 'and anyway, why would I? There isn't anything there for me now.'

He watched, then, as the Sensei's apparently innocent expression began to twist, until she was grinning at him with a particularly gloating kind of satisfaction. It made him instinctively want to shuffle backwards in his chair, away from her.

'It might interest you to know, Bluejay,' she said, 'that Ken's dragon pearl isn't the only Muralanian object within my collection. I happen to have a keen interest in the creatures and artefacts of Muralania more generally, to the extent that the Emperor, within the halls of her Palace, holds a vast array of Muralanian objects that I have helped her obtain over the years – with the help of my Lucky Crows, of course. In her immense gratitude, the Emperor has granted me free access to this collection, which happens to include none other than a vial of dragon tears. Do you know anything about the properties of dragon tears, Bluejay?'

Theo shook his head. As a Westerner from a land where the largest creature anyone had seen was probably a common kestrel, he could barely imagine that such formidable beasts existed, even behind the fabled walls of Muralania.

'Tears from a dragon,' said the Sensei, 'dropped over the sleeping eyelids of a human being, have the power to erase memories. Just a few drops could make past suspicions, fears and anger melt away, forgotten. Now, Bluejay, can you think of any use you might have for such a substance?'

Theo blinked. Of course he could. He was almost impressed – all the anger he'd felt just a moment ago now blunted, as he all but wanted to laugh at just how comprehensively she'd managed to corner him.

'How big is this vial?' he asked. 'What exactly is the extent of what it could do?'

'It contains enough tears to completely erase the recent memories of one human being. Might that be enough?'

Theo swallowed, silent, feeling almost frightened at what he might say.

The Sensei raised an eyebrow. 'I'm offering you a second chance, Bluejay,' she told him. 'It would be foolish of you not to take it.'

It wasn't a real second chance, he knew. Nothing could ever

bring back Seth, or undo the fact of his having killed a man – a man who'd meant the world to the girl he loved.

And yet, even just the feeling that it could theoretically be possible to return himself in Susanna's eyes to what he'd once been to her exerted an almost physical hold on him – and from the look on the Sensei's face now, she understood that, very well.

'I need some time to consider it,' he said. 'I need to get out of here. I need air.'

'I can't let you go quite yet, I'm afraid, Bluejay,' the Sensei said. 'Before you leave us, Ken here needs to install your Hourglass Tracker.'

Saito flashed him another grin, his teeth seeming to gleam conspicuously in the glow of the day's fading light. Theo actually did edge his chair back on the rug, then.

'My Hourglass Tracker?' he asked, not taking his eyes off Saito.

'Indeed.' The Sensei took a sip of her tea. 'It's a rather new invention, dreamed up by my clever scientists on the twenty-first floor. I think you'll be quite impressed by its capabilities. I certainly was. It is, of course, a tracking device – as the name would suggest – which allows me to keep track of all the people I have doing extra-special tasks for me.'

Saito was already on his feet, looming over Theo, blocking the last of the sunset's light and throwing him into shadow.

'Of course, though, it is far more than simply an ordinary tracker,' the Sensei continued, apparently oblivious to Theo's mounting discomfort. 'In fact, I gave it that additional name of *Hourglass,* because it also counts down your time – meaning, that is, if you have not returned to us within a week, both in possession of the pearl, and having dealt with these Kawakamis, it will release a deadly poison into your bloodstream.'

She paused here to take another sip of tea before continuing.

'You'll be interested to know, too,' she said, 'that the Hourglass Tracker also has the added feature of being particularly sensitive to the acoustic patterns of your voice, even from its position under your skin. If it does happen to detect a series of acoustic events that correspond to key words which suggest you could be in the act of revealing your mission to someone unauthorized – by which I mean anyone apart from myself, Hana and Ken here – that will also trigger an early release of the poison.'

'One week?' Theo repeated. He'd barely been able to focus on anything else after she'd said that. 'But how am I going to get them to trust me in *one week*?'

The Sensei shrugged. 'I suppose you'll just have to use those many *gifts* of yours.'

Theo started, and stared. She only smiled back.

'I warn you, the Kawakamis' home isn't easy to gain access to. I might, however, have a suggestion for an alternative means of infiltrating their circle. You'll have to do something about your clothes, though, first. I'm afraid that stolen jacket of yours won't do at all.' She yawned, then, looking suddenly tired of this whole business. 'You do accept the terms of the mission, don't you, Bluejay? I'm sure you'll acknowledge that I have been very fair.'

Theo didn't speak. Even without the threat of Saito's presence, he didn't know that he would have found his tongue any more easily.

'Good,' said the Sensei. 'Now, Ken – it's time for the Hourglass.'

As Saito began patting his jacket pockets, Theo sprang to his feet, backing away, off the rug.

'Do be a good boy and don't try to run,' the Sensei told him, 'or as I mentioned, Ken will have to break your fingers. There are also three heavily armed guards waiting outside the door with my granddaughter, who herself is a Ranjutsu blackbelt. Also this here,' she gestured at the dark glass of the windows behind her, 'is state-of-the-art, reinforced dragon-fire glass, so don't even think about trying to smash your way out. It'll only try my patience, and in any case, I think you'll agree that we are rather too high up for a daring escape through the windows. Don't forget that you have a lot to gain from this deal, too, Bluejay. If you only hold still, it'll be so much simpler for all of us.'

Saito advanced towards him. Theo didn't meet his eyes, but did as the Sensei told him, and didn't try to run.

'Bow your head,' Saito said, when he was in front of him.

'Think of the dragon tears, my dear,' the Sensei said, from the tea table.

Theo bowed his head. Within seconds, Saito had produced a device from his pocket that looked, to Theo's eyes, like nothing more than a fancy pen. Just as Theo was glancing up to get a closer look at it, Saito gripped him by the shoulder and stabbed the pen into the area of soft skin just behind and beneath his ear. Theo felt something small and hard enter his body and take up residence under his skin. Saito examined his handiwork, and gave a grunt of satisfaction, before finally relaxing his grip on Theo.

'It's done,' he told the Sensei, returning to his seat at her side.

When his body was his own again, Theo ran his fingers over the affected area. Though they came away streaked with blood, he wasn't able to feel any obvious wound – just a small, firm lump, about the size of a pea.

'Very good,' the Sensei declared. 'And I might add, Bluejay – don't even think about asking some back-alley healer to cut it out for you, either. The device attaches itself to your nervous system almost immediately. Only a very few people know how to remove it safely, and all of them work for me. A botched attempt to remove it would, of course, trigger a release of the poison. You'd be dead within a couple of days.'

She yawned, then, and pushed her teacup away from her on the table with an unmistakable air of finality.

'Now then,' she continued, 'it has been such a pleasure meeting you. I'm sure we'll catch up again before the week is over. Hana here will see you out.'

Theo stumbled around to see that the doors had slid open again, and the Captain – or the Sensei's granddaughter Hana, as he now knew her to be – was waiting there, as promised, together with several armed guards.

Fingers still worrying the lump behind his ear, Theo let himself be marched from the room. He risked a glance or two across at Hana as the doors shut behind them, hoping madly that she might offer him some help – like a clue, or at least some advice as to what to do if everything went wrong. She remained completely inscrutable, however, her dragon-fire glasses only reflecting his own worried face back at him as they walked over the thick, noise-deadening carpet to the elevators.

PART

PART II

IN THE SHADOW
OF THE PALACE

CHAPTER NINE

The Emperor's Garden Party

1.

If Toshiko had thought yesterday's Turning Leaf banquet had seemed extravagant, tonight's party to mark the launch of the ALISE bots was something else entirely. What must have been hundreds of guests, all dressed in diaphanous evening gowns, elegantly tailored suits and silk kimono, milled idly through a whole world lit up by the paper lanterns that winked from the branches of seemingly every tree in the garden to compete with the silvery light of the Three Sister Moons glowing overhead in the night sky. The air was scented with jasmine, and an ensemble of string players was set up on the ornamental bridge over the carp pond, releasing an ethereal music into the night quite unlike anything Toshiko had ever heard before.

Through it all moved the Emperor's staff, bearing wide, circular trays laid out with the most startling array of different types of food. Shiny little Service-bots on wheels rolled up and down the paths too, offering a variety of drinks almost wide enough to rival Mei's boba machine. There were also several tall, broadly smiling young women moving through the guests, bearing trays of drinks. They didn't seem like Palace stewards, as they were talking to the guests in a way that the ordinary servants here would have never been allowed to do. Yet those drinks trays clearly signalled that they weren't quite guests themselves – as did the fact that they were dressed identically, in sharply cut, sleeveless white dresses.

Toshiko found her gaze being drawn, repeatedly, over to one or another of these young women. There was something odd about them – something wrong, even. She watched one chatting brightly with an older man, handing him a glass of sparkling wine. Then she turned to look over at another, who was nodding attentively to something a woman was telling her, apparently at some length. At first glance, these women in the white dresses didn't seem to have too much in common, in terms of their features and general appearances, and yet as Toshiko continued to observe them, she began to notice several unlikely correspondences in their physical characteristics. They were all the exactly same height, for a start, and they all looked roughly the same age. Also, none of them blinked enough. With dawning comprehension then, Toshiko scanned the gardens, counting them. There were seven of them.

'Do you think that's them?' she whispered to Jun, next to her. 'Do you think they're the ALISEs?'

He nodded. 'We should try to meet one, before the evening is out.'

'I hope Mei gets the chance to scan one,' she replied. Then a sudden thought occurred to her. 'Do you think they're sophisticated enough to notice if they're being scanned?'

'Who can say?' Jun replied. 'Mei wouldn't take the risk, though, if she thought they might be. Or at least I hope she wouldn't.'

Mei had arrived a little earlier in the evening with her scanner in her pocket and a large laundry bag bearing Mochi in hand, to slip through the Imperial Palace's staff entrance. Toshiko hoped she was okay. For the first time in a long while, they weren't using the earpieces. They hadn't had time to figure out a discreet way to incorporate them into their outfits and accessories, and so until they all met up again back home at the end of the night, Mei was entirely on her own. Despite Toshiko's eagerness to show her siblings she could manage by herself, she was glad Jun had chosen to stick with her tonight. He could speak Vilmian so well that he would easily be able convince anyone that was where they came from. If all went smoothly, she might barely need to attempt a Vilmian accent at all.

She followed his lead now, in casually studying the rest of the guests who were filling the gardens. Among the aristocrats in their colourful designer outfits, she began to spot several people whom she strongly suspected of being Crows. As soon as she started noticing them, in fact, she found she couldn't stop seeing hints of gang tattoos under eveningwear, along with other small signs, like heavy rings clearly designed to do damage in a punch. The Crows here tonight all seemed to share a particular kind of alertness, too – as if they'd come here for work, not relaxation.

She shuddered, feeling suddenly vulnerable in her bright kimono. Even with Mei's admittedly very impressive make-up job – which her sister had completed with some light-brown hair colouring, and a pair of amber-tinted contact lenses – her disguise suddenly felt alarmingly flimsy.

'Well then,' Jun said softly beside her. 'I suppose we'd better get to work.'

Toshiko hurried to keep up with him in her wooden sandals as he strode deeper into the garden.

2.

It was the stranger again, from last night. The stranger who'd tricked Haru in the game with Mr Winter's ring, and had angered his mother so much. She was looking very different now, though. In fact, if Haru hadn't had his skill of being able to read people the way he could, he wasn't even sure he'd have been able to recognize her. He could really only tell for sure that it was her at all because she had exactly the same atmosphere about her – that same warmth and brightness of a lantern, burning steadily through the dark.

As he watched her point something out to the older man beside her – her father, perhaps, or her uncle – Haru considered whether it might be possible that she looked so different from how she'd done yesterday simply because she'd made the effort to get properly dressed up for this party. After all, even he probably looked a bit different tonight from how he usually did, wearing his embroidered blue robe with silver thread on the cuffs. And then of course, too, he was used to his mother completely transforming her appearance. At this moment, in fact, he knew she'd be shut in the Silver Laurel Room, painting on a new mask of make-up in preparation for her grand entrance later on, when she would make her speech about the new bots.

The stranger couldn't be an ordinary party guest, though.

Haru was sure his mother would never have invited her, after her behaviour yesterday. Could she, then, have come here tonight deliberately in disguise? A frisson of excitement passed through him as he considered the idea. Was it even possible, he wondered then, that she could have come here as a spy? The very idea was intriguing enough on its own, even before considering the bigger question of on whose behalf she might be spying. If he could only find out, Haru considered now, then he'd be able to pass the information on to his mother, and she would surely have to be impressed with him then, if he helped her to catch a spy. If that wouldn't be a sign of his finally living up to his responsibilities as Imperial Heir then he wasn't sure what would be. He began to follow the stranger at a distance, watching her closely.

It was amazing, he considered as he moved through the crowds, just what you could get away with as a child at an adult party. No one really wanted you there, and so they all chose to completely unsee you. Most people tonight moved aside as he passed them without even looking down at him. They simply carried on clinking glasses and holding conversations right over his head.

As he drew closer to the stranger and the man she was with, though, Haru began to realize that a few of the more imposing guests here – the ones with the tattoos and rings on their fingers like Mr Winter – did in fact seem to be paying more attention to him for once. He even noticed one of them saying something into the device on her wrist as he passed her by. He couldn't catch what it was exactly, but from the way her eyes fixed on him as she spoke, he was sure it had to be something about him.

He carried on through the party, keeping his head down now, and doing his best to avoid any guest with visible tattoos as he hurried after the stranger.

3.

Toshiko was still trailing Jun when he suddenly turned to follow a server bearing a tray of different types of maki roll. Jun stopped the server under the waxy emerald leaves of an evergreen magnolia tree, where two men in charcoal suits happened to be talking – and immediately, Toshiko realized that it hadn't just been the promise of sushi that had led Jun here. These two men were surely Crows. The younger one could maybe, at a push, have gotten away with being an ordinary party guest, but his older companion's suit was too short on the sleeves, and so didn't quite hide the edges of his tattoos. Both men, too, wore expressions whose seriousness seemed out of place in this atmosphere of luxury and celebration.

Jun popped a piece of sushi in his mouth and bowed his thanks to the server, who went back to doing his rounds of the gardens. Still chewing, Jun turned to face away from the two Crows, and said something to Toshiko in Vilmian, which of course she couldn't understand a word of. She nodded though, and pretended to be interested, while in actuality, she strained to hear the conversation of the two men behind her.

' . . . only the southern corner of the Crescent so far,' the older of the two was saying. 'No resistance. Or at least nothing to seriously worry us.'

'And they're on the barge now?'

'They are.'

'Gods,' the younger man said then. 'I don't know what the Sensei offered those boatmen, but I wouldn't sail out to Hanasaki Island for any money.'

'They'll be very well-compensated. And it may not even be all that dangerous, just to dump the captives there and go.'

'I don't know.' The younger man's voice had a clear note of unease in it now. 'It hasn't even been a year since the explosion. Definitely not long enough for the toxicity to have dissipated. You still hear stories about sea creatures and animals washing up dead on neighbouring shores.'

Both men fell silent. Toshiko risked a glance over her shoulder. The younger man was draining the glass in his hand while the elder looked on with an expression somewhere between disdain and concern. Pretending to be captivated by the lanterns in the tree, she pointed them out to Jun, who nodded vigorously and said something in Vilmian which sounded appropriately appreciative.

'Do you ever wonder,' the younger man continued, as soon as he'd finished the dregs of his drink, 'what will happen to all those people from the southern corner, on Hanasaki Island?'

'No.' The older man sipped his drink. 'I don't. Do you?'

'Not really,' his companion answered. From his tone, though, Toshiko wasn't sure she believed him. As she forced herself to nod and smile at something Jun was now saying, she saw this younger man sway a little and reach out a hand to the tree to steady himself. Clearly that hadn't been his first drink of the evening.

'It's best not to think about it too much,' the older man said then, a little more kindly. 'Trust me. And it's not like they could have stayed where they were, anyway. The city simply can't continue to sustain a place like the Keeper's Crescent, and it's no kind of life for anyone, living there. In the long run, this whole operation might even help people like them. If word gets out that this is what happens to those who arrive on our shores, people might stop coming in such numbers, and then ending up like they do.'

Toshiko couldn't listen anymore. She gripped Jun's arm and

guided him away from the two men, back into the more crowded
area of the gardens, under the ginkgo trees by the bridge. The
musicians had started playing something less ethereal now, with a
livelier melody. A few couples had even started dancing. Toshiko
shuddered. The music couldn't have formed a more jarring contrast with what they'd just heard.

'We shouldn't have come here,' she hissed to Jun. 'It was the
wrong decision. We should have gone straight to the Keeper's
Crescent. You heard what those men were saying. What have
the Crows done down there?'

Jun's face stayed perfectly composed as a group of women
sailed past, their sharp eyes assessing Toshiko, staring her
brazenly up and down to analyse her outfit, her bearing and
her face – and seeming to find everything wanting, given their
haughty looks. She knew Jun was doing the right thing in remaining so outwardly calm, as of course they had to maintain their
cover at all costs, but in that moment, she couldn't help but feel
absolutely frustrated with him.

'We have to go,' she insisted, as soon as the women had passed.
'The Crows have done something awful, I know it. What could
those men have meant, about that barge sailing to Hanasaki
Island? What's happening to those people from the southern
corner?'

Gently, Jun took her arm and piloted her closer to the band.
The music was loud here, and could go some way towards covering what they were saying from any curious ears.

'I'm as alarmed as you are,' Jun told her then, his face betray-
ing nothing of that alarm at all, only calm appreciation for the
song being played, 'but I don't think there's much we'd be able
to do, going to the Crescent now. For one thing, it would take
us a good while just to get down there, and anything could have

happened by the time we'd arrived. Here, if we play our cards right, we can find out exactly what happened, and how to stop it.'

Toshiko bit her lip, and tasted lipstick. What Jun said did make a kind of sense. It was true that the last time she'd rushed to stop the Crows with no plan, things hadn't exactly gone well. She couldn't just swallow her building horror, though, at having heard those words – *barge, Hanasaki Island,* and *the Keeper's Crescent.* It made her want to kick off these sandals that she still hadn't properly figured out how to walk in yet, and run straight to the Crescent's barbed wire, with all the power the pearl could give her.

'Trust me—' Jun began, and Toshiko so wanted to know what he was about to say next, as she truly hoped that it might throw water on the flames of her panic, and help her continue to navigate this party with something resembling composure. Before he could finish, though, Jun was interrupted by the approach of a young man.

Toshiko's eyes widened as she took in the fair hair, the slight figure and the ocean-blue eyes, and recognized the boy from Golden Moon Square. He was dressed completely differently now, his rough work clothes replaced by a dark suit with embroidered lapels, but it was clearly him. What did it mean, though, that he was here in the Palace gardens? Was their cover blown? She curled her toes, ready to discard her sandals and run. And yet even as she did so, she couldn't help but question again why he wouldn't have just handed her in to the Crows back in Golden Moon Square, if he had somehow seen through her disguise now, and really was with the gang. Why wait to approach her here?

'Good evening,' he bowed to each of them. Jun bowed back, while Toshiko simply stared. Jun gave her a nudge, and she remembered herself and bowed too.

'Do please excuse my niece,' Jun said, speaking Navishian now, but with a Vilmian accent – much more convincing than Mei's Aurian accent had been earlier. 'She is unaccustomed to events of this sort. All these people and this grandeur' – he laughed lightly – 'I am afraid she is a little overwhelmed.'

'Sorry to hear that,' said the boy with the blue eyes. 'Because I was just going to ask if your niece would like to dance.'

4.

He'd noticed the way she moved. Everyone else packed into the Palace gardens tonight seemed lumbering in comparison. She was taking small, careful steps in her wooden sandals, and yet instead of looking restricted, she seemed to Theo like a bird, every small contact with the ground light and percussive, the precursor to spread wings and flight.

Even though he knew this was all probably a distraction from his mission, Theo's eyes had been repeatedly dragged back to the sight of her red kimono with its swirling pattern of white birds catching the light, under the trees by the band. The graceful way she held herself did remind him a little of the girl from the square by the library – the girl whose face had surely matched the photograph that Hana had deigned to point out to him earlier, up on the screen in the Shadow Column's atrium – and perhaps, he'd decided, that was reason enough to try to speak to her. Gods knew, after all, that he needed to follow every lead he could find, however tenuous, with the Hourglass Tracker in his neck ticking down the minutes.

' ... I was just going to ask if your niece would like to dance,' he heard himself saying, before immediately cursing himself. Susanna had hated that, when people spoke to her via the men standing with her, as if she wasn't capable of listening and answering for herself.

'I can speak Navishian too, you know,' the girl said, as if on cue. 'Not just my uncle.'

Theo started at the sound of her voice. It was undoubtedly familiar – even more so than her movements. Surely it couldn't really be her, though? The Kawakami girl's eyes had been dark as onyx, while the eyes appraising him now were a light shade of amber. This girl's features were just completely different, too. And she was taller, surely, and seemed older. Her hair was even a different colour.

'Go on and dance,' the uncle was telling his niece. 'Have fun. Maybe you can ask some questions about life in Rainshadow City, and learn more about what all the fashionable people are discussing, these days.'

Now that Theo tore his eyes away from the girl's face to glance at her uncle again, he found he wasn't at all certain that he hadn't seen him somewhere before, too. He couldn't quite place where, though, and before he knew what was happening, the older man was ushering them off towards where the dancers were swaying, under the lantern-lit trees.

'Go on,' he was saying again to his niece. 'I'll wait for you here.'

She shot him what was unmistakably a glare in reply, but said nothing further, merely turning to bow to Theo before letting him lead her over to where more couples were moving now, hand in hand to the band's music.

'Could I have seen you somewhere before?' Theo risked asking her.

'No,' she replied, quickly.

'You seem very certain of that.'

'I'm from Vilmia. I only came over with my uncle today. For the party.'

'And yet you speak perfect Navishian.'

'I have a tutor.'

'But you haven't visited Rainshadow City before?'

'Not since I was very young.'

'It must be difficult, learning a language you have no occasion to speak.'

They were in front of the band now, and so he took her hands in his and began to lead her in a Navishian three-step. He didn't really know what he was doing – they didn't have dances like this back home. He was just replicating the movements of the other couples dancing around them. If she noticed anything wrong, though, she didn't point it out. Frankly, it didn't seem like she knew the steps to this dance, either. In spite of her natural grace, she kept stepping on his feet.

'Ow,' he said, as one of her wooden platform sandals came down particularly hard on the toes of his right foot.

'You're the one who asked me to dance. I don't think you're allowed to complain.'

He sighed. Whatever he'd been hoping for, this was not going well so far, by any measure. 'What's your name?' he tried asking her.

'Aya. What's yours?'

'Theo.' He saw no reason to lie. The Sensei, after all, seemed to have already learnt most of what there was to know about him, even in spite of his best efforts at keeping a low profile here on Rainshadow island.

'Theo?' Aya repeated, pronouncing the name carefully.

'Yes.'

'I've never heard a name like that before.'

'It's from a long way away,' he told her. 'From a place called Eardland.' He frowned. The name of his homeland sounded clumsy and ill-fitting amidst the Navishian words. 'Have you heard of it?'

Aya shook her head. The movement sent a loose strand of hair swaying past her chin, and Theo had to resist the urge to reach out to tuck it behind her ear.

'What kind of place is Eardland?' she asked him.

Theo considered the question while the song finished, and the band began on a new number. This time, the music was slower, and softer. Again, he mimicked the other couples around them, placing one hand on the golden sash around Aya's waist and copying their languid, spinning steps as he wondered how he might answer her question – and in pondering how he might capture something that felt so huge and complicated to him as Eardland, his home, in a sentence or two, he momentarily lost track of his feet.

'Ow,' it was her turn to say.

'Sorry,' he said. 'That time it was my fault.'

'And the other times weren't?'

'Not all of them.'

'As I said, though,' she told him, 'since you're the one who asked me to dance, I think that means all of this is your fault.' Her amber eyes were flashing, and he couldn't tell at all if she was joking.

5.

Jun wasn't overly keen on the idea of Toshiko being out in the party on her own, but the young man didn't look like one of the Crows, and it was true that the more they interacted with the guests here, the more they were likely to learn.

Keeping half an eye on his sister and the light-haired stranger as they wove their slightly awkward way through the other dancers, Jun headed through the chatting, laughing, feasting crowds to approach one of the ALISE bots, who would have looked like a perfectly ordinary smiling young woman in a white dress and with neatly bobbed hair, had her features not been so symmetrical, and so static – and had there not been a tell-tale group of interested observers gathered around her, too, of course.

When Jun finally reached the front of this crowd, the ALISE bowed her head to him. The sharply cut ends of her hair swept her chin as she did so, setting him off on wondering whether it would ever grow. She straightened up, fixed him with a broad but also blandly lukewarm smile – and then something unexpected happened. Her smile slipped, and for a moment, the ALISE stared at him with sudden intensity. Jun found himself reminded of someone taking a photograph. Then suddenly the smile was back, as if it had never left.

'Would you like a drink?' the ALISE asked him, proffering her tray.

'Thank you,' Jun replied, helping himself to a glass of lemonade.

She had freckles, he noticed. That was a curious touch of realism. She still hadn't blinked yet though, and her eyelashes were too long, and too thick.

And then he was pushed aside by the group behind him, all jostling and eager for a look at the new bot.

As Jun moved back through the crowds, wondering how he might learn more about these ALISEs and the Emperor's plan for their manufacture, he happened to pass a circle of guests in which it was impossible not to notice an older woman holding forth remarkably loudly on the subject of the LIFE-Hub. He sidled closer, listening.

From what Jun could make out, the Emperor's people had induced this woman to invest substantial quantities of her personal funds in the project, and now she was bent on convincing herself, along with as many others as possible, that this was both a delight and a privilege. She was dressed flamboyantly even for a gathering such as this one, in a multi-layered, pale pink evening dress that reminded Jun of a blancmange. In her right hand, she held an enormous, painted fan, which she waved enthusiastically to punctuate her words.

Perhaps, Jun considered, this was just the chance he'd been waiting for to really test out his skills as an undercover operator. Passing this woman by, he contrived to get in the way of her fan in the most natural-seeming manner possible.

'Goodness!' the woman cried out in alarm as the fan made contact. 'Goodness me. What an unfortunate accident.'

She certainly hadn't been shy in how vigorously she'd been waving it, and while it hadn't been an accident, Jun couldn't dispute that the collision did have elements of the unfortunate about it. He had to fight the instinct to rub a hand over his smarting cheek, in case it should destroy his painstakingly applied make-up job.

'Nothing to worry about, madam,' he said, as calmly as possible. 'I am quite uninjured.'

The woman, however, seemed more concerned with the fate of her fan. 'No damage. That's a relief,' she said. She frowned at him. 'I don't think I've seen you before. Who are you?'

Jun blinked. The brazen rudeness of Rainshadow City's ruling classes never failed to amaze him.

'I don't believe we've met before, madam. I'm here on behalf of my older brother – you may have heard of him? Jiro Ikeda – a gentleman of significance in the granitarium market.'

The woman's eyes brightened. 'In the granitarium market, you say? And you're here on his behalf? Is he not here himself?' She had started studying the crowds over Jun's shoulder now, as if a granitarium baron might pop up anywhere among them.

'Unfortunately, he is too unwell at present to make the journey to Rainshadow City, or I am sure nothing would keep him away. He is very much on the hunt for new investment opportunities, and, as it happens, the LIFE-Hub seems the perfect fit.'

'Oh,' the blancmange woman said, her face falling. 'The *journey* to Rainshadow City, you say? Just where is it, exactly, that your family is from?'

'From Vilmia, madam,' Jun told her.

The woman's gaze turned a few degrees colder. She swept a glance over her followers, checking they were listening, before turning back to Jun.

'Not just anyone can invest in the LIFE-Hub, unfortunately,' she told him. 'We were just now discussing the matter – only a moment before you crashed into my fan, as it happens. One has to be invited, you see. I myself was contacted personally by the Emperor's office.'

'In that case,' Jun assured her, 'it is entirely my privilege to have fallen in the way of your beautiful fan. Tell me, do you know when exactly we can expect the ALISEs to be fully rolled out? I've been trying to find out all evening, but no one here seems to have a clear idea.'

She ignored his question, having already turned back to her circle of admirers. 'As I was saying, before I was so inconveniently interrupted, the Emperor has been trying for years to create Service-bots sufficiently intelligent and adaptable to replace the more menial elements of our workforce. It was proving impossible, until she discovered the existence of a rather miraculous substance by the name of draconic ore, which seems to have changed everything. Just a fragment of draconic ore introduced into the body of a bot is enough to infuse it with a spark of genuine life.'

'Life?' interrupted a woman in a plum-coloured trouser suit, fixing the blancmange woman with a surprisingly shrewd look. 'But you can't mean that literally.'

'Oh, but I absolutely do. Emperor Asayo Soramoto – and she does confide in me, you know – tells me that the really amazing thing about the ALISE bots is that they are, to all intents and purposes, just as alive as you or me.'

'But that's impossible, surely,' insisted the woman in the plum-coloured suit.

'Oh I can't pretend to understand the ins and outs of it.' The blancmange woman gave an insouciant wave of her fan. 'But it isn't *impossible* at all – not with the help of this ore, as I say. The only drawback is that apparently it can only be found in the mountains of Muralania, which is of course a bit of a bore. Emperor Asayo does assure me, though, that she's brought enough of it over to our shores now to last us for years. So there's nothing to worry about there, as far as our shares in the LIFE-Hub are concerned.' At this, she nudged an extravagantly dressed older lady next to her, probably another of the Emperor's investor-confidants.

A man in a velvet dinner jacket cleared his throat, then. 'It seems a diplomatic risk, though, to take so much of anything from a territory not strictly within the Empire, let alone such a miracle resource as this draconic ore appears to be. I suppose our Emperor has done it all strictly legally, hasn't she?'

The woman in the blancmange dress only laughed, and gave another flick of her fan. 'Legalities,' she scoffed. 'Do you know, those primitives on Muralania never even thought to mine their own mountains? The ore should go to us, by rights. We'll make much better use of it.'

This was met with a slew of appreciative noises and laughter.

'What you say is fascinating, madam,' Jun tried speaking up again, as the laughter began to die down. 'I am curious – just how long ago did the Emperor bring the draconic ore onto Rainshadow island, if may I ask? And is it something that is easy to store, here? Or does it require specialist facilities?'

'Oh, are you still there?' The woman looked down her nose at him, which was something of a feat, considering she was at least a head shorter than he was. 'On Vilmia, a little bit of granitarium might be impressive, but when you come to the heart of the Empire' – she gestured expansively at the party around her – 'it's quite a different story, I'm afraid. You're not even a small fish in a big pond. People like you are the tiny tadpoles, just waiting to get eaten.'

All of those gathered around her fell quiet, but more than a few wore obviously amused expressions, and one woman couldn't quite stifle her laughter.

Jun retreated from the group, bowing a farewell to them in the most dignified way he could manage, before draining his lemonade and handing the empty glass to a Service-bot – which looked strangely old-fashioned, suddenly, as it trundled down the path on its wheels.

The slight may only have been directed at the person he was pretending to be, but Jun was under no illusions about how these people would treat him – the real him – if they were to somehow discover his true identity. Anyway, Auntie Reiko hadn't raised him to accept insults easily from anybody, and while he might be well practiced at not letting his emotions show on his face, inwardly, he burned now with indignation as he walked away, back towards the music and the dancers.

He didn't have long, though, to nurse his ire at the arrogance of Rainshadow City's upper classes, because almost immediately he found himself in another collision, although unintentionally, this time. At first, he thought he'd absent-mindedly walked into another party guest – until he straightened up to see the same ALISE with the bobbed hair, from whom he'd taken the lemonade, earlier.

'Here you are,' she said with that same, bland smile. 'I've found you.'

The apology froze on Jun's lips. This was only a bot, he reminded himself – and a new model, at that. She would likely be prone to glitches in her programming. Any number of things might be firing in the circuitry within her to make her say those words. It wasn't necessarily a sign of trouble.

On the pretence of brushing down his jacket, he reangled himself a little, trying to find Toshiko in the crowd. There she was – still dancing, apparently undisturbed. That was something to be grateful for, at least.

'It is my duty to escort you to the Palace, now,' the ALISE told Jun. 'The Emperor has much to discuss with you.'

'The Emperor,' Jun repeated, as cold panic began to wash over him. 'What an honour. Perhaps, though, you have mistaken me for another guest? I can't think what business Emperor Asayo might have with me, tonight.'

'There is no mistake,' the ALISE said.

'Well then, I'm afraid I might need a moment. I happen to have come down with rather a headache,' Jun stammered.

'Perhaps it is the crowds.' He began to back away, looking around himself for the exit that was nearest to both him and Toshiko – a gate at the end of the long avenue of ginkgoes. 'Will you excuse me if I leave you, for some air?'

Before he could turn away, though, the ALISE had shot out a hand to grasp his arm. Her grip was like iron. He wouldn't be able to wrest himself free without causing a scene. He briefly considered the merits of actually doing this for a moment, before deeming it too much of a risk. There was still a chance his cover wasn't completely blown – and he'd been seen arriving and exploring the party with Toshiko, as well. Any attention he drew to himself would ultimately endanger her, too.

With one last glance over to the dancers – Toshiko apparently still safe, dancing with the boy with the light-coloured hair – he nodded, and let the ALISE, who hadn't stopped smiling, lead him through the crowds.

6.

The other couples spun, and Theo did his best to copy them, gripping Aya's hands more tightly as the seemingly endless twists and turns of the dance set the patterned silk of her long sleeves flowing out behind her like folded wings.

'Do you still want to know what Eardland is like?' he asked her, when the spinning had slowed sufficiently for him to collect his thoughts.

'Yes,' she said. 'Of course.'

'Well,' he began, 'I suppose the trees are different there. And so are the flowers, and the air, and the soil.'

'How do you mean, different?'

'The flowers are a little less bright, and they're only out for a few months every year. The trees grow different fruit. And it's colder, even in the summer.'

'You don't make it sound very appealing.'

'No, I love it there, really. Or I did love it, anyway.'

He'd surprised himself with the words, and yet they'd come to him so naturally. The awful manner in which he'd left Eardland couldn't change the fact it was the only place he'd ever called home – and he did love its hills, and the mist in the mornings. He loved the warmth of the cottages in his village, with their thick, stone walls, and how the skies looked after the rain, pale and streaked with cloud. He loved the wildflower meadows, and the wooden temple in the forest with wild roses trailing its walls. And of course he'd loved Susanna, who had always seemed to him almost as much a part of the landscape as the shadows of the clouds, moving over the valleys. A cruel part of him wished she could see him dancing with someone else now, and wondered whether she'd feel anything like regret, in spite of what he'd done.

'What are you thinking about?' Aya was asking him now.

He hadn't realized he'd fallen silent. Somehow, even though he'd been lost in his memories, his feet had been managing to dance all on their own, keeping in sync with the music and her movements.

'If you really want to know,' he said, 'I was remembering someone I left behind.'

'I see,' Aya said, eyes narrowing. 'Was she pretty?'

Theo found himself startled again, this time at the directness of her question.

'Yes, she was,' he told her. 'Very pretty.'

'You're just saying that to make me jealous,' Aya replied, but she didn't sound genuinely irritated with him now, as she had when they'd first started dancing. Instead, her tone was light, even teasing, and in spite of the sadness that was threatening to wash over Theo now, at having finally let himself remember some of the things he did miss, so much, about home, he still found himself smiling back at her.

'So why did you leave Eardland?' she asked him then, abruptly – slightly warping its name in her accent.

'I didn't mean to,' he replied, not bothering to correct her pronunciation. 'It just . . . happened.'

'And you miss it?'

'Every day.'

'Tell me more about it.'

They spun faster and faster and faster.

'I lived in a small village in the hills, built around a sacred tree. The food is different there. We don't eat rice at all, for instance, and not nearly so much fish. It rains much more there, too. Sometimes every day, in winter. You would often see rainbows, especially over the rivers.'

'I like the rain,' Aya told him. 'It doesn't rain enough, here. I've never even seen a rainbow.'

And then several things happened at once. Maybe it was foolish – the influence of the music and the pace of the dance, or of the grace in Aya's movements as, in spite of her initial prickliness, she relaxed into its rhythms. Whatever the reason, Theo found himself wanting to bring a proper smile to her painted lips – an urge which set him reaching, against everything that seemed sensible, for the Gift.

Feeling like a flying gymnast stretching out fingertips for a beam just slightly beyond comfortable reach, Theo stretched for the vibrations of energy through the air towards the very edge of his awareness – before sending a surge of power out towards them, trying to draw in the rainclouds he could just sense hovering, distant, over the sea.

He opened his eyes again only to find Aya staring, her hand jumping to her throat in a gesture of surprise, as if she'd somehow felt what he was doing. That was surely impossible, though. Not even Susanna had been able to sense when he was using the Gift, and they'd been linked in everything, their thoughts perfectly in step – or they had been for a time, at least.

The music reached a climax then, and again Theo copied the other dancers, to send Aya in a whirling spin, away from him.

As he did, something bright flew from the neck of her kimono – and Theo's heart leapt to his throat as he registered a large, opalescent pearl on a golden chain.

7.

Haru pushed his way past the ballooning skirts of a woman's enormous pink dress, just in time to see the stranger whirling, caught up in the dancing, with Mr Winter's pearl flying out on its chain from the folds of material around her neck. As the pearl caught the light from the lanterns in the trees, he found himself suddenly struck by a flash of memory – a vivid recollection of how it had felt to touch it, in that brief moment during the Turning Leaf Festival last night, before Mr Winter had barked at him and smacked his hand away. It had felt a bit like swimming in the Palace's lakes in summer, maybe, or perhaps more like eating ice cream. Cool and fluid, and yet at the same time, charged with excitement.

Immediately, Haru changed his plan. Instead of finding out who the stranger was spying for – which he might still do; he hadn't completely abandoned the idea of impressing his mother – his new aim was to steal the pearl. After all, finding Mr Winter's pearl like this, without Mr Winter, was a golden opportunity. The stranger might be a spy, but she didn't seem nearly as forbidding as Mr Winter himself did, and she would almost certainly react more kindly than Mr Winter would, if she caught him. Besides, it was still his round of the game they'd started last night, wasn't it? And surely this could be the way he chose to play it. After all, when it had been her round, she hadn't properly explained the rules, and then she'd tricked him. It was only fair for him to play just a small trick on her now, in return.

8.

Watching the pearl fly out on its chain from Aya's neck, Theo immediately felt the distinctive jolt that was the Gift picking up on a high concentration of energy gathered around an object of power.

This was Ken Saito's dragon pearl – it had to be. It hummed with a vibrancy that reminded Theo of the sacred tree back home, as well as, in fact, the crates he'd hauled in last night at the docks. Unlike the crates, though, which had made him feel nauseated and confused, the force coming off the pearl made him feel light, like he wanted to dance right off the solid ground and straight into the air.

He was also hit by a more practical realization: here was the first part of his mission, swinging bright and clear before him. He need only reach out and grab it, and then he would have taken his first step towards halting the Hourglass Tracker, as well as earning that vial of dragon tears, the possibilities of which he couldn't help but be aware of, as much as he was trying not to let himself think of them.

His fingers began reaching for the pearl just as Aya snatched it back, to hide it again under the folds of her collar. Then, the musicians' song ended, and the rain that he'd summoned a moment ago with the Gift started to fall.

He'd hoped to bring just enough gentle, misting rain to catch the light of the lanterns in the trees and conjure a rainbow. He rarely used the Gift to change the weather, though, and clearly he'd misjudged the strength of force necessary. Instead of the light shower he'd hoped for, thick raindrops began to fall. They landed wet and hard on the warm paving stones, pattered off the metal hoods of the Service-bots, and threatened to soak the leaves, the lanterns, and all of the guests' carefully arranged outfits.

As the people around them began to cry out in surprise and alarm, Aya spun to a stop, dropped her hold of Theo's hands, and looked up at the sky with a look of horror that confused him. It was just a little rain, surely – and hadn't she just told him she liked the rain? Hadn't he brought this rain here just for her?

He watched then as the girl he'd thought of as Aya pressed her hands to her face, and they came away covered with a surprising amount of make-up. Already, now, in spite of the amber eyes, she was starting to look a lot more familiar. Before he could even begin to think, though, of what he might say to try and keep her here and win her trust, she had kicked off her sandals and was running away from him, through the gardens, her whole body infused with the grace of a bird taking flight.

CHAPTER TEN

Caught in the Rain

1.

For the second time in two days, Toshiko found herself running at full tilt through the Imperial Palace's gardens. Without consideration now for what Aya the granitarium magnate's daughter would do, she pushed her way through the clusters of people seeking shelter from the rain under trees and parasols. It was falling heavily now, washing away all the make-up disguising her face, along with the light-brown dye that Mei had combed through her hair. It rained so rarely in Rainshadow City that they simply hadn't thought to plan for it.

Cursing their carelessness, Toshiko found her way into a quiet area of the gardens, and from there, finally into the shelter of the Palace colonnades. If only, she thought now, there were

somewhere here where she might find a mirror. She needed to
see whether she still looked passably like Aya. If she didn't, she
was surely in danger. As she tugged off her socks – barefoot
seemed more practical, in case she needed to run again – and
then squeezed the rainwater from her kimono's trailing sleeves,
she began scanning what she could see of the gardens for Jun. His
disguise would surely have been just as vulnerable to the rain as
her own, and yet she couldn't see a glimpse of his blue jacket or
artificially silvered hair anywhere.

What she could see, though, was a group of four Crows, armed
and moving with purpose in her direction while being studiously
ignored by the few groups of guests nearby. Even through her
fear, she felt a stab of bitterness. Of course she couldn't rely on
anyone here to intervene on her behalf. The Emperor's acolytes
would never dare get in the way of anyone who looked as if they
might be from the Crows.

She shrank back behind one of the colonnades' pillars, trying
not to panic. She needed to think of a distraction fast, along
with somewhere to hide, or to run to. She couldn't possibly fight
all four of them now, without shoes and encumbered by a wet
kimono. Three were wearing katana on their belts, and she was
certain she'd spotted the tell-tale gleam of a throwing star held
between the fingers of the fourth.

She risked peering out again at them from behind the pillar.
They were far too close, and still she didn't have a plan. She held
her breath as they drew even nearer – only to let it go again in
surprise as they moved past her, to continue on down a path that
snaked around the side of the Palace.

She didn't understand it. Sure, she'd been trying to hide, but
the red kimono meant that she was anything but inconspicu-
ous. Like any typical purchase of Mei's, it drew far too much

attention. She could only conclude that perhaps those four Crows hadn't been looking for her, after all.

Edging completely out from behind the pillar now, she was just in time to catch the matching grim expressions on their faces as they turned the corner of the Palace wall, and disappeared from sight. Even if they hadn't been looking for her, they were clearly after somebody. Who could it be, though?

'Excuse me, madam, but are you okay?'

Toshiko was snapped out of her speculations by one of the party guests from across the gardens, calling out to her through the rain. It seemed he was suddenly only too eager to notice a young woman standing by herself in the shadows, now that it definitely didn't mean interfering the Crows. Again, Toshiko cursed the bright, bulky folds of Mei's kimono.

'I'm fine,' she called over her shoulder, as she set off again into the gardens to follow the Crows down the path that skirted the Palace's edge, her bare feet cold against its wide, flat stones.

Before long, she realized that she must be nearing the staff entrance of the building. Maybe, it occurred to her, if she could just find her way inside, then she might be able to find Mei, and Mei would surely know what to do about her unravelled disguise. She might even be able to hide her, and help her escape – or to find her a spare steward's uniform, at least.

After what felt like far too long of walking barefoot through the weather, she came to what had to be the staff entrance, busy with crowds of the Emperor's stewards, all rushing in and out to fetch rain coverings for the guests. None of them paid any attention to one dripping wet girl slipping inside, leaving a trail of damp footprints behind her.

2.

Ignoring the chaos brought on by the rain, the ALISE with the neatly bobbed hair and scattering of freckles marched Jun through the gardens. Never once did she relax her grip on his arm. As they walked, he was aware of two men dressed in the dark purple uniform of the Imperial Guard falling neatly into step on either side of them, quite as if they'd been ready and waiting to join them as they passed by. Praying to any God who might hear him that the rain wouldn't wash away his disguise and leave him completely exposed, Jun tried to keep up with the bot, as well as to maintain as much of an air of calm dignity as he could manage. The seven ALISEs present here tonight were such a focus of the whole event that walking beside one like this was certainly attracting plenty of stares. He knew he had to keep up the act of being Mr Ikeda, the Vilmian granitarium magnate's younger brother, if only to avoid drawing undue attention to Toshiko, with whom he'd been seen arriving and exploring the party. He scanned the gardens again, but couldn't see any sign of her now.

Before long, the ALISE was tugging him up the wide flight of steps that led to the towering, wooden doors of the Palace's entrance, which were carved with snaking vine patterns, and secured by a series of thick, metal bolts, which the Guards stationed at the top of the steps began to draw back at their approach.

'It is my duty to bring this man to the Emperor,' announced the ALISE again, addressing herself to one of the Guards.

'Um . . .' The Guard gave the bot rather a disconcerted look. 'I do know that, but I think she's about to do her speech, just at the moment,' he told the ALISE. 'Best to take him to one of the Generals for now, instead.'

The Guards pushed the doors fully open to reveal the long, shadowed, candlelit entrance hall within, a high-ceilinged space of smoky incense and gleaming dark wood surfaces, the edges of which were punctuated by carved wooden pillars. The ALISE tugged on Jun's arm, towing him inside. They were followed by the two Guards who'd accompanied them through the gardens before the doors swung firmly shut behind them all again, plunging them into an even deeper gloom. Jun tried not to wince as he heard the sounds of the bolts on the doors' other side being drawn closed once more.

All did not seem well in the Palace, he immediately noted. The hall seemed too deserted, when surely it should have been filled with Guards and officials. He could hear, too, the unmistakable sounds of shouts and running feet echoing from somewhere in the network of rooms beyond. He cast a look at the two Guards on either side of him. Behind their professional impassivity, he was sure they both looked tense now, too. The ALISE, though, seemed entirely nonplussed by the general sense of wrongness that was suddenly everywhere around them. She merely pulled on Jun's arm, and made to start off again, into the dim, flickering candlelight.

Abruptly, the sound of approaching footsteps drew nearer, and even the ALISE turned to look, as a door to their left flew open to admit three Imperial Guards into the hall, all of them out of breath and obviously agitated. The younger two, in fact, looked filled with a kind of wide-eyed panic that Jun had never expected to see from any Imperial Guard, given the way they'd always been so brutally in control throughout all his years on Rainshadow island so far. At first glance, the older man at the trio's centre seemed a little more composed, and Jun's eyes widened as he took in the silver braid and badges on the man's uniform, that marked him out as one of the Generals. And yet even this most senior member of the military was still showing surprising signs of agitation – his lined face was pale and tense, and his dark, silver-scattered hair was disordered, as if, not too long ago, he'd been running his hands repeatedly through it in worry. Now, in any case, he was keeping a hand held ready on the hilt of the katana he wore at his belt.

The two Guards on either side of Jun stood to attention immediately they registered the General's appearance.

'General Mori, sir!' they said in unison.

And yet General Mori seemed in too much of a hurry to acknowledge them formally.

'Good,' he only said when he saw them, sounding distracted. 'We need all the help we can get. I want the two of you to come with me now, to the Maple Wing.'

And then he set off again, striding down the hall.

'But . . . what should we do with the prisoner, sir?' stammered the Guard on Jun's right.

General Mori stopped, turned, and looked at Jun with an expression that made it abundantly clear that this was the very last thing he wanted to be dealing with, currently.

'It is my duty to bring this man to the Generals,' sang out the ALISE.

'He's one of the Kawakamis, sir,' added the Guard – and immediately, Jun felt any last vestiges of certainty and confidence dissolve in panic.

'How do you know that name?' he asked the Guard.

The Guard ignored him though, and simply carried on addressing General Mori. 'It seems like the invitation reached them, sir, just as planned. Though this is the only one we've found so far.'

Jun's eyes closed. It was true that Mei had found the image of the party invitation surprisingly fast, even given her hacking expertise. It was true, too, that perhaps their mock-up print-out of it had been accepted rather too readily by the Guards on the gate. They'd thought they were so clever – and now, it seemed, they'd done none other than walk straight into a trap. At least, judging by what the Guard said, it seemed that Mei and Toshiko were still safe for now.

General Mori only frowned, as if he had a headache coming.

'I don't have time for this,' he told the Guard. 'There are far bigger things unfolding in the Palace tonight which require our urgent attention. Take this Kawakami with you on the way to the Maple Wing and lock him in cold storage. We can figure out what to do with him later.'

And with that, the General turned on his heel and strode onwards, deeper into the hall's shadowed emptiness, the two Guards who'd been accompanying him following on his heels.

Before Jun could even think about trying to escape and warn his sisters, the Guards alongside him had seized his shoulders and wrested him out of the ALISE's grasp, to start after the General and his men.

'Walk fast,' said the Guard on his right, tightening his grip on Jun as they went. 'You heard General Mori as well as I did – we're urgently needed elsewhere, and every second you waste is one you'll be punished for later, make no mistake.'

Jun now felt certain, though, that under that veneer of toughness, this Guard was almost as frightened as he was.

There are far bigger things unfolding in the Palace tonight which require our urgent attention.

General Mori's words seemed to reverberate in the hall's polished emptiness as the Guards marched Jun to captivity.

They left the ALISE bot still standing by the Palace's entrance, smiling that same rather blank smile – just as she had been this whole time.

3.

'What do you think's inside this one?' Mei asked Mochi, holding a dumpling up to his nose for him to sniff.

They were holed up, just the two of them, in a small laundry room somewhere in the servants' section of the Palace. All around them was warmth, dim lighting and clean-linen smells, and between them was a tray of canapés – half of it filled with steamed, shell-shaped dumplings, the other half laden with a mix of vegetable and shrimp tempura.

Of course Mei had begun her time at the party by doing her level best to scan one of the ALISEs, but the bots were being absolutely mobbed by the crowds. She understood the enthusiasm, of course. They did look impressive. If she hadn't known beforehand, she might even have mistaken them for genuine humans – albeit humans who had been subjected to some weird Palace training programme which had taught them all to smile in a deeply unconvincing way. It was a shame, really, that the ALISE's smiles were all wrong. The motor programming of their facial muscles was imperfect, generally. Real people were a lot more expressive.

Mei had soon decided that there was no way a mere servant would be able to shove her way through the throngs for a closer look without causing undue kerfuffle, and so she'd spent a while simply handing out canapés like a regular steward. It hadn't been long, though, before she'd begun feeling sick with herself. What was she doing, actually helping the Emperor with her party? She couldn't imagine, in fact, how all the other legitimate stewards here could stand doing their jobs. Every day, they gave up their autonomy and moral principles to serve this woman who was, essentially, little better than a criminal-minded dictator.

And so Mei had quickly decided it was time for a break. Hence the laundry room, the canapés, and the cat. She would go back out there for another try with the scanner when people had got more used to the ALISE bots, and stopped crowding them.

Mochi gave the dumpling a dainty sniff.

'So they look like ordinary har gow, which would mean probably shrimp,' Mei deliberated aloud. 'But the food at this party is wild and I feel like I can smell something else, too? Maybe minced tofu and shrimp? Regardless, I'm definitely getting a hint of spring onion.'

Mochi sniffed again and meowed agreement, his squashy, flat little face registering cautious curiosity as he began to investigate more concertedly.

'Why don't I try it first?' Mei suggested. 'Hey, I could even be your official food taster. Always happy to do make sure nothing's poisonous for King Mochi.'

She took a bite out of the dumpling, and Mochi turned to glare at her – it was a classic, as far as his looks of appalled betrayal went.

'What?' she asked him, through an absurdly delicious mouthful of shrimp and spring onion. 'It's for your own good – I thought we'd agreed I was your food taster! And it's not as if there isn't loads more.'

She plucked a small piece of fried shrimp from inside the half-eaten har gow, and held it out for Mochi to nibble on. He turned away though, looking affronted.

And then the door to their little haven swung wide open, and

Mei dropped her dumpling on the floor. Framed in the doorway, the neat lines of her white dress looking sharper than ever in the corridor's bright light, stood one of the ALISE bots. This one had short, dark hair worn in a pixie cut, and bright green eyes which swept the small room to settle fixedly on Mei. Mei reached out a hand to settle Mochi, where he was busily picking the remains of the shrimp from the dropped dumpling's doughy wrapper.

She should have guessed something like this would happen, Mei inwardly berated herself. She should have just sucked it up and done her best at being a steward, serving the Emperor's guests. Now she'd find herself in trouble for sneaking off with a tray of fancy snacks, and would draw a level of attention to herself that could compromise her own and even her siblings' cover.

And yet, she considered, could this also be an opportunity? After all, here was an ALISE, somehow with no one else around. She got tentatively to her feet, and reached into her pocket for her scanner.

Then the ALISE spoke.

'Mei Kawakami,' it announced, with unmistakable, ringing clarity. 'You are a match for the wanted criminal – Mei Kawakami.'

Mei's eyes closed. *Of course.* She might be dressed as a Palace steward and wearing heavy make-up, but this was a bot. *A match*, it had said. The ALISEs had to have been fitted with facial recognition software. Why hadn't she thought of it before? *Stupid.* An unforgivable oversight.

She took a step closer to the bot. Mochi, having finished the fallen shrimp and finally realized something was up, began prowling beside her as she took one step, then another, raising her scanner.

'It is my duty to take you to the Emperor,' said the ALISE, still smiling brightly. 'You are the wanted criminal, Mei Kawakami.'

As the bot began to advance towards her, Mei flicked the scanner on and held it out. Immediately, the display went nuts as every light that could come on began flashing madly.

The ALISE advanced further into the room, the door swinging shut again behind her, closing them into a dim gloom which no longer felt remotely cosy. 'You are the wanted criminal, Mei Kawakami,' it repeated.

'Stop saying that!' Mei reached for a dumpling and threw it at the bot, marring the clean perfection of its white dress. The bot didn't react in the slightest, though, and only kept coming closer.

Feeling rather desperate now, and unsure of what she was doing, Mei pressed a sequence of buttons almost at random on her scanner. She'd primarily built it to detect electromagnetic frequencies from foreign objects, but she'd added some other features too, just in case she ever wanted to test how something might react to a blast of radio waves from an external source, for instance, or indeed to a strong magnetic field. She turned on both these features now, as the ALISE closed in – and just as the bot's hands reached out to seize her by the shoulders, she slammed the scanner right into the centre of its chest.

The first thing to happen was that, at last, the bot blinked. Mei hadn't actually noticed that it wasn't blinking until, finally seeing it perform the motion now, she realized what had been missing. Then, the ALISE began to glitch. While its arms continued to extend towards her, it couldn't seem to go so far as to grab her. It was stuck, instead, simply in this moment and action of reaching.

'It is my duty,' it repeated again, voice catching on the word. 'It is my duty.'

Mei lowered her scanner, turning off the magnet and the radio waves. Then she ducked out from behind the ALISE's reaching arms and began to circle it, thoughtfully.

Mochi followed her, looking thoroughly unhappy with the situation now, his fur all standing on end. *What did you do?* he seemed to be asking, his face angled up towards her.

'I think,' Mei said, considering, 'I think I must have damaged or disabled some sort of capacitor. Don't worry though, Mochi. She's not real. Just a bot – see?'

She approached the ALISE, tentatively. Still, it didn't move, and just kept on reaching out, to where Mei had been standing when she'd disabled it.

'It is my duty,' it kept insisting.

And then, with a low moan of what sounded like almighty physical effort, the ALISE turned on the spot, swinging its reaching arms around to where Mei was standing now.

'Please,' the ALISE said, its previously bright voice coming out grating now, sounding forced. 'Please,' it said to Mei. 'It . . . *hurts.*'

Mei's eyes widened. 'But it can't do,' she whispered back. 'I mean, you're a bot. You can't feel pain – can you?' She took a step back. 'How can you even be moving, after I disabled you?'

And then she noticed something new. The scanner, still in her hand, was blinking. Just one light, in the display – the same light which had come on, in fact, when she'd tried to scan the pearl last night, back in the apartment. She raised it closer to the ALISE, and the light grew brighter, with its blinking slowing in frequency, too. Mei held the scanner right up to the ALISE's chest, and the light stopped blinking entirely, settling into an unbroken glow.

'Please,' the ALISE gasped out again, its voice now coming out much lower, warped from its former pitch. 'Please. It hurts.'

'I'm . . . I'm sorry,' Mei breathed.

Then the door behind her swung open again.

'We've been alerted to irregular activity in this laundry room,' began one of the three Imperial Guards who were now standing, framed in the light of the corridor. Then his eyes fully registered the image of the ALISE, frozen and glitching, reaching out for Mei.

'Mei Kawakami,' said the ALISE, in her distorted, broken voice. 'Wanted criminal. It is my duty.'

'The Kawakami hacker girl,' said the Guard, eyes narrowing as he took in Mei. 'We were warned you'd be the Kawakami most likely to cause trouble.'

'Wait, what do you mean, you were warned?' Mei asked.

But she was distracted, still, by the ALISE. This all seemed so wrong to her. If she really had damaged a key capacitor, then the bot shouldn't still be able to talk. It shouldn't be behaving like this, at all. Even though its face beneath its pixie cut was still rigidly impassive, Mei couldn't shake the feeling that she hadn't just tampered with a computer at all – that instead, she'd caused someone genuine harm.

The head Guard of the trio now turned to his two subordinates. 'You take care of the bot,' he ordered one of them. 'It's valuable, and the Emperor will want it looked after.' Then he turned to the other Guard. 'You can help me take this Kawakami girl to the Generals.'

'My duty,' said the ALISE again. 'It is my duty.'

Mei didn't even try to resist as the two Guards seized her arms. She even dropped her scanner when they asked her to, her eyes still fixed on the bot.

'I'm sorry,' she said to it again as the Guards led her away, Mochi following, hissing in alarm. 'I didn't understand what I was doing.'

'It hurts,' the ALISE said again, its voice a little softer now as it turned to the Guard who'd been left there in the room to take care of it. Mei got one last look at its face – still calmly smiling, in spite of everything – before she was marched away, the door of the laundry room slamming shut behind her.

4.

Haru followed the stranger with the pearl and the red kimono all the way into the Palace, where he felt certain she wasn't allowed to be. He supposed this could be taken as yet more evidence of her being a spy, even if it did seem a little odd that she'd chosen the servants' entrance, which led through into the rooms where the staff cooked the food and laundered the clothes. A spy would surely want to spy on his mother, and his mother never came here.

The stranger was definitely up to something, though. That much was clear from the way she was moving so quickly, keeping to the shadows and looking around as if searching for someone. Haru couldn't help but feel a little smug that she hadn't yet noticed he was on her trail. He dodged out of sight as she turned to look over her shoulder again and congratulated himself on his subtlety.

It helped, of course, that the staff knew who he was. Unlike his mother, he was a common sight in this part of the Palace. None of them even thought to question him as he hid behind the large umbrellas, windbreakers and waterproof canopies that they were all gathering up to take outside, to the party. They all seemed in a terrible hurry. Maybe they were worried some of the guests out there would make complaints about them into their wrist communicators if they took too long, just as Haru feared they'd been doing about him.

He kept following on the stranger's heels through the narrow corridors, anyway, until they finally began to draw near to the doors which led out of the servants' area and into the main part of the Palace. It was here that Haru found himself struck, at last, with a good idea for how he might pull off his round of the game, and make the pearl his own. If the stranger continued up this corridor, she would soon pass the Palace's thermal baths – and Haru happened to know a way he might cut off a corner of her route, get to the baths before her.

At the baths, he told the servants there that he needed some towels, to take to the party guests. Of course, they immediately gave him a great big stack of them, no questions asked. He then placed these towels prominently in the middle of the corridor in which he knew the stranger would soon find herself, before hiding nearby in the long folds of a curtain.

It was from this point onwards that Haru's plan went even better than he could have hoped. It went so perfectly, in fact, that he felt it was almost as if the pearl actually wanted him to win the game. He watched, still tucked behind the curtain, as the stranger stopped, looked around, determined she was alone, and then bent to pick up a towel from the top of the stack. She dried her soaking hair first, before patting the worst of the rain from her clothes. Then she wiped off her face, which was a melting mess of all the make-up she'd been wearing. She looked much more like herself after that.

Haru continued to watch with mounting glee, then, as she began to dry her neck, and paused with the towel slung around her shoulders to pull the pearl from the folds of her kimono. She frowned at it, unclasped its chain, then crouched to fold it carefully into the next towel on the stack that Haru had left out for her. He had to stop himself from fully exclaiming in triumph then, as, leaving the pearl there to dry, she turned away from it to wrap her hair in the first towel, from around her shoulders.

Seizing his moment, Haru darted out from behind his curtain, grabbed the towel enfolding the pearl, and ran.

'Hey!' the stranger shouted after him. 'You get back here!'

Haru kept on running, even though he could hear her now, following behind. She might be fast, but she was also wet, barefoot and confused, and had a towel over her head – and of course she didn't know the maze of the Palace's interior like he did.

'I win round two,' he felt confident enough to shout to her over his shoulder as he went.

Still running, he dropped the towel and slipped the pearl safely into his secret pocket, near the collar of his robe. He found it hugely satisfying to know that though she may have managed to trick him once, justice was now restored. He was so pleased with himself, in fact, and running so fast through the Palace's winding, shadowed corridors, that he didn't notice the woman up ahead with the dark glasses and the long, black coat until he'd slammed right into her, and she'd grabbed him, clapped a hand over his mouth, twisted his arms behind his back, and dragged him sideways into a darkened room, which, in all his years of living in the Palace, he was sure he'd never been inside before.

CHAPTER ELEVEN

Trapped in the Palace

1.

That little sneak! was all Toshiko could think as she hurtled after the Emperor's son, paying no heed to where she was going, and feeling sluggish without the pearl's magic to help her. She was struggling in the kimono, too, its tapered length forcing her to take much shorter strides than usual. Hitching the material up to her knees, she rounded a bend in the corridor, only to discover that the boy had apparently vanished. She groaned aloud into the quiet emptiness ahead. This wasn't how tonight was meant to have gone, at all.

Looking around herself, she saw that she had found her way into a section of the Palace with an almost residential feeling to it – and which was definitely no longer part of the servants' area of the building. The corridor before her was lined with sliding doors of polished wood, all of which seemed to promise quiet, private rooms beyond, and everything, even the shining floor-boards beneath her bare feet, seemed imbued with the rose petal incense that the city's fashionable classes used to bring on sleep. Toshiko swallowed. It would be a dangerous thing indeed to be found here. What would the punishment be, for breaking into the Emperor's personal quarters? Several years of imprisonment? A lifetime? Worse?

Right on cue, she was jolted from her speculations by what sounded like a whole group of people approaching from some-where behind her. Cursing under her breath, she hurried over to the nearest set of sliding doors and chanced cracking them open.

No one was inside, thank the Gods. Instead, she was faced with only a small tatami sitting room, in which was arranged a tea table and some cushions. There were signs of its having been recently deserted in a hurry – most likely by Imperial Guards, given that a Guard's purple jacket lay abandoned next to one of the cushions.

Fervently hoping that the footsteps she could still hear coming this way didn't belong to some Guards returning for the jacket, Toshiko slipped inside the room and shoved the doors closed again behind her. She breathed a sigh of relief as, outside, the footsteps passed her by.

At the sound of murmured voices, she looked up to notice a second set of doors on the room's far side. While those she'd just slipped through were solid wood, these were made from paper, and were lit up with the lamplight of the room beyond. Through them, in fact, she could even make out a scene in silhouette, of several people gathered around a long table. The voices were muffled, but she could still hear odd words – *strategy, offensive, retaliation*. These, combined with the general authoritative timbre of the voices, made her immediately wonder if she'd somehow stumbled on a gathering of high-ranking Guards.

She crept closer, bare feet quiet on the tatami, trying to hear what was being said in more detail. She'd just counted eight people that she could make out around the table, when the conversation fell silent, each one of those shadow figures suddenly turning, now, to face in her direction. It was only then that she realized these paper doors surely threw shadows both ways. Her breath caught in her throat as one of the figures stood up from the table and began to stride towards her, the silhouette growing crisper and larger with every step.

Before she could hide or run or even get up from her knees and arrange her face in a suitable expression of contrition, the doors in front of her had slid open to reveal a man scowling down at her. He was dressed, just as she'd feared, in the distinctive dark purple and silver braid of the Imperial Guard.

Like holding an umbrella, was how she'd described the feeling of wearing the pearl to Mei. Well, now she felt as if she'd forgotten both umbrella and jacket, only to find herself in a typhoon.

2.

As Haru blinked into the gloom of the unfamiliar room that he'd been hustled and dragged into, the strange woman with the dark glasses who'd seized him and brought him here began to bind his wrists with some kind of rope. It felt worryingly strong, though quite light and thin. He began to yell, calling out into the room's darkness for help. Curiously, though, this didn't seem to bother the woman very much, even though they were quite near his mother's private quarters now, where there would surely be plenty of Guards around to hear him. As Haru shouted, she only kept on tying her knots, apparently unperturbed, and working so quickly even without any light that he could tell she'd done this many times before. He was still calling out for help when she tugged on the rope to test the strength of her handiwork, and then finally released her grip, apparently satisfied.

'There's no point in screaming,' she told him. 'This room happens to be soundproof. Also, you're giving me a headache.'

A lantern flared into life, transforming the shadowed, amorphous shapes around Haru into sights that made more sense. He was in a small room that happened to be entirely windowless – which he supposed explained the stale, musty smell. It had no furniture, and not even any ornaments, either, or anything else that might have made it seem more comfortable, because almost all of its space was taken up by the silver pipes and brightly painted, wing-shaped casing of the Imperial family's vast phoenix-wing harmonium. That must be why the room was soundproof, Haru realized.

He'd seen the instrument before, of course, but only when it was being wheeled out for special occasions. It hadn't occurred to him that it would have to be stored somewhere in the Palace, where the harmonium players would be able to practice on it.

Usually, seeing the harmonium made Haru smile, as he associated it with birthdays, and with other festivals filled with music and presents and dancing. Tonight, though, he only had a moment to frown at the instrument, confused, before a noise behind him drew his attention back towards the doors, which were sliding open again to reveal Mr Winter.

Mr Winter may have been dressed in an elegant suit for the party, but his expression was as grave and humourless as ever, his jaw set as his cloudy grey eyes settled on Haru through the half-light. Before Haru could even think to shout for help once more, Mr Winter had shut the doors again and fastened the latch. He greeted the woman next to Haru with a nod, before going to lean against the harmonium's colourful wooden casing. Haru felt his mouth turning dry under Mr Winter's stare, infused as it was with that distinctive menace of storm clouds.

'Thank you, Hana,' Mr Winter said to the woman who'd brought Haru here. 'You did very well to secure our little marionette so swiftly.'

The woman bowed in a sweep of her long, dark coat, receiving his praise – and Haru found himself so irritated, suddenly, by how the two of them were choosing to interact like this, over his head, that he finally found his voice again.

'Why have you brought me here?' he asked Mr Winter. 'And why are you hiding from the party like this, in this strange room, in the dark?'

'We're not hiding, puppet. We're waiting,' Mr Winter told him, with a flash of an enigmatic smile.

'What for?' Haru asked.

'News,' Mr Winter replied. 'News that should be coming from my associates any minute now.' He cast an impatient look at the device on his wrist, before returning his focus to Haru. 'How old are you, puppet?'

'I'm ten,' Haru told him. 'Why do you keep calling me *puppet*?'

Mr Winter ignored Haru's question. 'Ten years old,' he said, as if trying out the taste of the words on his tongue. 'A good age for you to be. Tell me, how would you feel about becoming Emperor sooner rather than later?'

'I don't want to be Emperor,' Haru said. 'Not yet, anyway. I want to go back to my room. Can I go back to my room now, please?'

'No,' Mr Winter said, softly. 'I'm afraid not, puppet.'

All of Haru's resolve to behave calmly and confidently in this situation abruptly disappeared, and he turned, sprinting for the door.

He hadn't managed more than a few paces before Hana caught him by the shoulders. As he wriggled in her grip, he felt the pearl pressing against his collarbone from where it was still hidden, in the secret pocket of his robe. Did Mr Winter know he had it? he wondered. Could that be what this was all about?

Briefly, he considered the idea of simply telling Mr Winter about the pearl, and giving it back. Yet he still felt it might be foolish to admit to having it at all, without first figuring out just how much Mr Winter knew. He began struggling even harder to break free from Hana, setting the rope she'd tied around his wrists rubbing harshly against his skin.

Mr Winter sighed. 'I told her to be gentle, you know,' he said, sounding bored, 'but if you're going to be difficult, we could easily change that. Show him, Hana.'

Hana's grip on Haru's shoulders suddenly grew so tight he felt sure his bones would crack under the pressure, and he couldn't help but yell with the shock of it. Only at a nod from Mr Winter did she finally slacken her hold again. Still gasping with the pain, Haru made no attempt to resume his efforts to get free.

'Did my mother ask you to do this?' he asked Mr Winter, instead. 'Is she still angry with me, for last night?'

'What your mother thinks and feels isn't important anymore,' Mr Winter replied.

'But . . . I thought you were friends,' Haru stammered.

'Friends?' Mr Winter's eyebrows went up. 'I don't have friends, puppet. Only allies. And your mother was a good ally. Really, she was. However, the most recent documents she signed for me made the construction of the bot-making factory – or the

LIFE-Hub, as she calls it – an Imperial order, and that, I'm afraid, was the last useful thing she could do for us. She wanted to use the factory to build nothing more than Service-bots, while my boss, on the other hand, has other goals and purposes.' Mr Winter shrugged. 'Our interests couldn't stay aligned forever.'

He glanced again at the device on his wrist, as Haru began to feel a new kind of dread steal over him. Yes, his mother was usually busy and always difficult to understand. One thing he did know for certain about her, though, was that she would never let anyone actually, properly harm him. If it was true that Mr Winter no longer cared what she thought or said, then it suddenly seemed to Haru as if he might be in serious danger.

'Are you going to hurt me?' he asked Mr Winter.

Mr Winter only laughed. 'No,' he said. 'Quite the opposite, in fact. We want to keep you as unhurt as possible, puppet. Our happy little marionette.'

As alarmed as Haru was, he found his attention suddenly diverted by an unusual sight, then – a swarm of little shadows had begun pouring out from beneath the phoenix-wing harmonium. He blinked as they made their way towards him, scurrying over and around Mr Winter's boots. Amazingly, Mr Winter didn't seem to have noticed them yet.

'So what will you do to my mother, if you can't be allies anymore?' Haru asked. While he was afraid of how Mr Winter might answer the question, it felt sensible to keep him talking and distracted from the small shapes that were still streaming around his feet, looking for all the world like a tide of shadow-mice.

'Your mother's time as Emperor is over,' Mr Winter said, bluntly. 'In the next few minutes, she will be assassinated. It may even have happened already.' He checked the device on his wrist again and frowned. 'You will inherit the Imperial title, and, as

Emperor, you will do exactly what we tell you. You'll be our happy little puppet. Understand?'

Haru made himself nod as Mr Winter's words seemed to echo unnaturally around the small room. He couldn't let Mr Winter panic him now. If the little shadows really were what he thought they might be, then he still had a chance of getting out of here, and of warning his mother in time to save her.

He swallowed down his fear as the mice-like shadows reached him and began to scurry around his own feet, running back and forth over his slippers and then climbing up his ankles, all the way to the rope knotted around his wrists. He chanced a glance back over to Hana, who was still loyally standing guard by the door, her eyes fixed on Mr Winter. Apparently, she was unable to see the little shadows, either.

And all at once, Haru began to feel almost reassured. The fact that neither of them could see what he could see was a perfect reminder that, in spite of what they may have wanted to believe, these people were not, in fact, in control of everything.

Tugging his wrists against the rope again, he found that it felt much looser now than it had at first. As he'd suspected, the little shadow shapes had been nibbling at the knots. He hid a smile. They were friends, then – and like Risu, surely. Sun Spirits, creatures made from Sola, come here to protect him.

The device on Mr Winter's wrist flashed then, and beeped. He glanced at it and swore, his expression turning even stormier – something that seemed as if it might be a good sign, to Haru.

'What did that noise mean?' Haru asked.

'You ask too many questions,' Mr Winter spat. 'You're going to have to get that habit under control if you're going to work with the Sensei. I don't know what your mother might have allowed, but you'll find the Sensei a lot less patient.'

Mr Winter's wrist device flashed once more, and as he looked down at it again, his scowl deepened. Haru chanced another tug at his bindings, and his heart leapt as they gave way, setting his arms and hands free.

Before either of his captors could realize what had happened, Haru was barrelling past Hana to the door. More little shadows were clustered around the door's latch, and as Haru hurtled towards it, the shadows moved as one. The latch flew up, and the door slid open.

And then he was running hard, the soles of his slippers slamming into the ground. A roar went up behind him – Mr Winter's voice, sounding furious.

'Find him and bring him back,' he was shouting at Hana. 'Then find out why the Emperor isn't dead, and how four of my best assassins managed to get themselves killed.'

Haru gulped. He had to warn his mother, as soon as possible. Even if Mr Winter's plan to kill her didn't seem to have worked this time, she was still in the gravest danger. He would look for her in the Silver Laurel Room, he decided. That's where he'd seen her last, getting ready to come out for her speech at the party. He just hoped he wouldn't be too late.

3.

'Go on, get in there,' said the Imperial Guard who'd brought Mei to join Jun in the Palace's cold storage cellar, giving her a light shove.

She stumbled forward, nearly dropping Mochi as she did so, who was curled up as a big, furry lump in her arms.

'Hey,' she shouted after the Guard as he slammed the door behind her, only to very audibly turn the key and draw several heavy-sounding bolts across the door's outside. 'I thought we were friends!'

Then she turned to flash Jun an ironical look, where he was shivering against the wall, watching her entrance from alongside a series of casks and barrels of wine and sake, as well as several large piles of something cloth-wrapped and pungent, which was almost certainly smoked fish.

'What?' she told him. 'I almost did think we were friends, as well. We ended up spending most of the evening together. First, he arrested me and tried to take me to the Emperor – but then something was wrong with the Emperor and everyone was busy, so we waited around together for *ages* until we found this old General guy, who sent us here. Plenty of time for a good conversation. He was practically my date for the night.'

Jun had to smile at that, in spite of his being so cold now, and everything having gone so wrong.

'I can't say I'm pleased you got captured, too,' he told his sister, 'but I am glad to see you.'

Mei grinned, setting Mochi down on the floor before coming over to sit next to Jun. As she did, he pushed his glasses up his nose to look at her properly. She'd discarded the steward's cap, and had somehow found time to pin her colourful, streaked hair back up into an artfully messy, half-up, half-down do, secured with a large, pink hairclip. He, too, had long since given up maintaining his disguise – and in spite of everything, he found that it did feel good not to be hiding anymore, and for the two of them to be looking fully and unapologetically like themselves again.

'I'm sorry,' he told Mei, now. 'This whole thing was a trap. They were expecting us. I should have seen it a mile off.'

'Hey, don't blame yourself,' she replied. 'I mean, it's possible that I may have missed a few small things, too.'

Jun blinked. That was a huge admission, for Mei.

'At least Tosh doesn't seem to be captured,' she continued now, giving him a nudge. 'That's something.'

'I hope she's okay,' he said.

'I know,' she replied, 'me too.' The concern that was in her expression now seemed a perfect mirror to his own. 'Any ideas about how we get out of here?' she asked.

Jun shook his head. 'That door seems pretty hard to get through, and it won't have escaped your notice that there are no windows in here, either. But I'm mulling it.'

The two of them watched in silence for a moment, as Mochi sniffed experimentally at the wrapped fish parcels.

'It could be worse,' Jun said, nodding over towards them. 'At least we've got supplies, for if we get hungry.'

Mei wrinkled her nose. 'I had a good amount of the food at the party, anyway. Did you try the shrimp dumplings? Weren't they amazing?'

Jun groaned. 'You had dumplings? I had maybe one piece of sushi the whole night.'

'Hey, it's like you said, though,' Mei replied, with an almost-convincing smile. 'There are perks to being staff. Turns out you can sneak food even before it leaves the kitchens.'

They both laughed, a little half-heartedly.

'Did you manage to get a scan of one of those ALISE bots, in the end?' Jun asked Mei. Her smile faded at the question – and, abandoning the fish parcels, Mochi came over for a stroke.

'There's something different about those bots,' was all she said as she scratched behind the cat's ears. 'Something that's more than just tech, almost. I don't know what it is, and I certainly don't know if I like it.'

Jun told her then what he'd learnt from the woman in the

blancmange dress, about how the bots were being built using draconic ore from Muralania, which apparently gave them 'a spark of genuine life.'

'You know, just a few hours ago I'd have dismissed all that as nonsense,' Mei said thoughtfully, when he'd finished. 'But now . . .'

She looked surprisingly hesitant for a moment, before seeming to shake off this uncharacteristic lapse into uncertainty.

'Hey,' she said, as Mochi wandered off again to sniff at the barrels of sake. 'That's something, though. You did manage to do a little undercover intelligence-gathering before being captured, and now we know what's in that warehouse, at the docks.' She frowned. 'Or we have a name for it, at least. I've never heard of draconic ore before.'

'There is one more thing that Toshiko and I discovered, too,' Jun began now, bracing himself. He found himself almost afraid to repeat out loud what they'd heard from the two men under the magnolia tree, feeling almost as if to do so might act as confirmation that it hadn't just been some sort of bad dream, or strange imagining of his own. And of course, he knew how upset Mei would be. He took a deep breath, before telling her: 'It sounds like the Crows cleared the southern corner of the Crescent, earlier tonight.'

'Wait, what do you mean, *cleared it?*' she immediately asked.

'Literally cleared it of people,' Jun said, rubbing his eyes. 'It seems like Tosh was right, and the Keeper's Crescent is the planned site for the LIFE-Hub. We heard two of the Crows talking. Everyone in the southern corner of the Crescent was put on some barge, headed for Hanasaki Island. And it sounded like the Crows would be back for the rest of the Crescent before long, too.'

'What?' Mei's screech was so loud that Jun was worried it would call a Guard to check on them.

'I know,' he said, slipping an arm around her shoulders. Of course he was upset too, but unlike him, Mei had been born in the Crescent, and had fully grown up there.

'But they can't take them to Hanasaki Island,' she said. 'They'll die there. They'll sicken and die.' She shook her head. 'I mean, I knew they didn't like us, but to want to wipe us out entirely ...'

'I know,' Jun said again, feeling useless in the face of her shock. He gave her shoulders a squeeze.

'We have to get out of here,' Mei said then, her tone suddenly steel. 'We have to get out of this stinking fish cellar, so I can find a way to get that barge back to the Keeper's Crescent, and make Emperor Asayo and the Crows regret the day they ever thought they could mess with us.'

She shook off Jun's arm, jumped to her feet, and began to prowl up and down in front of the room's locked door. Mochi, too, sprang down from where he'd been jumping between wine casks to land at her feet, apparently understanding that his presence was required once more. Mei gathered him into her arms, and from there, he climbed up into his customary position, draped around her shoulders.

'If ever there was a time to choose to fly above the river,' she said, seeming to speak more to herself than to Jun now, 'then this is it. There has to be a way out of here. Come on, Mei – think!'

4.

Looming over her in the open doorway to the lamplit room beyond, the Guard pulled Toshiko to her feet, and then gave her a shove, propelling her over the threshold and into full view of the group gathered around the table within.

At the head of this table, Toshiko was alarmed to recognize none other than Emperor Asayo – though she didn't look at all like her usual, polished self. The Emperor's face was scratched and stained, and her hair was tangled, pulled roughly back and tied with a basic rubber band. Her right eye was covered with a pale, gauze eyepatch, through which were soaking spots of what was unmistakably blood, while her left eye was smeared with a bruise-like mess of make-up. Her sapphire suit was creased, the sleeves shoved up to the elbows.

Toshiko's mind skipped back to those four Crows she'd seen out in the gardens earlier, moving toward the Palace through the rain with such purpose and menace. Surely this couldn't be their handiwork, though. The Crows and the Emperor were allies, weren't they?

Whatever it was that had happened to the Emperor here tonight, it wasn't only her appearance that was giving this gathering the definite impression of being some sort of crisis meeting. Everyone looked tense, and the room's refined décor – all high shelves filled with leather-bound books and plant pots – was undermined by the chaos of files, papers and pens that was strewn over the table's surface.

As Toshiko had guessed a moment ago while watching the silhouettes through the doors, most of the seats at the table were filled with men from the Imperial Guard, all wearing badges of high rank and carrying visible weapons on their belts. Among these officers was a scattering of people in dark business suits, who looked more like advisors.

'I don't care how timid she looks,' the Emperor said to the Guard holding Toshiko. 'Get some handcuffs on her, now. She needs to be secured.'

The Guard holding her did immediately as the Emperor

asked, pulling a set of cuffs from his pocket and snapping them over her wrists.

The Emperor then gave Toshiko a look which somehow conveyed with perfect, silent eloquence just how irritating and completely unimpressive she found her. Then she pushed the loose strands of hair from her face, and gestured to two of the Guards at the end of the table.

'She has Saito's pearl,' she told them. 'Search her.'

Immediately, the Guards rose from their seats to join the man who was already holding her, and all three began to completely invade Toshiko's personal space. Even as she shouted for them to leave her alone, they tore methodically at her kimono, ripping through its layers and seams. She didn't stop struggling as their hands ranged everywhere over her skin with a harshness that would be sure to leave bruises, but they were all so much stronger than she was that her efforts didn't have any effect. She had just begun to feel as if this awful search would never stop, when at last their hands left her, and they stepped away.

'There's nothing, Majesty,' one of them said, as Toshiko struggled to regain control over her own panicked breathing.

'That's not possible,' the Emperor said. 'She must have hidden it somewhere.'

At least, Toshiko realized, this must mean that the Emperor didn't know that the Crown Prince had taken the pearl – which also meant, crucially, that the boy hadn't given it to her. That was something to be glad of, at least. She wouldn't have liked to discover what kinds of enhanced abilities the pearl might give to someone like Emperor Asayo.

'How about I make you an offer for it?' the Emperor said abruptly to Toshiko then, interrupting her thoughts.

A ripple of surprise went through the group at the table. Clearly, it was far from usual for the Emperor to condescend to negotiate with prisoners. Toshiko raised her chin to meet her gaze, frantically wondering how long she might be able to keep her believing that she still had the pearl in her possession.

'If I am holding Ken Saito's dragon pearl in my hands within the hour,' the Emperor stated to Toshiko, 'then you and your accomplices will get to keep their lives.'

'My accomplices?'

'I don't have time for you to play stupid,' the Emperor snapped. 'I knew as soon as I saw you at that banquet yesterday with those foolish birds tattooed on your wrist that I'd finally found my culprits for the Granitarium Investments robbery. Yes, I know all about you now, Toshiko Kawakami. I know that you and your accomplices are far from being real citizens, too – a crime against Rainshadow City which would usually, as I'm sure you are aware, result in all of you disappearing rather permanently.'

'I don't know what you're talking about,' Toshiko stammered. 'I don't know anything about the Granitarium Investments robbery. I don't understand what you're saying.'

The Emperor turned a shade paler, her eyes flashing brighter.

'One of the key clerks involved with the case had a tattoo to match the one on your arm,' she told Toshiko. 'And I know this, because I have more spies than you've had days on this planet. In any case, the fact is that in addition to yourself, I have two more costumed fools locked up here in this Palace, both of whom share that same tattoo. Hand over the pearl, wherever you've hidden it, and they will live.'

'I don't believe you,' Toshiko said.

'Excuse me?' said the Emperor, as the Guards and advisors around the table shifted nervously in their seats.

'I don't believe you have anyone else locked up,' Toshiko told her. 'I think you're just trying to frighten me.'

'How much are you willing to bet on it?'

Toshiko opened her mouth to protest again, but the Emperor waved her into silence. 'I could even throw in an ID card,' she told Toshiko now, prompting more raised eyebrows from her advisors. 'A real one, with a proper entry in the Citizenry Database to go with it. You could go to the University, get a job. You could do anything in Rainshadow City you pleased, just like a real citizen. You'd like that, wouldn't you?'

Of course Toshiko would like that. It was almost too good an offer to refuse, on any terms, and Toshiko found herself wondering wildly now if there was some way she could still accept it, even though she'd lost the pearl.

'And the same for my family?' she asked the Emperor.

The Emperor barked a laugh. 'I'm afraid not,' she said. 'You're still young, Toshiko. Not much more than a child, really. It would be a shame to see you held back by the misdemeanours of your elders, but we can't have such crimes going completely unpunished. If you give me the pearl, your accomplices get to live – but it's back to the Keeper's Crescent for them.'

'It's not enough,' Toshiko told her, ignoring the tug she felt somewhere in her chest as she gave up this longed-for chance to be a real citizen.

The Emperor's make-up-streaked face twisted into a deeper scowl, as one of the advisors fully gasped at Toshiko's answer. Toshiko only bit her lip, unwilling to apologize. Of course that offer wasn't enough. The Kawakamis always stuck together, no matter what. It was the first principle of their family, and the first thing Reiko had taught each of them when they'd arrived under her roof.

'Not enough?' the Emperor said to Toshiko. 'Not enough? I'm being generous, offering you anything. Tell me, little girl. What would be enough? What's your price?'

Toshiko swallowed, and did her best to sound brave. 'I'll give you the pearl if you promise to stop what you're doing in the Keeper's Crescent.'

It was a risk, she knew, and she really had no idea what she'd do when the Emperor discovered that the pearl was no longer hers to give, but this was the only plan she had, and as long as the Emperor still thought she had something to bargain with, she was sure as anything going to keep bargaining.

'What could you know about that?' said the Emperor, her voice suddenly dangerously quiet.

'I know enough,' Toshiko told her. 'And I want you to stop. It's cruel.'

It was all Toshiko could do not to flinch as the Emperor slammed both hands down on the lacquered wood of the tabletop in front of her, sending pens and papers scattering. The Generals kept their faces studiedly blank, while the Imperial advisors at the table looked openly terrified.

'*Cruel?*' the Emperor thundered at Toshiko. 'Who are you to question me?' Her lipsticked mouth twisted into a snarl of bitterness. 'And I can't stop the clearance of the Keeper's Crescent, in any case. If you knew half as much about it as you pretend to, you'd know that it's up to the Sensei now, in all her wisdom.'

'But you could still stop her though, couldn't you?' Toshiko persisted. 'You could at least try. How can you just give all those people in the Crescent up to the Crows, again and again, when you know how the Crows will treat them?'

'You self-righteous little hypocrite,' the Emperor spat. 'As if you don't really agree with me, deep down, that those people aren't good for anything but being sent to Hanasaki Island. If you truly believed anything else, you wouldn't have deserted the Crescent the minute you were able to, leaving them all behind you.'

'That's not fair,' Toshiko insisted. 'That's not true.'

'I don't have time for this,' the Emperor said. 'I've made an effort to be generous, but if you won't accept my offer, I have other means of getting the pearl from you.'

She clicked her fingers, and five of the Guards stood up from the table to turn to face Toshiko.

'I need that pearl,' the Emperor said, a new desperation creeping into her voice, now. 'I don't just want it for myself, either, you know. It's for the whole Archipelago. It's the surest way to stop her, to protect the Empire's future.'

'Stop who?' Toshiko asked. 'Who are you talking about?'

The Emperor, however, seemed to have no patience left for conversation.

'Seize her,' she rasped, and the five Guards who'd been standing ready began moving towards Toshiko.

Toshiko spun and ran for the doors, only to find that they'd been closed and latched shut behind her. With her hands clumsy in the handcuffs, she spent a frantic, fleeting moment scrabbling to force the latch open, before being grasped from behind and pulled back towards the table.

Two of the Guards who'd searched her earlier were gripping her by the arms, while the others blocked any path to the doors. Toshiko struggled harder, her handcuffs cutting into sores they'd already made on her wrists, but the Guards easily held her secure, watching the Emperor for further instructions.

The Emperor got to her feet, stepping out from behind the table to advance on Toshiko with slow and deliberate steps. Standing, she looked both taller and tougher than Toshiko had expected – the scratches on her face and the streaks of blood on her jacket only serving to add to her general air of menace. Whatever it was that had happened to Asayo Soramoto tonight, it only seemed to have made her more ruthless, more determined, more openly ferocious.

'You must know where the pearl is,' she insisted, as she loomed over Toshiko. 'Tell me – what have you done with it?'

'I don't have it,' Toshiko finally admitted, her courage finally deserting her. 'Please, Emperor Asayo, please tell them to let me go.'

She was interrupted by the Emperor giving her a hard slap across the face. 'You dare do me the impertinence of addressing me by name? Who do you think you are? You're a criminal. An undocumented outlaw. You don't have the right to conceal the pearl from me. Tell me where it is, or my Guards will do a lot worse than restrain you.'

'I don't know where it is, anymore,' Toshiko stammered, fighting back tears now, more at the Emperor's words than at the pain of the slap. Of course she'd known that underneath it all, this was who Asayo Soramoto was. Part of her, though, had always yearned to believe in the Emperor's glamour – in her confidence, in her power suits and bright smiles. 'I lost it,' she told her. 'I'm sorry.'

Toshiko was in too much distress to think too carefully about what she was saying, but even if she'd had the leisure to consider it properly, she still probably wouldn't have been able to explain exactly why she didn't mention the Crown Prince. She owed him nothing, and then of course he was this woman's son, which surely meant he'd be shielded from her anger, at least to some extent. Perhaps some part of her simply felt that anyone with a mother like this deserved all the help they could get.

The Emperor leaned forward again, so close that Toshiko could see the different shades of red in the rusty specks of blood on her eyepatch, and in the lipstick stains on her teeth.

'I have an idea,' she said, her eyes narrowing. 'I think we should introduce our guest here to the oil tank.' She whirled to face the advisors and Guards still seated at the table. 'Don't you agree?'

'Yes, Majesty,' they replied, practically in unison, and in spite of all Toshiko's feelings of fear and helplessness, she experienced a flare of rage then, at these people's spinelessness, at their failure to recognize real cruelty when it was in front of their faces.

'It won't surprise you to hear,' the Emperor continued, turning back to where Toshiko stood, held by the Guards, 'that we host a great many ceremonial dinners and events here at the Palace, for which we are obliged to cater for large numbers of guests. In order to be able to do this easily, we keep a quantity of cooking oil within the estate – and, over the years, I have found that the most convenient way to store this oil is in one large tank. A tank takes up far less space than rows upon rows of barrels, after all, and it can also serve some useful secondary purposes, this being one of them. If anyone I encounter is stupid enough to lie to me, a few extended spells of being forcibly submerged in its depths does tend to do wonders for – if I may say so – *oiling* their rusty vocal cords.'

The tank's existence didn't seem to be news to anyone at the table. None of them looked even half as shocked now as they had done earlier, when Toshiko had dared to talk back to Emperor. One of the advisors even attempted a half-hearted laugh at the Emperor's pun, though she silenced him with a glare.

Toshiko had started to struggle again in the grip of the Guards, as the full implications of the threat began to sink in. 'You can't,' she said. 'You wouldn't.'

The Emperor only gestured to one of the Guards holding

Toshiko, and he clapped a hand over her mouth, cutting her off mid-plea.

Barely able to make a sound or even breathe behind his smothering hand, Toshiko cast her eyes around the room, looking for any possible sources of help. There wasn't much in the room that could realistically be commandeered as a weapon. There were the knives at the Guard's belts, but with the handcuffs still restraining her it seemed unlikely she'd be deft enough to grab one, even if she did dare take on all of the Guards in the room with a blade.

She had almost given herself up to panic, when by some absolute, impossible, Gods-given miracle, a heavy-looking clay plant pot on one of the room's high shelves started to shake. Toshiko watched as the shake turned to a judder, and then as the judder turned to a sway that sent the pot soaring off the shelf, straight into the forehead of one of the two Guards holding her.

His hands went instantly slack as he stumbled, crumpling unconscious to the floor in a shower of earth and broken pottery – and just for a second of surprise, the second Guard's hands relaxed, too. It was all Toshiko needed. She might not have the pearl anymore, but fear and adrenaline made her quick. She twisted out of his grip and dived for the shattered plant pot on the floor. Even with her cuffed hands, she managed to seize a broken shard from the mess, and swing herself around to fling it, for all she was worth, at the Emperor.

She didn't stop to see whether the shard had found its mark. Instead, she used the distraction of the sudden uproar she'd caused to turn and sprint for the doors – which, miraculously, were already sliding open to reveal Theo, somehow there and holding his arms out to her. She ran straight to him. There was no time to consider doing anything else.

As soon as he'd tugged her over the threshold and thrown the doors shut again behind her, he was grabbing her wrists, running his fingers over the handcuffs. Whatever he did somehow managed to spring their locking mechanism, and they fell with a dull thud to the tatami floor. She didn't have the chance to question what had happened though, because he was already rushing her out of the room, pulling her by the hand through the outer set of doors, into the lamplit corridor.

For a while, Toshiko simply let herself be piloted. She felt too shaken to think of doing anything else – even putting one foot in front of the other while avoiding tripping on her torn kimono was almost more than she could manage.

When they'd put what felt like a decent distance between themselves and the Emperor and her Guards, though, the fog of Toshiko's fear finally lifted a little, and she stopped dead, sending Theo stumbling.

'Where are you taking me?' she demanded of him. 'And why are you even in the Palace? Did you follow me?'

'Seriously? You're asking this now?' Theo tugged on her hand, trying to keep her moving through the Palace's network of disconcertingly identical dim passageways. 'I can get you to somewhere safe, and then we can talk. But we're not there yet.'

'Why should I trust you, though?' she asked him. 'I know virtually nothing about you.'

Theo was sighing now, a mixture of exasperation and urgency. 'I just followed you on a hunch, okay? I could tell something was wrong, out in the gardens, and I wanted to check you were all right. Happy?'

Toshiko stared. Of course she wasn't happy. None of it made sense. Who was he, that he'd been invited to the Imperial Palace tonight? And why would he care enough about a girl he'd danced with once to risk breaching Imperial Palace security?

'We can't stay here, or the Guards will find us,' he persisted.

He tugged again on her hand, and maybe that's what did it. She couldn't help but notice that he had good hands. They were strong, gentle, and warm, and felt just right to be holding on to now, when she needed so much to feel safe.

She nodded, just once.

Theo breathed out, relief visibly flooding his face. 'Okay then,' he told her, turning back to the corridor ahead. 'Let's go.'

5.

Haru had seen the whole thing from the Silver Laurel Room, watching through the crack in the doors. His mother had long since gone off to the Palace's healers, escorted by the full entourage of all her Guards and advisors, but still Haru found himself unable to move from where he'd crawled, out of pure instinct, to hide in the small, enclosed space under her dressing table.

There had been blood there at the end, and Haru had felt sick seeing the gash to his mother's leg through the tear in her suit, made by the sharp piece of pottery that the stranger had thrown. And yet, he realized, he wasn't worried for his mother anymore – not like he'd been when he'd run here, to warn her about Mr Winter and his plan. Everything had changed, and now, instead of being afraid for her safety, he was – he realized with a sharp, cold clarity – quite simply afraid of her.

He shook his head, trying to banish the memory of her cruelty to the stranger, and trying to forget, too, about how all the other people at the table, all those Generals and officials, had simply gone along with it. While he hadn't found himself too surprised to see General Kubo carry out his mother's commands, the sight of everyone there, without exception, just doing exactly as she ordered, had been chilling. Would they always do just as she told them, he wondered, no matter how brutal it was?

Haru squeezed his eyes shut, trying to block out the thought, only to find that the darkness seemed to make the images in his mind even more vivid. He couldn't stop thinking about the oil tank she'd mentioned. He'd never even heard of there being such a thing in the Palace before, and yet if the stranger hadn't escaped, the Guards would surely be forcing her into it right now, the slimy heaviness pressing in on her from all sides, to block her eyes, nose and mouth, and make it impossible for her to breathe without choking on oil. Just the idea of it made Haru want to scream.

Another thought kept sticking in his mind, too. The stranger could so easily have told his mother that he was the one who had taken Mr Winter's pearl – and yet she hadn't. Not even when it might have stopped his mother from saying and doing such awful things to her. She'd kept his secret while he'd watched and done nothing to help her in return, because he'd been too afraid – a coward.

Before today, whenever Haru had felt afraid of something, the feeling had always passed quickly. Now, he found that he still couldn't stop shaking, even tucked up like this in the silence, with the pearl clutched in his fist. Stealing it had been supposed to be a fun game. He'd never meant for everything to become so serious.

Opening his hand to look at it then, he found himself almost able to lose himself in its beauty for a moment, before all its colours blurred together, and he realized he was crying. A lot of this was his fault, he knew. He should have realized nothing good or fun could come of taking something that belonged to Mr Winter. Like the storm clouds Mr Winter so resembled, it was clear he caused nothing but misery.

And yet, Haru reminded himself, the pearl didn't only bring

trouble, because he was almost certain now that it was also what was helping him to see Sun Spirits, who were his friends. Even as he looked at it in this moment, too, he couldn't help but feel a little soothed by the swirls of blue, violet and gold which the shadows and light of the Silver Laurel Room were sending playing over its surface. The effect reminded him of touching various paintbrushes to the surface of a bowl of water, each one tipped with a different colour.

What had his mother meant by calling it a dragon pearl, he wondered now? Could it have something to do with the way the pearl appeared to have special powers? Surely it couldn't be a real dragon pearl – not like the ones Kei had mentioned when she'd told him about Sun Spirits. She'd said, after all, that dragons used their pearls to channel Sola, which definitely sounded important – and so if this really was a dragon pearl, then how could its dragon be managing without it? Haru frowned as he continued to watch the patterns of light shift over the pearl's surface. Having seen what his mother was willing to do to get her hands on it, he wasn't sure anymore that she'd care very much about something like that.

The pearl wasn't the monstrous thing here at all, Haru decided then. It was them – it was Mr Winter, and it was his mother. They were the monsters, both of them. When his mother had threatened the stranger in the way that she had, looming over her and ordering those men to hurt her, she'd looked to Haru like nothing so much as a demon from one of Kei's fairy tales, twisted and two-faced. He didn't even want to warn his mother about Mr Winter's plan anymore, he realized. In fact, he resolved then, he didn't want her to see him, or speak to him, or come anywhere near him, ever again.

Dashing the tears from his cheeks, Haru slipped the pearl into his pocket, gathered the last of his courage, and crawled out from beneath the table. Then he picked himself up and ran as fast as he could, tearing down the corridors far too quickly for any of the Palace staff to try to stop him.

He hurtled all the way outside into the rain, and kept going, running through the decked-out gardens, where all the guests were now being asked to leave amid whispered rumours that all was not well with the Emperor. Imperial Guards were pacing and patrolling in larger numbers than Haru had seen out here before, and all the paths and steps, even his favourite secret ways through the trees, were all guarded by armed men and women in uniform.

After the way he'd seen the Guards in the Council Room treating the stranger, Haru definitely didn't feel exactly at ease among them. At least there didn't seem to be any of those guests with wrist communicators to match Mr Winter's around here anymore. And he did know, too, that some of the Guards who hadn't been in the Council Room could even be quite kind – like General Mori, who'd given him a new temari ball when he'd lost his old one. He still couldn't bring himself to trust any of these Guards here in the gardens enough to ask for their help, though. Even the nicer ones would surely be on his mother's side – and he still wasn't sure, exactly, who was on Mr Winter's side. Who could he go to now, Haru wondered, when he didn't want to be on either?

Suddenly, it came to him. He had to find Kei. Of course he knew that she looked after him every day because it was her job to do so, but he also couldn't help but harbour a secret hope in his heart that they were true friends – and that the care she took of him might be about something more than her salary and position at the Palace. She would comfort him and listen to him, surely. And she would never side against him with his mother, would she?

And yet he didn't even know how to begin to find her. The gardens were still so crowded and disordered, and all the lanterns and decorations made everything feel unfamiliar.

He kept on running anyway, searching for her, his blue slippers getting soaking wet in the rain as he went, while branches scratched his face and hands. He felt too scared to call out her name, in case someone should hear him and notice him, and then take him to his mother, or worse – to Mr Winter.

He would have kept running like this indefinitely if he hadn't failed to see the loose edge of a paving stone up ahead of him in the dark. Haru fell hard, landing on his knees on the path and soaking his trousers in the puddles from the rain, as well as the hem of his robe. There were still party guests everywhere around him, along with Guards trying to get them to go home – and yet none of these people stopped to help him now, or even to check whether he was all right. Yes, he was still frightened of being noticed by them, but now that he had fallen and was all wet on the ground like this, the lack of a friendly helping hand felt almost too much to bear. A sob began rising in Haru's throat. Just a few hours ago, he'd been so triumphant, the winner of the game, and now the world was suddenly so full of terror that he simply didn't know what to do.

Forcing himself back up to his knees, Haru was on the point of giving up, and starting to cry properly, when he was met by the sight of Risu, crouched on the path before him. The wail Haru had been fighting to hold back died before he'd even made a sound, and suddenly he could only blink in surprise at the little flame-coloured squirrel watching him keenly with its gold-tinted eyes. As before, Risu seemed haloed in a warm, autumn kind of light, as if someone had drawn around his edges with golden ink that had bled out slightly into the world around him.

'Risu!' Haru cried, forgetting the soreness of his knee in his relief at the return of his disappeared friend. 'I was worried something had happened to you.'

Risu cocked his head, as if to note that, while nothing had happened to him, something had certainly happened to Haru.

'I know,' Haru said, looking down at his grazed, stinging palms and then tucking them under his arms before turning back to Risu. 'It's hard to explain.'

Risu gave him a firm stare. Then, with a flick of his bushy, amber tail, he turned and hopped away over the paving stones.

'Hey,' Haru called after him. 'Wait!'

Risu stopped to look back at Haru, then twitched his head to gesture onwards down the path. When he leapt forwards again, Haru understood this time, and followed.

Risu led him away from all the confused, gossiping, disgruntled party guests, into the quieter part of the gardens, near the servants' entrance. They wound their way under the colonnade where Haru had watched the stranger shelter earlier, before heading across the wide, damp lawn that stretched all the way to the laundry block.

And then Haru suddenly found himself laughing through his tears, as at last they rounded the block's corner to find Kei, framed in the light of its doorway. She had a full laundry basket in her hands, and was frowning out at the rain.

He hurtled towards her with no regard for what she was holding, or for how wet and dirty he probably was – and, blessedly, she didn't seem to care. The basket and all of its clean linen went tumbling onto the damp grass as she crouched to his height, and folded him in her arms. Haru's tears were mainly of relief now, and he felt almost brave enough to be embarrassed at the way he couldn't seem to stop crying.

'What happened to you, Princeling?' she asked. 'Are you okay?'

'Please, don't call me that,' he said into her shoulder. 'I don't want to be that anymore.'

'It's just a little nickname,' she said. 'And you are the Crown Prince, after all.'

He pulled back to look at her, swallowing his tears, steadying his breathing, trying to seem more serious than he'd ever seemed in his life. She was trying to soothe him, he could tell, but he needed to be helped, not soothed.

'I want to run away,' he told her.

She didn't tell him he was being silly, and she didn't tell him no. She simply looked at him, taking in his fear, his scratches, his soaking wet dirtiness, and asked – 'But why, Haru?'

'I'm so afraid,' he said. 'I'm afraid of all of them.'

Kei bit her lip. 'What happened?' she asked.

But Haru could only shake his head. He couldn't begin to imagine how he might explain it to her. 'I just need to get away from here,' was all he could manage. 'Please, help me.'

He watched the different thoughts flit across her face, like changing weather through a windy sky. For a moment it seemed she might argue, and he didn't think he could bear it if she did.

'Mr Winter locked me in a room,' he told her, all in a rush. 'And then when I escaped to find my mother . . .' He found he couldn't bring himself to finish.

In spite of his mother's coldness towards him, he had always been proud that she was the Emperor, and for all his life up until tonight, he really had believed that she was a good ruler. The fear and shame he felt now were just too new to properly express.

'She's a monster,' was all he could choke out. 'My mother is a monster. I've seen it.'

Kei gripped his shoulders, strong and steadying. 'It's okay, Haru,' she told him. 'You're with me now. You're safe.'

'You won't make me go back?' he asked her. 'You'll help me to run away?'

She looked more upset now herself than Haru had ever seen her before. 'Did you say Mr Winter locked you in a room?' she asked. 'Did he hurt you?'

'No,' Haru told her. 'At least, not really. There was a woman with him who tied my hands, but I escaped and tried to warn my mother. But then she—' Again, though, Haru found his words overtaken by ugly, shuddering sobs. 'You have to believe me,' he insisted. 'I have to run away from here. From *her*.'

'I do believe you,' Kei said, watching him closely. 'Trust me, Haru, I really do. But running away? That's huge. Are you really sure about this?'

'Yes,' he managed to say, as he tried to get his sobs under control. 'I'm certain.'

Kei bit her lip, then nodded. 'Okay,' she told him. 'Then we'll go.'

'Wait,' Haru said, his breathing finally steadying as her words sank in. 'Do you mean you're coming, too?'

'Of course,' Kei told him. 'What did you think? I'm not about to leave you now, am I?'

Haru felt another sob swell in his throat at the sheer relief and gratitude he felt now. It seemed almost too much to contain. He forced himself not to simply accept what she'd said, though, and to keep his voice steady, as he reminded her – 'But, Kei, if you left the Palace, my mother might not let you come back.'

Kei nodded. 'Don't worry about me,' was all she said.

He hugged her fiercely, hoping that she'd somehow understand the enormity of what he felt, to know now that she was really by his side, protecting him through everything.

'Now,' she continued, once he'd released her from the hug. 'I think I know somewhere safe we could go. I have a friend in the Keeper's Crescent. He'll be able to take care of us for a while.'

Haru took this in. He'd heard of the Keeper's Crescent before, of course, but only things about it which made it seem as if it wasn't a good place. That it was dangerous. Dirty. Filled with bad people. Hadn't his mother even said something like that about it earlier, when she'd been taunting the stranger? And yet everything he'd thought he'd known for certain had been turned on its head tonight. If his mother hated the Keeper's Crescent, then maybe that was enough for him to go there, and give it a chance.

'Thank you,' he told Kei. 'Thank you so much.'

'Come on.' She stood, and took his hand. 'We'd better go quickly, if we're going.'

'Can Risu come, too?'

'Risu?'

Haru gestured next to him, at the golden squirrel who was still there watching, his furry head on one side. Kei blinked and looked blank. She wasn't looking in quite the right place, Haru noticed – and then he realized that of course she couldn't see him.

'Risu,' he explained. 'My friend who disappeared. Remember?'

A slow smile spread over Kei's face. 'You can see Sun Spirits again.'

Haru nodded, feeling the pearl there, safe in his pocket. It had helped him to see Risu, and Risu had led him to Kei, and now she was going to look after him and take him away. The pearl was good, and on his side. He felt certain of it now.

As Kei led him through the dark gardens – Risu leaping alongside them, a bright ember in the rain-soaked night – Kei explained that all Sun Spirits, except for the dragons, were usually tied to a particular physical space. Haru's heart sank as he realized this would mean Risu couldn't follow them to the Keeper's Crescent.

When they reached the gates that led out of the gardens and into the surrounding Palace grounds, he stopped and turned to his friend – this squirrel, this tree spirit, this little force of nature who had been the spark of kindness and goodness he'd so badly needed in the lonely darkness of this place.

'Thank you, Risu. For everything,' he said. 'I'll come back to see you, I promise. Don't forget me.'

Risu twitched his nose, then dipped his head in an uncanny resemblance to a bow. Haru laughed, in spite of the sadness he felt at leaving him. 'I've never seen a squirrel do that before,' he said.

Risu pranced and flicked his tail, ushering them out of the gardens.

'He's right,' Haru said. 'Let's go.'

Risu leapt up onto the garden wall, and Haru turned to wave to the Sun Spirit as they passed through the gates. He felt so glad, suddenly, to have someone here to see him off like this, as he left behind everything familiar from his life up until now.

They found the wider grounds quiet, with all of the Emperor's staff having seemingly been recalled to the Palace, during the night's commotion. As Haru walked with Kei through the hushed darkness, he found himself completely unable to picture what they might find in the Keeper's Crescent. He liked the idea of the Keeper, at least, who had always seemed like one of the kinder Gods to him – being, as he was, a friend to the lost.

At last, they reached the deserted set of overgrown back gates which Kei had been leading them towards, and began to undo the bolts. This task done, Haru looked back one last time at the Palace's sloping roofs, still visible over the trees. Then he turned to face the path ahead, gripping Kei's hand as the two of them left behind all the sadness and fear of this place, as well as the shelter it had given them both for so long.

A friend to the lost, Haru found himself thinking again as they walked. He wondered if that might be what he and Kei counted as now.

CHAPTER TWELVE

Secrets Buried, Secrets Shared

1.

With her hand still gripping Theo's, Toshiko followed him through the Palace's labyrinth of sliding doors, dim corridors, low ceilings, incense and lamps. Keeping up with him was harder than she'd have liked to admit. Her bare feet felt cold and were beginning to hurt, what with all the running on these hard wood floors. Her kimono, too, continued to be a heavy, awkward encumbrance, still damp from the rain and always threatening to trip her. She still didn't completely trust Theo, either – which was why, when he suddenly spun to a stop and grabbed her shoulders, her hand shot out reflexively and slapped him across the face.

'Ow,' he hissed, rubbing his cheek. 'What was that for?'

Her arms had already flown up into a defensive Hido block,

which he completely ignored. Instead, he put his hands on her shoulders again, more gently this time, and tried to guide her onwards, down the corridor.

'What are you doing?' she demanded, wriggling herself free.

'Oh for the love of the Gods,' Theo pressed a finger to his lips. 'Can you not hear them?'

She stilled and listened. Footsteps – lots of them, moving in unison. It sounded like a whole patrol of Guards was coming this way. She stared back at Theo, unable to summon any more words, as she started to panic.

'Exactly,' he whispered. 'Now come on – we're not far.'

This time, she let him lead her onwards, both of them moving as quietly as possible until they reached a dark, panelled door to their left. He bundled them both through it into what turned out to be a sort of cupboard filled with pipes and levers, the functions of which Toshiko couldn't even begin to guess. He closed the door, plunging them into darkness.

'Stay absolutely quiet,' he murmured, making her jump, his voice closer in the dark than she'd expected. 'Don't move. Don't even breathe.'

He seemed to be following his own advice, at least – she couldn't hear a sound from where he was, next to her in the gloom. As the footsteps drew nearer outside, she sucked in a breath herself and held it, wondering what in the world she would do if the Guards were to open the door.

Then, from somewhere outside – somewhere near, but not too near – there came the noise of some kind of commotion. It sounded, in fact, like someone knocking over a whole shelf of books. The Guards' footsteps stopped, right in front of the door of their cupboard.

'That'll be her,' one of their voices rang out.

'Could it have come from the north reading room?' another Guard suggested.

'Only one way to find out,' a third voice said. 'What are we waiting for? Let's move.'

Toshiko slowly began to breathe again as the whole squad of stamping boots set off, leaving the corridor quiet.

'That was lucky,' came Theo's voice, through the darkness.

Something about the casual way he said it made Toshiko uneasy. It had been more than lucky. It had been nothing short of miraculous, in fact, but he didn't sound nearly surprised enough. Could he have known something was about to happen in the north reading room? It didn't seem possible. Anyway, there was something more pressing she needed to ask him.

'When I threw that shard of pottery at the Emperor,' she began, 'did you happen to see . . . ?' She let the question trail off. The possibilities seemed too awful to voice aloud.

'You got her in the leg,' Theo told her. 'She'll be injured, but you won't have done too much damage.'

Toshiko nodded, glad for the reassurance. She'd thrown that shard in a moment of unthinking terror. The idea of doing serious harm to the Emperor felt too unbearably huge to contemplate – apart from anything else, being wanted by the Imperial Guard for such an offence would have been the last thing she needed right now.

Theo had been rummaging in the cupboard's darkness, and was now pushing some folds of material towards her. 'I have something for you,' he was saying. 'I thought you might need this.'

'What do you mean?' she asked him. 'What is it?'

'It's a steward's uniform. I picked it up for you when I came looking for you here in the Palace. Don't you want it?'

Of course she wanted it. Now that she thought about it, a steward's uniform was precisely the thing she needed more than possibly anything else right now. And that was exactly the problem.

'Where did you get it from?' she asked him. 'Why are you helping me?'

Theo let out an exasperated sigh. 'We don't have much time.'

'We're hidden for the moment,' she told him, trying hard to sound as authoritative as possible while maintaining a whisper.

Her eyes were beginning to adjust to the darkness now, and she could see he was indeed proffering what looked like a folded pile of clothes, complete with a pair of slippers, sitting neatly on top.

'At least tell me this,' she demanded, then. 'Were you telling the truth when you said you were Theo from Eardland, or was all of that some kind of elaborate lie?'

'I was telling the truth,' he replied. 'Though I'm not sure you were, Aya from Vilmia.'

She sighed. Neither she nor her siblings ever revealed their true identities to outsiders, even at the best of times. And yet Theo had saved her life, hadn't he? And surely, someday, she had to be allowed to introduce herself properly to someone beyond her immediate family circle.

'I'm Toshiko,' she told him, 'not Aya.'

'Toshiko,' he repeated, and she was irritated to find that she quite liked the sound of her name in his voice. What he said next, though, ruined it all. 'Toshiko Kawakami,' he completed the name.

Her fists were up in an instant, ready to fight – though it was far from clear how that would actually work, in a space this small.

'Calm down,' Theo only sighed. 'I know you're one of them – one of the Kawakamis. I should have told you earlier. I'm sorry.'

'How do you know?' she asked. 'Are you working for the Crows?'

'I got your name from Crows intel, I'll admit it, but I'm not one of them. I don't work for them. I work for me.'

She laughed. 'No one in Rainshadow City works only for themselves.'

'You do,' he told her, and she found she couldn't argue.

'But still, why would you help me?' she asked.

'I'm a refugee,' he told her. 'I fled Eardland in a hurry, and now I live in the Keeper's Crescent. As you can imagine, Rainshadow City has very little love for me, and that's fine, because I have very little love for it, especially not for its Emperor. Before today, I had no quarrel with, or even any particular interest in you or your gang. I came here tonight for reasons of my own. When, though, I saw you were in trouble with my least favourite head of state, and after we'd happened to meet earlier, too, in the square . . . well. You seemed all right, and my enemy's enemy is my friend, if you know what I mean. I figured you could use some help.'

I had no quarrel with, or even any particular interest in you. Toshiko knew she had no rational reason to be upset by that, but still, she found it stung, a little.

'You're from the Keeper's Crescent?' she asked him now though, as something new occurred to her. 'Then you must know about what's happened, in the southern corner?'

He fell silent at that, and it was too dark for her to read his expression.

'Are people fighting back?' she prompted.

'They should be,' was all he said in reply, before thrusting the steward's uniform at her once again. 'Now, don't let me regret rescuing you. We're wasting time.'

'How did you get this?'

'Never mind that. Do you want it, or not?'

She had to admit that persisting with the sodden kimono would definitely make this whole situation harder than it needed to be. She took the uniform.

'You can't be in here while I change,' she told him.

'Excuse me?' Theo said. 'There are armed guards out there, patrolling the corridors.'

'Turn your back then,' she ordered.

He obligingly shuffled around to face away from her.

'And close your eyes.'

'Toshiko, it's so dark I can't see the wall in front of me.'

'I don't care, I'm not changing into this if you don't close your eyes,' she snapped. 'Are they closed?'

'Yes.'

'Good.'

Awkwardly, bumping into walls in the dark and cursing herself for even caring about feeling undignified in front of him, Toshiko struggled out of the kimono and into the comfortable tunic and trousers of the uniform. It was a particular relief getting her feet into the slippers, too, which, rather miraculously, happened to fit. She'd felt so vulnerable in bare feet.

'Thank you,' she said when she was done. 'This does feel better.'

'You'll be less conspicuous, too. All that red silk was a liability to both of us. We might actually have a chance of escaping now. Can I open my eyes again?'

'I assumed you already had.'

'Do you always assume the worst of everyone?'

Theo had just turned back to face her, when the two of them froze once again at the sound of more footsteps approaching outside. These weren't too close just yet, but were certainly getting closer – and they clearly belonged to another large group of people. It didn't seem like a patrol of Imperial Guards this time, though. For one thing, these footsteps weren't in unison, as the Guards' had been.

Before long, a low, grating voice, which Toshiko recognized only too well, rang out into the corridor.

'Keep searching,' Ken Saito was saying. 'There are only a limited number of places around here to hide.'

2.

Jun had been surprised when a trio of Imperial Guards had flung open the door of their prison in cold storage, only to comprehensively search him, Mei and Mochi, before marching them off, to leave them in a small, windowless room in the bowels of the Palace. He was fully alarmed when the door swung open to reveal Emperor Asayo Soramoto herself. Immediately, he sprang to his feet and, nudging Mei to do the same, dropped into a low bow.

'Sit down,' the Emperor said. 'There's no point in pretending you actually respect my authority.'

Jun considered a series of flowery assertions to the contrary, before deciding it was probably best just to follow the order and do as she said. He sat, and beside him Mei did the same. That was when he finally noticed how the Emperor looked.

The woman before them now seemed an entirely different prospect to the polished technocrat the island had grown used to. Flanked by two of the toughest-seeming Guards Jun had ever set eyes on, Emperor Asayo wore an eyepatch, was covered in small wounds and dirt, and looked, generally, as if she'd just come from some sort of brawl. As she advanced into the room, Jun noticed, too, that her right trouser leg boasted a large, ugly tear, revealing a thick, bloodied bandage around her thigh.

She eased herself into the chair behind the desk opposite them, folded her arms, and fixed them both with a glare. Faced with her now, Jun found he could well believe in all those hours of intensive military training she reputedly put herself through at dawn every morning. On either side of her, her two Guards drew matching, double-edged daggers from their belts and stood to attention – ready and waiting to do whatever she commanded to Jun, Mei or Mochi. At Mei's feet, Mochi began to hiss warily, his fur standing on end.

'Get that cat under control,' the Emperor snapped. 'Otherwise, I might well decide that cat fur is just what I need for some new winter gloves.'

Mei hushed Mochi, pulling him into her lap and stroking his head and ears. He did seem to settle at this, though Jun wasn't sure it would last.

The Emperor took a long moment to simply stare at them then, and Jun could positively feel how resentful she was, that for all the trials that her night had clearly held, it had ultimately come down to this – remonstrating with a couple of nobody orphans and their cat.

'My advisors assured me that luring you here would be the easy option,' Asayo Soramoto began, then. 'Why bother to give chase, they said, when I could just be the spider at the centre of the web? It seemed like a simple thing, to put an invitation in your way and wait for you to come to us. And yet you've caused so much *trouble* since I allowed you within my gates. *You*' – she turned her glare specifically on Mei – 'even hurt one of my ALISEs.'

Jun glanced sideways, and was surprised to see Mei looking suddenly guilty, even a little ashamed, under the Emperor's glare.

'I have suffered your presence here,' the Emperor continued, 'for one reason only – the dragon pearl that your associate had the temerity to steal from Ken Saito of the Lucky Crows, last night in my gardens. While Ken Saito himself might now deserve only my ire, and the sharp edge of a blade, his betrayal has only left me more determined than ever to get my hands on his pearl.'

Jun felt Mei start next to him. She was clearly just as surprised as he was, to hear the Emperor speak about Saito in these terms.

'I have already searched your associate, and so I know she doesn't have the pearl anymore,' the Emperor was saying now, though, 'and I am told that a search of both of you brought up nothing, too. All of which means that you lowlifes must have hidden it somewhere.' She leaned right across the table to glare at each of them in turn. 'In case you hadn't realized,' she said, 'this is the point at which you apologize to me, and tell me exactly what you've done with it.'

Jun sensed Mei stirring again, and laid a cautionary hand on her arm. He was afraid for Toshiko too, of course – especially since it sounded as if she no longer had the pearl to protect her. Voicing those worries out loud now, though, definitely wouldn't help anyone. He had always been adept at talking himself out of situations. It was time to see just how far those skills extended.

'The pearl is currently stowed somewhere, for safekeeping,' he told the Emperor. 'We can get it for you, but it won't be immediate.'

'How long will it take?' she asked.

'Well, that rather depends on you, Majesty.'

'Enough with this nonsense. You should be aware that I only need one of you two Kawakamis to tell me where the pearl is. To be blunt – one of the two of you is expendable. So think very carefully before you try to be obstructive.'

'We won't tell you anything,' Mei burst out then. 'Not unless you agree not to harm our associate. And neither of the two of us is expendable, either. I'd never tell you a thing if you hurt Jun, and he'd be the same, with me. We're family.'

'It's true,' Jun affirmed, trying not to look too closely at those two Guards, still poised with their double-edged daggers.

The Emperor only gave them both a slightly twisted smile. 'Do you know, I was prepared to offer your associate rather an attractive deal, and she chose to respond by trying to attack me. There's no way you can save her after that, I'm afraid. It would be simply irresponsible of me to grant any form of amnesty to such a violent individual. She is a security risk. I have my best people out looking for her now, and as soon as they find her, she's mine.'

The Emperor snapped her fingers to punctuate this last declaration. Next to him, Jun felt Mei flinch. He himself, though, breathed an inward sigh of relief to hear that Toshiko had somehow managed to escape.

'Fine,' he told the Emperor. 'We'll tell you where the pearl is. Just don't hurt us, please.' He cleared his throat then, desperately buying time as he racked his brains to think of somewhere convincing he could name as the pearl's hiding place, which might just help their cause. 'It's in the warehouse,' he said, at last. 'Down at the docks.'

It had been the best he'd been able to think up at short notice. Now, the only thing left to do was send out a silent prayer for luck to any nearby God who might be on his side. It was a desperate ploy, but it might yet work. After all, the Emperor was clearly distracted and frazzled – he just had to hope she was distracted and frazzled enough not to think too clearly about what he'd just said.

'The warehouse?' She glowered at him. 'What warehouse?'

'You'll surely be aware, Majesty,' he stammered, 'of a warehouse at the docks, currently storing a substance of interest, concerning your plans for the LIFE-Hub?'

'The Lucky Crows' warehouse,' the Emperor growled, her expression souring even further. 'Though that old witch and her jumped-up thugs won't have control of it for long.'

And then she blinked at Jun, suddenly seeming genuinely baffled. 'But why would you hide the pearl *there*, of all places? And how? You couldn't get past the Sensei's people. She has them guarding that warehouse day and night.'

Jun made a mental note of the female pronoun here to refer to the Sensei. That information was certainly new.

'If you look into the matter, you'll find there was a security breach at that warehouse in the early hours of this morning,' he said. 'That breach was our associate, depositing the pearl amid the crates. Of course, it would have been noticed in a heartbeat if she'd taken anything *from* the warehouse. But if she left something behind?' He shrugged. 'Why not hide the pearl in the one place no one would think to look?'

And then he threw up his hands, in a gesture of putting all his cards on the table.

'Look,' he said. 'The plan was to wait until all the fuss over the missing pearl had died down, and then to retrieve it, once security had slackened.'

The Emperor glared at him, her one good eye seeming to bore into him with laser focus, while the Guards on either side of her continued to look as menacing as ever. Then, at last, she nodded, and Jun released the breath he hadn't quite realized he'd been holding.

'If the Sensei is going through with the plan for the clearance of the Plains,' the Emperor said then, her eyes narrowed, thinking, 'her Crows will march on the Keeper's Crescent as soon as the sun sets tomorrow. I would, therefore, prefer the pearl to be completely under my control, and out of the Sensei's reach, as soon as is possible.' She straightened up in her chair, speaking now with more certainty and direction. 'The first priority has to be to conclusively wrest control of the warehouse from her. Once it is in my possession' – she turned to Jun and to Mei now, as if only just remembering that they were still there at all '– you shall retrieve the pearl from under its roof. My Guards will keep an eye on everything you do, and if either of you tries anything, and I mean *anything* different from what I've commanded, it won't just be your cat that I'll be turning into winter gloves. Understand?'

'Perfectly, Majesty,' Jun assured her. 'One last thing, though, if I may. You said you'd need us, once the warehouse is in your possession. What happens to us until then?'

'I don't give a damn what happens to you,' she growled, giving him a particularly hostile scowl.

'But you can't keep us in cold storage until then,' Mei piped up again. 'That could be ages. We could freeze to death.'

Although, privately, Jun did wonder whether that were strictly possible, he decided to run with it.

'It's true,' he said. 'And only we know where the pearl is, inside the warehouse. It's a big warehouse.'

The Emperor gave a groan of frustration which expressed, quite eloquently, just how little time or patience she had left for this. 'Then you can stay locked in here,' she told them. 'And be grateful it's not a lot worse. I won't tolerate any more trouble from you Kawakamis. Just remember – you don't need to be in good health, or even to have all your limbs, to direct my Guards to the pearl.'

She leaned right over the table then, treating first Jun and then Mei to another glare, which left nothing in doubt as to how little she cared for their well-being.

'I want that pearl,' she hissed. 'And you can't imagine how sorry you'll be if you fail to get it for me.'

3.

Listening to the ominous sounds of Ken Saito and his group of Crows coming ever closer, Theo found himself reaching reflexively for the Gift again. Before he could begin to consider how he might use it to help them, though, Toshiko had nudged him, interrupting his concentration.

'What's *he* doing here?' she hissed, speaking far too loudly for a girl who was meant to be hiding.

Theo's eyes closed as he wondered whether the Gods of Rainshadow island might actually have been trying to curse him in linking his fate with hers. If ever there was a way to make anything more dangerous, it seemed guaranteed she'd opt for it. He grabbed her arm, holding a finger to his lips for silence. This was salvageable, he told himself. From what he could tell, Saito was still quite a way down the corridor. Maybe he hadn't heard Toshiko at all over the sound of his footsoldiers' boots.

'Hold it. I think I heard something,' Saito said outside then, immediately shattering Theo's hopes. 'Everyone stop where you are, and listen.'

In the charged hush that followed, Theo couldn't help but be aware of Toshiko's fear. He hadn't let go of her arm – he wasn't feeling exactly relaxed himself, after all – and so could literally feel the tension rising in her, through his fingers.

'Spread out and search the area,' Saito was ordering his followers, sounding ready for the hunt. 'And if you see anyone from the Imperial Guard, use words before weapons, for now.'

At his command, footsteps seemed to swarm everywhere, with at least two sets of feet moving far too close to their cupboard door for comfort. Theo tried his best to stay calm as he listened to the Crows beginning to throw open doors, searching the rooms further down the corridor. Might he be able to use the Gift to divert them, as he had done with the Imperial Guard? Or might Saito be prepared for the Gift, even, and see right through any distraction immediately?

All at once, it came to Theo that, if he wanted, he could simply step out into the corridor. Because while it might feel like both he and Toshiko were hiding from the most terrifying man in the Crows, the reality of the situation was that that was only what she was doing. Saito wasn't after him. He might even be able to distract him, and lead him away. It could even be the most logical thing for him to do now, especially considering the extra complication he'd just identified a moment ago, in the dark.

Of course he'd kept his back turned while Toshiko had been changing, as she'd so firmly insisted. What he had done, though, was to risk using the Gift, to send his awareness out in her direction. Admittedly, it had felt maybe a little ungentlemanly to do this, but then with the tracker in his neck literally counting down his days left to live, he'd decided there was a limit to how gentlemanly he could afford to be – and he'd needed, more than anything, to find out what she'd do with Saito's pearl as she swapped outfits.

And yet two unexpected things had happened. The first, was

that he'd somehow managed to sense something of the energy flowing through her, in a way he'd never been able to do with any human being before, not even with Susanna. It had only been a hint of a feeling, but it had been unmistakable, all the same – something bright, like the flame of a candle, or a lantern, burning steadily in spite of the cold and darkness around it – and he'd been left reeling.

And then he'd noticed the second unexpected thing. The dragon pearl was missing. When it had flown out from Toshiko's kimono at the party, its concentrated power had been so intense that he hadn't even had to try to sense it. Now, he couldn't feel it anywhere – not around her neck, not in any of her pockets, and not anywhere near either of them at all, in this whole, accursed, cramped cupboard. If he let Saito find Toshiko and capture her now, the only lead he had to the pearl would be lost, potentially forever.

The sound of a door being thrown open really alarmingly close to them now jolted Theo from his thoughts. Next to him, he felt Toshiko jump at the sound, too.

'We only have to keep looking,' Saito was telling the Crows outside. 'I'm certain I heard someone nearby.'

Theo took a deep breath. He needed to take control of this situation, before it spiralled into being even more dangerous than it already was. He brushed down the lapels of his suit and ran a hand through his hair – it had got rather tangled what with all of the running and hiding – before reaching for the doorhandle.

'What are you doing?' Toshiko asked in what he supposed he might have counted as a stage whisper, if he was being charitable.

'They aren't looking for me,' Theo told her. 'It's you they're after. I can distract them. Wait here till I come back. It's too dangerous to go out there on your own.'

'I can look after myself.'

'I know you can, but the Emperor and the Crows are powerful. No one should face them by themselves if they can help it.'

He didn't have time to argue further. He just had to hope he'd done enough to avoid coming back to an empty cupboard.

'Wish me luck,' he whispered, before stepping out into the corridor with as much confidence as he could muster, and swiftly closing the door behind him, before Saito or any of his Crows could notice there was someone else inside.

'You,' was all Saito said on seeing him, somehow managing to infuse the word with a level of contempt surely sufficient to shrivel the pride of a God. 'It's only you.'

'Yes,' Theo agreed. 'It's only me. Would you ... fancy going for a walk?'

'A *walk*?' Saito couldn't have sounded less impressed if Theo had suggested a bathing trip to a poisoned swamp.

Theo cursed his own ineptitude in asking such a stupid question. It really had been the only thing he'd been able to think of at short notice, to lead Saito away from the cupboard, and Toshiko.

'I think you'll be interested in what I have to say,' he elaborated. 'It's regarding what we discussed earlier.'

Saito seemed to hesitate, and Theo seized upon that flicker of uncertainty.

'I have some important information to tell you,' he assured Saito, lowering his voice to a confidential volume, 'but it would be better discussed elsewhere, where we can rely on being away from the ears of the Imperial Guard.'

Saito fixed him with a firm glare, before throwing one last glance around the corridor, and beckoning his people to follow. 'This had better be good, Bluejay,' he growled before striding off, not even waiting to see if Theo would follow.

Saito seemed to have a thorough knowledge of the Palace's layout, and led the whole group of them on through its halls and passageways almost as if he were in his own home. The only real outward sign that he wasn't, in fact, was the careful hand that he kept resting the whole time on the hilt of the knife at his belt. He stopped, at last, in front of a set of heavy double doors, which he threw open to reveal a large library.

In contrast to the Palace's corridors, the ceiling here arched high overhead, lending the whole room a sense of air and space, which was only enhanced by the large bank of floor-to-ceiling windows in the far wall. The other walls were lined with leather-bound books, as well as with alcoves, holding stacks of scrolls. In the centre of the room was a spiral staircase, winding to a mezzanine. Theo could make out several glass cabinets up there, displaying objects that called for his attention with that same peculiar tug he'd felt from the dragon pearl earlier, as it had flown from Toshiko's collar as they'd danced. These, too, then, must be objects of significant power. Could the vial of dragon tears be up there, among them?

He squinted up at the mezzanine, trying to get a closer look, and had only just had time to make out the golden, filigreed casing of an overlarge scroll, together with an enormous grass-coloured jewel, before one of Saito's Crows kicked him in the back of the knee, forcing him to stumble further into the room.

Saito paced all the way up to the foot of the spiral staircase, before spinning on his heel to face Theo. His band of followers, on the other hand, fanned out in a semicircle behind Theo, blocking his route to the door. Turning briefly, Theo counted six of them, including the man who'd just kicked him. He swallowed. If he was going to make it out of this library in one piece, it would have to be by talking his way out.

'So tell me, Bluejay,' Saito began, 'what information do you have for me? Convince me I shouldn't just activate the Hourglass in your neck right now, for wasting my time.'

'Your boss gave me a job to do. Would you really kill me, before I've had the chance to complete it?'

Saito didn't bother to reply. He reached instead into his jacket pocket and pulled out a small switchblade, which he flicked open and began to twirl in his fingers with an unnerving, casual precision.

'I've found the Kawakami girl,' Theo told him, talking quickly now, 'but she doesn't have the pearl anymore.'

'Then where is it, Bluejay?' Saito hissed.

'I don't know – but I can find out.' He swallowed. 'Because she trusts me.'

He felt grubby for saying it. Did he even believe it was true, though, or was this all just playacting for Saito? Toshiko was prickly, difficult, and he'd barely been able to keep up with the questions she'd hurled at him while they'd been hiding together in the dark. He certainly wasn't sure his improvised replies had been remotely convincing enough to win her trust. What had she even meant, when she'd asked him about the southern corner of the Keeper's Crescent?

He was jolted back to the present by Saito abruptly hurling the switchblade in his direction. He ducked, eyes screwed tight.

When he opened them again, Saito was laughing, and Theo turned then to see the little knife embedded in the wood of the mezzanine balustrade, some ten feet above him. Saito hadn't been throwing to hit him, at all. He'd only wanted to watch him squirm.

'I need more time,' Theo said, trying to claw back as much poise as was possible. 'I can do it. Just let me keep working on her.'

'You have a whole week,' Saito replied. 'Is that not generous enough?'

'Wait,' said Theo then. 'What do you mean? Why did you come looking for her then, if I still have my whole week?'

Saito scowled. 'Believe it or not, Bluejay, searching for irritating little girls is not my full-time occupation. You'd do well to learn that not everything in this world concerns whatever it is you happen to be doing. Now' – Saito's eyes narrowed, assessing Theo. 'You still have the explosive device?'

'I do,' Theo nodded, patting the breast pocket of his jacket as, inwardly, he began to wonder who Saito could have been looking for, if it hadn't been Toshiko.

'Good,' Saito said, seeming to sharpen the edges of the word as he pronounced it. 'Because I've had enough of these Kawakamis. I need my pearl back, and I need the girl and her gang dealt with quickly.'

'Trust me, sir. I can do what you ask, easily. As the Sensei pointed out, I do have a certain unique skillset.'

Of course he had no idea, really, what Saito or the Sensei truly knew about the extent of that skillset, or indeed whether he was laying it on too thick with the 'sir'. Considering that Saito seemed to hold the power to activate the Hourglass and so to end his life, though, he figured he'd better try what he could.

'Show me, then,' Saito was saying. 'Demonstrate that the Sensei wasn't wrong about your chances of success. But hear this – plans of a far greater scale than you could possibly imagine are now in motion, Bluejay, and I will not have you getting in my way again.'

'I'm sorry for the misunderstanding, sir,' Theo told him, trying to smile reassuringly through the tight feeling in his throat. 'I promise I won't let you down.'

4.

After the Emperor and her Guards left, Jun and Mei simply sat for a moment in stunned silence, before Mei groaned, burying her face in her hands.

'What a mess,' she said.

'It could be worse.' Jun produced a handkerchief from his jacket pocket and wiped the beads of anxious sweat he had the leisure to notice now, trickling prodigiously down his forehead. 'We're still alive – for now, at least.'

'What are you talking about? She has Toshiko. And Toshiko's lost the pearl.'

'She doesn't have Toshiko. Weren't you listening? She said that she had her best people out looking for her, and that Toshiko would be hers *once she'd found her.*'

'Excuse me if I was too worried I'd be murdered on the spot to attend to the nuances of the conversation,' Mei snapped, though she did sound a little relieved. 'So she said she was searching for her. Is that really so much better?'

'Of course it is,' Jun said. 'Tosh has managed to escape.' He grinned. 'It looks like our little sister is a little too clever for the Emperor's people.'

Mei did concede a small smile at that. 'But what on earth were you doing,' she demanded, though, 'making up all that nonsense about the Crows' warehouse?'

'I just wanted to buy us some time, before she had us tortured or thrown in prison – or worse. As long as she thinks we have the pearl, or at least that we know where it is, she'll keep us alive.'

Mei seemed to consider this, stroking Mochi and maybe beginning to look a little calmer. 'So what do you think it was that happened, between the Emperor and the Crows?' she asked Jun, after a moment.

She sounded almost disbelieving, and Jun, too, found he hadn't even begun to properly process everything the Emperor had said about the gang yet. It was just so seismic a shift to the order of how things had always been done here, on the island.

He could only shrug. 'Maybe the Crows decided they wanted the LIFE-Hub and the ALISEs for themselves?' he hazarded. 'Though what they'd want a bunch of fancy Service-bots for, I don't know.'

Mei frowned. 'Whatever it is, I doubt it's for making tea, or doing the laundry. And regardless, it only means the same for the Keeper's Children, whether it's the Emperor or the Crows, or both of them together who want them gone.'

Jun nodded. Then he stood, and headed over to examine the room's only door. 'At least she kept us in here, rather than taking us back to cold storage. This door, you'll notice, only has one very normal-looking lock on it. It'll be a lot easier to break through.'

Mei looked more cheerful at that. 'You think you can do it?'

'I think so. I've picked up a few practical skills, what with all the years of heist fieldwork. And anyway, we're the Kawakamis. No one can keep us locked up for long.' He paused, as a new idea began to occur to him. 'Although there is one more thing, actually, that I think we need to do first.'

'First? As in, before escaping?'

'I think so, unfortunately. What I have in mind requires access to the Imperial Palace's closed security network – which, since we're in the Palace, I think we'd be best able to access from here. Now, you wouldn't happen to have a computer on you, would you?'

Mei raised her eyebrows. 'Who do you think you're talking to?' she said, pulling a large, pink, lacquered hairclip from her hair.

Mei twisted the hairclip until Jun was sure it would snap. Instead, it clicked open along a concealed hinge, unfurling like a flower to reveal a tiny keypad and screen. He grinned. Yes, the Guards had searched them on their way here, but they'd only been looking for the pearl or for obvious weaponry, and they could never have been any match, anyway, for his sister's enthusiasm for concealing tech in unlikely places.

'So,' Mei began, as she booted up her miniature computer, 'just what is it that you need from me then, Mr "Taking His Sweet Time To Escape Terrifying Captivity"?'

'I need you to hack into all the security systems at the warehouse filled with draconic ore. I know it's owned by the Crows, but I'm willing to bet the Imperial Palace network will still have a reasonable level of access to it, given that the alliance between the Crows and the Emperor seems to have fractured only very recently.'

'That should be doable,' Mei nodded. 'What am I meant to do once I have access, though?'

'Shut down the warehouse,' Jun replied. 'Lock it down as fully as you can – lock the doors, and change their entry codes. Do whatever you can to prevent them from ever opening again. Turn on any lasers or Fighter-bots stationed ready at the front doors, and make sure only you can turn them off again. Do whatever – just make it as difficult as possible for either the Crows or the Emperor to gain access to the place.'

'And why am I doing this, instead of escaping and finding our sister?'

'We will escape, and we will find Tosh,' Jun told her, reassuring himself in the process. 'My thinking, though, is that if the ore in that warehouse is so essential to the Crows and the Emperor, then surely it follows that without access to it, the LIFE-Hub can't go ahead. And if it can't go ahead, then maybe there's a small chance the Keeper's Children could be a little safer than they were before. Even if the Crows still attack anyway, locking down the warehouse could still divert some of their fighters away from the Crescent as they try to break back in – just as telling the Emperor that the pearl was inside might have done, as far as the Imperial Guard are concerned.'

Mei had begun tapping purposefully now at the keypad of her hairclip computer. 'I see what you're saying,' she said. 'And amazingly, it does make some sense.'

'Great,' Jun said. 'And then, after that, I'm going to need you to use your network access to set up a distraction on the other side of the Palace, to draw away the Guards while we escape. A simple fire alarm or something should do it, I reckon. The Palace seems in chaos tonight, after whatever Saito and the Crows have done. It shouldn't take too much to fox them.'

Mei nodded, still typing. 'I'll see what I can do. And what are you going to get up to, while I basically single-handedly save the day over here?'

'I'm going to pick that lock,' Jun told her. 'Speaking of which, you don't by any chance have any more hairclips on you? A real one, this time, would be preferable.'

Mei sighed, and without looking up from her work, pulled another grip from her hair. 'Let it never again be said that hair accessories are frivolous,' she declared, handing it to Jun.

He went straight to the door and crouched down by the lock, getting quietly to work.

'Where are we going to look for Tosh, after I'm done with this?' Mei asked, after some moments of quiet concentration.

'She'll have gone to the Crescent,' Jun said. 'I'm almost

certain. It was all I could do to stop her from dropping everything and running straight there earlier, when we heard about the barge. We'll go down there to ask if anyone's seen her, and that way we can warn them, too. Shutting down the warehouse might delay or weaken the Crows' attack, but it's still likely we'll be too late to stop it, and the Keeper's Children deserve to know what the Emperor just said – that as things stand, the Crows will be back for the rest of them at sunset.'

Mei nodded, her expression grim, and started typing even more quickly into her miniature keypad. 'Yes,' she said. 'We'll warn them.'

What exactly, though, the people of the Keeper's Crescent would be able to do with such a warning, Jun found he couldn't say for sure.

5.

Still sitting curled up in the gloom of the dusty cupboard, Toshiko snapped into instant alertness at the sound of light footsteps approaching, followed by a rap on the door. Theo, surely, was still the only one who would know she was hiding here. Certainly, he was the only person she could think of who might knock.

She stayed quiet, those last words he'd exchanged with Saito still echoing in her thoughts, most of her hoping he might simply go away. Unless of course it wasn't Theo outside at all, but actually Mei, having somehow found her. Mei, by contrast, Toshiko would be very glad to see.

As expected, though, the cupboard's door slid open to reveal Theo standing in the lamplight of the corridor. Her complete lack of surprise at seeing him seemed matched by his at finding her still there.

'You actually waited for me,' he said, sounding half-delighted and half-worried she might somehow contradict him.

'You're working for the Crows,' she said, blinking as her eyes adjusted to the light. 'You swore to me that you weren't.'

'And I wasn't lying. I'm not working for them.'

'But Saito recognized you, and followed you when you asked him to. *I have some important information to tell you.*' She felt her voice take on a childish, mimicking tone as she threw his earlier words to Saito back at him.

'But I led him away from you, didn't I?' Theo maintained. 'I was trying to keep you hidden. And amazingly, in spite of your best efforts, I seem to have succeeded.' He jerked his head towards the open doorway. 'Come on. Time to go.'

'So that you can take me to Saito, is that it?' She blinked as a new thought occurred to her. 'Hang on, was he the one who got the boy to steal the pearl from me?' she asked.

'What? No. What boy?'

Toshiko only shook her head. She didn't seriously think the Emperor's son was working for the Crows. He was only ten, and hadn't seemed like a bad kid, really. Also, there was simply no reason for him to be helping the Crows. She just felt so frustrated. It seemed like everyone was suddenly working against her.

'Come on,' Theo said again, holding out his hand to her. 'The Crows are taken care of for a while, and I've checked the corridors on either side of us. It looks as if the Emperor has moved the search to another part of the Palace, for now. We should be able to escape, if we go now.'

Toshiko only frowned at his outstretched hand, and didn't take it. 'What do you mean, the Crows are *taken care of*?'

Theo shrugged. 'I took care of them.'

She gave him her best sceptical look. 'I'm really supposed to believe that just some boy—'

'Hey, I'm nineteen,' he interrupted.

She rolled her eyes. 'Okay, I stand corrected. I'm really supposed to believe that some old, distinguished man of nineteen years old was able to disable the most formidable collection of gangsters on the island?'

'Yes,' Theo sighed. 'Look, I'm afraid we don't have time for this. The Crows and the Guard might be elsewhere for the moment, but that doesn't mean they aren't still crawling all over this place, like termites through a dead tree. I can't keep them away for long.' He paused, and then added: 'And after what I did back there to Saito, the Crows will be after me now, too. I can't cover for you again.'

'Just what did you do back there?'

'Let's just say I'm not Saito's favourite person right now,' was all he replied, with a grimace. 'Now, do you know of anywhere safe we could go? Because if you did happen to know of somewhere, we could go back there, and then maybe work on a plan to do something about what's going on in the Keeper's Crescent. About what you mentioned. In the southern corner.'

Toshiko had opened her mouth to keep arguing, but at this, she closed it again. She did want to do something about the southern corner attack, it was true. 'Not until you tell me what you did to the Crows,' she insisted.

Theo sighed again, lowering the hand he'd been holding out to her and then shoving both fists into his jacket pockets. It really was a very nice jacket, Toshiko noticed, anew – black velvet with mother-of-pearl detailing, and embroidery on the lapels. Where could a resident of the Keeper's Crescent, as Theo claimed to be, get a jacket like that?

'I wasn't going to tell you,' he said, then. 'But if it's the only way that you'll agree to come with me . . .'

He glanced up and down the corridor. All was mercifully silent and still, aside from the gentle flickering of the lamps.

'Before I show you anything,' he said, 'you have to swear you won't tell anyone. Not a soul,' he insisted. 'You have to promise.'

'Okay,' she said, confused now. 'I promise.'

'And you have to understand that I'm taking a risk, trusting you.'

'I won't tell anyone.' She frowned, confused at what could possibly merit such secrecy.

He stared hard at her for a moment, before stepping into the cupboard and sitting down opposite her. She expected him to begin speaking, but instead, he closed his eyes, laid his open palms on top of his knees, and took a slow, deep breath. Nothing happened, and yet he didn't do anything further, or even open his eyes. He just kept sitting there, cross-legged in the dust. As Toshiko waited, she found her eyes wanting to flick away from him, into the cupboard's darker corners. Watching him directly felt suddenly awkward. He seemed almost too vulnerable like that, with his eyes closed.

Suddenly, all the lamps outside in the corridor dimmed. And yet Theo didn't seem to register the changing light levels at all. He just carried on breathing steadily, his eyes still shut.

Worried now that the shift towards darkness might herald the coming of the Guard or the Crows, or something even more sinister, Toshiko reached for his arm, trying to warn him. Theo didn't react at all to her touch, though, his face remaining a picture of calm concentration.

That's when she noticed his hands. They were still resting, upturned, on his knees, but the air above each palm looked somehow different to that of the rest of the cupboard – as if, in fact, it were somehow faintly glimmering.

As she watched, this glimmer built to a soft glow, which then became a cluster of sparks above each palm, jostling and shifting like fireflies.

A slow smile spread over Theo's face as he gently brought both hands together, and the little lights followed, until he was holding a whole dancing cluster of them, bright and shifting within his cupped hands. Then his blue eyes opened, and he caught Toshiko's gaze through the sparks. She couldn't help but smile back at him, and as she did, she noticed that his blue irises were ringed with gold.

'What's happening?' she breathed.

Instead of answering, he opened his hands wide and blew gently on the sparks, sending them wheeling, twisting, scattering off into the corridor. They dispersed, leaves on an autumn wind, and a moment later the hallway lanterns returned to their original brightness.

She was surprised then to see him looking almost shaken by what he'd just done, dropping his gaze and blinking down at his palms, as if suddenly afraid of her reaction. And then, all at once, she remembered where she'd seen eyes ringed with gold before. Jun's eyes had looked that way, as he'd healed her shoulder.

'Wait,' she said to Theo now. 'Is this the pearl? Were you the one who asked the boy to steal it? Do you have it now?'

Theo did look up at her again at that, and she was surprised to see what looked like genuine hurt in his expression.

'Pearl?' he said. 'What could a pearl have to do with this? I've been like this my whole life.'

He'd spoken quietly, but she found herself taken aback by the emotion in his voice. All at once, she found herself wishing for a second chance to react. He'd trusted her in showing her something of himself, she realized now. And she'd failed him.

'I'm sorry,' she told him. 'I didn't mean that. I was just surprised, that's all. I've never seen anyone do anything like that, before. It was beautiful.'

'You really think so?' The ghost of a smile crept back onto Theo's face.

'Yes,' she told him. 'Of course.'

And although nothing definite had changed about Theo at all, she couldn't help but notice that he suddenly seemed completely different. All of his defensiveness – that air of skittish alertness mixed with a front of smooth confidence – had fallen away, and for a moment, he simply looked back at her, his smile widening.

'I can do other things, too,' he told her, then. 'Other things apart from just conjuring lights, I mean. I only did that just now because . . . well. I suppose I thought you'd like it.'

'I did like it,' she said. 'Thank you.'

He gave her a look, as if for some reason he could barely believe what she'd said, and then he laughed, so she laughed, too – until something in his face seemed to change, and his hand strayed to the left side of his neck again. She'd noticed that seemed like something of a nervous tell, with him. Suddenly, his expression seemed to close off to her again, as he recovered some of his old bravado.

'Like I said,' he told her, 'it's not just for pretty lights. I mean, you don't even *want* to know what I did to Saito back there—'

'That's how you broke into the University library, and stole the book,' she interrupted him. 'I didn't understand how you'd managed it, as that door should have been locked from the inside. But you used this . . . *power* to get past it. And to distract the Guards inside, I bet.'

For a moment, he seemed to be about to deny it. Then he hesitated, his expression turning sheepish. 'Good detective work,' he said.

She ignored his attempt at a smile, struggling to take in the extent of this new information, and to make sense of how it might fit into the already confusing picture she'd been forming of him.

'If it counts for anything, I also used it to make that flowerpot fall on the Guard holding you, back in the Emperor's rooms,' Theo told her then, abruptly. 'And I used it to make the rain come.'

'*You* made that rain happen? But why?'

Theo rubbed his eyes. 'I did it for you,' he said. 'So you could see a rainbow. I just didn't mean for there to be quite so much of it.'

Toshiko felt herself blush, and hoped it wasn't visible in the half-light of the cupboard.

'We should get out of here,' she said – to stop him talking now, as much as anything else. 'Before somebody finds us.'

'Excellent idea,' Theo said. 'Where would you like to go?'

Toshiko hesitated. Probably it would be most sensible to go home, to wait for Mei and Jun. The Emperor might have claimed to have them captured, but Toshiko hardly believed that was true. The Emperor had been saying anything she could to scare her, to trick her into handing over the pearl, and in five full years of living outside the law in Rainshadow City, Mei and Jun had never once even come close to being outsmarted by the Emperor or her Guards before. Probably, then, it would be best to say goodbye to Theo here, and go home to her siblings, so they could all pool everything they'd discovered at the Palace tonight and make a proper plan.

Then again, so much had changed since they'd set out for the party. Something terrible had clearly happened in the southern corner of the Crescent, and for all she knew, it could be getting worse even as she sat here, hiding. Now, too, in Theo, she had found someone new, who could do seemingly impossible things – and who also seemed strangely keen to help her. Having Theo at her side wasn't the same as having the pearl, but it was definitely something.

'Let's go to the Keeper's Crescent,' she told him. 'You live there, right? We can use your place as a base, and then see if we can find a way to use this power of yours to help the people there.'

'Don't you want to go back home, first?' he countered. 'Or does Toshiko Kawakami not require such foolish things as sleep?'

She rolled her eyes. All of his old annoying glibness seemed to be back now, as if the quiet vulnerability of just a moment ago had never been.

'We're going to the Keeper's Crescent,' she insisted. 'And if I get tired, I can just take a nap at your place.'

'I'd be delighted,' Theo told her. Then he stood, and held his hand out to her again. She took it this time, letting him pull her to her feet.

As he turned to check the corridor was indeed fully empty, she noticed his fingers go to his neck again, worrying the area behind his ear. Could it be a sign he wasn't quite as at ease with this new plan as he made out? She reminded herself that she couldn't quite fully trust him yet.

They left the red kimono behind in the cupboard. Mei definitely wouldn't be happy, but Theo had been right in thinking that the steward's uniform would be much more practical. It allowed her to move like a shadow at his side as they slipped through the corridors and passageways, and then into the Palace gardens, where they scrambled over the walls and out, at last, into the city.

PART III

TROUBLE AT
THE CRESCENT

CHAPTER THIRTEEN

Fried Eggs and Chicken Satay

1.

Haru hadn't realized how cold it became in Rainshadow City at night, even in early autumn. He was never usually allowed to be out of bed this late, after all, let alone outdoors. From the way the Sister Moons were setting while the stars were still bright in the sky, he guessed it must now be sometime around midnight.

He pulled his blanket more tightly around himself, and shivered. At least it wasn't raining here in the Keeper's Crescent, as it had been earlier at the Palace. And the fire was warm, too – that was something. The woodsmoke even blended with the scent of the nearby ocean in a way that made him think of adventures. He almost didn't mind that they hadn't been able to have the fire actually inside Kei's friend's house, where they would have been more sheltered. It was a very small house, with no chimney. Haru had never seen a house so small before, in fact, before coming to the Crescent tonight.

Kei's friend was called Ren, and Haru wasn't sure what he thought of him yet. Ren had greeted them with a wide smile and some jokes in Muralanian which Haru hadn't been able to understand. Then, though, Kei had explained who Haru was, and while Ren had looked alarmed at first, he'd switched to greeting Haru in Navishian almost immediately, and before long, his smile was back. His Navishian was good, generally, and judging by how easily he'd made the switch, it seemed like a language he and Kei spoke together much of the time. He was still quite young, probably somewhere around Kei's age, with creased smile lines around his eyes, and long hair that he'd tied back in a ponytail. He had strong hands that looked as if they'd be good at fixing things, and even though his house was so small – smaller, in fact, than Haru's bedroom had been in the Palace – he'd still decorated it with all sorts of hangings and flags, as well as with long strings tied with bright scraps of cloth, which Kei had called Keeper's Garlands. Now, Ren was frying them all eggs and sausages in a pan over the fire.

If Haru had heard all this without meeting Ren, he might have supposed him to be a fun, cheerful sort of person. Yet Haru couldn't help but notice that whenever Ren wasn't speaking to Kei, he tended to fall into a brooding sort of state, which made him seem even a little intimidating to talk to. Now, for instance, Ren was flipping sausages, but seemed barely aware of what he was doing. Really, he was staring into the fire, and Haru felt as if it might be interrupting something, to venture to speak to him now.

The deeper, more essential impression that Haru picked up

from Ren was in itself like fire, too – though not like the gentle blaze before them now, or even like the steady, lantern glow of the stranger at the party. To Haru, the nature of the life force within Ren seemed more like the flames that tore through the dry, dead wood of the bonfires at the Palace's Midwinter festival. A welcome, celebrated source of heat and light, but with the potential to turn wilder, too.

Sitting cross-legged next to Haru on the ground, Kei didn't seem to share any of the shy nervousness he felt around Ren. She had wrapped herself in a thick blanket similar to the one Ren had given Haru, and seemed perfectly relaxed, playing a stringed instrument of a type that somehow seemed quite familiar to Haru, though he certainly hadn't seen anything like it for years. It most resembled a wooden box, inside of which were eleven strings, tuned to different pitches. Kei was plucking and strumming these now so that the notes wove in and out of the tune she was humming, and as Haru watched and listened, he found himself almost sure that this instrument of hers matched the one in his hazy, early memories, being played by the shadowy, messy-haired figure of his father.

The stringed box also had another, unexpected feature that kept drawing Haru's eye, though neither Kei nor Ren was able to notice it. A mouse-like shadow was nestled under the strings, and kept popping its head out into the brisk night air during the lulls in Kei's song. Haru did try to catch its attention whenever it appeared, but it didn't seem as friendly as Risu, or was at least a little more wary.

'It's a weaver's harp,' Kei told Haru when he asked her, in a shy whisper, what kind of instrument this was. 'It's from Muralania. We grew up with our grandmothers playing these, didn't we, Honeybee?'

This was what Kei called Ren – and amazingly, for all his seriousness, Ren didn't seem to mind at all being given this nickname. In fact, he seemed to like it. The gloomy look fell away from his face again as he looked up at her. 'We did,' he confirmed, with a smile. 'I even brought this one from home.'

Haru wanted to tell Kei about the little Sun Spirit under the strings, as well as about the memories he had of his father. He felt nervous, though, at the idea of bringing such a thing up, especially with Ren around. He wasn't sure, after all, how people outside the Palace thought about his father. Did the rest of Rainshadow island believe he'd been a shameful waste of space, just like his mother did?

'Kei,' Haru asked, instead, 'did you and Ren come over from Muralania together?'

Kei shook her head, smiling. 'I came first, on my own. When I was twenty, I left Muralania and made it to Auria, which was the easiest island of the Empire to get to, back then, from Muralania. I snuck into one of the recruitment exams for Rainshadow City that run in the test centres there, and I passed – which meant I was allowed to come and work here.'

'But why did you want to leave Muralania?' Haru asked.

Kei's smile tinged a little sad, and she stopped playing the weaver's harp. The mouse-like shadow inside it raised its head under the strings again, as if it wanted to listen to what she would say, too.

'My mother was unwell and couldn't work,' Kei explained. 'We were struggling for money, and even being a servant in Rainshadow City pays far better than most kinds of work on any of the other islands – even Muralania.'

It could have been Haru's imagination, but Ren seemed to shake the frying pan a little more vigorously over the flames at that last statement of hers.

'I was all on my own here for five years,' Kei continued, 'sending money home. And then Ren followed me, didn't you, Honeybee?'

'Call it foolish, but I couldn't live without her,' Ren said, allowing himself a small grin.

'Did you take a recruitment test too?' Haru asked him.

'No,' Ren told him. 'That's why I live here in the Crescent, rather than up in Rainshadow City, like Kei.'

'Do you still like living here though, on the island?' Haru asked.

Ren seemed to focus on the cooking for a bit, studying the contents of the frying pan and poking at the eggs before answering. 'I like living near Kei,' he said. 'And I think she likes having me close enough to visit, too.'

'You know I do, Honeybee,' Kei smiled, and started softly plucking at the weaver's harp again. The little shadow ducked back into the body of the instrument, tucking itself into where the sound resonated, amid the wood.

'Besides, I kid myself that I can do some good here in the Crescent,' Ren said. 'There's important work here that needs doing.'

'You're definitely doing good,' said Kei. 'The Keeper's Crescent needs you, Ren.'

Haru didn't ask what work they were talking about. Generally, as a rule, he found adults frustrating when they talked about work. Instead, he simply carried on listening to Kei and Ren talk, finding himself increasingly fascinated by the warmth that flowed between them. When Ren had finished cooking, Kei put the weaver's harp aside to help him serve the food onto plates, and it was almost like watching a dance, Haru thought, to see the way their hands moved in perfect coordination, without either of them needing to say a word. They didn't seem at all aware that there was anything special about this, but Haru couldn't begin to imagine his mother, for instance, ever behaving this way around anyone, let alone with his father, whom she only ever spoke of with disdain.

'Thank you for bringing me here,' Haru told Kei, as she handed him his plate. The delicious aroma of fried food on the night air was making his stomach rumble. It felt like centuries since the party and all those fancy snacks that he'd sneaked off the servers' trays.

'Oh sweetheart, I hope I did the right thing,' she replied, looking partly worried, partly tickled as she watched him wolf his eggs. 'I hope you'll be safe here.'

'Don't worry,' he told her. 'Of course I will be.'

She chewed her lip. 'Are you ready to tell me any more about what happened at the Palace, yet?'

He shook his head, busying himself with his food.

Later, as Haru lay curled in blankets on a futon on the floor of Ren's main room, he listened to the sounds of people moving and talking in the Crescent outside, clearly audible through the house's thin walls. He reflected, as he listened, that he hadn't even been lying to make Kei feel better, when he'd said he was sure he'd be safe here. He really did feel as if he would be. Of course, this place did scare him a little, with all the sick people he'd seen begging out there by the roadsides, and the loud groups of teenagers, too, shouting to each other in languages he didn't understand – as well as all those curious, not entirely friendly glances that he and Kei had attracted, as she'd led him to Ren's door. He trusted, though, that Kei and Ren would look after him. And besides, he considered, as he nestled into the covers, he still had the pearl with him – tucked into his tunic, its chain now fastened firmly around his neck.

As he and Kei had walked here from the Palace, through the city and over the plains, he had seen hundreds of little shadow creatures, flitting in and out of the corners of his vision. It had seemed almost as if the Sun Spirits of the island had been sizing him up – judging whether or not they could trust him sufficiently to fully reveal themselves. He couldn't imagine how many more of them there might be, who had chosen to stay shy and hidden. Kei had told him, of course, that there were lots of Sun Spirits, and that no one knew how many existed, but he still hadn't expected them to be quite so ubiquitous. Even lying here now, he could make out a large hamster-like creature, sitting on top of the large tin box in which Ren kept his supplies of cooking spices, tea leaves and coffee grounds.

Haru shifted in his blankets, and then sighed as the creature seemed to notice he was watching it, and moved further back into the shadows. How he hoped that one day, all the Sun Spirits might grow comfortable with letting him see them. He couldn't wait to meet them all. He yawned then, and began to drift into a peaceful doze, thinking of just how amazing it was, really, that with the pearl around his neck, he need never be lonely again.

He didn't even feel worried when he surfaced from those first waves of sleep to hear Kei and Ren talking in low voices.

'It was the whole southern corner,' Ren was saying. 'If our spies are to be believed, too, it looks like we might have to face more of this – and soon. I hate to leave you here.'

'We'll be fine,' Kei was saying. 'It's just a meeting, isn't it? We can look after ourselves for an hour or two. You go. The Keeper's Crescent needs you.'

'I wish I could have warned you about this, though, before you came. And then, too, while there may have been fewer disappearances recently, they still haven't stopped. This is no place for children, really, for anyone who can help it. This is no place for you, Kei.'

'Wherever you are is the place for me,' Kei told him. 'And Haru and I stick together. I only wish we hadn't put you in danger, too, by coming here. The last thing you need is to be harbouring two fugitives.'

Haru felt a twinge of shame, that he hadn't even considered this before now. It didn't take long, though, for Ren to dismiss Kei's concerns.

'You haven't put me in much more danger than I was in already,' he told her. 'And if I was going to risk being accused of kidnapping the Crown Prince for anyone, it would definitely have to be you.'

Haru smiled to hear Kei laugh at that.

'I can't pretend we'll be ready to defend ourselves, though,' Ren said then, suddenly sounding more serious again. 'If the Crows come back for the rest of the Crescent, I don't know that we'll be able to stop them. I mean, I'm doing my best – but people are scared, and I can't in all conscience ask them to fight when it's almost certain we'd lose.'

'You won't lose. I know you won't.'

'They're not soldiers, Kei.'

'Neither are you,' she said. 'But you're protecting us, aren't you? And the Keeper's Children will do the same for their families, surely. For everyone else here.'

'A lot of them are sick. Or old. Or hungry. We need weapons. Money. Proper nutrition. This is happening far sooner than I thought it would.'

'They have you, Honeybee. And we have each other.'

Soothed by Kei's words, and by the way he felt a little included in that 'we' now, Haru began to drift off again. *Haru and I stick together*, she'd said. He was so glad she felt that way. The pearl felt warm against his heart now, and he was barely even aware of the sounds of Ren leaving the house as he gave into tiredness again, sinking fully into dreams.

2.

Theo had suggested finding a rickshaw driver to take them to the Keeper's Crescent, but with both the Imperial Guard and the Crows after them, Toshiko had felt safer walking. The Crescent, though, was the best part of an hour away on foot – through the city and along the island's coast – and even despite her impatience to get there, she did have to admit Theo had a point when, on reaching the city's waterside promenade, he pointed to a late-night hawker stand selling satay skewers.

'I know you aren't interested in sleep,' he said, 'but what about snacks? Are they allowed?'

'You get us some,' she said, giving him a handful of cloud credits. 'It would be best if no one saw my face. Just don't even think about using your powers to try and steal us extra skewers or anything. We've got enough people after us as it is.'

'And whose fault is that?' he replied, but without venom, already heading off towards the food.

They kept walking as they ate, but their pace slowed naturally as they gnawed at their skewers. Even with everything going on, Toshiko couldn't help but smile at the way the saltiness of the peanut sauce seemed to complement the cold ocean air, as if she were being embraced by the sea inside and out. Theo was looking a little more relaxed, too. He had rolled up the cuffs of his jacket and shirt, and his bright hair was wilder now, blown back by the breeze.

'Why did you leave Eardland?' she found herself asking him as they walked side by side along the concrete strip of the promenade. They'd barely spoken, walking here from the Palace, but now that the rain had stopped, the stars were out and they were eating together, it seemed wrong not to have some sort of conversation, and she found herself wanting to hear him talk about his home again.

He only laughed though, not cheerfully. 'Never one to avoid an awkward subject, are you?'

'Is it awkward?'

'You think I came to Rainshadow island on holiday, and ended up in the Keeper's Crescent because I admired the ocean view? I told you I'm a refugee.'

'I'm sorry.' Toshiko felt her face flush. 'I didn't think.'

'No, it's okay,' Theo sighed. 'Too many people here have a sad story for me to be precious about mine. It was actually all because of the power I have, that I showed you, in the Palace. People in my village didn't like it. Eventually, they hunted me for it. They said it went against our Gods. That it was evil.'

'I don't think it seems evil.'

Theo gave her a sly grin, before biting off a chunk of chicken satay. *'Don't think it seems evil,'* he repeated back, through the mouthful of food. 'What a vote of confidence.'

'I just mean that there are so many forces and things out there that we don't even know about yet. Like in all the traveller's tales from Muralania, for instance – the dragons people say live there, and all those ancient, powerful artefacts. And then – I don't know. Like how we discovered granitarium in the mountains.'

'Granitarium? How is that related?'

She shrugged. 'Maybe the world is full of new things we're just waiting to discover and understand. And what you can do is just another part of that.'

Theo was looking out at the ocean, not at her, as she spoke. Something about his expression shifted though, in response to her words.

Soon, they reached Starfruit Wharf, which tonight was lined with the moored boats of fishermen either too poor or too thrifty to pay for an indoor berth. The little crafts bobbed in the water, the breeze rattling their furled sails. Theo stopped walking to watch them as he chewed.

'She called it the Gift,' he said at last.

'Who did?' Toshiko asked, before realizing the answer with a jolt of a feeling that she wasn't quite ready to name, yet. 'The girl you left behind?'

Theo nodded. 'She said it was a gift from our Gods, to make the world a better place. And she said, too, that she thought it had been given to me, and not to anyone else in our village, because I was the one they trusted to know how best to use it.'

'Do you really believe that?'

'No,' Theo said. 'Maybe I did, for a bit, once. Not anymore.'

They kept eating for a while in silence. Waves washed against concrete, and ropes rattled against masts in the wind.

'What did you mean, when you talked about a pearl, earlier?' Theo asked, suddenly. 'You said a kid had taken it. A boy.'

'I didn't mean anything. I got mixed up.'

'I heard the Emperor talking, when her guards were holding you,' Theo continued. 'She said she was looking for a pearl that belonged to Ken Saito. That was the same pearl you were talking about, wasn't it?'

Toshiko sighed. If he'd heard this much, then she supposed there wasn't much point in lying to him. Besides, since she didn't even have the pearl anymore, it wasn't like she had much left to hide.

'Yes,' she told him. 'I stole it from Saito.'

He looked back at her with an expression she could only interpret as mingled exasperation and disbelief. 'But why would you
do something like that, though, when you know what stealing in
this city means?'

'I wanted to get back at him. He was threatening me. And I
hate him. He killed my aunt.'

'Oh,' Theo stared at her. 'I'm sorry. I didn't know.'

'Not my real aunt. Or – no. She was my real aunt. I only meant
that she wasn't my aunt by blood. She adopted me. And he killed
her, back when he was the Captain – just for standing up to him.'

'The Captain,' Theo said. 'This was back in the Keeper's
Crescent?'

She nodded. 'I grew up there, you know.'

'Did you come here to the island from somewhere else, then?'

She shook her head. 'I was born here, I think. Though I don't
know for sure.'

'But how can you not know?'

His questions, now, were sounding different to when he'd been
asking her about the pearl. Then, he'd been unpicking a problem.
Now, he seemed genuinely curious, the same way she'd been,
when she'd asked about his home country.

'I don't remember my parents. A Keeper's Child found me
abandoned as a baby on the Sandslip Plains, and took me to my
aunt. Or to the woman who became my aunt, anyway. Auntie
Reiko. She'd just taken in a child – the daughter of a neighbour
who'd suddenly died, and there'd been some talk that this girl
might be cheered up out of her grief by a sibling, maybe a sister
close to her own age. I was probably a bit young, but I still showed
up right on time.'

'And I'm sure you did cheer her up,' he told her.

Toshiko thought of Mei as she so often chose to be, holed up in her tech cave with her snacks, dreaming up scheme after scheme to campaign against the Emperor, the city, and the Crows – against the whole world, it sometimes seemed. She thought of the sharp acrylic nails Mei always insisted on wearing, of her many sarcastic barbs, and of her frightened fury earlier that afternoon, when she'd thought the cat had been put in danger.

'I hope so,' Toshiko only said.

'So how does a girl from the Keeper's Crescent end up at the Emperor's party?' Theo asked then, looking sideways at her.

'I could ask the same of you, couldn't I?' she replied, then sighed and stopped eating, to simply look out at the reflections of the Three Sister Moons on the dark waves. 'I don't know,' she said, then. 'That party. Did it make you feel—' She didn't know quite how to end that sentence, and so left the question hanging.

'Disgusted at the indulgences of the very wealthy?' Theo tried finishing it for her, speaking with his mouth full, chewing on his skewer. He was back to being flippant again, apparently.

'No,' Toshiko said. 'Or yes, kind of. But also – I don't know. Maybe just kind of blindsided to discover that there really are people like that, and places like that. Places as beautiful as the Palace gardens, so carefully put together, so curated, even – and that they exist simultaneously with the Keeper's Crescent, and the way life is there.'

'Was it really a surprise to you?' Theo asked, pausing in his devouring of the satay to turn to look at her.

'No, not really. Not in the way I think you mean. Of course I realized that those things must be going on, but I suppose I was surprised to find that it was all so beautiful – the gardens and the clothes and the music and just . . . all of it, really. And surprised at how angry I felt, to feel deliberately shut out from that kind of beauty.'

Theo shook his head and looked back out to the waves. 'That wasn't beauty, though,' he said. 'That was all just flashiness, and glamour – I don't know. It wasn't true beauty, anyway.'

'So what is true beauty, then?' Toshiko asked him.

Theo laughed, then looked away, seeming suddenly embarrassed. 'How did you manage to leave the Keeper's Crescent, anyway?' he asked, instead of answering her question.

Now it was her turn not to answer him. 'I'm afraid if I told you that, I would have to kill you,' was all she said.

She kept her voice light, so he'd know she was joking – which she was, of course – but it was also true that she'd probably already said too much.

'We're wasting time,' she told him then, eyeing the Moons, which were beginning to set over the water. 'Anything could be happening in the Keeper's Crescent by now. Come on.'

To his credit, even though he'd just taken a giant bite of satay, Theo followed her, matching her pace.

3.

That night, Haru dreamed again of dragons.

He had always imagined them to be solitary creatures, like the dragon in his dream from the Palace gardens, but there were three of them here together in the mountain lake where he now found himself. One had scales of a familiar bright turquoise colour, and he wondered if this could even be the same dragon as the one in that first dream. This lake was definitely different, though. A snow-covered peak towered above him, reaching into a flawless blue sky, while below stretched rocky slopes so craggy and sprawling that Haru couldn't even see as far down as this mountain's foothills.

The absence of mist up here, too, meant that unlike in his previous dream, Haru was now able to see all three dragons properly, and to watch as the scales of their long, fiercely muscular bodies caught the sunlight as they twisted through the lake's clear water. The turquoise and jade green of the two larger dragons of the trio shone vivid in the sun's brightness, while the third, smaller dragon's scales glowed an even richer, deeper blue, which reminded Haru of the night sky in summer. All three dragons had a single spine of flame-orange fur, too, which ran from the tops of their heads right down to the tips of their tails, which whirled in the water to whip up spray from the lake's surface. The same bright fur covered their broad faces, as well, reminding Haru of birds' feathers, in how the water seemed to slide right off it without ever soaking in.

Watching the three of them now, Haru found he could well believe what Kei had told him, when she'd said that dragons were the most powerful Sun Spirits. They seemed gigantic, in fact – the sheer scale of them maybe even a little daunting. The turquoise and the jade dragons were both well beyond the size of even the Palace's largest carriages, and the third, smallest dragon still looked big enough for at least two people of Haru's size to sit comfortably on its back.

They each had six legs, which were surprisingly short, given their size, and which ended in paws with tapering claws. All three dragons had very sharp-looking teeth, while the largest two had pointed horns curving up from the crowns of their heads, as well as long, orange whiskers adorning their jaws. The smallest dragon, whose eyes seemed larger and rounder than the eyes of the other two, had no whiskers yet, and only two little tufts of fur where, Haru assumed, its horns would one day grow in. All three dragons' eyes shone with a warm, golden, lantern-like glow.

As Haru moved closer to the dragons, walking up to them now along the lake's banks, he found his attention drawn to the natural collars of mirrored scales and gems that gleamed at each of their throats. He noticed, too, that at the centres of these shone single, gleaming pearls that did, in fact, look a lot like the pearl he was wearing now, around his own neck. Unlike his pearl, though, the dragons' pearls were fully glowing, illuminated as if from within by a cool, silvery light that reminded him of the Three Sister Moons.

While the dragons had certainly seemed like fearsome creatures to him at first, it dawned on Haru now that this was almost certainly a family group, with the two larger dragons the parents of the third, smaller one. It seemed to him as he watched them, too, that they might be playing. The smallest one kept chasing after the fish in the lake, or after the tails of its parents as they moved through the water, while the two larger dragons kept leaping above the lake's surface, sketching circles or figures of eight in the air, challenging their child to copy them. Haru suddenly found himself wanting so much to join in with these games, and even began running along the bank, quickening his pace towards the dragons, when the dream dissolved, and reformed again around him.

He was still by the mountain lake, and the three dragons were still there in the water, but now it was night, and stormy, and he was watching as a group of humans taunted and threatened the dragons, brandishing spiked spears so huge that each one needed two people to wield it. In spite of being so encumbered, though, many of these humans had already made it down the banks of the lake and into its shallows to advance on the dragons. Most of them, Haru noticed, were wearing jackets emblazoned with the same double-bird sign he'd often noticed people wearing in his mother's meetings.

It wasn't just the size of the spears or even their spikes that made them seem like especially cruel weapons, either – it was the fear they clearly engendered in the dragons. A chill went through Haru as he watched all three dragons rear and back away from the spears, even allowing the human invaders to break up their family group, in separating the largest of their number – the jade dragon – from the other two. It seemed strange to see such formidable creatures so cowed by something of human manufacture, and Haru began to wonder if the spikes of the spears might be coated with poison.

Seeming to gain confidence now that the two largest dragons were no longer together, a pair of men closed in, levelling their spear at the youngest, dark blue dragon, with the large eyes and the little tufts of fur in place of horns. The turquoise dragon surged forward to protect its child, displacing the lake's calm waters as it lashed out with its claws, and yet the men managed to dodge the attack, swinging their spear around to strike at the turquoise dragon's hide and rake an angry, red line through its glimmering scales. Blood swirled through the lake as the turquoise dragon roared with pain and anger – and Haru cried out then, too, calling loudly for the men to stop, even in spite of how afraid they made him.

The two men, though, ignored Haru's shouts completely. They were edging back towards the lake's shore now, their spear held low as they watched the turquoise dragon warily. Haru began to run towards them, hoping to try to stop them, somehow.

He'd nearly reached them when the wounded dragon's pearl flashed with new brightness, and as if in reply, lightning forked

down from the clouds clustered at the mountain's peak to strike
the banks of the lake – right at the spot where the two men had
been standing, just moments before. Thunder followed, resounding through the storm-filled sky, and Haru realized then, with a
shiver of awe, that the dragons could control the weather.

It wasn't only the storm they could harness to fight back,
either. Suddenly, the jade dragon's pearl shone, and the waters
of the lake around it were sent into turmoil. Haru stared as the
lake rose up into a whirling, liquid tornado that pushed back
the crowd of humans, and then surged up and over its banks
to engulf the two men who'd hurt the turquoise dragon, setting
them struggling and choking in the deluge of water.

It wasn't long, though, before another pair of humans charged
forward into the lake and caught the jade dragon's hide with the
spikes of their spear – and as the jade dragon howled, the churn-
ing wall of water subsided.

In spite of their injuries, the larger two dragons didn't stop
trying to protect the smallest one. They were flanking it now,
baring their teeth at their attackers. And yet they did both seem
considerably weakened, and were moving stiffly and slowly, in
a way that Haru knew surely meant their wounds must be filled
with poison.

The human raiders were swift, now, and precise. They used
their spears to drive back these largest two dragons, separating
them from their child.

Haru gathered all his courage then, and charged out into the
water. Even in spite of his fear, he knew that he had to do what
he could to protect the little dragon – and yet however hard he
tried to stop the attackers, it was of no use. None of these men
and women in their bird jackets seemed to be able to see him –
or even to feel him, as he did his best to tug them backwards. It

wasn't long before a whole group of them had managed to haul the little dragon out of the water and onto the banks of the lake, where they gouged a deep wound in its side.

Lightning slashed down from the mountain again, as the two larger dragons roared, from where they were still trapped behind the forest of poisoned spears in the lake. This time, one of the men was struck. His comrades didn't even falter, though. Leaving him where he lay on the ground, they continued in their efforts to subdue the small dragon, wrestling it onto its back and holding it down. Injured and with poison in its system now, it was clearly growing too weak to fight back.

Some new commotion started up then within the ranks of the dragons' attackers. They seemed to be parting to make way for someone, although Haru couldn't quite see through the throng who exactly this might be. Still trying to reach the little dragon, he pushed his way forward through the crush, and as he did so, he caught sight of this new person in flashes – glimpsing a pair of heavy, spiked boots, as well as a hand gripping the hilt of a long, curved knife, the fingers adorned with gleaming, heavy rings.

Finally emerging at the front of the crowd, Haru was just in time to see this man bearing down on the little dragon, with his curved knife raised. Haru tried to look away then, certain this man would surely kill the little dragon now – and yet the dream didn't let him, forcing him to watch as the man bent over the glittering, blood-slicked scales at the dragon's throat, and instead of stabbing his knife through them, as Haru had feared, used it to prise something out from among them.

The dragon howled, and the man gave a triumphant yell before turning back, exultant, to face his cheering followers. In that moment, the clouds parted, and Haru finally saw his face, lit up in the moonlight.

He was younger than Haru had ever seen him before, and his features were distorted with ugly, vindictive triumph as he held up what he'd ripped from the dragon's throat for his comrades to see. He was still, though, unmistakably Mr Winter, and what he was holding was an iridescent pearl, just the right size to fit comfortably in the centre of a human palm.

4.

It was only when Theo stepped onto the sandy, undulating grassland of the Sandslip Plains, beginning the approach to those familiar barbed-wire fences, that it really began to sink in for him that he was venturing back within the bounds of the Crescent. Even the smell took him back to his days of living here – salt from the ocean and fish from the docks, mingled with the scents of roasting meat and woodsmoke, as well as a faint whiff of open sewer. There seemed to be more smoke above the Crescent's roofs than usual tonight though, he noticed.

It didn't seem as quiet here, either, as he remembered the nights as being, in his days as a Keeper's Child. Through the fences, he could see many more people moving about the streets than was usual, considering the lateness of the hour. Voices were raised in conversation and debate, while lanterns and fires burned, casting flickering lights amid the shadowed hulks of the mismatched houses.

Avoiding the path leading to the nearest official checkpoint, Toshiko simply marched right up to the barbed wire – and after a nervous glance at the Guard tower looming a little way up the coast, Theo followed her. They were probably safe enough for the moment. The tower wasn't near enough for any Guard stationed within to recognize Toshiko's face, and anyway, the Guards were famously lenient about anyone entering the Crescent. It was leaving it again that was an entirely different matter.

Frowning, eyes wary, Toshiko leaned closer in towards the electrified wire that ran horizontally through the middle of the outer fence.

'Louder than I'd like,' she muttered. Then, in answer to his questioning look – 'What? Have you not worked this out yet?'

'Like I said,' Theo told her. 'I'm new to Rainshadow island.'

Toshiko blinked at him. 'The louder the hum off the wire,' she explained, 'the more worried you have to be. The fence will always give you a bit of a zap if you touch it, but if all the electricity's being stolen by people charging their computers or whatever, then it won't do you too much damage. When it's fully powered up, though, it's probably best not to risk it.' She leaned closer to the fence again, listening to the wire. 'Maybe they even gave it a bit of extra charge tonight, if they're worried about the reaction to what happened in the southern corner.' She frowned. 'How long did you say you'd been living here, again?'

'Only a couple of months.'

She didn't stop looking confused, but thankfully didn't question him further. Instead, she dropped to her front on the damp ground and began to wriggle right under the fences and through the narrow gap which, now that Theo really looked at it, didn't seem big enough for a fox to fit through, never mind a whole human being. Toshiko got to the other side easily enough though, her petite frame not even brushing the wire once. She looked like she'd done this a hundred times.

'Come on,' she called back, getting to her feet. 'It's fine if you're careful. And the earth even has a good bit of give in it tonight, after the rain. What are you waiting for?'

Theo steeled himself. He had to remember that things weren't the same for him now as they'd been when he'd lived here. Whenever he wanted to leave the Crescent again, there was every chance he'd be able to. He was on a mission from the Sensei, and with her authority behind him he'd surely be able to walk right out of any official checkpoint, no questions asked.

'What's wrong?' Toshiko called, clearly impatient to get going.

Absolutely no part of Theo wanted to try squeezing into that tiny space beneath the electrified spikes of barbed wire. And yet he'd told Toshiko that he lived here, hadn't he? And both times she'd met him, he'd been outside the Crescent. What method other than this would he be using to get in and out? He had to be fine with this, or he'd lose her.

'I'm just worried about what we'll find,' he said, stalling for a few moments longer. 'After all the talk of what's happened in the southern corner.'

Toshiko's expression relaxed and she extended a hand in his direction, stopping just short of the fence in front of her, almost as if she'd forgotten those layers of metal, sharp and humming with charge between them.

'I know,' she said. 'Me too. The sooner we've seen what we're up against, though, the sooner we can figure out a way to stop it happening again.'

Theo nodded, and deciding there was nothing for it now, he got down on his front in the dirt, copying her. She'd been right – the claylike earth did have the slightest bit of give in it. Abandoning any cares for his stolen eveningwear or his dignity, he inched his way forward along the ground, until first his head, then his neck slipped under the electrified fence. For once, he was glad of being so slight. While he might be useless at manually hefting crates, this was surely something he could do. Fighting every urge to twitch, or to try to look up, or even to breathe, he kept crawling forwards.

At last, after what felt like far too long – especially for someone meant to be adept at sneaking in and out this way – he was safely next to Toshiko on the other side. He did his best not to look too obviously relieved as he got to his feet, and began brushing the worst of the mud from his suit.

'Come on,' was all Toshiko said, taking his arm and tugging him with her, to plunge into the dark network of winding streets ahead of them.

Now that he was actually here, Theo couldn't help but wonder what really had happened in the southern corner. He'd lived close to that area of the Crescent himself, it being where the outcasts within this community of outcasts tended to live. Probably it was no accident, in fact, that the southern corner had been the first to fall victim to whatever misfortune was abroad tonight. With most of the Keeper's Children unlikely to risk themselves to defend it, it was one of the Crescent's most vulnerable zones. Most of the strange disappearances that had taken place during Theo's time here in the Crescent had been of southern corner residents, too.

The unsettled mood in the streets only augmented Theo's unease. Everyone around them seemed engaged in desperate preparations for impending misfortune. What exactly, though, did all these people fear might be coming for them? From the snatches of talk and whispers that he was able to pick up as they walked, it seemed to have something to do with the Crows – though this definitely seemed bigger than any of their usual rackets carried out under the Captain.

Through open doorways, in fact, he could see whole families now packing up their belongings by lantern-light – though where any of them would actually be able to go seemed unclear. Many people were walking the dark streets, too, stopping anyone they passed to ask if they'd trade a few credits for whatever they could afford to sell. Fires still burned in most of the fire pits outside the houses, as people sat up watching, talking, waiting – and eyeing both Theo and Toshiko with guarded suspicion as they passed.

Theo was used to being looked at with hostility, but Toshiko began to falter almost immediately at this unwelcome attention. Her confident strides turned to small, awkward steps, her arms coming up to curl defensively around her shoulders. Theo realized she was still dressed in the uniform of an Imperial steward – what had been the perfect disguise in the Palace was clearly not the ideal fashion choice for the Keeper's Crescent, especially on a volatile night like this.

He shrugged off his suit jacket – it wasn't like he'd paid for it, anyway – and folded it around her shoulders. She jumped at his touch, but didn't argue once she'd understood what he was doing. The jacket was big enough on her to completely cover the distinctive tunic bearing Rainshadow City's insignia – only the uniform's plain blue trousers and slippers were at all visible beneath its velvet. Pulling it around herself gratefully, Toshiko gave him a small smile. He only looked away, suddenly unable to meet her eye.

'Where are we going?' he asked, as much to distract himself from his thoughts as anything else.

'The café,' she said. 'On the Gods' Road. Mailee remembers me from when I lived here, and anyway I think it might be a good place for finding out exactly what's happened, and how we can help.'

Mailee. Of course Theo knew Mailee, too. Everyone who'd spent any time in the Crescent did, and she was definitely one of the more kindly characters he'd encountered while a resident himself. She'd always had a cup of her strange-tasting herb tea for him, and had once roundly told off a whole table of boys who'd been jeering at him in Navishian, throwing bits of trash at him and laughing. Would she recognize him? And if she did, would she buy the lie that he still lived here, despite the fact she'd seen no trace of him for at least ten months?

There was no time to worry about such things. They were walking down the Gods' Road before he could even think of a way to argue, with the café tent's distinctive cloth ceiling clearly visible up ahead.

When they finally ducked through the tent's doorway, though, there was no sign of Mailee at all. Her tea urns were still there on her usual table, and the café generally looked otherwise as Theo remembered it, with its chequered walls and shrine to the Keeper in the corner. And yet instead of Mailee and the usual night-time stragglers you might expect to see here at this hour, there was only a group of serious-looking Keeper's Children, clustered in a pool of lantern-light around some pushed-together tables.

'Hey,' Toshiko called to them, jogging the last few steps up to the gathering. 'Where's Mailee?'

One of the group – a man who looked to be somewhere in his thirties – turned and rose from where he'd been sitting, coming over to meet them. He had long hair tied in a tail at the base of his neck, and he looked tired, with dark under-eye circles tarnishing a face that would otherwise have seemed friendly and open.

'You've not heard?' he answered. Like many of the Keeper's Children, he spoke Navishian with an accent, but Theo still didn't know the Archipelago well enough to be able to place where his was from. 'She was visiting a friend in the southern corner when the Crows came. She was taken in the raid.'

Toshiko stared. 'But she can't have been taken. She remembered me. She was a friend of my aunt's.'

'She was a friend to a lot of people,' the man said. 'Many of whom were herded onto that barge alongside her.' Then he sighed, softening slightly at the expression on Toshiko's face. 'I'm sorry. It's a lot to adjust to. For all of us. You're not from around here, are you?'

'I used to be,' Toshiko said, before gesturing to where Theo was still hanging back, in the shadows. 'He lives here, though.'

Theo tried to look as collected as possible under the man's assessing gaze while, in reality, his stomach was now twisting in nauseous knots.

The man frowned. 'Haven't I seen you before?' he asked.

'Entirely possible,' Theo said, quickly putting his spiralling fears aside as he realized that if he didn't want Toshiko to discover he was a brazen liar, he would need to seize control of this interaction as swiftly as possible. 'I'm Theo, and she's Toshiko.' He gave the man a quick bow. 'It's good to meet you properly.'

'I'm Ren,' said the man, dipping his own head to the two of them.

'What's going on here?' Theo asked, gesturing at the table of Keeper's Children, still deep in conversation.

There were nine of them including Ren, Theo counted. They were all different ages and, at a glance, seemed like very different types of people, though they all shared the worn clothing and hard-bitten air common to the Keeper's Children.

Ren gave a bitter kind of laugh. 'This, Theo, is the resistance. I know it might not look like much, but I'm afraid it's what we've got.'

'The resistance?' Toshiko asked. 'To the Crows?'

Ren nodded. 'To anyone who threatens the lives of the Keeper's Children.'

'We'll join,' Toshiko said quickly, as Theo tried not to gape at her.

He couldn't join the resistance. The Crows would be furious with him, surely – unless the Sensei might interpret this as his becoming some sort of spy?

His fingers found the lump behind his ear again. They'd said it would pick up on his saying any key words that suggested he was spilling their secrets. What they'd not told him, though, was whether it would be able to detect what others were saying nearby, or even whether it was still listening to what was being said around it, when none of the words it had been programmed to recognize were being uttered. Giving the Crows a window into the plans of people only trying to defend themselves from disaster seemed to Theo like a whole new level of something he hadn't signed up to, and for a moment, he had the wild idea of demanding a pen and paper, and writing down a full confession of everything to Toshiko – begging her forgiveness, and asking what she thought he should do next. He swallowed down the thought. Even though the tracker wouldn't be able to hear such a confession, it was still far too much of a risk. What if Toshiko didn't forgive him, for one thing?

'I don't know,' he began to say, trying to back away. 'I'm not sure how much help I can be.'

'Any help would improve what we have already,' Ren told him. 'Take a seat.'

5.

Haru had fallen so far into his dreams that he didn't even wake at the sight of Mr Winter raising the pearl, ripped from the little dragon's throat, to show his followers. For a while after that, he only dreamed a formless churn of distress, until the tides of his emotion receded sufficiently for him to find himself in a new scene, on a cloudy, windy day, looking down at the dragons' lake from a new vantage point, higher up the mountain peak.

The jade-green dragon was circling overhead now, while the turquoise dragon was perched on an outcrop just ahead of him. It was looking down at something he couldn't quite see, over the ridge in the mountainside. The wounds to its side had healed now, though they'd left thick ropes of scarring through the scales.

Tentatively, Haru approached this turquoise dragon. He felt sure by now that it would never deliberately harm him, but he felt so small next to it, a mouse facing a tiger. It didn't move at all, though, as he drew closer, only kept its gaze fixed on whatever it was watching, down past the rocks.

Haru crept forward until he could look over the ridge too, to finally see what it was that this dragon was so focused on. He gasped to discover that it was the little dragon, lying sheltered from the worst of the snow and the elements in a hollow in the mountainside. At first, Haru was happy just to find the little dragon still alive after its ordeal at the lake, and to see that it had even grown a little bigger now, with small stumps of horns beginning to be visible on its head. And yet in spite of all this, it soon became clear to Haru that it was also surely gravely ill. Its blue scales had faded to a dull, washed-out shadow of their previous vibrancy, the lantern-light of its large, round eyes was dimming, and its breathing was slow and shallow.

Haru clambered down to it over the ridge, checking carefully as he did so for the reaction of the huge turquoise dragon. It still hadn't seemed to notice him, its attention entirely consumed by its child. Overhead, the jade dragon was still circling protectively, its trajectory unaltered in spite of Haru's approach. Haru dared to reach out his hand then, and to lay it as gently as he could on the scales of the little dragon's neck.

He was surprised to discover they were warm. He felt an answering warmth at his own chest then, and, reaching for the chain around his neck, drew the pearl out from his tunic to find it fully aglow – a beacon, flaring into life for the being to whom it rightfully belonged. Haru unfastened the chain, and held the pearl out to the dragon.

And then the sun broke through the clouds overhead to wash the whole scene in such blinding brightness that Haru flinched, and cried out in surprise. The brightness only increased, until he had lost sight of the little dragon completely, and indeed of everything else around him. Still holding the pearl out in one hand, Haru kept offering it up into the light, until his vision resolved just enough for him to be able to see the turquoise dragon again, diving down into deep water – into what looked like ocean waves, in fact, although a moment before, they hadn't seemed to be anywhere near the sea.

The turquoise dragon rose back up through the water, breaking the surface. Seafoam clung to its whiskers and to its magnificent orange fur, as it fixed Haru with the warmth of its golden gaze.

'*I'm on my way,*' it told him – and it seemed to Haru then that he *felt* the dragon's words as it spoke, rather than heard them. '*Wait for me.*'

And then everything grew so bright again that this time, Haru was forced to close his eyes.

When he finally opened them once more, the dragons had gone, and he was awake, out of breath and drenched uncomfortably with sweat, lying on a futon on Ren's floor, with the pearl a burning, heavy weight against his chest.

As his breathing calmed, Haru shook off his blankets and pushed himself up to sit, fishing the pearl out from under his robe to take a good look at it. It was glowing – although only in a very faint echo of how it had shone in the dream.

'Except it wasn't only a dream, was it?' Haru whispered, half to the pearl, half to himself.

And all at once, Haru understood what he needed to do.

CHAPTER FOURTEEN

What Could People So Small Do About Something So Big?

1.

'New volunteers,' Ren announced to the Keeper's Children gathered around the pushed-together tables in the café. 'Toshiko and Theo.'

Theo winced as Toshiko grabbed his arm again to tow him over to join Ren and the resistance. She pulled up two chairs, sat down, and gestured for him to do the same, all while he searched his brain furiously for a believable way out of this that wouldn't spook her. Coming up with no plausible excuses, though, he found the only thing he could do was sit, too, and try to look calmer than he felt. The others around the table nodded to them in greeting and acknowledgement, but no one ventured an introduction of their own. They all seemed too busy and too worried for pleasantries, or even to study Theo's Eardlandian features with the usual curiosity.

Ren might have called this group of people the resistance, but Theo couldn't help but notice as he scanned their faces now that three of them were surely on the older side of sixty, and that none of them, apart from maybe Ren himself, looked convincingly the part of a warrior. Instead, wrapped in coats and blankets against the night's chill, they looked to Theo just like a handful of regular people who did regular things – like working and cooking and taking care of children. They wore matching expressions of worry, and the way their eyes all seemed to flick reflexively towards Ren seemed to signal clearly just how much they relied on him, as their leader.

Theo thought back, then, to his visit to the Shadow Column – to the black, dragon-fire glass of its walls and windows, and to those floors upon floors of gang members, all working for the Crows' machine. He thought of the Sensei's calm callousness, and of Ken Saito at her side, in all of his ruthlessness, power and violence. He couldn't help but think that if the Sensei could see this resistance now, it would only make her laugh.

'Can you tell us what happened in the southern corner, properly?' Toshiko was asking the group now, though. 'I've only heard bits and pieces.'

Ren's expression darkened. 'The Crows came in force after sundown. First, they just destroyed the place. They smashed walls, furniture ... everything they found. They burned anything that would burn. Then, they gathered everyone who lived there – close to three hundred people, by our estimates – and forced them onto a barge they had waiting at the docks, which immediately sailed out to open sea. We can only assume it's headed to some sort of prison camp. And that's not the end of it, either. We have spies watching the coast who tell me that four more similar barges have arrived, in the hours since.'

Theo stared hard at the little coloured squares of the chequered tablecloth in front of him, as he tried to make sense of Ren's words. This was on a whole different scale to anything he'd ever heard of happening in the Crescent before – far more extreme than a few people vanishing in the night.

'So what's in the southern corner now?' he asked Ren. 'What did they leave behind?'

Ren shrugged. 'Nothing much. People got the fires under control pretty quickly, so they didn't spread, but there's nothing habitable left in that whole section of the Crescent. Just rubble, smoke and ashes.'

The little house that Theo had briefly occupied there would be gone, then. His old neighbours, too, would have been rounded up and cleared from their homes, treated like nothing more than cattle. He found himself picturing Mailee again, prodding him hard on the shoulder and telling him he needed to stand up for himself, when the other Keeper's Children poked fun at his foreign features. Mailee, who was on that prison barge, too.

'And you haven't figured out where the barge is heading, yet?' said Toshiko, her voice hard.

Something about her tone jolted Theo sufficiently out of his own shock to pay attention.

Ren only frowned. 'Nowhere good, is my only guess.'

'It went to Hanasaki Island,' Toshiko told the group. 'I heard two of the Crows talking about it, earlier tonight.'

Everyone was staring at her, now. Theo registered their various expressions of horror – and the fury, too, that had suddenly ignited in Ren's eyes.

'What does that mean, to Hanasaki Island?' Theo ventured to ask. 'I'm new to the Archipelago. Only arrived two months ago.'

The woman next to him turned to study him then, with narrowed eyes. She wore a battered waterproof jacket and a red scarf over her hair, and was one of the youngest of the group, maybe somewhere in her late twenties. 'Pretty good Navishian, for a blow-in of only two months,' she said, her tone tinged with mistrust.

'It was never officially reported in Rainshadow City,' Toshiko began to explain, 'but just over nine months ago, there was a disaster on Hanasaki Island – some kind of lab explosion. It's known that the Emperor has labs all over, carrying out experiments for the LIFE-Hub, and given the effort she seems to have gone to in suppressing knowledge of what happened, it does seem like this lab could have been one of hers. Even with my sister's excellent computer hacking skills, it's difficult to find out much about what was really going on in there. Whatever it was, though, the explosion burned the land and poisoned the soil, as well as the air. All the crops and vegetation were destroyed, and those who escaped being killed directly in the blast got sick too, most of them dying pretty quickly afterwards. There are stories, now, of their ghosts haunting the island. People on passing ships have seen figures walking the shoreline. Figures that don't look quite human.'

'Everyone who could leave, did so,' Ren cut in then. 'A few arrived here, in the Keeper's Crescent, even though the journey from Hanasaki Island takes close to two weeks – the furthest you can travel within the Empire. It's no credit to us, I'm afraid, but they weren't exactly welcomed when they got here. People were afraid of them – worried they might carry something of the sickness they'd fled on their skin. And so, many of them ended up in the southern corner.'

'How very cruel,' spoke up an elderly man in a thick, wool-lined jacket and fingerless gloves. 'To send them back to what they believed they had escaped.'

Theo's chest felt suddenly tight, as if there wasn't quite enough air here in the tent for everyone to breathe.

'The one thing that's certain,' Ren continued, 'is that Hanasaki Island is still in the grip of the poison. Sailors who've passed by that region all give accounts of a curious, almost certainly toxic mist hovering over the island, obscuring all but the very edges of the coast from view. It seems, too, that any living creature to venture near its shores surely perishes. You hear of things. Scores of dead gulls washing up on Aurian beaches. Whole shoals of cloudy-eyed fish found floating belly-up in the nearby ocean, clearly having strayed a little too close.'

'And that's where they're sending the Keeper's Children,' Toshiko said, her voice quiet now, charged with anger. 'That's where all those people on that barge are already on their way to.'

A headache was starting up behind Theo's eyes and he couldn't tell if it was a sign of the Hourglass Tracker beginning to make its presence felt, or if it was just his body reacting to this latest revelation about the corruption of the Rainshadow Empire. It suddenly seemed laughably naïve that he'd ever thought the introduction of the ALISE bots could even be a good thing for the Keeper's Children, in saving them from doing some of the more dangerous jobs around the city. How he hated this place – hated it more with every passing second.

'Is there some way we could follow the barge?' Toshiko was asking now. 'Some way to stop it, and capture it back from them, even? We have to rescue those people.'

Ren was shaking his head. 'We haven't forgotten them,

Toshiko, believe me. But I just don't know what the nine – now eleven – of us can realistically do to help them at the moment.'

Toshiko opened her mouth, looking like she was about to argue, but Theo interrupted before she could speak again.

'Four more barges,' he said. 'You said earlier that your spies had seen four more barges, moored at the docks. You think those are for everyone else, don't you? For the rest of the Keeper's Children. Meaning that the Crows are coming back.'

Ren glowered into the heart of the lantern set up on the table in front of him. 'I think it would be stupid to assume anything else,' he said.

The expressions of the others around the table sank into even greater seriousness at his words. For a while no one said anything, and Theo became acutely conscious of the sounds beyond their little circle of lamplight in the café. The night outside was filled with the shouts and calls of Keeper's Children – all of whom had experienced so much disaster and loss in their lives already – as they scrambled to prepare as best as they could for this new danger.

'I know why they're doing this,' Toshiko said, breaking the silence. Everyone turned to look at her.

'So do I,' said the young woman with the scarlet headscarf, next to Theo. 'It's obvious. The Crows hate us. Everyone on the island hates us. We're a blight on their precious coastline. They don't even care about the Keeper, whose protection we're supposedly under. They just want us gone.'

'Lina, come on now . . .' Ren began, with a pained look.

A glance around the table though showed just how much the resistance agreed with Lina on this point. Each of their faces, in fact, reflected a different version of the same pain and anger Theo had felt so often himself, at the way he was always treated here on Rainshadow island – as an outsider, a nuisance, a blight.

'What I meant to say,' Toshiko tried again, speaking a little more gently, 'is that I know why the Crows are doing this *now*, specifically.'

'Go on,' said Ren, though he, like everyone else around the table, still looked sceptical of there being anything more to these attacks than a simple desire from the rest of the island to see them all annihilated.

'It's the Emperor's LIFE-Hub,' Toshiko said. 'The bot-making complex, for the ALISE bots. I think she's enlisted the Crows to clear the Crescent for her, so that she can build it on this land. I'm certain of it, in fact. Everywhere else on the island is already completely covered by the city, or the granitarium mines.'

'She always does use the Crows to do her dirty work,' said Ren thoughtfully, beginning to nod, now. 'And I couldn't figure out, either, why the Crows would decide so suddenly they wanted us gone, in spite of the labour racket they've got going here, and the way they bleed so many credits from us with their so-called taxes, too. This would make a certain sense.'

'I think I preferred believing it was driven by hate,' the old man in the wool-lined jacket said then, his voice wavering. 'At least then it felt like we mattered a little to them all. Now we're just inconvenient clutter on the land, being cleared to make space for Service-bots.'

They were interrupted then by a woman striding in from the night through the cloth flaps of the café's doorway, and immediately shattering any hints of plaintive mournfulness in the atmosphere with the sheer force of her presence.

This new arrival to their circle was walking ferocity – tall, strong, and with Crows gang tattoos snaking all the way up her neck, over her scalp, and around the sharp lines of her undercut, clearly signalling a rank far higher than footsoldier. And yet she wasn't one of the Crows, Theo immediately knew – because he recognized her. They all did. She was one of the Jetsam.

The Jetsam were people who, once upon a time, had been recruited by the Crows from among the Keeper's Children, just as he himself had been. For whatever reason though, life with the Crows hadn't worked out for them. And so, maybe after a few months in the gang, or after a year, or even after much longer, in some cases, they'd risked breaking the gang's vows of loyalty to return to their lives in the Crescent. That was where the name 'Jetsam' had come from, referring, as it did, to the bits of rubbish discarded at sea which had then washed back onto the shore.

The transition between the Crescent and the Crows wasn't an easy one to make in reverse, though, and as the name suggested, these returnees were never welcomed back into the Crescent's community with open arms. Some of them, after all, had been doing the Captain's work here during their time in the gang – and that was hardly easy to forgive, or forget. And so the Jetsam had learnt to stick together, and while their name might have originally begun as an insult, it had always seemed to Theo that the group now used it among themselves almost as readily as everybody else did. It was as if they'd decided that having a name for themselves, as a group, dignified them with some sense of belonging here, however ambiguous.

The Jetsam were tolerated if not welcomed in the Crescent, because they sold goods that were hard to come by via any legitimate means. When Theo had lived here, he'd often seen this woman, in fact, out trading on the Gods' Road, and had even scrubbed her boots a few times in return for candle-ends.

And it hadn't just been candle-ends she'd sold, either. She, in particular, had always had the best and most essential goods on offer – firelighters, cuts of meat, even coats and new clothes, sometimes. He'd always assumed this must mean that she still had strong links with the Crows, or at least with some of their number. Those black-market goods couldn't have come out of nowhere, after all.

'I hear you need fighters,' she surprised him by saying to Ren now, raising an eyebrow in a way that seemed part question mark, part challenge.

'Are you volunteering?' Ren asked her, sounding almost as incredulous as Theo felt.

The Jetsam woman flicked her hair over one shoulder, exposing the tattoos winding over the shaved section of her scalp, and fixed him with the full ferocity of her glare.

'Yes, if you're actually serious about the idea of resistance,' she replied. 'If not, we can make our own arrangements.'

'You do realize that we're talking about the Crows, here?' said Lina, next to Theo, frowning at the woman as if certain this was some kind of trick. 'You do understand you would be fighting your old friends?'

The woman scowled. 'I realize the situation,' she hissed, 'and this may come as a surprise to you, but I have more reason than most to fear the Crows, in spite of what I know you all think.'

'We don't think anything,' Ren said, to an undercurrent of sceptical murmurs from the table around him. He leaned forward now. 'What's your name?'

'Ava,' replied the woman. 'What of it?'

'Well, if we're going to be working together, Ava, then we should know each other's names,' Ren told her, evenly. 'I'm Ren.'

'I know who you are,' Ava said. 'I live in the Crescent, just the same as everyone else here. Even though most of you might like to pretend otherwise.'

Ren, though, seemed unfazed by this barb. 'A moment ago,' he said to her, 'you said *we can make our own arrangements*. But who did you mean, *we*? Are you volunteering on behalf of all of the Jetsam?'

Ava tilted her head to one side. 'Only some,' she told Ren. 'We find ourselves in different situations, you understand, regarding our former employers.'

'So how many people could you give us?' asked Ren.

'Twenty-six,' Ava said, looking around to take in the whole assembled gathering of the resistance now with her gaze. 'Most of us have weapons, and we're all good fighters. Trained by the best, you might say.'

She gave an ironic sort of grin at that, which only made Theo feel more uncomfortable in her presence. Could the resistance really trust such an offer, coming from someone like her?

He chanced a sideways glance at Toshiko, trying to gauge what she might be thinking. She seemed to have coiled into herself, watching Ava through suspicious eyes, her lips pressed shut. He found himself wondering whether she would look at him that way too, if she were to discover his own involvement with the Crows. The idea of that felt a lot more uncomfortable to him than he would have liked.

'I'll consider it,' Ren was saying now, though. 'While twenty-six is certainly not nothing, I'm not sure it would be enough to tip the balance of an armed conflict in our favour. We're talking about facing possibly hundreds of armed Crows here. I'm not even sure fighting is our best strategy at all, considering how few people in the Crescent are trained to fight.'

'*Strategy*,' Ava repeated, with a low, scornful laugh. 'Don't be absurd. Fighting is the only strategy left to you now. You don't have a choice.'

The glare she cast around the table at this was only met with uncomfortable silence.

'Fine,' she told them. 'Whatever. Think about it. You know where to find me.'

All the determination in Ren's expression seemed to fade as he watched her go – and just for a moment, Theo thought he'd never seen anyone look more uncertain, or exhausted.

Theo turned back to Toshiko then, to notice that she had turned decidedly pale, and was shivering. It wasn't too surprising, he supposed. It was very late, the Moons having long since set outside, and it was cold in the tent, too – far colder than either the fire in the corner or the jacket he'd given her really had the power to mitigate.

'Are you sure you don't just want to go home?' he asked her, in a voice low enough that the others wouldn't hear.

She shook her head. 'This is where I'm meant to be,' she told him. 'I was raised a Keeper's Child, and if I can help them now, I'm staying.'

He nodded, trying to ignore the frustration he felt – not, now, at anything to do with the Sensei or the pearl, but simply at the unerring knack Toshiko seemed to have for putting herself in dangerous situations, and the complete lack of care she seemed to give the question of her own safety.

2.

Sitting alone at the edge of the café, Toshiko stared into the fire, sighed, and took a sip from the cup of herb tea that was warming her hands. It tasted slightly different to how she remembered – an unwelcome reminder that Mailee hadn't been the one to brew it. Mailee who had recognized her, and been kind to Mochi, and bound her injured shoulder. *No need to worry about me, Reiko's girl*, she'd said. Toshiko could hardly believe that such a stalwart of the Crescent could now be trapped on the Crow's barge bound for Hanasaki Island, apparently beyond the reach of help.

Everyone had dispersed from the tent for now, either going to try to recruit those willing to fight from among the Crescent, or simply to go home and rest, to conserve whatever strength they could, for the struggle to come. Even Theo had ducked out into the night, to get them some blankets. She'd offered to go with him, but he'd insisted she stay in the relative warmth of the café instead. The point of the blankets was to warm her up, he'd insisted, not to make her even colder in going out into the night to look for them. She took another gulp of the tea, trying to stop herself from shivering. Five years away from this place had made her forget just how cold it was, at night.

She looked up from her cup just in time to see Theo reappearing, ducking through the café's doorway with a pile of blankets in his arms. He handed them to her, and then pulled up a chair next to her by the fire, his blue eyes reflecting its light.

'I'm sorry,' she said to him, then.

'What?' He turned to her, obviously confused. 'Why should you be sorry?'

'I didn't mean me, specifically. It's just … your home. You'll lose everything, if the Crows come back here.'

'Oh,' he said, and shook his head. 'You shouldn't worry about me.'

'Why not, though?'

'Because no one should,' he almost snapped. 'Least of all you.'

Then he rubbed his eyes, and turned away. 'Gods,' he said. 'I'm sorry. I just ... didn't expect this.'

'Expect what?'

'Just for you to be so ...' He looked back up, and for a moment he seemed almost angry – though not at her, she could tell. At something in their wider situation, maybe. His expression soon softened again though, and he even smiled. 'You know,' he said then, 'it seemed crazy to me, at first, the way you run right into danger, every time. I mean, it still does seem crazy to me, honestly. I would never do that. I'm not like you at all. I hide from things, and do what I can to survive. But you – you always find another option. Another way of doing things. You don't let anyone convince you that the only way to be is hiding, and surviving. And in spite of growing up here in the Crescent, and everything I know that means, you still didn't let any of it warp what you were willing to do, or stop you from fighting for what really matters to you.'

She reached out then, across the narrow space between them, to take his hands in hers, finding that they felt as cold as hers did. He started, as if surprised, but didn't draw back.

'Above the river,' she told him then.

He blinked. 'What?'

'It's something my family says – something my aunt told us. It means that you always have to remember that you have a choice. Instead of getting caught up in a river's current, you have to learn to fly above it, like the birds.'

'But what if it's too late to learn, though?' he asked, his voice little more than a whisper, now. 'What if you messed up, really badly, and now the current is too strong. What if doing what you have to do to survive really is the only option left to you?'

'But you didn't mess up,' she told him. 'You're here, now. With the resistance.'

'You don't understand,' he began, just as she reached out to stroke his cheek. His skin felt too hot, in spite of how cold his hands were, almost feverish.

And Toshiko didn't know what she was doing now, at all. She felt herself to be in entirely new and uncharted territory – and yet he seemed so desperate and lost, and who knew how long they had left together. Anything could happen to them when the Crows came back to the Crescent.

And so she leaned across, and kissed him.

Theo froze, lips cold against hers, and for a moment Toshiko was sure she'd made an awful mistake. She began to draw away again, poised to blurt out an apology, when he leaned in, and kissed her back.

The moment seemed to last forever to Toshiko, and yet to still be over in an instant. As they drew apart, she found she could feel, too, a new and almost miraculous lightness and energy flowing through her. She almost expected to see the same golden sparks he'd conjured in the corridor earlier scattered through the air around them, lighting up the dark chill of the tent. When she opened her eyes to smile back at him, though, his irises were clear blue, not gold. And then suddenly, Toshiko didn't feel cold anymore at all, and she didn't feel scared of anything – because she had a new idea. An idea that could be a source of hope for them all, now.

'Your power,' she said to Theo. 'Could you use it in some way, to help? Could you use it to fight the Crows?'

He seemed to falter again though, his expression shuttering back over as he turned away, to look into the fire. 'I've thought about it,' he said, 'but if the Crows come back in the same kind of numbers as they had in their attack on the southern corner, I don't know that the Gift would be much use. I've only used it to fight once before.'

'In Eardland?'

He nodded. 'At the time, it felt like the only way to save myself, but . . . I completely lost control, honestly. I escaped with my life, but I almost wish I hadn't.'

He looked so cut off from her, suddenly, and from everything around them. It was such a contrast to how open he'd seemed just a moment before, and Toshiko almost hated herself, for keeping on pushing him like this. If there was any chance it could give everyone here in the Crescent a better chance at survival, though, then surely she had to keep trying.

'What if you could use the Gift in some sort of different way, instead of just fighting?' she suggested. 'I mean, you changed the weather, back at the Imperial Palace, didn't you?'

'Not in the way I meant to. Besides, how am I meant to fight the Crows with a rain shower?' He gave a sad kind of laugh. 'I doubt they worry as much about getting wet as the city's pampered classes clearly do.'

'But then you faced the Crows on your own at the Palace, too,' she persisted. 'You were annoyed when I didn't believe you'd taken on Saito and the rest by yourself. What's changed?'

But Theo wouldn't meet her eye at all now, and just kept watching the flames. 'That was different,' he said. 'That was trickery, or sleight of hand. In a stand-up fight there's not much room for smoke and mirrors.'

And maybe she would even have given up on this whole line of questioning, if Ren hadn't appeared just then, ducking under the chequered awning of the café with two new people at his side – or two not-quite new people, in fact. While Toshiko was sure she'd never seen the young woman before, the little boy she was leading by the hand, however, she would have recognized anywhere.

3.

Haru couldn't help but gape at the sight of the stranger from the Palace. It was definitely her, though, sitting here in the Keeper's Crescent, next to her light-haired friend from the party in the Palace gardens. In fact, she seemed perfectly at home here, in what Kei called the café – though really it was more of a tent filled with chairs and tables, as well as two old Sun Spirits who looked like hares standing guard beside a pair of enormous tea urns.

The stranger seemed surprised to see him, too. He didn't think she looked too angry with him though, at least.

'He had a nightmare,' Kei was telling Ren, now. Haru had already tried to explain to her that it had been more than a simple nightmare, but she'd seemed distracted, and hadn't understood what he'd meant.

'He shouldn't be here,' Ren was replying. 'Neither of you should be. Really, you should both leave the Crescent while you can.'

'I'm not leaving you,' Kei said to Ren. 'Not now. Not ever again.'

Ren only shook his head.

The stranger's friend with the light hair by the fire was confusingly unreadable, Haru noticed then. When he'd first seen him, at the party, Haru hadn't been able to pick up much of an impression from him then either, but he'd assumed that had been something to do with there being so many people between them. Now though, at close quarters, this young man remained just as much of a blank as ever. In fact, Haru wasn't at all sure that he trusted him – and not just because of not being able to sense any clear impression from him, either. As Haru continued to watch, he noticed how the young man's gaze kept skittering away, flicking towards the dark street beyond the café, as if he felt trapped in here with them all.

The stranger had jumped to her feet now though, and was approaching them. Unsure of what she might say about the pearl, Haru found himself edging closer to Kei, shrinking into the folds of the long coat she'd thrown over her Palace uniform.

'What? What's up?' Kei asked him, but he could only shake his head.

The stranger kept coming until she was right in front of Haru. Then she did something that surprised him – she squatted down to his height, and gave him a warm smile.

'Hello,' she said. 'I'm sorry we didn't get off to the best start. I'm Toshiko.'

Toshiko. A reassuringly normal name. Not a cold, towering title, like *Mr Winter*, or *Majesty*.

'I'm Haru,' he told her.

She smiled. 'It's nice to meet you properly, Haru,' she said. Then she straightened up again to talk to Kei.

As the two women introduced themselves to one another, Haru stared down at his slippers, knowing it was only a matter of time before Toshiko brought up the pearl. He could always lie, he considered. He could tell her he'd lost it, or given it away, or that someone else had taken it from him. Would she believe him, though? Haru wasn't the best liar.

At last, Toshiko crouched down again to his height, to look at him properly. 'I have something to ask you,' she said. 'And I'm not going to pretend it's a game this time, and I'm not going to try and trick you. That pearl you took from me earlier gives power to whoever possesses it. In fact, I think it works by enhancing what you're already good at, making you extremely, almost magically good at it.'

Haru nodded. What she was saying made sense. He had always been able to intuit something of the nature of the life force that radiated from the people and living things around him, but with the pearl, he could fully see Sun Spirits. He could talk to them, even.

'I'm asking you,' Toshiko continued, 'I am begging you, Haru – to give that pearl over to the resistance. I think we might be able to use it, to help everyone here in the Keeper's Crescent. I think it might give us a fighting chance against what's coming for us.'

She did seem completely serious, with no more joking or trickery. In fact, she looked almost desperate.

The kind of desperation written over her face now, though, seemed of an entirely different order to the grasping kind of desperation his mother had shown, ordering her Guards to search Toshiko for the pearl. It was completely different, too, from the desperate triumph that had distorted Mr Winter's face in his dream, as he'd held the pearl up for his followers to see, after prising it from the little dragon's throat. Toshiko's words seemed rooted in concern – in bone-deep worry, in fact, for the Keeper's Crescent, ramshackle place that it was. And she was *asking* for the pearl, too, not trying to take it from him.

Haru looked up at Kei, unsure of what he should do. He'd only just arrived here, and he wasn't even sure what all the adults were so worried about, or what Ren had meant, either, when he'd told Kei it might be dangerous for them to stay here. If giving the pearl to Toshiko might help Ren and help Kei though, then maybe he should do it, even if it meant losing the chance to find a way to return it to its dragon – even if it meant losing his ability to see Sun Spirits, too.

Of course, as soon as he'd learnt that the pearl had been

stolen and needed to be returned, Haru had understood that he wouldn't be able to keep his ability to see Sun Spirits forever. And yet he would still be so sad to have them disappear from his life again so soon, and to lose so immediately the sense they'd given him of another, more ancient and more wonderous world he hadn't even known still existed, beneath Rainshadow City's skyscrapers and grids of built-up streets.

The Sun Spirits weren't his only true friends anymore, though. He had Kei, and he had Ren – and now maybe Toshiko would become his friend, as well. He could still sense her life force there, like a lantern, burning steadily through darkness. It would be good to have a friend like that.

'What does she mean, Haru?' Kei was asking him.

Haru swallowed, and made his decision. For an answer to Kei, he reached to unfasten the chain from around his neck. He heard her breath catch as he drew out the pearl from the folds of his robe – heavy, shimmering, iridescent – and held it out to Toshiko.

4.

He was so much better than his mother, Toshiko reflected, as Haru held the pearl out to her, gleaming at the end of the gold chain hanging from his small fingers.

'Thank you, Haru,' she said, as she reached out, gently, to take it.

Immediately she held the pearl again, she felt, once more, the soothing promise of its strength and protection. She didn't have time to enjoy it, though – or to consider the many questions now crowding her mind, about what on earth the Crown Prince was doing in the Crescent, and what the Emperor might do, too, if she were to find out he was here. She didn't know when the Crows might be back, and there wasn't a minute to be wasted. She turned away from Haru, Ren and Kei to stride back towards the fire, to where Theo was still sitting, watching her with something that seemed almost like dread, now.

'The pearl makes whatever natural abilities we have stronger,' she told him. 'You said you weren't sure the Gift would be enough to help us against the Crows, but what if this could change that?' She held it out to him. 'It could make the Gift stronger, couldn't it?'

He didn't come forward and take it, as she'd hoped he would. He only stayed where he was, staring up at her, looking for all the world like an animal caught in a trap.

'You can't hide from what you can do, Theo,' she insisted, the pearl still held out to him in her open palm. 'Maybe your powers really were a gift given to you by the Gods, to make the world better.'

'No,' he insisted, his voice shaking now. 'She wasn't right, the girl who told me that, and even she knows that now. Please, just ... don't ask this of me, Toshiko. I don't want to make this choice.'

He was even sitting on his hands, everything about him begging her to stop this. And yet she couldn't – not after having seen what he might be capable of.

'But you could help,' she told him. 'And people's lives are on the line here. You always have a choice to fly above the river, remember? This is a choice you have to make. So make it.'

'I'm sorry, Toshiko,' Theo whispered then. 'I'm sorry I couldn't be better.'

And she found she could only stare as he snatched the pearl from her open palm, sprang to his feet, and ran for the café's doorway.

He was gone before any of them could react, vanished into the Crescent's enveloping darkness.

5.

After all the complaining about being cold and hungry which Mei had done during the walk from the Palace, Jun was surprised to see her settle into an unfamiliar quietness – a calmness, almost – as they made their way at last through the winding streets and alleyways of the Keeper's Crescent. The mood here was tense, but Mei strode through it undaunted, with Mochi at her heels, just as if neither of them had ever left this place.

Though Jun and Mei had spent so much of their childhoods together, and of course Jun irrefutably thought of Mei as his sister, he could see now more clearly than ever that she, unlike him, had been born here, and had watched her mother die here – that she'd lived here for years, in fact, and through all sorts of enormous things, before he'd washed up at the docks. She truly was a Keeper's Child, through and through.

She'd decided that they should head for Mailee's café, it being the closest thing the Crescent had to a focal point, and Jun had readily agreed, glad of the chance to see Mailee again. Apart from anything else, he was more desperate now than he'd have cared to admit for someone else – someone older, reassuring and reliable – to finally take charge of deciding what they should do next.

When they stepped inside the café, though, there was no sign of Mailee. Jun had just begun to wonder if there might be something wrong, when he caught sight of Toshiko, sitting in a loose grouping of people by the fire. She was dressed oddly, in a Palace steward's uniform, worn under an embroidered suit jacket and fringed blanket – but she seemed safe and well, thank the Gods.

'Tosh!' Mei called out, as Toshiko looked up.

What had seemed, momentarily, like clouds of care and worry on Toshiko's face parted as she sprang to her feet, and began to run towards them. And then Jun and Mei were running too, until at last the Kawakamis were finally reunited – the three of them wordlessly enveloping each other in the kind of group hug that makes everything feel better while it lasts. When the hug broke apart, Mei didn't let go of Toshiko, holding her instead at arms' length, inspecting her.

'Are you okay?' Mei was saying now, checking Toshiko over as if searching for visible damage. 'The Emperor didn't do anything to you, did she? You're not hurt?'

While Toshiko did seem physically fine, Jun couldn't help but feel, as he studied her more closely, too, that something still seemed to be seriously wrong – that she seemed heartbroken, in fact.

'What is it, Tosh?' he asked. 'What's happened?'

She only shook her head. 'I don't know,' she said. 'I'm not sure. We' – she corrected herself – '*I* lost the pearl. Again. I gave it to someone. I shouldn't have trusted him.'

'*Him*?' Mei screeched, as Jun hushed her.

'It's okay, Tosh, don't blame yourself,' he told her, and then, sensing her reluctance to explain anything further at the moment, he added – 'You can fill us in later.'

He turned to look around the tent more fully then, finally registering the presence of what was unmistakably the Emperor's young son, amidst the cluster of anxious-looking people who were all standing watching them now, from by the fire. Jun was obviously confused as to what the Crown Prince's presence here might mean, and yet he couldn't think about it properly at all, because he was distracted by a growing sense of unease.

'Where's Mailee?' he asked the tent at large.

Toshiko only looked more upset at the question. 'I'm sorry, Jun,' she said. 'Mailee's been taken.'

'Taken?'

Toshiko nodded. 'By the Crows.'

Jun's eyes closed. The thought of his old mentor being finally overcome by the Crows, after so many years of standing strong and apart from them, felt almost impossible to understand. And he'd needed her here, too – he'd needed her to help him, and to tell him what to do in the face of all the terrible things that were now threatening them.

He took a deep breath, and opened his eyes. This didn't mean he could just give up though, he knew. In fact, it meant precisely the opposite – and he and Mei had come here tonight with an important message to relay. He stepped back from his sisters, to address everyone gathered in the café.

'We've come with news,' he told them all. 'And it's not good news, I'm afraid. The Crows are coming back.'

'We know,' Toshiko interrupted.

'But we know *when* they're coming back,' Jun continued. 'They're coming at sunset, tomorrow. We have until then to be ready for them.'

6.

If Toshiko still felt lost after Theo's betrayal, Jun's deadline seemed to give new purpose to everyone else, and soon, the core of the resistance was gathered around the café tables again. Mei and Jun were at the group's centre this time, while Ren took a moment away from being at the helm to sit slightly off to one side by the fire, with Kei and Haru. Toshiko could see him watching them all closely, listening and thinking – perhaps trying to work out if Ava had been right when she'd told him there was no choice left but to fight the Crows, unprepared for combat as they were.

'Paper,' Mei demanded, and someone produced a sheet from somewhere, along with a pen.

Mei neatly wrote out the heading, *'Resistance Planning Meeting'* at the top, then double-underlined it.

'First things first,' she said. 'We're the resistance, yes? So what do we know about who we're resisting?'

'It's the Crows again,' Toshiko answered, a little sulkily. 'It's always been them. The Crows with the Emperor hiding behind them.'

'Wrong,' Mei unexpectedly said then though, with a slight shake of the head. 'Or not entirely correct, anyway, because there's been a development. I did think you may have missed it.'

'What kind of development?' asked Ren.

'The Crows and the Emperor are' – Mei glanced in Haru's direction – 'no longer friends.'

'What do you mean, *no longer friends*?' asked Lina, clearly growing impatient, fiddling with the cuffs of her waterproof jacket.

'Well . . .' Mei began, still looking over at Haru, clearly unsure of how to continue.

'It's okay,' Haru surprised everyone then by speaking up. 'When you say, "the Crows", do you mean Mr Winter's friends?'

Kei nodded to him. 'Yes, Haru. Mr Winter's real name is Ken Saito. He works for a gang called the Lucky Crows.'

Haru nodded, digesting the knowledge. 'Mr Winter tried to kill my mother,' he said, after a moment. 'He – or the Lucky Crows, I suppose – tried to kill her and to kidnap me, to make me their puppet. I only just escaped.'

The table dissolved into gasps and murmurs at that, even Mei and Jun looking surprised at the full extent of Haru's news. Kei, next to Haru, drew him into a fierce hug which left him looking a little embarrassed. This seemed to be the first she was properly hearing of all this, too.

'So the bad news,' Mei continued, 'is that the Crows still want to destroy your homes, to make way for the LIFE-Hub. They're still planning to use those barges too, as far as we know, to take all the prisoners to Hanasaki Island. What's changed for certain though, is that they won't be doing this on the Emperor's behalf anymore. They seem to want the LIFE-Hub and the bots it'll produce for themselves – for their own reasons, whatever those may be.'

A new note of alarm entered the already fearful murmurs that were moving amid the group now, and Toshiko found herself shivering again, though this time it had nothing to do with the cold. Whatever the Lucky Crows might want with such a resource, just the idea of the gang possessing anything so powerful was alarming in itself.

'Clearly, then, we need to stop the Crows,' Mei said, writing out a new heading on the paper as she spoke. 'So what ideas do we have so far, about how we're going to do that?'

When she'd finished her double-underline, she looked up and around the table. Toshiko followed her gaze, but instead of the pragmatism or inspiration she knew Mei would have hoped for, she saw only worry and fear.

'Come on,' said Mei, with a flick of her streaked hair. 'Surely some of you have some ideas. Jun and I have done something already, even.'

'What have you done?' Toshiko couldn't help but take the bait and ask.

'I hacked into the security systems of the warehouse in which the Crows have stored all the draconic ore, and I locked the whole place down. No one is getting in there for at least five days, I'd guess, and with no access to the ore, the plans for the LIFE-Hub will suffer delays. There's a chance that could buy us some time – or that it could keep the Crows and the Guard divided and distracted, at least.'

Toshiko grinned. She should have known her siblings would figure out some sort of plan. They always did.

'So as I said,' Mei continued, 'that's something. But it's far from being enough. What else can we do to save the Crescent – and to bring home this barge, too, before it gets to Hanasaki Island?'

Toshiko looked around again. After Mei's example, she was expecting a little more spark, even some signs of hope. And yet even now, no one seemed ready to suggest anything – all of them still just looked scared.

The resistance's eldest member, the old man in the wool-lined coat, spoke up then.

'It's good that you came back here to help us,' he told Mei. 'And we appreciate you trying, we really do. But all this talk of the Lucky Crows, and even of the Emperor herself . . .' He shook his head. 'I think I speak for all of us when I say – what could people so small ever do about something so big?'

From the expressions of several of the others around the table, Toshiko saw clearly that he spoke for more than just himself. The old man blinked, and looked away – shuffling his feet a little, as if ashamed by what he'd said.

He was right to look away. Mei's expression conveyed outrage as only Mei could, and Toshiko couldn't help but feel a shiver of awe for her sister then, as Mei slammed both hands down on the table, and swept a glare around the assembled group.

'What can you do about something so big?' Mei replied, addressing herself to all of them now, not just to the old man. 'You can do everything, that's what. You can do everything, if you want to. You don't need to be caught up in any current, or to let anyone else tell you what happens to you.'

She pushed her chair back, to gesture around the café – up towards its roof, which was high and arching, even if made from oilcloth, and then over towards the Keeper's Shrine, and the tea urns, and the fire.

'Look at where we are,' she said. 'It's no accident we all came here tonight, out of everywhere else we could have gone, because did Mailee ever live her life like a small person? No, she made this whole place for us, to be the heart of our Crescent, and a home for the God who takes care of us. And did she ever go along with the Crows' way of doing things?' Mei continued. 'Did she accept that we didn't deserve healing, only kakogan dust to tranquillize pain until we died? Of course not. She took care of each and every one of us, because she knew we were people who mattered.'

Complete silence had fallen among the others at the table. Some looked as if they desperately wanted to believe what Mei was saying. Others were still avoiding her gaze, as if they knew they should try to listen, but still couldn't quite convince themselves that she was right.

'Mailee might not be here to look after us right now,' Mei said then. 'And we might be managing, too, without so many others who we relied on to take care of us, taken from us before their time by the Crows, and by the Emperor.' Her voice cracked a little here, but she only slammed her hand against the table again, and kept on going. 'All of that only means, though, that we now have to do our best to think and act as courageously as they always did. Listen to me—' The old man who'd first asked

Mei the question lifted his eyes again as she turned to address him, her voice growing ever more insistent – 'You asked me what people so small could ever do about something so big, but *you are not small*, do you hear me?'

Still no one spoke as Mei's words rang out through their circle and beyond, seeming to resonate out into the night. She simply glowered at them all for a moment, and then sat back down in her chair, gazing around at the group with something that was almost sadness in her eyes now, shaking her head as if to say that in looking at all of them here – and in really *seeing* each of them, too – she was only hit by new disbelief at what the old man had said.

'None of you are small,' she told them again. 'Absolutely none of you are small.'

PART IV

KNIVES AND
LIGHTNING

CHAPTER FIFTEEN

From Out of Shadows
and Nightmares

1.

The Crows began arriving on the Plains just after dawn, echoing their namesake birds, dark-winged, and gathering in anticipation of carrion. They came piecemeal, as individuals or in groups, their black jackets rendering them not much more than silhouettes in the mist-scattered light rising over the waves. They stayed beyond the barbed wire for now, not bothering the Keeper's Children yet, only watching. From within the Crescent, Toshiko watched them right back, as they smoked, or talked, or simply stared – eyeing the territory they'd been called here to take.

She found herself wondering how many of these men and

women had started out as Keeper's Children themselves. It was well known that the Crows recruited here. Did any of these gang members looking in from the other side of the wire feel regret for this place? Or had all of them who'd started out here gladly resigned all care for the Crescent when they'd walked away from it, just as the Emperor had accused Toshiko of doing herself?

The Crows kept coming as she watched, some even cycling in with bicycle rickshaws and carts filled with building materials – shovels, bricks, wooden slats and bamboo scaffolding – which they deposited on the Plains alongside the wire. They were preparing for afterwards, Toshiko understood, getting everything ready for the next phase, which could start just as soon as these homes had been destroyed, and their inhabitants either slaughtered in the dirt in front of the wreckage, or sent to a slower, more drawn-out death on Hanasaki Island.

She shivered and pulled her blanket tighter around her shoulders. It was the blanket Theo had handed her last night, and she hadn't taken off his jacket, either. She would gladly have discarded both, purging any comfort he'd offered her, except that the day hadn't heated up yet, and she'd been thoroughly chilled overnight.

Jun approached then, coming to stand next to her where she'd stopped mid-step to watch the Crows on the Plains. The two of them were meant to be working together this morning, following what the resistance had settled on as the only possible plan – recruiting as many of the Keeper's Children as they could before sunset, to meet the Crows in battle.

Only Mei had stayed behind in the café, where she was using her hairclip computer to hack into the Crows' networks. Having already gained access to several of the Crows' Comms-Discs when she'd built the Birdcatcher database, she'd had a good amount of practice at this already. If she could build on that work now to fully breach the Crows' closed network, she could work to scramble their attempts to send each other crucial logistical messages, and could send out false orders, too. She could try commanding, for instance, all the Crows to leave the Crescent in order to defend the locked-down warehouse from the Imperial Guard instead.

There still wasn't any plan, though, for rescuing the one barge that had already sailed for Hanasaki Island, and while Toshiko did understand the need to focus on saving everyone in the Crescent, she still found she couldn't keep her mind off those people, Mailee among them, who were even now crammed into that vessel on the water. She hoped they'd have no idea yet of where they were being taken. Knowing the destination would surely only make the voyage even worse.

'It's best not to watch them,' Jun told her, nodding over at the nearest group of Crows on the other side of the barbed wire, standing with their arms folded, their expressions entirely un-readable as they watched the Crescent. 'My advice is to worry about what we're doing, not what they're up to.'

'Don't they say it's a good idea to know your enemy?' she re-plied, not taking her eyes off them.

'Yes, but Mei's covering that for us. Stare at this lot too long and we'll lose our nerve.' He was smiling, but Toshiko could tell he was far from joking.

She nodded and, pulling the jacket and blanket more tightly around herself again, turned away from the Crows to face back towards the familiar maze of streets, stretching all the way down to the barbed wire on the Crescent's other side, by the docks. Even though she might not be able to see them from here, the Crows' barges were waiting there, she knew – moored and ready.

Trying to keep her thoughts from dwelling too much on those barges for now, she looked further out to the waves, whose saltiness permeated the air everywhere here in the Crescent, and then up to the early-morning sky. The Three Sister Moons were visible there above the water as they sometimes were during the day, glowing a delicate, pale gold in the reflected sunlight. Toshiko felt herself smile, then, at the sight of those three golden crescents, all of slightly different sizes. When she, Mei and Jun had been little, they'd sat in the yard in front of their house, not far from here, and had tried to decide which Kawakami would be which moon. How she and Mei had laughed at the idea of Jun being one of the Three Sisters. One afternoon, Toshiko remembered now, Auntie Reiko had been out there with them too, stirring a pot of soup on the fire. She had interrupted their laughter to suggest that she be the third moon in their game instead, if the idea of Jun being one of the Three Sisters was so ridiculous to them. *But you can't be a moon,* Jun had told her, with immediate dismay. And when she'd asked him why not, he'd said, with such certainty, *because you're the sun, of course.*

In all their years of living with her, and in spite of all the hardship they'd had to endure in the Crescent, Toshiko never once saw Auntie Reiko cry. She was sure she'd come close to it that afternoon, though. Jun had always been the kindest of them.

'What exactly happened, last night?' he broke into her memories now, by asking. 'You said you'd trusted someone you shouldn't have trusted.'

Toshiko didn't reply immediately, just kept watching the Three Sisters – and yet Jun didn't prompt her. He simply waited, ready to listen. She only fiddled with one of the embroidered sleeves of her jacket, and shook her head.

'I don't know,' she told him. 'I think maybe I've always been able to rely so much on you and Mei, that I can tend to trust people too easily. I'm not sure I want to discuss it.'

She wasn't looking directly at him, keeping her focus trained on the Moons. In her peripheral vision, though, she could still see the concern in his expression. Usually she told him everything, but this felt different. Taking her at her word, he didn't push for more details.

'I think being open to trusting people is a good thing,' he only said, after seeming to consider what she'd said for a moment. 'Sometimes they'll let you down, but maybe more often than that, trusting other people is the only way forward. We'll all have to trust each other when we're facing the Crows later today, after all. And sometimes, just showing you trust someone can bring out the best in them.'

Toshiko only kicked a foot into the dusty ground beneath them. 'Except when it doesn't,' she told him.

Jun nodded at that. 'Except when it doesn't,' he agreed.

2.

If the Crows were paying attention to the location of Theo's tracker today, they would surely be curious as to what in the world he was up to. He'd walked the distance from the city's commercial district to the Shadow Column four times, and during the course of those back-and-forth journeys had spent long stretches of time simply standing still. Most often, this happened when he was by the ocean, outside the Shadow Column. Only once during the late morning did he stop in the Old Town, in front of the University café in Golden Moon Square. He didn't go in to buy anything.

No discernible messages appeared for him from the Crows though, either via the tracker in his neck or by any other means, so Theo had to assume they were all too busy to concern themselves with some quietly erratic behaviour from one of their minor agents. He didn't like to think what they might be busy with.

If Toshiko had been right, then the Crescent was now top of the Crows' agenda. She'd seemed so determined when they'd last spoken not to even try to escape, but would she change her mind now, after what he'd done? Without the pearl, she would be almost powerless against the Crows. It would be irrational, surely, to insist on staying.

Then again, he knew all too well that that just wasn't the way Toshiko thought. She was the kind of person who held fast to her principles, even if it meant putting herself in danger. Suddenly, even the simple task of putting one foot in front of the other came to feel overwhelming, and so Theo stopped walking, right in the middle of the waterfront promenade – causing several well-heeled citizens to glare as they were forced to dodge around him. Today, he considered, he probably did deserve those hostile looks.

A small part of him tried to insist then, defiant, that it was just too much to expect everyone to be like Toshiko, and willing to sacrifice their lives out of altruistic principle. It was far too high a moral standard to which to hold the whole of humanity, surely. And yet he also knew of course that it wasn't just a moral principle he'd betrayed. He'd betrayed everyone in the Crescent, and worse, he'd betrayed Toshiko personally. He'd left her in danger when maybe, just maybe, if only he'd been better and less afraid, he really could have done as she'd said, and used the pearl to protect her.

He tried to shake off the thought, and made himself start walking again, following the ocean to the Shadow Column.

It was late afternoon when he found himself back beneath its black glass frontage. The scene around him here certainly carried no signs of anything untoward. The wide, stone steps leading down to the ocean from where he was standing were populated with languid-looking citizens engaged in lazy afternoon wanderings, or idle chatter. None of them seemed to have any more pressing demands on their attention than the enjoyment of the early autumn sun, as well as of a variety of snacks from the food vendors, whose stalls formed a fragrant promenade in the shade of the waterfront's line of cherry trees, their leaves already turning red with the season.

Something about the seeming ease of these people, and their enviable, impossible freedom from any serious fears pushed Theo to finally come to a decision. Turning his back on them and all of their thoughtless ease, he made his way up the steps to the Shadow Column's entrance.

'Eleanor Minami sent me,' he said to the Crows on the door, and this time, he wasn't surprised to be ushered through into the building's gleaming interior.

3.

General Mori of the Imperial Guard had a headache. He knew and understood that her Imperial Majesty had also had a difficult time of it since the Crows' attempt to seize power, but the way she was behaving now was hardly helping them to restore any sense of order and calm to the Palace.

'No access? What do you mean, no access?' she was shouting now at a timid-looking, clipboard-holding aide, who had appeared at the sliding doors of the Council Room to interrupt this meeting of the Ten Generals with the news.

'All the security systems have frozen, Majesty, and none of the usual passcodes or override systems are working.'

'Passcodes? Override systems?' The Emperor couldn't have seemed less impressed. 'Can't we just send a squadron of Guards to smash the damned doors down?'

'With respect, Majesty, those doors are reinforced Muralanian dragon-fire steel, secured with bolts of the same material, as well as a state-of-the-art Iron Fortress combination-locking system. And even if we could get through them manually, all the laser systems on the warehouse floor are armed, while the maps we held of those lasers' layouts and trajectories have been corrupted. Any Guards would be fried, within the first steps they took inside.'

Tearing at her hair, the Emperor gave a wordless yell of frustration – the sound of which sent a pulse of agony through General Mori's temples. He pinched the bridge of his nose and tried to divert himself from the pain by considering whether he'd ever actually seen someone literally tear at their hair before. He didn't think he had. He'd always assumed it was a figure of speech.

'It's the Sensei, it has to be,' growled the Emperor – seeming even more in the mood to jump to conclusions than usual today, Mori noted. 'She knows we'll be coming for the dragon pearl and the draconic ore, and so she's got those computer meddlers of hers at the Shadow Column to lock us out – to lock *me* out, in point of fact, when we were both meant to have access to the ore, the whole time. I don't care who happens to own the deeds to that warehouse – the ore belongs to the Empire. It was never hers to hoard like this.'

Her scowl only deepened as she swept her gaze around the Ten Generals, as if daring any of them to challenge her. Of course, no one did.

'She's made a mistake, though,' the Emperor continued, after being met with only silence. 'Because try what she will to keep us out of that warehouse, the plain fact is that she doesn't have an army. She only has a band of amateurish gangsters and hooligans, ill-equipped for real pitched combat – and even if we haven't got the dragon pearl to help us yet, we can still expect to exceed their capabilities. I will not put up with anything more from that old witch.'

The aide was still hovering in the doorway, clipboard in hand, clearly unsure of whether to stay where she was, or to leave without the Emperor's formal dismissal. General Mori caught her eye and gave a discreet nod towards the door. She gave him a quick, grateful bow and vanished back the way she'd come. The Emperor didn't even seem to notice.

'I want troops sent to that warehouse within the hour,' she declared, 'with orders to take no prisoners if they're met with any opposition from the Crows. We need to send a clear message. The Sensei and her gang of bandits are dead in this city.'

It seemed a rash idea to Mori – especially the part about taking no prisoners. As a military man, he'd accepted killing as an occasionally necessary part of his job, but he certainly had no love for it. To his disappointment, though, several of the other Generals were already nodding their approval at the Emperor's words. It was no surprise to see that upstart General Kubo among them.

Kubo was one of four younger officers whom the Emperor had promoted into the Circle of the Ten Generals in recent months, retiring, in the process, four good men and women who hadn't been much older than General Mori. To General Mori's mind at least, Kubo was undoubtedly the least suitable of these new appointees for the role. It hadn't been much more than a few months since he'd been a mere lieutenant, his sole qualification for promotion being an irritating tendency to agree indiscriminately with all of the Emperor's schemes. Kubo was worse, too, than simply being a barefaced sycophant. Even at that rank of lieutenant he'd had a habit of inserting his own, overly bellicose opinions into the deliberations of his superiors, seeming to believe that violence, intimidation and subjugation were the answers to every diplomatic situation. The forceful belligerence and ideological zeal with which he'd consistently voiced these views had always disconcerted General Mori. Kubo, after all, could hardly be much older than thirty, and Mori knew for a fact that, however strongly held his convictions seemed to be, they certainly weren't backed up by much real experience in the field.

'To put forward a suggestion, Majesty,' General Watanabe spoke up then, much to Mori's relief. Watanabe was a member of his own generation, and a stalwart of the military whose judgement he respected, even if they did have the occasional disagreement. 'I realize how keen you are to launch an imminent attack on the warehouse,' Watanabe continued, his voice measured, the deep lines of his face arranged in his typical expression of dependable sobriety, 'but might I ask you to consider the alternative of waiting until after dark?'

'But why would I want to wait?' growled the Emperor. 'The Sensei needs to know she can't get away with defying me like this, and, more to the point, the dragon pearl is hidden in that warehouse. Why not seize it imminently?'

'I agree that the pearl is an important potential asset, Majesty,' Watanabe replied. 'Indeed, if we had managed to obtain it from the Kawakamis tonight as we'd initially hoped to do, then it could have made all the difference to the strength of our force.

As things stand, though, the unnecessary gamble of risking a head-on confrontation with the Crows could cause numerous casualties, even deaths, among our troops. Our intelligence agents report that the Lucky Crows are now gathering on the Sandslip Plains, for all the world as if the Sensei is planning to go ahead with the sunset raid. Why not wait, and take the warehouse by stealth then, while the Sensei and the Lucky Crows are distracted by their attack on the Crescent? We could even use a smaller force with elite training, and supplement them with Fighter-bots.'

General Mori nodded his appreciation at Watanabe's words. Watanabe could be brash sometimes, and he was overly fond of Fighter-bots – which, in General Mori's opinion, often caused more trouble than they were worth – but his overall argument was sound, and Mori was grateful for a colleague who dared talk sense to the Emperor when required. Surely none of them here, even Kubo, would want to risk the lives of their soldiers so casually.

'I will do nothing by stealth,' the Emperor spat, leaning over the table to Watanabe, her eye which wasn't covered by the eyepatch livid and flashing, amid its dark smears of eyeshadow. 'I am the Emperor of the Rainshadow Archipelago, while the Sensei is an old woman at the head of an undisciplined mob of delinquents. I will have her broken.'

'Of course, Majesty,' Kubo said then, his head bobbing obsequiously, eyes flashing behind his round glasses. 'I, for one, completely agree.'

Inwardly, General Mori groaned. Clearly, he would have to say something to support Watanabe's attempts to be the voice of reason at this meeting.

'With respect, Majesty,' he began, copying the deferential

formulation of words used by the timid aide just moments before, 'I do think Watanabe's suggestion might be worth considering. After all, we won't look weak once the Crows' warehouse is firmly in our possession.'

Slowly, the Emperor turned herself around to face him. He could see the individual, uncombed strands of her hair standing out from her scalp to catch the light of the lanterns, as well as the bloodspots on her eyepatch, which had darkened to an unsightly brown.

'We cannot take Watanabe up on his clever suggestion,' she began, leaning sarcastically on the *clever*, 'because we will be busy elsewhere tonight. This evening, as the Lucky Crows raid the Keeper's Crescent, we will not be capturing their warehouse by stealth as Watanabe would have us doing, because we will already have won it back from them. We will, instead, be gathering Rainshadow City's full standing army, and, with the dragon pearl on our side, we will be marching on the Crescent ourselves.'

The Emperor pulled herself to her feet – clearly something of a struggle with her injured leg, though she was fighting not to show it.

'Today, we will publicly destroy the power of the Crows in battle,' she announced. 'We will kill the filthy betrayer, Ken Saito, and we will finish the clearance of the Keeper's Crescent, claiming the land for ourselves. Then, tomorrow morning, we will begin building the LIFE-Hub, as planned. All will be well again, and it will be clear as daylight to every soul in the Archipelago that anyone who thinks they can plot against me will find whatever power and influence they think they hold in this Empire as swiftly removed from their grasp as a mother's breast from the gums of a thieving, alien child. Have I made myself clear?'

General Kubo broke into spontaneous applause. The other Generals around the table were less effusive in their enthusiasm, but under the Emperor's gaze all of them did murmur their assent, even Watanabe. Mori rubbed his eyes and added his voice to the chorus of agreement. What else was there to do?

Another knock came, then, at the sliding doors to the Silver Laurel Room, and the Generals turned to see, once again, the waiting silhouette of the clipboard-holding aide.

'Come,' growled the Emperor, heaving herself back into her chair.

The doors slid open.

'Majesty,' the aide began, 'with respect, I have more news.'

'With respect,' the Emperor mimicked. '*With respect.* You shouldn't need to tell me – the respect should be obvious. What? What is it? What is your news?'

'It's your son, Majesty,' the aide stammered. 'The Imperial Heir, Crown Prince Haru. No one can find him anywhere. He's missing.'

'Missing?' The Emperor's voice was barely louder than a whisper, but she sounded even more dangerous now than she had done all evening. 'She's taken him,' she said, fury vibrating behind every syllable. 'I'll bet that witch has taken him. How *dare* she?'

She slammed both hands on the table, and Mori was glad to notice he wasn't the only one of the Ten Generals to jump at the sudden noise.

'You will win possession of that warehouse as soon as possible,' she commanded them now, 'and then you will prepare your troops for full battle with the Crows at the Crescent, at sunset. I will ride with you, at the head of the Imperial Army. With the dragon pearl to help me, I will be invulnerable.'

'With respect, Majesty—' began General Watanabe.

'Silence!' the Emperor roared. 'The next person who tells me they are contradicting my judgement *with respect* will spend the next three days of their life failing to breathe *with respect* in the oil tank. Get out of my sight, all of you. You have a war to win.'

Mori pushed himself to his feet, and followed the others as they made their way out of the Council Room. Everyone seemed to be trying their best to look dignified, despite the fact they were jumping to the tune of such clearly ill-advised orders. Only Kubo looked genuinely pleased at what had been decided.

It worried General Mori, too, that the Emperor didn't seem to have any clear plan for rescuing the Crown Prince, beyond simply destroying the power of the Crows. General Mori, after all, had always been rather fond of the little boy, whenever he'd had occasion to see him. He was so different from his mother.

4.

Far more of the Keeper's Children had signed up to fight the Crows than Toshiko had expected. She felt her stomach flip with something between fear and excitement as she swept a look over the gathered forces filling Mailee's café, sitting on the rugs and mats spread out over the floor. They'd pushed all of the tables and chairs to the sides of the tent – it had been the only way to fit everyone in.

Ava was here too, along with all twenty-six Jetsam she'd promised to the resistance last night. They were sitting bunched together in the café's far corner, expressions wary as the other Keeper's Children either pretended they weren't there at all, or shot repeated hostile glances in their direction.

For her part, Ava seemed to have come to the meeting fully armed, with two daggers on her belt and twin swords worn crossed on her back. Her arms were bare today too, showing off the tattooed vines, corvids and snakes trailing all the way up to her shoulders from her wrists. She wasn't the only one among the Jetsam here with obvious weapons or gang tattoos either, and Toshiko couldn't help but think how vulnerable the rest of the Keeper's Children were here in this tent – largely untrained, unarmed, trusting these fighters from the Jetsam to stay loyal, and relying on Ren and the resistance's small circle of organizers to keep them safe.

She watched Ren making his way to the front of the crowd then, to stand facing them in front of the Keeper's Shrine. Next to him lay the small pile of spare weapons the resistance had managed to gather at short notice – a handful of knives, three bows, and a single quiver of arrows. Beyond this, the Keeper's Children wouldn't have much more at their disposal than blunt kitchen knives and household utensils.

Despite the fact Ren was almost literally standing in front of an audience, Toshiko still felt as if she were witnessing something private as she watched Kei approach and stand on tiptoe to kiss the lines of care seemingly etched into his forehead. Toshiko looked away, only turning back when Ren cleared his throat and raised up his arms for silence, ready to address the gathered crowd.

'We'll meet the Crows in three groups,' he began. 'Group One will occupy the roofs, armed with stones and rocks with which to attack the invading Crows from above. Group Two will need to be confident with hand-to-hand fighting. You'll meet the Crows on the ground. It's a tall order I know, but Group One will cover you from the rooftops, which should help some. Group

Three, you'll hang back when the Crows first appear, and then filter around to cut them off from behind, once they've entered the Crescent. You'll attack from there, so they'll be fighting us on two sides. Now, this is important – anyone with training in any martial art, or with experience using a blade,' – he cast a pointed look in the direction of the Jetsam, who all stared stonily back – 'I want you in either Group Two or Group Three. Leave the rooftops and Group One to those who haven't fought before. Are we clear?'

Perhaps it was sleep deprivation, but Toshiko found she didn't feel very clear at all. Her mind, in fact, felt as if it were only very loosely grasping the reality of what Ren was saying. It seemed unreal that they might be fighting the Crows in just a few hours. Last night, she herself had volunteered to help teach Groups Two and Three some of the fundamentals of Hido, but the whole thing seemed insane to her, suddenly – this group of mostly civilians, facing hardened gangsters trained in street combat, all on only a couple of hours' training. All at once, she felt too warm in the café. The sun's heat was beating down through the cloth ceiling above, while at the same time, the fear, anticipation and anger coming off the gathered Keeper's Children seemed to thicken the air, until it felt hard to breathe.

Ren was still speaking, though, his voice now charged with a new intensity, a fire of determination burning beneath each of his words. 'Many of you here today, I know,' he said, 'would never have chosen the Crescent for your homes. You came here in the worst circumstances, having suffered unimaginable losses, only to face imprisonment within these bounds of barbed wire – only to be both used and ostracized, too, according to the whims and conveniences of the corrupt powers that run this island. And yet in spite of it all, you built yourselves a true home here, in the

Keeper's Crescent. And, more than that, far from being a disparate group of exiles, we the Keeper's Children are a *people* now, in our own right. A people with a right to exist. We'll show them the truth of that, tonight. We'll show them that we are so much more than just an inconvenience, to be cleared from the land whenever they choose. That this is our home, not some resource for them to exploit as they please, and that we, the Keeper's Children, will stand together, with the Keeper's blessing, to protect one another.'

A cheer went up from the massed volunteers, and even Toshiko found that she felt a little less doubtful, at his words. Of course the people here deserved so much more than the Crescent's life of restrictions and enforced poverty. And yet Ren was right, too. The connections between all of them here might originally have arisen from harsh necessity, but what now bound them to each other as Keeper's Children was something bigger than all the hostile forces that had forced them together. And while none of them had ended up here by choice, that didn't mean they shouldn't all now be proud to stand shoulder to shoulder with each other, and show both the Crows and the Emperor that, in creating the Crescent, they had in fact created something that had moved far outside of their control – a people and a place that could not now be destroyed at their whim.

As the cheers died down, Ren was suddenly all business again, clearly aware there was no time to waste. He ordered everyone to their feet, instructing them to sort themselves into the three groups.

Toshiko used the opportunity to slip out through the café's doorway, into the cooler air of the light breeze, blowing over the Gods' Road. It was unusually quiet, here – the usually bustling heart of the Crescent almost deserted. By now, there wouldn't be a Keeper's Child left who didn't know the Crows were attacking at sunset. Everyone had either gathered in the café to fight, or was hiding, preparing for the Crows' arrival in whatever small ways they could.

Just showing you trust someone can bring out the best in them, Jun had said, this morning.

Well, in handing Theo the pearl, she'd certainly shown him she'd trusted him. And yet the horizon at the top of the Gods' Road remained empty, and the curve at the road's other side stayed deserted, too. Was he really capable of abandoning her – of abandoning all of them here – like this? Young and inexperienced she might be, but she couldn't believe she'd imagined everything between them. It had all felt so real, hadn't it?

She rubbed her eyes, which were tired and painfully dry after the long hours during which she'd subjected them to the amber-coloured contact lenses, and then gazed one last time up and down the Gods' Road's empty reaches. Then she turned back to the café's doorway, away from the road and from her hopes. She would be needed soon, she knew, to help train the groups for the fight.

As she ducked beneath the chequered oilcloth, she was surprised to catch Haru's eye. He was sitting at the other end of the tent with Kei, close to where Ren had been addressing the crowd, and yet, despite being so deep in the thick of all the tent's activity, his gaze had been hovering around the café's entrance. He gave Toshiko a small smile, but she could tell from his disappointed expression that she wasn't the person he'd been hoping would appear.

Interesting, she noted. It seemed, then, that she wasn't the only one in this café who was on the lookout for someone else to arrive.

5.

Every time Haru caught sight of Toshiko, he wanted to kick himself for having been so foolish in giving her the dragon pearl. He knew he couldn't really blame her for what had happened, when she so obviously hadn't meant for her friend with the bright hair to run off with it – and yet that was still the way things had turned out, and now Haru wouldn't get the chance to give the pearl back to the little dragon, to whom it really belonged.

Without the pearl, too, his ability to see Sun Spirits was waning, and it didn't feel now as if he were losing his new friends for any reason that was worth it. He could still see the hare-like creatures by the tea urns, but the little shadows he'd spotted earlier, dancing in the embers of the fire, were fading – to his eyes, at least. He could only be sure they were still there at all through the few glimpses he caught of them in the very corner of his eye.

He supposed he was lucky he could still see any Sun Spirits at all, with the pearl gone. Last night, Toshiko had told him that both her and her brother's special abilities had disappeared, the moment they'd let go of it.

Toshiko was making her way through the crowds now, though, towards him and Kei. He would have to prepare himself to talk to her, and pretend he wasn't annoyed. He didn't want to make her feel worse, after all, when she already looked as worried as she did.

All the adults seemed worried, here in the Keeper's Crescent. They all talked as if they could win this battle, but their confident words didn't match their expressions. Haru had pretended not to notice, but he couldn't deny that this mismatch scared him. Earlier this morning, Kei had even handed him a small pocket knife, telling him to keep it secret, and to hide it in one of the sturdy boots Ren had given him in place of his slippers. He could even feel the knife in there now, its wooden handle and sheath heavy and uncomfortable against his ankle. Kei had said she was sure he wouldn't have to use it, but if she'd been telling the truth, then why give it to him at all?

But now Toshiko was here, saying hello, and so Haru did his best to stop thinking about all his fears and to nod politely back.

'Are you waiting for someone else to arrive?' Toshiko asked him then, unexpectedly.

'No,' he replied, keeping his voice as casual as possible. 'Why? Are you?'

'No,' she replied. 'Of course not.'

She did look a bit shifty though, Haru thought, and he wasn't completely sure he believed her. Although he was hardly being very truthful now either, he supposed.

I'm on my way, he could still hear the dragon saying in his dream, after all. *Wait for me.*

6.

As soon as Theo was past the security scanners and into the Shadow Column's sweeping foyer, he was met by two Crows in dark suits and earpieces, who wordlessly accompanied him to the elevators. In contrast to when he'd last been here, the foyer was almost deserted. The Crows who'd met him, too, were both small women, and noticeably older than the more typical gang members he'd grown used to. Of course, these two certainly still could have some surprising combat expertise up their sleeves, but he did feel a creeping unease, wondering where all the more obvious fighters of the gang had disappeared off to.

Once in the elevator, one of the women reached into her jacket pocket and produced a small silver key, which she slid into a corresponding lock on the side of the elevator keypad. She gave the key a sharp turn to the right, and, to Theo's surprise, they started moving down, instead of up.

Before he could even begin to wonder what a place like the Shadow Column might keep in its basement, the doors had slid open, and the two Crows were flanking him, each with a firm hand on one of his shoulders, to direct him out into a shadowed corridor, where they were met with a powerful smell of damp, and a distant dripping sound. The same woman who'd produced the key pulled a torch from another pocket, which she turned on to illuminate the corridor immediately in front of them, revealing a network of rusting pipes on the walls, chasing their ways over and around creeping patches of mould.

The two Crows marched Theo through the gloom to stop in front of a secured metal door, by which time he was feeling increasingly unsettled, half-convinced these Crows must have brought him down here to have him murdered. The only thing that kept him relatively steady as his two minders drew back the bolts on the door was the knowledge that if the Sensei had wanted him dead, there was surely no particular reason why she couldn't have simply had him killed in broad daylight.

At last, the door swung open, and they stepped into the room beyond. It was long, narrow, and dim, lit only by lanterns suspended from brackets in the wall, close to its high ceiling. Although it was definitely better-kept than the corridor they'd just vacated, it was still far from being as luxurious as all the other parts of the Shadow Column Theo had seen so far. He immediately got the impression of this being some kind of work-shop, or lab – a behind-the-scenes type of place, not intended for show.

Wooden work benches lined one end of the space, and Theo shuddered to see them scattered with what at first glance looked like severed body parts. Quickly, though, he made out that these were, in fact, surely bot-parts, which had simply been sculpted and meticulously painted to resemble the human body. He found himself abruptly, morbidly transfixed by a female head – hairless, with beautiful amber eyes – as well as by the hand, perfectly jointed, which lay alongside it on the bench, its fingernails five neat ovals.

The two Crows who'd brought him here didn't let him pause to stare, marching him instead deeper into the workshop's shadows, towards where two figures in white lab coats sat at a long, wooden table, facing away from Theo and his minders. The surface of this table in front of them was heavily scarred with chemical burns, and scattered with papers showing a mixture of mathematical calculations and complicated graphs. Amidst them stood an uncommonly large silver coffee pot, along with two small cups crafted in matching style.

Instead of attending to any of these items on the table, though, the two figures were watching a third – a woman with long, dark hair falling to her waist, who was standing before them on some sort of plinth. She was dressed only in a loose, white robe, and had no shoes or jacket, or anything else to keep herself warm. Even as one of Theo's minders announced their approach with a strategic cough, this figure remained utterly still, her expression a perfect blank. The two figures at the table, though, stood and turned to meet them.

Theo felt his throat tighten as he recognized the Sensei – just as small and unassuming a figure as he remembered, with her short, silver-grey hair neatly combed, her spectacles worn today on a mother-of-pearl chain around her neck, and a hint of a beige cardigan visible beneath her lab coat. He knew enough now not to be deceived by her appearance.

He was fairly certain that he'd never seen the man who was standing next to her before. He was in early middle age, and from the way he was watching the Sensei for her reaction to the newcomers, he seemed to be some sort of underling, very much in her thrall.

The women on either side of Theo stopped walking then in unison, sending him stumbling forward a step before they yanked him back into line.

'My thanks to the two of you,' the Sensei said to them both. 'I am happy to entertain our friend myself, from here.'

The women released Theo's shoulders without objection, bowed to the Sensei, and turned to walk back to the door. The Sensei smiled. The man next to her shifted awkwardly from foot to foot. The woman in the robe still didn't move an inch.

'You too, Rico,' the Sensei continued, addressing the man in the lab coat. 'I'll speak to the Bluejay alone for a moment.'

Alone? In a surreal moment of terror, Theo found himself wondering if he was the only one present who could see the woman up there on the plinth at all – and then Rico's eyes flitted over to her, and Theo was flooded with relief that, whatever else might be going on here, at least this man could see the silent, white-robed figure, too.

'Ms Minami,' Rico began then, his voice unsteady. 'You'll appreciate my reluctance to leave the side of my creation at such a critical time ...'

The Sensei gave him a smile, but it was the kind of smile that people crossed roads, cities and even oceans to avoid. 'This is important, Rico,' she said. 'Don't worry, I'll take good care of your beloved lady friend in your absence.'

A look of mingled frustration and embarrassment crossed the man's face, but he bowed low, and turned to follow the two women from the room.

The Sensei waited for the door to shut behind them all, before she spoke again.

'In the wild,' she began, 'bluejays have remarkably unpredictable migratory patterns. No one knows why they come and go as they do. You are beginning to behave rather too much like your namesake, Bluejay. Why have you come to see me now, while the Kawakamis are still living?'

Theo swallowed, trying to push away thoughts of Toshiko. He needed to stay alert. Far from being reassured by the lack of visible gang muscle around the Sensei now, it only made him feel as if there must be something here that he was missing. His eyes flitted back up, again, to the woman on her plinth, where she loomed behind the Sensei, remaining as still as a statue.

Who – or what – was she? Theo's brain seemed to have begun working on this puzzle without his direct permission. And then, remembering the human-looking bot-parts he'd seen on the work benches near the doorway, he started to understand.

'Can she move?' he asked.

'Not yet,' the Sensei replied, her gaze turning almost wistful as she glanced over at the woman – or at the bot, as she surely must be. 'She has yet to be given the gift of life.'

'Is that a fancy way of saying she hasn't been switched on yet?'

'No,' the Sensei said. 'It isn't.'

Theo frowned. 'So what does it mean, then?'

The Sensei looked at him through narrowed eyes. 'Always curious, aren't you, Bluejay? You're just the kind of student I used to enjoy teaching, back when I still did such things. If it'll stop you quaking in your boots, though, I can assure you that she can't see or hear us at all. She is merely an inert shell. Rather beautiful though, don't you think?'

Theo shivered. The body looming before him was unnerving, unsettling, uncanny – certainly striking – but 'beautiful' was not the word he would have chosen. Still, it didn't feel wise to disagree with the Sensei – and so he nodded, and the Sensei laughed.

'Her beauty is intentional, you know. It'll make her a more effective soldier. Are you aware that many of the Archipelago's islands still recruit only men into their Guards? All those men won't know what to do, when faced with an army that looks like mine. How will they even begin to allow themselves to admit to feeling threatened by a horde of beautiful women?' She smiled. 'Over the years, you see, I've learnt that there is considerable power in allowing oneself to be underestimated.' She gestured at the bot. 'This here may only be one vessel, but once the LIFE-Hub is under my control, it won't be long before I have my army. And then we will take the whole Archipelago, and so begin its transformation.'

Theo swallowed. The Sensei had plans, it seemed, far bigger than anything he'd imagined. And yet despite the immensity of what she was saying, she spoke almost dreamily, turning now to reach out and stroke the bot's calf, rather in the same way someone might stroke a favoured pet. The folds of the bot's white robe shifted at her touch, while the body, of course, didn't move an inch. It looked so human, so real, that Theo found himself struggling to accept that it could be a fully created thing, built from machine parts. While the skin was certainly uncommonly smooth, it still looked unmistakably like human skin – and then the face, too, while being eerie in its perfect symmetry, did definitely still look like skin, muscles and ligaments over bone. It could be illusory, but to look at the bot now, Theo found it difficult to believe that face wouldn't be just as capable as that of any ordinary human being, in the matter of expressing thoughts, and even emotions.

It won't be long before I have my army. The phrase seemed to move in whispers through Theo's mind, as he studied the bot. He wondered, too, what the Sensei could have meant by the Archipelago's *transformation*? Any kind of transformation to these islands with her at its helm didn't bear imagining. He'd hardly been keen on the Emperor's plans for the ALISE bots, but this vision of the Archipelago's future seemed undeniably more nightmarish.

Would she really be able to capture the whole Archipelago with an army of bots like this one? He wasn't sure, but it didn't seem impossible. Beneath the folds of the robe, the bot's body did look strong. If it had been animated, Theo had no doubt it would easily have been able to do him some considerable damage, in a fight.

When the LIFE-Hub is under my control, the Sensei had said, too. Of course, he'd known that the Crows were planning to take the Crescent, but hearing as much from her lips made it a lot harder, now, not to think about what could be happening back there, to Toshiko and the others.

Theo bit down hard on the inside of his cheek, tasting blood. He had to focus, and worrying about the Crescent, and even wider the fate of the Archipelago, was all distraction. He'd made his choice hours ago, and he'd chosen to live – or to do what he could in that direction, anyway. The Crescent wasn't his home, and it wasn't his problem, and neither was the Archipelago as a whole. He refused to feel any obligation to become some kind of martyr to these places that had treated him as if he were worth less than the dirt on the roadside. It was time to get on with why he'd really come here today.

'I have the dragon pearl,' he all but blurted out.

7.

The Imperial Guard captured the locked-down warehouse from the Lucky Crows. The victory, though, felt anything but glorious to General Mori. It had been too hard-won, worlds away from the easy confrontation the Emperor had promised.

The Crows had been uncoordinated and chaotic, yes – shouting into their Comms-Discs, apparently struggling to communicate – but they had also been vicious, highly trained martial artists, armed to the teeth and prepared to fight dirty, never hesitating before wounding or killing. The only reason the Guard had triumphed at all, Mori suspected, had been the simple, practical fact of their having been mounted on horseback, while the Crows had fought on foot.

He reached up to stroke the mane of his horse, Red Pine, and took a moment to contemplate the site of the battle around them. All of his Guards looked ragged, many of them wounded. The sad fact, too, was that these were the lucky ones. They had lost sixty-eight good soldiers over the course of the battle – all of them brave, loyal men and women. Some had been General Mori's personal friends.

The sense of loss pervading the afternoon was only compounded by the fact that, even after so much sacrifice, the Emperor's people still hadn't managed to break through the warehouse's doors. As Mori contemplated those closed doors now, he found himself unable to believe that anything it might hold – whether it be all the draconic ore in the world, or even a thousand dragon pearls – could be so exceptional as to genuinely merit the loss of so many good people's lives. He wondered how many of his Guards, here, would share that belief. Of course, though, none would ever dare voice the thought aloud – not in the Emperor's presence.

'Get up,' he could hear her calling now to the troops, as they tried to recover from the battle.

He turned to see that she was already mounted again on Lightning, her chestnut-brown mare, and was riding up the waterfront towards him, rallying the scattered groups of Guards as she went. Lightning was agitated and restless, clearly picking up her rider's mood, her head tossing as if railing against her bridle's constraints.

'We've spent too long already, trying to get through these doors,' the Emperor called from the saddle to her soldiers, as they tried to tend to the injured and take care of the dead. 'We'll just have to proceed without the help of the dragon pearl. We can't afford to waste more time.' As Lightning reared, she pulled hard on the reins, and continued to roar at her troops. 'I'm meant to be leading an army, not a circus. If you value your lives and the lives of your families, you will get up and onto your mounts. We're not finished with the Crows yet. We're going after them – we're going to chase them down to the Keeper's Crescent, and take the Crescent back for ourselves.'

Further along the waterfront, Mori could see General Kubo already beginning to round up his troops with a zeal that felt impossible to understand, given the number of comrades they'd just lost.

Even as General Mori followed the Emperor's orders, pulling himself back into Red Pine's saddle, he found he couldn't quite swallow the bitterness rising in his throat. He looked again at those warehouse doors, and then over at the sight he'd been trying to avoid since the battle's end – the long line of bodies they'd have no time to bury, now, laid out under the fading sun, to be picked at by birds.

8.

Sitting next to Mei at her table in the Keeper's Crescent's café, Jun was the first to notice the change in her expression.

'What?' he asked, as she looked up from her little hairclip computer. 'What's wrong?'

'It's the Crows,' she said. 'I may have stopped them getting any communications through to each other via the Comms-Discs, but I can still see the messages they're trying to send.'

'And what are they trying to send?' Jun asked, trying to keep his voice calm. He'd rarely seen Mei look so rattled, and was surprised by how much it unsettled him. At the tone of her voice, even Mochi had roused himself from the oblivious snooze he'd been enjoying around her shoulders.

'They're saying the Imperial Guard is coming after them, and so they're changing plans. They want to invade the Crescent immediately, before the Guard can get to them. They're not waiting for sunset.'

Jun found he could only stare at her.

'I've blocked off most of the Crows' network,' Mei was saying, 'but I'm not infallible, a few messages will still get through. And I can hardly stop them from literally speaking to each other, in person. They might be more disorganized without full use of the Comms-Discs, and it might be less of a coordinated attack, but if the messages say that they're coming now . . .' she trailed off, the colour draining from her face.

Jun looked at the scene in the café around them. Several of the Jetsam were training a large group of Keeper's Children in how to disarm an opponent, while another group was assembling piles of rocks, meant for throwing from the rooftops. Many of the volunteers weren't even here. They were out, scattered through the Crescent – training, or making preparations.

'But we're not ready,' Jun stammered, his voice coming out as little more than a whisper.

9.

Toshiko looked up at an unexpected shout. It died away as quickly as it had come, returning the still air of the Keeper's Crescent to the same state of hushed expectancy that had dominated the afternoon, becoming ever more suffocating the closer they drew towards sunset. She hadn't been able to make out any words in the shout, or even any defining details of the voice. It sounded, though, like it had come from somewhere among the buildings behind them.

She'd brought a group of fifteen resistance volunteers here to the southern corner, hoping to teach them the basics of Hido. She had to admit it was a bleak location in which to train, filled as it was with the wreckage of demolished houses, but it was also the one place in the Crescent she'd been able to think of at short notice with enough open space for this number of people to practice. Perhaps part of her, too, had wanted to focus her students' minds. She didn't have time for anyone to posture or show off in an effort to demonstrate their strength, or aptitude. If this training was going to be any kind of help at all, it was essential everyone here understood the seriousness of the situation.

'What was it, do you think?' asked Lina, whose blocking technique Toshiko had been in the middle of critiquing when the shout had distracted them. For all Lina's tough and determined talk in the resistance meetings, she looked fearful now and was watching Toshiko wide-eyed, as if she might somehow have answers.

'I don't know,' was all Toshiko could tell her, as Kenji, one of the other volunteer fighters, dropped the stance he'd been practising, and began to stride away from the southern corner's emptiness and rubble towards the line of deserted houses that marked the beginning of the territory the Crows hadn't cleared yet.

'Hey,' Kenji called. 'Who's back there? Are you okay? Give us a shout if you're okay.'

Toshiko followed behind him, along with Lina and a handful of the other resistance fighters, the group of them rounding the line of buildings to see a small girl running towards them, barefoot. She couldn't have been more than eight years old.

'Help!' the girl cried as soon as she saw them, stumbling as she half-turned to gesture behind her, at something over her shoulder. 'You have to help!'

'Come on, sweetheart,' called Lina, as she rushed forward towards the girl. 'Keep running. Come over here now, over to me!'

Toshiko wondered at the sudden urgency in Lina's voice, and then saw what Lina had surely noticed already – a plume of smoke, curling from the cluster of buildings behind the girl. Lina had reached the girl now, and was seizing her shoulders, hustling her back, towards the others.

'What is it?' she kept asking the girl as they went. 'What's happened?'

But her questions were unnecessary. A pair of Crows was emerging from behind one of the buildings – a small woman with dyed red hair worn short and spiked, her hands glittering with the razor-sharp blades of miniature throwing stilettos, and a much taller man with a loose grin and loping gait, swinging a machete. Toshiko noticed, with a start, that its wide, silver blade was patterned with what looked like fresh blood.

'Crows!' Kenji began calling out – and then his eyes caught on the man's blade. 'What did you do?' he cried, and began running towards them, fists raised.

'No, Kenji, stop!' Toshiko shouted after him. 'It's too dangerous!'

She was too late, though. Moving with the swiftness of a trained fighter – a swiftness Kenji and the others still sadly lacked – the woman drew back her left hand and hurled one of her blades, sending it spinning right for Kenji.

The stiletto's point reached its target easily. It pierced Kenji's shoulder, sending him recoiling and stumbling, his feet still trying to keep running even as his body was thrown back with the knife's momentum.

The other resistance fighters ran to him, tugging him to his feet, pulling him back as he gasped and blinked at the new reality of the dagger's curved, black hilt protruding from his fragile flesh. Toshiko, however, found herself immobile and unbelieving, unable to do anything other than stare at the two advancing Crows.

You're not meant to be here yet, she found herself wanting to insist. *You were meant to wait until sunset.*

Then the red-haired woman raised her remaining stiletto, and at last Toshiko came to her senses. She pulled out the dagger Ren had lent her, and lowered herself into a Hido crouch, ready.

'Run!' she ordered the group around her. 'Get the message to Ren and the others. Tell them that we're out of time. The Crows are here already!'

10.

'They don't care if we're ready or not,' Mei was telling Jun in the café tent, her voice charged with a horrified kind of finality. 'They're here. We've run out of time.'

Then, sending Mochi into full, hissing alarm, she swept her computer to one side, jumped up onto the table, and yelled to the resistance at large.

'The Crows are coming. They're coming now. The battle is starting. Go, quickly, get into position.'

Jun just managed to catch sight of the pained expression on Ren's face, before the whole gathering of volunteer fighters descended into chaos. Keeper's Children and Jetsam alike were shoving and trampling each other in their urgency to get to the café's doorway and out into the Crescent to do something – anything to meet this existential threat to their homes and families. Ren was hovering, seemingly on the point of following them all out onto the Gods' Road, when Mei shouted his name, and he turned to look back at her.

'Be careful out there,' Mei called over to him. 'I don't know how the Crows figured this out, but they know that you're our leader. The messages they're trying to send through the network identify you as the main target to hit, along with Ava. Somehow they know about her, too. The Sensei's got rewards on both your heads.'

'How much?'

'Fifty sun credits for her. Sixty for you. Dead or alive.'

A cold tension gripped Jun's heart at the words. Those rewards were seriously substantial sums, whichever way you looked at them, and he didn't doubt that any number of Crows would be keen to try their luck at securing one or even both of them. From the moment he stepped out there today, Ren would be fighting for his life – as Ava would be, too.

Ren only nodded at Mei's announcement, in spite of the seriousness of its implications.

'Thanks for the heads-up,' he told her, shortly. 'I'll get a message to Ava.'

Then he turned and ran after the Keeper's Children, ducking out of the café's illusion of shelter, and into whatever was happening beyond its deceptively cosy, chequered walls.

Jun could already hear shouts out there, along with the echoing sounds of destruction. He was sure, too, that he could smell burning. For a moment, he almost ran after Ren, to try to pull him back. As their leader, he needed to stay safe. What would happen to the resistance if he were killed?

And then Jun's mind went to the other resistance fighters, the ones who hadn't been here in the café when Mei had yelled out the news. They were still dispersed around the Crescent, and wouldn't even know what was happening. There was a group gathering more stones by the river, for instance, and a group doing Hido training with Toshiko.

Toshiko, Jun thought, finally snapping into action, jumping to his feet and running for the doorway, hurling himself out of the café and into the press of people outside.

Immediately, he was thrown to one side by the crowd, his glasses jarred and knocked from his face. Blinking through the sudden blur and disorientated by the overwhelming noise, it was all Jun could do to reach down and scrabble for his fallen glasses on the ground amid the stampede of feet. He'd only just managed to seize them between grasping fingertips before he was carried away down the Gods' Road by the crowd's momentum.

Jamming the glasses back onto his face, the world seemed no

less chaotic for his being able to see it more clearly. It was a place of screams and running feet, of crowds of people, pushing and shoving and surging in all directions – a place where low sunlight struggled to break through the columns of smoke already rising from the Crescent's outskirts, and where storm clouds were gathering over the sea.

An hour earlier, Jun really had begun to believe that the Keeper's Children might be able to hold their own in this fight and defend the Crescent. Abruptly now, he let go of that dream. He had to find his little sister, and then he would find Mei, and once they were all three of them together again, they would escape this place, slipping under its barbed wire just as they'd done once before. Surely that was the only real option left to them, now.

11.

Haru heard the start of the commotion at sea first, before anyone else – which made sense, because he was the one listening for it. From inside the café, he heard the thunder and the waves breaking loud over the wooden slats of the docks. He heard the ocean wind rattling the Crescent's houses, tearing through the fluttering Keeper's Garlands and battering at the café's cloth ceiling above him. He heard screams, and he smelled the bitter, mineral quality to the air as a huge gust swept a storm in from over the water, and the café's canvas doorway flew wide open, as if the whole tent around them were drawing a gulp of the evening into its chequered lungs. Haru broke free of Kei's arms then, and ran right out into the storm.

He'd known there was a battle happening out here, of course, and he'd been prepared for it to be awful, but it was

still a shock to discover just how awful it really was. Homes
were burning, and everywhere people were bleeding, crying,
and screaming for mercy, or attacking each other with huge,
glinting blades.

And yet, Haru knew that he had to somehow look past all of
this, because the battle wasn't the only thing happening now, outside here in the Crescent. He forced himself to dodge and weave
his way through the fighting on the Gods' Road, and then down
through the lines of burning houses all the way to the barbed
wire that separated the Crescent from the beach.

The fighting might be quieter down here, but the world was no
less in turmoil. Beyond the fences, the sea had risen into a twisting, elemental tower of mingled water and air currents, of gust
and seafoam, salt and spray, that reached high into the storm-
darkened sky. Even as fresh cries rose from the fighting behind
him, and the smell of smoke on the wind grew stronger, Haru
stayed frozen in place, his eyes fixed on this whirling, surging
pillar of elements – as, in a scatter of blue and white lightning,
something enormous burst from its heart.

Lightning flared, briefly rendering the creature a silhouette,
before a flash of sun broke through the cloud overhead to splash
its huge, uncoiling body with a scattering of light. And Haru's
breath caught, then, at the sight of a dragon – the dragon from
his dream, somehow suddenly really here before him, emerging
from this storm of water to fill what seemed like the whole sky
with the vivid brightness of its turquoise scales, its flaming orange
fur, and the glowing light of the pearl at its throat.

In any other circumstance, Haru would have revelled in
this creature's magnificence. And yet, he knew all too well just
how badly he'd failed it. He'd given away the little dragon's
pearl – surely the one thing it wanted and needed so much, and

which it had travelled all this way for, from Muralania, at the Archipelago's far edge.

He also understood, though, that the fighting behind him was turning more brutal by the moment. The resistance was struggling, and he had to do what he could to help – for Kei, for the Keeper's Children, and simply for what was fair, and right.

Feeling very small, suddenly, in the face of so much elemental vastness, Haru raised his arms, and began to wave up at the dragon.

CHAPTER SIXTEEN

A Storm Over the Gods' Road

1.

It was a remarkable sight – this giant, turquoise serpent of air and water, soaring in from the sea to circle the battle from overhead, weaving in and out of the gathering storm clouds over the Gods' Road. Everywhere, Keeper's Children looked up in shock at its sudden appearance. Cries of awe, and then of alarm rose from their ranks, as people began to scatter and run, fleeing the dragon's immense shadow. No creature like this had been seen near Rainshadow island for generations.

Curiously, Toshiko noticed, even as she sprinted down the Gods' Road with the Crows on her heels, the dragon didn't seem to have wings, although it was undoubtedly airborne. Instead, it seemed to be navigating the sky using currents of air, churned up by the storm. It reminded her of how it had felt to wear Saito's pearl, and to sense the air around her as a web of golden threads – any one of which could catch and carry her.

The thought was shattered by a flying stiletto landing point-down in the earth next to her, dangerously close to her right foot. She spun to face her assailants, and was just in time to dodge a throwing star's spinning blades. It flew past her face, cutting the air with sufficient force to set the loose strands of her hair flying. She shivered. Had it caught her, it could have been lethal.

The worrying truth was that most of the Crows were fighting to kill, now. Their initial strategy of forcing everyone onto the barges seemed to have evaporated in the face of the Keeper's Children's determination to fight back. Toshiko had seen several broken, bloodied bodies lying by the side of the Gods' Road as she'd run here, pursued by the two Crows who'd ambushed her in the southern corner.

Gritting her teeth, she turned to face them now, her dagger raised as she tried to keep her eyes on both of them at once – on the red-haired woman with her throwing stars, and the tall man with the loose grin and the blood-soaked machete.

The man lunged for her first, his huge blade swinging. She managed to parry the blow with her much smaller dagger, but the force of the collision jolted and jarred her arm, all the way to the shoulder. She staggered, only to find herself face to face with the woman, who had another stiletto in hand, and was levelling it in her direction.

Operating purely on reflexes now, Toshiko used a Hido block to knock the woman's hand aside. Then, switching her dagger to her left hand, she drew her right hand into a fist, and aimed a fast punch at the woman's throat.

The woman took the blow square in the larynx, her eyes turning wide with shock as she reeled off to one side.

The man with the machete grimaced. 'You're a tricky one, aren't you?' he said, raising his blade once again.

Then, abruptly, Toshiko panicked. Faced with such naked violence bearing down on her, she curled into a crouch, both arms thrown over her head – as if that could possibly protect her from a blade as large as this one. And yet even as she cowered, a surefire target, the blade didn't fall.

She chanced a glance back up. The man was still standing over her, his machete still raised, but he hadn't even begun to bring it down, and he looked tense now, suddenly cautious.

That was when Toshiko noticed the hand on his shoulder, and saw the fingers, gleaming with distinctive, heavy rings. She swallowed, hard, as the familiar form of Ken Saito emerged behind him, out of the smog of the battle – a forbidding figure in a Lucky Crows jacket.

'Leave this one,' Saito told the man with the machete, in a voice that sliced through the clamour around them as easily as rock through water. 'She's mine. She has something that belongs to me, you see.'

The other Crow lowered his machete, his free hand held palm-up to Saito, as if to say that whatever this was, he wanted no part in it. Toshiko watched him nod to the red-haired woman, who had stopped midway through readying another bladed star, her eyes warily on Saito. The two of them stepped back, giving the top General and consigliere of the Crows his space.

In his right hand, Saito held the curved knife that Toshiko knew only too well. As she watched, he began swinging it round and around, mapping a lethal circle.

'Hello again, little girl,' he said. 'I'd have thought you'd want to thank me. After all, I believe I did just save your life. And yet you look almost as frightened as you did five years ago, when I came to visit your aunt.'

All at once, Toshiko found herself filled with such rage that she hardly knew how she was able to get to her feet, raise her dagger, and look him in the eye. How dare he return so brazenly to the Crescent, after doing so much harm here during his years as the Captain? It was as if he believed he stood apart from humanity, less like a man than a God.

As she stood, ready to face him, Toshiko welcomed her anger. And as Saito lunged for her, his grin twisting into a scowl, she let her fury fill her completely, leaving no room for fear. Some part of her understood, perhaps, that her anger would be the main thing she'd have going for her in this fight, without the pearl's power to help her.

2.

The Keeper's Children reacted to the dragon's arrival with immediate fear. They were a people, after all, who were all too used to being under threat, primed by life to assume the worst, and at the sight of this new potential menace from the sky, what little order there had been within the groups of resistance fighters began to crumble. As Jun pushed his way through the Crescent, calling out for Toshiko, he became aware of those around him breaking ranks, stumbling for any kind of cover they might be able to find amidst the fistfights, knife fights, and burning buildings.

Then, amidst the escalating chaos, he heard Ren's voice on the wind. The resistance's leader was still alive, and sticking loyally with his troops.

'Listen to me,' Ren was saying. 'Don't run from the dragon. We'll be lost, if we scatter now. Stick to the plan. Keep dividing into the groups!'

Ren probably was right, Jun realized, as he ducked behind someone's half-destroyed house to hide from a pack of armed Crows. Keeping to the agreed strategy might well give them their best chance of survival, seeing as the Crows did still seem to be the biggest threat here. They were far less distracted by the dragon than the Keeper's Children were, and were easily numerous and coordinated enough to threaten the life of every single Keeper's Child within the Crescent, despite Mei's work in scrambling their Comms-Discs. Even as Jun watched, two heavily armed Crows ran past his hiding place in the ruined house, shoving a Keeper's Child hard into the wreckage as they went, without breaking their stride. The young woman's head slammed against the edge of a metal sheet in the debris, and she fell hard, exposed to the battlefield.

'Stick to the plan,' Jun could hear Ren still shouting. 'We are the Keeper's Children, and we will protect one another!'

Amazingly, Ren's words did appear to be having some effect. As his voice reached more of the resistance, the shoving and panic began to lessen. Fewer people, too, seemed to be trying to desert the defensive formations that Group Two had begun forming around the buildings.

'We can survive this,' came Ren's voice again on the wind, 'but only if we stick together, and stick to the plan!'

Jun looked up and down the Gods' Road on either side of him once more, still hoping to see some sign of Toshiko. In front of him, the young woman the Crows had thrown against the house's wreckage was still collapsed on the ground – though no further Crows seemed to have noticed her, yet. *Get up!* Jun silently willed her, from behind his shelter.

The defensive ring of resistance fighters nearest to Jun seemed to be managing to hold firm now, even in the face of an onslaught from the Crows. He could see two Jetsam among them – who, it seemed, hadn't deserted the Keeper's Children at all, though so many had doubted their loyalty. Instead, they were sticking to the strategy and standing by their comrades – doing the very opposite, in fact, of what Jun himself was doing, he realized then, with his plan to find his sisters and to run.

He hesitated. Of course he still wanted to escape all of this terror and violence. Of course, too, he still wished that he and his sisters could be a simple unit of three again, with no loyalty owed to anyone beyond themselves. And yet ... and yet.

'For the Keeper's Crescent,' Ren was shouting now, sounding ragged, his voice turning hoarse, but not giving up. 'We can win this!'

Maybe, Jun considered, it had been wrong to think that the Kawakamis had ever really been a unit of only three. Maybe that had simply been a necessary lie they'd told themselves, as three children doing what they could to survive. They weren't children anymore now though, and Jun knew he could do better for these people than to abandon them again.

With one last glance up to the dragon – still an ominous shadow overhead, the coils of its body weaving through the storm – he took a deep, steadying breath, and stepped out from behind the ruined building.

He did have one useful skill, gifted to him by Mailee, who might be trapped on the Crows' barge, but whose lessons and values could still be here, in some way, through him. He might not know the first thing about fighting, but he did know a little of how to take care of the injured, and there were already Keeper's Children everywhere throughout the Crescent who needed his help. He wouldn't run – he would stay, and do his best to save them.

The air was thick with weapons now – with throwing stars, flying arrows, spinning knives and daggers. Staying alert to all of these threats, and keeping himself hunched low, Jun made his way over to the young woman he'd seen the Crows attack, still crumpled in the rubble. Her eyelids fluttered open as he laid a gentle hand on her shoulder, but her gaze seemed worryingly unfocused. A trail of blood tracked down her temple by her left eye, from where it had collided with the metal.

'Hello,' Jun told her. 'My name is Jun Kawakami, and I'm here to help you.'

She blinked, looking confused, then began to move, shifting herself up off the fallen wall. Jun helped her, taking her weight as she moved herself away from the debris.

'I'm sorry, but you can't stay here,' Jun told her. 'Do you think you can walk, if I help you?'

He offered her his hand, and after only a moment's hesitation, she took it. He hauled her upright, and then, slinging her arm around his shoulders, began to lead her, still unsteady on her feet, back up the Gods' Road.

He would take her to the café tent, he decided, where he would find the medical supplies Mailee had always kept there, and then round up some resistance fighters with healing experience to take care of her. Then, he would take a bag of Mailee's medical kit himself, and head back out onto the battlefield, to do what he could for all those who needed help out here.

'We have to keep together,' he heard Ren shouting, again. 'We have to stick to the plan, and look after each other!'

The injured young woman seemed to rally a little at the sound of her leader's voice. With what seemed like a huge effort of will, she pulled herself more upright, suddenly less of a dead weight on Jun's shoulders, and began to walk forward a little more steadily, as if Ren's words had convinced her to keep defying the Crows, even if that was now only by fighting for her own survival.

3.

Further down the Gods' Road, Toshiko fought Ken Saito. He was controlled and vicious as ever, but she was a cyclone of anger. Some memory of the pearl seemed to have embedded itself in her limbs and her muscles, and though she could no longer sense and use the flows of air around her, she still felt faster and stronger than ever as her borrowed blade parried his.

'What have you done with my pearl?' Saito snarled, accompanying each word with a slash of his knife.

Toshiko dodged and wove, before aiming her own blade up towards his throat. He deflected the blow, and laughed.

'You realize your odds aren't good,' he said. 'I'm not even trying yet.'

'Then try,' she spat, hating how she had to shout her throat ragged just to be heard over the battle, while his graveyard tones seemed to sail over the noise so effortlessly. 'I'm not afraid of you.'

'Don't be stupid,' Saito said, as his left hand reached around to grab her ponytail. 'Of course you are.'

He pulled hard on her hair, and Toshiko screamed in spite of herself as he dragged her in closer towards him, scalp-first, to hold his knife against her throat.

This was the second time in as many days that Toshiko had felt its sharp edge against her skin. Almost every instinct was telling her to struggle, yet she held still, careful not to move and accidentally brush the blade.

'Clearly, you don't have the pearl anymore,' Saito said, his breath repellently warm on her cheek as he gripped her. He sounded faintly amused. 'Your combat skills have suffered. Perhaps you can tell me what happened to it.'

'And then you'll cut my throat, anyway?'

'I won't cut your throat if you tell me, how's that? I can't promise you'll be allowed to live, but I can promise that much.'

'What's that meant to mean?' Toshiko tried to seem defiant, but the question only came out sounding worried.

'It means,' Saito replied, the knife still held steady, 'that I, personally, can let you go if you tell me where the pearl is, because I'm not the one with orders to kill you.'

'So who does have orders to kill me?'

Saito replied with a swift, painful kick to the back of Toshiko's knee, sending her collapsing forwards, towards his knife.

He caught her shoulder at the last instant – in time to save her life, not in time to stop the blade from drawing blood. It was only a shallow cut, but Toshiko could feel panic rising, draining the force of her anger.

'I don't know where it is,' she all but screamed, in her desperation. 'I don't have it. Let me go.'

Saito only tightened his grip on her shoulder, fingers squeezing until she cried out with the pain of it, tears sparking hot in her eyes.

'If you really aren't going to tell me, I do have other ways of tracing the pearl,' he said. 'And while in some ways I'd like to spare myself the act of taking yet another life, what is just one more, really? One more little life, added to a lifetime of blood? I could end you so easily.'

'I don't know where the pearl is. I promise I'm telling the truth.'

He gave her another kick, straight to the small of her back, and she couldn't stop herself from lurching forward again, grazing the blade of his knife.

'It was stolen,' she burst out then, hardly aware of what she was saying now in her fear. 'A boy called Theo took it. He has light hair and blue eyes, he's nineteen, and he lives somewhere in the Crescent.'

At last, Saito lifted his knife from her throat, Toshiko's breath coming out in a rush of relief even as he shoved her, letting her tumble to the ground.

As she pushed herself back up to her hands and knees in the dirt, though, she felt something bright within her flicker and fail – some small light she'd been holding on to and nourishing abruptly wink out. She'd betrayed Theo. Saito would go after him now, and he would have no warning.

Still on her knees, Toshiko found herself in the perfect position from which to plead with Saito, to take back her words and insist she'd been wrong – and she was ready to, as well, and surely would have done, had he not knocked the words right out of her mouth with what he said next.

'Bluejay,' he growled, eyes darting up over the battlefield to the horizon, as if Theo might appear somewhere there. 'Why hasn't he brought the pearl to me, then? And why did he leave you alive?'

4.

'I have the dragon pearl,' Theo said, again. The Sensei seemed not to have heard him the first time, absorbed as she was in contemplating the bot.

'Good.' The Sensei turned her attention back to him. 'I was

hoping that would be the case. You could have no other reasonable excuse for demanding an audience with me, especially
considering you've made no progress on the second part of our
deal. The Kawakamis are alive.'

'I realize that,' Theo said, 'but the pearl was what this was all
really about, wasn't it? And now you'll have it back. Surely that's
the most important thing?'

'You've still got six days until your time is up, Bluejay. There's
no reason why you shouldn't accomplish your whole task.'

Instead of replying to her, Theo reached into his jacket pocket
for the pearl, and held it up, so she could get a good look at it.

'I won't kill the Kawakamis,' he stated, and it felt good to
say the words out loud, even as he understood that, in finally
declaring this, he'd definitively forfeited any chance of his ever
earning the vial of dragon tears. 'But I will give you the pearl, if
you guarantee you'll let me live.'

The Sensei actually began to laugh. 'Here you are, in the
heart of my power, surrounded by people who follow my every
command, in a basement you can't escape without a unique key –
and you dare try to *bargain* with me?'

'I was hoping to appeal to your sense of reason, and perhaps
to your better nature,' Theo said, even as his mouth turned dry.
'I've brought the main thing you needed, and surely no one wants
more lives on their conscience than absolutely necessary?'

The laughter died on the Sensei's lips. 'The number of lives on
my conscience, Bluejay, is none of your business.'

'Please. I can't kill them,' he told her, feeling ever more desperate then as a memory came to him, unbidden, of Toshiko smiling
back at him through a handful of golden sparks. 'I can't do it. But
this – the pearl – this is what you want, isn't it?'

The Sensei's gaze flicked from Theo's face to the pearl in his hand. Steeling himself, he took a small step back, away from her, and then another, and then closed his fist tightly around the pearl.

'Look,' he said, speaking quickly now. 'I don't care about the dragon tears anymore. I really don't. I don't even care about going home. But please, if I give you this, will you take the tracker out of my neck? Will you let me live?'

He held his breath as she seemed to consider him from behind her gold-rimmed glasses. Of course he knew how reckless, foolish and desperate it had been to come here and ask her this, but as he'd walked back and forth through the city today, searching his thoughts for some other solution, he hadn't been able to think of a single one. Of course he didn't want to end Toshiko's life, but neither did he want to have to give up on his own, ill-deserved as it might be.

The pearl felt uncomfortably heavy in his fist now, and he suddenly felt so tired, too, of the endless games of survival that Rainshadow City demanded he play so relentlessly, just to buy another hour or two of existence on its shores.

'Look,' he told the Sensei. 'I've done everything I can. Please' – he opened his palm and held out the pearl to her. 'Just take it. Take it and let me live.'

5.

Jun managed to get the injured young woman to the café tent. It was the obvious place to look after those who'd been hurt in the fighting, being the most heavily defended site they had, and Jun hoped others would share his instinct in making it the place where they brought all those who needed help.

He realized all too well now that in the process of rallying the resistance to face the Crows, they'd not made a proper plan for how to take care of the wounded. They'd just been so rushed, and it had also perhaps felt a little too much like bad luck, to start making concrete plans for the harm that the Crows would do to the Keeper's Children's bodies, inevitable as that harm had probably always been.

Clutching a bag filled with Mailee's medical supplies, Jun left those resistance fighters he'd found in the café with instructions for how to look after head injuries, stab wounds and broken bones, and set out again, into the battle. There were wounded people everywhere now, and before more than a couple of minutes had passed, he'd applied a tourniquet to a worrying leg wound, and had sent several more injured Keeper's Children back to the café, helped by comrades.

He kept on down the Gods' Road, moving through the fighting carefully and sticking to the fringes, hoping to stay out of the thick of the violence himself, while maintaining a vantage point from which he could identify those in need.

'Take the wounded to Mailee's café,' he shouted to the Keeper's Children as he went, trying his best to spread the word. 'There are healers and supplies there.'

He'd not gone far, though, when he found himself suddenly halted by a pair of Crows. It took him a moment to recognize the same two young men who'd so nearly captured him before, at the docks – Hiroto and Daichi Santos, the brothers from the ruins of Hanasaki Island.

'Hello again,' said Daichi with a grin and a casual wave, which revealed a full handful of gleaming, spiked rings. 'You seem to be developing a habit of getting in our way.'

Hiroto, next to him, hefted and gripped the chain he was carrying, this one with a sharp-looking sickle swinging forbiddingly from one end. Daichi took a step forwards, curling his hands into viciously barbed fists – and Jun realized then, too late, that he was standing with his back to the corrugated iron and splintered wood of a caved-in house. The Santos brothers as good as had him cornered.

'You don't need to do this,' Jun tried. 'Didn't we already agree to be friends?'

'I gave you one chance,' Hiroto spoke up then. 'That was it. I said so, at the time. One chance to get away and take care of your family. And then you used that chance to come here, and join up with these resistance fighters?'

'You seem to be giving orders, and everything,' Daichi added. 'Are you some sort of leader now?'

'Hang on,' Jun began. 'That's not what's going on here—'

'Don't even try all that bullshit with me again,' Hiroto said, beginning to swing his chain, gathering momentum, the sickle slicing a menacing arc through the air. 'If you really cared so much about your family, then why come back here to the Crescent, of all places, when it's so clearly a lost cause?'

'It's not a lost cause,' Jun shot back. 'It can't be. Too many people's lives are at stake. You lived here yourselves once, didn't you? Is that the calculation the two of you made when you joined the Crows? That the Keeper's Children were a lost cause?'

Daichi only stared back. Hiroto, though, looked away. 'You have no right,' he said to Jun. 'You have no right to tell me that, when from what I hear, you yourself once made a very similar call.'

'And yet here I am,' Jun told him, 'on this side of the battle, today, with a bag full of medical equipment. And there you are, facing me with your weapons, standing on the wrong side of history.'

Hiroto gave a short laugh, filled with scorn. 'Spare me the self-righteousness,' he said. 'If you'd suffered what I've suffered – what my brother and I both suffered, back home on Hanasaki Island, then you wouldn't care a damn about sides of history. You'd just want to survive.'

Perhaps this was true, Jun honestly wasn't sure. Curiously, though, Hiroto didn't look fully sure of the truth of his own words, either. His chain had fallen limp in his hands, and for a moment, doubt hung, palpable, in the air between them. Then the moment was shattered by Daichi.

'Quit talking to this goon,' he told his brother. 'And quit listening to him, too. He's our prisoner. Since when did you listen to prisoners?'

Hiroto turned sideways to look at Daichi – and that instant of distraction was all Jun needed. He barrelled towards the brothers, Mailee's medical bag held protectively in front of his face. If luck was on his side, he'd be able to shove his way between them and out of this tight spot, before either of them could react.

He hadn't quite made it back to open ground, though, before Daichi grabbed for him with his handful of spiked rings. They were as sharp as they looked, and even though Jun was moving fast, Daichi still managed to catch his upper arm, the rings slicing through Jun's jacket to his flesh.

Daichi struggled to get a firm grip as Jun kept trying to pull away – until at last, with a painful wrench and tear away from the rings, Jun finally managed to slip Daichi's hold. He kept running even as he felt the blood begin trickling down his arm. As he went, he heard Daichi exclaiming behind him, sounding almost in shock at what he'd done.

Had Daichi ever properly hurt someone like that with a weapon before? Jun wondered. Perhaps, until now, it had all been simple posturing. How would the experience take him? Would he be any less casual in his attitude towards violence, or would he get a taste for it?

Jun didn't linger to find out. He kept moving, dodging through the hand-to-hand fighting, not letting himself stop to check his wound, though it was beginning to throb now, the warm stickiness of blood soaking his sleeve in alarming quantities.

He was still stumbling his way through the bitter chaos of the Gods' Road, when his eyes caught on a tide of movement in the crowds up ahead. A charge of resistance fighters was running at full pelt towards a group of Crows holding a clutch of Keeper's Children prisoner. With a sudden shock of recognition, Jun saw that it was Ren himself at the front of the charge, leading it with sword in hand.

'Those people are freer than you'll ever be, with your oaths of loyalty to your Sensei,' Ren shouted to the Crows, as he ran to meet them. 'The Keeper's Children will never be your prisoners!'

Just before Ren's sword clashed with the blades of the Crows, Jun abruptly found himself knocked to one side by a Keeper's Child hurtling seemingly out of nowhere, fleeing an attacker – and he fell heavily in the dirt.

He clutched for his bag of medical supplies, desperately trying to keep his grip on its reassuringly sturdy handle as he struggled to regain his feet – and by the time he had, Ren's resistance fighters and the Crows were fully embroiled in their clash. Jun couldn't see Ren himself anymore, but he could hear the captured Keeper's Children cheering, and could see several of them now trying to resist their captors.

'Fight for your freedom,' Ren's voice came through the fray. 'The Crows are cowards. They surrendered their own freedom long ago, to a faceless leader who cares nothing for them. They have nothing to fight for. We can beat them!'

Jun was jogging towards Ren's voice, hoping to help in any way that he could – when, in the melee, he saw one of the Crows whirl around, sword extended, to run a Keeper's Child straight through the heart with the blade. The woman crumpled instantly to the ground. First, a hush descended. Then, the screams began.

Without questioning what he was doing now, Jun increased his pace, running at full tilt towards the fallen woman even as the blood still poured from his own arm. He had to help her, even if it was only to hold her hand as she lost her grip on life.

He had almost reached her, when he was knocked from his feet again – and, this time, the handle of Mailee's medical bag slipped from his fingers. He pushed himself to his knees, looking wildly around for Mailee's bag, only to find a huge man in a Crows' jacket grinning down at him, with a mouth full of glittering gold teeth.

'Lost something?' the man growled. Then he seized Jun's arm, tugging painfully at his wounds as he manhandled him to his feet.

Jun managed one last look back at the fighting behind him, before his captor hauled him away. In that flash of a moment, through the shifting, mounting horror, he finally caught sight of Ren. The leader of the resistance was on the ground, the Crows were advancing on him from all sides, and he was clutching at his leg, his face contorted with pain.

6.

Haru felt the dragon's attention fix on him like a spotlight from out of the sky. He kept waving even as it stopped circling the battle, changing its trajectory to begin the descent right towards where he was still standing watching it, by the barbed-wire fences next to the sea.

Before long, its three pairs of clawed feet were touching down in the dust before him. As the dragon landed, in all its vast, turquoise and bright orange magnificence, Haru took a deep breath.

'I'm sorry,' he began, before the dragon had even had the chance to settle itself fully on the ground. 'You came for the pearl, but I don't have it. I gave it to someone because I thought it would be safe with them, and I was wrong.'

The dragon levelled its gaze at Haru, holding him in the glare of its lamp-like eyes.

And yet I can still feel its magic coming off you, it said.

Haru found himself reeling, then – not at the sound of the dragon's voice, but at the peculiar quality of it. The dragon spoke just as it had done in his dream, in fact, with the words resonating not out loud, but somewhere inside his own consciousness.

If I can still feel the pearl's magic on you, it continued, *that means it cannot have been gone long, at least.*

'It was taken almost a whole day ago,' Haru admitted.

The dragon dipped its glowing gaze at that, and although Haru realized it was probably foolish to try to read human emotions into its expressions, he was sure he could see disappointment, and perhaps even betrayal, written across those fierce, unfamiliar features.

Then you must have a remarkably strong affinity with Sola, to have held on to the power for such a long time, was all it said, though.

Haru pictured the little dragon as it had been in his dream, with its deep blue scales, and miniature, tufted horns. It had seemed so vulnerable in its sickness – and it had trusted him, too, allowing him to lay his hand against its warm neck.

'I'm sorry,' he choked out again. It felt like so far from being enough, and yet he knew, too, that he had more to ask of this dragon. He had good reason for having watched for its arrival all afternoon. He just had to work up the courage.

'I don't know where the pearl is, but I do know who took it,' he began. 'And I can help you find them, but first . . .' He swallowed. It felt so wrong to bargain with the dragon like this, when he had failed it so badly, but what other choice did he have? All around him, blameless people were fighting for their lives. 'But first, will you help us, please? I can't leave my friends like this.'

Only then did the dragon seem to fully register the battle unfolding around them. Haru waited, tense with worry, as it reared, stretching its body to look over the houses behind him, in the direction of the Gods' Road, where he knew the fighting would be fiercest. He tried again to read its reaction as its golden eyes swept their surroundings, and yet, this time, the dragon remained inscrutable.

The people who tortured me and took my child's pearl away, it said. *They wore this same symbol, this sign of two birds. Why have they come to destroy this place?*

'They're the Lucky Crows,' Haru explained. 'And they came to steal my friends' home, and use it for themselves.'

The dragon's eyes flashed. *And the man who took my child's pearl. Is he among them?*

'I think so,' Haru said, with a shiver of fear at the idea that the man he would always think of as Mr Winter, even though he now knew his true name, would surely be somewhere close by. 'Yes, he'll be here.'

The dragon bared its teeth, sharp and jagged as cliffside rock, before lowering itself towards the ground once more, this time dipping its heavy, furred head all the way down to Haru's height.

Climb up, it told him.

Haru could hardly believe what it was asking of him. Hesitant, he reached out. The dragon didn't flinch away. It appeared, in fact, to be waiting.

He laid his palm against its side, taking care to avoid the ropes of raised scar tissue that still criss-crossed its flank – echoes of the wounds carved by Mr Winter's knife. Its scales felt smooth and warm, exactly as the little dragon's had felt, in his dream.

There seemed nothing for it except to try to clamber up. The dragon even helped him, giving him a foothold with one of its clawed feet, and soon, Haru had managed to swing a leg over its neck, shuffling around so that he was sitting with his fingers twined in its bright orange fur.

You know the field, the dragon said. *You will inform my strategy from the sky.*

Haru held on tightly as the dragon began to uncoil itself again, stretching towards where the storm was darkest, over the heart of the Crescent.

7.

Jun was in a clutch of Keeper's Children, being herded down the Gods' Road by the Crows. They were a long way from the main body of resistance fighters now, separated from them by what felt like an uncrossable ocean of conflict. The Crows could only be taking them to one place, Jun knew – to the docks, and to the waiting barges, bound for Hanasaki Island.

The Crows used swords and machetes to keep the Keeper's Children packed close together and moving fast – and these blades were far from being an empty threat. Moments before, a teenage boy armed with nothing but a blunt kitchen knife had been cut down where he stood, and the Crows had left him bleeding out on the ground, his body simply abandoned there to be trampled by all those fighting and fleeing around them. A woman – his mother, Jun had guessed – had launched herself at the man who'd killed him, only to have her throat sliced open, almost casually, as if she'd been nothing more than a piece of fruit. She'd been standing not far from Jun, and he'd been caught by her blood as she'd fallen. He couldn't tell how much of the red soaking his jacket now was hers and how much was his, from where Daichi had gouged him with those rings.

He'd wanted so much to help that woman and her son. He wanted to help everyone here who'd been harmed by the Crows – all of whom now seemed willing to take human life without a second thought. And yet, instead of being the heroic battlefield healer he'd wanted to be, and who would have made Auntie Reiko and Mailee proud, he'd never felt more like a scared kid – too young, frightened, feeble and untrained to take on the responsibility that somebody here surely needed to shoulder. He just hadn't been ready for it, it seemed.

His disordered thoughts strayed again to what Hiroto had told him, in the moments before Daichi had torn into his arm.

If you'd suffered what I've suffered, then you wouldn't care a damn about sides of history. You'd just want to survive.

Was it true? Jun wondered then. He didn't like to think so, but with every passing second that he didn't do anything to stand up to these Crows who were now herding them to the docks, he felt he understood Hiroto's words a little better.

And then from behind him, there came the sounds of a commotion. He whirled on the spot just in time to see Ava appear seemingly out of nowhere, forcing the Crows holding them prisoner to part as she launched herself at the whole group of them, a sword in either hand.

The Crows immediately stopped moving forwards, their focus shifting away from the captured group of Keeper's Children and onto this new attacker. The man with the gold teeth who'd captured Jun swung his blade at Ava in a brutal, hacking motion, like a man trying to fell a tree with an axe.

Even as Jun cried out in warning though, Ava met the blow with her twin swords crossed – and the sound of the clash of metal on metal was harsh enough to split open the afternoon.

Jun watched then, breath held, as Ava managed to heave the Crow's sword back, away from her, and then to spin and parry the blows of two others.

The man with the gold teeth recovered his balance. Flanked by two more Crows, both wielding machetes, he lurched once more for Ava, sword swinging.

Jun watched as she whirled, her swords raised, to deflect all three of their blades in a fast, two-handed motion that looked almost effortless – all while aiming a kick behind her at a fourth Crow who Jun hadn't even noticed, coming up behind her.

She'd discarded her long coat somewhere in the battle, meaning her gang tattoos were now fully on show, the snakes and vines of them rippling with sinew and muscle as she fought relentlessly against these people, to whom she'd once written allegiance all over her skin. Jun felt a stab of shame, then, that he'd been so squeamish earlier about fighting alongside her and the rest of the Jetsam.

'A little help, here?' Ava yelled out as she whirled past him and the other Keeper's Children, a blur of swords and flying hair.

Her words broke the spell of shock that had descended on their group. Two young women broke from the front of their cluster, screaming an improvised battle cry as they brandished their weapons at the Crows around Ava, as if galvanized by her courage. The rest of the captured Keeper's Children surged after them, Jun among them, ready to seize this chance at survival.

And then Jun saw the woman from the Crows who was suddenly coming up behind Ava, sprinting for her, machete raised.

'Ava!' he screamed out.

Ava reacted only just in time, hurling herself forward, away from the blade, and then into a cartwheel kick that caught her assailant on the chin. She flailed her right sword out, stumbling for balance as she tried to keep two more Crows at bay, while at the same time swinging her left blade up, to parry the woman's machete again.

She had almost managed to recover her former poise and control over the melee, when the same blank-eyed young Crow who Jun had noticed amidst their ranks earlier darted forward, too quickly, and slashed his knife up the length of Ava's side, slicing a deep laceration up the right side of her ribcage.

'Fifty sun credits!' he cried out, his free hand punching the air in triumph, as he flicked his knife up and away from her, the blade dripping with blood.

Ava's breath suddenly seemed to be catching in her lungs – she seemed, in fact, to be choking on nothing but air, her expression shifting from one of battle focus, to one of cold panic. And then she was stumbling, struggling even to hold up her swords as she gasped for breath.

The young Crow who'd cut her began to laugh. 'Looks like I've just made my fortune,' he said, preening himself before the others.

Both Ava's swords slipped from her hands then, sharp edges flashing as they tumbled, blades skittering over the dirt. Her hands flew to her wound, fingers turning immediately slick with blood as she pressed on it, and then crumpled to her knees. She still managed to spit on the young man's shoes as she fell – and her saliva, Jun couldn't help but notice, was flecked with an alarming amount of blood.

Her attacker only laughed again, and lifted the foot she'd spat on to kick her in the stomach. 'Traitor,' he said. 'I feel only pride at bringing you down.'

'Wait a minute,' interjected another of the Crows then – an older, taller woman, with a tattoo of a spider on her cheek. She had fully turned away from the Keeper's Children now, and was squaring up to the boy. 'Who says that it was you who brought her down? The Sensei would have to take your word for it.'

Most of the other Crows around them seemed to be having similar thoughts now too, their attention shifting away from the captured Keeper's Children and onto the young Crow who'd hurt Ava, as the reality of the full fifty sun credits began to dawn on the group at large. As if that change in the Crows' focus had been the starting gun to a race, three of the Keeper's Children broke away from the other prisoners, taking their chances in a sprint up the Gods' Road.

'They're getting away,' cried the woman who'd attacked Ava with the machete. 'Don't forget what we came here to do. Get them to the docks, now, or Saito will be wanting our blood.'

This invocation of Saito's name seemed to restore discipline among most of the Crows. And so, even as Ava lay defenceless, eyelids fluttering, at the feet of the last four Crows who wouldn't give up on the fifty sun credits even when faced with the threat of Saito's anger, Jun and the others were herded into an even tighter group and marched, once again, with a bristling forest of Crows' weapons trained on them, towards barges at the docks.

Head bowed, Jun let himself be led away with the rest of the group, leaving the fallen leader of the Jetsam behind. Ava had tried to come to their rescue, and now she was gravely wounded, defenceless and in the hands of enemies, all staking their claims on the reward placed on her head. She deserved their help, he knew. And yet what could he and this small group of untrained, virtually unarmed people do, without forfeiting their own lives? It seemed wild to him now that he'd supposed he could be a leader, a hero – or even just someone who might be able to make the smallest bit of difference to how this battle would go. *If you'd suffered what I've suffered, then you'd just want to survive.*

He realized then that in all of the danger and confusion of the battle, he'd forgotten there was a reward on Ren's head, too. His mind flitted back to the last sight he'd had of the resistance's leader – injured on the ground, with the Crows closing in on all sides. He hadn't heard Ren's voice on the wind for a long while, now. Was it simply a question of distance, and of the storm and the battle being too loud? Or had the promise of sun credits sealed Ren's fate, too?

8.

Haru clung to the dragon's back as it uncoiled its serpentine body, stretching into the currents of the storm. From up here, he could see clearly over the row of houses that had separated him from most of the fighting. So many buildings seemed to be burning now, and yet that suddenly seemed like a small thing, in comparison with the numbers of wounded who were now haunting even the Crescent's narrowest and most peripheral streets.

When everyone had talked about fighting in the meeting earlier, Haru had never quite pictured it like this. He hadn't thought about the burns, or the torn-open skin, or the screams. He could never have imagined the weeping of parents as they held on to broken children – children who had been whole and healthy just moments before.

'My mother should be here,' Haru said aloud. He wasn't even speaking particularly to the dragon anymore. He was simply giving voice to thoughts he felt sure would overwhelm him, if he were to keep them inarticulate. 'She should have come here, to help. She might not understand it, but these people are her people. Lots of them were born here, on the island – and even if they weren't, they probably came here from other islands in the Archipelago, in her Empire. And even if they didn't, it doesn't matter. This is their home, and it's a real place in her city. She has a duty to be here, to protect them. And she isn't.'

Mothers aren't always able to do everything they'd wish to protect their children, the dragon's voice spoke up then, in Haru's mind, surprising him.

'But my mother never protects the right people,' he replied, only realizing just how true the words were as he said them. 'In fact, I think all of this is mostly her fault.'

He wiped the tears from his eyes with his sleeve. Feeling almost unable to bear the injustice of the horror unfolding below him, he turned his gaze up towards the storm instead, looking into clouds that were now crackling with building lightning. And as he did, a new thought occurred to him.

'Are you the little dragon's mother?' he asked.

I am, the dragon said.

'What's the little dragon's name?'

Almost without Haru's realizing it, they had begun to rise even higher over the battlefield. All of the dragon's front feet had left the ground now, and it was continuing to stretch skywards.

Kiri, the dragon replied.

'Kiri,' Haru repeated, trying to keep himself calm as even the dragon's back feet left the ground, sending dust swirling around them while they began to surf the currents of the storm. 'You must be a good mother to have come all the way here, to get his pearl.'

Perhaps, said the dragon, with sadness in her voice.

'What's your name?' he asked. 'I'm Haru.'

And I am Hiranaya.

'I've never heard a name like Hiranaya, before.' Haru was having to shout now, over the wind. It was so strong up here, tugging at his clothes and sending sparks of rain into his face and eyes.

It is an old name, the dragon said. *From the mountains of Muralania.*

'Kei's from Muralania.'

Who is Kei? A friend?

'Kei's better than a friend. I think I trust her more than anyone else in the whole world.' Haru chewed his lip. 'I hope she's okay.' He looked down to the battle again, searching the ground below him for any sign of her.

He had an even clearer view of the Crescent as they rose higher. So many people were hurt. Haru watched as they wept and called out, desperate for help that wasn't coming. There were even people who had simply collapsed, reduced to crumpled forms under the feet of the fighters. He shivered at the thought that he could now be, unknowingly, looking down on the dead.

He could also see several large groups of Keeper's Children being marched through the streets as the Crows' captives. All of these groups were heading in the direction of the docks, where he could see those four barges Ren had talked about, waiting for the prisoners. Haru's eye caught then on the group closest to the docks, and he was sure he could make out Toshiko's brother among them, his blue jacket turned half red with blood.

There were so many people who needed his help – too many to reach, all at once.

'It's hopeless,' Haru said to Hiranaya. 'What can we do, when so much harm has already been done?'

9.

All half-formed thoughts of pleading for Theo's life now vanished, Toshiko dropped to the ground, rolled swiftly away from Saito, and then jumped to her feet, dagger held out protectively in front of her.

Saito smiled, the motion of his jaw stretching the scar on his cheekbone, turning it a livid white. 'You didn't know, did you?'

He laughed – a joyless, grating sound – before stepping neatly to one side as she slashed her dagger uselessly in his direction.

'How trusting you turned out to be.' He shook his head. 'Or perhaps Bluejay deserves more credit. He does have a reputation for being a good liar.'

'I don't believe you,' Toshiko told him. 'It isn't true.'

'Fine,' Saito said. He sounded bored, now. 'Believe what you want. You've told me what I needed, and look' – he sheathed his knife – 'I was telling the truth. I really don't have orders to kill you. I don't even particularly want to. You're not important, and why not spare myself the bad dreams, if Bluejay can take the hit for me?'

Toshiko still didn't dare take her eyes off him for a second. Surely this was only some kind of trick, to distract and weaken her.

Saito really did seem to have lost interest in her now, though. He was looking skywards instead, to where the huge, turquoise dragon was visible once again, rising from the direction of the sea. His eyes narrowed as he watched it. 'I've wasted enough time on you, little girl,' he said, never taking his eyes off the dragon. 'I have another old ghost from my past to attend to.'

With all of Saito's attention still trained on the dragon uncoiling in the heart of the building storm, Toshiko began, slowly, to back away. When, finally, she judged herself to have put a decent stretch of distance between the two of them, she whirled and began to run.

'That's right,' she heard his graveyard voice carry after her as she fled. 'Run away, little girl. But just you wait and see what face death wears, when it does come for you. You might even find yourself charmed by its unusual blue eyes.'

She kept moving, dodging past Crows and Keeper's Children alike, her vision blurring with tears that were falling fast now. She swiped at them as she went, with hands that were streaked with dirt and with blood. Saito had to be lying, she told herself. Theo couldn't belong to the Crows. After all, the Crows were vicious, and senseless, and empty of everything that was good and beautiful in this world. He couldn't be one of them. He just couldn't be.

10.

Haru's sense of hopelessness only increased as he looked down on the battle from the heart of the storm. And then his eyes caught on the part of the Gods' Road where the fighting was at its most dense, and his heart seemed to drop in his chest at the sight of Ren, fallen to the ground, with Crows closing in around him. Ren was swinging his sword wildly at them, keeping them off for the moment, but he didn't seem able to move one of his legs at all. There were some others from the resistance nearby, trying to protect him, but the Crows were repelling them almost effortlessly, all of their attention reserved for the leader. There was only so long, Haru realized, that Ren would be able to survive like this.

'Ren!' Haru cried out, though there was no chance of Ren hearing him, from all the way up here, in the storm.

He thought then of Ren addressing the whole crowd of resistance fighters in the café tent – of all those upturned faces watching him, waiting for him to tell them what the next step was, and trusting him with their lives. He thought, too, of how seriously Ren took the trust these people placed in him. He thought of Kei, calling him *Honeybee*, smiling and playing the weaver's harp as Ren cooked their food by the fire. Even if things were too overwhelming and even hopeless, this was surely somewhere to start.

'Can we help him?' he called to Hiranaya, pointing down to where Ren was still repelling the Crows' blades, though his thrusts with his sword were looking weaker.

Yes, Hiranaya told Haru. *Of course we can.*

The great dragon closed her eyes then, and as her pearl began to shine even more intensely, the storm built to new heights around them. Soon, Haru was sure he could actually feel the Sola surging through it, and Hiranaya channelling that Sola, twisting and compressing it, to almost unbearable pressures.

He clung on, digging his fingers into her fur, as the wind tore at him. His breath caught as the water particles within the swirling cloud around them began to crackle with blue and bright white electrical charge.

Haru had completely lost sight of Ren and the Crows below now. He could only see the battle in flashes, through the storm – the flash of a blade, the slickness of blood on the earth, the crying face of a child. He bent his head to wipe his eyes on his sleeve again, and as he did, the group of Crows surrounding Ren came into view. There were eight of them now, and while they hadn't got to Ren yet, they were close.

The Sola storm continued to build in intensity around them until Haru felt it to be almost unbearable. Then all at once, Hiranaya let go its power, releasing all of the storm's gathered energy in a multi-pronged electrical charge that surged down as lightning, zigzagging towards those same eight Crows below.

Haru closed his eyes just before it struck.

11.

An almighty peal of thunder racked the Crescent, leaving screams and panic in its wake – and then Jun heard a 'cheer beginning to go up, apparently from among the Keeper's Children. It seemed an incongruous sound at first, so wrong in this disaster of a battle as to be almost nightmarish, until one of his fellow prisoners turned to him with the news that had been spreading through the Crescent: the lightning had hit only those wearing the black, logo-stamped jackets of the Crows.

The possible implications seemed almost too huge to fathom. Had it just been luck, or could the dragon really be on their side?

Jun had no leisure to consider the question – a sudden shock of impossible light and then heat surged down to fill the whole world around him, knocking the air from his lungs and throwing him off his feet. Reflexively, he threw his arms up over his eyes, and yet even still, his vision felt as if it were being scorched by an immense brightness, blue and white, as a roar of thunder shook the earth beneath him.

In that moment, and even as the light and the heat subsided, Jun felt certain he'd been struck. He couldn't hear a thing anymore of the battle's tumult – only a muffling blankness, permeated by a faint ringing. His eyes, too, felt as if they'd been seared into permanent blankness by the lightning's brilliance.

And then he became aware that he was still conscious and breathing, and able to crawl and then even to push himself up to his knees. His hearing was still gone, but when he did finally force his eyes open, he found his sight beginning to recover.

On the ground around him were his fellow prisoners – all in similar states to him, struggling up to their hands and knees, blinking in dazed confusion. The Crows who had held them captive, however, were crumpled, their bodies so clearly broken by the force of the multi-pronged strike, their skin covered with burns.

Before Jun knew what was happening, he was being helped to his feet by a Keeper's Child who he hadn't seen before. A whole influx of resistance fighters, it seemed, had come to the aid of the prisoners, charged with new hope and energy by the lightning.

Jun took the man's arm and let himself be led, stumbling, away from the peril of the docks and back up the Gods' Road, towards where the resistance was strongest.

Lightning flashed again, followed by more thunder, which Jun, with his hearing still damaged, only felt as a pulse of pain in his ears. He ducked, hunching as he ran – and yet he needn't have. The lightning had struck elsewhere in the Crescent this time, further inland.

By the time they reached the ring of resistance fighters around Mailee's café, Jun's hearing had recovered sufficiently to be able to hear all the speculations and conjectures that were passing among them now, with fevered energy. Up there, so the rumour went, riding on the dragon's back, was the Emperor's son – the boy who most of them, if not all, had begun to accept as their own in spite of his parentage, having seen how Ren and Kei cared for him.

The Prince has brought us a dragon, they said. *He's brought us a dragon to fight the Crows.*

There was a new sense of purpose among the resistance, now. Everywhere, Jun could see Keeper's Children rushing to stamp out fires, or to help comrades who were still struggling with Crows. And he was still alive, against the odds. He had escaped the horror of a prison barge to Hanasaki Island, and had survived his brush with the dragon's lightning.

He heard a familiar voice rising then, over the mingled disorder of the battle and storm, and he turned to see Ren coming towards them, out of the chaos on the Gods' Road. He was limping, held up on either side by two young men from the resistance, and his right leg was clearly twisted and badly injured, but he was alive, and he still wasn't giving up.

'For the Keeper's Crescent!' Ren was shouting. 'We can win this!'

As Jun and all those around him took up the cry, the sounds of all the mingled voices blurred in Jun's storm-damaged ears, until he couldn't even recognize his own voice in the collective roar.

'For the Keeper's Crescent,' they chanted together. *'We can win this.'*

With his eyes lifted to the sky, then, up to the terrifying, formidable, wondrous creature who had miraculously stepped in on their side, Jun finally began to believe it might be possible.

CHAPTER SEVENTEEN

Making Choices

1.

The Sensei drew closer to Theo, and still he kept holding the pearl out to her, in his open palm. Her eyes narrowed, studying him. At last, apparently satisfied that this was no trick, she reached out and took it.

Theo blinked. The pearl was out of his hands now, literally – he'd finally given up the responsibility of deciding what to do with it. Surely he should feel nothing but relief? The Sensei, for her part, seemed almost jovial as she slipped the pearl into her cardigan pocket.

'It's Ken Saito's, isn't it?' he found himself asking her. 'What will he do with it?'

'It doesn't belong to Ken,' she told him. 'It belongs to me – as, in fact, Ken himself belongs to me. I let him keep it, though, because he will be the one to use it. And also because it helps him.' She looked almost melancholy for a moment. 'Ken deserves as much, after everything he has done on my behalf.'

'When you say that he'll be the one to use it,' Theo asked, 'what exactly do you mean?'

'Goodness, Bluejay. More curiosity. You really would have made an excellent student.' She gave him a particularly sharp sort of look. 'Perhaps you still might.'

Then she walked back over to the table to lift the enormous silver coffee pot with a surprisingly steady hand, and pour herself a cup. She didn't offer any to Theo. As he watched, she took a careful sip before sighing, contentedly. Then, she gestured up at the bot woman, still looming above them.

'When I said that she hadn't been given the gift of life yet, I wasn't being poetic,' she told Theo. 'These bots will be alive, in all ways that matter, because they will run off Sola. You've heard of it? It's the same force that flows through all living things, giving them life. The only difference between my bots and any other living creature, will be that the Sola won't flow into them naturally, as it flows into me, for instance – or indeed into you. Instead, it will be installed industrially within them, in the factory in which they are birthed. We have a source, you see. A mountain ore uniquely rich in Sola. Just a fragment of this ore, inserted into the heart of each bot, will be enough to render it almost as much of a living being as you or I.'

'That's what was in the warehouse,' Theo realized, then. 'That's why I felt so drained, lifting it. And so sick, just being near it.'

'Yes, Bluejay,' she said. 'It wouldn't surprise me at all if you had a peculiar sensitivity towards the ore. You asked me, though, what my consigliere will do with the pearl. The dragon pearl is a conductor of Sola. It allows whoever possesses it not only to sense the Sola around them, flowing like water, but also to conduct and manipulate that Sola – or, we might say, to build dams and channels to guide its flow.'

'Is that how the pearl enhances the abilities of whoever is holding it?' Theo asked, thinking now of what Toshiko had said, back in the Crescent. 'Is it true that it can do that?'

'Indeed.' The Sensei gave him a thin-lipped smile, as she continued to sip her coffee. 'The fact is that many people do happen to have a particular skill or talent, which they access from a highly focused, almost meditative state – a state, that is, in which they are particularly attuned and connected to the flows of Sola in the world around them. The pearl, as a conductor of Sola, serves to heighten this kind of state, and that does, usually, lead to an enhancement of the original skill.'

'So what does the pearl enhance for Ken Saito?'

The Sensei gave Theo a calculating look over her coffee cup. 'I should have thought that would be obvious. My consigliere is famous throughout the island for his ruthlessness, for his lack of compassion, and for his willingness to do anything, no matter how brutal or barbaric, if it achieves my desired ends.' She shrugged. 'The pearl enhances all of these traits, by helping him to forget. I wasn't lying, when I told you it blocked out the nightmares. It's partly why he's so very keen to get it back.'

Theo shuddered, his eyes flitting to the cardigan pocket where she'd slipped the pearl. It seemed almost outrageous that something so comparatively small could achieve something so awful, in the wrong hands.

'I have also been training Ken to use further aspects of the dragon pearl's power,' the Sensei continued. 'And he has, in

recent years, become quite expert in the whole business of ma-
nipulating Sola for many different ends, achieving a level of skill
which will even allow him to use the dragon pearl to tap into the
force flowing through the hearts of my bots. Like this, he will be
able to command the bots simply with his thoughts, and with his
will.' She gave a small, self-satisfied shrug. 'Every conquering
dictator needs a worthy General in the field, after all.'

'Of course,' was all Theo could bring himself to say. Ken Saito,
the remorseless, psychic commander of an army of formidable
bot soldiers. The mere idea was awful enough – and in returning
the pearl to the Crows, he had just facilitated the reality.

The Sensei either didn't notice his disquiet, or didn't care
much about it. 'You were right to prioritize the dragon pearl,'
she told him. 'It is, as you see, quite crucial to our plans, and in
getting it back to us so quickly you have proved your usefulness.
You have not, though, fully earned your freedom – as I'm sure
you realize. As a result, I will keep the tracker in your neck, but
I will take away the countdown.'

With that, she set her coffee cup on the table, and shook back
her right sleeve, to reveal one of the same Comms-Discs that all
the Crows above the rank of footsoldier wore on their wrists. This
one certainly looked like a fancier model than Theo had seen
any of the other Crows wearing, though. It had more buttons,
switches and dials even than Ken Saito's, as well as a shining,
lacquered wood buckle on its strap.

The Sensei frowned down at it, and for a moment, she seemed
to all appearances like a harmless older lady, perplexed by some
new item of technology. Then she pushed a series of buttons,
and her Comms-Disc emitted a triumphant beeping sound.
Immediately, Theo could have sworn he felt better – less like he
carried imminent, impending death within his veins.

'That's done,' she told him. 'The countdown has now stopped.'

'Thank you,' Theo said, only narrowly avoiding the indignity of openly gasping with relief. 'How can I tell for sure, though?'

'The same way you could tell it was counting down,' the Sensei replied. 'You'll have to take it on trust. And don't thank me yet. The tracker is still in your neck, after all, which means you'll have to continue proving yourself useful to me. You won't be escaping my influence any time soon, I'm afraid.'

She smiled. It was a reassuring-looking smile, completely at odds with the words she was to utter next.

'Be assured that I can activate the Hourglass's poison at any time,' she said, 'however far away from me you try to run.'

2.

Ken Saito may have said that he wouldn't be the one to kill Toshiko, but he was a bloodthirsty double-crosser, and Toshiko didn't trust him an inch. She only kept on running, trying to get as far away from him as she possibly could through the racket and turmoil of the fighting, and the chaos brought on by the lightning.

Her eyes found a knot of Keeper's Children up ahead, beating Crows back from a house that was already being eaten by flames. Setting her sights on the relative safety of the group, she put every bit of strength and speed she had left into the sprint.

As she drew nearer, she noticed something odd. Even though, just moments before, the Crows had seemed so completely in control of this battle, the Keeper's Children now appeared to outnumber the Crows in this fight. She saw then too, as she ran, that there were now Crows lying fallen everywhere around her – lifeless, twisted into impossible positions, and with gaping, ragged wounds on show.

And then suddenly, a man's body was sprawled on the ground right in front of her, blocking her path. First, she saw the black jacket of the Crows. Then she saw the scorch marks, and the livid, branching pattern of damaged blood vessels standing out dark against his skin – something that could only have been the work of the lightning. Finally, she noticed how young his ruined face still looked.

She stepped over him carefully, her pulse thudding in her ears and nausea rising in her stomach. This man had been the enemy, she knew. He had come here today to burn homes and to kill the Keeper's Children. Even if his young face had still been animated with life in this moment, even if he'd been begging her for help, it would still have been her duty to the Crescent to leave him here, on the ground – wouldn't it?

She walked on without looking back, despising her own thoughts even as she watched one of the Crows in the fight around the burning house reach forward with both hands to snap a female resistance fighter's neck, as if it were the easiest thing in the world. How she hated this.

And then she realized that at the sight of the dead young man on the ground behind her, she'd completely forgotten to keep running.

She whirled, dagger held at the ready, expecting to see Saito slicing through the smoke and the rain with his curved blade, and ice-cold stare. And yet he wasn't there. He didn't, in fact, seem to be anywhere near her.

The hand holding her dagger began to shake. As she raised her other hand to steady it, she began to wonder if perhaps Saito really had been telling the truth when he'd said he wouldn't follow her. And yet, even as she became aware of her breath starting to come in huge, trembling gulps, as her body registered that she'd somehow managed to escape him, she felt strangely distanced from these physical reactions – far too conscious of the dead, suddenly lying all around her, to experience anything close to genuine relief.

Still holding on hard to the hilt of her dagger, even though she was now shaking far too much for it to realistically be of much use, she turned and jogged the last few yards up to the resistance fighters, still locked in combat with the Crows around the burning house. She'd meant to help them, when she'd started running over here. Now, she'd never felt less eager to fight in her life – and they seemed to be doing okay without her help, anyway. There were a couple of Jetsam among them, fighting hard and fast on either side of the formation.

Instead of joining the defensive arc around the house, she ducked behind it, to join those who were working to put out the fire. Even through the flames, she could see that, like many of the Crescent's dwellings, this house shared its rough layout with Auntie Reiko's old home – a back room for sleeping, a front room for eating, and two windows looking out onto a front yard. Blinking, coughing and squinting with the smoke and the heat, Toshiko tried not to think too hard about the extent of the damage that had already been done to this little home, or about whether those who'd lived in it would even still be alive to return to it, if this nightmare ever subsided. Instead, she seized a sandbag from a nearby pile, and began throwing its contents over the flames.

Only now, absorbed in this desperate yet repetitive activity, did Toshiko let herself think back once more to what Saito had told her, in response to her desperate confession that Theo had stolen the pearl.

Perhaps she'd known for a while, and had simply chosen not to see it. It would certainly explain why he'd run away, anyway.

Did it explain everything, though? Did it explain the warmth of his lips on hers, or why he'd given her this jacket she was still wearing, and told her about his homeland as they'd eaten chicken satay by the sea? Did it explain why he'd found blankets for her when she'd been cold? And why he'd hesitated, too, when she'd offered him the pearl, sitting on his hands and asking her to stop trying to get him to take it?

Why did he leave you alive? Saito had questioned. She found herself desperately wanting to know the answer to that now, too.

The flow of her thoughts was cut short by her sandbag finally running out of sand. She turned away from the heat of the blaze to grab another, and in doing so, found her eyes drawn back to a shadow on the ground, just a few feet beyond the fighting. Looking at it from here, it could have been anything – a discarded coat, a pile of trash, some sort of animal. Toshiko knew, though, that it was the body of the young Crow she'd stepped over on her way here, dead after being struck by lightning.

She found herself sending her thoughts out to that crumpled body, through the afternoon storm light. *Why did you join the Crows?* she wanted to ask. *And once you had, was there any part of you left that was still just you, not belonging to them at all?*

Her questions, of course, were answered only by the sounds of the battle, as the living still fought with each other for the ground on which the dead young man lay.

3.

Even from high up like this on Hiranaya's back, Haru still wasn't quite able to avoid seeing the deaths on the ground below. The Crows seemed willing to kill anyone who got in their way, and of course, they weren't the only ones dealing out death anymore, either. The triumph he'd felt as Hiranaya had first summoned the lightning had curdled to sickness at the sight of the twisted little bodies of the Crows whom that lightning had actually struck, their upturned faces like a scattering of teardrops through the wreckage down below.

And yet he didn't beg Hiranaya to stop. He didn't even suggest it. He only clung tight to her flame-orange fur and looked on, even pointing out another group of Crows, clustered around a crumpled shape he couldn't avoid recognizing as Ava.

The lightning did its work. As it subsided, and Hiranaya soared on to find new targets below, Haru saw one of the Jetsam running over the scorched ground to Ava's side. He realized then that he hadn't seen Ava move at all since he'd spotted her – not even when the lightning had blasted all around her. He could only hope this help hadn't come too late.

He found himself thinking, again, of the bodies of the Crows, and of how not so long ago, Ava had been a Crow herself. How was he to know that those people whom Hiranaya's lightning had just killed hadn't been capable of change, like her? It suddenly felt like far too much power to be able to make the choice of saving her life over theirs, as he'd just done. And yet, if he were offered that choice again, he wasn't sure he'd do anything differently.

He just hoped so much that Kei would think he and Hiranaya were doing the right thing up here – or, failing that, that they would at least be able to keep her safe. He kept his eyes trained on the ground, searching for her with renewed focus, even despite how much he wanted to look away from all the horror still unfolding down there. He would never forgive himself if she were in danger and he missed the chance to protect her.

Fighting the Crows had become about more now, too, even than protecting Kei, and all the individual people he knew among the Keeper's Children. The Keeper's Crescent felt important to him now, simply for its own sake. Back when he'd been wearing the pearl, he'd been able to see so many Sun Spirits here – more of them in this small space than he could imagine living anywhere else on the island.

Normally, too, he was only able to pick up impressions from people. The longer Haru stayed in the Crescent, though, the more he found that he was able to feel a clear atmosphere coming off this whole place. It was a little different to the feelings he usually got from individuals – more mixed up – but it was still undeniably there. It was sea salt, and lighthouses, and safe harbours in storms. It was shelters on mountainsides, footsteps to follow and guiding hands. It was hope. And it was, Haru was beginning to understand, something that had been baked into this patch of land by everyone who called it home – and by everyone who had done so, too, in generations gone by. Maybe, he thought now as he kept watching from above, through the raindrops blurring his vison, maybe that's what it truly meant, when people said this place was under the Keeper's protection.

This new feeling and understanding had kept the protests from his lips, anyway, when Hiranaya had sent down the lightning. It even guided him now to point out another group of Crows, running towards a small, wooden house with flaming torches in their hands. Of course Haru didn't want to kill anyone, but too much hope had been poured into this place by generations of Keeper's Children for him to watch what the Crows were doing to it now, and not try to fight back.

He still kept his eyes screwed tight shut though, as Hiranaya drew on the Sola of the storm once again, to send more lightning down to strike those Crows. He only reopened his eyes when he could feel her moving on – and yet he was still in time to see that

none of them had made it to the house. He found himself wanting
to scream as the last of the group still standing fell forward onto
his knees, the burning torch in his fingers following the pattern of
those of his fellows as it tumbled to the ground, and winked out.

As Hiranaya flew onwards, Haru wondered then if this was
what it would feel like to be Emperor – and if this was how it felt
for his mother, even, every day. This feeling of finding yourself
doing awful things, when all the while, you'd only hoped to do
what was right. And of facing decisions, too, in which there were
only bad options, and yet still having to choose one option and
act on it, because to do nothing would be even worse.

4.

'You have more tasks for me, then,' Theo said to the Sensei.

His fingers found the lump of the tracker under his skin
again – still there, still threatening his existence – as something
like despair scuttled over his heart.

The Sensei nodded. 'I will have, yes.'

'But I don't have to kill the Kawakamis?'

The Sensei shrugged. 'Events have moved faster on that particular front than I anticipated. In all likelihood, the Kawakamis
are already dead.'

'You can't know that,' Theo said, his throat tightening as he
wondered if it were true. Had the Crows reached the Crescent
already? And where was Toshiko now?

'Oh Bluejay,' the Sensei said, giving him a shrewd kind of look.
'I hope you didn't get too attached.'

Suddenly then, Theo felt as if he could see his situation with a
new kind of clarity – a clarity that had eluded him, ever since he'd
joined up with the Crows. He was still alive, yes, and was now more

likely to live beyond the end of the next six days. And yet he would always be at the Sensei's mercy – something that had arguably been the case even before Saito had put the tracker in his neck, dependent as he had been on the Crows for his continued survival in the city. Now, this situation would never end. He'd betrayed the trust of people he cared about, only to prolong his precarious existence in what essentially amounted to a state of slavery. And not only that, either, but he'd helped the Sensei build an army that could inflict Gods knew how much more suffering on the world.

Perhaps Toshiko had been right. Perhaps there were more important things in this world than simply staying alive at all costs.

He studied the Sensei carefully now. She was still fiddling with the Comms-Disc on her wrist, tapping at the buttons as if trying to exit whatever mode she'd got it into, to disable the Hourglass. While she was absorbed in this, the fingers of her right hand brushed the cardigan pocket containing the pearl, and the ghost of a satisfied smile danced over her face.

'I must say,' she said as she continued to tap at the Comms-Disc, 'it was very useful of you, too, Bluejay, to infiltrate that rebel meeting last night. The acoustic data from your Hourglass enabled us to identify some of the Crescent's key ringleaders, as well as to find a young woman – a traitor from our ranks by the name of Ava Song – who we've been hoping to eliminate for years.' She looked up then at last, fixing him with a particularly penetrating look. 'I was able to offer some quite appealing rewards, which should mean that these agitators are eliminated by the end of the night. And it was all thanks to your help, Bluejay. What I would like to know now, though, is whether or not that help was deliberate? Did you mean for us to listen to that meeting? Or was the intelligence-gathering you did there rather more accidental?'

She went back to tapping her Comms-Disc, seemingly in no

rush for an answer. The rush of shame Theo felt at her words, though, made him reckless. She might be the ruthless boss of an organized crime syndicate, but she was also a little old lady with no bodyguards present – and she was momentarily distracted, too. It was surely now or never.

He'd made the wrong decision in coming back here, and giving her the pearl. He knew this now, beyond any doubt. And he knew, too, that he had to do everything in his power to set things right. He lunged at her, going for the cardigan pocket, and for the pearl.

5.

The gashes Daichi had gouged in Jun's upper arm were still bleeding. Ducking into the café in search of a bandage, as well as to check on all the wounded here, Jun was glad to spot Mei sitting on the far side of the café from the entrance – still safe, and absorbed in her hairclip computer. She was sitting, in fact, at exactly the same table at which he'd left her, Mochi now dozing at her feet.

Around her, Mailee's café had begun to fully transform into an improvised field hospital. There were injured people everywhere, stretched out on blankets and futons, as a small but busy team of Keeper's Children used Mailee's salves, bandages and wound washes to help as best as they could. It was just like Mailee, Jun considered now, to have provided the means for the Keeper's Children to look after one another, even when she herself was so far out of reach. The only thing her supplies would lack would be the kakogan dust she'd so openly despised. With a stab of guilt at even having the thought, Jun did wonder if they could have used some of the painkiller, now. Many of these Keeper's

Children were clearly suffering badly, many so gravely injured that kakogan dust's long-term addictive qualities sadly seemed a very abstract thing to be worrying about, in their cases.

Scanning the lines of wounded, Jun noticed, with a jolt of relief, that Ava was there among them. By some lucky chance, it seemed the Crows hadn't beaten her, after all. She was lying on a stretcher close to the fire while a woman tended to her wounds – and though pale and unconscious, she was breathing.

As Jun took a moment, then, to bind his injured arm, he couldn't help but notice that even as the very air within the café tent grew thick with all this urgency and suffering, Mei didn't seem at all interested in helping any of these people around her. His exasperation only ticked up a level, too, to see the small pile of the resistance's weapons – including the only three bows they had in their possession – still lying on the ground beside her, where they'd been left behind, in all the confusion of the Crows' early invasion. After everything he'd seen outside, Mei's apparent obliviousness to something so crucial as these weapons felt like a direct affront. She could at least have given them to a resistance fighter to distribute.

With his arm finally bandaged, Jun marched right up to her table and, with an effort, managed to bite back any direct accusations, simply asking her instead:

'What are you doing?'

'I suppose you realize you're covered in blood,' Mei replied, not even looking up from her screen. 'I would be concerned, but seeing as you've got enough energy left to be annoyed with me, I'm guessing that not much of it is yours.'

He'd tried his best to keep his tone neutral, but apparently Mei knew him too well for that. 'And what if I'm right to be annoyed?' he ventured.

'Oh, spare me,' she replied, still typing, before finally looking up at last with an exasperated sigh. 'Look,' she told him then. 'We have different areas of expertise, remember, brother?'

Confused, Jun only blinked at her sullenly.

'You're good at working with people, while I prefer computers,' Mei said, as if addressing a difficult child. 'Ask me again. Ask what I'm doing, but ask it genuinely this time.'

Jun sighed. Only Mei could still manage to tell him off in the midst of a literal battle. 'What are you doing?' he said again, and this time, his voice was free from any hostility.

'I've hacked into the barges waiting at the docks.'

He must have still looked confused, because she rolled her eyes and said, 'You remember? The ones that were meant to take us off to our miserable, painful deaths on Hanasaki Island? Well, while they're mostly manually operated, powered by sails and ropes and all the usual ship-building stuff, they also all happen to have computerized navigation systems – which is interesting on two counts.'

'And why is it interesting?' Jun asked, in obedience to Mei's arched eyebrow.

'Why thank you for asking. One' – Mei held up a finger – 'it suggests that whoever has been tasked with sailing them to Hanasaki Island needs the help of a computer to find their way there. And two' – she held up a second finger – 'it's especially interesting, because these computerized navigational systems are all conveniently linked into the Crows' network.'

Slowly, understanding began to dawn on Jun. 'When you say the Crows' network—' he began.

'I mean the same network the Crows use for the Comms-Discs that I already hacked into, to mess with their communications – which is something I'm still doing, by the way. You're interrupting me.' Mei's eyebrow ascended even higher, a perfect arc of disdain. 'But back to the barges,' she said. 'I managed to access their navigation systems, and to scramble their coordinates. So even if it does all go to hell outside, and we do all end up on a charming boat trip out to the north of the Archipelago, whoever's piloting us will have a hard time finding their way to Hanasaki Island now, at least.'

All indignation vanished, Jun felt his face break into a grin.

'You're a genius,' he told her.

'I know,' Mei replied, going back to her computer.

She typed a few more commands into the keypad, pressed 'Enter', then sighed. 'Although, for once, maybe I'm not quite genius-like enough. I still can't reach that barge that already left for Hanasaki Island, at all.' She bit her lip. 'It must have a matching navigation system to the four barges at the docks, but it's out of range of the City Web. And I can't figure out what to do about that.'

'You've still done a lot more to help against the Crows than I have,' Jun told her. 'I've been trying my best, but out there it's just ...' he trailed off. Trying to make Mei understand the full extent of what was going on in the battle wouldn't help her to concentrate, he realized. And she needed to concentrate, if she was going to keep going in this work that really was serving the resistance. 'I just ... think what you've managed to do already is amazing enough,' he finished.

'Yeah, well. I'm not sure Mailee and everyone on board that first barge would agree,' Mei sighed.

Jun watched his sister work in silence for a few moments longer, before shaking himself. This battle was far from over yet.

'I'm going to see what I can do to help some of these people,' he told Mei, gesturing over at the lines of wounded, resting on stretchers and blankets around the fire.

Mei seemed so absorbed in her work that he thought she might not even reply. She did look up from her screen then, though, and when she did, her sangfroid only faltered a very little as she asked, 'All that blood on your jacket – I was right, wasn't I? It isn't really yours, is it?'

He shrugged. 'I'm fine,' he told her. 'Don't worry about me.'

She gave him a long stare then, as if trying to bore through his eyes and search his mind for the truth of this statement. A bystander might have thought she was angry with him. He knew enough about Mei, though, to finally see how afraid she was.

'I'm fine, really,' he said again, a little more gently this time. 'I'll be just over there. There's a ring of resistance fighters outside the café, too, circling us. We'll be okay.'

Mei nodded. 'Just … don't do anything stupid,' she said. 'They kept bringing in more broken people – dead bodies, even, sometimes.' She shook her head, looking fiercer than ever. 'I was here on my own,' she continued. 'And you're so terrible at fighting, Jun. I was terrified that sooner or later, one of them would be you.'

6.

Lunging at the Sensei, Theo didn't even manage to make it within arm's length of her before a sharp agony unlike anything he'd experienced exploded through his skull. He collapsed to the floor with a yell, dimly noticing that she hadn't even glanced up from her Comms-Disc. The pain continued, beating at his temples from within, in fresh, excruciating waves – until he found himself literally writhing and screaming on the floor as she tapped at a few last buttons, nodding in satisfaction.

At last she looked up, turning her attention back to him, and the pain abruptly stopped. Theo let out an involuntary gasp of relief, but found himself incapable of doing anything more for the moment, other than lying flat on the blessedly cool floor. The pain had only lasted a few seconds, but he could feel his whole body now clammy with sweat.

He was aware of the Sensei blinking down at him as he tried to summon the strength to get back to his feet.

'Did you do that?' he managed to choke out, through his shock.

'Still asking questions, even now,' the Sensei observed. 'I have to say, I almost admire you, Bluejay. I would admire you, in fact, if your curiosity wasn't coupled with such obvious idiocy.'

Theo groaned. 'I don't know,' he replied. 'I feel like that was my first real moment of non-idiocy, so far as you're concerned.'

At last, he managed to push himself to his hands and knees, and to shove his hair back, out of his eyes. It was hardly a formidable show of strength, but at least he could now face her from a vaguely upright position.

Immediately, even though the Sensei hadn't even so much as glanced down at her Comms-Disc, he felt another wave of pain assault his temples. He sagged on his knees and clutched at his skull, but managed to stop himself from falling fully back to the ground this time, at least. This pain was perhaps a little less acute, but it also somehow seemed more pervasive. It was a kind of agony that felt as though it could endure.

'How are you doing this to me?' he asked, between gritted teeth.

'I've told you I used to be a teacher. Did you never wonder what I was a teacher of?' said the Sensei, in reply. 'For someone so curious, it seems a fairly elementary question to have failed to ask. I happen, Bluejay, to be a teacher of the manipulation and control of Sola – something that means that I am somewhat expert in the matter of controlling the Sola flowing through you and around you, and can easily guide it to suit my needs.'

Even through the throbbing in his skull, Theo began to feel his thoughts splinter and reform, as something close to a revelation began to inflict itself upon him.

'Wait,' he stammered, 'just what is it that you mean?'

'Did you never suspect this could be my subject area?' the Sensei continued. 'How did you think my consigliere became sufficiently expert in the art of using Sola to control a whole army, using simply his mind? For years, now, Ken has been my only student, but in my youth, I taught many a gifted mage to use their power. I wasn't lying when I said that in many ways, you'd have been an ideal student, Bluejay. You were born with the requisite abilities, after all.'

Theo forced himself to look up at her properly then, through the pain. He found himself both utterly shaken and yet also somehow now entirely unsurprised to discover that the light grey irises of her eyes were ringed with gold – with the very same gold that he'd seen before, in fact, illuminating his own eyes.

'Are you telling me that you have the Gift, too?' he asked, reaching for the words through his agony.

The Sensei raised an eyebrow. 'Well, I would never refer to my abilities by such a foolish name, of course. And I'm doing a lot more now than simply *telling* you, too. Surely you don't think this headache is natural?'

'But why didn't you say something before?' Theo all but cried out then, in reply. 'I thought I was the only one, in the whole world. You let me believe it.'

'Ah,' said the Sensei, with a new coldness in her voice. 'But what did I owe, to you? You're still only a footsoldier, Bluejay. Don't forget it.'

'And what about Ken Saito?' Theo found himself unable to stop asking, even as the pain surged. 'You said you were teaching him. That you've kept him within your control, ever since he was a child. Is he like me, too? Does he also have the Gift?'

'No.' The Sensei shook her head. 'I didn't train Ken because he was a gifted mage. After all, only a fool would appoint a General who could ever come close to rivalling her own power. I trained him because I trust him completely, and also because I have more important things on which to focus my mind and my abilities than simply issuing instructions to my troops. You see, Bluejay, with the help of an object like the dragon pearl, it is possible to train even those who aren't born with any clear abilities in the art of channelling Sola. They just need to have some level of latent natural aptitude – and most people do tend to, you know. Those with no sensitivity at all to Sola are almost as rare as those born truly gifted.'

The pain in Theo's skull built further until it began to feel simply too much, impossible to bear. He yelled out in protest, and tried to lunge for her again, even though he could barely see, barely move with the pain – thinking only now to try to make her stop.

The Sensei took a small step back, dodging his flailing efforts with little difficulty.

'You'll forgive me if I now secure you a little more thoroughly,' she said. 'And you'll be glad to know that once your new restraints are in place, the pain in your head can stop. Some of my operatives will then shortly be along to escort you to the torture suite. I can't promise your stay there will be pleasant, but it's a fair penalty, I think, for the disobedience you've chosen to show towards me this afternoon, Bluejay.'

Almost before she'd finished speaking, Theo began to feel as if the very air surrounding him had acquired greater mass and density, and was pressing in on him from every direction. Soon, he could barely move. Even breathing properly seemed to be becoming difficult.

And then, at last, the pain in his head stopped – just as suddenly as it had begun, as if the Sensei had simply flicked a switch.

Immediately, Theo began to struggle against the invisible pressure she was using to restrain him – and yet he found it to be even more intense than he could have imagined. It took all of his strength just to move his fingers and toes.

He sent his gaze darting back and forth throughout the room, searching for anything at all that might help him to escape from this terrible position in which he'd found himself, kneeling and trapped by the kind of power he'd come to believe he would never find – and yet which gleamed out at him now, unmistakable, in the bright gold malevolence of the Sensei's eyes.

7.

Haru clung on tightly as Hiranaya wove amid the fighters on the ground. He'd persuaded her to descend from the skies, certain he'd seen Kei down here, and wanting to whisk her up to relative safety on the dragon's back. And yet, now that they were actually down here, there seemed to be no sign of Kei anywhere, anymore.

'She has to be somewhere nearby,' Haru insisted. 'I'm sure of it.'

Hiranaya kept moving through the fighting, using her claws and whipping tail to sweep aside any Crows still threatening the Keeper's Children, and working to break their resolve with her roar and her bared teeth.

'It's the Emperor's son!' the Keeper's Children called out, as they saw Haru perched up on her back. Either that, or – 'It's the Keeper, come to save us!'

And Haru supposed it was true that he must look a little like the Keeper, still in his blue robe from the party in the Palace gardens. The idea that these people might mistake him for a God would have made him laugh, though, if he hadn't been feeling so shaken up by the violence of the battle around him to do anything of the sort. As it was, he was just grateful to see their smiles as they caught sight of him and Hiranaya, as well as to see that same hope he'd felt emanating so strongly from the Crescent sparking to life again in their eyes.

Where was Kei, though? He needed to know she was safe. And, more than that, he needed her reassurance, and the warmth and shelter her arms could always provide, whatever terrible things might be happening beyond their circle of protection. And yet there were so many people out here, and Hiranaya was now moving too quickly for him to see anything clearly as she snaked through the crowds, rushing to defend any Keeper's Children in trouble.

Haru was just going to ask her to slow down so that he could look for Kei more carefully, when she jolted to a stop anyway, nearly throwing him from her back as she let out a roar of un-mistakable pain and rage.

'What is it?' he asked her. 'What's happened?'

She didn't answer, only turning, instead, to face the cause of the problem. And there, grinning up at them, was Mr Winter. He held a gleaming, curved knife in his hand, and fresh blood was dripping from the blade.

'What luck to find you both here,' he said, before looking up to grin specifically at Hiranaya, his teeth like a row of tombstones. 'You remember me, don't you?'

Before Hiranaya could respond, though, he'd raised his knife and slashed at her flank. Haru half expected to see the blade simply glance off her scales, as he'd seen the weapons of the other Crows doing, as they'd moved through the fighting on the ground. Instead, though, Mr Winter's knife sliced a bloody gash into Hiranaya's flesh. From where he was sitting, perched up by her neck, Haru had to cling tight to her fur as she reared, howling, whirling her tail in Mr Winter's direction. Mr Winter merely stepped back, moving almost elegantly to allow the muscled, spiny mass of it to fly past him harmlessly, causing nothing more than a slight ruffle of his hair.

Haru didn't understand why Hiranaya was suddenly so clumsy and uncertain. She'd been so fearless with the other Crows, and yet now she was cringing, almost, before Mr Winter, sinking low to the ground. He could even feel her muscles trembling beneath him, as if she were losing the strength to hold herself upright. The lightning storm she'd built overhead was waning, too, the clouds beginning to clear to reveal a lurid sunset as the light of her pearl grew dimmer.

She roared again – a sound of pure, frustrated anguish – and at last Haru understood what was wrong.

'His knife!' he began to shout, pointing to Mr Winter, hoping one of the nearby Keeper's Children might hear him. 'Get his knife! It's poisoned!'

Either no one could hear him over the noise of the battle, or the task of challenging Mr Winter was a greater one than even the bravest resistance fighter was willing to take on.

'It's nothing to worry about,' Mr Winter said then, catching his eye, making Haru shiver. 'It's only poisonous to dragons, and even then, it isn't lethal – or it probably isn't, at any rate. She's worth more to me alive, you see, for the moment. This coating on the blade just makes it a little easier for me to get what I want. She remembers it, I'm sure. Don't you, you hideous beauty?'

Hiranaya made a swipe for Mr Winter with her claws, but he dodged easily. The poison had made her slow, while Mr Winter's own reflexes were as alarmingly quick as ever.

'Don't even think about it,' he said now, bringing his knife down again to slice a long, curving cut down the length of her side. Blood filled the wound, dripping down Hiranaya's flank, and Haru cried out in dismay as she slumped fully forward, falling hard in the dust, the glow of her pearl now fainter than ever.

Still clinging to her neck as she lay suffering, Haru had never felt quite so small or so useless before, unable to help this glorious being of air and water, after she'd saved so many of his friends' lives.

'You can't do this,' Haru cried out anyway, to Mr Winter. 'I won't let you.'

And yet Mr Winter didn't seem to be listening. He was suddenly distracted, glancing around at the nearby Crows, all of whom were acting oddly, too. They'd begun backing away from the Keeper's Children, gathering in groups and shouting things to each other that Haru couldn't quite hear through all the battlefield's commotion. Mr Winter began furiously tapping at the communicator on his wrist. It didn't seem to be doing what he wanted it to though, and eventually, with a yell of frustration, he tore it off and threw it to the ground.

'It's the Imperial Army,' Haru finally heard one of the Crows shouting. 'The Imperial Army is coming!'

The Imperial Army – that meant his mother, surely, or her troops at least. Could she really be coming here? For what reason?

Haru didn't have time to wonder further. Mr Winter's expression had hardened with new resolve. Carelessly, without even seeming to think about the pain he was causing, he slashed at Hiranaya one more time, tearing another angry gash through her hide, and sending more dark red blood gushing out, to mar the triumphant turquoise of her gleaming scales. She howled where she lay – fully flat on the ground now, seemingly unable to muster any strength to try to resist, or even to move.

Not even pausing to survey the damage he'd done, Mr Winter strode towards where Haru was still sitting, up on her back. Moving fast, he reached up to seize the loose material of Haru's blue robe and tugged, hard. Haru realized he couldn't keep holding onto Hiranaya without pulling painfully on her fur, and so he let himself slide down to land hard in the dirt at Mr Winter's feet. Before he could even rub his bruises, Mr Winter had hauled him to his feet.

'I'll be back for you later,' Mr Winter spat in Hiranaya's direction. 'When this is done, I'll have your pearl for my collection.'

Then he was off, his grip cutting into Haru's right arm as he dragged him roughly through the battlefield, moving so fast it was all Haru could do not to stumble.

8.

In spite of all his efforts at struggling against the Sensei's invisible restraints, Theo remained stuck on his knees in front of her. The sudden pressure of the air that she'd sent to press in all around him was simply too intense to resist. Even with a maximum of effort, he found himself unable to achieve more than the smallest twitches of his muscles – it was difficult, even, to blink. And yet he was increasingly aware, too, that with every second that passed, the Crows she'd summoned here to take him away to her 'torture suite' were surely getting nearer.

The Sensei, for her part, appeared to be rather enjoying herself now that she'd got him safely secured. It didn't seem to be costing her much exertion, at least, to maintain these restraints. As he watched, she reached for her coffee cup again, leaning against the table's edge as she sipped from it delicately.

'Oh dear,' she said, gazing back at him as a small smile played over her lips. 'Poor Bluejay.'

The curious thing, Theo realized then, was that she did sound almost genuinely disappointed, although certainly not disappointed *for* him. Instead, she sounded disappointed *in* him, as if she'd expected better – and just that hint of a feeling was enough to shake Theo out of his mounting alarm, and to give him an idea. Clearly, he was approaching this situation in the wrong way.

First, he forced himself to stop struggling, and to slow his breathing. Then, when he felt as if he might just be physically calm enough for it to work, he closed his eyes and tapped into the Gift. Immediately, he was able to sense the vibrations of energy in the bonds that the Sensei was using to hold him. He was surprised to discover that while they might be strong and dense, they were also far more fluid than he'd expected, the energy within them washing around him almost like water. Having acknowledged and explored the bonds in this way, he coaxed his mind to ignore them, just for a moment, as he used the Gift to reach further out into the room, trying to find something here that might help him.

The other frequencies in the room weren't so very unusual in themselves. He could feel the movements of the air, for instance, and the gentle vibrations of the wood of the table and work benches, as well as the low hum of the stone floor. This was all more or less as he would have expected – especially given the lack of windows, the closed door, and the fact of there being no other living things present here, other than himself and the Sensei. What certainly wasn't expected, though, was the way all of these currents of energy seemed to be bending and gathering around the Sensei. It was as if she were a magnet, pulling them all towards her.

Experimentally, Theo isolated one of these golden, arcing air currents, and gave it a gentle tug. It yielded only slightly, before snapping back into place around her, with its fellows. She grinned.

'You're understanding a little better now, I see.'

'So you were born with the Gift, too?' he said, still hardly believing the words as he said them. 'You really are like me?'

The Sensei laughed – a jarringly light, almost musical sound. 'No, I am not *like you*,' she replied. 'At one time, many years ago, I may perhaps have resembled you a little. Since then, though, I have spent many decades honing and understanding my powers, while you, on the other hand, seem to have chosen to spend your short life using your abilities for little more than moving furniture.'

'But you said you used to teach people,' Theo persisted. 'Does that mean there are others like this too, who were born with abilities? Where are they?'

The Sensei took another sip from her little silver cup as she considered his question, then gave a nonchalant shrug. 'Well, Bluejay, I would imagine that they're all over the world, just like any other randomly chosen set of people. Many, I'm sure, conceal their abilities to fit in with their peers – as you might have done, had you been wiser. Equally, I've heard of some mages disappearing from their communities completely, and living alone in the wilds. Many, though, do manage to find themselves a teacher, particularly if they happen to be born somewhere where their abilities are encouraged, rather than ostracized.'

'A teacher like you, you mean?' he asked.

'Yes,' she affirmed. 'A teacher like me.'

She drained her coffee, and set the empty cup on the table. The gesture seemed worryingly final, to Theo. He wondered how far away those Crows were now, coming here to take him away. His mind returned again to those words of hers – *torture suite* – as he remembered, too, how the Emperor had threatened Toshiko with the oil tank, back in the Palace. He had no doubt that the Crows' methods would be worse than that, by far.

As he'd been talking with the Sensei, he'd let his perception of the room's frequencies dwindle. Now, with an effort, he tuned back in to them again – except that this time, instead of sending his awareness broadly outwards, he focused in on the bonds holding him, paying attention to the particular rhythms of their movement and flow. To directly resist something this strong would surely only lead to failure. If he could divert the flow of the energy within them, though, by offering it an easier, alternative route to follow, instead of around his limbs, then that might just work, he was almost sure of it. He would have to be quick, though. As soon as the Sensei figured out what he was doing, he was certain she'd find a way to block it.

'So where are these places, in the world, that have lots of teachers of Sola?' he asked her now, hoping to distract her with the question.

'There are pockets of teachers everywhere,' she answered. 'Anywhere where mages are permitted to practise their craft in the open. There are many, for instance, behind the walls of Muralania.'

Theo's eyes were open, as if focused on her, but he was barely listening to what she was saying now. Instead, he was concentrating furiously on visualizing a pathway – something golden, wide, free-flowing, easy. A road drenched in sunlight, winding gently downhill. *Here it is*, he silently urged the Sola flowing thick and oppressive around him. *Take the easier route. Doesn't it look lovely?*

'Pockets of teachers?' he said, aloud. 'Does that mean there are schools?'

The Sensei almost guffawed at that. 'Nothing so ridiculous. But sometimes a group of mages band together, or develop a distinct and shared approach to our art, which they choose to pass on to their students . . .'

It was working. The energy binding him was flowing away down the path he'd created for it, and Theo couldn't keep the grin from his face as he felt the space around him finally beginning to lighten.

At last, free of the Sensei's restraints, he jumped to his feet – and how satisfying it was to see her staring at him with an expression approaching genuine shock.

'How did you do that?' it was her turn to ask.

'Must be all that practice moving furniture,' he replied.

9.

The house Toshiko had been struggling to save had finally stopped burning. Far too much damage had been done, with all the furniture and belongings within well beyond salvaging, but she hoped, still, that there might be something left here in the ruins that could be built upon. Feeling exhausted, suddenly, and light-headed with smoke inhalation, she found it was all she could do to sit on the ground and stare at the wreck of it – a burnt-out shell surrounded by ash and sand, and mud formed by the run-off of water that they'd hurled at the flames. A circle of resistance fighters still surrounded the site, but for the first time all after-noon, this defensive measure didn't feel necessary. The Crows were backing off, retreating into groups, shouting to each other. For a moment, Toshiko thought a miracle had happened – that the Crows were leaving the Crescent, and the Keeper's Children had won the day. And then, she heard what they were saying.

'The Imperial Army is coming!'

Getting to her knees, she forced herself to look beyond the immediate wreckage around her, to study what the Crows were doing in more detail. They seemed disorganized and confused, with none of their Comms-Discs seeming to function properly – likely as a result of Mei's work. Some of the leaders, though, had begun verbally shouting orders to their footsoldiers, rounding them up, urging them now to leave the Keeper's Children, and to gather . . . where?

With what felt like an immense effort of energy and will, Toshiko got to her feet, shouldered her way out from behind the ruined house's defensive cluster of Keeper's Children, and began to follow the Crows. She did her best to stay out of their sight as she did so, ducking behind the wreckage of buildings, and keep-ing her head down. None of them so much as glanced over in her direction as they went, though, the news of the Imperial Army seeming to have subsumed their focus entirely. They were more coordinated now, in spite of the malfunctioning Comms-Discs, all of them heading west, moving parallel to the ocean.

As Toshiko stumbled over charred wood, over smashed glass, around bodies and over stained, discarded Keeper's Garlands, the mass of Crows she was following only grew.

'Everyone to the Western Gate,' roared one of their

commanders, an older man with full gang tattoos. He held his knife in the air, a beacon for attracting attention. 'They're coming from the west.'

The storm had eased, at least, and the rain had stopped, which allowed Toshiko to see the faces of the Keeper's Children around her. She was surprised to find her own confusion reflected back in only a very few – most were showing a hard-won survivor's capacity to adjust fast to new peril, rushing to gather children and belongings, preparing to run again.

And perhaps they were right to do this, Toshiko considered, dimly – perhaps that was even what she ought to be doing now, too. She should probably at least be trying to find Mei and Jun, so they could be ready to escape together. And yet still, she kept following the Crows as they snaked their way through the smouldering streets and out onto the open plains that extended alongside the sea, all the way to Rainshadow City.

Why the Imperial Guard should be coming here now, to the Crescent, she didn't know. It couldn't be to help the Crows. Not after they'd tried to kill the Emperor. And then the Crows around her, too, seemed almost as wary of this army's approach as the Keeper's Children did.

At last, she came to the Crescent's western border, where she saw with a sudden jolt that everything here was almost un-recognizable to her, because the whole of the Crescent's Western Gate, along with a wide section of the barbed-wire fences that had run alongside it, had been torn down. Until now, that gate and those fences had seemed an unchanging, unalterable reality to Toshiko – and yet here they were, lying in fallen metal sheets that looked even larger to her than she would have imagined now they were laid out like this, flat on the ground.

A squadron of heavily armed Imperial Guards was standing

to attention in the wreckage, clearly responsible for the job, with each of the soldiers holding a grappling hook attached to a long length of rope. For a wild, optimistic moment, Toshiko wondered if the Emperor could have come here today to liberate the Keeper's Children from the Crows. After all, her son had surprised everyone with his compassion and selflessness. Surely she must have some of that goodness within her too, even if it was buried very deep.

And then Toshiko stumbled to a halt, her hopes faltering as she finally registered the thunder of approaching hooves shaking the ground beneath her, and she looked out beyond the torn down fences, to the wide expanse of the plains.

The Imperial Army really was coming in force: hundreds of Guards riding hard towards the Crescent in an arrow-shaped attack formation, an oncoming tide of dark purple on horseback. They were heading straight for the break that their advance guard had made in the fences – and Toshiko found she couldn't possibly interpret this as a rescue party. There were just too many of them, approaching with too much open aggression.

Back on her side of the fallen fences, on the strip of scrubland now scattered with battle debris, extending beyond the last of the Crescent's houses, the Crows were gathering, preparing to defend their claim to this land. Their commanders seemed fully in control once again, and were marshalling their troops into straight, defensive lines to face the Imperial soldiers across the plains.

Toshiko's breath caught then as she noticed Ken Saito at the front of the Crows' ranks, gripping Haru before him as an obvious hostage – his long, curved knife held to the boy's throat. Haru looked terrified, but his eyes weren't actually on the blade. Instead, they were raised up, fixed on the approaching Imperial Army – not more than a few thousand feet away now.

The storm clouds may have partially dispersed, but dusk had finally fallen, and so it took Toshiko a moment to see that it was Haru's mother, the Emperor herself, riding at the head of the Guards' attack formation, forming the very tip of its arrow. She was dressed in full combat uniform now, and while her left hand gripped the reins of her horse, her right held a long, straight sword, unsheathed and upraised. She was riding low, moving at a gallop, and, as Toshiko watched, she dug her heels into her horse's sides, urging it even faster. She began to pull away from the rest of the group, racing over the last stretch of ground on her own, directly towards the waiting army of Crows.

And then came the moment that would sear itself like a brand across the evening. As the Emperor drew close enough to the fallen barbed wire for Toshiko to see her bloodied eyepatch, as well as the sheer fury in her expression, she raised her sword skywards, and with a wordless yell, hurled it straight at Ken Saito.

The sword flew, flipping over and over itself in the air to soar over the plains in a lethal wheel of sharpened metal.

Shock must have caused Saito to loosen his grip on Haru. As Toshiko watched, breath held, the boy managed to break free, dropping to the relative safety of the ground and rolling away, just as the sword's journey came to its spectacular end – slicing deep into Saito's flesh, just above where his neck met his shoulder.

The feared consigliere of the Crows merely looked surprised for a moment, his eyes watching the sword as it fell, and tumbled to his feet. And then at last, blood finally bloomed, spurting from the ragged laceration above his collarbone.

Saito clutched at it before removing his hand again, fast, as if he'd been burned. For a moment, he simply stared down at his fingers, wet and slick with gore. Then he stumbled, and began to sway. Along with everyone else gathered there, Toshiko looked on, transfixed, as this young man who had always seemed so invincible – who had taken so much from her, and from her family – finally fell to his knees and crumpled, a broken thing, the blood and life flowing out of him like water into the dirt.

CHAPTER EIGHTEEN

Emperor of the Archipelago

1.

Lying where he was, flat on his stomach in the dirt by the Keeper's Crescent's fallen fences, Haru seemed first in line to get trampled beneath the hooves of his mother's horse.

He screamed as she tugged on the reins, pulling so hard it looked painful for Lightning. Thank the Gods she did, though. Lightning stumbled to a stop, then whinnied and reared, front hooves kicking wildly in the air before finally slamming down into the mud, mere inches from the far edge of the collapsed fence in front of Haru.

Haru scrambled to his feet and ran. He ran from Mr Winter, from his mother and from Lightning, slipping through lines of the Crows, who were all still standing watching Saito in shock.

His first, barely conscious thought had been to return to where he'd left Hiranaya, but he soon realized there were far too many Crows around him now to be sure of being able to make it all the way back through their ranks. They might currently seem paralysed without their leader, but it would only take one of them to decide to take matters into their own hands for him to be taken hostage again.

Still running and trying not to panic now, Haru sheered off to one side, heading away from the Crows towards the area of scrubland where the fences still stood, leading down towards the Crescent's southern corner. The Crows' ranks didn't extend far beyond the break in the fences, and as soon as Haru had moved past the massed ranks of them, he felt his feet beginning to stumble, and his breath starting to come in huge, shuddering gulps, as all the fear he'd suppressed in his escape finally surfaced.

He didn't feel able to keep running, and yet he knew he couldn't stay where he was either, out in the open like this. Looking around himself at all the debris and ruins that were everywhere here, from the battle, he dived behind the first thing he saw in the wreckage that seemed as if it might serve as a kind of shelter – an abandoned bicycle rickshaw, half-mangled and collapsed on its side.

It was only when he was crouched behind the rickshaw, his breathing steadying again, that Haru properly registered that neither Mr Winter nor anyone else was coming after him anymore. It seemed that he'd managed to get away, while the Crows were all distracted by the turmoil of his mother's arrival – and then, too, Mr Winter was clearly in no condition now to pursue him anywhere.

In fact, Haru found he could barely bring himself to look across to where Mr Winter was lying all twisted up on the ground with various Crows clustered around him, trying to help. Haru thought he recognized Hana amidst them – the woman who'd captured him, back in the Palace. She was still dressed in the same dark glasses and long coat, but looked desperate now, and was shouting something to Mr Winter as she bent over him, getting increasingly covered with his blood.

It terrified Haru, to see that anyone could lose so much. He could even hear the wet, choking sounds Mr Winter was emitting – hideous and impossible to shut out, in spite of the roar of the wind, and the shouts of the Crows, and the thundering hooves of the approaching Imperial Army.

Averting his eyes, at least, from the sight of Mr Winter's suffering, Haru turned his gaze towards his mother. Still on the other side of the dismantled fences, she was sitting proud on Lightning, surveying the massed ranks of Crows. She might be a figure of terror, but in spite of the fear Haru still felt towards her, he could also understand now how she could be seen as a figure of strength. It took bravery, after all, to face the Lucky Crows like this, almost on her own, with her army still riding hard to catch up behind her. She looked even more unkempt than when he'd last seen her, spattered as she was with dirt, and also with what he could only assume must be blood. And yet, the wildness of her appearance suddenly seemed almost appropriate to Haru, now that she was out on the plains on horseback, dressed in the military clothes he normally only saw her wearing when she trained in the very early mornings.

He began to wonder if it was possible that he could have misjudged her completely, and misunderstood everything – even the fearsome pitilessness that he'd seen in her, back at the Palace. After all, he himself had done things today in the battle that he wasn't sure could ever be right – and yet he'd still done them, and had kept doing them, because to do nothing would have felt even worse. And here she was, after all, arrived with her army at last, surely to help them all against the Crows. She had even saved his life from Mr Winter.

She ignored her troops as they finally drew up to stop behind her, choosing, instead, to focus her attention on the Crows.

'The Sensei is old,' she bellowed out to their ranks, her voice soaring over the battlefield, clear all the way to where Haru was hiding, behind the fallen rickshaw. 'She is absent and tired, and the man she relied upon to command you is as good as dead.'

With a flick of her reins and a kick of her heels then, the Emperor set Lightning ranging up and down the length of the break in the fences, moving back and forth along the lines of Crows, to address as many of them as possible as she continued to speak. The Crows, for their part, continued to seem uncertain of what to do without their leader to guide them. They were still bristling with clear hostility, weapons raised, but at this very moment, at least, the Emperor seemed safe from attack.

'The footsoldiers you had guarding the warehouse have been defeated,' she told them. 'Some of them have been killed, and the draconic ore is fully mine now, as it should have been from the beginning. The Sensei has lost. *You* have lost. Surrender now, or I will storm the Crescent and take this land from you by force. Surrender now and you might live to see another morning.'

The Crows didn't lower their weapons, but Haru noticed subtle movement in their ranks, and heard the murmurs too, carried towards him on the wind, of those who were considering their options.

'Lay down your weapons and bow to my soldiers,' the Emperor commanded, 'or die on this Godsforsaken stretch of land, fighting for an old woman who isn't even here to see your sacrifice, let alone to stand alongside you. That's your choice.'

The noise from the Crows built louder, and Haru risked peeking further out from behind his rickshaw to watch them. Some now looked almost ready to do as his mother said, while others still seemed unyielding.

'What do you think she'll do with us, if we do surrender?' Haru heard one of the Crows at the nearest edge of the gang's formation saying to his comrade. 'Give us citizenship, and positions in the Imperial Guard? No chance. We're dead either way. Better to go down fighting.'

The Emperor brought Lightning to a halt, and then turned in the saddle to gesture towards the spot where Haru was hiding. 'My son and heir,' she said, 'will be allowed to leave the Crescent unharmed, to join my troops.'

Immediately at her words, the eyes of all the assembled gang members turned towards Haru – the full focus of the Crows shifting to fix on him in one awful moment. And yet still none of them seemed to dare make any move forward. Perhaps the calculation his mother had made would hold, and the threat of her army really would be enough to keep them in place.

'I will send General Mori of the Imperial Guard to escort my heir back to safety,' she continued. 'My General will also go unharmed.'

At that, there was some movement in the troops behind her, and the ranks parted as General Mori rode forward to her side – a stocky figure in his dark purple uniform, mounted on a steady, strong-looking horse with a glossy red coat. Haru had always liked General Mori, and was glad his mother had chosen him for this part of her plan – even if, from the look of concern he thought he saw etched, now, in the lines of the General's usually friendly face, it seemed possible she hadn't consulted him about it in advance.

The Emperor shifted again in her saddle to look at Haru, and though she only had one good eye, and was staring through the barbed-wire fence in front of him, as well as over the churned-up debris from the battle, he still felt her glare on him like the light of a burning sun. He swallowed, reminding himself that sometimes, Emperors needed to be fearsome.

'Come, little one,' she called to him. 'It's time to go home.'

'Home?' Haru said, edging out from behind his rickshaw, and beginning to walk towards her.

'Come on, little one,' she said, again. 'It's time to go back to the Palace. You'll be safe there.'

'But what about my friends?' Haru called back to her, straining his voice to make himself heard over all the distance between them.

'Friends?' His mother's voice dropped suddenly in temperature.

'Not the Crows,' Haru hurriedly clarified, realizing how she might have interpreted his question, given that he was now virtually embedded in the Crows' ranks. 'I meant everyone else here, at the Crescent. Haven't you come to help us?'

'Help you?' his mother asked, sounding perplexed. 'You're the Crown Prince. You're my heir, and the future of the Archipelago. Of course I've come to help you.'

'But what about the others?' Haru tried again. 'What about the Keeper's Children?'

His mother laughed. 'Don't try to tell me you like this place. No one does. It's a disgrace. Get out of there and we'll build something better.'

'A new Keeper's Crescent?'

'My LIFE-Hub, for my ALISEs,' she said, before turning to

General Mori, who hadn't moved from behind her, his face a mask of impassivity. 'Now, go on,' she said. 'Get in there and fetch back my heir.'

As General Mori bowed his head in assent, Haru began to feel all his fragile hopes begin to crumble again. He stopped walking and simply stared at his mother as she continued to beckon him, from Lightning's back. Of course she had only come here because she wanted this land for herself. Of course, too, she had only saved his life because he was the Crown Prince, and therefore a necessary part of the machinery of her leadership. He wanted to cry. He wanted to shout at himself for ever trying to believe better of her.

And in his distress, he turned away from her, looking wildly around for somewhere else he could go – and that was when his gaze happened to catch once more on the convulsing, blood-soaked form of Mr Winter, where he was still collapsed by the fallen fences, with Hana and a knot of other Crows clustered around him. As Haru watched, one of Mr Winter's hands shot out to land heavily on Hana's shoulder. It was a pale hand, streaked with blood, but its grip seemed strong enough. And then Mr Winter let out a sound somewhere between a yell and a growl as, using Hana as a willing support, he hauled himself into as close to an upright position as a man in his state could manage.

It could only have been a matter of minutes since he'd attacked Hiranaya with his poisoned knife, but those minutes had wrought a transformation far more dramatic than Haru had ever seen in anyone before. All of Mr Winter's considerable strength had visibly drained away, to be replaced with nothing but the cold violence of fury. Every feature in his face was twisted up with it, so that it seemed to be almost all that was keeping him upright. His skin had turned as pale as paper, too, which only seemed to emphasize to Haru that this was all Mr Winter was now. This feeling. This rage.

Raising his hand from Hana's shoulder, and pushing aside another Crow who'd been trying to stem the flow of blood from his neck, Mr Winter hauled himself around to face the Emperor, letting the blood tumble freely now.

'We won't surrender,' he insisted, voice ragged. 'This is not your Empire – not anymore.' And then he turned to point a shaking finger towards where Haru was still standing, hesitant, in plain sight of everyone here on the battlefield. 'Seize him. Seize the Imperial Heir. He's ours.'

Hana immediately darted forward, her short, dark hair and long coat flying behind her as she lunged to fulfil his command – and behind her dark glasses, Haru could see now that her face was stained with blood, dirt and tears. Before he could think to run or shout, or do anything to protect himself in any way, she'd grabbed his upper arm with that familiar grip like a metal vice, and brought her dagger to his throat.

2.

The Sensei's eyes flashed, showing real anger now at how Theo had managed to throw off the restraints that she'd placed on him. She shook back both sleeves, raising up her arms – and all of the papers on the table behind her rose into the air.

Theo stared, unsure of how to respond, as each individual sheet began to fold itself into a small, origami bird. The floating formation of folding paper was a surprisingly beautiful sight, and as he watched, he found himself almost wanting to copy the Sensei, to see if he might be able to use the Gift to do something like this, too. Before long, the birds were complete. They hovered, over a hundred strong, in a cloud above the Sensei's upraised arms. Then she gave a flick of her wrists, and all of them turned to face Theo. He realized what was going to happen about a split second before the birds descended.

Whatever the Sensei had done to them, their beaks certainly felt sharper than any ordinary folded paper. Arms flailing now as he tried to fight them off, Theo fled back towards the work-benches, hardly knowing where he was going as the whole cloud of birds followed after him.

Ducking behind the nearest bench, he seized one of the bot arms lying on its surface, only to almost drop it again, recoiling in instinctive revulsion – the arm in his hands felt just as he would have imagined a severed human limb might feel. It seemed exactly the right weight, somehow, and had the very same light hairs and texture of skin as a human arm would – even the same folds at the elbow.

And yet there wasn't time to be squeamish. The Sensei might only have been lounging against the edge of the table, watching his distress with an expression of mild interest, but her birds were still descending everywhere around him in a torrent of little stabs of pain, their beaks beginning to draw blood.

Raising the bot arm into the air, Theo waved it like a baton, trying to beat them back. The birds, at least, didn't seem suffi-ciently intelligent to distinguish between him and the arm, and he found some brief respite as they attacked it with abandon, shredding its almost-human flesh into a bloody, mangled mess of meat. Clearly, though, this wasn't a sustainable way to fight back – and the expression on the Sensei's face had even turned to something almost like amusement as she watched him.

With an almighty effort, Theo marshalled his thoughts back into something like clarity. The Sensei had used the air to restrain him earlier, and he'd managed to understand enough of how she'd done that to be able to undo it. Perhaps he could use what he'd learnt to help him again now.

Dropping the ruined arm, he threw his own arms over his face in a partial, if largely ineffective shield against the birds, and closed his eyes to once again access the Gift. Making himself ignore the pain of the birds' attacks, he thought back to those flowing streams of dense energy with which the Sensei had surrounded his body, and considered how he might copy them.

He began by pulling the air currents tightly in towards himself. Then, when he'd gathered as many as he felt he could possibly hold, he let them go again, firing them out like elastic to send a dense wave of air away from him, in all directions.

It collided with the birds spectacularly, blowing them back and scattering them, to land broken and torn in the room's far corners. And even through his fear, Theo couldn't help but feel the excitement of having learnt to use the Gift in a completely new way. He almost grinned, even, as the Sensei gave a frustrated yell, jumping up to alertness from where she'd previously been leaning so nonchalantly against the table's edge, the very picture of smug composure.

Theo's triumph, though, proved to be short-lived, as the Sensei's eyes flashed brighter gold, and the same terrible pain she'd used on him before began to start up again, behind his eyes.

Acting on pure instinct now, he reached once more for the air currents around him, and encouraged them to flow around himself this time, to form a kind of shield. Amazingly, it seemed to work – the agony in his head immediately fading to a dull ache. His shield certainly wasn't impenetrable, but for as long as he could maintain it, it seemed able to deflect at least a portion of the torment the Sensei was trying to send his way.

Feeling increasingly desperate now, as well as perhaps a little curious as to what else he might be able to achieve with the Gift, Theo reached up to pluck one of the last few origami birds to have survived his attack out of the air. It struggled, trying to peck at his hand, but he kept a tight hold of it between finger and thumb. Then he steadied his breathing, and attempted to do something he'd never even thought to try before – splitting his awareness to use the Gift for two different things at the same time. Keeping his mind as clear and as focused as possible, he just about succeeded in maintaining his shield, while also probing into the workings of the bird.

Splitting his mind like this wasn't an easy thing to sustain, though. It felt to Theo rather like singing one tune at the same time as trying to play a different one on an instrument, all while not being fully sure of either melody. It didn't help that he was aware the whole time, too, of the Sensei's eyes on him. They seemed to burn with golden fire now, her usually mild expression twisted into one of ever-increasing fury as, with her arms out-stretched, she threw the full force of her strength into her efforts to break through his shield. He couldn't quite deflect all of her attacks, and several spikes of excruciating pain did reach him as his shield flickered and faltered.

And yet, with an immense effort of will, Theo did still manage to stay focused on studying the origami bird. The working the Sensei had woven around it seemed too complex for him to be able to do much more now than simply alter it in quite a crude way – and yet, he considered, that might just still be enough to give him the help he needed. Acting fast now, he unpicked and restitched the bird's magic as best as he could, before opening his hand to loose it at the Sensei, sending it flying straight for her cardigan pocket, which held the pearl.

Before the bird had even reached her, though, the Sensei had thrown up her arms again – and this time, the silver coffee pot on the table behind her began to hiss and rattle, its lid blowing off in a cloud of steam as it rose into the air. Before Theo knew quite what was happening, it had flown towards him, and he was being pelted with a rain of unnaturally scalding coffee, which seemed, somehow, to be able to circumvent his shield without difficulty.

He yelled as the heated liquid burned his skin, and yet still tried to keep his attention trained on his little bird, which had reached the Sensei's pocket now, and was beginning to peck at the material.

It managed to pull a few threads loose, before she reached down and seized it, her golden eyes flashing with outrage as she crumpled the bird in her fist, and then opened her hand to let it fall, crushed, to the floor – a simple piece of paper once again.

The boiling rain kept falling, the last few birds kept pecking, and the pain in Theo's head was mounting rapidly too, with his shield increasingly in tatters. And yet those few threads that the bird had picked loose had given him a new idea. He gritted his teeth, and stared hard at the wool of the Sensei's pocket.

'Stop trying to think of a way out, Bluejay,' she told him as he did. 'There isn't one. And would it really be such a bad life, being my servant? You show enormous promise. I could even teach you, once I knew I could trust you to be obedient.'

He didn't reply, only kept trying to detect the exact weave and composition of the material of her cardigan.

At last, he felt sure that he had it – and, using the Gift with more precision and delicacy than he'd ever managed before, he began to encourage the wool of the pocket to unravel. For a moment, he thought it wouldn't work. Then, the threads started to unwind and come loose, and the pearl fell to the floor with a clatter.

He dived for it, throwing himself painfully onto the flagstones. The Sensei was nearer, though, and turned out to be surprisingly fast, in spite of her age – and Theo let out a yell of frustration as she snatched it up in quick fingers.

He heard a light rustle of material then, coming from somewhere up ahead of him, and he pushed himself onto his elbows from where he'd landed on the hard floor, just in time to see the bot woman stepping off her plinth to approach him, with pale arms reaching, outstretched.

For a moment, Theo didn't understand what could be happening. The Sensei had insisted this bot was a mere shell, and while of course he'd never trust her to tell him the whole truth, he was also certain that had there been any Sola currents flowing through this body, he surely would have sensed them earlier, himself, when he'd scanned the room with the Gift.

His incomprehension kept him unmoving as the bot stalked towards him. Even now, it seemed far from fully alive. Its face was completely blank – not dead, exactly, but certainly not living – and then there was the particular way it moved, too, with such slow, jerky and deliberate steps. It reminded Theo of a puppet, he suddenly realized – as if this body was being piloted from the outside.

With an effort, he tore his gaze away from the bot's approach, looking back over to the Sensei, only to find that her eyes were now blazing an even brighter gold than before, her gaze fixed on the bot as she held the pearl before her in both hands. She was, it seemed, finally drawing on its power. The pearl was luminous, in this moment – lit from within, pulsing with something like moonlight.

Theo shook himself out of his paralysis to scramble backwards, away from the bot. And yet it kept coming, its pace steady, its eyes blank, its long hair swinging in dark curtains on either side of its face. The white robe lent its movements an eerie quality, too, as if underneath, the bot really might be gliding, instead of taking real steps on real feet. Theo was aware of the Sensei beginning to laugh – a wild sound, charged with the dragon pearl's power.

He forced himself to his feet, and continued to back away. As he did, he reached out with the Gift once more, probing the bot, searching for some way that he might be able to halt it, or redirect its movements. He was just beginning to wonder if that last option might be possible, when the Sensei's laughter rose to crystallize into a harsh, commanding yell – and the bot ran at him, full pelt, hair flying and robe billowing, to fasten its strong, fleshy hands around his neck.

3.

Hana's dagger was just inches from Haru's throat as she gripped his arm tight below the shoulder, so that he couldn't struggle free. While Haru did feel terrified, trapped like this under her blade, he found that his terror was mingled now too with something else – a new feeling of disappointment so deep it was almost exhaustion. Disappointment in his mother, and in everyone at the Palace who followed her orders every day. Disappointment in the whole world, even, for being such a tangled, corrupted mess.

The ranks of Crows around him, in contrast, seemed bolstered and encouraged by Hana's boldness in seizing him, as well as by his mother's lack of immediate retaliation. She was watching Hana fixedly, and Haru knew the kinds of considerations she would be weighing, now – just how far might she be able to push the Crows, before Hana would simply relinquish her advantage in holding him hostage, in taking his life?

'Archers, ready on my command,' the Emperor eventually called to her troops, her voice taut with calculation. Behind her, hundreds of Imperial bows were immediately loaded with arrows and levelled at the Crows. 'Take aim – and fire!'

Haru tried to duck as a storm of arrows flew overhead, straight into the gathered mass of Crows behind him. A whole battery of cries went up from their ranks, and in spite of the proximity of Hana's knife, Haru risked turning his head just slightly to look over, to see what had happened. All order in the gang's formation had abruptly begun to collapse. Most of the Imperial arrows seemed to have found their marks, and men and women were now crumpling and falling everywhere through the lines of fighters. Hana's arm began to tremble as she saw this too, her blade hovering ever closer to the delicate skin of Haru's throat, but still she didn't act on the threat. This time, at least, it seemed Haru's mother had made the right calculation.

'Should I hurt him, Ken?' Hana was calling to Mr Winter now, though. 'Should I hurt him in retaliation?'

And yet Mr Winter seemed in no condition to issue further instructions. Bent over, his hands on his knees, he only coughed wetly and hawked up blood that spattered his shoes and the muddy ground around them. None of the other Crows seemed ready to issue Hana with any kind of order either, with their ranks still in turmoil, more of them still falling, suffering, to the ground, or bending to help their comrades.

And then, suddenly, above the sounds of their distress as well as the combined roar of the waves and the wind and the horses, Haru heard his name being called – a distant shout from some-where in the direction of the Crescent.

'Haru!' the voice was saying. 'You have to let him go, please!'

It was Kei, Haru realized, and even amidst all this bloodshed, he felt a small spark of gratitude ignite within him to know that she hadn't abandoned him, and would even dare take on the Crows in order to look after him.

'Kei,' he called out in reply. 'I'm here – I'm here! Help me!'

Hana, though, somehow made her grip on his arm even tighter at that, and he broke off his cries in a yelp of pain.

'Harm my heir and none of you will survive this day,' the Emperor cried out then, and Haru could hear the frustration in her voice at having found herself in this deadlock. 'Your forces are outnumbered, and if you harm him, I will order my Guards to fight to kill.'

'As if you would ever tell them to do anything else,' Hana yelled back. She was sounding less in control now, though – increasingly uncertain, even anguished. Her eyes kept darting between the Emperor and Mr Winter, who was still doubled over and visibly struggling to breathe. And then Mr Winter choked and fell to his knees, and with a cry Hana turned towards him – her grip on Haru's shoulder slackening as she did so.

That moment of inattention was all Haru needed. He twisted away from her, wriggling out from under her dagger, pulling himself free.

He began to stumble away, over the mud of the battlefield, searching around himself for somewhere to run. Everywhere, though, it seemed there were more Crows, or fallen barbed wire, or scattered debris. He spun, feeling increasingly helpless, and then froze at the awful sight of Mr Winter lurching up and away from Hana now, beginning to stagger and then career towards him, through the battle's wreckage, his ghost-white hands stretching wide. He was still bent double, and was covered in gore now, coughing blood that ran over his lips and down his chin in thickening rivulets.

Haru tried his best to dodge away from him, but Mr Winter still managed to grasp a handful of his blue robe – the same robe he'd put on what felt like years ago now, for his mother's party – and Haru's stomach flipped, then, at the sight of that soft, familiar material soaking in so much of Mr Winter's blood. He began to struggle harder as Mr Winter leaned down to look him in the eye, seeming to fill his whole world with the twisted fury and hatred that so clearly roiled and churned within him.

'You,' Mr Winter choked out, his blood flecking Haru's face. 'You think you're the future of this Empire, yet the Sensei has plans you couldn't even dream of.'

And then, keeping a tight hold of Haru's robe with one hand, his other hand began to scrabble at his belt for his knife.

'Let me go,' Haru cried, as he tried his best to wriggle free of the robe.

Mr Winter saw immediately what he was trying to do though, and only shifted his hold to grip him by the shoulder. Haru didn't stop trying to pull away, but even with all his injuries Mr Winter was so much stronger than he was.

'If my life ends here today,' Mr Winter said, sounding now as if he were forcing each word through a haze of pain and ruin, 'then the Imperial line ends, too.'

His other hand did find his knife then, and Haru began to struggle even harder as, with a series of unsteady, jerky motions, Mr Winter finally drew the long, curved blade from its sheath.

Haru knew, now, that everything depended on his being rescued within the next few seconds. He could still hear Kei calling to him, but she didn't sound close by enough yet to be able to help. He was sure he could hear Hiranaya roaring, too – but she had been grounded and weakened by the poison, and in any case she was all the way back behind the Crows, towards the heart of the Keeper's Crescent. His mother was yelling with fury on the other side of the fallen barbed wire, and General Mori, too, was starting to ride towards him – but neither of these adults was near enough to rescue him, either.

Mr Winter swung his knife wildly, and Haru screamed, lurching even closer in towards him, in spite of all the blood and horror, in his efforts to dodge the blade. He managed it, but it was all too narrow an escape. Had Mr Winter's sword arm not been so unsteady with his injuries, there was no way Haru would have been able to evade an attack at such close quarters. As things were, he would need more than luck to escape a second time.

As Mr Winter prepared to swing his knife again, Haru realized, all at once, that he couldn't rely on an adult to come and save him. Hardly knowing what he was doing, he reached into his boot for the pocket knife Kei had given him before the battle. Being uninjured, he was faster than Mr Winter, and managed to pull out the little blade and unsheathe it before Mr Winter could rally his strength behind that second swing of his knife.

There was no time for Haru to hesitate, or even to prepare himself. With a cry, he thrust out the knife, screaming as it made contact with Mr Winter's jaw, and then as he slashed it downwards, to cut a jagged line through the sinews of Mr Winter's throat.

Haru's fingers, suddenly so slippery with blood, soon lost their grip on the knife's smooth, wooden hilt, and he dropped it, letting it fall out of his reach to Mr Winter's feet.

Mr Winter was choking and convulsing now, his eyes slipping in and out of focus as blood fountained from his throat, as well as from his existing shoulder wound. Somehow, he still managed to raise his blade, making as if to swing it once more towards Haru – and then his arm gave way, sending his knife clattering down as well, to land on the ground next to Haru's.

Haru began to struggle against Mr Winter with renewed determination, trying once more to get free. It seemed, though, that the harder Mr Winter fought to breathe, the more tightly his fingers twisted into Haru's shoulder.

'Let me go!' Haru cried out, his voice now shrill with pain and fear.

Mr Winter hung grimly on, forcing Haru to stay with him even as his eyes bulged and rolled, and more blood poured from his wounds to soak them both.

Finally, after what felt like lifetimes to Haru, the light went out in Mr Winter's eyes and he slumped, lifeless, to the ground at Haru's feet. Even then, Haru had to struggle to pry himself free from the dead man's grip.

He was aware that somewhere nearby, Hana had begun screaming – a desolate howl that soared up over the battlefield. Stumbling, shaking, and feeling sick, he looked up again only just in time to see her running towards him, dagger raised, slicing through the air with new, uncontrolled fury.

He turned and ran from her, heading this time straight into the ranks of Crows, back in the direction of the Crescent.

'Kei!' Haru cried out as he dodged his way through them. 'Where are you, Kei? I'm here. Help me.'

None of the Crows even tried to stop him. Now little more than a disorganized rabble of uncertainty, injury and distress, they were all still too focused on those among them who'd been hit by the Guards' arrows to care much about what Haru was doing. So many people were lying dead, and so many more were clearly suffering and screaming out for help.

For a moment, as Haru wove his way through the throng, he had the strange experience of feeling almost as if he were at one of his mother's parties again, darting unseen through adult guests at waist height. Then, finally, he was through, bursting from the lines of black-jacketed men and women to emerge where the remaining forces of the resistance had gathered – and it seemed so marvellous to him then, that in spite of everything the Keeper's Children had faced in the battle, they were still here, still determined to protect their home from all invaders.

'Haru!' he heard Kei's voice call again.

He whirled, looking first amid the resistance fighters, and then up and past their ranks until at last he saw her, running towards him from the westernmost streets of the Crescent.

'Kei!' he called out, and as the resistance parted to let him through, he sprinted the last muddy stretch of land to meet her.

In one seamless movement, Kei dropped down to his height and gathered him into her arms, squeezing him tight.

'Thank the Gods,' she whispered. 'I'm so glad you're safe.'

'Me too,' he told her. 'But glad about you being safe, I mean.'

'I'm never letting you out of my sight again,' she said. 'Or at least definitely not so you can go riding dragons into battle.'

Haru burrowed his head into her shoulder, inhaling the familiar, slightly soapy scent of her hair. Even though of course he understood that they were still far from being properly safe, he suddenly felt so cared for – so loved, even – that for that moment, it felt as if nothing could ever break through the walls of protection that she had built up around them both.

As he had nestled into Kei's embrace, Haru had squeezed his eyes tight shut. He blinked them open again now just in time to see, over her shoulder, the curious sight of Toshiko's sister climbing up the side of one of the little Keeper's Crescent houses in front of him. She was using its windows and drainage channels as handholds and footholds, and seemed to be heading all the way up to its corrugated metal roof. In one hand,

Haru noticed, she was holding one of the three bows that Ren had gathered for the resistance, and on her back was a quiver of arrows.

4.

With its fingers and thumbs around Theo's throat, the eerily human-looking bot didn't hesitate even for a second before it began choking him, pressing in hard to crush his windpipe.

Theo felt his limbs and torso begin to spasm at having his breathing cut off so suddenly and with such force. He found his body wanting to choke on its own saliva, only to discover that even this was impossible, with the bot's hands squeezing him so tightly. He tried to fight it off, scratching at its back and tugging its hair, but he felt weak and flailing, and in any case, it didn't seem to experience physical pain – or to react to it, anyway. He needed to cough and to breathe. He needed to be sick. He needed to think of some kind of plan, or he would die like this.

Then he heard the sounds of rusty bolts being drawn back, and hinges creaking open – and over the bot's shoulder, he saw the two women who'd brought him here, stepping in through the lab's doorway, their expressions matching studies in frightened obedience.

The Sensei turned to them, and in that moment of her concentration being broken, the pearl's light dimmed, and the bot's hold on Theo loosened. He exploded out of its grip, coughing, gagging, retching, tears streaming from his eyes as he gasped for breath. It felt as though his lungs would never be able to inflate properly, as if they would never again work as they should.

Through all of this, he swept a look around at what was facing him – the two Crows at the door, the bot, the Sensei. He was outnumbered and outmanoeuvred, and he had no doubt that as soon as these two new arrivals figured out what was really happening here, everything would abruptly get even worse. There was no more time to think. Instead, he forced himself to crawl over the flagstones to the table, where he seized hold of the huge, silver coffee pot – and then, with an almighty effort, lurched to his feet and hurled it straight at the Sensei's head.

5.

Haru continued to watch as, with a clatter of the arrows in her quiver, Mei managed to haul herself onto the roof of the house. She jumped to her feet, her boots hitting the corrugated metal with an echoing slam.

He wanted to call out to her, to tell her it wasn't safe to climb up like that, in full view of the Guards and the Crows – and up onto a metal roof too, even while storm clouds lingered overhead, potentially still charged with lightning. The look on Mei's face, though, kept Haru silent. She seemed so determined and sure of herself up there that she looked almost serene as she straightened the quiver on her back, and adjusted her grip on the bow.

'Mori,' he heard his mother yell then, from the head of her troops. 'Speed it up. I want my son back, now.'

Haru heard hoofbeats and the sound of a horse whinnying, as the resistance fighters in front of him parted to reveal General Mori, riding straight for him.

Everyone, in that moment, was focused either on him, or on the General, or on the Emperor. He was the only one who seemed to notice Mei up there on the roof, as she loaded an arrow into her bow, and raised it, angling it beyond the fallen fences of the Crescent's border towards the Imperial Guard on the scrublands. He kept watching as she rolled her shoulders, and then shut one eye to take closer aim.

And all at once, Haru realized he knew almost for a certainty what she was about to do.

Mei's arrow flew so fast he could barely make it out as it soared through the dusk, towards where his mother was still at the front of her troops – mounted on Lightning and with the full focus of her attention now trained, Haru realized, on him. One moment, she was sitting tall in her saddle, hollering orders over to General Mori. The next, Mei's arrow had caught her hard, square in the throat, right above the collar of her uniform.

Haru cried out, and a general roar of confusion and disbelief went up from the battlefield as everyone – Crows, Imperial Guards and Keeper's Children alike – began to register that this seemingly impossible thing really had happened. Everyone was now trying to see where the arrow had come from, and Haru even noticed a few Imperial Guards pointing over to where Mei was still standing, on the roof. All of the Guards were shouting to each other, disbelieving and confused, and were calling to his mother, too, asking her for orders that just weren't coming, given that she now seemed unable to speak. Haru saw, in fact, that she was choking – her eyes bulging – and that she was struggling even to keep her grip on Lightning's reins as she stared fixedly over the plains at her assailant.

Haru followed her gaze then, to look back towards Mei. Mei's hands were steady as she lowered her bow, her shoulders were square, and when she spoke, her voice sounded calm and assured, carrying clearly through the shocked hush that had begun to descend over the battlefield.

'That's for my Auntie Reiko,' she called to the Emperor, as all eyes on the battlefield turned towards her now. 'That's for my family, and for every family you let suffer and grieve, because you hoarded power. That's for all the Keeper's Children, and for everyone you kept shut out and excluded from Rainshadow City. That's for all those who you condemned to suffer in poverty, and at the hands of Lucky Crows – for everyone whose lives you decided didn't matter.'

Even before the end of this speech, the Emperor had fully collapsed in her saddle, to slump against Lightning's neck. Mei didn't wait around to watch anything further. Dropping her bow with a clatter, she turned to jog the few steps to the rooftop's edge, before leaping down to disappear amidst the Crescent's winding streets.

6.

The heavy silver coffee pot arced its way through the air towards the Sensei's skull, and in that moment, Theo saw genuine shock flash over her face as he felt her gather in all of her power to block the pot's trajectory. As she did so, the bot, together with the few origami birds she'd managed to keep airborne, collapsed inert to the ground.

She managed to halt the pot in mid-air, just inches from the tip of her nose. While she'd been distracted, though, Theo had scrambled towards her, over the floor. He dodged the pot as it fell, and then, as it landed with a hard clang on the room's stone floor, he sprang up to deal a swift yet brutal upper-cut to the bottom of her jaw.

The Sensei's head snapped backwards, and as the two Crows at the door yelled out protests, Theo grasped again for the Gift, sending out a wall of dense air to hold them back and keep them from interfering as he snatched at the Sensei's closed fist, holding the pearl. He caught her wrist and squeezed hard – increasing the pressure until she cried out and at last her fingers loosened, the pearl slipping from her grip. Its iridescent surface gleamed in the lantern-light as it tumbled to the floor. Theo landed another blow to the Sensei's temple, before diving for it.

The Sensei was slumped now, dazed, against the table. Her bot was still lying lifeless on the floor where she'd left it, and the wave of air Theo had sent out with the Gift had managed to push the other two Crows all the way back to the lab's doorway. No one could beat him to where the pearl lay, still dimly glowing. Seizing it, he leapt over the spreadeagled body of the bot, and then ran straight for those two underling Crows by the door, using the Gift as he did so to disperse that wall of air he'd thrown in front of them.

Choosing one of them at random, he seized her in a headlock and held the pearl to her temple in what he hoped to all the Gods was a convincingly threatening manner. It worked only too well – she screamed, the sound echoing loudly through the lab. Rattled by the sudden noise, and beginning to panic slightly himself now too, at how little he felt he knew what he was doing, Theo slapped a hand over the woman's mouth, sending her eyes widening in even greater terror.

He turned then to the other Crow, giving a nod towards the pearl. 'This thing can amplify my powers a hundredfold,' he told her, his voice coming out scratchy and painful after the bot's attempts to strangle him. 'You've seen I have power. You've felt it, even. Imagine how much more damage I could do, with this pearl to help me. Now, we're going back to that elevator, where you are going to use that special key of yours to get me out of this basement, or I swear by all the Gods on this island that I'll melt her brains before you can even call for help.'

He was almost surprised when this second Crow recoiled from him, with what seemed to be genuine fear. He really must look quite a sight, he supposed – still gripping his hostage as she struggled, and then also with his clothing all torn from the birds, too, and his skin covered in still-bleeding cuts from their beaks as well as with burns and stains from the Sensei's rain of scalding coffee. He wondered if the inevitable bruising from the bot's efforts to strangle him was coming up yet, on his neck.

The Crow he was holding on to tried to speak then. With his hand still clamped over her mouth, it was difficult to make out exactly what she was saying, but it did sound, blessedly, as if she were urging her colleague to obey. The second Crow nodded, and cast a worried glance over in the Sensei's direction. The Sensei had slipped down from where she'd collapsed against the table, and was lying sprawled alongside the body of her bot, looking entirely insensible. The Crow gave a quick, fearful nod, and then turned to exit the room with fast footsteps – heading, Theo hoped, for the elevator.

He was just about to follow her, when the Sensei stirred, pushing herself up from the flagstones to blink, somewhat groggily, at the Comms-Disc on her wrist. At the sight of her awake again, the woman in Theo's grip began to struggle with renewed energy, clearly afraid of the Sensei seeing her like this, so completely subdued by an enemy. The Sensei, though, ignored both her and Theo completely, remaining focused, instead, on her Comms-Disc.

Something at the back of Theo's mind immediately began urging him to do something then: to abandon his hostage and try once more to knock the Sensei unconscious, maybe. Instead, he only watched as she frowned at the Comms-Disc's screen, and pressed a few buttons.

She did look up at him after that, and even despite the blows he'd dealt her, she suddenly didn't seem groggy at all. Her eyes were completely clear, while her features – not remotely grandmotherly anymore – were warped into an unmistakable expression of triumph.

And then Theo was hit by a sudden flash of pain. It shot all the way down the left side of his body before disappearing again, there and gone so fast he could almost have imagined it. It left him blinking and disorientated – and realizing, too, that the sounds of his hostage's screams were now ringing freely through the lab once more, the hand he'd used to cover her mouth having instinctively flown away from her, up to the tracker in his neck.

He pulled his wits together with an effort, and turned his focus back towards the Sensei. And yet her gaze was already losing its terrible focus, turning slack. As he watched, her eyelids dropped and she slumped at last into unconsciousness, her head hitting the stone floor with a painful-sounding thump.

For a wild moment, Theo thought she might be dead. Then, a flicker of her eyelids and a murmur from somewhere deep within her stupor told him otherwise, and dimly, he registered an un-expected gladness to find he hadn't killed her. She'd surely been wrong, back when she'd told him that killing would only become easier. The relief he felt at those flickering eyelids told him more clearly than anything else that, for as long as he lived, he never wanted to kill again.

He also now realized very clearly that he had to get out of here fast, before she could wake up again. He was aware, too, that he'd probably left that other Crow on her own outside in the corridor for far too long. Pulling himself together, he swung the pearl back towards his hostage, who was still in his grip, using the Gift as he did so to send just the smallest pulse of light towards its opalescent surface. In response, the pearl flared with a brightness that surprised even him. The woman whimpered with terror, squeezing her eyes shut against its glare.

'Come on,' he told her, feeling a stab of revulsion towards himself now, as he let the pearl's light subside again. 'I just need to get out of here.'

She came willingly, and together they finally made it out through the heavy doors of the lab.

The second Crow, thank the Gods, was waiting for them at the open doors of the elevator. She looked frightened too, her eyes fixed on the pearl in Theo's fist.

With an inward sigh at how almost everything he did seemed to turn into something shameful, no matter how good his intentions, Theo brandished the pearl in her direction, and sent another pulse of light through it, making her flinch.

'Let's go!' he ordered as he ran down the corridor towards her, tugging his hostage with him.

The waiting Crow had already been gripping her little silver key, and as he and the hostage hustled awkwardly past her into the elevator, she slipped it into the relevant slot in the control panel.

It was only when the elevator doors had finally closed behind them all that Theo let himself think back to what the Sensei could have been doing with her Comms-Disc, in those last moments before she'd lost consciousness. He was still alive, so perhaps that meant she hadn't triggered the poison after all, and it had only been a ploy to frighten him back into doing her bidding. And yet he couldn't ignore that awful surge of pain he'd felt emanating from the tracker as she'd tapped at those buttons.

He considered what she'd told him about how the poison worked after being activated, back when Saito had first installed the tracker in his neck.

You'd be dead within a couple of days.

Could that really be all he had left to him now? Theo swallowed hard, feeling the effects of the bot's attempts to strangle him as he did so, in the dull, pulsing ache of his throat.

As soon as he'd escaped this skyscraper of nightmares, he resolved, he was going straight back to the Keeper's Crescent. He would throw the explosive device Saito had given him to kill the Kawakamis into the sea, once and for all, and then he would find Toshiko and her siblings. He would return the pearl to them – or even better yet, he would find a way to use it himself, to help them, and finally do what Toshiko had asked of him, when he'd made the wrong choice and deserted her.

Moments ago, almost unthinkingly, Theo had asked these two Crows to imagine what someone with powers like his might be able to do with the pearl's help. Then, he had simply been trying to frighten them into doing as he asked. Now, he really began to wonder. The Sensei had said that there were people with powers like his all over the world. She'd told him, too, that among these people, there were many who'd never even thought of suppressing their powers, and who, instead, were actively learning to use them. Even back in Eardland, in the good days when he'd had Susanna's help, Theo had never really stopped feeling wary of the Gift. Perhaps it was time he conclusively put that fear aside, and found out what he was capable of.

7.

Haru twisted in Kei's arms to look back at the limp form of his mother, slumped against the neck of an increasingly restive, frantic Lightning. The shaft of Mei's arrow was still clearly visible from here, where it was buried in her throat. Was she dead? It didn't seem possible. She'd always been such a fixed presence – not only for him, in his own life, but for the whole Empire. Surely someone like her couldn't be extinguished so easily.

Kei tugged gently on his arm. 'Don't look,' she tried to tell him.

Haru knew she was probably right, and yet still he couldn't stop staring as his mother lost her grip on Lightning's reins entirely and tumbled from the horse's back, falling all the way to the muddy ground. He couldn't even look away as Lightning suddenly reared in wide-eyed panic, and then landed, her hooves crashing down onto his mother's spreadeagled form. Haru did close his eyes then, hearing the crack of bones.

'It's okay,' Kei said, sounding so worried that he never would have believed her, even if he had followed her advice and kept his eyes shut the whole time. 'You're okay.'

Haru realized he was crying now, and clinging to Kei so tightly he must have been hurting her. He forced himself to slacken his grip and draw back from her a little, just in time to see General Mori dismounting from his horse in front of them and gathering the reins in one hand, his lined face grave but composed. Haru had only just begun to blink away his tears when the General did something very surprising indeed: he removed his helmet, revealing his silver-flecked hair, and knelt before Haru in the dirt and mud of the battlefield.

'My Emperor,' he said to Haru. Then he bowed his forehead all the way to the ground.

Haru could still only sob and gulp in response. He didn't understand, didn't *want* to understand what was happening. He wished General Mori would stand up and get back on his horse. Far from doing that, though, the General didn't even straighten up from his bow, and before long, a wave was passing through the Imperial Army, as each of its hundreds of soldiers echoed

General Mori's actions, lowering their weapons, dismounting, and bowing to Haru – all of them ultimately choosing to follow the General's lead, although some did act more quickly and eagerly than others. The resistance fighters, too, were beginning to join them, and another sob rose in Haru's throat at the sight of all those brave Keeper's Children whom his mother had treated so badly, trusting him now to be better.

'*My Emperor.*'

The words resonated through the battlefield, not quite spoken in unison, but seeming to mean more, for the fact that each voice sounded fully individual, as if each person truly meant what they said.

And yet Haru still felt completely unsure of how to respond. Of course, he'd known that one day he would inherit the Empire, but he'd expected that to happen in many years' time, when he was older and ready – not now, not like this, on a battlefield, and when he was so tired and young and unprepared.

A roar like a thunderclap sounded somewhere behind him then, and a gust of wind swept over the plains as Hiranaya soared above the Crescent to once again dominate the sky over the battlefield. Her cuts from Mr Winter's poisoned knife still bled freely, the blood coming off her in red ribbons which curled out into the air around her. Haru couldn't help but notice, too, that her pearl wasn't glowing nearly as brightly as it had done before. And yet, in spite of all this, she still looked, in that moment, every inch the triumphal vision – all brightness and strength. A cheer went up from among the Keeper's Children at the sight of her rising up again like this, and Haru felt his heartbeat start to steady.

'What should I do?' he whispered to Kei, then.

'Why not do something new, and bow back to them all?' was her suggestion, in his ear.

He stumbled forward, and managed to bow to the resistance fighters and the Crescent, before turning to bow to General Mori, and then to the whole Imperial Army. Whispers, then, began to start up everywhere, sounding to Haru like a breeze moving through leaves.

And then the solemnity was shattered by a broken cry, emanating from where the Crows were still gathered, uncertain without Mr Winter to lead them. Haru squinted into their massed ranks to see Hana – still consumed with fury, still standing with her dagger raised.

'Seize him, seize the new Emperor!' she was shouting.

And at last, as if waking from a dream, the lines of Crows began to surge forward, back into the Crescent, towards where Haru was still standing, next to Kei. The Keeper's Children raised their weapons in response, as Kei and General Mori both immediately jumped to their feet to take defensive positions in front of Haru. Hiranaya landed in a gust of wind on the narrow strip of scrubland behind them all.

Haru turned and ran to the dragon, throwing his arms out to embrace her. When he pulled back, he saw just how strained and ill she still looked, her face tense with the effort of fighting the effects of the poison from Mr Winter's blade. She bared her gleaming teeth in a smile for him, even so.

Perhaps another flight would be a good idea now? she suggested, her voice resonating inside his mind. This time, Haru didn't hesitate to scramble up and swing his leg over the thick muscles of her neck.

'Can Kei come, too?' he asked Hiranaya. 'I want her to be safe.'

Of course, the dragon told him. *Although I do not know how long my strength can last, carrying two humans.*

'You'll rest soon,' Haru told her. 'I promise.'

He held a hand out to Kei, and she ran to climb up behind him. Hiranaya launched herself skywards, just as the first of the Crows reached the front line of the Crescent's resistance fighters.

As Haru looked down to the battlefield, he realized that he could see Ren. Ren's leg was bandaged, but he was still limping forward through the ranks of the resistance to meet the Crows, ready to defend the Crescent from attack, as courageous and determined as ever. Haru could see the Imperial Army more clearly from up here, too – a sea of dark purple made up of hundreds of soldiers, all mostly remounted on their horses again now, prepared once more for battle. And yet they all seemed to be looking up at him, Haru realized, as if awaiting direction. Suddenly, he understood what needed to be done.

'Can you fly over them?' he asked Hiranaya.

Wordlessly, she turned in the air to carry them up and over the Crescent's borders, to hover directly above the Imperial Army.

'Drive the Crows away from this place,' Haru ordered the Guards, hoping his voice would carry well enough over the wind. 'Don't kill them. Take prisoners if you have to, but don't kill them. Not unless they're about to kill you. Just make them go away, and leave the Crescent alone. Do everything you can to protect the Keeper's Children and their homes.'

Down on the other side of the battle lines, Hana was giving orders too, to the Crows.

'We stand firm and fight,' she was shouting. 'We can't let those of us who died here today die for nothing, and the Sensei has plans for this land. We can't leave until it's ours.'

The Crows as a whole, though, seemed far from as committed as she was to persisting in carrying out the Sensei's orders. To stay here and fight, after all, would now mean facing an army of trained Imperial soldiers, all armed with tall, powerful bows and mounted on horseback – an army that also had a dragon on its side. Some of the Crows were turning to run already, breaking off from the ranks of fighters to flee through the Crescent, heading for its more distant gates.

The Imperial Army advanced then, crossing over the fallen fences into the Crescent, as General Mori rode his huge red horse through the disordered forces of the Crows to meet them and ride at their head.

'You never fail to surprise me, little Emperor,' Kei said in Haru's ear, as they flew on Hiranaya's back to join the Imperial troops. And even though he'd seen and done so many terrible things today that he feared he'd never be able to sleep easy again, Haru still smiled, and reached to take her hand.

PART V

HORIZONS
AND SHORES

CHAPTER NINETEEN

Binding the Wounds

1.

The Imperial Guard made short work of driving the Lucky Crows out of the Crescent. The Crows were wearied, as well as disorganized without Ken Saito to lead them, and it wasn't long before they gave up the Crescent and dispersed.

Once it was clear they really had left, Haru told most of his Guards to return to the barracks in the city proper, to rest and await further orders. He asked only one regiment to return as soon as possible, bringing medical supplies for those who'd been hurt in the fighting.

It felt strange to Toshiko to be relying on Imperial Guards like this, when for so many years they had been one of the two faces of the enemy, just the sight of their dark purple uniforms enough

to set her nerves on edge. She found herself doubting the level of
control that Haru really had over them now, half-expecting them
to turn on him at any moment, and rebel. It simply seemed too
much to believe that these fearsome spectres of her childhood
should be so swiftly tamed by a child.

And yet, as Haru issued his orders, she couldn't avoid seeing
what was surely relief on most of the Guards' faces. Perhaps more
of them than she'd suspected had doubted their former Emperor's
judgement. The idea that anyone could follow such orders as
to march on the Keeper's Crescent still made her feel furious
though, even as a small voice reminded her of how difficult it was
to stick to any principles and still survive, in this city.

On this occasion, anyway, in spite of her fears, all of the
Guards did as Haru told them. They left the Crescent to carry
out his instructions under the command of two Generals, named
Watanabe and Kubo.

General Mori and his regiment volunteered to stay behind,
to guard the Crescent against any possible further attacks,
something that Haru and also Ren had agreed was a good
idea – even though Ren clearly shared Toshiko's wariness of
the Guards. Toshiko supposed she also could see the sense
in a regiment remaining behind, in spite of that wariness. As
much as she didn't like to admit that they could still be in some
danger from the Crows, her long experience of the gang told
her it was best not to take any chances. No one, for instance,
had managed to capture the young woman who'd seized Haru
in the battle, and who'd been so insistent, too, on following the
Sensei's orders to the end. And then there was the Sensei herself,
who, as far as anyone knew, was still alive and well somewhere
in Rainshadow City.

Although General Mori and his Guards certainly couldn't

stay here protecting the Crescent forever, their presence for the moment allowed the Keeper's Children to focus on what was currently the most urgent concern – helping the many people who'd been injured in the fighting.

The situation only grew more worrying as night fell. The wounded had already been gathering in the café during the battle, but now, in its aftermath, so many more people were arriving at its doorway all the time, in search of medical help – Keeper's Children, Jetsam and Guards alike. There were even some Crows among them. No one, of course, was particularly keen to help this last group. As a rule though, the Crows coming to them for help were all so badly injured that it simply felt wrong to turn them away. Toshiko herself had even admitted a pair of them into the tent earlier: two young men, clearly brothers, the older holding up the younger, who'd been bleeding heavily from a brutal gash in his side. Of course she understood that these two must surely have done terrible things in the battle, and yet in that moment of seeing them outside the café's doorway like that – the older man's face so drawn and haunted at the extent of his brother's injuries – she hadn't found it in her to tell them they weren't welcome here.

The café's fire did something to keep the little world under its red, chequered roof warm and welcoming for everyone arriving here in search of help, but in practice, the blaze could do little to dispel their pain or their fear, not to mention the mounting worries of those tending to them.

The problem wasn't the lack of capable healers. Many Keeper's Children had some basic healing knowledge, and they had Jun in charge of them now, who'd been taught by Mailee, as well as several of the Imperial Guard who had experience of treating battle wounds. There was also a small army of volunteers here helping, who might not have had much expertise, but were willing to do their best with the menial tasks. The problem was the lack of medical supplies and equipment. It was likely to be several hours until the Guards who'd gone into Rainshadow City to fetch these things would return, and the supplies Mailee had kept here in the café were already running perilously low. There was far from enough to treat a whole battle's worth of wounds, and there wasn't even an adequate supply of clean water – all the water they used had to be carried over in containers from the river, before being boiled clean in pots over the fire.

While Toshiko might not be a natural healer like Jun, she'd still volunteered to stay in the café and do what she could to help. On Ren's instructions, she carried on meeting the new arrivals at the tent's doorway, directing them to whichever healer seemed best able to help them. In between, she did whatever else might assist the healers with their work – heating water and boiling the rags they were having to use in place of bandages, or drying these out by the fire and distributing them. She had to keep doing her best, she told herself, even if every new injury she saw only deepened her growing fears that, for many of these people, the most that anyone here would be able to do for them tonight might still be far from enough.

Even while busy with all these tasks, she kept a close eye on Jun as he worked. He seemed powered by a new fire of determination, which she'd never quite seen in him before. She was proud of him, of course. And yet as she watched him, she still couldn't help but think, too, of how much more good he'd have been able to do here, if she hadn't lost the pearl to Theo.

As she headed back from boiling rags by the fire to greet more new arrivals, she was handed a tray filled with cups of herb tea by another Keeper's Child, who was also here helping the healers.

She handed these out as she continued over to the café's entrance, offering tea to anyone who still looked well enough to drink it, hoping that it might offer some warmth and comfort, even if it didn't taste quite the same as Mailee's had used to.

She handed the last cup on the tray to a Keeper's Child who she found shivering outside the tent's entrance. The woman was freezing cold and nearly grey-faced with pain, but none of the healers was able to do anything for her yet, because there seemed nothing more urgently wrong with her than a broken leg. Toshiko gripped the woman's hand briefly, muttering something to her about how strong she was, which sounded trite and useless even to her own ears. The woman, though, managed to give her a weak smile – and that smile was almost harder for Toshiko to bear than the sight of the worst of the injuries here. It was far too filled with trust, gratitude and hope, none of which felt at all merited, given the growing sense of chaos and desperation in the tent, as more and more people clamoured for the healers' attention, and the medical supplies ran ever lower.

Retreating quickly from the woman, Toshiko was unable to do much more than stand still in front of the fire for a moment, trying to regain her composure. She found herself picking again at the loose threads of the jacket she was wearing – still Theo's, seeing as it wasn't like she'd had time to change it – as she tried to fight the hopelessness that was on the verge of engulfing her.

Her eyes flicked reflexively over to the café's doorway, and instead of seeing more new arrivals, jostling for help, for a moment there was only Mei there, with Mochi at her feet. She was standing with her back to the scenes inside the tent, just looking out, into the night. As Toshiko watched, Mei lifted Mochi to curl around her shoulders.

This was the first moment since the battle that Toshiko had

seen her sister alone. She'd been hailed as a hero by the Keeper's Children for what she'd done, and had been surrounded ever since by admiring resistance fighters, vowing to keep her safe from any reprisals, as well as by those who simply wanted to be close to her, to shelter in the strength she'd shown.

Toshiko wondered what on earth Mei might be thinking now, as she looked out into the darkness – and for the first time in their lives together, she found herself questioning whether her sister was fully all right. Mei had always been so much older and stronger, and always so formidably on top of things. How did it feel to kill an Emperor, though? How did it feel to kill anyone, for that matter?

Since the battle's end, she hadn't felt at all able to reach Mei, through all of the people surrounding her. She'd barely had the chance to talk to her, in fact, and wasn't even sure what she'd have said, or asked, if they had been able to speak. The truth was that she couldn't help but see Mei, now, a little as it seemed the rest of the Keeper's Children saw her – as a steely young woman, capable of bringing down an Emperor, apparently without breaking a sweat. She just wasn't sure how to square this with the fact Mei was also meant to be her big sister.

Even still, Toshiko began to weave her way towards Mei through the tent's desperate churn of activity. Before she'd managed to reach her though, Ren called out for her sister's attention back in the café, and without even noticing Toshiko there behind her, Mei turned to go over to him, to speak to the injured resistance fighter he was currently looking after. A lot of the wounded wanted to speak to Mei, Toshiko had noticed. They seemed to draw strength from her – and, watching Mei crouch down next to the injured man and take his hand, Toshiko realized that the hope Mei was able to give to these people might just turn out to be one of the most important healing resources they still had left at their disposal here.

Left alone now to hover uselessly in the café's doorway, Toshiko steeled her nerves, preparing herself to return to the world of blood, fear and suffering in the café behind her. And as she did, she looked out over the Gods' Road, taking in the sights of the battle's aftermath.

The rain had stopped, the Moons and stars were out, and the background susurration of ocean waves, ever-present in the Crescent, seemed somehow louder than usual. It was cold, too, and she rolled the sleeves of her jacket down, pulling it tighter around her shoulders as she watched the Keeper's Children out on the road. Everyone out there was moving as if dazed, their hands working busily to clear debris, while their faces, caught in the moonlight, showed only various kinds of hollowness, or grief.

Toshiko wondered then how Mailee was doing, and whether she knew yet where it was that the boat she was still trapped on was heading. Was she was hoping for a rescue, or had she given up?

Toshiko was just turning to go back inside again, when her gaze caught on a figure rounding the bend of the Gods' Road, coming from the direction of the coast – and though he was still quite far away, there was no mistaking who this was. There weren't many other people around here, after all, with hair that would shine gold like that, when caught in the flashes of light from the Keeper's Children's lanterns.

Toshiko's heartbeat skipped, then quickened at Theo's approach, and she couldn't tell whether this was out of anger, or something else. Those words of Saito's still haunted her. *Why did he leave you alive?*

2.

'I think I can use the pearl to bring back the barge that the Crows sent to Hanasaki Island,' Theo told Toshiko all in a rush, before she could even begin to consider what to say to him. 'I think I can bring those people home.'

His voice was completely hoarse, and she couldn't help but notice, too, that he looked awful – covered in scabs, streaked with blood and dirt, and with a collar of angry purple bruising visible around his neck, even in this light. He was still dressed in the shirt and trousers he'd worn to the old Emperor's party, but they were barely recognizable now, they'd become so worn and ragged. He seemed ill at ease, too, sinking his hands deep into his pockets, and not quite meeting her eye. Was it only guilt at having betrayed her? Or did she still have to worry about any orders he might have concerning her, from the Crows?

Toshiko wanted to shout at him, for abandoning them all. She wanted to ask him why he looked like that, and what had happened to him since he'd left. And yet, she simply couldn't ignore the implications of what he'd just said to her.

'What do you mean, you think you can bring the barge back?'

'I used the Gift to manipulate the weather before, remember?' he said, looking up now, tentatively meeting her gaze. 'I think that with the extra power the pearl could give me, I might be able to change the direction of the wind and maybe even the tides, and turn the boat around like that.'

'You really think that's possible?'

He shrugged. 'I think so. I mean, it's definitely *possible*. I can't say for certain it'll work. That barge left more than a whole day and night ago now, so it'll be quite far out to sea already. And then I haven't actually tried using the pearl at all since I – well.'

'Since you stole it,' Toshiko finished for him. 'Since you abandoned us, taking the one tool that could have helped us in a seemingly impossible situation.'

Theo rubbed his forehead. 'That's fair, I suppose.'

'You lied to me. You were working for the Crows the whole time.'

He didn't deny it. 'I'm not working for them anymore,' was all he said. 'And don't you think this is worth a try? If there's any kind of chance we could save Mailee and the others, surely we have to take it?'

Toshiko badly wanted to ask him just who he thought he was to tell her this, when he'd failed so completely to take the chance of helping them all before, in the battle. She didn't, though, because a new idea was beginning to flare in her mind now, like an ember from a fire she'd assumed had gone out long ago.

'Where's the pearl?' she demanded, holding her hand out for it. 'I need it, right now.'

'Don't you want me to try and bring the barge home?' Theo asked, only blinking back at her. 'I'll need to do it soon, if I'm going to.'

'Of course I want you to,' she said. 'But there's something else we need to do first.'

She kept her hand held out for the pearl, waiting. 'Did you really come back to help us?' she asked. 'Or was it only to tend to your ego?'

He seemed to be about to argue, then nodded and pulled the pearl from his pocket. As he held it up to show her, in spite of everything, Toshiko couldn't help but feel a shiver of sheer wonder then, at its otherworldly magnificence – at its marbled surface, reflecting the moonlight and the lanterns in the night around them, and at that inner glow it always seemed to have, too, even when its power wasn't being used.

Theo tipped the pearl into her palm, and as she closed her fingers tight around it, she almost laughed at the surge of sheer relief she felt to hold its power like this once again. She allowed herself a small, tight smile, and Theo, infuriatingly, managed to shake off the conflicted look he'd been wearing since reappearing, to grin fully back at her.

'What?' she scowled at him.

'It's just good to see you, is all.'

She only rolled her eyes, and before he could say anything else, began towing him by the arm back towards the doorway into the café.

'I'm giving the pearl to my brother,' she explained, as they went. 'We don't have any proper medical facilities here, but he can compensate for that, with the pearl's help. You can make yourself useful, too, while he's working. How are you with cleaning cuts?'

'I ... I'm not sure.' Theo let himself be led through the café's doorway, to look around himself as if dazed at the scenes of mounting distress that were everywhere, here. 'I suppose I can try.'

Toshiko did feel a certain grim satisfaction then, at how genuinely shaken he looked to be plunged like this into the world of suffering inside the tent. *Good*, she told herself, as she pulled him over to where Jun was still hard at work. *Let him see what he abandoned us to.*

3.

Further down the Gods' Road from the café, in the direction of the sea, Haru found he couldn't stop the tears leaking from his eyes as he and Kei worked together to tend Hiranaya's many battle wounds.

Every time in Haru's life when he'd cried before, the way he'd felt on the inside had matched the crying on the outside. He'd never thought, in fact, to consider the two things as separate – they had always seemed seamlessly interlinked. Now though, as he took care to soak the cloth he was using to clean Hiranaya's wounds in his bowl of steaming hot water, before dipping it again into the second bowl of cooler water that he was using to wipe the blood and dirt from her scales, he found that his tears no longer seemed at all connected to what was happening within him.

This was because, despite the fact that he certainly was crying, all Haru could seem to feel was a new, muffled kind of blankness. This blankness had begun, perhaps, as a sort of scream in the moments after he'd killed Mr Winter. This scream had then expanded as he'd watched his mother die, slumped over her horse, until it had filled his mind entirely – and it hadn't paused since then, not even to draw breath. It was so unvaried in its seeming endlessness, in fact, that it had now managed to settle into a new kind of nothingness, in its own right.

Hiranaya opened her golden eyes to watch him as he wiped the layers of dirt from a deep gash that Mr Winter had gouged in the side of her neck. Her breath was coming shallow, and her pearl, which had shone so brightly when she'd first appeared above the battlefield, was now casting only a faint, sickly light – so dim that Haru didn't think he'd have been able to see it at all, had it not been so dark out here on the Gods' Road. Even the sheen of her scales seemed to have dulled. Her golden gaze was steady, though, as her voice sounded once more in his mind.

Haru, she said, *now that you are Emperor of these islands, you will be needed at the Palace. You should be going there, to secure your authority, not looking after me, here.*

This wasn't the first time tonight she'd tried to tell him this.

Haru only shook his head as he wiped away more of the blood still seeping from her wound. He noticed Kei casting him a concerned look at that head shake. He forgot, sometimes, that she couldn't always hear what Hiranaya was saying to him. He didn't feel in any mood to relay the dragon's words to her, though. She would probably only agree with them, and then he would have to argue with her as well, because regardless of what anyone might say, Haru knew he didn't need to be at the Palace at all. He needed to be here with Hiranaya, making her better, so that she could find the pearl and take it back home with her to Muralania, to Kiri.

I do see that the burden of being ruler of the whole Archipelago is a heavy weight to lay on such young shoulders, Hiranaya's voice resonated through his thoughts again. *I am not trying to pretend that it is an easy thing to face.*

'When do you think you'll be able to fly again?' Haru asked her, instead of properly replying. 'We have to find Kiri's pearl. He's waiting for you.'

Hiranaya's golden eyes closed again, and immediately Haru regretted reminding her of this. Of course she knew very well that Kiri was waiting, without him bringing it up.

'I'm sorry,' he said immediately, before she could answer. 'You'll be well again soon, I know it. And then we'll look for the pearl together. Everything will be fine. I promise.'

The poison is strong, Hiranaya told him. *I healed from it before, but not quickly. I am not so young as I was then, either, and my wounds are more extensive this time. Even if I can recover, it might take seasons. And Kiri cannot wait for seasons.*

The blankness that still reigned within Haru had muffled all of his own feelings to such an extent that he immediately recognized the flood of grief he experienced at these words of Hiranaya's as something that belonged to her, and not to him. It was as if his mind hadn't been able to fully process in language what she'd been trying to express – as if he didn't yet have the vocabulary to translate such feelings into an adequate form of words, and so had been left simply with the sensation of her sadness, as something too enormous to articulate.

'You won't take seasons to heal,' he told her. 'We'll find some way around it. We'll make the healing faster.'

She opened her eyes again then to fix him with the steady glow of her gaze. *If I do not recover,* she asked, *will you find Kiri's pearl on my behalf, and take it to him?*

Haru shook his head. He didn't mean to say no, he was just unable to accept what she was asking. 'You will recover,' he told her. 'I'm the Emperor now. I have power, and people who will help me, and I'll do everything I can to make you get better.'

Healing does not always work that way, Haru, Hiranaya told him. *And if you want to be sure of your rule as Emperor, you should return to the Palace.*

Haru wanted to block out her voice, even though he knew it was impossible, what with its resounding inside his own mind. Abruptly then, he realized that the flow of tears from his eyes had become so strong that he could barely see what he was doing anymore, dipping his cloth into the bowls of water.

'Haru?' Kei sat back on her heels to look over at him. She seemed so obviously anxious that Haru dropped his own cloth into his bowl of hot water, and went to give her a hug.

'Everything will be okay,' he told her, trying to sound reassuring, even though he wasn't even sure what it was, exactly, that was concerning her now, when there were so many huge and terrible things weighing down on them. 'I'm the Emperor now. I can make sure everything's okay.'

She held on to him tightly. 'You'll be a wonderful Emperor, Haru. I know it.'

He nodded into her shoulder, and tried not to think about the vast empty space in the world where his mother should be. Almost everyone seemed to want him to fill that space now, and of course he didn't want to disappoint them. It just didn't feel right, though, to simply step into what she'd left behind. To do that would feel almost like trying to remake the world as if she'd never been in it at all, and in spite of everything, Haru still wasn't sure that he wanted to do that. Whoever she'd been, after all, and whatever she'd done, she'd still been his mother.

4.

As soon as he fastened the pearl around his neck, Jun was beset by a clamouring crowd. The rumour of his enhanced healing abilities had spread fast, and now, before he'd even got started, everyone was demanding help for themselves, or for loved ones. Immediately, Ren and two of the Jetsam stepped in.

'He'll see only the most serious wounds,' Ren insisted, his face grave as he turned away those with sprains, broken bones, minor burns – with anything, in fact, that was of no immediate threat to life.

Watching the faces of those being turned away, Jun couldn't help but feel heartbroken. He knew Ren was right – there were Keeper's Children here whose lives were hanging by a thread, and he needed to see them first. But that didn't stop him from wishing things could be different. Back in the thick of the battle, he had struggled to help anyone the way he'd wanted to. Now he was getting a second chance to do some good for the Keeper's Children, and he was still already falling short. He wasn't even sure the pearl would work for him as it had done before, when he'd healed Toshiko's shoulder wound. And yet, he had to try.

The two Jetsam fighters flanked him like bodyguards as Ren led him to those who most needed his help.

They went first to a young man of about Jun's own age, who was struggling to breathe with what looked like a punctured lung. Pushing aside all his doubts about the pearl and whether he would even be able to make it work again, Jun knelt by his patient's side and placed his hands gently over where the damage to the lung was worst.

He sent an inward prayer to the Keeper, asking for help, begging the child-God for the strength, now, to do what he must. And then he tuned into the terrible knotted threads of the young man's pain.

5.

Toshiko had explained to Theo that the pearl would enhance her brother's natural gift for healing. Theo probably should have been prepared, then, for seeing what Jun would be able to do with the pearl. He still found himself completely astounded, though, to watch Jun work.

Even from the outside, it didn't look easy to heal the young Keeper's Child with the punctured lung. It was a task that seemed to cost Jun something, the intense effort it demanded clear in the furrowed lines that etched themselves into his expression as he focused. Theo noticed, too, more pale grey strands emerging amid Jun's dark hair as he worked – and yet in spite of all the obvious strain, Jun continued on, determined, until the wounded young man drew in a deep, shuddering gulp of air, then dissolved into tears of gratitude, weeping like a newborn at being able to breathe again.

Even then Jun didn't pause for a break, simply letting Ren lead him on to the next patient.

He wasn't able to save everyone. Some of the Keeper's Children still lost their grip on life under his care, and yet even when this happened, Jun got back up to his feet and went to the side of the next person in desperate need of his help, relying on Ren to stay behind and explain to those who were grieving that there were still limits to this power, and he couldn't bring back the dead. Before long, Jun looked exhausted, his face grey, his hair streaked distinctly with white. Yet he still kept on going – and, slowly but surely, he saved one life, then another, and then another.

Theo felt more than a flicker of shame, knowing that in all his years of living with the Gift, it had never once occurred to him even to try using his powers for this purpose. And yet, he also found that watching Jun gave him hope, too – and not just because fewer lives were going to be lost here today than had at first seemed inevitable. The fact was, Jun's healing work showed him, definitively, that at its best, the Gift really could be an instrument for good – because he was certain, now, that Jun was most definitely using something very close to the Gift, as he did this healing work. The Sensei had explained, after all, that most people did have some natural aptitude for channelling Sola, which could be enhanced by the pearl, even if they hadn't been born with any obviously unusual skills, and Jun's eyes had turned a lighter, softer version of that same, tell-tale gold that Theo had seen earlier, in the Sensei's eyes as she'd fought with him, and that of course he'd seen reflected back in his own, too.

At Toshiko's bidding, Theo boiled rags, fetched bandages and collected supplies from the Keeper's Children who were bringing whatever they could from their homes to help those in the tent. And as he did, he caught himself wondering whether things might have been different back in Eardland, had this type of healing come naturally to him. Would his powers still have been regarded as the Devil's work, if he had used them in this way?

There was still so much grief and desperation everywhere here, especially from those who had to watch as people they loved moved beyond the point at which Jun was able to help them. No one here, though, was showing anything like the suspicion Theo had met with in Eardland, whenever he had used the Gift openly. For one fleeting moment, as he sorted a new batch of donated supplies into what was usable and what wasn't, Theo allowed himself to imagine what it might be like to return home, only to find himself treated with this same level of acceptance. Then he shook his head, dismissing the daydream. It was a far more hopeful one, after all, than he had any right to entertain – especially given that even if he were to now run straight to the docks and jump on the first ship sailing in Eardland's direction, it seemed increasingly unlikely that he'd live long enough to make it more than a few days into the voyage.

His thoughts drifted then, inevitably, to the idea of asking Jun for help, himself. There were so many other people here, though, who were all in much more urgent need than he was – people who, in all likelihood, were also far more deserving. And then, too, what if the Sensei had been right, when she'd told him that the efforts of any healer would only speed up the poison's effects?

'Only the most serious wounds,' Ren kept on insisting, still having to wave people away even in their suffering, to reserve Jun's time and energy for those for whom it could mean the difference between life and death. Jun was still working hard, his eyes still lit with gold as he looked after a woman with a deep chest wound, but he looked increasingly exhausted.

No, Theo resolved. He shouldn't even be thinking of asking Jun to use his strength on helping him, when he'd come here to finally focus on helping others, for a change. And so he turned away from watching, as Jun made far better use of the ability to channel Sola in just a few hours than he himself probably had done in his full nineteen years – and he got back to work, helping Toshiko as best as he could.

6.

Eventually, after what felt like hours of near-miracles from Jun, and relentless, back-breaking work from the rest of them, the pain and fear that had been constant in the café since Theo had first arrived finally gave way to simple tiredness. Far too many lives had still been lost in the battle, but, thanks to Jun, they'd managed to bring more people back from the brink than ever would have seemed possible, earlier in the evening.

And yet, the presence of the dead hanging over everything tonight still left Theo with a new kind of hollowness. Earlier, he'd had the disconcerting, strangely desolate experience of seeing the body of Daichi Santos, laid out with the dead. Apparently, the younger of the two Santos brothers had somehow ended his life here, back on the other side of the divide between the Crescent and the Crows, which he and Hiroto had seemed so eager to leap over for good.

Theo hadn't seen any sign of Hiroto, but Daichi, in death, had been wearing Hiroto's watch – which Theo had always assumed must be a family heirloom, in being far nicer than anything any lowlier member of the Crows would typically be able to afford.

Daichi's wounds had been cleaned by somebody, too, and Theo didn't think any healer from among the resistance would have taken the time to do that for one of the Crows, when there were still Keeper's Children's lives to be saved. Perhaps, then, Hiroto had come and gone, wanting his brother to be laid to rest here – not among criminals like himself, but alongside the shrine of the Keeper, who took care of the young, and the lost.

Theo was still turning over these thoughts, shivering by the fire over a cup of herb tea in the new quietness that had settled over the tent, when Toshiko appeared again at his side.

'Jun's finished for now,' she said. 'This work ... It's taken a lot out of him. But he's helped a lot of people, tonight. In fact, I don't know what we would have done, if he hadn't had the pearl.' She hesitated. 'Thank you for bringing it back.'

Theo only shrugged. 'Oh, you know me,' he ventured then, with a weak attempt at a smile. 'I'd never dream of doing anything that wasn't entirely selfless, where that pearl is concerned.'

That only earned him a look of outright disdain. He supposed he couldn't blame her. Probably it was far too early to be making jokes about what he'd done. He was feeling really quite light-headed now though, which seemed to be making him inappropriately flippant. He sighed and, steeling himself for what was surely coming next, took one last sip of hot tea before setting his cup down on the floor.

'Are you ready, then?' Toshiko asked him, right on cue.

More than just light-headed, he was also feeling slightly nauseous, and so weary he wasn't even fully sure he'd be able to get up from this chair again, never mind drag himself down to the waves to wield power over the ocean and sky. And yet Jun had never let up, all night – never pausing in his efforts to help while he was still needed, even in spite of how much it clearly exhausted him. And now, the Keeper's Children imprisoned on the barge needed Theo's help, as soon as possible. He was all too aware that the further away the barge was allowed to travel on the open ocean, the more difficult it would be for him to find it, using the Gift.

'I've never been readier,' he told Toshiko.

Then he braced his arms against the sides of his chair, and managed to push himself to his feet.

She didn't return his attempt at a smile, only stared hard at him, as if searching his expression for some sign that he really could do what he'd promised her. Eventually, though she still looked far from being satisfied, she reached into her jacket pocket for the pearl, and held it out to him.

This time, he didn't hesitate before taking it.

'Thanks for trusting me,' he told her.

'Yes, well,' she replied, without a shred of lightness in her voice. 'You'd just better not mess this up.'

CHAPTER TWENTY

Lighthouses

1.

During his long walk back to the Crescent, Theo had had plenty of time to consider the pearl, sitting so unassumingly in his pocket. Of course he had wondered, just a little, how much power it might truly hold when used in combination with the Gift.

At the time, he'd definitely felt he'd been doing the right thing in ignoring the temptation to experiment, and try to find out. Now that he was actually wading into the cold, dark shallows of the ocean, though, being buffeted by the salt and spray on the breeze, with the pearl swinging from its chain around his neck and already emitting a dim glow as if in sympathy with the moonlight, he began to wonder if allowing himself just a little practice with it in advance might have been more practical.

He'd thought that wading deep into the ocean like this might help him become better attuned to its rhythms and currents, but he was only in up to his shins, and already his whole body felt in shock at the unexpected iciness of the water. Deciding that this would just have to be deep enough for his purposes tonight, he stopped and turned, to look back towards the shore.

A lot of people are counting on you, Ren had said, back in the café tent where he was still taking care of the wounded, when Theo had explained just what he was going to try now. *You're their last hope.*

As if Ren's words hadn't made this situation feel daunting enough, many of the Keeper's Children, including Toshiko and her siblings, had actually gathered along the coast, to watch. They were sitting wrapped in blankets, either along the wooden platforms of the docks, or in clusters along the strip of beach beneath, to form an audience that radiated hushed expectancy. Many of them probably had friends and family on the barge, Theo was only too aware.

In an attempt to look more confident than he really felt, he gave these assembled spectators a wave, now. A few people waved back. Toshiko wasn't among them.

The new Emperor returned his wave at least, as he made his way out onto the beach through the Crescent's Southern Gate, to join the expectant crowd of Keeper's Children. He raised a hand to Theo in a hollow sort of way, before turning back to the enormous, injured dragon, now limping, very slowly, behind him – a creature Theo had last seen collapsed on the scrubland, apparently insensible.

On the road back to the Crescent, Theo had found many a traveller eager to tell stories of the Crown Prince flying over the battle on dragonback, as well as to exclaim over what an auspicious sign this dragon's blessing surely was for his reign. Actually faced with the Emperor now, though, Theo couldn't help but think that if he hadn't recognized him from the telecasts, he'd never have suspected that this was the same boy as the one in all of those heroic tales. He simply looked too small and fragile to be Emperor, as he shuffled down the moonlit beach, pulling his robe tight against the ocean breeze, while shooting looks of concern at the dragon next to him, as she struggled along the sand – the dragon who, laid low as she was by her injuries, seemed almost as unrecognizable from the war stories as the Emperor, in spite of her size, claws and enormous teeth. Theo noticed the pearl, then, glowing amidst the crusted jewels at her throat – an uncanny copy of the one he wore on the chain around his own neck.

He dropped the Emperor a low bow, though the boy didn't look in any mood to care about such formalities, and then bowed to the dragon, too, for good measure, only to struggle to pull himself upright again. The cold currents of the ocean seemed to be conspiring both with the grainy silt beneath his feet, and with his own dizziness, to tug him downwards. He only managed to finally stand up straight with immense effort, after which he turned hurriedly away from the watching crowd to face the horizon again. It was time to get started. He didn't know, after all, how much longer he could last out here. He drew in a deep breath, trying not to wince as the cold, salty air scoured his bruised throat. Then he closed his eyes, reaching out with the Gift to study the forces around him.

He felt the pearl's effects immediately. Throughout his life so far, using the Gift had always seemed like listening carefully for different frequencies. He felt now, though, as if he didn't even need to listen like that anymore, because somewhere deep inside himself he already simply *knew* all the ways in which Sola might flow through every natural thing.

Eyes flying open again, he found that he could literally see it happening, everywhere around him. The whole world was suddenly lit up in patterns, in golden channels of energy that arced through the sea and the skies overhead, forming what looked like the beams and arches of a vast, cosmic cathedral. There were new beings everywhere, too – creatures resembling nothing he'd ever seen before, bobbing in and out of the waves, or dipping their wings through the golden currents of air curving overhead. Unlike ordinary birds and animals, these creatures shone with astonishingly high concentrations of Sola's golden light, even seeming to radiate it themselves, as if they could somehow be made from it. Theo blinked at the sight of one of these beings, flitting just beneath the ocean's surface, surprised to see that its shape appeared almost human – and then he found himself distracted, immediately, by a crowd of small, bright silver creatures leaping through the water like flying fish.

He had to remind himself that he couldn't afford to waste time marvelling at this newly revealed splendour. Mailee and the others on the barge were relying on him, and even through the vibrancy of all this life that he could now see and feel so fully, he could also sense his own body struggling against exhaustion – and possibly against something worse, too, in the form of the Sensei's poison, which even now could be taking hold within him.

He used the Gift, then, to reach even further into the ocean, chasing the currents, cold and warm, shallow and deep, through swells and over rocks – far further than he'd ever tried to stretch his awareness before. And then, at last, he found the barge, an unmistakable knot of pure dread on the waves.

2.

With the chill sea breeze on her face, Toshiko shivered and nestled deeper into the scratchy wool of the blanket that she'd pulled around her shoulders. It felt strange to be allowed to sit on this stretch of sand outside the Crescent's confines, which she'd only been permitted to look at through barbed wire for most of her childhood. Despite all those years of yearning to be out here, she found she was far too anxious and too cold now to even begin to enjoy the experience.

She wondered if everyone else out here on the beach felt as freezing as she did. It seemed a sign of just how much silent hope they all shared that they'd chosen to sit out like this – and so late into the night, too, when all of them were in desperate need of rest, following the battle. She hoped she hadn't misled them in insisting Theo had a good chance of succeeding.

'Still nothing,' Mei said, next to her, tapping at the keypad of her hairclip computer and ignoring Theo, out in the waves. 'It's so frustrating,' she continued. 'I just can't seem to be able to do anything, with the barge out of range of the City Web.'

'What would you do, if you could reach it?' Jun asked her then, from where he was sitting on Toshiko's other side, wrapped in a blanket and looking like he badly needed sleep, instead of a freezing night out here. He'd insisted on coming with them though, saying he couldn't rest until he knew what had happened with the barge, and his old mentor Mailee.

Mei shrugged, glancing up from her screen just long enough to give Mochi a scratch behind the ears. 'I don't know. Not without having had a proper rummage through its navigational systems. What I do know, though, is that I trust myself to help those people much more than I trust that thieving betrayer, with his magic jewel.'

Toshiko rolled her eyes at that, even despite the new shyness she still felt around Mei, following the battle. Perhaps Mei did have a point, though. Theo had certainly seemed sincere ever since coming back – but then again, he'd seemed sincere to her before, too, hadn't he?

She squinted out to where he was standing now, in the ocean. She couldn't see much from back here on the beach, in the pale moonlight – only an indistinct, shadowed figure looking out to the horizon, holding himself very still in the waves.

She heard Haru pipe up behind them. 'Do you think it's working?' he was asking Kei. 'How can we can tell if it's working?'

'I'm not sure we can tell,' Kei replied. 'I think we just have to trust that he's trying his best.'

'What if that's not enough, though?' Haru persisted.

'We can only wait and see,' Kei told him. 'Here, you should take another blanket. You're shivering.'

Toshiko turned back to Jun, next to her, only to find that he was shivering, too. She hated how much of his hair had turned white from his efforts with the pearl, so afraid it might signify that some greater, deeper harm had happened to him as a result of the work he'd done here tonight.

'You should go to the café and get some sleep,' she told him, feeling the strangeness of now being the one trying to take care of him, when it had always been the other way around. 'That barge has been sailing away from here for more than a full night and day. There probably won't be anything to see for a long while yet.'

Jun nodded, and yet stayed where he was. She followed his gaze out to sea, and out towards Theo again, who suddenly seemed very small to her out there, amid the ocean's vast, heaving darkness.

3.

Theo hadn't been sure if he would recognize the barge, but the deep currents of fear he felt emanating from it made it impossible to mistake. Immediately, he found himself wanting to call out in fear – or even to forget the whole idea of bringing it home, and to simply run away. Fighting that urge, he forced himself to focus on the air, filling the barge's sails.

Trying to do this while blocking out the terror and seasick misery emanating from those on board wasn't easy, but eventually he managed to begin reangling the sails, edging them into a position he hoped might guide the whole vessel around, back towards the Crescent.

It still didn't feel like nearly enough, though. Even through the heightened awareness that the pearl granted him, he could still feel his body growing weaker by the minute. The sails were moving too slowly, and the bow of the barge hadn't even begun to shift its course away from Hanasaki Island. Impatient, now, Theo did his best to replicate how he'd split his awareness while fighting the Sensei – dividing it, this time, between the air in the sails and the currents of Sola moving through the ocean.

The light from the pearl around his neck flared with the effort, and he was dimly aware of his legs beginning to feel unsteady beneath him. Trying to ignore this, he probed deep into the ocean, only to discover that Sola behaved differently here to how it moved through the air. He'd never really used the Gift within water before, never mind on the open sea, and he hadn't expected all the currents of it to feel so densely interwoven, and so complicated, with each strand of energy so dependent on all the others, in a mesh of waves and tides and changing temperatures. It was beginning to feel like simply too much for him to handle.

Fighting rising panic, he began tugging on the currents of Sola flowing around the barge's hull, trying to wrench them into some new shape which might turn the boat around. The harder he pulled, though, the more unwieldy they seemed to become, growing ever more tangled, and ever more difficult for his weary mind to comprehend. With a yell of frustration at his own clumsiness, Theo gave up on these strands, and, instead, sent all of his energies deeper underwater, to give the currents around the boat's keel an almighty wrench.

Immediately, he regretted it. Hadn't he learnt, after all, that using the Gift was always a delicate dance of encouragement and suggestion, and that simply trying to force currents of energy into compliance would never work? He fought to slow his breathing, and had just resolved to puzzle out the patterns of the sea more patiently, when, with a lurch somewhere deep inside his stomach, he felt the unthinkable happening, as the barge began to sink.

He threw all his remaining strength into trying to steady it again, giving everything he had towards stopping its descent. And yet it wasn't enough – not nearly. Theo screamed aloud in frustration as, still fighting to grasp hold of the barge with the Gift, he fell to his knees in the water.

4.

As Theo collapsed in the waves, a cry went up from the Keeper's Children gathered on the beach around Haru. They weren't the only ones to respond to the sight, either. Suddenly, the ocean and sky were filled with creatures. *Sun Spirits*, Haru realized with a jolt of wonder that finally did something to break through the numb emptiness that had been so dominating his mind. He looked round quickly, but no one else on the beach seemed at all aware of the Sun Spirits appearing. Perhaps the time he'd spent in proximity to Hiranaya's pearl was now making it possible for him to see what no one else could, now unfolding in the waves.

More Sun Spirits were gathering in the shallows around Theo than Haru could ever have imagined existing within this small patch of sand and ocean by the Crescent. Soon, the air above Theo too was filled with beautiful, birdlike creatures, with long, feathered tails which flashed in the moonlight – and other winged beings were joining them too, who looked more like bats or pterodactyls, or even like humans with feathered wings. The Sun Spirits filling the ocean, as well, were just as various as those of the sky – a haphazard assembly of the finned, scaled and furred. And, as Haru watched, and with all these creatures now supporting him, Theo began to straighten up again. At last, he managed to get back to his feet. He was still clearly under a lot of strain, but he was steady now, with all these beings of air and sea clustered around him, helping him, holding him upright, and adding their strength to his.

And then Haru became conscious of Hiranaya beginning to stir next to him, on the sand – and all at once, the blankness still in his mind was lanced through with white-hot fear, as she began to drag herself, still limping, down the beach to join the rest of the Sun Spirits in the waves, splashing to Theo's side in the shallows.

'Hiranaya!' Haru called after her, wishing his voice were more authoritative, like the voice of a real Emperor. 'You have to come back, to keep resting. Please! You're poisoned.'

He sprang to his feet, and began to chase after her.

Suddenly, Kei was there, grasping his arm, trying to stop him – but he tugged himself free from her grip.

'Haru!'

He was dimly aware of her following him now, as he went.

'What are you doing? *Haru!*'

5.

Toshiko discarded her blanket on the sand and ran down the beach into the freezing water to join the little chain which Theo, Hiranaya, Haru and Kei had now formed in the shallows. Theo and Haru were on either side of the dragon, their hands resting on her scales, while Kei was gripping Haru's hand. All of their eyes, not just Theo's, were shining with a brighter version of the gold that had lit Jun's as he had healed the wounded in the café – and Toshiko realized that they must be sharing the load of saving the barge. If there was any chance that she could help, too, then of course she knew she had to take it. After only a slight hesitation, during which she gave herself a fierce inward talking-to for feeling awkward about something so trivial as taking Theo's hand, when so much was at stake, she reached out to lace her fingers with his.

Immediately their hands touched, the world exploded with light and colour in a supercharged version of what she'd been able to sense before, when she'd fought with the pearl's help.

She gasped to see, too, that it wasn't by any means just the five of them who were linked together there, in the water. All around them, in the ocean and sky, were creatures of all kinds, shining with life force and energy – and all of their eyes were glowing gold, too, fixed with determination on the horizon. Trying her best to remember how it had felt to bend and alter the currents of air around her when she'd last worn the pearl, Toshiko took a deep breath, and fully attuned her awareness to theirs.

First, she felt a shock of nauseated fear, completely at odds with the bright world around her. Then, suddenly, she realized that it was the barge that she could suddenly feel, far out on the ocean. It was pitching in the waves, unsteady, but the combined strength and effort of those in the chain around her seemed to be just about holding it above the waves. It had turned away from Hanasaki Island now, too, and was facing back towards home.

Of course, she realized then, as she let the full extent of the fear felt by those on board wash over her. This rescue wasn't just a question of winds and tides – there were Crows on the barge too, fighting to frustrate Theo and the others as they wove Sola through the sails and around the hull. She closed her eyes, letting herself visualize the barge more clearly, and joined her energy, fully, to that of the others.

It wasn't long before she sensed Jun joining the chain next to her, gripping her free hand in his. As he did, she felt the strain she'd been bearing lift a little. On her other side, Theo was on his knees again, but his grip seemed a little stronger after Jun's arrival, too. Soon, she was conscious of splashing in the shallows behind her, as still more others came to help them, grasping hands to extend their chain of people, until it stretched wide in both directions through the cold water.

As more Keeper's Children joined them, they seemed to attract more of the bright creatures, too. These beings were now emerging not just from the sea and from the air, but also from the Crescent itself, behind them. Even as she kept her focus trained on the horizon, Toshiko managed to catch sight of a large creature with grey fur and whiskers, quite unlike anything she'd seen before, lumbering down the beach to join hands – or paws, she supposed – with a member of the Jetsam on one side, and a young Keeper's Child on the other.

These were the deep spirits of the Crescent, she began to understand. They were the Gods of this place, even if no human had ever granted them that name – beings born from the deep flows of energy that moved through everything here. The ruling classes of Rainshadow City may have disowned and mistreated the Keeper's Children, but in the presence of these spirits, Toshiko saw now that this island wasn't just defined by the politics of its ruling class. After all, these Gods of the Crescent were far more deeply connected with the true, natural life of Rainshadow island than the Crows or the old Emperor had ever been. And here they were tonight, choosing to stand with the Keeper's Children, hand in hand.

And then she heard a snatch of laughter – the voice sounding very much like that of a young boy – as, in the corner of her eye, she saw a flash of bright blue. A child was running down the beach from the Crescent, dressed in a blue robe not dissimilar from Haru's old one. She could just make out his leaping figure as he splashed into the shallows, setting the water sparkling in the moonlight as he waded over to join the end of their chain, too.

It was hard for Toshiko to make anything out for certain, what with keeping so much of her attention fixed on the barge – and yet, in her heart, she felt sure she recognized this little figure who had just joined them all in the waves. How could she not, after all, when she'd pictured him watching over her, and over all the people here in the Crescent, for as long as she could remember?

Even while the Crows on the barge kept fighting back, their chain of humans and Gods on the beach continued to share the strain of the barge's rescue, weaving Sola through the wind and the water with a gentleness that Toshiko was coming to learn held just as much power as violence.

Little by little, the actions of the Crows on board started to feel increasingly small, and Toshiko's heart began to lighten.

6.

The Lucky Crows' hold over the barge faltered in the early hours, just after the Moons had set. As the first streaks of dawn appeared on the horizon, its sails became visible. A cheer went up, then, from the people and Sun Spirits around Haru, and he became aware of some of the Keeper's Children breaking off from either end of their chain to run back into the Crescent, probably to spread the news.

Although Haru was deeply tired and cold here in the ocean, the deadening scream that had filled his head since the battle seemed to have finally receded. It simply felt as if there were no room left for it within him, now that his whole being was taken up with the warm feeling of being linked to all these people and Sun Spirits, through golden threads of energy. He'd been lonely for so much of his life, and now, connected to everyone and everything around him, he found he could barely remember what loneliness felt like. Next to him, too, Hiranaya's breathing was steadier, the light of her pearl shining brighter, and Haru couldn't help but hope that she might be feeling better, too.

The barge kept coming closer, until he could make out the slick gleam of its dark wooden bow in the waves. Before long, he could even see small figures moving about on its deck.

'Stand ready,' came General Mori's voice, behind him.

'Yes, sir,' Haru heard a chorus of Guards reply.

He was relieved that someone had thought to bring General Mori to the beach – General Mori, who had always been kind to him, and who had bowed to him first. General Mori, who, crucially, too, hadn't been present in the Council Room alongside those other Generals, when his mother had tried to capture and torture Toshiko.

At last, the barge was fully looming up from the horizon, to make its final approach to the shore. It looked far larger and heavier even than Haru had imagined, during all the hours of sensing it out there, on the sea. Soon, it had drawn close enough that he could make out the figures on its deck more clearly, and his heart leapt to see that none of them looked like Crows. Some were even holding oars, and were using them to help, rowing hard for the Keeper's Crescent.

There were a number of people in Lucky Crows jackets, in fact, tied up with ropes to the barge's masts, while others who were surely Keeper's Children stood guard over them. The Crows on board, it seemed, had been definitively beaten. Even so, none of the Keeper's Children on deck seemed to be celebrating – and Haru found himself so wanting to wave at them, to welcome them and reassure them that everything would be okay now.

The barge wasn't quite here yet, however, and he knew he couldn't let go of Hiranaya until it was fully home – especially as their chain of people was now beginning to fragment, with people dispersing to make space for the barge to come into shore.

At last, Theo and Hiranaya sent one final pulse of Sola into the waves, and the barge surged forward into the shallows. Only then did Haru feel Theo finally let go of that first thread of Sola that had served as their anchor throughout this whole, long night, holding them all together. Theo collapsed fully into the water as he surrendered it, and Haru turned towards him in alarm – and yet already Theo was being lifted out of the ocean by the helping hands of Keeper's Children, who carried him safely back up onto the sand.

As Haru blinked, trying to bring himself back into full aware-ness of the world around him, he saw that Hiranaya's eyes were now returning to their usual soft golden colour. All around them, too, everyone who'd stood in the chain together was rubbing their eyes – some were hugging each other, while others simply stared around themselves in disbelief at all the Sun Spirits. Many people, it seemed, were now able to see them too, in this brief moment after they'd all been linked together.

A new thought occurred to Haru then, and he turned to look through the crowds of people and shining Sun Spirits for any sight of a blue robe, somewhere in their midst. During the night, at some indeterminate hour long before dawn had become visible on the horizon, he was sure he'd seen a Sun Spirit who'd looked like the Keeper himself, coming down from the Crescent to help them all.

There didn't seem to be any sign of the Keeper anywhere now, though – and, Haru realized, he didn't have time to search more thoroughly just at the moment, because the Keeper's Children on the barge were all looking increasingly apprehensive at the sight of General Mori and his Guards splashing into the waves, heading towards them. These people had spent their lives fearing the Imperial Guard, Haru realized – and then there was also the question of what they might make of the fearsome sight of Hiranaya, here to greet them all with her enormous teeth and sharp claws.

And so he finally obeyed his instincts and raised up his arms to wave at all those Keeper's Children on the barge's deck, and as he did, he called out, 'Hello, friends! Welcome back!'

The others on the beach around him began to follow his lead, waving and calling friendly greetings, and the Sun Spirits even joined in, too. Haru wasn't sure if any of the Keeper's Children on board would be able to see the spirits, but he hoped that the warmth of their welcome might still reach them as an emotion or atmosphere, regardless. At last, tentatively, everyone up on the barge's deck began to wave back – and the sun seemed to light up, then, in Haru's heart.

Springtime, clear skies and light for the future of the Archipelago. That was what his name was meant to mean, and for most of his short life, Haru had never felt that it had suited him. In this moment, though, he suddenly felt as if it fitted perfectly – that he was a beacon, or a lighthouse, bringing everybody home.

7.

The Crows on board were arrested immediately by the Imperial Guard. After that, the Keeper's Children flooded the barge to help the hundreds of people still down in its hold to safety. The sick and wounded were taken straight to the café tent, where, in spite of Toshiko's concern at what it might mean for her brother's health, Jun would put in another shift of healing with the pearl.

She knew that in spite of her worries for Jun, she should probably be feeling triumphant now. After all, they'd accomplished what, only last night, everyone had considered impossible – they'd defended the Crescent, and had rescued the barge.

They never would have been able to do that last part, though, without Theo – and now he was lying, unconscious, on the sand, next to where she was sitting watching him with increasing unease. He was still breathing steadily, but he was looking concerningly pale and depleted, even as the warm sunlight played over the planes of his face. The pearl was still glowing its faint, moonlit glow around his neck, and it was starting to seem, to Toshiko, like the only thing about him that still radiated any light or life at all. Even with that whole chain of people and spirits helping him, she knew that he'd still taken on the lion's share of the strain.

Soon, Lina was here, asking for the pearl so that she could take it to the café tent, where Jun was setting up again. Of course Toshiko understood how important the pearl was for her brother's healing, and wouldn't have dreamed of stopping Lina from taking it. Yet she still felt a pang of resentment as she watched her walk away with it, taking its power and its light away from Theo, leaving him looking even more drained.

The Keeper's Children who'd lifted him out of the waves had wanted to take him straight to the café, and maybe it hadn't been the most medically thought-out decision, but she'd instinctively asked them to leave him here, on the beach, promising to keep an eye on him until he woke up. She'd wanted him to stay out in the warmth of the sunlight until Jun was ready. He just looked so pale, and his hands were so cold.

She was busy trying to rub some warmth back into them, when his eyelids fluttered open.

'Toshiko,' he said. 'You're here.'

She jumped at the sound of his voice – still so strained and rasping – and immediately dropped his hands.

'How are you feeling?' she asked.

He frowned, blinked, and even managed a one-shouldered shrug. 'I guess I could be worse.'

He attempted a smile. She forced herself not to smile back. She might be glad to see him conscious, but that didn't mean she'd forgiven him.

'I'll go tell Jun you're awake,' she told him. 'He'll come and check on you.'

'No, don't,' Theo said. 'Please.'

With a groan, he pushed himself up until he was sitting opposite her on the sand. She looked over her shoulder then, to follow his gaze to the barge, where its former prisoners were still climbing down from the deck, to be greeted with smiles and hugs and helping hands.

'I just ... want to stay here for a moment,' he told her. 'I want to sit, like this, and watch what we managed to do. Stay with me?'

Toshiko hesitated. 'I should go, now that you're awake,' she told him. 'They need my help in the café.'

Yet, when he didn't say anything further, and just kept watching the Keeper's Children as they finally escaped the barge, she found herself shifting around on the sand so that she was sitting next to him, watching it all too. For a while, they simply stayed like this – not touching, not talking, just witnessing, and taking in the momentousness of each and every life they had managed to save.

'Do you think it feels like coming home to them?' Theo asked after a while.

'How do you mean?' She turned to him. He was wearing a curious expression – a happiness that wasn't quite devoid of pain. He looked to her like someone who'd woken from a pleasant dream only to feel more keenly what was lacking in his waking life.

He seemed to be about to answer, when a cheer went up from over by the barge, and they both looked around again towards it. They were just in time to see Mailee emerge onto the deck from the barge's hold. She was leaning on a young woman's arm for balance, but she looked otherwise as full of life and health as ever, and was smiling broadly as she made her way down the steps from the deck to finally wade through the shallows, back up onto dry land.

It seemed now like everyone still out here on the beach had turned to watch her return – and to celebrate the homecoming of this woman who, for so many years, had stood at the heart of the Crescent, looking after most of them here since childhood, and whose café, even in her absence, had been their safe haven during the battle.

'You go,' Theo told Toshiko then. 'Go on. Welcome her back.'

Toshiko saw that, without realizing it, she'd half-risen to her feet, as if to run and greet Mailee with the others – a true Keeper's Child turning towards this stalwart of the Crescent, as a heliotrope towards the sun.

'What about you?' she asked. 'Are you strong enough to walk?'

'I'll be all right,' he said. 'I want to stay here just a little longer.' He seemed to hesitate then, as if he wanted to say something more.

And suddenly, Toshiko felt, again, like a girl hovering at the borders of a new land. She sensed, somehow, that anything he might say next could force her into a decision that she wasn't quite ready to make. Should she turn back and return to everything she already knew, or should she risk stepping over that border with him, into uncharted territory?

Before he could speak, she got to her feet, brushed the sand from her clothes, and ran away from him along the beach to where she could see Mei now, at the centre of the group clustered around Mailee in the barge's shadow. As Toshiko watched, Mei threw her arms around the older woman, hugging her tightly.

'Reiko's girls,' Mailee said, turning to greet Toshiko, too, with a broad smile. 'I knew I was right to pay attention to that cat of yours the other day. He has your auntie's good judgement, you know.' She pulled Toshiko in for a hug as well. 'Mei here has been telling me what you've been doing, since my capture. And you can take it from an old woman who knew your auntie well – she would be thrilled to know that you've grown up to be so brave.'

Mailee was soon drawn away by more Keeper's Children

wanting to welcome her home, and so Toshiko turned to Mei, who was still standing next to her on the beach. She had to say something to her sister now, she decided, to break this unnatural, uncomfortable awkwardness that had set in between them since the battle.

'Didn't fancy helping us with the barge at all then?' was somehow the question that came out.

Mei shook her head. Toshiko anticipated a sarcastic reply, but for once her sister only looked thoughtful.

'That dragon pearl and I just don't seem to get on,' Mei said. 'I mean, I have nothing against it, I guess, if it can bring about stuff like this' – she gestured at the rescued barge. 'But it still just doesn't make any sense to me, how and why it works. And that makes me uneasy. I thought that if I tried to join in that line with all of you, I might even stop it from working. Besides, I had other things to do.' She waggled her eyebrows mysteriously.

There was no resisting Mei's mysterious eyebrows. 'Like what?' Toshiko had to ask.

'Like waiting for the barge to come within range of the City Web, so I could send a message to the Keeper's Children through all the screens and loudspeakers on board, saying we were rescuing them, and would very much appreciate any help they could provide towards that end themselves. How else do you think they got it together to mutiny against the Crows on board and seize control of the oars?'

Toshiko had to smile at that. 'I should have known that was you,' she said.

'Exactly so, sister,' Mei grinned back. 'You know you can always trust me to make trouble for the Crows.'

As Toshiko, Mei and a few others walked Mailee to her café, Toshiko looked back, just once. Theo was still sitting just as she'd left him, except that now his gaze was fixed on the sea. She hovered, undecided as to whether she should run over to him and insist he come with them, to ask Jun for help. Then Mei called to her, telling her to hurry up, complaining she was lagging behind. And so Toshiko turned away from Theo again, jogging to catch up with the little group of Keeper's Children. He would be fine on his own, she told herself as she went.

CHAPTER TWENTY-ONE

The Emperor's Choice

1.

When Jun stepped out of the café tent and into the sunlight that was washing the Crescent with all the brilliance of a storm's aftermath, the morning was still relatively young. His second session of healing with the pearl had been far easier than the first – especially with Mailee at his side, cheering him on. In spite of having only just escaped the barge herself, she'd immediately taken charge of overseeing everyone doing healing work in the tent.

Many of those who'd come off the barge had been weak from exhaustion, dehydration, seasickness and emotional upset, but relatively few had had serious injuries. There had really only been minor cuts, burns and sprains to deal with. Jun did know, of course, that these Keeper's Children would need a lot more than their superficial wounds patched up and a few hours of rest to recover from their ordeal, but at least their physical scars wouldn't linger too long.

'You've done very well today, Jun,' Mailee had said with a smile when he'd looked up from his final patient, finished in his work with the pearl at last. And just for a moment then he'd been able to see himself anew, through her eyes – and the unmistakable pride in her gaze had finally allowed him to see some of the good he'd done here, instead of just focusing so completely on everyone he'd failed to help in the battle.

Looking around himself now at the morning unfolding on the Gods' Road, he began to wonder where he might find Toshiko and Mei. They'd both disappeared from the café tent a couple of hours ago – he could only assume to get some rest. It was remarkably quiet out here in fact, with the whole sunlit world seeming infused with the particular kind of hush that he would usually associate with early mornings at the very start of spring.

It was odd – while he was certainly tired, and the white streaks in his hair hadn't regained their colour, he wasn't feeling particularly drained at all anymore. He definitely couldn't feel anything like the absolute, bone-deep exhaustion that had afflicted him earlier, after using the pearl to heal the Keeper's Children who'd been wounded in the battle. He even wondered if there could have been something healing for him in that process of rescuing the barge, and of being linked to all those people, and streams of golden light, and creatures and spirits. As if, in that moment of connection, a power far bigger and more fundamental than anything he'd yet encountered had managed to untangle and restitch part of the damage that had been done within him, as a result of the exertions of healing.

He rubbed his eyes. He would probably start feeling tired again soon enough, regardless. In the meantime, he decided, he was simply going to stand here for a moment, to enjoy the warm sun and the gentle breeze on his skin.

'Toshiko's brother!' he heard a small voice call then, and turned to see Haru bustling towards him down the Gods' Road with Kei at his side.

Jun gave them both a smile. Even though Haru was the Emperor now, he seemed to have such little regard for the rituals of Imperial protocol that it seemed possible he didn't even know what most of them were.

'The name's Jun, actually,' Jun told Haru, giving the little Emperor a mock-offended eyebrow-raise. 'You are indeed correct, though. I am Toshiko's brother.'

Haru nodded impatiently. 'Yes, yes,' he was already saying. 'Jun. I knew that. You have the dragon pearl, don't you?'

Jun nodded.

'Hiranaya needs it. Hiranaya the dragon, I mean – that's her name, you know. It belongs to her son. He'll die without it!'

Jun blinked, taking in this new information. Although he'd realized, of course, that he wouldn't be able to keep the miraculous healing powers the pearl gave him, it had never occurred to him to consider the pearl as stolen property. Suddenly, it felt absurd to him that neither he, nor his siblings, nor any of the Keeper's Children, had thought to properly question the pearl's origins. Perhaps the powers it had granted them had simply felt too valuable to invite much curiosity on the subject. It wasn't a very comfortable thought, and he shivered in spite of the sun's warmth.

'Of course Hiranaya can have it,' he told Haru. 'Where is she? Or should I just give it to you, to take to her?'

Haru shook his head. 'You need to come, too,' he told Jun. 'I think she's nearly well enough to fly home, but she needs help with her injuries before she can risk the journey.'

'Hang on,' Jun said. 'You want me to try and heal a *dragon*?'

Haru shrugged. 'It can't really be all that different from healing humans, can it?'

Jun considered the idea. 'I don't know,' he told Haru. 'It might be very different. I have no idea if I can do it.'

He stopped talking, though, at the shadow that had started to fall once more over Haru's expression. After the battle, Jun had been concerned at how shaken the little Emperor had obviously been. He'd been glad to see him looking so much better after bringing home the barge, hopeful that Haru might have experienced a similar healing effect in the process of the rescue as he himself had done. He certainly had no wish to bring sadness back into the young Emperor's eyes again so soon.

'You know, though,' he said hurriedly, in a bid to bring the light back to Haru's face, 'I suppose I didn't realize I could heal humans, until the day before yesterday. I could certainly have a go at dragon healing.'

He followed Haru and Kei as they led the way through the streets that wound down to the sea. Arriving at the Crescent's southern perimeter, he was startled to see that a whole stretch of the barbed wire had been pulled down, and that Keeper's Children and Imperial Guards were working together along the beach, using grappling hooks, rope and whatever improvised tools they had to hand to keep pulling down more of the fences. At the demise of these towering metal spectres that had dominated so much of his childhood, Jun felt a weight lift from his heart that he hadn't quite realized was there. With a nod to those working to tear down the remaining fences, he followed Haru and Kei through the gap in the wreckage where the Southern Gate had once been, onto the beach.

Haru, for one, seemed largely oblivious that he was crossing any kind of significant boundary at all. Once on the beach, the little Emperor took off, running ahead of Jun and Kei towards the vivid turquoise hulk of the dragon coiled up by the waves.

'It's good to see the fences coming down,' Kei said, though, echoing Jun's thoughts as the two of them followed more slowly behind. 'It feels almost like the beginning of a new world.'

Having lived in the Crescent for as long as he had, Jun was always instinctively wary of any rash expressions of hope concerning its future. Nevertheless, he couldn't help but agree that the scene around them this morning did feel different. As well as those pulling down the fences, there were plenty of Keeper's Children simply gathered here on the beach, relishing the chance to finally enjoy what had so recently been a completely forbidden space.

Many of these people were sitting and talking in clusters, their voices loud with relief and exultation as they shared stories of how they'd survived the past day and night. Aside from all the lively groups, there were also a few people sitting alone out here, watching the ocean. Jun recognized Theo, sitting cross-legged close to the waves, and felt his own smile fade a little as he watched him lift a stone from the beach and hurl it out towards the horizon. He wondered, then, why Theo hadn't come to him with his injuries, given how beaten up and worn out he was looking now. Theo seemed, in fact, almost like part of a different world to the hopeful, sunlit one currently being enjoyed by everyone else on the beach.

Jun was just considering whether to go over and ask Theo whether he wanted some help, when Haru waved to them from all the way down the beach at Hiranaya's side, calling for them to hurry up.

'Come on,' Kei said to Jun, picking up her pace to a jog. 'We'd better hurry. He's been so worried about whether Hiranaya will be able to get home.'

While of course Jun had stood alongside Hiranaya as they'd rescued the barge, he still couldn't help but feel a little dazzled by her now, as he approached. Close up, in full daylight, just the sheer scale of her was overwhelming, never mind the way her smooth, electric turquoise scales stood out so vividly against the amber grittiness of the sand. He tried his best to mirror Haru's air of ease and trust around the dragon as she lifted her enormous, furred head and bared her considerable teeth at them in what Jun very much hoped was a smile.

Jun might have assumed that, after the last couple of days, nothing much would be able to surprise him anymore. He still found himself reeling, though, as a voice began to speak to him – definitely from somewhere inside his own head.

Hello, Jun, it said. *I'm Hiranaya. We've not met properly, but I've heard about the good you've done for so many people. Thank you for agreeing to help me, too.*

Jun's wonder at the way she seemed to be able to communicate through thought alone immediately gave way to awkwardness. She might be thanking him, but he was only able to heal like this with the help of the pearl that had been stolen from her child.

'I didn't think to use my abilities for you, though,' he managed to say in reply. 'I'm so sorry that I didn't help you earlier.'

Hiranaya only shook her head, whiskers trailing in the breeze like seagrass underwater.

But you did help me, she told him. *All of you did. I had been badly poisoned, and yet the Sola that flowed through all of us as we rescued the boat was so bright and so strong that the poison simply could not persist, and was purged from my wounds. Can you not feel the effects, too, of having had such goodness flow through you?*

'I suppose I can, yes,' Jun answered. 'But how can I help you, then, if the poison is already gone?'

The poison may have left my wounds, but the wounds themselves are still there. Healing from cuts in the ordinary way takes time, and time is one thing that, at present, I am unfortunate not to have. I must return to my child. He cannot last for much longer without his pearl.

Jun nodded, swallowing down his guilt. 'I'm so sorry that it's me who has it now,' he managed to tell her. 'And I wish I'd asked you, too, before I used it. It's yours, of course, to give back to him.'

Thank you, Jun, Hiranaya told him. *I know you meant no harm.*

Haru and Kei had been watching them carefully throughout this exchange, and Jun realized from their expressions that they hadn't been able to hear a word of what Hiranaya had been saying.

'I'm going to try and seal her cuts,' he managed to explain.

He took the last few steps up to Hiranaya, in all her enormous, vivid unfamiliarity, and hovered his hands above a long, angry gash to the side of her neck. Next to her like this, she still seemed a formidable creature, but there was an unexpected softness to her, too. Her huge, golden eyes, set wide amidst her blazing fur, seemed to radiate an empathy that Jun hadn't quite expected to see from the being who'd harnessed the lightning so fearsomely during the battle.

'May I?' he asked, his hands waiting just above her torn scales.

She gave a slow blink, then nodded.

Laying his fingers on the cut as gently as he could, Jun took a moment to grow used to the feeling of her warm, dry scales on his fingers, then let himself sense the patterns of energy weaving over her skin, searching for the snags and tears in these patterns, which formed the wound.

And as he did this, Jun realized, he didn't feel drained at all.

Because, as it turned out, both he and Haru had been right, in different ways. The process of healing dragons was similar to that of healing humans in some respects, but it was also completely different, because Sola didn't just flow through dragons – they *were* Sola itself, in being physical manifestations of its energy. For Jun, now, tuning into the rhythms of Sola in Hiranaya felt like nothing more than stepping into the warm, clear light of an unfamiliar sun.

2.

Haru hung back, watching anxiously as Jun healed Hiranaya's many cuts and lacerations from the sharp edge of Mr Winter's knife. He couldn't help but wince as Jun came to a particularly nasty wound, and Hiranaya let out a soft whine.

'Do you think she'll be strong enough to fly home, when her wounds are better?' he asked Kei, trying to speak quietly so Hiranaya wouldn't hear him. He knew just how desperate she was to start the journey back to Kiri.

'I suppose she can rest and recover fully at home,' Kei whispered back, 'once she knows her child is safe.'

'But what if she can't make it all the way there?' Haru asked. 'Isn't Muralania very far away?'

'She'll make it,' Kei said, and Haru so wanted to believe her.

At last, after what had felt like an impossibly long time, Jun was raising his hands from Hiranaya's hide and stepping back from her. Haru was pleased to see that he even looked as if he might have a little more colour in his cheeks than before – as if the process of helping Hiranaya might also have helped him.

'How does that feel?' Jun was asking the dragon.

Hiranaya stretched her long neck, beginning to uncoil from where she'd been curled on the sand, and Haru could feel her drawing currents of air towards her again as she raised herself off the ground to her full height. A few of the people on the beach still seemed a little uncertain about the idea of a dragon looming over them like this, looking increasingly nervous as Hiranaya gave a celebratory-sounding roar.

Jun was laughing, though. 'Good,' he said. 'I'm very glad.'

Then he unfastened the clasp of the pearl's chain from around his neck, and held it out to Haru.

'I think you ought to be the one to give her this,' he told Haru. 'I should go and find my sisters.'

Haru shuffled forward to take the pearl, and then Jun was bowing to him, and to Kei and to Hiranaya too, before walking away down the beach.

A curious sense of the momentous seemed to settle over the three of them, left together there on the sand. Haru approached Hiranaya, holding the pearl out to her. Its iridescent surface caught the sunlight, breaking into a wash of different colours, and Haru saw, then, that Hiranaya's eyes were beginning to turn misty with tears. He felt the need to say something, to complete the sense of the pearl's having finally been properly returned, and yet he didn't know the first thing about making speeches. Still, it felt like too important a moment to let slip by without saying something of what needed to be said.

'On behalf of the Rainshadow Empire,' he ventured, 'here is Kiri's pearl back again. It was taken from him wrongly, and I am very sorry that it ever happened.' He frowned. That had been important to say, but it had come out sounding impersonal, maybe even a little prim. 'Please also tell Kiri hello from me, when you give it to him,' he added. 'I hope that he feels a lot better, very soon.'

Hiranaya curved her long and sinuous neck until her huge head was level with Haru's. Very carefully, she took the pearl's chain in her teeth, then hooked it gently around one of her claws.

Thank you, Haru, she told him. *You'll be a better Emperor than your mother ever was, I'm sure of it.*

And large teardrops began to fall, then, from her golden eyes.

'Please don't cry,' Haru burst out. 'Kiri will be all right now, won't he? Why are you crying?'

Unlike humans, Hiranaya told him, *we dragons only weep very rarely, in moments of great happiness. These are the first tears I have shed since Kiri's pearl was stolen.*

It still upset Haru to see her crying though, and without thinking, he reached out to wipe them for her.

Careful, little Emperor, Hiranaya's voice had a sharp ring to it now that made Haru pause, hands held out, not quite touching her. *My tears carry an unusual power. Just a few drops on your skin could begin to wash your memories away.*

Haru took an instinctive stumble back from the large, sparkling droplets that were still falling from her eyes to soak into her fur . . . and then he stopped, thinking.

'What if there was something I wanted to forget, though?' he said.

It felt wrong to be asking her this, when this moment was meant to be about finally giving something back to her, instead of taking something more. And yet Haru still couldn't help but think of the instant when Mei's arrow had pierced his mother's throat, and he'd watched her fall forward, onto her horse. It seemed an endless, repeating moment now in his memory – one that would never finish for him, as long as he lived. And then, too, there was the endless scream that had occupied his mind since the battle. It was true he'd been feeling a lot better since being connected to those wonderful streams of light that had burned the poison out of Hiranaya as they'd rescued the barge, but he knew, instinctively, that the scream hadn't gone away. It was still there, just waiting inside his head for the right moment in which to resurface. He sensed how patient it could be, too, in its unendingness.

It is true that you are very young to have seen so much these past few days, Hiranaya said, seeming to understand his thoughts. *If you really do want to forget, you may collect my tears. They work best when dropped onto sleeping eyelids.*

Haru blinked and looked away, aware of her golden eyes watching him carefully, as well as of Kei also studying him with concern. He suddenly felt too exposed, trapped by the weight of being considered like this as he made his choice – and so he turned away from them both, towards all the Keeper's Children gathered on the beach.

Apart from Theo, who was looking over at Hiranaya, watching her now with a peculiar fixity Haru didn't really understand, everyone else on the sand had gone back to being absorbed in their own conversations and stories. Haru could see so much happiness and love in these little gatherings – so much joy at simply having made it to this bright morning after the battle, with this place, the Crescent, still theirs to call home for as long as they wanted it. He could hear the music of that gladness in the Keeper's Children's voices as they were carried over to him on the breeze.

When Haru had first arrived in the Crescent, even though he'd been grateful to Kei and to Ren for sheltering him, he'd still thought of it as somewhere alien and frightening. He'd since learnt, though, of the huge importance of this narrow strip of land – of how generations of Keeper's Children had turned what might once have been little more than an open-air prison into a unique place, layered with history and stories. There were just so many Sun Spirits here, born from all the years of care, suffering and love that had infused into the Crescent's bones. Haru himself had been connected to those Sun Spirits as they'd rescued the barge, and in those moments of connection he'd been able to sense something of the hard stories which had given rise to their bright lives. Although many of the stories were far from happy ones, he found now that he would never want to forget them. They were important – and an important part, too, of this island which, as Emperor, he now needed to look after. He wanted desperately, in fact, to remember everything he'd come to understand of the painful, complex process by which the Keeper's Crescent had become the place it had.

Also, there was the fact that he had only properly met Hiranaya yesterday, in the thick of the battle. While the fighting had of course been terrible, his memories of it were inseparably mingled with the only memories he had of her. And then, he realized, deciding to forget the last few days might also mean having to forget Risu, too. It might even mean having to forget that there were Sun Spirits at all, when he was still only just getting used to the idea they existed – only just learning, too, that the world, in reality, was a place filled with so much more life than the built-up, concrete landscape of Rainshadow City had previously led him to believe.

Haru took a deep breath before turning back to Hiranaya and Kei, and shaking his head.

'There are too many things I don't want to lose,' he told

Hiranaya. 'And I'm the Emperor now. I should be brave enough to remember all the bad things, along with the better ones. Emperors have to make terrible choices every day, almost, and they have to understand difficult things. How could I be Emperor if I couldn't live with that?'

Kei frowned, taking his hand and giving it a squeeze.

'But you're still so young, Haru,' she told him. 'The most important thing is for you to be happy.'

Although Haru gripped her hand back, he wasn't quite sure that Kei was fully correct when she said this. It seemed unlikely to him that things could ever be quite so simple again. From all his years of watching his mother, it had always seemed clear to him that there were far more important things for Emperors than being happy.

There is a chance, Haru, Hiranaya said then, as if reading his thoughts, *that an untroubled Emperor could be a stronger one.*

Haru shook his head more definitely this time, before stating the one thing he knew with absolute confidence to be true in this moment.

'All my life I've dreamed of meeting a dragon,' he told her, 'and you are more amazing than I ever could have imagined. I don't want to forget you.'

Hiranaya bowed, tears still falling from her eyes, dripping from her fur to soak freely into the sand. Haru wished so much that he could hug her, and yet wary of the power her tears held, he only bowed. He began to feel a rising dismay, then, as he realized there wasn't much left for any of them to say now, other than goodbye.

'I wish I could come with you,' he told her. 'I wish I could come to Muralania, to see you return the pearl to Kiri myself.'

Hiranaya bared her teeth in another smile, though her golden eyes were turning sad. Haru noticed her tears had stopped falling.

I wish that were possible, too, she told him, *but you are needed here, little Emperor. If you don't claim your power over the Archipelago now, then someone else surely will in your place, and I very much doubt whether they will have as kind a heart as you.*

Haru nodded, suddenly a little frightened at the idea of her leaving him here, with all of his mother's old Generals and ministers. It had felt so much more possible to issue orders and take control when he'd been soaring over all of them on her back. How would he fare without her to help him?

'Can we come and visit you, though, on Muralania?' Haru turned to Kei, then. 'Can we go together, like you said before when you told me you might take me to Muralania one day?'

'Of course,' Kei told him. 'If Hiranaya says it's all right for us to visit her.'

When you're ready, Hiranaya said, *I am sure that Kiri will be keen to meet you. We will keep an eye on the horizon for you. Goodbye, little Emperor.*

Her pearl was alight again, and Haru was aware of more air currents gathering around her now, disturbing the sand and lifting her higher. Many of the Keeper's Children on the beach looked up from their conversations and began to wave.

'Goodbye, Hiranaya!' Haru cried out, desperately, waving as hard as he could now as the dragon soared on the air currents down to the waves and then launched herself into the water, finally beginning the long journey home.

How Haru wished he could follow. How he wished he could travel with her, amidst the ocean currents all the way to Muralania, where she would soar above the island's high walls and then over its forests and rivers and lakes until, at last, she would reach its high mountains. Amidst those snowy peaks, Haru knew, Hiranaya would surely find her child waiting for her, and she would finally restore his shining pearl to him – the pearl that, from the beginning, had always been rightfully his.

3.

As Hiranaya disappeared, moving eel-like beneath the surface of the waves, Theo let his waving hand drop. He felt as if he'd been bidding farewell to far more, even, than this seemingly miraculous being who'd stepped in to save them all, when he'd failed so spectacularly to rescue the barge on his own. He wasn't even thinking about the pearl and the extra power it had given him. He was thinking, of course, of Hiranaya's tears. The sight of them, falling thick and sun-spangled onto the sand, had sent his thoughts chasing over the ocean in the opposite direction to where she'd been headed – all the way back to Susanna, wherever she might be, amid Eardland's hills and forests.

And yet, as he'd watched Hiranaya weep, Theo hadn't found himself wanting to rush to the dragon's side to beg for her tears. Perhaps it was mainly just that there wouldn't be much point in his possessing such a thing as dragon tears anymore, what with the poison from the tracker ravaging its way through his body at this very moment, as he did know in his heart that it surely was.

It wasn't just the reality of the poison, though, that was stopping him from coveting the tears. Having watched Jun's work with Sola be greeted with such gratitude and acceptance here in the Crescent, and then after everything else that had happened in the past few days, too, Theo found that he wasn't even sure anymore that he ever wanted to go back to Eardland. He certainly wouldn't want to return to Susanna's side, if his place there could only ever be founded on deception, and the dragon tears' theft of her memories. He'd never truly wanted that, at all. He'd only latched onto the idea of the tears out of desperation – as a way of holding on to one last thread of belief that it might still be possible to return to his old life, and to see love light up Susanna's eyes again, just for him.

That version of him that she'd loved was long gone now though, he knew – and not only because killing Seth had destroyed it. He'd lost so much in leaving home, and had since gained so much, too, that he felt now as if the life he'd shared with her was a dream that belonged to some other, different Theo. A Theo who was, for better or worse, consigned to the past. He'd never be able to fit himself back into the contours of that dream now, whatever he did. Not even if he were to be miraculously transported home and cured from the poison.

A wave of heaviness swept through his limbs then, and he lay back on the sand, closing his eyes against the sun, which was now almost directly overhead. He supposed there wasn't much point in worrying about whether its rays would burn his skin. A bit of sunburn seemed laughably benign, compared to the poison eating its way through his insides.

It was too late to ask Jun for help, with the pearl getting further away by the minute, held in Hiranaya's claws. Could he try to turn the Gift inward, and use his own powers to heal himself? The idea only filled him with exhaustion. He wouldn't even know where to begin. He sighed. He didn't want anyone to see him like this, so weak and useless and self-pitying. It was time for him to go.

He managed to sit up, and then to haul himself to his feet, and was just beginning to make his staggering way down the beach, when a shout behind him caused him to stop and look back.

Toshiko was running over the sand to meet him. He hadn't been able to recognize her voice properly through the ringing that had just started up in his ears.

'My brother's worried about you,' she said, gesturing back to where she'd been sitting with her siblings and the enormous grey cat he'd seen her with that first afternoon in the square. 'Why didn't you go to him for help? You look awful.'

Theo managed a shrug. 'Thanks,' he said.

That earned him a sarcastic look, which didn't feel quite fair. As far as he was concerned, it was a miracle he'd managed even a hackneyed stab at humour, given how he was feeling.

'Where are you going?' she asked.

'Just away somewhere. Probably back to the city.'

'You don't want to stay here? Everyone's grateful, you know. For the barge. I mean, you could have a home here, if you wanted it.'

Theo shook his head, then immediately regretted doing so, as the motion made both the headache and nausea worse. 'No one has anything to be grateful to me for. I would have completely messed all that up with the barge without everyone's help,' he said.

She was still frowning at him, looking disappointed.

He sighed. 'And whatever you might think, I'm not leaving because I don't care about the people here,' he added. 'Or because I think I'm better than them.'

'I didn't say that.'

'You didn't have to.'

He rubbed his eyes. At some point during the past few hours they'd started feeling really quite painful, all scratchy and irritated. He really didn't want to argue with her, especially not when there was a chance this could be their last conversation.

There would be a lot of last things now, he supposed. He may even have lived through quite a few of them already, without realizing it.

'I'm sorry,' he managed to say. 'I should go.'

He turned away again, continuing his trudge along the sand. It was probably far too cursory a farewell. Not saying goodbye properly, though, gave him the pleasant illusion of leaving things open, even if his life was starting to feel increasingly like a closed book. Toshiko probably wouldn't want any kind of elaborate goodbye, in any case. Very likely, she was still angry with him.

'Hey,' she shouted after him though, when he'd just begun to assume she must have gone back over to her family.

He turned to squint at her through the sun's glare.

'If—' she began, then stopped, shook her head, and started again. 'Will you come and let me know you're okay, when you're recovered?'

She'd said it like a challenge, with nothing really at all in her tone of voice or expression to indicate that she was anywhere near forgiving him. And yet, suddenly, Theo found it just that little bit easier to stand up straight. He even managed a smile.

'I'll be sure and do that,' he promised.

For a moment, she looked as if she might say something further. When she didn't, he just nodded and turned to continue his slow walk down the beach.

CHAPTER TWENTY-TWO

New Horizons

1.

As soon as their bicycle rickshaw stopped beneath the magnolia trees of the Palace gardens, Haru threw open the door and scrambled out as quickly as he could. He'd been nervous, earlier, as he and Kei had said goodbye to Ren and the others in the Crescent – afraid of how it might feel to be back in this place, so linked as it was to his mother's memory. The gardens seemed just as welcoming to him as ever, though. Perhaps it was because his mother had come out here so rarely, unless it was to host some special event, restricted as she'd been to the confines of the Palace's halls and corridors by all the work she'd had to do as Emperor. Really, this little world out here in the fresh air, with its frog pond, avenue of ginkgoes and miniature bridge over the water, had always been Haru's more than it had been hers.

It would be difficult, too, for these gardens ever to feel haunted, when everywhere you looked, there were luxuriant green leaves, fountains of running water and the scented, bright blooms of late summer flowers. Haru wandered over to the nearby patch of grass beneath the magnolia trees where, what felt like a lifetime ago now, he'd fallen asleep and first dreamed of Hiranaya moving through the mist.

At the thought of Hiranaya, he couldn't help but be reminded that it could be years, even, before he saw her again. He tried to push the notion away, and to think back instead to the bright, golden feeling of rescuing the barge – and then, too, of how it had felt to have Ren pull him aside for an awkward hug in the moments just before he'd stepped into the rickshaw with Kei, to set out from the Crescent. *I'll be here whenever you need me*, the leader of the Keeper's Children had told him. *With the two of us working together, Haru, this could be the start of a new world.*

Kei was still thanking the rickshaw driver when a flash of gold in the ginkgoes' canopy caught Haru's eye, and all of his more melancholy thoughts were chased away at the sight of who was coming towards them through the trees.

'Risu!' he shouted, full of gladness as he ran to meet the little squirrel, who had now scurried down a tree trunk and was skipping up the path to meet him. While Haru's ability to see Sun Spirits had returned after being so closely linked to both Hiranaya's and Kiri's pearls while rescuing the barge, he'd noticed that it was already beginning to fade again, with fewer and fewer Sun Spirits appearing to him in the Crescent. While he had hoped that he'd still have enough time left to see Risu here, he hadn't dared to feel certain of it until now.

'You see, I did come back,' he told Risu. 'Just like I said I would.'

Risu twitched his nose, looked at Haru with his head on one side, and then ran to leap up Haru's arm and sit on his shoulder.

Risu had always been shy before, never even letting Haru stroke him, and Haru couldn't help but beam with pride at having the little Sun Spirit choose to sit on his shoulder like this. Risu really must be pleased to see him home.

And then Kei burst out laughing, and Haru suddenly realized just how strange he must look to anyone who wasn't able to see Risu. After a moment, the thought of that made him laugh, too – his first real laugh since the battle – and even Risu joined in with a happy chirruping sound.

'Why don't we go for a walk in the gardens?' Haru asked Risu and Kei as their laughter began to settle, seeming to fill the air around them with new warmth and light.

'I think that would be a wonderful idea,' Kei told him, as Risu chirruped again.

Haru was just about to lead the way towards the gravel path that wound all the way around the Palace and back to Risu's golden-leafed maple tree, when he noticed Kei suddenly tense up next to him. He turned and followed her gaze to see General Mori approaching, striding down the main path from the Palace's doors to meet them, flanked by two more Imperial Guards, both of whom Haru recognized as being from General Mori's own regiment. Haru reached up to stroke Risu, just in case the arrival of these new people should unsettle him. For his own part, Haru could feel the tension beginning to rise within him again as they drew nearer.

General Mori and the Guards bowed low as they met him on the grass. Haru bowed too, unsure of what was proper for him to do now as Emperor, and also feeling rather as if he were playacting being an adult.

'We have much to discuss, Majesty,' General Mori told him as soon as they'd all straightened up. He had tired eyes, Haru noticed, and a deep furrow etched between his eyebrows that seemed at odds with the bright freshness of the gardens. 'I have done my utmost to keep the Ten Generals and all of your ministers satisfied while you've been away in the Keeper's Crescent, but I cannot pretend that all of them have been contented. General Kubo, especially, has been causing me some difficulty. He unfortunately has the loyalty of the colonels in his division of the Guard, which means he could be a dangerous man to ignore. We must now determine the most prudent way in which to proceed.'

Haru nodded. Hiranaya's repeated warnings to return to the Palace as quickly as possible had prepared him for the possibility of there being some difficulties of this sort here. He shouldn't have been surprised, either, that General Kubo was the one stirring up trouble.

'Okay, I understand.' Haru nodded to General Mori. 'What do you think we should do?'

'Perhaps this is something that would best be discussed indoors, Majesty,' General Mori said, with a glance around the sunlit gardens. 'Since the death of your mother, General Kubo has developed a habit of wandering the Palace and its grounds, often with a tendency to appear nearby wherever I have tried to conduct conversations on your behalf regarding the affairs of state. I do think it would be better, overall, if I could update you on current proceedings in a more private atmosphere.'

Haru frowned. 'Of course,' he assured General Mori. 'I'll come right in, after our walk.' He gestured to Kei, and up to Risu on his shoulder, momentarily forgetting that to General Mori, Risu would of course be invisible.

General Mori only coughed gently, clearly uncomfortable. 'I am sorry to press the matter, Majesty,' he said, 'but a comparatively long stretch of time has already passed between the death of the previous Emperor and your arrival today at the Palace to attend to affairs here. I must admit that it has been a challenge to keep even those Generals who profess loyalty to you content.'

Next to him, Kei crouched down to Haru's height. 'We should go with the General now,' she whispered in his ear. 'We can walk in the gardens afterwards.'

'But I might not be able to see Risu by then,' Haru told her, probably speaking too loudly, but not really caring if General Mori and his Guards heard what he was saying. This felt far too important. 'I don't know how much longer I'll be able to see Sun Spirits,' he explained. 'It's been hours, now, since I last touched Kiri's pearl, and hours, too, since I was last near Hiranaya's. I don't want Risu to disappear forever, while we're stuck in a meeting. I want to say a proper goodbye.'

Kei gave him a sad sort of smile. 'Even if you can't see Risu anymore, Haru, you know he'll still be here.'

Haru followed her gaze then, up to General Mori and his Guards, who were all staring resolutely ahead, as if they couldn't hear this conversation, although he knew they most certainly could. They didn't realize Risu existed, he reminded himself. They probably didn't even know about Sun Spirits. How would it look to them now, if he refused to come and help?

Feeling rather as though he were surrounded by walls that had begun to close in on him, even though he was still outside here in the open, Haru turned away from the Guards to stroke Risu's fur.

He watched Risu wriggle with contentment at being stroked, and tried to fight the rising panic he was feeling at the idea of this magical friend being taken away from him, after so little time together.

'Couldn't Risu just decide for himself that he wants me to see him?' he asked Kei. 'Couldn't all the Sun Spirits?'

Kei shook her head. 'I'm not sure it works like that,' she told him. 'Though maybe you could learn. There are mages on Muralania who have taught themselves the skill of seeing Sun Spirits, and you clearly have a talent for it. Maybe they could teach you?'

'On Muralania? When we go to visit Hiranaya?'

Kei smiled. 'Yes,' she said. 'When we go to visit Hiranaya.'

Kei always knew what to say, to send a little sunlight through the clouds. How lucky he was to have her at his side. Haru gave her a hug, being careful not to upset Risu on his shoulder.

'You'd best be quick now,' Kei told him, with a pointed look at General Mori and the Guards.

'I'll be two minutes,' Haru told them, before grabbing Kei's hand and towing her behind the row of magnolia trees.

He knew hiding away like this would probably only make him seem childish in front of General Mori, but he didn't want to have to say goodbye to Risu while being watched by people who couldn't even see him, and who didn't understand the first thing about him at all.

When Haru crouched down to the path, Risu seemed to know what to do. He ran down his arm and hopped off onto the gravel. Perhaps he'd been listening to everything they'd been saying. Even if Risu might not use human language to communicate, Haru was sure he had a knack for understanding it.

'Goodbye, Risu,' Haru told him. 'I'm so sorry that soon, I

won't be able to see you. Will you still come and visit me some-times, even though I won't know you're there?'

The squirrel gave a melancholy chirrup and bobbed his golden-furred head.

'Thank you, Risu. Maybe one day I'll learn how to see you again.'

The squirrel blinked its golden eyes, dropped Haru what looked very much like a bow, and then turned to leap up the trunk of the nearest magnolia tree. Haru watched Risu as he ran along a branch and then sprang over into the next tree, further down the path. For a moment, the flame colours of his coat stood out, bright against the green leaves, then he leapt sideways into a large fir tree and disappeared amidst its shadowed branches.

'Well done, little Emperor,' Kei told him, smiling, though she sounded sad. 'Ready to take your throne?'

Haru wiped away his tears, and nodded. 'Let's go,' he told her. 'I'm ready.'

2.

A full two days had passed since the Kawakamis had finally returned home to the apartment, and in that time, Toshiko had showered, washed her hair, eaten about a week's worth of food, and slept for a very long time.

Now, it was getting on for evening and, dressed in a shirt and trousers that were blessedly clean and not meant to be any kind of disguise, she was sitting on one of the high-backed chairs at the Kawakamis' dark wood dining table as two of Mochi's Mouse-bots chased each other around her feet. The table in front of her was set for dinner, and the iron candelabra was lit, giving Toshiko the feeling that the little circle of space around her was its own little world of light.

Across the room, Mei was sitting on the couch with Mochi on her lap. She was working her way through a mango bubble tea as she frowned down at a letter from Haru. She'd arrived home not five minutes ago, and in contrast to Toshiko, she was definitely not dressed in clean clothes, her jeans and boots covered with dust from long hours of hard work in the Crescent. Her air of being worn out by the day, though, was balanced by a quiet kind of contentment that Toshiko didn't think she'd ever seen before in her sister. However much Mei had claimed, previously, to enjoy the idea of being in a gang, it clearly suited her much better to be channelling her talents into helping the Keeper's Children, instead of into a life of crime.

Mei hadn't paused in her work for the Crescent at all, in fact, not even for a few days' rest. Thinking several steps ahead of everyone else, as usual, she'd persuaded both the Guard and everyone in the Crescent of how important it was to get all the draconic ore that was still in the Crows' old warehouse off the island. It still had the potential to be very dangerous, she'd reminded them, so long as it was within reach of the Sensei – or of anyone else on Rainshadow island, for that matter, who might find themselves interested in using its immense power for their own ends. She'd even come up with a plan for how to get rid of the ore, inspired by her hacking of the Crows' barges during the battle. After a lot of frustrated tapping away at her hairclip computer, she'd finally managed to find a way of remotely piloting the barges beyond the range of the City Web – which meant that she would easily be able to send all five of them back to Muralania. She'd spent the day today working with Ren and Ava to lead a combined crew of Keeper's Children, Jetsam and Imperial Guards to unload the full contents of the warehouse onto the barges, ready for them to set sail tomorrow morning.

From what Toshiko had been able to glean from the casual
shrug Mei had given her when she'd asked how the day had gone,
the plan was working well so far. Toshiko hoped it was a good
omen that these three groups, which had previously existed so
fractiously alongside each other – Keeper's Children, Jetsam and
Guards – were able to cooperate like this and work together with
the common goal of keeping their island safe.

This wasn't the only thing giving Toshiko tentative hope for
the future, either. Haru had announced that he was granting
citizenship to all the Keeper's Children, and was also sending
Guards and money to the Crescent, to help rebuild it into an
area just as well-provisioned as any other in Rainshadow City.
The Keeper's Children would be able to stay living there if they
wanted to – or, as full citizens now, they would be free to make
their homes anywhere else in the city they chose.

The word was, too, that Haru planned to grant citizenship to
any footsoldiers from the Crows who needed it, on the condition
that they gave up their involvement with the gang. While Toshiko
wasn't at all sure how she felt about this, she couldn't forget how
the Jetsam had helped them all in the battle, and knew it was
possible a lot of the Crows' footsoldiers weren't really so different.
She was glad, too, to think that the new policy meant Theo would
qualify for citizenship now, if he wanted it.

And then there was Haru's letter, which Mei was in the process of reading – still with a frown. It had arrived this afternoon,
hand-delivered by an Imperial Guard, and both Toshiko and
Jun had read it already.

Kei and I can't leave the city yet, the letter had said, after some
general greetings to all three Kawakamis, including Mei, and
hopes for their good health (Toshiko suspected that Kei might
have helped Haru with that part of the writing of it).

There is far too much for us to do here, even to leave the Palace very much, and while General Mori is a big help of course, he is often unwell with headaches, and Kei says he is under too much strain as it is. I am therefore writing to ask for your help. Not all of the Generals and Ministers agree, but I am determined to found a Parliament for the Rainshadow Empire. Ren says a Parliament would help make things much better and fairer for everyone, and I feel certain he is right, as it would involve people coming from all the other islands to have a say in how the Empire is run. Would you like to be my ambassadors, and travel from island to island, to explain the idea of the Parliament to everyone?

You would have a nice ship, with proper sailors and some Guards from General Mori's regiment to go with you, and it would be filled with plenty of food and things. You could also bring your cat if you like, as this will be good for stopping rodent problems on the boat.

We can discuss this more in person if you accept, but perhaps you would also be able to travel to Muralania, where Kei and Ren are from, and where Hiranaya the dragon lives – and where, too, I have recently learnt that my own father came from. I am trying to learn more about him from General Mori, and while I know that Muralania is beyond the reaches of the Rainshadow Empire, I would still like to find out if I still have any family left there.

I hope that you will say yes. You would definitely be the best people to do the job. After everything at the Crescent, I know how I can trust you.

After this message from Haru, there were several more pages of writing – first in Kei's flowing script, and then in General Mori's more careful and orderly style – explaining all about the plans for the new Rainshadow Parliament, the ship they would have, and the route through the Archipelago they would take.

Mei didn't look any happier by the time she'd finished reading the letter. 'I suppose it's nice he asked all three of us,' she said, 'seeing as he couldn't even look at me, back there in the Crescent.

I suppose he thought if he asked me, too, we'd be more likely to say yes. We obviously can't though. I mean, I can't leave the Keeper's Children – not now. Ren just asked me today if I would lead the Rebuilding Committee, along with him and Mailee. He wants me to help him install a proper electricity supply for the Crescent, and set up all of the computing infrastructure.'

'That's great, Mei,' Toshiko told her. 'You'll be great at doing that.'

'Hang on,' Mei's eyes narrowed. 'Why are you looking at me like that? You want to say yes to this, don't you?' She flapped the letter, sending Mochi's ears twitching grumpily as the resultant breeze unsettled his fur.

Toshiko shrugged, shifting uneasily in her seat under Mei's glare. 'I've never travelled, or seen any of the other islands. And this could be a chance to do something really important.'

'But I'm already doing something really important,' Mei growled.

'You wouldn't have to come with us,' Toshiko said quietly, then.

'What?' Mei's reply came out close to a shriek. 'What do you mean, *us*? You're not telling me Jun wants to do this, too?'

At her words, Jun stepped in from the kitchen, blinking as clouds of cooking steam cleared from the lenses of his glasses. The apartment wasn't big, and he'd clearly been able to hear everything they were saying. His hair, with its new white streaks, was pushed back into the band he always wore to keep it out of his eyes while in the kitchen, and the almost comical way it was sticking up at all angles contradicted the seriousness of the expression on his face.

'I'm sorry, sister,' he said to Mei. 'It's a chance to see the whole Archipelago. To actually meet people from all the other islands, instead of just messing around here, reading about the languages and cultures of places I never get to visit. I might even be able to go to the Mainland again, and see where I was born. Don't you ever get curious about Auria, to see where your mum came from?'

Mei only scowled and pulled Mochi in for a disgruntled hug.

'Besides,' Jun continued, though his voice was softer now. 'I really think I could do this job well. I'm good with people, remember?'

Mei sighed. 'Different areas of expertise,' she said.

Toshiko had an idea, then. 'Couldn't you use the same technology you're using to pilot those barges remotely to help us keep in touch, even when we're out of reach of the City Web? If you could figure out some way that we could send messages to each other, no matter how far away from Rainshadow island we were, then it would be almost like we'd never gone away.'

'No, it wouldn't,' Mei snapped. 'But I suppose I might be able to work something out with the tech. I just thought we were meant to stick together. I mean, it's what we do. It's what Reiko wanted for us.'

'So come with us,' Toshiko said.

Mei shook her head. 'Haru doesn't want me to. Not really. How could he? And anyway, I'm not leaving the Keeper's Children. Haru's a sweet kid, but he clearly sees no reason why the citizens and Keeper's Children won't just all be friends, nice and easy, once everyone has citizenship and the Crescent has been rebuilt. I mean, it's enough of a struggle just to get the Keeper's Children to work with the Guards and with the Jetsam at the moment, never mind with the citizens. And I don't even blame them, really. Ava can still barely move with all her injuries, and yet just this morning she nearly pulled all the Jetsam out of unloading the warehouse. She'd somehow got it into her head to argue with us all, insisting that we should keep the draconic ore for ourselves, and try to sell it – as if there weren't a million ways that that could easily backfire . . .' Mei shook her head as if to clear it, and sighed. 'The point is,' she continued, 'things feel volatile enough as it is, and they'll only get trickier once we introduce the citizens into the mix. For years, they watched and did nothing while people struggled in the Crescent, and I don't think the Keeper's Children are about to forgive that. I'm not sure the citizens will be happy to suddenly welcome all the Keeper's Children into their neighbourhoods, either – and don't even get me started on this new idea of giving footsoldier Crows citizenship. We still don't even know, either, who was responsible for disappearing all those people from the Crescent over the past couple of years. What if it wasn't the Crows at all, but someone else, from among the citizens?' She sighed again. 'Haru's just so young, is the problem. And he's spent most of his life sheltered, up in that Palace. He just . . . he thinks the world is simpler than it is.'

She rubbed her eyes and took an almighty gulp from her tea. Suddenly, she looked almost ready to go into battle again, her expression was that fierce.

'You can't fix all that stuff, though,' Toshiko told her. 'It's too much for anyone to fix.'

Mei didn't look up from scratching Mochi's ears as she said, 'I have to try, though. And I have to do what I can to protect the Keeper's Children, most of all. I'm one of their leaders now. They need me.'

Toshiko nearly laughed at the grandiosity of the words, before she realized that they were true.

'We're still a family,' Jun said then. 'Wherever each of us is, it'll always be the three of us, and we'll always look out for each other. And this won't be forever.'

Toshiko nodded, and after a moment, Mei did too. 'And I don't care if your ship gets infested with rats,' she told them. 'Mochi stays home with me.'

Neither of them would have dreamed of arguing with her.

'So who's ready for dinner?' Jun asked, leaning on a reliable method of cheering Mei up.

'What have you made?' asked Mei, unable to keep a note of curiosity from her voice.

'Chicken donburi, wakame salad, and miso soup,' said Jun. 'And I made some dashi-stewed kabocha pumpkin on the side.'

Mei sighed. 'That's another thing,' she said. 'What am I going to eat, when you're not here?'

Jun shrugged. 'I suppose you're finally going to have to learn how to cook.'

3.

Once they'd eaten and washed up the plates, the Kawakamis went to sit in the circle of soft lamplight around their squashy blue sofas. Normally, at this point in an evening, Jun would start mending a jacket, Toshiko would open a book, or Mei would slope off to her tech lab. Tonight, though, by some unspoken agreement, they did none of these things.

Jun spent a moment rummaging around in 'the dressing-up box', and then brought through his picture of Reiko, along with his old sketch of the Keeper, a little table, a box of matches, the incense sticks and their stand. He set the table up between the two sofas, and then placed both the image of the Keeper and the por- trait of Reiko on top of it, where they were visible to all of them.

Then, kneeling on the rug, he lit the first incense stick, before shaking out the flame to send the smoke, with its familiar smells of mandarin peel and cinnamon, floating out into the room.

'One for our beloved Auntie Reiko,' he said, as he placed the stick in the stand. 'We miss you still.' He did the same for a second incense stick. 'Another for the Keeper,' he said. 'Thank you for looking after us since our childhoods.'

They watched as this second trail of smoke began to rise.

And then, for the first time in years that Toshiko could remember, Jun lit and extinguished a third incense stick, placing it carefully in the stand beside its fellows. 'One for Hiranaya, brave dragon of Muralania. May our prayers reach you over the seas. I hope you found your child safely.'

And then he lit a fourth. 'One for all the Gods of the Keeper's Crescent,' he said as he shook out the flame, and the smoke began curling from its tip. 'Great and small, young and old, known and unknown. You came to our aid when we needed you, and for that you have our eternal gratitude.'

The three Kawakamis sat in silence for a moment, each lost to their own thoughts as they breathed in the scented air.

'So,' Mei eventually broke the silence. 'Did we do it? Did we get "real revenge", as you called it, Toshiko?'

Toshiko sighed. She was sitting cross-legged on the sofa next to her sister, with an oversized kawaii cushion in her lap. She rested her chin in its marshmallow-like softness as she considered the question.

'Yes, I think we did,' she said, eventually. 'Saito's gone. And what happened to Reiko, and to us, couldn't happen to anyone in the Crescent now.'

'Do we really think the Crows are well and truly over?' Mei asked.

'I hope so,' Jun said. 'Haru seems pretty serious about dismantling them.'

'He still hasn't found the Sensei yet, though,' Toshiko reminded him. 'Or that woman with the dark glasses. Not even after that raid on the Shadow Column.'

'They'll be in hiding,' said Mei. 'The Sensei is far too clever to try staying at the Column, or to go back to any of the Crows' old haunts, now that the Guard are after her. You know, I'm hopeful that we won't hear too much from her for a while. The only reason she was so powerful before was because the old Emperor allowed it.'

'That's another thing that won't happen again now,' Jun said.

'Thanks to Mei,' Toshiko added. 'Thanks to both of you.'

'And you,' said Jun.

Toshiko shrugged. 'I don't know. I feel like I just chase after the two of you all the time. Like I try to keep up with everything you're doing, but just end up making a mess, mostly.'

Both of her siblings turned to look at her then.

'What?' said Mei. 'That's ridiculous. You were the one who started this whole thing off.'

'By messing up the mission with the ring?' said Toshiko.

'By telling us all to think bigger,' said Jun. 'By forcing us to stop hiding, afraid in the shadows, and persuading us to do something substantial, to really change things. "Real revenge" was your idea, remember?'

'It was Mailee's idea, strictly speaking ...' Toshiko began, before Mei threw a cushion at her.

'Stop arguing with us,' Mei said. 'We're trying to be nice about you for once. And he's right: none of this would have happened without you. Even messing up the mission and stealing the pearl was part of that, really. You weren't afraid to properly take them on, from the beginning.'

If it had been anyone other than Mei saying this, Toshiko would have thought it was just an attempt to be kind. Mei never wasted words on social niceties though, and as she considered what her sister had said, Toshiko found herself smiling. Perhaps she really was starting to hold her own in this family.

'Thanks, Mei,' she told her. 'Everyone did it together, though. Not just the three of us either, but all of the Keeper's Children. And Haru and Kei – even Theo. All of us here who knew things needed to change.'

'A bigger picture in a different sense,' Mei said, a little sadly. 'Maybe it's not just about the Kawakamis anymore, but all of us who were abandoned, or shut out by the city. The orphans of Rainshadow island.' She ran a hand over the tattoo on her wrist, of three birds, flying over water.

'And maybe Reiko always knew that,' Jun added then. 'Maybe that's why she took us in, when we were just tiny strangers to her.'

Toshiko sighed. 'Real revenge is one thing, but – I don't know. It's not as though it's made losing her feel any easier.'

'No, but she would be proud of us now, I think,' Jun said, and Mei nodded. After a moment, Toshiko nodded too.

The seriousness of the mood was broken by Mochi, who'd been in the process of stalking a Mouse-bot when the cushion Mei had thrown at Toshiko tumbled off the sofa, straight onto his back. The surprise sent him yowling forwards to leap on the bot, which promptly malfunctioned and spewed out a whole pile of cat treats onto the rug. The Kawakamis laughed at Mochi as he alternately pawed through the pile of treats and prodded the now inert Mouse-bot, to see if it might produce any more.

'You know,' Mei said then, 'after all of you brought the barge back, I asked Hiranaya if she thought she could sense anything special about Mochi. Like, whether he could maybe be related to those creatures you all say you saw in the water that night – the Gods, or the Sun Spirits, you know. I was so sure she'd say he was descended from them or something, but she actually just laughed at me. I hadn't even known that dragons could laugh. Turns out he's just a regular cat.'

'It doesn't surprise me,' Toshiko told her.

The Mouse-bot blinked back into life, and they watched Mochi chase it a little longer, before Jun broke the silence again.

'I wonder what will happen about the ALISE bots,' he said. 'We're getting the draconic ore off the island, so they won't ever be manufactured again on the scale the old Emperor intended, but there were still those first bots she made – the ones we saw at the party. They'll still be around, somewhere.'

He visibly shuddered, and Toshiko felt a tingle of unease creep up her own spine at the memory of those bots, smiling their matching, wide smiles.

'Maybe there's a way to reprogramme them,' Mei surprised her by answering. 'I mean, the bots can't help their own programming, can they? We can't even blame them, if they're still loyal to the old Emperor. They're not in charge of what their internal commands make them do. In a way, they're just as much orphans as we are, now. I mean, maybe I could even help them. Or at least take a look at their programming – if Haru wouldn't object to me visiting the Palace.'

Toshiko gave her a look. 'Since when can bots be orphans?'

Mei seemed to consider the question, giving it more thought than Toshiko had expected. 'I just ... I think there are different kinds of magic in this world. And those bots are a kind of magic too. A new kind, maybe. Plus, none of this was really their fault.'

Toshiko couldn't help but smile at that. Her sister never lost the capacity to surprise her.

'Maybe,' Jun cut in then, 'once they've been reprogrammed, Haru can find jobs for them, too.'

Mei laughed, though her laughter had a slightly bitter edge to it. 'Maybe he can send them all off on a sea voyage of their own,' she said. 'I mean, for someone so young, he does seem surprisingly good at finding jobs for everyone.'

'I think it's a good thing we have proper jobs now,' Jun told her. 'We never wanted to be criminals forever.'

'We never wanted to be criminals at all,' said Toshiko.

Looking at Auntie Reiko's picture then – that perfect image Jun had captured of her laughing in the sunshine, in the doorway of their old house – Toshiko did finally feel she could say for certain that Reiko would be proud of her, and of how she lived her life. She felt, too, as if she was only just now beginning to understand the full extent of what the notion of flying above the river might really have meant to their beloved auntie. Jun had been right, when he'd said that the three of them owed their lives to Reiko's determination to always pay attention to how the choices she made worked in connection with those of the people around her. To fly above the river then, for Reiko, hadn't just meant fighting to be who she'd wanted to be, in an individualistic sense. Instead, she'd lived her life with a bigger picture in mind, striving to become someone who would help the world to grow into the place she'd wanted it to be. It was a philosophy that seemed so evident to Toshiko now, in that decision Reiko had made to take in three parentless children and raise them as her own.

So while a small part of Toshiko did still wish the three of them could be going off now to realize the individual dreams they'd each held for their lives, throughout their childhoods – that she could be going off to study at the University, while Mei went to work for a tech company and Jun took a job at the hospital – she knew, too, that they had opportunities now to do things that could be even better, in being connected to something broader than simply their own private ambitions.

'Above the river,' she said to her siblings then, as they both turned to look at her. 'We've really managed it – I think. To fly above the current.'

She shuffled forward on the couch to reach for their hands.

'Above the river,' both Mei and Jun repeated, as all three grasped hands together.

To Toshiko, it seemed then as if the words resounded out from their circle, to rise up through the incense smoke, filling this little home they'd made for themselves, before continuing on, beyond their apartment, out into the city. She imagined the words reaching all of the Rainshadow orphans out there, known and unknown to her, who suddenly had a new chance to reshape this island city of theirs into somewhere that, one day, might truly feel like home.

4.

Of all the places in Rainshadow City where Theo could have spent this afternoon, he didn't quite know what had made him choose the steps outside the Shadow Column, leading down to the water. And yet here he was, sitting watching the terns dip their wings over waves that glittered in the low sunlight as he listened to the cries of street vendors selling food he still couldn't afford, and probably wouldn't even be able to swallow now, anyway, given it seemed certain he was dying.

Had he come here for answers? If he had, the impulse hadn't been logical. The Shadow Column didn't even belong to the

Crows anymore, after the raid on it yesterday, carried out by Haru's Imperial Guards. A squadron of Guards was still standing at the door now, while more of them, Theo knew, were inside, working their way through its many floors and rooms, uncovering what they could of the Crows' secrets. Maybe there really was a cure for his condition somewhere in there, but even if it did exist, it seemed likely he was long past the stage at which it could have fixed him.

He had hardly expected the poison to be kind, and yet he still found himself surprised by how quickly his body had declined over these past three days, since his fight with the Sensei. Even his vision had begun to fail, with bright spots of light and blinkering darkness working in tandem to obscure his surroundings. He had run out of cloud credits this morning, and wouldn't be able to pay for his room tonight – and yet the way things were going today, it was starting to look as though that wouldn't be much of a problem.

He sighed and stretched out his legs on the steps below him, still managing, in spite of everything, to reap some last moments of pleasure from the sight of the afternoon sun on the surface of the water. It would be sunset soon, and from the shades of pink that were already bleeding into the sky, it seemed likely to be an especially good one. That was something, he considered, given it would probably be his last.

Just as he'd decided that he might as well give himself up to self-pity, seeing as there wasn't much else left for him, his thoughts were disturbed by the sight of something small, dark and strangely familiar tumbling over the stone steps alongside him. He assumed, at first, that it was just another caprice of his failing vision. Then, a gust of wind brought it closer, and he saw that it was, in fact, a perfectly straight, black feather. It danced and twirled on the breeze, eventually reaching his boots.

Despite a vague apprehension of dread, he leaned forward to pick it up between finger and thumb. He'd just about managed to persuade himself it must be some sort of leftover of the Crows' presence at the Shadow Column, when he heard footsteps approaching, and two figures came to sit on either side of him on the steps.

Even in spite of his deteriorating vision, and the fact she'd covered her hair with a scarf in what he supposed was a gesture towards disguise, Theo couldn't fail to identify the Sensei, on his left. She had some faint bruising around her forehead and jaw, but otherwise, remarkably, she seemed none the worse for their last encounter. She was, in fact, sitting on the hard stone steps in apparent comfort, smiling mildly out at the ocean.

It took Theo a moment to place the much younger woman on his right. Her long, dark and incredibly smooth hair was fastened in a loose knot halfway down her back, she wore a simple white dress, tied with a sash at her waist, and she sat with her pale hands resting neatly on her knees. It was the hands Theo recognized first.

'You're that bot,' he choked out. 'You're that bot who tried to strangle me.'

His voice had only gotten hoarser since he'd last seen these two, and he found himself hoping, rather irrationally, that in hearing it they both might feel at least a little sorry for what they'd done to him.

'Now, Bluejay,' the Sensei tutted. 'Don't be rude. Rei here wasn't herself yet when that happened. I was the one who tried to strangle you. I simply borrowed Rei's body, before she was using it.'

The bot blinked at Theo, then politely bowed her head. 'It is very nice to make your acquaintance,' she said.

Theo simply stared back. It was eerie to see this face animated with something like shy curiosity, when he'd last seen it staring so blankly down at him, as its hands had squeezed tighter and tighter around his windpipe. He shuddered.

'Have I offended you?' said the bot, face falling.

'Do try to be polite, Bluejay,' said the Sensei. 'As I said, she's perfectly alive now, and as fresh to the world as a newborn baby. What kind of impression of things do you want to give her?'

Theo only shook his head, before shifting himself back round to look at the Sensei. 'I'm sorry,' he said, 'but how can she be alive?'

The Sensei tutted. 'Bluejay,' she said. 'Don't be slow. I explained to you all about the properties and capabilities of draconic ore.'

'I remember,' he said. 'But that ore was in the warehouse, which the Imperial Guard captured from you three days ago. And they emptied it today, completely. They got all the ore off the island. I watched the boats leave this morning.'

The Sensei chuckled. 'That was only the ore intended for industrial use, for this iteration of the bot-making factory. It isn't as if I don't have further supplies. You didn't think we imported a whole warehouse-full of ore from Muralania without first having seen how well it could perform? How did you think my scientists developed the idea of living bots in the first place?'

'Wait,' Theo said, frowning. '*Your* scientists? I thought living bots was the old Emperor's idea.'

'Well,' said the Sensei with a shrug, 'it was a collaboration, really. And anyway, Asayo only wanted to use her bots as glorified servants, their sole aim and purpose being to wait hand and foot on her spoiled citizens. I was the one with the vision to conceive of our bots as warriors for a wider, worthier cause.' She sighed, lost in thought for a moment before seeming to return herself to the present. 'But I suppose, Bluejay,' she said, 'that you'll have been wondering why I came to see you today.'

'Not really. I mean, you've clearly come to gloat.'

The Sensei tutted. 'Surely we know each other well enough by now for you to realize I would never bother with anything so useless? No, I have a job for you.'

Theo had to laugh at that, though his laughter swiftly turned into a fit of painful coughing. 'What job could I possibly do for you now?' he asked, when he'd recovered himself enough to speak again. 'Is the job just to die quietly, by any chance? You've left me in no condition for anything else, I'm afraid.'

He coughed again, then spat blood into his palm. Next to him, he felt Rei recoil, while the Sensei cast him a disappointed look, as if he were being unnecessarily distasteful.

'I would ask you to excuse me,' he snapped, 'but I'm afraid all this is both of your faults.'

'Really, Bluejay,' the Sensei sighed. 'There isn't any need to be quite so dramatic. You haven't even heard what the job is yet.'

'Ask someone else to do it,' he told her. 'I'm done working for you.'

'I would, gladly, have asked anybody else. However, after the death of my consigliere and the loss of the pearl, it unfortunately seems that you are the only one left at my disposal with the qualifications such a job would require.'

The Sensei reached into her pocket and produced a glass bottle so small it could have disappeared completely into even a child's fist. It had a silver stopper and an elaborate pattern of golden fretwork around its neck. It also happened to be filled with a dark red liquid, whose lurid colour only seemed to deepen as it caught the evening sunlight. It looked to Theo exactly like blood.

'You don't suppose,' she told Theo then, the ghost of a smile stealing into her expression, 'that I would poison such a valuable asset as yourself, without having a cure within my possession?'

Theo tried not to react. Very likely she was bluffing, just taunting him further. Probably it really was blood in that vial, or water, with a few drops of dye.

'It's an antidote, in case you were wondering.' The Sensei treated him to a casual raise of her eyebrows, before slipping the bottle back into her pocket, out of sight. 'And it's yours, too, if you accept my offer.'

Theo picked at the barbs of the feather he was still holding in his fingers. Even if she was lying, he supposed, it wasn't as if he had very much to lose.

'Just because I'm listening,' he told her, carefully, 'that doesn't mean I'm saying yes.'

The Sensei smiled. 'You may have heard rumours that there are ghosts on Hanasaki Island, following the laboratory disaster?'

'I've heard the stories,' Theo told her. 'Shades of those killed in the explosion, haunting the shores and calling out to passing ships. I can't say I believe any of it.'

'Well,' the Sensei said, 'you should. Or you should believe some of it, anyway. There absolutely are strange figures stirring on Hanasaki Island, except they aren't the ghosts of the dead. They're bots.'

Theo blinked at her. 'Excuse me?'

'They're what we call Yurei bots,' the Sensei smiled. 'Just like Rei here,' she nodded over at the bot on Theo's right. 'Except that while Rei was grown in the Shadow Column of course, those other Yureis were made on Hanasaki Island. You see, it wasn't just a simple lab which Asayo and I were running over there. It was a full first attempt at her LIFE-Hub. We built it there in the years before she felt it was safe to set up here, on her own shores.'

Theo stared. 'And yet it was safe enough for Hanasaki Island? Didn't it turn the whole place into a poisonous wasteland? Didn't it kill hundreds of thousands of people?'

The Sensei waved away his outrage. 'Sometimes, the broader progress of society requires great sacrifice,' she said. 'In any case, the Yurei bots currently haunting Hanasaki Island's shores shouldn't now be shunned, just because the method of their manufacture turned out to be rather more destructive than initially anticipated. After all, they are perfectly serviceable. They are simply earlier versions – prototypes, if you will – of the ALISE bots. The metal and circuitry design of those ALISE bots, in fact, was simply a compromise arrived at between Asayo and myself, after she insisted the process by which we gave life to the Yureis was too volatile to continue. Personally, though, I did always prefer the Yurei model. It has so much more potential.' She sat back a little on her step, the ocean breeze tugging gently at the edges of the scarf in her hair as she looked out at the waves.

Theo turned again to the Yurei next to him, only to find she was staring right at him, her eyes alive with curiosity. He couldn't help but instinctively recoil to see such animation in her features – she was so close an imitation of a human being, and yet clearly something else entirely. He turned back to the Sensei.

'But if both the Yureis and the ALISEs were designed as living bots,' he asked, his mind whirring now, 'just what is it that makes one so different from the other?'

He looked back at the Yurei. She gave him a shy smile.

And then the inevitable dawned on him. Perhaps he had known all along, since he'd first seen her back in the Shadow

Column's basement lab. 'She's organic, isn't she?' he asked the Sensei. 'She's made of flesh and blood.'

The Sensei grinned. 'Well spotted, Bluejay,' she said. 'She is indeed made from organs, muscles and sinews – all laboratory grown, you understand, and only from the most carefully chosen cells. Indeed, we had such a broad and extensive cell-harvesting resource in the people of the Keeper's Crescent that we were able to be highly selective, in terms of the traits we chose for our Yureis.'

'Wait,' said Theo, beginning to feel sick now in a way he knew had nothing to do with the poison. 'You harvested cells from Keeper's Children? Without telling them what you were doing?'

The Sensei met his horror with a level gaze. 'It's not illegal,' she said. 'They have no rights or protections under Rainshadow City law.'

'That's why people kept getting taken,' Theo breathed, re-membering, now, those fearful nights in the Crescent, the shouts of alarm as yet another Keeper's Child was discovered to have vanished. 'And that's why the ones who came back had all those scars.'

The Sensei inclined her head. 'Yes, we did try to return as many as we could to the Crescent. After all, simple stem cell extraction doesn't cause much harm. It was the subjects whose brain cells we needed who couldn't be preserved, unfortunately.' She shrugged with an air of mild regret. 'The result of the process is, anyway, that Rei's body is now stronger and better optimized for all sorts of things than the majority of human bodies that are born naturally, while she can also still benefit from the significant advantages of being made from flesh, instead of metal. Really, Bluejay, I thought you might have noticed all of this sooner, con-sidering you've actually felt her hands on your skin. It's amazing, though, what even quite intelligent people can deliberately avoid noticing. I suppose she makes you uncomfortable.'

'Uncomfortable?' Even in his weakened state, Theo managed to scramble up several stone steps away from Rei as the truth of what she really was fully sank in. 'Gods. That's one way of putting it. You grew her from stolen cells. From people you kidnapped. People I lived alongside.'

'Settle down, Bluejay,' said the Sensei. 'Apart from anything else, you really don't have time for theatrics. My antidote can do a lot, but it can't revive a dead body, and I haven't even finished telling you, yet, about the job I'm offering you.'

'No time for theatrics?' Theo said, still gaping at Rei, who only blinked back at him, looking hurt. He brandished the black crow's feather in his hand in the Sensei's direction. 'Then what the hell was this meant to be?'

The Sensei chuckled. 'Touché. Can I assume, though, that you've calmed down sufficiently now to listen properly? You do surely acknowledge that this would be a very stupid way to die?'

Theo rubbed his eyes, which, after the exertion of scrambling up those steps, were rapidly filling with bright spots again. 'Just what is it you want me to do?' he sighed.

'Well, Bluejay,' the Sensei said. 'As you might well have guessed, I haven't quite given up on the idea of my bot army.'

He groaned, and slumped back on the steps behind him. 'Why not, though? I mean, what is it all *for*? You've lost your power – or most of it, anyway. Why keep trying to accumulate more?'

She gave him a curious look, at that. 'Has it never occurred to you that I might want something more in this world than simply power, Bluejay?'

'Like what?' he asked her.

But she only gave him a thin-lipped smile. 'Perhaps one day, I'll tell you. For now, all you need to know is that the Yurei bots of Hanasaki Island are a resource of vast potential, that, currently, no one is claiming. You see, like their cousins, the ALISE bots, they can be easily controlled by someone familiar with the practice of channelling Sola.'

'So you want me to go to Hanasaki Island and round up the troops for you,' Theo stated.

The lack of any change to the Sensei's expression told him he was entirely correct in that assessment. He shivered. It seemed ironic, and so deeply unfair that she would send him to Hanasaki Island, after everything he'd done to save all those people on the barge from the very same fate.

'Why don't you go yourself?' he asked her. 'You may not want to suffer a slow and drawn-out death from poisoning, but here's news – neither do I. I mean, why shouldn't I just carry on dying here, instead? It would be simpler. And quicker.'

'Oh but I will be going there myself,' she told him. 'As will Rei here, and my granddaughter, Hana. You do remember Hana, don't you? In any case, what I'm asking now is for you to come with us. And we won't be poisoned by Hanasaki Island's hostile atmosphere because I can use my knowledge of Sola to shield us. I could even teach you how to use Sola to protect yourself. I could teach you lots of things, Bluejay. I'm sure you'd be quick to learn.'

'You would teach me?' he asked.

She nodded slowly.

'Didn't you say, though, that you would never teach someone with strong natural abilities, like mine? What's changed? How do I know you're not lying?'

She gave a quiet laugh. 'Almost everything has changed, Bluejay. Surely you can see that? You yourself observed, just a moment ago, that I have now lost most of what I once had. I have lost my headquarters, with its labs and offices. I have lost my Imperial support and funding. I have lost the majority of my draconic ore, as well as my most prized artefact, the dragon pearl. I have also lost Ken, as well as most of my footsoldiers.' She gave him a thin smile. 'It seems that the new Emperor's promise of citizenship for those of them who choose to defect is turning out to be quite popular.' She shrugged, then, before turning to look out over the harbour again, shading her eyes. 'Don't think that I don't care about these losses, Bluejay,' she continued. 'I do understand, though, that over the years, life has given me a lot, and so it only seems balanced that sometimes it should take from me, too. It has, however, given me one interesting thing recently. It has given me you.'

'I don't belong to you.'

She made a non-committal noise. 'We'll see. I think I've learnt enough about you by now, Bluejay, to feel fairly certain of your coming around to my way of thinking.'

'You're lying to yourself.'

'I have never knowingly lied to myself before, and it seems a little late for me to start now, don't you think? While you, on the other hand—'

'Just what is it exactly that you're really suggesting?' Theo cut across her, not keen to spend any more of what could be his last moments listening to the Sensei's pronouncements on his weakness of character. 'You'll give me the antidote, and train me to use the Gift, if I go with you to Hanasaki Island to gather these bots, is that right?'

'There is just one other small thing,' she said.

He laughed – carefully this time, trying not to descend into uncontrolled coughing. 'I knew there would be. Go on. What is it?'

'One quick task for you and Hana to accomplish first, before we set out on our voyage.'

Theo grimaced at the thought of working with the Sensei's granddaughter, remembering her unfeeling glare.

'Is she a mage, too?'

The Sensei shook her head. 'Unfortunately not. If she were, I wouldn't need you. Talent for Sola can be passed through the generations, but it seems she failed to inherit it.' She shrugged. 'Hana is not without many other talents to recommend her, though. I am sure you will find her a helpful accomplice.'

'In doing what?'

'You will break into the Imperial Palace, find the collection of Muralanian artefacts I procured for the former Emperor, and steal a selection of the most powerful of them. I will of course give clear instructions to you both on which these are. I have decided, you see, that continuing to pursue the dragon pearl is more trouble for me than it is worth. We will still need something, however, to amplify our abilities such that we can wield control over a full army of Yureis. Even my gifts will require some assistance, to maintain such a feat.'

Theo's mind flitted back, then, to the room that Ken Saito had led him to in the Palace, when he'd been hiding with Toshiko – the library, with its spiral staircase and cabinets filled with objects of power, lurking just out of reach.

'I think I know where the artefacts are,' he said.

The Sensei gave him a sidelong look, and then a broad, satisfied smile.

Then she rose to her feet, dusting off her trousers. 'Good,' she said. 'A most excellent start. I'm so glad we are beginning to understand one another.' She clicked her fingers at Rei, prompting her to rise, too. 'Now, Rei and I have an awful lot to organize, and really must be on our way. Arranging a secret sea voyage is no simple task, I assure you. I'll just leave the antidote here for you.'

She slipped the bottle out of her pocket again, and placed it carefully down next to where Theo was sitting on his stone step. He tried not to look at the deep red liquid, made redder by the light of the sunset.

'I have to warn you,' the Sensei told him, 'it does taste foul, but you really should drink it down in one. You'll start to feel better within a couple of hours. Then Hana will call for you in a few days, when you're properly up and about, and we'll be able to get started.'

She turned and began to walk away from Theo, up the steps, the bot following faithfully behind her.

'Wait,' Theo called after them. 'What do you mean, Hana will call for me?'

The Sensei sighed, stopped and turned, looking irritated with him now for keeping her. 'Perhaps I didn't make myself clear. A choice to take the antidote is a choice to take the job. Of course, I suppose you could still decide to ignore it and leave it there on the steps. I feel certain, though, that you of all people, Bluejay, would never do something so heedless. Because, you see, I know you agree with me that life is far too sweet to simply throw away.'

She turned again and continued her progress up the steps.

'Wait,' Theo called after her once more, his voice getting increasingly ragged now with the effort of all this talking. 'How do you know I'll even still be here, on the island? I could run away.'

'You couldn't, though,' the Sensei said, over her shoulder. 'Hana would always find you. She's a sharp girl, and anyway you're forgetting just how easy you are to trace, with that tracker in your neck.'

'But I . . .' Theo sighed, feeling increasingly defeated. 'I've run out of money,' he told her. 'I can't pay for my room. I mean, I thought I'd be dead, before it mattered.'

Without turning round, the Sensei took Rei's arm and muttered something in her ear. The bot nodded, eagerly, then rushed down the steps back to Theo, holding out a coin from her pocket – a shining, silver moon credit.

Theo only stared at her as she blushed and bowed, still holding out the coin.

'With the Sensei's compliments,' she told him, eyes respectfully lowered as she waited for him to accept it.

For a moment, Theo considered dashing it from her fingers, down the stone steps to the harbour. Then he reached out to take it. He found himself unable to repress a shudder, though, at the familiar, fleshy feel of her hands as his fingertips brushed hers. If she really was just as much flesh and blood as he was, he found himself wondering then, was *bot* even the right word for her? Or was she something else entirely?

He flinched away from her, the coin held tightly in his fist, and was startled to see a curious expression pass over her face, almost of pain. Was he imagining it, or could she really be giving him a look of reproach? Before he could study her further, though, she'd turned away and was hurrying back up the steps to the Sensei's side.

He glowered after the two of them as they walked away, before looking down at the moon credit and at the crow's feather, which he still held in his hands. He waited until the Sensei and Rei had completely disappeared from view, then pocketed the credit. It wasn't the same thing as accepting her offer, he told himself – money was money, after all, even if you were dying. He spent another moment twisting the black feather back and forth in his hands before dropping it, letting it fly away on the breeze.

And then he turned to crouch next to the tiny glass bottle on the steps. Was it really true that he couldn't run from the Sensei, or from Hana? Surely, if he used the moon credit to buy a berth on a fast ship heading out of the Archipelago, then they wouldn't bother to chase him across the sea? The Sensei would always know where he had gone, that was true, but was he really so valuable to her plans that she wouldn't let him escape? He rubbed his eyes as his vision filled again with bright white spots. It was possible. She had lost a lot, as she'd said. He probably was one of her main assets now – one of her last chess pieces on the board.

He glowered at the red liquid in its vial, and yet it stayed, of course, completely enigmatic. He didn't even know if it would work.

He groaned aloud, and then pulled the moon credit from his pocket again. One side of the silver coin showed Rainshadow City's crest – the trident crossed with the fishhook – while the other showed a ship in full sail. He laughed, softly, at how apt this seemed. If the coin landed crest-side up, he decided, then he wouldn't take the antidote. He would die here, sometime in the next few hours, on Rainshadow island. If, however, the coin landed on the reverse side, showing the ship, then he would go with the Sensei on her voyage.

After a quick prayer for wisdom to any God who might be listening, he positioned the coin between finger and thumb, and tossed it.

Feeling as unwell as he was, though, his balance was off, and the coin flew up at an unexpected angle. Time seemed to slow down as Theo watched it spin through the air, its trajectory shifting towards the glass bottle holding the antidote. He could picture the collision in his mind's eye – the horror of that little bottle smashing uselessly against the stone steps.

He lunged for it, forgetting the credit and snatching the bottle up in quick fingers with a covetousness that surprised even himself. And then the credit landed, nowhere particularly nearby at all. It sparkled in the evening light, almost as if it were laughing at him. The Rainshadow City crest was facing upwards.

Theo eased himself back down to sit on the steps again, and stared deep into the vial of red liquid that he now held in his fingers. He still didn't have to swallow it. He could listen to the coin. He could smash the bottle against the steps himself, or walk right down to the harbour and throw it into the sea. Either way, it would be the work of a moment to remove its temptation, and then he could die a free man – as the person who'd chosen to do what was right, and leave the Crows behind.

He turned the vial over and over in his hands, before finally looking up into the breeze, at the red and gold streaks of setting sun over the water. He thought, then, of green hills and turquoise dragon scales – of Eardland's sacred tree and of the Keeper's Shrine in Mailee's café. He remembered the feeling of cold seawater on his feet, as well as that of the power which had flowed through him as he'd worked with the others to bring the barge home. He thought of Susanna – and not, for once, of the terrible look she'd given him on the night he'd killed Seth. Instead, he found he could picture her as she'd been before, in the life they'd shared together that was still kept safe in his memories, even if there was no going back to it now. And then the image seemed to fade and dissolve as, with a wave of confusion mixed with something else – something painful and joyful and expansive, all at once – he found himself thinking of Toshiko. Of how she'd told him it was *beautiful* when he'd gathered all those sparks of light into his palms, in order to show her the Gift.

Life is sweet, the Sensei had said, and for all that he hated her and wanted to scream his frustration out at the waves, he couldn't help but admit that, in just this one respect, he did agree with her, wholeheartedly.

ACKNOWLEDGEMENTS

My huge thanks and gratitude to my wonderful literary agent, Peter Straus at Rogers, Coleridge and White, who responded to my seeming to give up on having any kind of writing career at all by quietly suggesting I have a go at a completely different kind of book – and so ignited the first spark of what became *The Rainshadow Orphans*. Huge thanks to Peter, too, for his tireless work in supporting both me and this novel through every stage of the process, from draft 0.1 to publication. Without Peter's wisdom, insight, tenacity, kindness, direct honesty, left-field sense of humour and true dedication to books and literature I don't know where I'd be.

Huge thanks to everyone else at Rogers, Coleridge and White who also helped me and *The Rainshadow Orphans* from behind the scenes. You're all wonderful, and I'm so indebted to you all. Thank you especially to Emer Walsh, as well as to Claire Wilson for reading an early draft. Huge thanks also to Emily Hayward-Whitlock at The Artists Partnership.

My thanks are due, too, to editors Charlotte Trumble and Joe Monti, who acquired *The Rainshadow Orphans* for Simon & Schuster, and so completely changed my life – thank you so much! Thank you both so much, too, for reading my work with such meticulous care and thoughtfulness. Your combined editorial guidance really helped me to understand both the writing process, and the whole fantasy genre in far more depth. Thank you too to Gemma Creffield for taking the series on into the future – I'm excited to be working together!

Thank you to all the other brilliant people at Simon & Schuster working tirelessly and brilliantly to make books like this one happen. Huge thanks to Amy Fletcher and Ben Phillips for the truly amazing work in foreign rights. Thank you to Katherine Armstrong for heroically stepping into the breach when we needed you, and for all your brilliant work in looking after this book at the publishing house. Thank you to Suzanne Baboneau for your kindness when *The Rainshadow Orphans* was acquired, and for being so welcoming both to me and to this novel. Huge thanks to India Minter for the beautiful work on the covers, and also to Weston Wei for the stunning cover illustration and Virginia Allyn, the fantasy cartographer. It really is such a dream to see Rainshadow City brought to life so wonderfully in visuals.

Huge thanks are due too to Gail Hallett in Editorial, Karin Seifried in Production, to Polly Osborn, Sarah Jeffcoate, Kate Kaur, Laurie McShea and Joe Christie in Publicity and Marketing, and to everyone in Sales: Madeline Allan and the Online Sales team, Olivia Allen, Rich Hawton and the Regional Sales team, Nicholas Hayne and the International Sales team, Heather Hogan, Jonny Kennedy and the Non-Trade Sales team, Katie Sormaz and Alice Twomey. Thank you as well, of course, to the members of the Finance, Contracts and Operations teams who supported this book's publication. On the US side of things, huge thanks to Caroline Tew and the rest of the team over at Saga Press.

Thank you so much to all the brilliant international publishers who took on *The Rainshadow Orphans*. Your enthusiasm and belief in the book really carried me through the tougher parts of the editorial process, and it's such an incredible privilege to be able to share this story with people around the world, through all of you. I'm hugely grateful to you all, and delighted and excited to be working together.

My thanks to the brilliant friends who helped me directly with this project. Thank you to Nick Bradley and to Rhian Williams for your help with the translation of 'above the river', and the Kawakamis' name (I hope I haven't stretched poetic license too far with how it ended up). Thank you so much too to Mina Ikemoto Ghosh for your support as a friend, and for your very thoughtful sensitivity read and advice regarding all the folkloric and cultural elements of the book which were borrowed from real-world cultures. Thank you to Theo Steele for all of the fun conversations about worldbuilding and physics, and for being such a brilliantly thoughtful person to throw ideas around with, in general – I'm excited to see where these conversations go for books two and three of the trilogy. Thanks too to W. Y. Dobson for the chats about yōkai and invented martial arts, and to Juanita Jordan, surely the best physiotherapist ever, who kept neck and shoulder pain at bay and also kept me smiling through the long days and weeks of typing.

A particularly extra special thank you is due to Alex Allison, who read this novel in the deepest, darkest phase of the editorial process, when I'd essentially taken it to pieces and then completely lost sight of how to reassemble it again into something publishable. The comprehensive editorial notes Alex gave me in double-quick time were like nothing I'd ever experienced before in their levels of care, insight, ingenuity and razor-sharp clarity, and the subsequent conversations we had, too, were crucial to the development of this novel and its characters. Thank you so much, Alex – working with you on this was such a joy, and taught me so much. Everyone should go and read Alex's brilliant novels immediately! And special thanks of course to Isabel, too, who I'm told was doing some crucial cheering on, behind the scenes.

Huge thanks to all of my friends more generally, for all the kindness and fun you bring into my life as well as for the support you gave me while this book was being written – you know who you are, and you're all brilliant. Thanks especially to Louisa Dawes for the unerring friendship and support, as well as to Jenny Mustard and to Jakob Tanner, both of whom I feel like got a particularly blow-by-blow account of this particular book's journey!

Huge thanks to everyone I've taught, both in school settings and beyond. A particular mention has to go to the marvellous 7H of 2022–3 – you know who you are. Really, though, to all of the students I've taught, this book was in large part written for all of you. You all inspired me so much with your brilliance, strength and bravery, with your loyalty to one another, your resilience and energy, your humour and, of course, your undying love of bubble tea. All of you together were the inspiration for the Kawakamis, and I really hope you enjoy meeting Toshiko, Jun and Mei. Thank you for having me as your teacher, and for being the inspirational humans that you are.

Thank you to all of my own teachers, especially to my English, Drama and Creative Writing teachers, without whom I never could have got to this point of being a writer today. Particular thanks are due to the formidably talented Chris Barton, who only taught me for two years, but filled them astonishingly full with so many things which would go on to define and guide my life: from how music and literature can speak to each other, to the different ways in which the creative process can work – and then of course there was going to visit elephants in South Africa, too. I wish so much that I'd got back in touch to say how important all of that was to me, before it was too late. Sending huge thanks and love too to Dee Shulman, Max Barton and Addison Axe.

Finally, huge thanks to my family, for all your patience and support. Thank you to my parents, Kazuo and Lorna Ishiguro, for your support and encouragement, not just with this book but with all the writing I've subjected you both to (of extremely variable quality) over the decades. Thank you for raising me in a house and a world of books, and for showing me by example what it might look like to forge a life as a reader and a writer.